The King's Grey Mare

D1397539

About the Author

Bestselling author both in the UK and North America, Rosemary Hawley Jarman was born in Worcester. She lived most of her time in Worcestershire at Callow End, between Worcester and Upton on Severn. She began to write for pleasure, and followed a very real and valid obsession with the character of King Richard III. With no thought of publication, she completed a novel showing the King in his true colours, away from Tudor and Shakespearian propaganda. The book was taken up almost accidentally by an agent, and within six weeks a contract for publication and four other novels was signed with HarperCollins. The first novel, *We Speak No Treason*, was awarded The Silver Quill, a prestigious Author's Club Award, and sold out its first print run of 30,000 copies within seven days. *We Speak No Treason* was followed by *The King's Grey Mare, Crown in Candlelight* and *The Courts of Illusion*. She now lives in West Wales and has recently published her first fantasy novel, *The Captain's Witch*.

The King's Grey Mare

ROSEMARY HAWLEY JARMAN

TORC

Cover illustration courtesy of The Bridgeman Art Library

This edition first published 2008

Torc, an imprint of Tempus Publishing
Cirencester Road, Chalford,
Stroud, Gloucestershire, GL6 8PE
www.tempus-publishing.com

Tempus Publishing is an imprint of NPI Media Group

© Rosemary Hawley Jarman, 1973, 2008

The right of Rosemary Hawley Jarman to be identified as the Author
of this work has been asserted in accordance with the
Copyrights, Designs and Patents Act 1988.

British Library Cataloguing in Publication Data.
A catalogue record for this book is available from the British Library.

ISBN 978 0 7524 4563 2

Typesetting and origination by NPI Media Group
Printed and bound at Nutech Photolithographers

Foreword

In the few biographies of Elizabeth Woodville, she is shown either as a helpless woman subject to the terrible vicissitudes of fifteenth-century fortune, or as a cruel dynast obsessed only by the welfare of her own faction.

In this novel I have endeavoured to portray her as the victim of circumstances, no worse and no better than many others of her time; a woman blessed with outstanding physical beauty and incredible luck. She gambled, won and lost, and was often influenced by others more evil than herself.

Acknowledgement should be made to the Reverend S. Baring Gould's book: Curious Myths of the Middle Ages, in which he touches briefly upon the legend of Melusine, the water-witch from whom the Woodvilles claimed descent. Whether this was merely wishful thinking on their part is immaterial. Few can quarrel with Elizabeth's fitness for the. role of enchantress.

All characters, with a few minor exceptions, really existed. 'Mistress Grace, a natural daughter of King Edward' is mentioned in contemporary records as the chief mourner at Elizabeth's funeral.

R.H.J.

Prologue

1492

The little flame burned beneath a gilt-headed statue of the Virgin. It quivered in the draught that crept in the corners of the great chamber; it burned up and down, shining upon worn tapestries. At times its radiance stung the eyes of the woman in the bed. She gazed feebly away and up to the dim, vaulted ceiling, then down again at the two or three weary faces that had come to watch her dying.

Then she gazed at the statue until her sight was tired. They had begged her to sleep, but there would be time enough, an eternity of black, velvet sleep. If God were merciful. No stars for her, no gold crown. And, cried her consciousness, O Holy Virgin, O blonde, remote-faced Virgin! No Hell.

The time was near and she knew it. During the long weeks on the hard bed of the Abbey guesthouse at St. Saviour, Bermondsey, an unseen stranger had stood in shadow, courteously waiting, like a foreign emissary. Now, he made his subtle presence known. She saw how his breath stirred the little flame. She moaned and closed her eyes and immediately there came vision after vision, clearer than truth. A procession of ghostly beings, a pale lisping child who plucked at her gown and offered a nosegay; a blind boy, singing. A priest who fumbled with his breviary and cast a frightened glance towards her. A gypsy woman with her throat torn out by hounds, blood dropping like slow rubies.

A tall man, roaring with laughter, and a fair-haired girl, weeping. Then a beloved face, a face long-dead, with a tender mouth and eyebrow quirked in sweet good humour. Next a black-clad knight, his face resolute and stern. Lastly, a thin face beneath rich jewels. Famished eyes and a tight line of mouth. It smiled so dreadfully that she dragged herself from the vision with a cry. One of the watchers sprang out of a doze, embroidery slipping from her lap.

'Madame, only a dream ...'

'A dream,' she repeated weakly, as they raised her on stonehard pillows, proffered an undrinkable tisane of reeking herbs. Then, lucidity struggling to return: 'What time is it? What month? What year?'

'Past midnight, Lady. They'll soon be ringing Matins.' And, as if obedient, a bell shattered the feverish quietness.

'Tis June, Madame. The seventh year of his Grace King Henry the Seventh.'

'His Majesty,' reproved another. Kings had a new title now, fitting the divine dynasty of Tudor.

'And who am I?' – fixing the speaker with glittering blue eyes that were oddly alive in the perished face.

'Why, Madame, who but our dear lady Elizabeth,' said the woman.

'Plain, unadorned Elizabeth?' A mechanical touch of the old hauteur here; enough to make the flame shiver and sigh.

'The Queen's very dear mother, Madame. Queen-Dowager, no less, sovereign lady of King Edward Fourth, whom God assoil.' Queen-Dowager, Queen-Dowager. The title was mouthed, breathed, with a snigger in the breath, half-hidden. They whispered it in a dying fall of whispers, and she sank back on memory. With her own painful breath, the light beneath the fair pale Virgin guttered and rose. Hearing the sparse, obsequious voices she thought: I am Elizabeth, one-time Queen of England, and these wenches are all I have left to cherish me on this last journey. Once there were a thousand to do my bidding alone. The flame muttered of death's inexorable advance, and of times older than any of those remembered by the vigil-weary women about the bed. Times sweet and sour; times lived through, somehow, with a divided heart.

She was Elizabeth, dying. She of many names would be but a cold inscription, and soon forgotten. What did they call me? She mused. Elizabeth Woodville; and then, the widow of the virgin's face. Later, it was Bessy; lovesome, bedsome Bessy. A King called to her; she saw the great golden face engorged with longing, felt the striving hands. She thought: in the time before the heart ceased to have any value, I had another name.

7

A dead Queen, faery-like, danced before her closed eyes. The frozen tears of pearls garlanded her hair. 'I shall call you Isabella!' – a phrase like a song. 'And you shall choose your own husband, *ma toute belle!*' Consciousness waxed and ebbed; her life's review. So, I was Dame Isabella Grey. Grey, that most beloved name, so cruelly translated into a jest by the common folk. They never loved me, as they loved the King. Her hands clutched air; old thoughts of vengeance renewed, shaming her in a fresh vision's sad, drawn face. Ah, she thought: he was handsome, but he mocked me too. The face advanced, in time with the sonorous plainsong from the chapel nearby. 'You destroyed me, Elizabeth,' the face said, softly.

Shifting like mist, the years crept back. Unheralded there came another name, black with heresy, and with it, her mother's face, whose ancient raddled beauty the grave had left unmarred. Together they stood beside a forest pool. Under a little moaning wind, the mother's insistent voice spoke.

'See, child, see! Remember her! She'll never fail us, so pray to her ...'

The water rippled. All around trees seemed to shrink in fear, shrouding their trunks with foliage. In the depths of the pool, something evil, beautiful, rose darkly, and the old voice said: 'She lives in us. From time's beginning, we have shared her power.'

Elizabeth, one-time Queen of England, shrieked aloud, then, swiftly as it had engulfed her, the elemental terror withdrew. Dimly she knew that someone prayed; through tear-stung lashes she looked to see who had come to kneel by the bed. Gold hair shimmered in her sight, green eyes, a fresh young face, tragic, loving. She tried vainly to sit upright.

'Majesty ...' she said. 'My daughter?' The ill-matched words tailed off, suffused by the mumble from the corners of the room, the click of rosary beads. They were all praying. Jesu, mercy. Jesu, mercy. *Ave Maria, gratia plena.* Mercy everlasting, on her soul.

'She thinks you to be the Queen!' said one, breaking off her prayer. Mirth tinged her voice as she spoke to the newcomer, who leaned forward, frowning, bending near the stricken face.

'Sweet Madame, 'tis Grace,' she murmured. 'Sleep a little; I'll not leave you.' And she blinked tears away so that the others should not see, for they were gossips, jealous, fickle, and iron-hearted for all their feigned duty. And the Queen-Dowager was sleeping, the anguish passing from her face like a rain-cloud from the stars. She was growing young again, a child greeting womanhood, when each morning, hung with birdsong, brought her to the eager day, and each day was itself the morning of life. Death's pale flame swirled about her, but she knew nothing of it. She was fifteen years old.

PART ONE

The Flower of Anjou

1452–61

'Vanité des vanités, toute la vanité!'
Queen Margaret of Anjou

She lay in her secret place with thoughts of love. This was a nook
where none could find her, hidden by the deep flank of clustering
willows and bounded by high reeds that grew around the edge of
the little lake. One hand supporting her cheek, she lay comfortably
against a bank of kingcups. Her feet were tucked beneath her gown,
and she herself was like a willow, with her long hair, more silver than
gold, reflecting the trees' dappled greenness.

She could stay thus, motionless, for hours. A bright bird had settled
near her sleeve and, an armslength away, two brindled trout sunned
themselves in the shallows. Unseeingly she gazed at them, with
eyes as clear and impersonal as the water, their blue merging with
its gold and green; eyes that were still yet charged occasionally with
passionate, half-formed thoughts. Virginal, receptive to the rippled
message of the lake and bland as an artist's new canvas; such were
the eyes of Elizabeth Woodville as she dreamed, of sweet, unreal love
sucked like honey from old romances; the Chronicles of Froissart,
the magic tales of the Chevalier de la Tour Landry, and Chaucer's
high, gaudy myths. Love idealistic, love unfeigned, as in the far days
of Eleanor of Aquitaine, when knight and lady lay on either side
of a naked sword, only their souls communing. Kisses grew beside

the kingcups. The trout, rising, plashed a courtly old song into her
drowsy mind.

Je loe amours et ma dame mercye
 Du bel acueil qui par eulx deux me vient ...

She bit off the unsung tune midway. A song of Burgundy, the
enemy of France, yet a good air, mellow and sad. She sighed, nibbled a
shining strand of her own hair, smoothed the plain silk of her bodice.
Courtly love, courtly dances filled her heart, but her dress, two years
old, fitted her no longer, and was fast wearing out. The Woodvilles
were by no means poor, but it was known that Elizabeth's mother
would have them richer.

'God's curse on this paucity of our estate,' Jacquetta of Bedford
had said lately. Then, with a rare and very secret smile, seemingly for
Elizabeth alone: 'Yet we have other things, to make us wealthy beyond
the stars.' That beautiful and mysterious smile had lingered with
Elizabeth. Would her mother be smiling now? Elizabeth wondered;
for an hour folk had been calling, searching for her fruitlessly. First,
like the bellow of an ill-played shawm, the voice of her nurse, then the
chaplain whinnying in a voice unused to anything but the mumblings
of the Mass, and lastly her sisters, primly, dutifully crying her name
and giggling as they ran up and down the pleasaunce paths.

She parted a strand of willow and peered across the garden, now
deserted. What she saw gave her small gladness. It meant little that
since 1168, when William de Wyvill enjoyed the tenure-in-chivalry of
Grafton land and the favour of King Henry the Second, Woodvilles
had walked these same velvet lawns and had culled from those borders their simples and condiments. The fennel, the rosemary, bryony
and St. John's Wort, ampion, vervain and rue; the herbs sweet and
sour, the good herbs and the evil herbs, for fever and madness and the
soul's easement. The plants to hide rankness or add spice to a festal
dish; the gillies and violets for table-dressing, and the reeds, amongst
which she lay, for strewing on a dusty floor. The sheltering yews and
the one great oak in the garden's heart failed to move her. Likewise
the manor itself, with its timbered gables flanking the soaring roof
of the great hall and its chapel tower rosily tipped by sunlight. For
Grafton Regis represented learning, nurture, discipline, and held
her from that world for whose romantic splendours she yearned. At

London, there was a French Queen, by rumour wildly fascinating, with a court, maybe, like that of fair Eleanor of Aquitaine ...

The sisters came into view again, running from behind the high stone wall that bounded the stableyard and bakery. Shrill and anxious, their voices called her. Catherine, her favourite, broke from the others and ran alongside the stream towards the lake. She wore a well worn murrey gown. A gleam of plump flesh showed through a split seam. Round, where Elizabeth was slender, she ran, dodging the tussocks of reed. Elizabeth raised her arm above the banked kingcups and waved, watching her own white hand and the way the green folds of her sleeve belled about her wrist in an outworn elegance. At the French court, their sleeves were like great bladders, sewn with pearls and miniver to glisten in the dance. She knew; she had seen paintings. All her undanced dances faded as Catherine plunged towards her.

Her sister's small coif was trimmed with tarnished gold, below which her fair hair spread itself in a tangled cascade. All the sisters were blonde, but none bore the colouring of Elizabeth, whose hair, silver-gilt and falling to her knees, was a shining mist in candlelight and under the sun seemed woven of rare and precious thread. Sir Hugh Johns had looked long at her hair; there had been tears in his eyes.

Breathless, Catherine threw herself down, crushing bright blossoms. The trout, frightened, flicked away into the depths.

'Oh, Bess!' Catherine gasped. 'We've searched for you for hours – Margaret tore her gown and Martha fell – her nose bled. We are all going to be beaten. Dame Joan is wroth.'

Elizabeth frowned. Dame Joan was their crabbed old nurse and Elizabeth loathed the humiliation of beatings. Sometimes wheedling could bring lenience. Today, however, the weather was warm; Joan would be sweating and merciless under the old-fashioned houpeland that encased her girth like a knight's harness. Catherine rattled on.

'Bess, I pray you, come.' Her round bosom strained dangerously at another seam. 'The whole house is upside down. Anyway – ' curiously – 'what do you *do* here all this time?'

'I think.' Elizabeth chewed on a sour-sweet grass, gazed at the lake, diamonded by sun. 'I muse. I dream.'

'About Sir Hugh Johns?' Catherine looked archly at her. 'Oh, sister, imagine. You'll soon be a wedded lady ... the first of us. Come now, and talk of Hugh to Joan, it'll cool her temper. I'll miss you when you go,' she finished wistfully.

'I'll go nowhere,' said Elizabeth, biting the stem in two. 'With him, at any rate.'

Catherine's plump jaw dropped. 'Don't you like him?' she said incredulously. 'We all thought him a sweet and gentle knight. When he laughed at talk of your dowry and said he would almost be content with you alone, we were enchanted ...'

'Fool's prattle,' said Elizabeth. A brief vision of Sir Hugh's plain pleasant face assailed her. She had asked him of fashions, of the latest airs and dances, and he had stuttered incoherently. He had never even spoken to her of love, had merely excused himself to seek her mother's bower, where they conferred stiltedly about monetary matters. Sir Hugh was well purveyed of money. Was that what her mother had meant, speaking of their future with that strange little smile? Somehow she thought not. Somewhere, there was love, its colours unknown. Love the stranger, to be instantly recognized. Hugh Johns was not love, nor ever could be.

Catherine's voice went on, complaining: Bess was all over green stains, Bess would have them all beaten. It was hard to be one of many unwed sisters. The brothers were in livery service at noble households. Lionel was destined for the Church, Edward for the sea. They were only young yet. Nearest Elizabeth's age, Anthony was the best. She loved his slender elegance, his learning, his chivalry. He could translate any poem, Greek, Latin or French, into something better than the original. Soon he would be able to best any other stripling knight in the tourney. She wished he had been present at the interview with Sir Hugh. He would have made him blush rosier still, with his subtle, adult wit. There had only been seven-year-old John, pulling faces at the stammering knight's back. That had earned him a beating that day ...

Anthony would have been able to comfort her. 'Do what you will, sweet sister,' he would have said. 'None can drag you to the altar!'

It was not as if the Queen had commanded the match. That would have lent a different colour to the affair. Elizabeth knew that her mother had the Queen's ear through their mutual French birth. Jacquetta of Bedford's first husband had been Regent for King Henry the Sixth in France; Tante Isabel was married to the Queen's uncle, Charles d'Anjou. Thinking again of Queen Margaret, Elizabeth almost choked with frustrated longing. There was clodpoll Sir Hugh, lusting to bear her off to some distant manor, as tame and *ennuyeux* as

Grafton Regis, while the lovely London court frolicked carelessly; for there had been scant talk of war since Jack Cade's uprising two years earlier. York, the turbulent Richard, also seemed quiescent, despite his wearying aspirations and his stirrings of Burgundy. It was an old quarrel; York and Lancaster sporadically at each other's throats like feast-day mastiffs. She was sure they would not talk of policy at the court. There would be only music and courtly love, in the royal palaces with their enchanted names: Greenwich, Eltham, Windsor, Sheen, the shining one.

'The chaplain says,' said Catherine pompously, 'that your soul is wayward, wanton ... faugh!' She shifted to another patch of reed. 'My dress is soaking. Why do you choose this dismal place to hide in?'

Elizabeth whispered: 'I love the lake.'

Catherine said uncertainly: 'Will you come now? Madam our mother, as well as Joan, will punish you.'

'Mother knows?'

'Yes, she came down to welcome the party from Calais. Our father's here.'

'Imbecile!' cried Elizabeth, springing up. 'Why did you not tell me?'

Her beloved father was home, and she not there to greet him. She ran, across meadow and lawn, past the falcons' mew with its rank, raw-meat smell – under the archway into the ward and, skirting the chapel building, up the worn stone stairs to the children's apartments. There the chaplain met her, muttering prayers or imprecations. Within the solar, the nurse fussed grimly among the sisters; Jacquetta, Eleanor, Anne, Martha and Margaret; toddling, preening or playing about the floor, according to their age and disposition.

'Well, my lady,' said the nurse sourly, motioning to a tiring-maid to unfasten Elizabeth's laces, 'may you find mercy, though you don't deserve it. Hurry, now. My lord waits for you below.'

Elizabeth shivered at the cool touch of a clean linen shift. She danced impatiently on the spot, itching to run to the oriel through which she could hear the stamp and jingle of many horse, the deep voices of men, a breath of song. *He* could sing better than any man in England or France. How long of him had she missed already? Sometimes he only stayed a day, to enchant them all with a tale of courtly prowess. Then he would depart, leaving the manor even more dull and lifeless than before.

She was dressed at last in a high-waisted Italian silk patterned with red roses, its tight sleeves trimmed with marten. Catching the sun through an embrasure, her hair gleamed like thistledown. She descended the stairs to the Hall, followed by the sisters who were old enough to attend her, and she knew that she outshone them, as a silver candle shames a tallow dip. The Hall was full of courtiers, knights, wearing her father's blazon. A royal herald stood stiffly by the fireplace. The colours on his tabard, the leopards and lilies of France Ancient, leaped to her glamour-hungry eyes like a blaze; she heard bright, soundless music.

The tables, flanking three sides of the Hall, were laid for supper and at the knights' dais at the northern end sat her parents, talking with a tall boy. Anthony! Unexpectedly home on leave from his livery service. For the first time she cursed the seductive, solitary lake that had made her miss so much joy. She went forward to the dais and knelt.

After the long obeisance, she looked into eyes blue as her own. The eyes of Sir Richard Woodville, Earl Rivers; Knight of the Garter, Privy Councillor, Knight Banneret and leader of men; yet first, her own father, and deeply, possessively loved. He raised her, kissed her, beckoned to a henchman who came forward with a long package wrapped in hessian. Inside was a thick, shining-swathe of cobwebby lace.

'From Alençon,' said her father, smiling. 'One of the many perquisites of my captaincy there. For my fairest daughter.'

She looked at him, at the way his russet hair was threaded with silver and curled on his broad shoulders; how the rich blue velvet doublet fitted him like a skin. The old collar of 'S's, worn by all knights in the service of Henry of Lancaster, gleamed on his chest. He was called by many the handsomest man in England. She thought, gloriously: they are right! Then, while she gloated over the lace, he turned again to talk to his wife.

'Bordeaux has fallen,' he said. 'The French conquest of Aquitaine is complete.'

'Ah, Jesu,' said Jacquetta of Belford. Totally noncommittal was that little prayer, yet there was a triumph in it. England for the English, they said; yet Jacquetta's heart was bred and nurtured among the French, and Lancaster was her watchword.

Young Anthony winked at Elizabeth. He had a golden fineness, too, she thought, in his gay scarlet habit and shirt of fair Rennes cloth. She mused again on Sir Hugh, already running to plumpness; she had been spoilt by father and brother for beauty in other men. Thinking of Hugh put her in mind of her mother's yet unheard opinions. Disquiet crept over her. Had a decision been reached, while she was dreaming by the lake? And what did her father think of Sir Hugh? She listened closely to the conversation; still they spoke of policy.

'As Seneschal of Aquitaine, I had a great force,' said Sir Richard. 'Two thousand bowmen, three hundred spears. And then I kicked my heels at Plymouth, revictualling a fleet which none seemed minded to use. The King, Jesu preserve him, sometimes seems ...'

He ceased abruptly. Other conversations buzzed in the Hall; behind a screen one of the minstrels discreetly plucked his lute. Jacquetta's face was impassive as she listened, waited for her husband to resume. Elizabeth studied her; it seemed this day as if she were seeing them all for the first time.

Duchess of Bedford in her own right, daughter of Pierre, Duke of Luxembourg and Marguerite del Balzo of Andria, Jacquetta Woodville still owned much of the legendary beauty of her youth. Her eyes were lustrous, her features clear and proud. The narrow band of hair revealed at the edge of her coif was still a rich coppery gold. She wore many rings, and about her neck lay a ruby and diamond reliquary reputed to hold a bone of St. James. She was holding a parchment letter from a personage of some note, for from it dangled a great seal like a gobbet of wet blood. A letter newly arrived; Elizabeth knew suddenly that it concerned herself. Her eyes flew to her mother's, and were held in a strange, perceptive gaze. Her heart beat hard. Good or ill lay in that parchment.

The gamey scent of the roast peacock wafted to her nose, but her stomach fluttered fretfully. Now she would be able to eat nothing, even in her father's honour. Not all Anthony's wit could sharpen her taste, until she knew the content of that roll.

Still Jacquetta's eyes, all-knowing, fathomless, held hers, as the clarions sounded for supper.

Early morning sunlight pierced the chapel windows and gleamed upon paten and pyx and chalice.

Confiteor tibi in cithara, Deus, Deus meus; quare tristis es, et quare conturbas me?

The chaplain watched Elizabeth constantly, while he tongued the Mass by rote. The words meant little after years of repetition and left his mind free to wander. He marked her trembling as she took the Host; this was in itself the sign of conscience, as was the way she bent her head to draw comfort from her missal. Soul, why art thou downcast, why art thou all lament? A tear crept softly down her cheek and the chaplain's stern mouth relaxed. So the eldest Woodville maiden was penitent. She rued the disgraceful scene in Hall last evening, caused by a letter which, thought the priest, should have been hailed meekly and with gratitude.

The eldest Woodville maiden was, however, weeping not in penance but with renewed rage. She murmured, choking: '*Spera in Deo, quoniam adhuc confitebor illi ...*' Wait for God's help ... my champion and my God! The painted saints about the altar studied her coolly. Everywhere there was a candle, starred by her own tears, cold as the light in her father's eyes when she had run from the Hall last evening.

They had given her the letter to read aloud. Its heavy seal had fallen across her wrist, the writing was powerful and black. Sir Richard had stretched himself in his chair, jewelled goblet in hand, prepared to enjoy his daughter's pretty voice. At first, reading, she had been proud, then incredulous, and upon reaching the fierce, swarthy signature her tongue had trembled in fury. In the body of the Hall there had been whisperings. A young page, waiting near the dais with his dish of venison frumenty, had started to grin. Amid this growing interest, this knavish amusement, she finished the letter, and the echo of its words fed a sudden, incredible anger.

To Dame Elizabeth Woodville:

Right worshipful and well beloved, I greet you well, And forasmuch as my right well beloved Sir Hugh Johns, knight, which now late was with you until his full great joy, hath informed me how that he for the great love and affection that he hath unto your person, as for your great and praised virtues and womanly demeaning, desireth with all his heart to do you worship by way of marriage, before any other creature living as he saith.

I, considering [– the lordly *I*! here she heard her own voice becoming high and strained] I, considering his said desire and the great worship he had which was made knight at Jerusalem ... And also the good and notable service he hath done and daily doth to me, write you at this time, and pray you effectuously that ye will condescend and apply yourself unto his said lawful and honest desire, wherein ye shall cause me to show unto you such good lordship [here her tongue tripped over immoderate rage] as ye by reason shall hold you content and pleased, with the grace of God, which everlastingly have you in his blessed protections and governance,

Signed: Richard Earl of Warwick.

That name made folk tremble. Warwick was a living legend, hand in glove with half the crowned heads in Europe. It was said that he used Richard of York as his mammet, driving the Duke, his cousin, willy-nilly into uprisings, and lording it in England and in Calais, where Elizabeth's own father was second-in-command to the Earl of Somerset. Warwick used folk to his own ends; some even said that Warwick's word was law! She had always disliked the sound of his arrogance, his power. And now, here was Warwick, treating the whole business of her betrothal as a *fait accompli* – foisting his ditch water-dull liegeman upon her as if to bestow the greatest favour! Reading between the lines, the letter was tantamount to a command.

The words burned. 'Wherein ye shall cause me to show you *such good lordship* as ye by reason shall hold you content and pleased!' Reason left her. She would not suffer his good lordship. She would not be Warwick's chattel, to marry to whom he thought fit, not even for the grace of the God he invoked so confidently. She was Elizabeth and none other. In that moment she felt that not even her parents, not even the King and Queen could command her, bend her ferocious, adamantine will. The nurse could beat her and the priests pray. She was Elizabeth, who would not be bidden! In that terrible moment of madness she had tried to tear the thick parchment across, had crumpled and ground it beneath her little shoe; all this under the company's astonished gaze and her father's mounting wrath.

Rising from the dais, he had shouted at her: 'Dame, have you lost your wits? Is this the way to treat a fair offer? Earl Warwick ...'

She had screamed back like an eelwife. 'Warwick! Pox take Warwick! And you hate him yourself, my lord, for his treasonous talk against the Crown!'

Even Anthony, behind his father's chair, had blanched, for there were several visiting Yorkist partisans in the Hall, dining in precarious amity. Sir Richard's face had turned the colour of Clary wine.

'God's Passion, is this the speech of my daughter?' he cried. 'Madame, go to your room. Before this, I was not of a mind for you to marry Hugh, but by Christ, he shall have you now! And may Our Lady give him grace to tame that temper!'

At that instant the grinning page had laughed out loud, through sheer nervousness. Maddened further, she rounded on him and caught him a stinging blow across the cheek. The boy, who was the son of one of King Henry's courtiers and new to the Woodville household, set up a noise like a pig being butchered. Two great hounds leaped roaring from under the table, and Sir Richard hurled his goblet across the chamber. Only Jacquetta had remained calm. Recalling the scene like a nightmare, Elizabeth realized that her mother had not spoken one word.

The Mass was over; she touched her lips to the Book. The chaplain rose, and, followed by a hobble of aged chantry priests and the singing-boys, came down the nave. She intercepted him in the porch.

'Father, I wish to be professed as a nun,' she said. Her lips were trembling. He looked at her not unkindly. 'Nay, my daughter.' He made to walk on. She caught at his vestment and he looked down, surprised.

'I am in earnest,' she said softly. Anything, rather than be used, be bidden. Anything so long as she, Elizabeth, could choose. In some convents life was, she believed, almost gay. She would be admired by her sisters as the fairest nun in Christendom.

'No, my child,' repeated the chaplain.

'You yourself said,' cried Elizabeth, 'that my soul was wayward. For my soul's good, Father, please ...'

The chaplain smiled palely, twisted his gown from her grasp.

'Your reasons are wrong, daughter,' he said, as if he read her mind. 'And do you consider yourself fit to be a Bride of Christ?'

The choir filed past. Standing abjectly in the porch, she heard the chaplain say to an acolyte, 'My lady is to wed Sir Hugh ... by the Rood, Jack, this chalice needs scouring; 'tis foul with fingermarks ...'

The nurse escorted Elizabeth back to her apartments, where she was in durance with no company but that of the baby sisters. They had not allowed Anthony to visit her, and he was leaving that morning, bound again for the house of his patron in the south. Since last evening she had set eyes on neither parent. She sat down before her tapestry frame and began to work with short vicious needle-stabs. Appropriately the picture was one of St. Jerome lecturing some maidens. Elizabeth pushed her needle through his eye. Through the half-open window she could hear voices and the jingle of a bit as a horse tossed its head. She stole a glance at Dame Joan; the woman was drowsing, oblivious of a summer fly crawling on her neck. Elizabeth rose, crossed to the casement and pushed it wide. In the court-yard below a few of the guard lounged, gossiping. A saddled horse waited. Anthony was within the house, making his farewells. The few short sweet hours were over, unshared by her. Again she cursed Earl Warwick's insolence. Hated Warwick! the fault was his. Warwick, powerful, remote, had, without even setting eyes on her, caused disap-pointment and grief. Dispiritedly she leaned from the window and listened to the men talking. Policy, of course, the old war-talk that bored her so; the familiar names: York, who last year had returned from Ireland ready to do battle with the royal House of Lancaster. He had been pacified only by a seat on King Henry's Council, and the King's declaration of trust in him. Beaufort of Somerset, under whose command her father had once been at Calais; true knight and liegeman of the King and especially of his Queen, Margaret. Hated by York, for some reason, more than any other man. Now they spoke of the Queen; the free, fortunate, beautiful Queen.

She would never see the Queen. Soon she would be cooped, brooding, on Hugh's manor, bearing the customary child a year, Hugh himself doubtless flaunting off to Jerusalem again in the serv-ice of his lordly master Warwick. Perchance Warwick would visit her during her husband's absence. Odious thought! her fancy saw Warwick inspecting her household, appointing her servants; her imagination all but endowed the unknown Warwick with horns and a cleft beard. Tiny drops of sweat broke out on her face; she clenched her hands and wept.

Anthony came down the steps into the courtyard, an esquire fol-lowing him, and grasped the waiting horse's bridle. The sun touched gold from his uncovered head. Elizabeth dared not call, even with the nurse snoring behind her. Instead she threw a rosebud down; it dropped on the horse's saddle. Anthony looked up at her white face and small, imploring hands.

'Ah, sweet sister,' he said very softly. 'God send you good fortune.' He rode up to the window; by stretching up he could almost touch her hand. She glanced across the courtyard. Most of the guard had dispersed, but three were dicing on the cobbles outside the mew. Anthony's esquire wandered over to join them.

'Take me with you,' she whispered. 'Take me away!' Before he could answer, she had nipped up her gown and was sitting on the sun-warmed window ledge. Her feet hung down a yard from the horse's ears. Anthony's face looked up, pale and troubled. The cobbles seemed a long way down. She had visions of her skull crushed, every bone in her body smashed to pieces. Yet in that instant she jumped, slid, fell into her brother's arms. The horse reared in fright at the sudden burden and bolted, hooves ringing on the stones. Anthony struggled to hold her across his saddle-bow, while she began to laugh like a madwoman. They careered through the gate, swerved under the arch and raced across the meadow. Anthony was swearing, calling on the saints. Eventually he brought the horse to a bouncing halt.

'Sweet Jesu!' he said, rubbing a strained wrist. 'You could have been killed! What a fool's game!'

They were near the water, and her secret place. The shimmering willows seemed to listen as they argued, he shaking his head despairingly, she crying, pleading.

'Take me away,' she begged. 'Grant me this one favour, and I will repay you, if it's the last thing I do in life.'

'Come, sweeting,' he said, looking suddenly like a frightened child (he was little more). 'It's not your death. Sir Hugh is kindly, biddable. I doubt not you'll have your way with him in the end. Come,' disentangling himself from her arms, 'make the best of it.'

Still she sobbed and besought him.

'Where would I hide you?' he said uneasily. 'I ... I should get into trouble.'

She recognized from his last sentence that he was as young, as powerless as she. She dismounted slowly into the reedy grass, her hair awry, her face drawn and miserable.

'Go, then,' she said dully. 'I know you would help me if you could.'

'Aye!' he answered, eager to be off. 'Saint Catherine keep you; we'll meet again soon.'

'Farewell,' she said, turning away.

He gathered up his reins. 'Bess, use our father kindly,' he said. 'You shamed him sorely last evening.'

She walked away, hearing the scudding hooves of his departure and his shout of farewell. In utter resignation she descended the moist green slope to where the bank of kingcups made a pillow and the same two trout lay basking under sun-kissed water. She sank down, curving her body beside the shady willows, and let sadness engulf her. Then came the unmistakable feeling that she was not alone. Someone was watching her. A chill enveloped her as she thought of ghosts of the reedland, bogies that changed themselves to water-birds; the Lord of Evil himself, inhabiting, for sport, this lonely, sunlit place. Then the uncomfortable feeling was broken by a calm, a beautiful voice.

'Weep no more, daughter,' said Jacquetta of Bedford.

Astonished, Elizabeth saw her mother sitting unattended on the other side of the willow tree. Green-latticed sunlight lapped at her steady profile. For all this rustic departure, she was attired with customary fineness. Her headdress was of silver cloth, stretched over a little pointed horn of starched damask. Small jewels winked in her ears and upon her white bosom. She wore dove-coloured satin and a high embroidered girdle. Her little shoes of clary velvet were stained with mud and rushes. Otherwise she was immaculate. A hand wearing a pearl-and-ruby rose, beckoned through the hanging frond of leaves.

'Tis like the confessional!' said Jacquetta, with a tinge of laughter. Elizabeth crept closer.

'And truly I would beg forgiveness, Madame.'

'Be still, Elizabeth.' The strong white hand took hers, and mother and daughter sat silent for some minutes. In that clasp a force was born, communicating itself from the older woman to the younger. It was like the moments before a storm strikes, and there was in it also warmth, power, something so all-consuming that Elizabeth tried vainly to withdraw her hand.

'Do you think,' said the Duchess, 'that I would have you wasted on any paltry Yorkist cur?'

Light rippled on the water. The leaves shook themselves at the incredible words.

'You did not come to me,' said Jacquetta, 'being content instead to rave in unseemly fashion at my lord, which put him in a passion I have taken all night to still. Yet stilled he is,' with a tiny smile of triumph. 'You have much to learn of the ways of men. Obstruct them with rough speech, rantings, and, like a hog's bladder kicked by boys, they grow more resilient. Yet, apply a sweet pinprick, a loving word, a sigh, a tear, and you cause them to think, and think again, and grow womanly, and do your will.'

She released Elizabeth's hand, and uprooted a reed.

'Or this, a better allegory-' twisting and bending the stem brutally. 'Force will not master this pliant reed. Yet - ' splitting the green tip with sharp fingernails - 'apply cunning, art - ' the reed began to peel in layers - 'some deviousness so slight 'tis scarcely there at all-' the stem flaked, showed hollow - 'and your adversary is undone. So it is with men, and policy, and love.'

The hypnotic voice ceased. From the further shore of the lake there came the whirring of wings as a brace of wild duck rose and made for the freedom of the forest.

'So they fly,' murmured the Duchess, watching. 'And so they escape the *ennui* of Grafton Regis. How fair the female is, with the sun on her wings!'

She knows my every thought! marvelled Elizabeth. And, mother of mine though she is, I know her not at all. The past years had done little to bring them close. To Elizabeth, Jacquetta had been a distant, awesome figure, spending much time in Calais, London, Rouen, and almost yearly *enceinte* with another Woodville child. Jacquetta had seen the London court many times. Yet it was not she who had whetted Elizabeth's fancy with tales of its glory; these had been gleaned from grooms, maidservants, and were often inaccurate. In all her fifteen years, Elizabeth had had only formal speech with her mother. The Duchess was talking again of Sir Hugh Johns.

'The knight is pleasant enough,' she admitted. 'But his policies sour my stomach. No Yorkist shall have *my* daughter.' Her pearly face was suddenly savage, then she laughed. 'This day I will send word to the great lord Warwick declining his liegeman. Not even a King could gainsay me in matters of the heart! No upstart scion of York shall bid my blood!'

Intrigued, Elizabeth slipped through the screen of willow to kneel at her mother's feet. The Duchess studied the upturned face. So perfect was its symmetry that she looked, spellbound, for longer than it took for a white frill of cloud to drift across the sun, and for the light to return, blindingly gold. It shone upon Elizabeth's broad brow, small full mouth and pointed chin. Her eyes reflected back the sky; her hair was silver and gold, utterly unreal in its beauty. By the saints, Jacquetta thought: she is fairer even than I was, and men would maim one another for a smile from me!

She said: 'It is time you knew my history. My life with Bedford was happy, almost to the time of his death, some sixteen years ago. I say almost; for, when Suffolk was my husband's captain – (aye, Suffolk, butchered by *Yorkists* on Portsmouth strand two springs ago!) – I was with the army in France. Our captains were there, of course. There was one ... ah, Jesu! it comes once in a lifetime.'

'The handsomest man in England,' said Elizabeth.

Jacquetta smiled. 'Aye Sir Richard Woodville and none other. The first sight of him was like a strong blow to my heart. Thereafter came pain, the pain of partings. The pain,' she said softly, 'of loving, and of being bound to another man.'

She lowered her voice even more.

'I believe, Elizabeth, that strong desire can cut through destiny; that even the planets can be turned in their courses by thought; worlds shaken by it, consummation achieved. For ... my lord of Bedford died.'

She took Elizabeth's hand again. Again the feeling of shattering power was born, and mounted.

'There was no need thereafter to quell our longings, our hungers. There was no need for me to avoid Sir Richard's eyes or run from his voice. He had been knighted by the child king Henry at Leicester, yet his lineage was not so high as my own. All the same, his was the face I had been born to look upon. It was the *coup de foudre*, the power and glory of the heart.

'We were married full secretly, for my dower had been granted upon Bedford's death by a patent of the King. I was pledged to do fealty to my uncle, the Bishop of Thérouanne, the King's Chancellor in France. I was forbidden to marry without the King's edict, given under the Great Seal of England. Yet soon I had no choice but to throw myself upon Henry's mercy. I was great with you then, Bess. My uncle fumed and my brother, Louis of St. Pol, declared himself outraged by my disobedience. So I wooed the King. I besought him to extort whatever fine he wished, while my kinfolk railed at me. They threatened your father and me with all manner of punishment.

'We were fined one thousand pounds. I smiled at the young reed of a King, I put him to my will. I knelt to Cardinal Beaufort, offered him my manor of Charleton Canville, and looked into his soul. He paid my fine; yea, gladly. Then your father was appointed to the royal commission of Chief Rider of the Forest of Saucy.' She pointed. 'Over there, Elizabeth, where your desires lately flew, in the guise of a wild duck!'

Her gaze wandered across the lake. A fish jumped, suddenly silver.

'You love the water, Elizabeth,' said the Duchess, her voice changed. Closed within her hand, Elizabeth's fingers felt a throb, a vibration that encompassed flesh and veins, striking at that which was hidden, and deep.

'In all water,' said the Duchess, 'there are spirits. In all fountains, meres, rivers, the sea. One spirit above all. Omnipotent. We are part of her and she of us. You knew it,' looking at Elizabeth with a fierce tenderness, 'My blood runs in you, my wit and will are yours. My shameful secret, Elizabeth, you were once, carried within me through anger, and born triumphant. Now, my fairest, my eldest. My Melusine ...'

She was the Jacquetta of youth, burning-bright, all-powerful. Eyes closed, Elizabeth listened to slow, mystic words.

'I am of the royal House of Luxembourg. I am of the blood of a water-fay, who ensnared Raymond of Poitou. Melusine met with Raymond by her home, the fountain in the forest, and took his wits away. She asked Raymond for as much of the land around the fountain as could be covered by a stag's hide; she cut the hide into ten thousand strips so that her land extended far beyond the forest. There she built Lusignan. She bore Raymond children: Urian, with his one red and his one green eye; Gedes, of the scarlet countenance (for him she built the castle of Favent and the convent at Malliers); Gyot, of the uneven eyes (for him she built La Rochelle); Anthony, of the claws and long hair; a one-eyed son; and lastly, Geoffrey of the Tooth. He had a boar's tusk.

'She obtained an oath from her husband that she would be left alone each Saturday in strictest privacy. Raymond kept his word, though his courtiers swore that Melusine betrayed her lord with fiends. But one day he weakened and sought her out, deep in the heart of a lonely lake. There he saw that her nether parts were changed into the tail of a monstrous fish or serpent. He spoke to none of this, nor did Melusine betray that she had been discovered. One day, however, news came that Geoffrey of the Tooth had attacked the monastery of Malliers and burned it, putting to death his own brother and a hundred monks. So the house of Raymond rose against itself, and Raymond cried to his wife: 'Away, odious serpent! Contaminator of my noble race!'

'At this Melusine replied: 'Farewell. I go, but I shall come again as a doom. Whenever one of us is to die, I shall weep most dolorously over the ramparts of Lusignan; whenever tragedy strikes a royal House, I shall do likewise.' So she departed, after suckling once more her two youngest sons, holding them on the lap that owned scales shining like the moon.'

Elizabeth opened her eyes. The Duchess said: 'This, then, is our heritage. We can fear naught with this immortal ancestry. Raymond, like all men, was a fool. Melusine is our strength. She lives in us. She fortifies us. Receive her power. From the time I bore you in my womb, Elizabeth, I knew you would be a fit child of Melusine, and fair enough to grace the ramparts of Lusignan. It was all written, long ago.'

'Two days hence, you and I will say farewell for a while.'

Elizabeth, confused, said: 'Madame, you are leaving us?'

'Nay, it is you who will go. The time is full for you to visit the court. Queen Margaret will receive you into her service, she loves me well. Bear yourself discreetly; do the Queen's will in all things. Now come, and beg your father's pardon for last evening.'

Joyful, amazed, Elizabeth followed her mother. A summer storm was rising, gathering light from the lake. The Duchess of Bedford moved on under luminous clouds. The water rippled obeisance to her light passing. Her face was like a mask, beautiful, with a beauty that was worn, and knowing, and strong and evil.

> My lady's fair eyes
> Put Dame Venus to shame
> I drink to her name
> In mine own tears and sighs.
> I shrink from her scorn,
> Though 'tis sweet as her breath;
> Wellaway! I was born
> To a love sharp as death.

The scrap of verse, as usual unsigned, had been concealed in Elizabeth's dancing slipper. Reading it, she smiled impatiently; she knew from whom it came. Jocelyne de Hardwycke of Bolsover was constantly leaving such ditties in her path. She would find them tucked beneath her platter; they would flutter from her missal in the royal chapels of Westminster or Greenwich. These were the undying messages of courtly love, of which she had once dreamed so avidly, and which now, ironically, left her stifled with boredom. For Jocelyne only served to remind her of Grafton Regis, left far behind. Only a week after her arrival at court, she had looked up from her place at the board among Queen Margaret's gentlewomen straight into the lovelorn eyes of her childhood neighbour. Mary have mercy! she thought, letting the note fall to the floor; I played Hoodman Blind with him when I was six years old! She continued the slow contemplation of her reflection in the polished oval of bronze. Her hair, as she sat, hung almost to the floor. She combed with long, languorous strokes; the silvery mass crackled like a hundred small fires. The Queen would soon be summoning her and the others to wait on her for the evening. Behind Elizabeth, there was whispering; from Ismania Lady Scales, with her long upper lip and snapping dark eyes; from the ladies Butler and Dacre, both pretty, with simpering, vacuous mouths. They disliked her, and she did not care. Margaret Ross was there also; kindly Meg, the arbiter in squabbles. Elizabeth combed and combed, while the hostile air in the chamber sang like a lute. Ismania's face appeared, distorted by the mirror, behind her own.

'Dame, *we* would like to complete our toilette,' she said frigidly. Covertly Elizabeth watched her retrieve, and read, the dropped note. One of the ten little maids who were part of the Queen's personal retinue stood near, holding a bowl of rosewater, and Ismania flung herself round to face the child.

'By St. Denis! Renée! Do you know no better than to bring such as this into the chamber of virgins?'

Renée had been bribed by Jocelyne to secrete the note. Elizabeth watched while the child's eyes filled with tears. Ismania was the last to talk of virgins. Everyone knew that she had been jilted recently by a gentleman from Ireland and, desperate, had paid the herbman extortionately for a special receipt a fortnight ago.

'Corrupt, vile trash!' Ismania cried, tearing up the note. 'It is surely meant for none here.' She looked spitefully at Elizabeth's straight, slender back. 'Mayhap it is, though ... I've heard that in Northamptonshire virtue hides in the pigsty.'

Margaret Ross said, 'Hush!' and glanced anxiously at Elizabeth, who turned, smiling from the mirror and held out her hands to the bawling Renée.

'Dry your eyes, chuck.' Anger seethed within her like a hidden fiend, yet still she smiled. She pushed a dish of sugared violets towards the child. 'Fill your purse, sweeting, and then you may put up my hair.'

Renée crammed comfits into her mouth, knelt eagerly, gathering up the gilt fall of Elizabeth's hair. Dexterously she set to coiling the shining mass and covered it with a heartshaped, horned cap waiting on its stand by the mirror. Elizabeth rose at last from the only chair in the room. Her dress was of scarlet sarcenet, billowing below a gold cincture. Tiny marguerites, the Queen's device, were powdered on the skirt. The low bodice revealed a silken swell of flesh and the shadows between Elizabeth's breasts. On her first finger she wore the pearl-and-ruby rose, a parting gift from Jacquetta of Bedford. A single jewel hung from the veiling at her forehead; her eyes blazed blue fire. Ismania glared like a gargoyle.

'That is a most unseemly gown,' said Lady Dacre in a voice of hoar-frost. 'I beg you, Dame, raise the bodice a whit. The sight of all that flesh will turn me from my dinner!'

'Nay, leave it be,' said Ismania unexpectedly, and strangely agreeable. 'It is rumoured that the King will dine tonight.'

Elizabeth studied her ring, feeling uplifted. At last she would see the King, and not before time either, she thought. During the weeks she had been at court there had been that empty throne. She conjectured on the King's appearance. He must be at least thirty, yet surely handsome. Was he not the son of Harry of Agincourt?

'Where does the King go, these long whiles?' she asked Margaret Ross. 'To France? Ireland? Has he been negotiating about the war with York? What manner of man is he?'

Lady Ross was bathing her large hands in rosewater. 'The King is holy,' she said quietly. 'He knows naught of war. He has been to the shrine of Our Lady at Walsingham, and to Canterbury to gaze on the relics of blessed St. Thomas. As for his manner – you will see for yourself.'

There was a tap on the door. The Queen's page, Thomas Barnaby, was revealed.

'Mesdames, her Grace commands your presence in her bower.' Oddly smirking – 'King Henry's back.' His eye travelled over

Elizabeth's tight bodice and the milky upswept bosom. He gave a whistle. '*Ma foi*! Dame Woodville might be well advised not to ...'

Ismania rose quickly. 'Your pardon, Master Barnaby, but it grows late,' she cried. Like a full-sailed carvel, she surged across the room and out of it. 'Come, ladies!' she called over her shoulder. They followed her to the next apartment, where the Queen sat under a canopy of blue cloth-of-gold. There, the women knelt to kiss her hand. When the turn of Elizabeth came, she raised the hem of Margaret's gown to her lips in an especially gracious gesture.

The bower was airy and well appointed, but in other parts of the Palace of Westminster the hangings were in tatters and the furniture broken with age. The court was poor. By now Elizabeth had heard tales of the Queen's financial hardship. Although Margaret had come as a French princess to wed Henry of England, she had pawned her silver plate to buy food for her retinue on the journey through Mantes, Pontoise and Rouen. King Henry himself was in debt to the tune of ten thousand marks.

Yet this evening Margaret of Anjou was dressed in all her available finery. She was small; the hand with which she beckoned the women from their knees was scarcely larger than a child's and bore five heavy rings. Beneath a delicate diadem of fleur-de-lys gold, her fair hair hung free. From her purple mantle shone a broken mist of pearls. Pendent pearls wept on her sleeves and skirt forming a repeated motif of marguerites. In her mellow southern accent she greeted her ladies, while her small strong hand rested upon that of Elizabeth. She made no effort to conceal this mark of favour.

'*Bon soir, ma toute belle*,' she said. '*Tu es ravissante ce soir.*'

Elizabeth tried a discreet compliment in return. Margaret laughed.

'*Moi*' she said. '*C'est vanite!*' – disparaging her own beauty as a man might mock his certain vigour. Her face glowed. Elizabeth thought, romantically: Love for her returning lord illumines her.

'Dame Isabella–' still she addressed Elizabeth. 'This is your courtly name, and so we shall call you.'

She looked at the hand, with its one bright jewel, in hers. 'So! My pearl and ruby, which I gave to your mother, returns to court! *La sage Jacquette* served me well. Will you be as loyal, Isabella?'

'Always, Madame.' Elizabeth heard a tiny hiss of chagrin from Ismania standing behind her, and tried to check a smile.

'Ah, you laugh!' said the Queen. 'Doucette, I fear you are too gay for this dull court. We must find you a husband. Now, where is there a knight fittingly endowed for Isabella?'

Though the Queen spoke teasingly, Elizabeth's spirits fell. Sir Hugh Johns was now wed to a stout wealthy lady named Maud, but there could be others as glum and tiresome as he.

'I have seen Jocelyne de Hardwycke at Mass,' pursued Queen Margaret. 'At no time does he follow the holy writ; his eyes wander over to what he deems earthly Paradise. He is well-purveyed of lands, and the Stag, his father, grows old ...'

'Madame, I pray you,' said Elizabeth, disturbed. 'Jocelyne pays court to all. He loves only love!'

She should not interrupt the Queen, yet Margaret showed no annoyance. She said only: '*Bien*, Isabella. Perhaps it is better that you should choose your own husband. Your mother loved me well; I kept her close to me. *Sainte Vierge*! I above all, do not wish to lose you!'

She leaned and kissed Elizabeth, who thought, incredulously: the Queen does my will! My thanks, Mother, for the tale of your own love-match, of which Margaret must know. As she walked behind Margaret towards the great staircase leading to the Hall, she felt, for a moment, the stirrings of omnipotence, blinding and transient as a lightning flash.

A seneschal cried open the way before them, the clarions began their blazing fanfare. The Hall was crowded; Elizabeth, excited, had difficulty in matching her steps to the Queen's slow tread. At the door she fell back so that Sir John Wenlock, the chamberlain, could escort Margaret to the chair of estate. Elizabeth walked beside Ismania, who smiled sweetly. Carelessly, she smiled back.

'Since your are so beloved, Isabella,' whispered Ismania. You must take my place at the board. I'll sit lower down.'

She urged her forward, saying, still smiling: 'Sit nearest the dais; thus you will see the King's Grace better.'

They proceeded the length of the crammed Hall, between the trestles set to seat two hundred knights and ladies as well as the esquires, bishops, priests and clerks who by various means had contrived an invitation to the King's homecoming banquet. To right and left jewels and velvet shimmered, threadbare tapestries billowed under the gale of courtiers bowing in reverence to the Queen's passing. To the left of the throne, servers scampered in and out of the buttery with loaded dishes. Queen Margaret seated herself in one of the two chairs of estate. The other was still vacant. Close behind her seat stood three of her chief ministers: Piers de Brezé, the great French general; Lord Clifford, arrogant and black-browed, and the old white-haired Earl of Shrewsbury, the Great Talbot. Beneath the cloth of estate and further down was another empty chair.

'Tis the Queen's wish.' Margaret Ross leaned forward to whisper. 'In memory of Suffolk.'

Yes. Suffolk, butchered by Yorkists on Portsmouth's strand. Jacquetta's voice had held vehemence. For the first time Elizabeth wondered about war. If the Queen's heart were sore enough to honour thus one dead captain, might she not seek revenge on York? Was Richard of York as quiescent as his recent oath of fealty would have men believe? The clarions brayed again, as if for a call to arms.

'Way for the King's Grace! Here enters his Grace King Henry the Sixth, lord of England and Ireland ...'

Down the Hall came a small procession of men. Elizabeth craned to look. Here was the King; none was crowned, but she picked him out. His hair was quite grey; he was tall, broad, slim in the waist. A white scar on his cheek, and eyes so dark a grey that they were almost black. Bronzed skin, and an ironic, humorous mouth. So handsome; a fit mate for Margaret. He wore sapphire velvet, and the Lancastrian collar of 'S's gleamed goldly on his chest. The King – or was he the King after all? – knelt before Margaret and remained in obeisance, as did two younger men, whose faces were hidden. Another, whom Elizabeth had not even noticed, ascended unsteadily to the Queen's side. He might, she thought, staring, have been some humble clerk drawn by mistake into the royal party. He was thin, bowed, solemn, and clad entirely in dusty black. His narrow head and ears were covered by a cap of the same black stuff, his only jewels a great tarnished reliquary swinging at his breast. In a milk-white melancholy face, grey, lustreless eyes surveyed the company disinterestedly. From her close proximity, Elizabeth watched him with disbelief. Could this be the heir of Agincourt? She watched the Queen take one of his limp pale hands and kiss it.

With difficulty she dragged her gaze away as food was set before her; steaming breast of partridge with a sweet pepper sauce, eels stewed in almond milk. Thomas Barnaby filled her hanap with the wine of Anjou. Across the Hall, Jocelyne de Hardwycke lifted his cup and blew a soundless kiss towards her. Ismania Lady Scales leaned back in her chair and called, over the tumult of resumed conversation: 'Do you see the King, Isabella? Does he see you?' Then she laughed, a knowing, dangerous laugh. Elizabeth felt a surge of annoyance. The King, she observed, had given no sign of seeing her yet, and she resolved to make him look at her. He would acknowledge her finery, and devil damn Ismania!

The King was talking in a loud voice that contrasted with his frail appearance. The handsome scar-faced man knelt smiling at his side.

'By St. John!' said the King. 'What a throng are here this day! I am weary from the pilgrimage. At Walsingham they have phials of Our Lady's blessed milk—' he crossed himself '—but I had no money. All last night I lay before the shrine. By St. John! I had me much ghostly comfort from it. Nay, nay,' waving a steward away. 'No wine. Wine makes madmen and fools.'

The knight with the scar poured the Queen's wine; she smiled at him, while the King maundered on, glancing over the Hall as if in a dream. Elizabeth sat up straight. She dipped a bunch of grapes in wine and ate them sensuously, her eyes fixed on the dais, and at last caught Henry's attention. He looked long at her, then, his face whiter still, beckoned her nearer. With one triumphant backward glance at Ismania she moved gracefully forward, and sank deeply before the King in homage.

'Who is this?' he said in a high, querulous tone. The Queen answered softly: "My kinswoman, Isabella Woodville, does you solemn duty here, your Grace.'

Elizabeth raised her eyes and smiled at the King. She could see the large smudge of ash on his forehead. So he did penance – for what? She realized suddenly that he had no smile in answer to hers. He rose slowly, eyes bulging. With a shaking finger, he pointed at the silken square of Elizabeth's bosom, exposed in the candlelight.

'Forsooth!' he cried. 'Look! Look!' he commanded the whole company. 'My court becomes a nest of harlots!' Eyes still riveted to Elizabeth's bosom: 'Forsooth, have you no shame? By St. John!' He shook his finger at Elizabeth, who drew back, gasped, and burst into tears.

Henry turned upon the Queen. Tears stood in his eyes, his voice became a shriek. 'And ye, madam! Ye be much to blame!' To Elizabeth, who was weeping copiously: 'Whore of Babylon! Blasphemer!'

Elizabeth turned and ran down the Hall, and the King sprang from his dais and, crying aloud, rushed in the opposite direction, disappearing through the buttery. She did not linger to see where he went. Tears streaming, she fled, past Ismania's smile of utter triumph, away from Jocelyne's sympathetic face, and out from the Hall, through the ranked heralds and guard. She ran upstairs and along cool stone galleries until she reached her chamber.

Behind in the Hall, the scar-faced man bent to Queen Margaret and whispered. When she nodded, her face troubled and angry, he turned to one of the young esquires who had, throughout, been hovering near the steps of the dais.

'By St. John!' he mocked. 'John, is she not fair? Think you that you can comfort her?'

There was no mockery in the young man's answer.

'For the rest of my life,' he said softly. 'Now, I'll not trouble her, she is too distressed. Yes, she is fair.' He glanced at Margaret with a lifted eyebrow, a peculiarly sweet smile. 'Fair as a Queen.'

Long after it had grown dark, Elizabeth sat on the floor of her chamber. The tear-stained scarlet dress lay beside her and she wore an old grey gown, high at the throat and pinned with a brooch which stabbed her neck whenever she moved. All was deathly quiet. For the past hour there had been faint sounds ascending from the Hall; the sweet wail of the viële, the rasping reed of the cromorne, and occasional half-hearted laughter. Now the revel was over, but the other women had not returned. She felt cold; the river mist was rising around the Palace and there was the first touch of autumn about. It seemed to penetrate the chamber, deepening her humiliation with its dank breath.

At first she had imagined wildly the whole court discussing her. She endowed the blaze of gaping faces with cynical smiles, she saw them asking one another her name and dismissing her with the deathly sign once used above the arenas of Rome. Then, as time passed and her panic gave way to sorrow, fury at Ismania, and finally numb despair, she realized that her fears were possibly groundless. The whole disaster had been over swiftly; she had knelt before the King only for as long as it had taken Queen Margaret to consume a handful of sugared rose-leaves. She had not even taken a full reconnaisance of the other faces around the dais; their reaction was unknown. A fleeting image of the scar-faced man nudged her mind; from him she had caught a flash of real appreciation, from a man who loved pretty women in gay dresses. Mary have mercy! Realization struck at her. A normal man. Again and again she saw the chalkfaced King, a film of spittle on his lip, eyes protruding as if he were being strangled. In God's name, what kind of a King was he? That crust of ashes on his forehead marked him as a saint, yet he had accused her vilely, unjustly. He had railed likewise at his Queen. 'Madam! ye be much to blame!' Margaret's face had darkened swiftly; she had dashed one glance towards the scar-faced man. Though he had come from pilgrimage with the King he had seemed apart from Henry, he had served only the Queen with wine. She wondered vaguely at his name and lineage. Now she would never know, for the King would surely dismiss her from court. Ismania's laughter rang silently in her mind. For the first time she longed for her mother; the austere comfort, the powerful presence, Jacquetta's strange philosophies.

'Melusine.' She spoke the name aloud.

The room became quieter still, as if it waited for an answer. Then, far below, the river's lapping voice grew louder, surging about the thick walls, drifting on mist. She rubbed her wrists, her flesh stared in points of chill. Somewhere a night-bird cried mournfully, and it seemed as if the dark chamber were full of swirling fog. She thought ardently upon Jacquetta's rune-like wisdom. *She lives in us. She fortifies us. Receive her power.*

'Melusine,' Elizabeth whispered. 'I am your child.'

A shudder assailed her. From the time when she had been old enough to lisp the responses in the Mass, she had been familiar with the punishments awaiting heretics. The fiery eternity of torture, justly applied by a fierce God. Heat stronger than ten thousand candle-flames. Even on earth, they burned you if you forsook the old saints, the law-givers. Folk said that that pain was over quickly, if the faggots were green and the smoke thick. Not so with the fires of Hell. There, you burned for ever.

And then the strength and horror of these matchless doctrines ebbed utterly into the silence, a darker deeper silence through which she said softly:

'I need one to protect me.' Because she spoke to an empty room she laughed, to chase fear. She thought of Jocelyne de Hardwycke more seriously than ever before. He was the son of a powerful lord, and none would insult her with Jocelyne as husband. He was well-favoured and courtly, and he was for Lancaster. Truly, she had dreamed of love, the *coup de foudre*, the unmistakable face of love; but love was only a small part of life. She might well wed Jocelyne. The Queen would raise her brows at this *volte-face*, but she would doubtless be pleased after all.

'So, send me a husband, Melusine,' she said more boldly. The night-bird cried again. In her mind, she added: And let him be kind, and let me be loved more than any woman.

The feeling of cold had left her. Almost banteringly she continued, her voice thrown back from the stone walls: 'And bring Ismania a punishment for mocking me; only a light one!' she added hast-ily. Although this was but a game, played for comfort's sake, even games could go awry. A sudden banging on the door sent her to her feet. In the doorway, ringed by light from the fiery cresset he carried stood the page, Barnaby. He called: 'Anyone there? Ho! Dame Woodville?'

He entered, warily looking about him, and saw her.

'All alone, my dame?' He looked her over, smiled foolishly. 'You've changed your gown. I liked t'other better.'

'Spare me your likes and dislikes, Master Tom,' said Elizabeth stiffly. 'Where are the ladies?'

'Below, playing at cards with your love-lorn knight,' he replied. 'As for your gowns, *I* tried to warn you of the King's humour.' He yawned, losing interest. 'Come with me now. God's nails, I am weary worn.'

'Come with you where?'

'To the Queen. She commands it.'

Renewed dismay filled her. Margaret was enraged. And was the King with her, ready to shriek fresh dreadful words? Trembling, she asked the page. He laughed raucously.

'Nay, sweet dame. He's in chapel and likely to be there all night. Saying a novena, he is.'

She bound up her hair while Barnaby held the light steady before the mirror. She straightened her gown and followed the page through long passages with arched vaulting and faded gilt columns to where the guard stood drowsily to attention outside the Queen's apart-ments. They passed through the outer chamber of reception and through another door into the Queen's retiring room, where she chose to renew herself with entertainment, or conferred with her ministers. Beyond yet another door lay her bedchamber. Elizabeth entered uneasily. The Queen was seated on a carved chair of Spanish walnut and she had changed her gown to a pale azure robette. Ermine fringed her throat, her face was pale. Two men, of which one was the knight with the scar, stood behind her, studying a parchment loosely held on Margaret's lap. Master Francis, the Queen's physician, mixed a draught at a side table, and Margaret Chamberlain, the royal dressmaker, was folding the purple mantle into a coffer. On cushions near the Queen's feet a maiden of about nine years sat alone with a chessboard.

Elizabeth knelt. Barnaby, self-possessed and slightly truculent, prostrated himself before the Queen and said, with his face against the parti-coloured tiles:

'My liege, here's Dame Woodville. And I can't find your dog.'

The scarred man said quickly: 'Her Grace's dog is lost?' Margaret smiled wistfully. 'Yes, my lord. Dulcinea, the lovely bitch you gave me. She was frightened by the clarions and ran away.' To the page: 'Barnaby, go. Search further.' Then she beckoned Elizabeth. There was the Queen's hand under her lips, a smell of jasmine, kindness.

'My poor Isabella!'

The Queen was not wroth. She bade her rise. Ashamed no longer, she looked squarely about, at the men behind Margaret's chair, and at the chess-playing child. Hers was a strange face; long and aware; the small, snapping black eyes were old in wisdom. The Queen said:

'My lords, I would present my most affectionate kinswoman, Dame Isabella Woodville. His Grace, James Earl of Wiltshire' (tall, swarthy, a saffron tunic – he kissed her in courtly fashion) 'and my dear cousin–' the Queen's voice became heavy, as if her throat pained her – 'Edmund Beaufort, Earl of Somerset.'

The scar added to his attractiveness. He, too, kissed Elizabeth, and drew back smiling.

'*Ma foi*! there's naught so lovely as a blonde maiden! But even your Rhineland fairness, Dame Isabella, cannot quench the daisy-flower!'

And his smile was turned on the Queen, as he fingered the gilt marguerites he wore about his neck. Elizabeth thought: so this is Beaufort, York's chief enemy. Warwick, so men say, hates him too. I shall therefore love him as if he were my kin. The old-faced child got up and stood beside her.

'This is my niece, the Lady Margaret Beaufort,' said the Earl. Playfully he pinched the unsmiling little face. 'The cleverest mortal alive. Lucretius, Tacitus, Suetonius, Sallust; all are her bedfellows. Dame Isabella, my gold collar for your neck if you can beat her at chess!'

Solemnly the Lady Margaret set the ivory men in the initial position. Elizabeth hesitated. There was something to be said first, expiation to be made for her dress, her flight from the Hall.

'Your Grace, permit ...'

The Queen read her troubled face. 'Nay, Isabella, it was no fault of yours. The King...' She paused. Suddenly she looked paler, and ill.

'The King is holy,' said Beaufort of Somerset. He turned to the physician. 'Master Francis, is her Grace's draught ready?'

The doctor presented a small vial. Beaufort forestalled the Queen's hand, and swilled a little of the potion round his mouth.

'Camphor and poppy, naught else,' said Master Francis. 'Her Grace will sleep soundly.'

'Two drops,' said Beaufort. 'Two drops only. The rest is danger.'

The physician bowed and quit the chamber, and the dressmaker, her work finished, went also. Elizabeth fidgeted. Lady Margaret was waiting, eyeing her shrewdly from the spread chessboard.

'Shall I play, your Grace?'

The Queen looked absently up from Beaufort's hand, which still held the little vial.

'Yes, Isabella. I sent for you because you were sad. Now you must be happy. The King ... the King is frail, and prone to shocks that others do not comprehend. We must protect the King.' Her eyelids dropped again. Her gaze rested on Beaufort's bronzed hand.

Elizabeth sat on the cushion opposite Lady Margaret, and, looking into the sharp eyes, knew instinctively that she would be beaten. The child went to the game with ice-cold foresight, like a military campaigner, while above their heads, the Queen held a conversation with her two ministers. It became apparent that they had forgotten the existence of both Elizabeth and Beaufort's young kinswoman.

'By God's Passion! He lost his gown again at Canterbury,' Beaufort was saying. 'He gave it away to a poor friar, a thin fellow who took such a liking to it that half my money went in its recovery.'

The Queen drew in her breath, as if she were in pain.

'*Pardieu, le pauvre Roi!*' she said softly.

'*La pauvre Angleterre,*' muttered the Earl of Wiltshire, and bit his lip. Lady Margaret moved her King to the right, and almost smiled.

Elizabeth sat, her eyes fixed on the chessboard, listening.

'I mentioned to him once more Richard of York,' continued Beaufort. 'He's dangerous; I'll not forget his face when he saw me in the King's tent at Blackheath; by the Rood!–' he laughed arrogantly – 'York was sure I had been banished. The King's Grace knew not what he did when he summoned me once more. I thought that York would fall in an apoplexy, that day last February.'

'Nay, he knew not what he did,' said Margaret slowly. Elizabeth advanced her pawn two squares and looked covertly at the Queen's troubled face.

'Better than York have failed to quell me,' said Beaufort of Somerset with a chuckle. 'Yet he is far from conquered, and so I told the King, who replied: 'By St. John! Richard Plantagenet gave me his word, in holy St. Paul's, to keep the peace, to raise no troops, and be forever obedient. All the saints witnessed his sacred oath.' Then it was that he bestowed his mantle on that puling friar.'

'Is the Duke still at Fotheringhay?' asked James of Wiltshire.

'Yes. My scurriers report his standard flying there. His Duchess is again with child.'

Lady Margaret Beaufort, taking advantage of Elizabeth's inattention, put her King in safety and brought her Rook into play. The Queen sighed.

'So Proud Cis is *enceinte*,' she murmured. 'Doubtless with another son. Well, Isabella?' She had caught Elizabeth's eyes upon her unguarded face. Guiltily, the other answered: 'I was but musing, Madame.'

'Musing on what?' the Queen said stiffly. Elizabeth babbled: 'Why, your Grace, husbands ... I thought, if it should please you, I will take Sir Jocelyne after all.' It was the first refuge she could think of. The Queen's face eased instantly. Beaufort of Somerset laid a light hand on Elizabeth's shoulder.

'Isabella,' he said. 'Marriage is but a licking of honey off thorns. You will have many eager to plight their troth. Wait a little while.'

The Queen rose. 'I am weary,' she said. 'This evening was not a glad occasion. We must devise some entertainment – a fair, a joust. Yes, a joust!'

The two Earls agreed heartily, and Elizabeth, who had never seen a tournament, was overjoyed. The anticipation lingered, after she had bidden the Queen good night, and had congratulated the impassive little Lady Margaret on her victory. Light-hearted, she made her way back to her own apartments. Beaufort walked some little way behind her; she was embarrassed in case he did not wish for her company so went faster, her small shadow and his tall one thrown in wavering procession on the walls.

At the staircase she saw Queen Margaret's dog. A slim little whippet that had been frightened by the noisy trumpets, and cowered and snarled as she bent to pick it up. Beaufort came quietly up behind her.

'I will take the beast,' he said, quite roughly, and scooped it, thin and trembling, up into his arms. He began to walk slowly back towards the Queen's chambers. The torches were flaming brightly and the Palace was quiet, so that Elizabeth saw how he buried his face in the little dog's neck and heard his broken, passionate whisper.

'Marguerite! My Marguerite!'

Barnaby met Elizabeth at her door. He was in a fury. He had been awakened from snatched sleep to summon the leech to Ismania Lady Scales, who was vomiting and purging. They could find no reason for her malady. It was quite unaccountable, like the work of some mischievous spirit.

She rode to the jousting ground in a litter with the Countess of Somerset and Lady Margaret Beaufort, and she was pleased that the other ladies were somewhere behind in the entourage, more subordinate than she, the Queen's chosen lady. That evening in Margaret's private apartments was a covenant of favour which none could gainsay. Her mind often returned to it; to the soft, quicksand conversation going on above her head; to the Queen's kindness; to her own extraordinary witness of Beaufort in the passage giving way to the festering wound of a forbidden emotion. She held that scene in her heart, like the tales of the old Court of Love.

Upon the rough road the litter swayed suddenly and she was thrown against the stiff brocade side of the Countess of Somerset, who smiled dreamily. What would you say, my lady, if I told you that your lord loves the Queen? She knew, without asking, the answer: We all love her, Dame Isabella. God strengthen her.

'Is this your first tourney, Madame?' Lady Margaret Beaufort's pompous voice broke through. She sat, small and composed, with a massive brow and those dark eyes that probed calmly. Beside her, her aunt the Countess looked ruffled and homely; sweat gleamed on her pink cheek, for it was warm in the litter. The Beaufort maiden continued to study Elizabeth. To avoid the penetration of that look, she bent her head and gazed through the window let into the side of the barrel-shaped carriage. London Bridge, with its row of felons' heads rotting over the drawbridge, lay seven miles behind, and the sparkling river had coiled beside them and finally withdrawn. Now the procession passed on down the long rutted road to Eltham. The way was divided by quickset hedges; fields sprawled on either side, peopled by scores of peasants. They watched as the royal train, with its banners and blazoned arms, went by. They dragged off their caps and knelt in duty as the King, black-clad as usual, rode mournfully past; but as the litter bearing Queen Margaret rolled by, a man, tall, ragged-bearded, took one pace forward and spat covertly towards the daisy-flower emblem. The Countess of Somerset was leaning back with closed eyes, but Lady Margaret Beaufort missed nothing.

'The fellow is a madman. None the less, had I the power I should have him instantly beheaded.'

Elizabeth glanced at her and could well believe it.

'It is because the Queen's Grace is too *French*,' pursued the diminutive maiden. 'Doubtless that churl's father fought at Agincourt. Now that our French possessions are well nigh lost, he feels the sting.' With a candour that made Elizabeth gasp, she said: 'And of course, the Queen has no issue to set on England's throne. She'll not find favour until such time as she bears a prince.' Musing, she said again: 'Yea, I would have that oaf butchered where he stands. Or better, have his tongue out so he can spit no more.'

She seemed set fair for a long homily. Elizabeth frowned. She would rather not hear of tongue-cuttings and butchery; her spirits were high. Her gown was a poem in dull pink and gold, she wore a new curved cap given by the Queen as a reward for one of Jacquetta's old receipts. Lately the Queen had been smitten by pains in her breast.

'Take woodsage and horehound equally much. Stamp them and temper them with wine and drink it three days fasting.'

This leechcraft she had shown to the Queen, and Margaret had been pleased. She had been raising the cup to her lips when Beaufort of Somerset entered. As before, with the sleeping potion, he had nipped the vessel from her hand to taste it with a fierce concentration. Then, nodding, he had thrown one of his bronzed smiles in Elizabeth's direction, and had allowed the sovereign to drink.

'If my lord has an evil of the breast, I can cure it,' Elizabeth said, nervously jesting. 'My mother swears on this draught.'

'And for a pain in the heart?' Still Beaufort smiled, but as if the smile hurt him. 'Has *la sage Jacquette* simples to drive that ill away? Potions to steady the weight of government upon a frail head? Herbs against the canker of a realm divided?'

'My lord?' She had looked at him, only half-comprehending the reason for his sudden savagery. Then unexpectedly, King Henry had entered the chamber with John Faceby, his own doctor and the inevitable retinue of sombre-clad priests and monks. He had shuffled across to take the Queen's hand as a child might seek the clasp of its mother. He had given Elizabeth one glance that held no recognition of the fact that she was even female, much less that the last time she had so desperately offended the eye. He was, she thought, an enigma.

The procession halted at the tiltyard. At the head of the line, Henry was squired from his horse. This day they had managed to part him from his black skull-cap, and a thin diadem on his head caught the sun in a sad little flash of fire. He murmured to himself, a prayer, and his eyes roamed to the great loges which had been built for the spectators on either side of the lists, to the flaring pennoncelles surmounting each pavilion, and to the royal standard above his own state canopy. He looked, and murmured, then cast his eyes down at the velvety grass, where his gaze remained.

'Come, your Grace,' said Beaufort crisply. Henry stood, pointing to something in the grass, visible only to himself, for all the lords peered, mystified. Then, urged, he took one faltering step, and another, and walked towards the royal loge, while heralds sounded his advance.

Elizabeth stood poised upon the step of the litter, stunned by the gaudy scene; the surging colours of tapestry and standard, the tall pavilions flinging round shadows on the emerald grass. A small figure in her wild-rose dress and golden cap, she gazed at the panoply of mock war; the great destriers caparisoned to the hoof in cloth of gold and silver, the knights already armed for the tourney, unwieldy yet magnificent in their ceremonial harness; the hundred different arms displayed on bright shield and pennon. The King, now joined by Queen Margaret in slow procession across the ground and seeming comforted by her presence; the Queen herself, divinely encompassed in a mist of teardrop pearls and silver tissue. Beaufort and his son Edmund; Piers de Brezé, James of Wiltshire, the Duke of Buckingham, and the Great Talbot, with his white head and veteran armour. Elizabeth looked only at the royal pair, the principal courtiers; those who stood in shadow went unnoticed. She did not see, very near and fixed upon her, the unknown eyes of love.

The young man in the sky-coloured tunic had waited long, yet at the shattering moment of seeing her emerge from the litter he felt the impact so keenly that he actually shivered and signed his breast with the Cross. Had any asked his reason he might have laughed, muttered that he was safeguarding his soul from too much beauty; or that he summoned the saints to protect this woman from all ill; or that he invoked the blessing of God, Our Lady, and even the pagan Venus, upon his own heart-tearing love.

That she had never noticed him, and indeed had not done so on the night when she had fled weeping from the King's displeasure, did not trouble him unduly. So often had he possessed her in his mind that already it seemed she was wholly his. Had he been told otherwise, he would have been inconsolable, and bemused as a dreamer roughly roused. He was Beaufort's esquire, he was just twenty years old, and he had never been in love. The posturing amours of court life were to him empty and meaningless. Likewise he had so far escaped the more serious affair of a politic marriage, shaped for the annexation of property and the enhancement of family power. His enthusiasms had lain with soldiering; his horsemanship, unequalled among his peers, and his courage bordering on rashness, were celebrated. Until the night when he had returned with Beaufort from escorting the King's pilgrimage, his mind had been steadfastly applied to the pursuit of knighthood. Although, unlike many of his fellow esquires, he owned no crazy lust for blood, he had followed with interest the machinations of the House of York, in the vague hope that one day he might show his prowess in battle. Given a stout horse, he fancied himself, not without a little wry humour, leading a victorious charge. Beaufort inspired him, although the Earl, it seemed, had come close of late to breaking his knightly word. He had promised to send his esquire to Calais as emissary and scurrier, for there was information to be gleaned there regarding the humours of France and Burgundy, and the prospect was inviting. Yet this promise had been given a twelvemonth ago, and was not yet fulfilled.

Now, Calais meant nothing. Life was changed utterly, and it was Beaufort himself who had been the catalyst. For the Queen had sent word of her new gentlewoman, and Beaufort had been inspired to speak of her beauty to others. The reality of Elizabeth had been a shock; she was fairer than rumoured, as the vision of a saint out-matches the written legend.

He had never seen a saint, but he had seen Elizabeth, and found in her the distilled essence of his unimagined dreams. Now, at Eltham, she passed before him for a second time, and the whole scene wavered into mist around her, leaving her as the jewelled core, twice as bright, twice as lovely, and the bringer of soft tears.

So did John Grey, son of Lord Ferrers of Groby, stand with the filmed eyes of love, to watch his lady shining in the sun.

She descended from the litter with the Countess and her niece. Outside the jousting ground, folk had come to watch the sport through knotholes in the palisade. There were a few mendicant friars, a cluster of sore-ridden beggars, and some amateur entertainers, jug-glers, a bear stumbling on a chain. Near the entrance were a half-dozen gypsies, darkeyed and filthy. One, a woman, broke from the rest and ran towards Elizabeth. Thomas Barnaby cursed her, dealing blows from his staff, but she dodged him and threw herself down before the three ladies.

'Your future, worships, for a handful of silver!'

'Silver be damned,' growled Barnaby. The woman knelt upright, eyes knowing and unafraid, rat-gnawed kirtle stained with berry juice. Lady Margaret Beaufort held a muskball to her nose against the gypsy's earthy reek. Yet Elizabeth looked for a moment into the strange eyes with their courage and calmness, and heard the woman say, softly:

'Why don't you wear your proper token, my lady?' The eyes were set upon Elizabeth's brooch, the tree-root emblem of the Bedfords, enclosed in a pearl frame. The woman moved closer, emitting the scent of woodsmoke and rank herbs.

'The serpent,' she whispered. 'The beautiful serpent. You have her face. Earth, Fire, Air, Water; the last is yours.'

Elizabeth turned to Barnaby. 'Give her money.' The gypsy spoke again, unhesitatingly; a little rhyme.

'A royal prince, fair lady, shalt thou wed,
But troubles dire shall fall upon thine head.'

She turned from Elizabeth, but it was still for her that she spoke.

She looked at Lady Margaret, haughty and fretful, and at the smiling, docile Countess of Somerset. Then her glance went to the royal standard, and finally back to Elizabeth.

'Bone of they bone shall by a future fate,
With blood of these three houses surely mate.'

Then she clawed the coin reluctantly given her by Barnaby into her bosom and darted back into the swell of people. Disappointment filled Elizabeth. The rhyme had come too glibly. It was all nonsense, and a waste of silver. Barnaby was pulling her out of the path of a dozen horses, ridden by brilliantly armoured knights and surging towards the tiltyard. The breeze fanned banners to a blaze. Barnaby cried: 'Tis the Tudor knights!' They walked on across the green towards the loges and Barnaby said: 'My lord Edmund, and my lord Jasper. Owen, the third brother, sports not.'

'Owen is a monk,' said Margaret Beaufort's clipped voice. 'So he jousts only with the saints. Edmund, Dame Isabella–' she turned with great dignity – 'is my future husband. It is arranged. He is the King's half-brother, as you know.'

All knew, but Margaret could not resist pressing the point. One of the popular scandals was the old love-tale of Owen Tudor the elder, the humble Welsh esquire who had wheedled his way into the chamber of Queen Katherine, the widow of Harry of Agincourt. Owen had a singing voice to shame the birds, and bright gold hair. Folk said that Queen Katherine had a taint of madness; her father, Charles the Sixth of France, had been utterly lunatic. Thus they acquitted her fall from chastity. Her kingly son, the holy Henry, now made all well. Here were the Tudors, fruit of that old treasonous coupling, riding to the joust, welcome at the court. They had inherited little of their father's comeliness; both were thin and sallow and Jasper's mouth was cruel. They gave fair greeting to the King and Queen, who sat beneath their canopy while the contestants finished arming in the pavilions below. Taking her seat near the royal loge, Elizabeth heard the King's clear brittle voice.

'By St. John! I behold all my household knights! Why have we no foreign guests here this day?'

Beaufort, his foot upon the stair of the loge, said gently: 'There was little time to send ambassadors, your Grace. The Queen devised this tourney for your pleasure.'

'Yes, 'twas kindly thought,' said the King vaguely. 'By St. John! Let not the sport be too rough, though. Men have been slain in joust.'

Margaret leaned to him. 'Sire, will you give the signal?' The marshals were waiting with their white wands poised and the line of heralds had trumpets at shoulder height. The King nodded, and was about to raise his hand in which he held a gilded staff, when a commotion at the entrance to the lists diverted him. The whole company grew instantly alert; they rose a little from their seats, they whispered. They turned to one another and then back again to look, with expressions of incredulity, anger, and mirth, at the mounted men who rode on to the green. There were three knights, and the standards borne above them flaunted as if they bragged a challenge into the teeth of the wind. The snap of their colours drew all eyes; around the lists the whispers became a murmuring roar. Followed by a few esquires, the three cantered across the sward, and the banners leaped above them. Blazoned upon the air-flung silk was the fetterlock of York, next to it the device of Lord Salisbury, and, flaring so that its shadow ramped towards the royal dais, the snarling Bear and Ragged Staff of Warwick. Over their half-armour the three knights wore mantles starred with the White Rose of York.

'Here,' said Beaufort to the King, 'would seem to be your foreign guests, my liege.'

Henry rose uncertainly and sat down again. The Queen showed anger. Briefly all her beauty vanished, leaving an expression of keen malevolence; her eyes became suffused with blood and the sweetness of her lips assumed a vitriolic line. A dangerous face; even as it faded and was replaced by her customary calmness, its memory was awesome. Slowly the three knights dismounted and walked towards the royal loge. They drew off their velvet caps and knelt. Warwick's mantle parted to show two crests; two helms facing each other, one bearing the Beauchamp Swan for Warwick the other the Griffin of Montagu, for Salisbury. Richard of York came forward first to kiss the King's hand. He was small and slight, with a high-boned, determined face. Dark hair with reddish lights fell to his shoulders, and his eyes were a clear, fanatical blue. Salisbury behind him was blond, more obviously Plantagenet, with great height and breadth of shoulder. Warwick, with the sureness of one who draws all eyes, came last to the dais. Like his father of Salisbury, he was tall and strong. His adamantine will was apparent in the long, clean-shaven chin and the grey eyes which, though large as a woman's, had a glittering, hawkish fire. Through a long silence the King spoke doubtfully.

'God's greeting to my lords. Why are you come? I fear we are all unready for you.'

Barnaby, picking his teeth, said, in a voice loud enough to make heads turn: 'God's Tongue! Why does he speak thus, unwarily? There's much truth in *politesse* ...'

Warwick rose toweringly. His rose-dappled mantle swirled; black hair curled on his brow. Everything of him was puissant and challenging and might have said: Behold us! We of the blood royal, of Edward the Third ...

'My liege, we heard there was a joust,. and have humbly come to see the sport. Also–' he paused, enough to weight his words – 'we wondered eagerly on your Grace's health.'

'The King is well.' Queen Margaret answered, swiftly, coldly.

Warwick turned smiling to the Duke of York, 'Then, our hearts rejoice, eh, Dick? These rumours should be hanged at birth, like wantless pups ... 'twas said your Grace was ailing.'

'News of this joust has travelled fast,' said Beaufort of Somerset slowly. 'It was arranged very recently; a privy affair.'

Warwick said, into the wind: 'My lord of Somerset is skilled in knowledge of privy affairs. So much that others–' he indicated Richard of York – 'reck not what transpires in the royal Chamber of Council, though they have every right! And the fancies that are spread! for one, that in England, fair women rule ...'

Beaufort's face turned to angry chalk. But the King answered, amiable, artless: 'By St. John! I know not what men say! At Walsingham lately I had a sign. If my lords do but love one another, all will be well. Will you ride in the tourney, my lords? Some of my knights lack an adversary. My lord of Somerset is keen to pledge a great spear against a worthy opponent.'

'Nay, my liege,' said Warwick easily. 'This day we are not equipped. But I'll touch steel with you, my lord of Somerset.' The breeze blew his hair into serpent coils and his jaw tensed. 'Another time. Gladly.'

The King laughed, a high, irrational sound. His eyes wandered mazedly over the three knights. He said suddenly: 'And Richard of York? Well, cousin? How does your lady wife, the Rose of Raby?'

Again, Warwick was the spokesman.

'Thriving, both long and large,' he said lovingly. 'There's no more goodly sight than a fair woman great with child!'

And his eyes travelled insultingly over the Queen, her weasel waist and boyish breasts. She sat up straight, whitefaced as Beaufort, and the tear-drop pearls on her bodice quivered with her hard breathing. Warwick said musingly:

'Children! they are strange creatures, my liege. Why, only lately, my cousin of York's young son, Edward of March – but ten years old – talked of leading an army ... all fancy, certes, yet what fiery blood! As if the spirit of dead warriors moves the child!'

The Countess of Somerset gasped. 'Jesu!' she whispered to Elizabeth. 'The dogs make no effort to hide their aspirations to the Crown. Why does the King suffer this goading?'

Henry said gently: 'Will you be with us long, my lords?'

Richard of York answered in his mellow, distinct voice: 'Alas, your Grace must give us leave to ride as soon as the sport is finished. I must to Fotheringhay again.'

Salisbury added, laughing richly: 'Yes, Sire. We save our strength. I promise you shall see us riding, armed, one day!'

'For God's love, start the tourney,' breathed the Countess of Somerset. She looked appealingly at her husband and motioned towards the marshals, waiting with their white wands. Beaufort nodded and bent to whisper in the King's ear. A look of utter blankness crossed Henry's face. He looked up at the banners, the horsed knights waiting, their rich armour winking strongly at each pavilion. Esquires hung desperately on the bridles of excited horses. The King looked down at the green grass, as if seeking a sign, and was dumb.

'Will you be seated, my lords?' said Queen Margaret, in a voice like frozen rain. Warwick, Salisbury and York bent the knee again and withdrew. Elizabeth saw them advancing towards her own loge, Warwick growing bigger, taller, filling her sight. She shrank closer to the Countess, her eyes riveted upon the enemy's steel and velvet, the reddish aureole of York's flowing hair, Salisbury's strength. Her disquiet grew. Mary have mercy! Warwick was taking his place in the loge beside her. She turned her face away, while the Countess, shaking with indignation, inclined her head stiffly and murmured a cool greeting to the Earl. Then, she heard him say:

'Madame, you do not present me to this lady?'

She heard the 'Countess's reply. Because there was no help for it, she turned and looked straight into Warwick's eyes. Yes, she said inwardly; this man is danger. This powerful renegade is truly my foe.

'Dame Woodville. So, Madame, we meet.'

He was that rarity; a man who looked at her without admiration.

'I had hoped,' he said deliberately, 'to have had a reply to my letter in your own hand, not your mother's. I had imagined also that it would be far different from the one I received.'

So Jacquetta had given him a straight answer. Haughtily Elizabeth replied: 'Sir, I thank you for your interest in my affairs, but the matter is closed.' She looked again towards the royal loge, where Beaufort and the Queen bent to King Henry, who gazed dreamily still at some mystery in the grass. It was an ant, carrying an egg on its back, and he appeared to be talking to it.

'The King seems *distrait*,' remarked Warwick.

On the sward below, the first contestants, James Earl of Wiltshire and the Duke of Buckingham, sat their horses, holding great foil-tipped lances couched. The breeze fluttered the destriers' housings, and the Earl's beast pawed with a massive hoof. The trumpeters waited, silent. And suddenly, Richard of York laughed. It was a merry, sweet laugh, but all the danger in the world was in it. Queen Margaret moved swiftly. She rose, taking the royal wand from Henry's lax hand. She shimmered, pearly and slender; the white oval of her face was savage, anxious. Her clear voice carried over the emerald sward.

'I, Marguerite, as Lady Paramount, give the command. Earl Marshal, let the tourney commence!'

Under the scream of the clarions and the yell of '*Laissez aller*!' Warwick said, with a studied insolence. 'So it is true! Fair woman *do* rule England this day!'

Elizabeth slewed to stare at him. As the roaring thunder of hooves mounted and the two knights approached one another at a gallop, she knew that Warwick had not done with tormenting her.

'Do not imagine I have forgotten the slight you offered my liege-man, Dame Woodville,' he said, almost amiably.

She looked away again, pretending to be absorbed in the joust. With a splintering crash, the two destriers met on either side of the palisade. Wiltshire's lance, held crosswise at an angle, found its mark in the ornaments on Buckingham's helm. Simultaneously,

Buckingham's point lodged in the decorations of his opponent's gorget. Both knights were unhorsed. The riderless horses thundered on, one of them plunging into the barrier dividing the lists from the spectators. The air was rich with cries.

'You could have had my good lordship, Dame Elizabeth,' said Warwick softly. 'Yet you called down a murrain upon my person.'

One of the combatants was cast like a beetle on its back, helpless in his heavy armour. Esquires rushed to aid him. Elizabeth saw herself again in the hall at Grafton Regis, crying: 'Pox take Warwick!' and the outraged faces of the visiting Yorkists. Evidently they had lost no time in relaying her insult to their chief. She stared unseeingly at the lists. The contestants were horsed again and riding, faster this time, lances held loosely, ready for the moment of impact and the hard high thrust.

'So, Dame Woodville,' pursued the inexorable voice, 'a knight of Jerusalem does not suit your lady's palate. Likewise my patronage is to be spat upon ... did you think it wisdom to make an enemy of me?'

The assault of his eyes drove into her. Under that terrible look the high preparation of words cringed and died. She feared and loathed him. Then the Countess of Somerset, who had been listening closely while feigning interest in the joust, saved her. Turning, she said kindly: 'They fight like lions.' (Wiltshire and the Duke were on foot, hacking at each other with broadswords.) 'Isabella, is the sport too rude for you? Jesu! you are trembling. Will you not rest a while in our chariot? Barnaby – where is the boy? – will escort you.'

'*Merci, merci, madame*,' whispered Elizabeth. How clever of the Countess! A little of her courage returned and she cast one bitter glance at Warwick as he rose to allow her to step down from the loge.

'Yes, my lady,' he said softly. 'You run from me. How fortunate are women – they may run while men must fight. Run, Dame Woodville. We shall meet anon.'

Barnaby gave her his arm and she leaned on him, affecting faintness as they walked down the tapestry-hung passage between the loges, to where there was calmness and birdsong and the air was sweet with crushed grass and blossoms. Barnaby grumbled all the way; he had been enjoying himself. She dismissed him.

'Will you be safe?' he said. 'God's Eyes, I never thought to play wetnurse. Go rest then, lady. I'll see you later! He ran off, eager to witness the next joust, which was to be between Lord Clifford and the Great Talbot. He had laid heavy wagers on Buckingham's victory and was furious at missing the outcome.

Elizabeth could see the litters drawn up by the roadside, with grooms and pages sleeping in their shadow, but she did not go to them. Instead, she turned and walked down a little leafy road, where Eltham's crumbling palace stood among great oaks. There was a small stone archway through which she passed to find herself in a garden so beautiful that she stood entranced for a moment. Two or three tame peacocks bowed and danced upon the clipped lawns, yew hedges bounded the abundant rose-beds, and there was a large lake, white with lilies, their delicate stars nestling on broad flat leaves. Between the flowers the water was so clear that she could see every detail of her pale reflection. She knelt, and the pallid Elizabeth wavered up at her and smiled softly, with teeth like white seeds between scarlet lips, and eyes still shadowed with a remnant of disquiet. The friendly water welcomed her image. Far away, she heard the distant clarions' scream and the rumble of hooves, like noises heard in a dream.

Still Warwick's pressing menace cast a cloud on beauty, even as the breeze blew a cloud across the lake to hide the sun. Melusine, she said wordlessly, where is my protector? For I need one now, if ever. I have made an enemy of Warwick. Where he is concerned, even the Queen must look to her protection. A feeling of doom made her shudder, and the mirrored Elizabeth shuddered, her body long and wavering in the water. Melusine, Melusine, have you forgotten me?

Then brightness came again, but in the lake beside her image, a shadow remained. A young straight shadow that moved forward and became defined. A face that took gold from a sunbeam and mirrored itself brightly; a curving mouth that spoke of sweet temper and good sense. Straight features; one eyebrow set in a quirkish lift. Eyes that grew large in the lake. A face to cherish and to trust. A face to look upon for ever.

She gathered her skirts and rose slowly to face him. He wore a tunic of sky-blue satin and knelt instantly at her feet. When he raised his face, with its innocent mouth, all ready to do her homage, she thought, without surprise: *So this is he. He is here at last. Love, I have waited, and now the waiting ends.* She heard his quiet voice murmuring an apology for startling her. His lips were warm on her cold hand. He knew her name, he said, he had watched her progress from the lists.

She knew him not, he said: John Grey, son of Lord Ferrers of Goby. And then the courtly conversation ceased, and they looked at one another, as if they had thirsted for the looking since time began.

'*She met with Raymond by her home, the fountain in the forest, and took his wits away.*'

The *coup de foudre*. The power and glory of the heart. These were mere words, inadequate tools to describe the joy that was almost pain, the feeling of bodily dissolution, spiritual ecstasy. Words to skim only the surface of the deep water, the sure and sweet experience of mutual worship, the certainty that now the nucleus of the world breathed and lived.

There had been no need for coquetry or wooing. Within five minutes of that first meeting, all was equal. Reality made nonsense of her one-time cherished tales of romance. Those chroniclers knew naught of love, love's real implications. Only Chaucer, perhaps, had come a little close.

> The lyf so short, the craft so long to lerne,
> Th'assay so hard, so sharp the conquering,
> The dreadful joy, that alwey slit so yerne,
> Al this mean I by love ..

The dreadful joy. The essence of pain, instinctive, unfathomable. A host of new, half-understood fears. Fear of the knowledge that this person, now so dear, was only mortal and would, one day, cease to breathe, to kiss, to laugh and sorrow with her. The dreadful joy of realizing that she was split in two, that half of her went with him through the world, into danger, or sadness, so that all his pleasures were hers and all his griefs, her misery. For the first time in her life, Elizabeth longed for self-abnegation. Pride slipped away; she wished to be fluid, invisible, to crawl inside his heart and be one with him for ever. If he were sad, she wept. If he rejoiced, she knew childlike gaiety. To her eyes, the sky seemed hard, a bright sapphire, and every flower, tall icy lily and blood-red rose, met her with an almost physical shock. Wherever she looked she saw his face, in searing beauty and fondness. His voice called her in the wind and the birds' song, his very existence sharpened her senses. His name was a talisman, a comforter. The *coup de foudre*. So had Jacquetta named it, the passion few had known. Now Elizabeth held it in her heart, and was daily amazed, for she had not thought herself capable of such love.

She became careless, forgetful, smiling gently whenever the other women spoke to her; she fell in with their plans where once she would have been obstructive and tantalizing. She kissed Ismania on the cheek and offered to tire her hair in the new Italian fashion. She loaned Lady Dacre the pearl-and-ruby ring. Only when rumour of her attachment crept through the Palace, coming to roost in the women's chamber, was this new madness explained, and they laughed. Only a little, for John Grey was truly noble, favoured by powerful lords. Bradgate Hall in Leicestershire, the inheritance of Petronilla de Grandmesnil, whose father Baron Hinckley was tenant *in capite* there to the Conqueror himself, had been handed down to Lord Ferrers of Groby; Bradgate, therefore, was a fine drop of honey to lick from the thorns of marriage! The reason for their jealous laughter was chiefly Elizabeth's mien; she epitomized the love-lorn maiden of song and ballad. She heard their mockery through an amethyst haze; she looked upon the world with gentle uncaring joy. When without warning the bubble burst, and Beaufort ordered John to accompany him to Calais, it seemed an evil trick of fate.

On a day when autumn had cursed the trees leafless, John sailed, and Elizabeth went sadly about her duties. Going to the Queen's bower, she passed the guard; one of the elderly knights chaffed her gently, saying that she looked like a maid preparing for death; her inborn swift anger, fettered for weeks by happiness, rose, an ugly beast. She tongued a cruel retort that brought the blood to the old man's face.

The Queen was alone save for a viol-player scraping a lonely French air, and, beside him, two seamstresses repairing a gown. The window was half-open and banged restlessly under the assault of the wind. Margaret looked once at Elizabeth; it was enough.

'What troubles you, Isabella?'

'Your Grace cannot wish to learn of my small affairs.'

A little impatiently Margaret beckoned her nearer. The Queen looked unwell; her face was puffy, her eyes bright with unease.

'Tell all, Isabella,' she said. 'I pray you, attend my hair. Take off this cursed headgear. My brow has an iron band around it.'

Elizabeth lifted off the little coif which was like a crescent moon, webbed with tawdry veiling. The pale hair fell free; she set the comb to the Queen's small head. The two faces wavered together in the mirror. The comb moved down like a fish through sunlit water. Margaret's expression was distant, troubled. Elizabeth thought suddenly: Can the Queen ever have loved as I do? All her world encompassed in that saintly, wandering King. She has been wed to him for seven years. Would to God that I were wed. John, ah, John.

'Tell me,' the Queen repeated. She took a strand of hair over one shoulder and began to braid it deftly. Sighing, Elizabeth said: 'As you will, Madame. It is an old tale ever repeated. I have met the man I would marry and he has gone away.'

'His name?' said the Queen lightly, and Elizabeth told her.

It is a good choice,' said Margaret. 'Grey will be wealthy, and he is strong for Lancaster.' She went on braiding, with delicate, unerring twists, talking almost to herself, like a man who names captains, deploys armies.

'So, he is of the Norman blood. *C'est vrai!* I believe the title comes through an heiress of Blanchemains to the line of Ferrers Groby. And Bradgate is a prize ... their demesne stretches far ...

Elizabeth said, proud of her own extravagance: 'Madame, I'd take him were he a beggar.' And then her voice began to tremble. 'For I love him. I loved him before I was born and I shall love him when we are both dust. With every vein of my heart and every hair of my head, I love him, sore.'

There was no showmanship in this last speech which astounded even herself. It left her weeping, trying to nudge away tears with the bell of her sleeve. She looked into the mirror and found the Queen's blurred face. Its expression was indistinguishable.

'And does he, too, love you with this so hot passion?' enquired Queen Margaret in a strange voice. Her hands had ceased braiding and lay twisted in her lap.

'Ah yes, Madame!' cried Elizabeth with joy. 'Yes, and yes, and more!'

'Then you have everything!' said the Queen. She sprang up, and took two or three frantic running steps towards the window, as if to cast herself out, and down. She turned as swiftly to show a haggard face, one unfinished braid coming apart, and the eyes of a trapped wolf. She's ill, Elizabeth thought, appalled. She made a movement of dismissal to the sewing-women and they left hurriedly; the viol-player tucked his instrument under his arm and crept out after them. She searched for words to calm Margaret.

'Sweet your Grace, I am sure ...'

'Naught is sure!' cried the Queen wildly. There was anger directed at Elizabeth in her eyes and voice. O Jesu, thought Elizabeth: how have I offended?

'Madame,' she stammered, 'you yourself advised me to choose my own husband. This I have done, and I ask your royal assent to my marriage with John Grey of Groby. Madame, as you have ever been kind to me, I ask you this.'

The dreadful thought occurred to her that Margaret, for some reason, might withhold her consent. Very well; she would approach the King, as her own mother had done (a sigh, a tear, a loving look. I bent the young reed of a king to my will!) She would go in ashes and mourning rather than give up John. Then Margaret said shrilly:

'You shall have my royal assent. You shall marry John Grey. I shall watch your children growing strong about you. I shall see you loving and loved. *And I shall curse you for it.*'

Then she wept, and caught blindly at Elizabeth's hand like a woman sinking in quagmire. After a long time, she was calm and said, looking through tear-washed eyes: '*Doucette*, some demon led my tongue. Envy is the deadliest sin of all It eats the heart. Isabella: is to love and be unloved crueller than love returned yet forbidden?'

'Your Grace should not speak thus to me,' Elizabeth said uneasily. In her mind she saw Henry, lack-lustre as a winter bird, and fleeing the flesh; and Beaufort, whispering of his bitter passion to a dumb beast.

'Why not?' said Margaret sharply. 'You who will have everything, can you not help me bear my pain? You will have love, like few women. You will have sons, like all women ... She bit her lips and the wolfish, haunted look returned to her eyes. 'Richard of York's wife ... *la maudite* ... mark you how they taunted me with the news that she's with child again? *Sancta Maria!* My life, my throne, is threatened through love ... lovelack!' She caught Elizabeth's hand again and dragged her to a prie-dieu in the corner of the room, where a small bright flame burned fitfully against the wind.

'Pray with me,' she commanded. '*Maria, Maria, Sancta Maria*, thou who wast Mother to Our Lord, hear me. *Jube, Domine, benedicere* ... Lord, grant a blessing: a son!' Inarticulately her prayers lashed upward about the flame, while Elizabeth added her own. To Saint Bernard, patron of childbirth; and in secret, to Saint Valentine, patron of lovers. Praying, amid Margaret's tumult, for herself. That she and John should marry ... that Beaufort should bring him back home, soon. The room was suddenly quiet. Margaret stared dazedly at the wall. Elizabeth whispered: 'Madame, my lord of Somerset ...'

The Queen flinched and trembled perceptibly. 'What of him? He is in Calais.'

'Where he commands my own dear lord,' said Elizabeth softly. 'Summon them home, my liege.'

Queen Margaret looked at her. 'Yes,' she whispered. 'Yes. And may God answer all our prayers.'

Little and lovely for all her ravaged expression, she knelt before the prie-dieu and looked steadily at Elizabeth, who saw, unknowingly, the revelation of things to come. The Queen's eyes were soft with love but the sacred flame, reflected obliquely, gave them the aspect of two fair cities, burning.

And she was happy again. The millrace of her joy moved fast through the remnants of autumn, laughed in the grip of winter, and bubbled over at the holy season of Christmas, when the court assumed a modest gaiety. Though the King spent more and more time in prayer and meditation, the Palace pleasured itself as extravagantly as Margaret could afford. Throughout the twelve days there were plays and disguisings, mostly of a sacred nature for the King's approval. On the final evening, when the Lord of Misrule had capered an introduction, Richard Bulstrode, the revelsmaster, presented a pageant of his own contriving: the Passing of the Hours. Elizabeth played the Queen of Night. In a gown of clinging black tissue, with her unbound hair crowned with stars, she was borne into the Hall on a painted litter, dramatically lit by cressets. Lithe and rounded, she was carried high, the proud coin of her perfect profile luminous against the flames, the arrogant blue eyes meekly downcast, the silken, star-twined hair blowing gently in her wake.

She felt the heat of the torches warm upon her cheek, and close; she feared nothing, not even fire. She was immune, this night, and glorious. The procession approached the dais where Margaret sat with Beaufort kneeling at her side and where the King observed the secular scene with a gloomy primness. Beaufort's brown hand rested near the Queen's small foot. Little details sprang forth; the faces of servers and henchmen, the glint of a peacock feather stuck like a sword in the picked carcass; the ragged hem of a tablecloth There were glances too; the rapt looks of unknown men avid for beauty and caught in unconscious lust; the women's faces tight with jealousy. She saw John, he stood a little apart from the dais. He was stamped with an almost sacred emotion: the look bestowed by a father on a cherished child, or a good priest on the Eucharist.

There was nothing priestly about him later. Intoxicated by the thunderous applause after she had said her few trite rhyming words and been borne again from the Hall, she sought him out, where he waited for her on the gallery. She cut short his courtliness, his murmured words of adoration, and flung her arms about his neck. Unwittingly she lit dangerous fires, whispering, teasing, turning her smooth cheek to meet his. Was I not fair, my lord? Did you hear their cries? He kissed the bubbling speech to silence, holding her tightly enough to hurt. He gathered handfuls of her shimmering hair to kiss, and she felt his power, the bruising inevitable harbinger of possession. Although she loved him and melted to him for an instant, a little cool corner of her mind whispered: Hold back. So she withdrew, seeing the candle of his eyes grown large with longing, leaned tiptoeing again to kiss each longing, lightly, and slipped away to stand apart from him against a pillar.

He groaned. 'O Jesu, Isabella. Can one love so and still keep sanity?'

He followed her, kissing her hand, her sleeve, the hollow of her throat. Again she retreated, to stand in half-light. Above the black gown her face was pale, a disembodied candle-flame.

'I love you, my lord, and trust have kept my wits.' She tried to speak lightly. He was not to be put off, however. In his arms again, part of her succumbed to the sweetness of his mouth. The other part, away somewhere, watched and measured and warned. Hold back. Even the flame of his hand upon her breast was tempered by that coolness. He whispered of love, and incautious, impetuous suggestions: she lay with the other ladies of a night, did she not? And he, God's curse on it, was bound to serve Beaufort of Somerset, should he be needful or wakeful; but there were ways, friends who would do duty for him, be it for gold or other favours. By the Mercy of Christ, Isabella! 'I must have you this night, or die!' And the heat of her leaped in gladness towards this consummation, while the wary, sea-cool essence of her, of Melusine, who lay apart from her husband every Saturday, writhed and gave tongue. A sweet rebuke, damning and promising in a breath.

'Are we not then to be wed, my lord?'

Instantly he was contrite. It was a churlish, unforgivable thought, yet her beauty was wholly culpable. 'Can you blame me? A king, an emperor, would want you. Do you think I don't crave our wedding-day as much, more than you? I would wait for ever. The waiting would make of me an old man. An old, old man, for ever and ever in love ...'.

There were tears in his voice. He rose from the knee so swiftly bowed before her. He stood tall and slender; she reached up to touch his cheek with her soft white hand.

'I give you my life,' he said. 'My little lovesome wayward Isabella.'

'Am I, John?' she said, intrigued. 'Am I all those things?'

He took her hand and kissed the palm. 'Lovesome,' he said, each word a kiss. 'Little, yes. Wayward? Nay, love, I wronged you. Yet ...'

'Go on, my lord.'

Deeply he looked into the large eyes with their innocent, hidden power. When he spoke it was hesitantly, doubtful words strung out like beads.

'I know little or naught of women. I would be a fool to say I understand them. Yet you, Isabella, are beyond all understanding. I feel ... I feel that when I hold you in my arms I am on the boundary of a foreign country ... You are strange, my love. You are a wonder.' Inflamed by thought, he clasped her to him. 'I would gladly enter that strange land. My Isabella, you rob me of my soul!'

She swayed to him, sinuous, enchanted and enchanting. The sound of distant music, a sweet high pagan wail, filled her ears from the Hall. Eyes closed, she saw visions. Rippling water, shapes sporting in a fountain. Almost she saw the face, the glittering hair like waterweed, the monstrous shining tail. *I am strange. I am a wonder, and he feels it.* She held him gladly. When he asked the measure of her love, she answered, in reverence and perfect truth: 'My heart, you are my other self, and I am yours.'

'Speak to the Queen,' he said, trembling. 'Desire her Grace to appoint our wedding-day.'

Within a few days, she did as he asked, and found Margaret strangely distrait, with a desperate air of indecision about her. She was surrounded by rolls and registers all awaiting the signet of the King, who had not been seen for days. Eventually she gave Elizabeth her attention.

'I have your marriage settlement drawn, Isabella,' she said. 'I will give you all that I can afford. Two hundred pounds from my privy Purse. Would Jesu it were more. You have served me tenderly.'

'Your Grace is more than generous.'

'Then repay me,' said Margaret.

'How, your Grace?'

'By staying at court until the spring. I need you, for there are few worthy of my trust. They are all about me with their greedy spying eyes, ready to do me duty until a better bargain shows itself. I would have you close to me these next few weeks. For the love I bore your mother and now bear you – will you stay? Will you share my chamber o' nights, share my griefs, my passions?'

Elizabeth looked steadily into the Queen's eyes. There was no mistaking her intent. Beaufort of Somerset's image shone fatally from those hungry, longing eyes. Neither was there any mistaking the implications, the dangers.

'The King, Madame ...'

Margaret gave a short laugh. 'He has a new pastime, my poor Henry. As he has spent so much on Masses, he must have the alchemists work night and day at the Philosopher's stone. Only by conjuring gold from dust can he afford the prayers against his constant maladies, his vapourings. O Jesu! I came from France laden with joy – to a royal prince – to empty barrenness!'

Wildness rode her face. Elizabeth said swiftly: 'Do not trouble further, sweet Madame. I will stay as long as you need me. But I would marry in the spring!'

'You shall. When you have served me, and not only me. The Crown, and royal Lancaster! Did you know,' she said with soft anguish, 'that York's wife did bear another son! On the second day of October last; a puling sickly wretch they call Richard. Another son! Edmund, Edward, George, Richard. The Yorkists multiply ... so stay by me, Isabella. Be loyal, discreet, and loving, and I'll not forget you when my dynasty is strong.'

Eyes lowered, she felt the Queen's kiss on her brow, and nodded fervently. She would defer her own raging longing for John. Only for the Queen, whose words were half-comprehended, and at the same time, terribly clear. For Lancaster, and England – and for love? A web was growing, drawing her to Margaret, and woven of audacious fancies best sealed in silence.

The day following, Queen Margaret gave orders that she desired only the company of Dame Isabella Woodville in her chamber at night, and dismissed the guard from her door. The King, she said, had taken it upon him to seek her counsel late of nights, and she would not have him hindered. I am full of trust, she said, and will not be harmed by isolation. The court fluttered a little, shortly forgot, and was still.

It did not happen nightly. More often than not, the Queen slept tranquilly with Elizabeth close by. She in turn learned to anticipate the Queen's whim; to read to her should she be restless, to serve her with wine or play the harp in the soft dark hours. And to withdraw gently, eyes blinded by duty, into the adjoining chamber when the tall figure, with his soldier's step muted, entered like a ghost and passed through to the Queen.

The echoes of their love enhanced her own. Nightly she dreamed of John, and ached for the spring.

I love. He is mine. I love more than my own life, more than all pleasures, persons, dreams that I have known. This love is my whole world. She shivered suddenly, frightened by the dreadful joy, the fear of tempting demons with such utter bliss. Then his eyes smiled into hers, and she dismissed the fear. She studied his face, the face to look upon for ever; the crooked brow, the curving mouth, the firm, clean-shaven chin; the bright, new-coin hair so properly dressed upon his straight shoulders. John, I love. He for his part thought: She is mine. The fairest woman in the realm. Mine to cherish while life lasts, to have and love through long years. Until we are both white-haired ancients to whom that hot young love is but an unremembered mystery. Then, I lie. I shall remember, should I be ninety years. Oh God! he thought, let me have all those years with Isabella.

It was a day when every tree unfurled tiny green banners. It was the day when Dame Elizabeth Grey and her husband rode at last from the court. After the long ceremony in the Royal chapel, when the singing boys lifted their voices to heaven and candles painted the vaultings with softest light; after the nuptial Mass, the vows taken under the Queen's smiling gaze, they did not delay in London even for a night. Standing with the holy water crystalline upon her flesh and with her hand in John's, she whispered: 'Let us to Bradgate, my lord, at once!' He, bemused by love and joy, had nodded, murmuring: 'Sweet, we must share a void with the Queen before parting!' So they pledged Margaret in sweet hypocras, oblivious of the other courtiers standing about them, almost unconscious of the Queen's presence. 'To our years,' John whispered. 'To our happy years!' Drinking from the cup which Elizabeth's lips had touched, he felt the weight of those unlived years hang on his fancy like a sweet ripe fruit. Drunk with the future, he embraced it to the end, smiling again at the thought of himself an ancient man, spent and satisfied with love. It was an impossible thought. Then fleetingly, he thought of another old man, fallen just lately.

There had been mourning in the Palace. The Queen had wept openly and King Henry had ordered Masses for the soul of the Great Talbot, Earl of Shrewsbury. He had been killed in Guienne, fighting with all the miraculous strength of his eighty years, for England against France. Yet he was pledged to a French-born Queen! John's bridal heart carelessly saw wry humour in it. England had lost the better part of France; yet they had a daughter of France reigning. Lovely, generous ... his warm eyes surveyed Margaret as he prepared his farewell. God preserve her. The slender body was now rounded, and John, in innocent male awe, fancied he could hear that second heart beating within ...

For the Queen was with child. Proclamation had been made to the assembled court. Henry had occupied the dais solitary, twitching his gown between thin dusty fingers, looking about him as for an ambush. When the Esquire of the Body, Richard Tunstal, came down the Hall, parchment in hand, the King had started up as if at foulest tidings. As Tunstal began to read, the glad cries from the court drowned any response from Henry, who quietly left the Hall. He returned to make it known that the said Tunstal should receive an annuity of forty marks from the duchy of Lancaster.

'Because,' said the King like a schoolboy, 'he it was that made unto us the first comfortable relation and notice that our most dearly beloved wife ... was *enceinte*.' Here he paused and blinked at some parchment notes he held. 'Aye, to our most singular consolation, and to all true liege people's great joy and comfort.' So saying, he got up, sat down, looked worriedly about him, and gave a great sigh.

The Palace hummed with triumph. The news was dispatched to York, to Canterbury, to Ireland and to Calais; and more especially to Warwick Castle and to Fotheringhay. Night and day prayers were offered that the Queen should, in November next coming, bear a son. Margaret took the ladies Ross and Scales to her chamber at nights, and the guard was reinstated, to cherish her doubly precious person. Thus was the most secret campaign concluded, and Elizabeth, Dame Grey, was free to go.

Richly clothed against the spring breezes, they rode together through sun, and showers up the long furrow of Watling Street. Although John had furnished a litter for his bride she scorned it, and rode with him, saying they should not be parted so soon. A strand of her hair tickled his face as he leaned to kiss her. They laughed and sang, riding hard towards Bradgate, and leaving the few pages and women who escorted them far behind on the road. The wind blew back their song and mingled it with that of the calling birds, until it was like the high pagan gaiety of spirits. John raised his voice:

'Who shall have my fair lady?
Who shall have my fair lady?
'Who but I, who but I, who but I?
Under the leaves green!'

And Elizabeth answered with shrill note:

'The fairest man
That best love can,
Dandirly, dandirly, dandirly, dan,
Under the leaves green!'

Each passing moment was a target for laughter. John recalled one night in Calais, when the others had fed him so much wine that he had danced on the table and thought that he could fly.

'It's love, not wine, that gives us wings!' he cried. 'Watch me, my love!'

He put his restive horse at a quickset hedge. Elizabeth reined in, sat watching. The horse's glossy quarters bunched in power. John's hands were strong and light; fluidly anchored on the reins. His chestnut head bobbed against a tapestry of green leaves. He wore a red cloak; it tossed about him as horse and rider reared for the leap, rising until it seemed they would merge with the sun. They were silhouetted in blinding brightness, and John's mantle glowed like fire. Fire? No, blood! He was clothed in blood. Elizabeth flung up her hands over her eyes, suddenly, senselessly demented. Thus blinded, she sat like stone. A timid touch stirred her sleeve. Renée, the little tiring-maid who had been given to her by the Queen, spoke softly:

'What ails my sweet lady?'

She opened her eyes. John was trotting back down the road, patting his horse's foamy neck. His cloak was rich red velvet, her own wedding gift, and fell in orderly folds about him to his stirrups. That was no vision, she told herself. I am fatigued after the ceremony. And I do not have visions. To Renée she said: 'Tis naught; go ride with the others.' None the less, she kept John closely within her sight thereafter. When she caught his hand and kissed it passionately, he looked at her with a little wonder and much love; he lifted her from her horse to his, singing anew:

'The fairest man, Dandirly, dandirly, dandirly dan!'

'How much further to Bradgate?' she asked.

Two days' journey, he said, if the roads were good. Incredulously he saw her pleading face. 'Sweet, would you have us ride through the night?' He kissed her, saying: 'Nay, we must lodge tonight at some holy house.'

'Must we? Can we not ride on? It would be one night less without Bradgate.'

Something in the name called to her. She craved Bradgate, needed it. In its image there was strength. A rock, a haven redolent of John's heritage and the timelessness of their future together. She begged for speed as the day grew old along the worn greenness of Watling Street. She was not weary, would never be weary. Finally John gestured towards the flagging entourage behind. 'Look at your women and my pages, sweet cruel wife! We may be strong and adventurous, but they would fall on the road. And there's our resting-place ahead.'

The tented roof and towers of an abbey glinted in the sun's last rays. Elizabeth pouted, feigned displeasure. When they were admitted by a porter she had a little, unlooked-for vengeance. The Abbot showed her to the women's guesthouse and John the men's quarters. Useless were his protestations – 'Father, we were only married today!'

The Abbot looked hard at him. 'Fitting, then, my son, that you should spend the night in prayer. I too will ask a blessing on your union. We are a poor house ...' he said mechanically. John beckoned for gold from his esquire. He turned back to Elizabeth with such a comical expression of dismay that she choked on laughter. She whispered, while the Abbot stood severely by, swinging his keys: 'It's best, love. I would not begin our honeymonth within a cloister. My heart–' still jesting, happy and sad – 'what's one night, more or less?'

Her first sight of Bradgate was like a blow to the heart. They came upon it suddenly, riding down a path through densely wooded parkland. A tiny stream accompanied their progress and the boles of elms shone on either side. Banks of primrose and violet grew at the foot of ancient oaks; through a clearing there was a glimpse of bluebells like a still sheet of azure water. Wild orchids grew in profusion; rabbits fled nimbly for cover. Above the treetops arched in a lacy green cavern, filled with the song of throstle and blackbird and the mockery of the cuckoo. Crushing flowers, the little company galloped down the path and, amid a flurry of startled wings, around a bend where Bradgate lay in welcome.

Its lattices gleamed like noonday stars, its merlons seemed, to quiver. The standard of Ferrers Groby sprang and billowed from the tower. The fortified manor stood with its feet in flowers, clothed in rich ivy among a splendour of green lawns. Spreading westward was a lake that made the pool at Grafton Regis a murky puddle by comparison; a lake crowned with a distant drift of swans and fringed by bright willows. A little waterfall spilled through an aperture in the low wall girdling the manor. Elizabeth looked again at the lake; a breeze kissed the water and silvered it to fire. There were shallow steps leading down to the waters of her heart's desire. Tears filled her eyes.

'Do you not like it?' said John softly.

Words could only dispel the depth of her feeling. John, the lake, and love were one. She turned and kissed him and clung, saying: 'Aye, my heart. I like it well.'

She dressed with care for the evening. The scarlet sarcenet was revived, with no fear of gloomy Henry's curses. She bade Renée brush her hair and leave it loose to befit the maidenhood soon to be willingly relinquished. Shy little Renée, made bold by her mistress's gaiety, chattered, exclaiming: 'Like a queen, madam, like a queen!' Incongruously the face of the dirty gypsy at Eltham returned to her, and she smiled. A royal prince, fair lady, shalt thou wed! She had proved the woman a charlatan, and was glad of it. She turned to embrace Renée briefly, crying: 'Yes! I am a queen! Queen of Bradgate! My king is John!'

'You are my prince,' she said later to John. They sat at their own high table, surrounded by friends, eating spiced heron. Elizabeth had been drinking deep of the deceptively flowery Rhenish. The well-wishers were admiring her, envying John.

He said, a little gloomily: 'Sweet, it's as well I am your prince. For myself, I am not even knight as yet. I pray I may be sent on campaign, where I may be dubbed ... Calais again, though 'tis quieter there than for many months ...

She said aghast: 'Already you talk of leaving me!'

The company roared. John smiled adoringly, foolish. 'Not yet, my lady, and not tonight, certes.' He, the obliging host, began to sing.

'Sweet mistress mine, ye shall have no wrong,
But as yet grant me, sith we be met,
That fair flower that ye have kept so long,
I call it mine own as my very debt ...'

Under the applause, the laughter, he looked at Elizabeth and felt his manhood falter in awe. Sitting there in the candlelight with her pure pale face and shining hair, she seemed unfleshly and remote. He motioned for more wine, feeling a kind of anger at the sight of this spirituality; it made his own desire seem crude and unchivalrous.

His steps were a little unsteady as he followed her up the flaring shadowed spiral to their chamber. He was weary from the journey, from wine and joy. The company bade them a merry good night, before themselves retiring to envious beds. The proud, fey delicacy of Elizabeth was apparent to them all; thus they refrained from all but the mildest of marriage jests, called from the stair-foot. Alone with Renée, she was unrobed of the scarlet dress and attired in a loose white *robe de chambre*. In the adjoining room John cursed under the ministrations of Giles, his page, a shortsighted youth who fumbled with knotted laces and mislaid his master's bedgear.

Then John sought Elizabeth and found her chamber empty save for Renée, sparkling nervously, arms full of discarded garments. He knew a swift irrational dismay, and thought: I imagined it all; the wedding was a dream, the ride here, her face against mine at the table. There is no Isabella; she was but my own desire made flesh. Renée saw his sadness and said gently: 'Sir, my lady has gone to the . chapel to pray.' He smiled again, and gave her a gold half angel. She merged with shadows and left him alone.

He walked to the window-embrasure and looked out. A full white moon shed its weird light on the lawns, the sleeping flowerheads, and turned the lake into crystal. He stood breathing in the spring light, unaware that the scene on which he looked was the same which had caused Elizabeth, moments earlier, to quit the chamber murmuring of prayer. He wondered whether he should join her in the chapel, to give thanks for this, the greatest of his life's blessings, yet he was loath to leave the whiteness, the stillness. Then, at the edge of the lake, something moved. He craned forward with a stifled exclamation at sight of it. It was small and shimmered; it caught the moonlight and blazed in it like a slim white flame. He began to tremble. Others of his acquaintance had seen spirits, wraiths that played in the moon's full and could take a man's wits away for ever. He had scoffed at these tales. And yet, this thing was real, fixed in his sight. It walked on air; it stepped among the reeds, dipped until it was one with the water and indistinguishable from the silvery ripples. He felt real fear, for himself, and for Isabella. Before she returned from the chapel, he must drive away whatever it was that sported in Bradgate's lake.

He cast a fur robe about him and went swiftly downstairs. Moving quietly through the sleeping manor, he came upon the two great wolfhounds which he kept for game. Almost his hand went to their chains. These beasts would tear the throat from any enemy. Then he thought; should this enemy be of Hell, the creatures would die of terror. So he went steadfastly and alone into the garden scented by gillyflowers, and strode down towards the little watergate where the cataract bubbled and sang.

His sight had not lied. Something played and plashed in the shallows, its outline diffused as if it were clothed in light. It slipped in and out of the water; it floated a white flower on the surface. Its shape lengthened and it raised two drifting arms, gathering handfuls of water, letting them trickle down like jewels. He took all his courage and stepped forward, saying firmly:

'In the Trinity's Name, be gone!'

The shape gave a soft cry, a laugh, and began to glide towards him. Disbelievingly he heard it call his name, in the note of the falling fountain, in the high shrillness of the nightingale that sang from the trees.

She rose naked from the water and came to him, her wet hair shrouding her body like a tumult of silver weed. Anger at her outrageous folly, and pure delight rose and fought within him. Delight won, swelled by the sight of her flesh, diamond-glittering in water and moon. This was Isabella, his bride, no longer the image of an untouchable saint, but wanton, mischievous, maddening. The reprimanding words were stillborn in his mouth. All he could say was: 'Sweet heart, you will be chilled to death!' He snatched up her robe, discarded on the ground, and sought to wrap her in it, while she whispered, excited, irresistible:

'Forgive me, my sweet lord. It was the lake! Oh, the lake!' And she came closer so that drops from her tender, lithe flesh trembled on his own clothing. His hands let fall the mantle meant to robe her and reached instead for the slender, damp body leaning eagerly towards him. He was losing himself in the cold glittering torrent of hair, lifting and carrying the luminous creature into the shade of a willow. The moss was soft beneath them. And here was the strange, beloved country, its long-besieged harbours opening for him.

A single cry, like a night-bird, rose, shivering from her lips.

'John! My one true love!'

The lake rippled gently and was still.

'It was an evil day,' said Jacquetta of Bedford.

Elizabeth glanced about her while her mother talked. The court had changed little in two years. Here at Sheen, the once-beloved palace of Richard of Bordeaux, burnt for grief after his wife's death and later restored, the trappings were familiar. The hangings were perhaps a little shabbier, the wine they were drinking a trifle sourer. Otherwise there was no sign of the holocaust that had so nearly demolished the Queen's party. Drinking from a dingy hanap, Elizabeth sat by her mother in the window-seat. Outside birds chirped merrily under the May sun, reminding her of Bradgate.

'Two Augusts ago ...' said the Duchess.

'Had his Grace been ailing before?'

Jacquetta shrugged. 'You saw how he was. Always half in the next world, but well enough. Then, with no warning...

The King had dined at four, frugally. There had been only a few courtiers with him; the Duchess and Sir Richard Woodville had been invited by the Queen. His Grace had eaten a small portion of roast sturgeon, and had seemed himself, morose and fey, sitting close by the Queen, giving halfvoiced answer to all that Margaret said. There was nothing about him to show that he was possessed. All went well until an ambassador from Calais arrived. The ambassador was slow and soft-voiced and Margaret, seeing that the King appeared to be half-asleep, herself descended from the dais to take the dispatches offered. In her high-waisted gown and with her proud carriage, the presence of the royal babe was very evident. Her belly, said Jacquetta, burgeoned like a ship's prow. Foolishness even to mention this, for all knew of the joyful condition, none more than the King. Yet there had been a sudden starting up from his chair, that familiar pointing finger, quivering and stabbing at the Queen. All had heard the King's shrill cry, broken off short.

'Forsooth! ...'

Forsooth what, Our Blessed Lord only knew, for the King had sunk in a rapid swoon, falling headlong across the steps of the dais, his black robes hitched about his lean thighs, his dusty head and hands suppliant, down-pointing. Folk rose in dismay to succour him.

The King came to himself after a few minutes, when it was discovered that he could not speak. Stricken and mute, he looked uncomprehendingly at whoever addressed him. He was carried to bed, where he lay, his head turned to one side, gazing at the floor. The court was frantic. Master John Faceby had no rest for days and nights on end, desperately brewing simples or studying the planets' courses for a reason for the King's malady. Doctors were summoned privily from all over Europe; even a filthy wise-woman was consulted. This was August, and by Christmas the King had not uttered one word, nor had he lifted his eyes, even to survey the new Prince, England's heir.

'They carried the babe to him over and again, so that he might bless it,' said the Duchess. 'But it was useless. The King only moaned a little, and kept his eyes down. It was a terrible malady, a madness, carried in the blood. The King's grandsire, Charles of France, was likewise stricken.'

The disaster was so close kept that half England remained in ignorance of it. Yet the agents of York and Warwick were no less vigilant than in times past. That very Christmas a deputation headed by Warwick arrived at court with the time-honoured, sardonic request to know how the King prospered. There was no help but to reveal Henry to them, and the secret was no more. One look at that face as empty as a dry well, those quivering drooping eyelids, coupled with his silence, and they knew then that the King wandered in some private world, alone among shadows.

'There was naught to be done,' murmured the Duchess. 'Cursed York and his claim ... he was appointed Protector of the Realm, being the nearest of the blood. A great triumph for Warwick. The Queen was nearly demented.'

'Yet she had her son,' said Elizabeth softly.

Out in the pleasaunce the birds were singing louder. Elizabeth dreamed of Bradgate, and folded her hands over the slight mound clothed by her green satin gown. Soon she would hold her own babe. She thought of John. He had ridden north to Groby to oversee some of his deceased father's estates; he was bound for London soon, to join her. A little smile curved her mouth. 'The fairest man, that best love can!' Fairer than fair. The memory of all their days and nights together laid a veil over Jacquetta's alarming narrative. All this talk of policy meant little, it seemed like the jousting of knights, spectacular but harmless. Lancaster had worn the crown for sixty years. What if the line did come only from Edward III's fourth son, John of Gaunt? What if York, as he was ever at pains to stress, did descend directly from Lionel of Clarence, the third son? Lancaster was supreme – Agincourt had proved it. She sighed, and stroked again the little roundness below her narrow embroidered girdle. She could see her reflection in a sunlit pane of the oriel. Fair, I am fair. She cast a little sly smile at her mother. Fair enough to grace the ramparts of Lusignan! Then she said, dutifully:

'And when did the King recover from this storm?'

'The following Christmas. He awoke and was himself again. They rushed with the babe to his bedchamber and he cried: 'By St. John! I bless this child. For it is surely one conceived by the Holy Ghost!''

Thus York's brief power was ended. He and Warwick were banished from court with threats and unsheathed blades. Beaufort of Somerset (whom they had used cruelly, said Jacquetta) was reinstated. People rejoiced. 'Yet I feel,' said the Duchess soberly, 'that the people only love the Queen while Henry lives; were she alone, I fear that my sweet Marguerite ...' She left the sentence and looked through the window as if searching for an enemy. 'There will be war,' she said. 'I feel it.'

Elizabeth sat comfortably in the warm sunlight, trying to share the Duchess's precognition, and failing. Again in secret she stroked the slight curve of her belly. The babe should be born at Bradgate. She turned to her mother, saying: 'Madame, how much longer? When can I leave court? There is much to see to at my home.'

'When the Great Council is over,' said Jacquetta sternly. 'Marguerite
... the King wishes all his loyal friends to hear him.'

Then Thomas Barnaby, graceless as ever yet oddly dear to Elizabeth,
knocked and entered the solar. He grinned, gaptoothed; she smiled
at him, remembering the day he had escorted her to the garden
at Eltham. 'Ho, your Grace! Ho, Dame Grey!' he said. The Queen
awaited them, he said, and grinned, and mopped, and Elizabeth
marked his face down for some reason that meant nothing, as a
face she might see again somewhere, and she put the fancies away.
They went in procession to the Queen's chambers. Margaret was
standing with her face to the window; she was much thinner. Her
waist looked nothing, her shoulders were spare and taut. Elizabeth
knelt, with her mother, and presently felt the Queen's kiss on her
brow. Bright and young and arrogant, she looked up, and saw that
Margaret was changed. Hard lines were limned about her mouth,
her eyes had a fervent glitter and her cheeks were colourless. Beside
her stood Beaufort of Somerset, his hair whiter now, with. Piers de
Brezé, James of Wiltshire, all the Queen's trusted favourites.

Shyly Elizabeth addressed the Queen.

'Felicitations, most noble Grace, on the advent of England's heir.'
Instantly the strained white face sprang to bloom, and Margaret
seized her hand. 'You would see him? You would see my son?'

An armed guard surrounded them both as they climbed tight
spiralling stairs and halted before an oaken door, upon which one of
the henchmen beat with his halberd. Inside, a group of white-coiffed
nursemaids doted on the infant prince. Tall for his age, he wandered
forward to lay a tiny hand on Elizabeth's skirt. She knelt in homage;
the hand dropped to the toy dagger in his belt. His large dark eyes
studied her as she murmured, 'Most princely Grace,' and a shower of
quick baby-talk which awakened no reaction in the impassive small
face. There was an oldness and wisdom about him. One conceived
by the Holy Ghost? Rising, she said to Margaret: 'Madame, he is
the proudest, most winsome child,' and was startled by the Queen's
expression. Love, conceits, all the aspects of a mother were there, but
overshadowed by a kind of ferocity. She devoured the prince with
her eyes; her breath came quickly. On their knees, the nurses followed
the child wherever he wandered, hands outstretched lest he should
fall. Four doctors were present, two tutors, and outside the chamber

came the faint slither of the halberds crossing. The Queen sank to her knees before her son. She said:

'Proud! Yea, Dame Isabella, he is proud! His name is Edward, after the great founder of Lancaster. His device is the Silver Swan. Bright and puissant, the heritage of might. And mine! My dynasty's joy and hope!' Her voice quivered and dropped almost to silence. '*Ma fleur d'Anjou!*'

The flower's face creased in a subtle discontent. '*Reine ... ma reine ...*' he lisped, pawing Margaret's trembling hand.

'We, through *him*,' continued the Queen, through clenched teeth, 'shall conquer. Our succession is secure. York can threaten, the devil Warwick can sneer, but we are fast on England. Does he sleep easy?' she demanded of the nurses. To the tutors she said: 'Let him read and write soon. Give him all knowledge, learning, power.' To the doctors: 'Your heads on a platter, messires, if any malady seeks him out.' She turned again to the little Edward, taking his face between her hands, loosing a torrent of French endearments, the mother vanquishing the dynast for a little space.

They went by river to Westminster Hall, where the Great Council was to be held. Between her father and mother Elizabeth sat watching the swell of waves about the painted craft, and seeing disinterestedly the cranes dipping all along the river from Blackfriars to the Tower. Perfume and spices wafted from the ships from Italy and the East. At the Vintners' Wharf casks of wine were being unloaded. Yet trade was sparse, men said. England was a country to beware. Denuded of her French possessions, she had an untrusted Queen, a demented King reigning.

Close, Elizabeth felt her father's warmth. It was good to be with him again. Broad and handsome, he inquired as to her health and that of John. Jacquetta of Bedford sat enjoying the voyage, her head dipping to the rhythm of the lapping waves. And there was another passenger aboard, one who frowned at each miscast stroke of the oarsmen with the dignity of an octogenarian, who closed her nose with a herb-sprig at the stench of cod wafting from the fishmonger's alleys: Lady Margaret Beaufort. Fully twelve years now, she sat, eyes on a sacred manuscript, but now and then looking about with a passionless, all-seeing gaze. Elizabeth ventured to ask her: 'Are you wed yet, my lady?' and the dwarfish maiden answered: 'Next year, Dame Grey. To Edmund Tudor. The King so decrees.' She bent again to her reading with one chilling, complacent look.

At Westminster Hall a host of knights and nobles were gathered, all wearing the Lancastrian 'chain of 'S's or the flower of Marguerite. The Queen was already seated at the head of the throng, with Henry, gaunt and shadowy; the little prince, toy dagger occupying his hands, sat on a red velvet throne. The oaths were taken, the principals of the Council took their places. The occupants of the Hall accommodated themselves as best they could, some leaning against the walls. To Elizabeth, crushed behind three tall knights and their ladies, the Queen was a blur, the white face a little flame, the spare small body straining upwards. Beaufort of Somerset presided. On the faces of the councillors there was triumph, hardly veiled. Many were richly robed; in his poor gown, the King looked like some wantwit peasant come to solicit alms. Elizabeth twitched her father's sleeve. 'Why are they all so proud?' she whispered. 'I never saw my lord of Buckingham smile like that before.' Buckingham was a tall dour knight who cared little for ceremony. Sir Richard Woodville leaned down to murmur: 'It is a great day for Lancaster. Look about you!'

She glanced before and behind at the massed courtiers. Every face bore the same look; smugness, arrogance. Lady Margaret Beaufort, all but smirking, knelt on a prayer-stool near the dais, while beside her stood her betrothed, Edmund Tudor, and his brother Jasper, thin and sallow and haughty. Colours made a mosaic of the Hall; gowns red and green and yellow, the brown of a friar's habit, the black robes of the tonsured clerks, who, quills and parchment ready, waited on the Council's words. Sir Richard leaned again to his daughter.

'There are no Yorkists present, Bess. And should any come, they will be refused entry. This is the Queen's new Council. Today she pits her might against those puny adversaries. Listen to my lord of Somerset, Bess! See the tide turning!'

His blue eyes blazed with satisfaction. Nowhere was there a sign of the White Rose, the Bear, the Falcon, the Fetterlock, the Griffin. There was a scuffling at the great door, where guards with pikes conducted a whispered argument with someone outside. One who demanded admission, and pressed on the door so that it swung open; who doffed his grimy cloak to reveal a tunic studded with marguerites. Elizabeth swung round quickly to see the newcomer, now jesting with the apologetic guard, slip in under the raised halberds. He was tall and slender and copper-haired. The fairest man ...

'John!' she cried, earning a frown from her father. Heedless, she ducked and writhed through the press of people, treading on feet, feeling her sleeve tear on the hilt of a dagger. Then she was at his side, feeling his strength, his velvet doublet smooth upon her throat and breast. She, a wife of two years' standing, should neither feel nor act thus, hut feeling, like a whirlwind, swept her, overcame her; tears dissolved his face when she looked at him. He bent and took her mouth hungrily, released her, hugged her to him again. She said, over the sound of Beaufort in strident proclamation from the dais: 'Ah, my lord, my lord! How I do love you!' Around them heads turned, though not in annoyance. For in those ageless words was something to make those long past love remember, and be kind.

They whispered together like children, holding one another close. Silly loving words: why had he tarried so long? She died by inches when he was away. It was her fault, he said, there had been many complex matters in the Groby estates for his eye, his seal, on which he could not stay his mind for thinking of Isabella. Six weeks, six whole weeks. Did she prosper? And the babe? In the shadow of a tall squire's cloak, his hand slid to caress her belly. Joyful tears stained her cheeks; he wiped them dry with his fine linen kerchief. Beaufort's voice rose and fell, filling the Hall with meaningless words. What had her father said? That this was the tide turning? Let them talk and talk. Her own tide was turned this very day. Her ship was anchored in the sweet slack harbour of love.

Then John said: 'I may have to go to war.'

Her racing pulse slowed. The grey arched pillars of the chamber rose high above her. She felt her body suddenly cast in their image; stone-cold and stiff, supporting the great weight of new trouble as they upheld the faded gilt roof ... It would be madness to swoon. All men went to war. Their women harnessed them, remembered them in the Mass, and waited for their returning, or their non-returning. Or did they swoon, the weaker ones? Only at the reality of death, not at a word. She had never succumbed to such fits in her life. It must be the babe that made her head ache and grow light as a puffball. John's arms pulled her back from a blinding greyness. Stinging heat rose in her eyes. She heard him say:

'Listen, sweeting, to the Queen. She is going to address the Council.'

Margaret's pallor held all eyes. Her diadem caught the light, and her little teeth gleamed in a wolfish smile. King Henry looked up frailly at her, and the little prince ceased toying with his dagger and took his mother's outstretched hand. He walked, well-schooled, with her to the edge of the dais, and stood, his white silk mantle falling to the floor about him. Margaret said clearly, fiercely:'My lords and loyal subjects! Behold our salvation! This day I give to you the emblem of our royal House, destined to be anointed with the Chrism. Born of my body to defend our throne. My lords! The Prince Edward!'

Like a shipwrecking sea, cheering split the air. It lasted long minutes while Margaret stood, surveying her son. The King muttered, startled, and looked towards heaven, while Beaufort moved to the prince's side, placing a bronzed hand on the small shoulder. Nearly all the councillors were tall, but Beaufort, in that moment, looked like a giant. The Queen began then to speak in earnest, her accent growing heavy, tortuous like a saw-edged knife, commanding like a mace. She lit the imagination and the loyalty of all. Even the sycophants who had squandered the King's treasure while he prayed were moved. She lashed them with her own ambition. She spoke with French oaths, calling on the saints and all her ancestors to witness her renewed hope, her strength, in the presence of England's heir. Her vengeance stirred a great wind in the Chamber, especially when she spoke of Beaufort.

'Remember, my lords, that when Richard Duke of York forced himself upon this realm as Protector, he had our dearest cousin imprisoned in the Tower? Is this protection? To use thus one who has earned our favour through his great and laudable counsel at all times? Is this loyalty? To our royal and beloved husband? To me?'

King Henry raised his eyes.'Forsooth, nay,' he said.

'Gentlemen,' continued the Queen, 'we are weary of this false pretentious claim of York and all his minions. We will suffer him no longer.' Her lips were slick with froth. 'My lords! If you are my loyal and noble Council, you will this day order an assemblage of all our military. For the purpose of safeguarding our person against all enemies. Messires! Will you array yourself accordingly?'

John's arm closed tighter about Elizabeth. 'This is a formality,' he whispered. 'We are out to frighten the Yorkists ... sweetheart, be calm.' But his own voice was far from such, and full of excitement. A roar answered Margaret's challenge. Already armed men were issuing from the adjoining chamber. Beaufort was down on one knee before the King. He proffered a sword. Uneasy and wistful, the King took it, weighed it, nodded an acceptançe, then bowed his head over the gleaming steel, tracing the cruciform hilt with a devout finger.

'Is the King to fight also?' Elizabeth found this hardly credible.

'There'll be no fighting; the Yorkists will run,' said John, as if he rued the prospect. 'And the King must show himself. He'll lead one of the levies. To Leicester.'

So he knew all the time, she thought sadly. Even the venue for the marshalling of the troops. I must be brave, like all other women. Yet no other woman loves as I ... The hall was hot with talk, the throng dispersing. Hand-clasped, she and John slipped out into the corridor. Already there was the chill sound of sharpening steel on stone from the neighbouring courtyard where there was an armoury. Sick with longing, she said: 'Pray Jesu you need not leave this very day.'

He laughed, lifted her off her feet, kissing her throat and bosom. 'Nay, sweet, my arms are in good order! All this franticking to prepare I'll leave to those who let their gear go rusty. Oh, Isabella!' He shrugged his body in the travelstained velvet. 'I'm not fit to kiss you. Lead me to a bath, and dinner!' She looked at his eyes and knew with gladness that the bath would be cursory, the dinner rushed through. Warmth flooded her. My love, she thought. And more; my saviour and my friend.

She awoke once in the night and cried out, full of some obscure image, a dream of shadows and dark places. And he was there instantly, drawing her down in his arms, so strong that her bones felt like a kitten's. The scent of him lulled her to sleep again before his murmurings of comfort had ceased. She dreamed again, that life itself was a dream, and that they walked together through drifting roses, their heads touched by the sun. There were flowers on every bush. When she bent to pluck the flowers she saw that they were really jewels, sapphire periwinkles, primroses of beaten gold. The rainbow blossoms were searing hot to the touch. She awoke laughing at the nonsense of it all, awoke to John's warmth and his drowsy amorousness. And the old dance of love again, to greet the morning.

The royal army left for Leicester three days later. Henry wore a purple mantle over ill-fitting armour. A great cross he wore made a weird clanking sound as it jounced on his cuirass. He scarcely seemed to know why he was so attired. Margaret knelt before him, kissed his hand, and he looked down upon her with a vague tenderness.

'Fie, my lady, why all this pother?' he remarked. 'If my lords do but love one another, all will be well.' He turned to look out of the window on to the Thames, which sparkled under the May sky.

Beaufort came then to the Queen. His harness was scoured to a mirror sheen. As if he were going to a tourney, he wore the daisy-flower, tucked into the join at his gauntlet.

'God speed you, *mon cousin*,' said Margaret. The King was still at the window, gazing and muttering.

'Look to his Grace,' she said.

'With my heart's blood,' replied Beaufort of Somerset. 'I would die a thousand deaths before he should come to harm.'

'And I will cherish our heir,' said the Queen, giving Beaufort her hand. He held it tightly, tears in his eyes. At that moment a messenger, spur-blood on the hem of his cloak, was admitted. He offered a sealed roll, which Margaret waved away. 'Speak!' she commanded. 'All here are my friends and advisers.'

'Your Grace,' complied the courier, 'I bring news that the Duke of York and his followers are encroaching upon Leicester. They march south, together with Lord Salisbury and his men. They are hot to defend themselves against what they call slander ... they come in peace, they say, to do homage to the King.'

'Force!' said Margaret coldly. 'Is this loyalty? Is this homage? And what of me? What of my beloved heir?'

The messenger said unquietly: 'Your Grace, the Duke of York would be Protector of the Realm again.'

'*Nom de Dieu!*' cried the Queen. 'I have had my belly full of York's protection. Sir, get you gone. Keep me informed. My lord—' to Beaufort, who rose from his knee— 'I wish you good fortune'. She took a large beryl from her finger. 'May this token aid you.'

Beaufort kissed the jewel, patron of soldiers and of love. He extended his arm to the King and together they left the chamber. Elizabeth was alone with the Queen, whose eyes were hard and gleaming, like the beryl. Fearsome eyes.

'Would Jesu I could go to war,' said Margaret softly.

A blackbird began its virile song outside the window. Elizabeth knew, as surely as if the Queen had told her, that it was not possible for her to leave for Bradgate yet. And the trees would be a foam of pink and white; the lake would be patterned with lilies. Her sorrel mare would have foaled and there was a new troupe of minstrels to play for dinner. Listening now to the diminishing tramp of mailed feet, the rattle of the drawbridge, she walked in fancy through her own manor. There was the hall, with its hearth fragrant with resinous logs struggling to burn against a joyful finger of sunshine through the lattice; the south wall covered with her favourite tapestry – Goliath and David, marvellously worked and lifelike ... the polished oak staircase. The chamber above with its great tester bed, empty now. The vast stone kitchen ... the servants would be idling – the steward too, who needed a firm hand and was in love with the cook.

Margaret's voice startled her, saying: 'I had it fashioned especially.'

A page knelt before the Queen, pieces of a suit of harness strewn about him. The cuirass sparkled, its convexities points of shattering light. The greaves were delicately wrought and chased, and the casquetal, darkness showing through its eye-slits, bore a plume of proud mantling. The Queen motioned to Elizabeth, who helped unfasten Margaret's robette. Without a word, the page, eyes on the floor, armed his sovereign. She was swiftly transformed into a figure of light. Small, mysterious, with the casquetal fitted over her head, she became half-human, neither male nor female. In her hand she took a heavy sword. The page fell back as Margaret took a few clumsy, weighted steps. Then she lifted her helm's visor. The face of a pale savage youth looked at Elizabeth.

'*Oui!*' she said. '*Comme La Pucelle d'Orléans!* I, Marguerite, should be with them this day!'

Then she laughed, her stern face softening, and lifted the helm gently from her head. 'But I do not go,' she said. 'I stay to guard my son, my hope, my pride.'

'Madame,' Elizabeth said nervously, 'John says there will be no fighting; the Yorkists will run.'

The Queen was swiftly disengaging herself from the cumbrous armour. With a sudden gaiety, she nodded, she even broke into a snatch of song.

'Your handsome lord speaks sooth, Isabella,' she said. 'The rats will run. So, I have indulged my fancy. We will to Greenwich, where I am always happy. Make ready the Prince. Come, Isabella, you shall entertain us. We'll drink to Lancaster. And to France,' she added, so softly that her words drifted almost unheard.

Elizabeth covered a sigh. No returning to Bradgate yet. Bradgate must wait, as it would always wait, secure and fair, gracious haven. For the twentieth time she opened the manuscript of verse and read aloud:

'*Benedicite*, what dreamed I this night?
Methought the world was turned up so down.
The sun, the moon, had lost their force and light,
The sea also drowned both tower and town.
Yet more marvel how that I heard the sound
Of one's voice saying: "Bear in thy mind,
Thy lady hath forgotten to be kind."'

The Queen loved this poem, and Elizabeth read it sweet and true. Yet Margaret sat silent, and, looking up, Elizabeth saw sadness on the pale face. Half to herself, the Queen said:

'*Nom de Dieu*! I have been kind. I have given him an heir to support his weakness. I have upheld him in all adversity. *Henri! Le pauvre!*'

'Sweet your Grace,' said Elizabeth, 'be easy. My lord of Somerset will look after him.'

She stretched her dull limbs. She would have loved to walk across the green pleasaunce to where beds of blossom flourished. There was a pool, too, where moorhens paddled from bank to bank. Yes, Greenwich was beautiful; but it was not Bradgate. Although she had been at Greenwich for only a few days, it seemed like years. Margaret's nervousness harassed her. Sitting daily under a May sun growing fiercer, the Queen would talk, in English, French, and Latin, and sometimes to herself, with determination, with disquiet. And there was no question of Elizabeth leaving her yet. Although Bradgate called in a torrent of memory she must sit, reading, or singing in her boyish treble little airs treating of God and the heart. She could not play with the little Prince; his mother kept him close confined, and besides, he was not the kind of child one played with. Daily Elizabeth felt the burgeonings of her own fruitful body, suffered discomforts that the Queen never noticed. Daily the minstrels who had been engaged to plumb King Henry's madness twanged and scraped in gallery and garden. *Ennui* dragged at Elizabeth. Once she had craved the court above all. Now she would have given blood for a sight of Bradgate.

Jacquetta of Bedford had returned to Grafton, and Sir Richard Woodville had ridden with the levies to Leicester. Elizabeth thought of her brothers and sisters. She had not seen Anthony for months. He would be almost a man, ready for such knightly exploits as those on which his father and John rode today. Poor, sweet John! frustrated by his lack of knighthood. Perhaps if he acquitted himself well in putting the Yorkists to flight, the King might rouse himself to honour him. Then there would be more lands, more fee-farms, to augment Bradgate. She dared not ask the Queen when the army might be returning with their tales of Richard of York's humiliation. Her only task was to divert the Queen from such thoughts. So she sat burned by the Greenwich sun, and read aloud.

'To complain me, alas, why should I so,
For my complaint it did me never good?
But by constraint now must I shew my woe,
To her only which is mine eyes' food,
Trusting sometime that she will change her mood ...'

The Queen was not listening. Elizabeth left the verse in mid-air and beckoned to one of the yawning lutanists. 'Sweet Madame, will you not sing with me?' Anything to relieve that *distrait* watchfulness. Margaret turned, smiling distantly. She sipped from the scarcely touched hanap of wine at her side, and suddenly looked almost gay.

'I will sing them all to perdition!' she announced, but she melted from her strait position and came to sit, sisterly, on the cushions with Elizabeth. A page, heartened by the sovereign's changed mood, poured more wine and drove away a wasp. The lutanist struck a sweet chord: The *Roman de la Rose,* in a setting by Antoine Busnois.

'Bel Acueil le sergent d'Amours,
Qui bien scait faire ses exploitz
M'a ja cite par plusieurs fois ...'

They looked at one another, broke off singing, and for no reason save the release of tension, both began to laugh.

'Oh, Isabella!' cried the Queen. 'I well remember the time when you first came to court — so little, so *vierge* ... abashed by my poor Henry's humours. Now, you possess yourself well, and do I understand you are *enceinte*? May your son be as brave and proud as mine!'

At last the Queen had noticed. 'Sweet Madame!' Elizabeth bent gratefully to kiss the small hand, and in that same moment felt it grow stiff, actually felt the blood leaving it so that it was icy, like a dead hand. She looked up, and followed where the Queen's eyes stared across the lawn. A man was running towards them. Running wearily; he stumbled twice and all but fell; he clutched at his side. His surcoat was ragged, its once-gay colours dirty. Half his mail was missing; he still wore steel gauntlets and part of his cuirass, but his legs were clothed only in torn and filthy hose. Down one thigh there was blood, seen clearly as he came nearer at that gasping, tripping run. His head was bare, and the sun tipped its familiar tawny with raw light. Elizabeth rose, freeing herself from the dead weight of the Queen's hand. She took a step forward but did not run to him. The despair on his face slowed her feet. With him he brought fear that almost vanquished the sharp joy of seeing him again.

'John, my lord,' she whispered. The blood was crusted on his thigh; it doubled her fear. He came on, running, the figurehead of a terrible catastrophe. Now he filled their sight; he fell before Margaret, fighting for breath.

'Your Grace,' he said, and retched, turning his head aside. In her own body Elizabeth felt the torment of his outraged lungs. The Queen had risen and was standing straight, her wine-cup overturned. The red liquor soaked the grass.

'Madame, your Grace,' he said. 'The news is dreadful. I beg leave to acquaint you with most dreadful news.' This sort of thing he said, over and over. Whatever he has seen, Elizabeth thought, terrified, it has addled his wits. She cried shrilly: 'What, John, in God's name?' And went to him and caught him in her arms, seeing the dried blood flake off against her gown. 'Oh, Christ, my love, you're wounded ...' He looked down, saying tersely: 'It's not my blood. Would Jesu it were.'

Not his blood. Oh, thank God, he is whole and sound, mine still, his beauty untouched. She clung to this, while his dreadful news came pouring out. The Queen's face seemed to put on years, a year for each word he spoke, until she was eternally old even past death.

'The Yorkists were magnificently arrayed, with a great force. All the

Nevilles and their mercenaries; Salisbury's troop alone outnumbered ours ... they fought like devils. We were trapped, we had no chance. Your Grace, your lords have suffered ... will you hear who died?'

'I will hear,' said Margaret.

'Lord Clifford,' said John, trembling as with ague. 'Northumberland, and Buckingham's son. Dorset, Devon and Buckingham were grievously wounded and taken prisoner. God knows where Wiltshire is; he fled the field. Sir Richard Woodville ...'

'Yes?' said Elizabeth. She bit her lip; it bled.

'Escaped by the hair of his head. He is safe, Isabella. Christ's Passion! They were waiting for us, ready ...'

'What of the King?' said the old woman that was Margaret.

'They are bringing him back to London. They will not mistreat him, they say, because he is the King. But they proclaim their power, Madame. Your captains are hacked to pieces.'

'And my lord Beaufort of Somerset?'

Jesu, she is calm, thought Elizabeth. It is not meet for her to be so calm. She frightens me. John looked down again at his stained hose.

'This is his blood, your Grace. I was close by him when he fell. Beaufort is dead.'

Still the Queen showed no emotion. She said: 'Where did this encounter take place?' Her voice was like a chafed thread.

'At St. Albans. We fought up and down the heart of the town.'

Then Margaret began to scream. She threw herself down upon the grass, and the spilled wine soaked her gown until it was bloodily red like the imagined corpses of those she loved, and she screamed.

'Cursed be the name of St. Albans!'

John, his face sweated and grief-torn, went on talking compulsively, while the Queen's shrieks faded to dry sobs and silence against Elizabeth's breast.

'The king is unharmed,' John a vain comforter, repeated. 'He ...' he laughed, a short, madman's laugh. 'He even jested with his captors. Love thine enemy, he said. He ... embraced my lord of York.'

The Queen raised her head. Blackness ringed her eyes, as if she had been struck in the face.

'I will make York to stink in the King's nostrils,' she said. 'Even unto death.'

The victorious Yorkists came to London with a show of peace, demanding their inheritance. Sternly they insisted upon a voice in the Council. They confronted the Queen, who was for a time powerless. And so a fretful kind of peace obtained, shot through with bloody risings from Margaret's party. And Bradgate shared this mockery of peace.

Like a cradle, the little boat tipped at its moorings in the willow's shade. It was an old boat discovered by Elizabeth during her lakeside ramblings. John swore it to be unseaworthy, yet she had ordered the leaks repaired with pitch and plaited rushes, and now, with mischievous triumph, shepherded her family into it for an afternoon of water-sport. She lay back comfortably in the stern. Her second son, Richard, slept in her arms. Three-year-old Thomas was pretending to fish. Renée who was not enjoying the outing, crouched miserably at her mistress's side. John, stripped to his shirt, had been glad to tie up the boat and rest, shipping the oars he had unskillfully plied across the deep green water.

'Well, my lady,' he said, loving and cross, 'I told you I was no mariner.' He rubbed his upper arms. 'This crossing has crippled me. Renée! Look to young Thomas! I did not get sons to see them drowned!'

Undisciplined as a fiend, Thomas romped between his parents in the boat, falling flat as the wind-stirred ripples rocked it, bawling and laughing at the same time. Renée clutched at him. She was water-green with fear, and as the boat pitched under Thomas's leaping, let out a muffled scream. Elizabeth spoke, a sharp rebuke, and the child quietened; with the silly young wench he could do as he pleased, but when his mother used that tone, it was time to act discreetly. So he sat down and treated her and his baby brother to a charming smile. Elizabeth thought him a lovely child. Wayward, yes, but so like John, with coppery chestnut hair and straight features. She cradled the baby closer. He too was lovely, and she had named him for her father, the best Richard living. The dappled sun touched her face. She trailed a hand in the water, feeling it cool as silk. Through the trees she saw the distant merlons of Bradgate, and closer, the face of John; eternally comforting, eternally fair. A wave of love filled her and unconsciously she smiled, a smile so dreaming and seductive that it was almost unearthly.

It was four years since the dreadful day at Greenwich; only a vague memory which she held best forgotten. Now that she had her sons,

John's frequent absences were less painful, and always short. Bradgate entwined itself deeper and deeper in her heart. It was a surrogate John, who was often summoned to Calais, where there was a new master. Loathed by the Queen's party but proud in his suzerainty as Captain of Calais, the Earl of Warwick sat with the Channel under his hand. Like some hideous spider, thought Elizabeth, and was thankful not to have witnessed Margaret being forced to accede to the appointment. She could imagine the Queen's face and voice, and the fancies brought unease. John was speaking of London affairs now, and she sighed, for the green day was fair, the water deep.

'This is the nub of the matter,' he said. 'The merchants and traders. The common folk are more powerful than a score of royal or rebel forces. The people want peace at any price. London is full of gossip and the Queen is the butt of most shameful ballads. Even John Hardyng – you remember him, he writes good verse – felt moved to express himself against the evils of the day.' He fumbled in his pouch for a scrap of paper. 'A copy was pinned to the door of St. Mary Woolchurch. None can punish Hardyng, for it's only the truth.'

Elizabeth took the slip and read.

In every shire with jacks and sallets clean,
Misrule doth rise and maketh neighbours war;
The weaker goes beneath, as oft is seen;
The mightiest his quarrel will prefer;
The poor man's cause is put on back full far,
Which, if both peace and law were well conserved,
Might be amend, and thanks of God deserved.

She said silently: I know naught of poor men. My neighbours don't war against me. Yes, I pity the weak but am glad I am not as they are. My needs are met; do not speak of things I do not understand. She handed the *billet* back to John without a word.

'The people hate Margaret openly now,' said John softly. 'They will never forgive her for what Piers de Brezé did at her command, two years ago.'

The Duchess of Bedford had brought that particular piece of news, smiling sardonically. The Queen is like a raging devil since Beaufort was murdered, she said. Now John said the same.

'You would not recognize Margaret; she has become a fiend. That is why she allowed Piers to land and burn Sandwich to the ground. A country invading itself! That pretty little port! I swear, Isabella, the world goes mad.'

A cloud crossed his face. He had been there, in the aftermath. He had seen children tossed into the flame, heard the screaming. The cobbles had been awash with firelit blood.

'They raped the women; they impaled infants on pikes. I remember Sandwich well.'

Elizabeth saw Renée's face grow sickly with dread. Tom, too was listening. 'Hé, Master Big-Ears!' she cried. But still John talked.

'The citizens of London are hot for York. They have heard Margaret's oath: that she will pillage and burn and ravish to secure the supremacy for her son. King Henry is like a dead man but the people are still loyal to him. It is the Queen they loathe. They offer up prayers that York will deliver England from the French she-wolf. They cry the Prince Edward bastard, saying that the Queen lay with James of Wiltshire, or Beaufort of Somerset. In York's Parliament, the boy was disinherited.'

Elizabeth looked at the water's depths, where dank reeds writhed. She felt the cool lapping turn icy against her fingers and withdrew them.

For the first time she felt and understood the tingling infective madness of Margaret's hatred. John said: 'They will not harm the King. York only wishes to be named heir when Henry dies. Warwick ...'

'Warwick!' Again, that name, clouding her summer's day..

'He has vast power. His exploits in the Channel are famed abroad. The merchants adore him. He has a way – proud and yet humble – that enchants the common man. His generosity excels.'

'Pox take Warwick!' cried Elizabeth, right in Renée's shrinking ear. Then she began to laugh, remembering that other time, not so long ago, when she had cursed Warwick accordingly. Had Warwick had his way she would be wed to Sir Hugh Johns. She threw the sleepy baby up and kissed him. John did not share her laughter.

'Sweeting, you would be safer at Westminster,' he said gravely. 'While I am away, Margaret's men could descend on this place and kill you all. She is recruiting the men of the north, and the Scots, who, by my faith, are Antichrist itself.' Renée stifled a moan. 'I think it best you come back with me to London.'

'Leave Bradgate?' cried Elizabeth. 'You'll have to bind and carry me. Besides, Margaret loves me, she would do me no harm. I will never leave Bradgate!' And she folded her red lips on the subject, while John gazed at her, thinking how little she knew. She had not seen Margaret, as he had, the last time; the ghastly, insane face, the eyes suffused with blood. Margaret's mercenaries ravaged where they would and Margaret, obsessed with hatred, had forgotten whom she loved.

'We shall none of us be touched,' said Elizabeth, with a heart-stopping smile. 'We are under Divine protection.' From the lake's centre a fish rose suddenly, like a warning light. An odd thought struck her, a thought of Melusine. Was Melusine ever jealous of God?

'The Duke of York has sons,' said John. 'Edmund, Edward, George, and the little, sickly one, Richard. Edward is Earl of March, Edmund Earl of Rutland. I saw Edward, the warlike one. He is taller than any man I know, and but seventeen. He says that if his father falls, he will rise like a phoenix in his stead. The Queen has sworn to have his head on a pike.'

For the sake of Thomas's perked ears, he forebore to describe what else the Queen had promised for Edward of March, and continued: 'He has a head of golden hair, and piercing blue eyes. A great broad fellow. I wish,' he said sadly, 'that as King Henry is so often wont to say, these lords could love one another. For when I saw Ned of March … enemy though he be, I liked him.'

She said sharply: 'Have sense, for God's love! York and all his sons are our sworn foes. Usurpers and pretenders!' John's fair skin reddened.

'Are you quarrelling?' asked Thomas with interest. John ruffled his hair. 'Nay, child, just husband and wife. When you have a wife, you must beat her often!' They all laughed, and Elizabeth asked, as a diversion: 'How does Lady Margaret Beaufort, and her noble Richmond Tudor?'

'Didn't you know? She wed and buried him almost within the year. She has a son, Henry, two years old. Poor Edmund never saw the child.'

'Holy Jesu! What killed him?'

'Margaret's terrible learning, so they say,' chuckled John. 'With her philosophy and Greek, her disputations and dissertations, Edmund, unsure of his own wit, pined and died. But Margaret will be married again soon. To Henry Stafford. She is proud of the babe,' he added.

'Now being nurtured by his uncle Jasper, in Wales.'

Secretly he thought of Margaret Beaufort with distaste. She flaunted at court as if her descent were of the most royal. Her bravado made no pretence at covering old history. The Beauforts were merely descended from John of Gaunt and his mistress, Kate Swynford. Bastards all, legitimized by Richard II with the proviso that none of the line should ever aspire to the Crown. Yet Margaret strutted like an Empress; her small black eyes could intimidate. There was something unnatural about her. He yawned, suddenly weary of all these heavy thoughts. Isabella sat opposite him in her white and saffron dress and Tom was pestering to catch some fish. John unhitched the boat and pushed off. They floated around the lily-pads, and the sun was bright.

Later, the sun down, the moon high, there were no wars in the whole world. Within the great tester bed there was no room for fear or cruelty, King or Queen. In that warmth was sanctuary, fair as a flower and sweet as honey.

She dreamed the jewelled dream again and turned to him in sleep, smiling like a happy child.

The following Christmas, snow fell. Snow the like of which defeated men's memory, so thick and violent were the storms. The snow came like a silent white army from the shapeless sky. For an hour or so it would cease, when the close-packed whiteness seemed watchful, aggressive. Crisply it covered the frozen ground, the sleeping plants beneath. The lake was patched over by stiff ice, the lilies visible only as sad pale shapes. Then a fresh fall would descend, until the drifts climbed knee-high against the walls of Bradgate and each gargoyle on the buttresses wore a high white helm. In the surrounding meadows, the hirelings dug out frozen sheep. Men cursed and battled against the whirling white flakes, and struggled in sodden jerkins through days which seemed to last only a lead-grey hour until nightfall.

Elizabeth felt unbearably cold. She ordered great pine-log fires to be lit in every room; she wrapped herself in fine wool and fur. At night, rather than be prey to the draught which savaged the bed-curtains, she took Renée and the baby to sleep with her. They lay close-hugged under every available bed-cover, and still she was cold. Part of the chill was born of John's absence. He had ridden north on the King's service and this was the longest separation she had had to endure. She pictured him encamped somewhere on an icy wind-ravaged field, and his distress enhanced her own. No word came from him; the roads were almost impassable. The only person to get through to the manor was an old beggar, solid in death on the doorsill one morning, his beard pointing upward almost comically, like a jagged ice-sword.

The cold shortened her temper. It irked her that she could not wander the estate. A quicksand of white surrounded her, its great drifts hiding dead cattle. The servants went quietly about, their voices like the hush and drip of soft snow from the eaves. Although she knew her ill humour would pass with the sunshine, she crouched sadly by the roaring fire in the hall, with the cradle close at hand and Thomas snivelling from the inglenook, with a heavy cold. He was becoming more wayward, openly disobeying his nurse and tor- menting the servants. Once, he even disobeyed his mother, staring insolently. She smacked his face; he did not weep, only went with a dangerous look to do her bidding.

Christmas came too soon. Elizabeth paced the house, bitterly dis- appointed that there was none to share the merriment engineered by Jakes, her long-faced fool, and that of the pages he had trained to bring diversion over the holy season. On Christmas Day she knelt before the altar in the little chapel, her face flowerlike in the light of a score of festive candles. She whispered: *Blessed Christ, let John come home before the Twelve Days are out. Let him be here to make my season bright, bringing his own sun that melts snow* ... The candles flickered, coldly dispassionate. Her chaplain turned and watched her curiously. He thought her fair but unpredictable. He could not know her mind, her sudden discovery: that no feasts, no comfort or gaiety could satisfy in John's absence. All was empty as air. Only Bradgate remained, her fortress and her rock, and even that like a hearth without a flame.

She thought of Christmas at Grafton Regis. The little sisters would be grown. Did Catherine miss her? Was Anthony home, full of wit, fashioning new games for them to play in the Great Hall? Lionel, let out from his clerkly studies? Edward, with his sea-coloured yarns? Was Sir Richard seated at the laden table, his colour deepening in firelight and wine? She did not even know if her father rode on campaign this Christmas. No messages; not a word, and only the hush of the deepening snow.

The steward and his wife were hungry. Far away down the hall, the pinched faces of her henchmen looked cheered as the roast peacock was borne in, its tail feathers spread in an iridescent fan over the meat. The venison frumenty was glazed with savour. Elizabeth set Thomas in the chair beside her, and warned him to behave well. She motioned to Jakes to dance, tell a story. In the gallery minstrels set up a sweet cold wailing. 'A toast, Madame,' said the steward gallantly 'To our beloved mistress, this holy season.' The wine in his cup was a jewel; an old memory sprang from nowhere. Queen Margaret, spilling her wine, a bloody stain upon her gown. Her screams. Elizabeth wrapped a fur tippet closer about her throat, and forced a smile.

'To Bradgate,' she responded, and the small company raised their goblets. She was suddenly renewed. This was her demesne. Never would she lust for anything more. Grafton Regis might be filled with a gay family; but she would dine with servants in Bradgate and count herself fortunate. Yet still she felt cheated, and angry with the Presence behind the cold white candles in the chapel. The Twelve Days were passing like a fugitive, and John was not there to share them.

There came a thaw. Water dripped from the gargoyles and cascaded down the towers. The stiff reeds on the lake became pliant like the swords of a vanquished army. The lake itself swelled, black and dangerous. The thaw was followed by freezing, virulent gales carrying more ice from the north, scattering the hard powdery snow-pellets everywhere. The steward slipped on fresh black ice and broke his arm. He lay agonized for days, and Elizabeth brewed the dried root of mandragora for his easement. Thomas grew naughtier and the babe more handsome. The treacherous roads yielded and John came home, as if at the whim of some spiteful force, now that the revels were over, the wine drunk, and the rich food a memory.

He came by night. Through a dream she heard the stamp and jingle of horses, the swish of hooves crossing melted snow. She awoke instantly. Her first thought was of Queen Margaret's mercenaries, earlier so gaily dismissed, and with it came the chilling realization that Margaret's love for her might indeed have waned. For was not she, Elizabeth, the sole witness to that which Margaret must most ardently conceal? The knowledge that the prince, the Flower, was neither conceived of the Holy Ghost nor of King Henry, but of Beaufort of Somerset? She began, in a heartbeat, to count the servants reliable enough to wield cudgel and axe for her protection. She slipped from the bed and ran to the window, snatching the baby Richard from his cradle. Outside it was broad moonlight, and passing through the courtyard were dark horsed shapes. More riders were silhouetted on the edge of the lawn, their mounts' hooves churning the snow-filmed grass. Someone swung a lantern high. She heard the great door below reverberating to a mailed fist, then the steward's shuffling feet. There were voices, strong and wide awake, the rasp and groan of keys. The hounds were snarling and raving. Suddenly their threatening note changed to bays of joy. Only for John did they make that keening, loving sound. She laid Richard down again and flung a robe about her. The moonlight whitened her hair; it hung to her knees. She ran along the gallery and stood at the stairhead, looking down upon a hall swarming with men. They were a weary, unshaven company, and most of them were harnessed. Pages were hurling logs on the half-dead fire, and plying bellows. Someone was calling for wine, and the steward was shouting at servants who ran with candles, flagons.

Drawing the robe close, she descended the stairs, her hair blowing in an icy draught. John came to the stairfoot holding out both hands. The rest of the company turned to look upwards. As one man they went upon their knee, a startling, pleasing gesture. She made a little, queenly motion bidding them rise. Then she was in John's arms.

'Sweet Jesu! You're wet through!' she cried, feeling damp soaking her thin robe. 'William! Gervase! Bring fresh garments, and see to that fire!'

'Once, my lady, I felt you likewise,' he said, with a little smile. 'Oh, the lake! How I love the lake!' He mocked her lovingly, but his voice was blank with weariness. His face was drawn and hag-ridden under a stubbly beard.

'These are my friends.' He indicated the men behind them. 'They have fought and ridden hard with me ...' He wavered and clutched the banister. Elizabeth led him to the fire; he dropped into the ingle-nook. She turned to offer hospitality to his followers, seeing bloody bands around a head, a wrist. While the servants scurried with meat and bread and mulled possets, she sat close beside John, while the hounds fawned on him. He had lost flesh; he closed his eyes and there were blue bruises under them. As he took a steaming cup, his hand shook like an ancient man's. She said, whispering: 'My love, my lord, you are sick.' He replied. 'Nay, only weary unto death.' To her distress he began to weep silently, tears issuing from beneath his closed lids.

'Tis a strong fatigue that I can mend, she told herself. The herbal my mother gave me; Valerian, Our Lady's balm, the juice of the cherry to bring tranquillity ... She rose from his side murmuring: 'Forgive me, love, I'll not be long.' He held her hand, fast.

'Give thanks that you are a woman!' His hard voice surprised her. 'Lord God, the sights that I have seen these months, and this last week! Well, Isabella! Your Queen has her heart's desire.'

He opened his eyes. 'York's head upon a pike. And Salisbury's. And Edmund of Rutland. Seventeen years old, that one. In York, on Micklegate, those three proud foolish heads stare out, still bloody. The Queen's men placed paper crowns about their brows. So York, the king that never was, now overlooks the town of York.'

Gladness welled in her. Now the wars would be over, and John with her always. She said, excited: 'And Warwick? Where is his head?'

The man with the bandaged head spoke. He was a great sergeant-at-arms, with bull-shoulders.

'Warwick's head still adjoins his body. He remained in London, to oversee the government.' He spat into the fire, and Elizabeth's brief satisfaction faded. It would have been such a sweet, private triumph. Still, with York dead, Warwick must surely abandon his cause. John, cold hand warming in hers, began to tell her all that had happened during the past months.

Soon after John left Bradgate in July, Warwick, Salisbury and Edward of March advanced on London. Spurred on by the chroniclers and balladeers, the City welcomed them like paladins. The magistrates of London loaned them a thouand pounds to equip their force, the merchants extolled them. Weary of the Queen's dementia, the King's fogged image, the citizens upheld their new salvation, who rode to Northampton, gathering men as they went. There, they joined battle wth the royal army and in less than an hour were victorious. Again Margaret's lieutenants suffered sorely; the Duke of Buckingham, not long since released from prison, the new Earl of Shrewsbury, Lords Egremont and Beaumont were slain. Again the King was taken in courtesy to London, where York claimed the throne by hereditary right. This denouement fanned the flame of Margaret. From the sanctuary of Harlech Castle she set about recruiting fresh troops; the wild northerners, the rampant Scots, the fanatical Welsh. And in the blinding snow that fell over England, that had struck cold in even Elizabeth's young bones, the crisis was reached, at Sandal in Yorkshire.

As Christmas approached, the Lancastrian party and the Duke of York's men agreed to hold a truce for the holy season. Cold and weary, the Duke retired to his castle at Sandal, while a few leagues away the royal army encamped at Pontefract. A quiet descended, John said; an eerie, snowfilled quiet that no great fires or forced mirth could dispel. Victuals were scarce, and tempers like bowstrings. The royalists, minds filled with their Queen's frenzy, sat tensely staring through the greyness towards Sandal. And on the thirtieth of December, something broke in the hearts of those men. The captains ordered an immediate advance. Violation of truce it may have been, but there was no gainsaying that brutal decision.

York was almost alone in his fortress. Half his men were out foraging; the rest slept exhaustedly.

'We killed the guard and the troops stationed outside the castle, and we burst into the Hall. Young Rutland got away after York was slain, but he was pursued to Wakefield and struck down. Salisbury was killed almost at once.'

The Yorkists had made a pitiful attempt at jollity, hanging holly and mistletoe, and soon those green boughs floated in a sea of blood. Dead and dying littered the courtyard. And the following day the Queen's men followed her command to the letter: crowned with paper and straw, they were impaled, the stricken heads of Rutland, Salisbury, and York.

Elizabeth said softly: 'Then this ends our sorrow. The Queen may rest easy. Oh, my lord ...'

He turned on her violently. 'Jesu! Madame, you talk like a child! Think you that York's kin will suffer this loss mildly? Have you forgotten that Warwick goes unscathed, and that in the West, gathering more armies, rages Edward of March? Like a phoenix, he said! And like a phoenix, he will rise against the Queen! The citizens pray for his victory. Don't you know that even now Margaret's men march southward, raping and burning! They sack churches, murder nuns and priests ... Do you think that Edward of March will forgive his father's and brother's death?'

In all their time together he had not rebuked her thus. My lord is sick ...' she whispered. 'Weary ...!

'Weary of war.' He closed his eyes again. 'This old, damned weariness. What a fashion in which to spend one's life! When there is beauty and truth and learning to enjoy, I must ride, by day and night, chafed by my harness, rain upon my head, blood on my hands ...'

He lifted his lids to show tenderness. 'All I ever asked was you. To sit in peace with you, on my own manor, to lie in peace o' nights with you in my arms. Even a knighthood matters little now, my love, my Isabella.'

He rose from the fireside stiffly. In every corner of the shadowy Hall men were asleep, heads pillowed on saddles or garments, faces blank with exhaustion.

'To bed,' he said, staggering. 'We must be up betimes; tomorrow we have many leagues to cover.'

'Tomorrow!' she cried, awakening one of the sleepers. 'Yes, we must ride southerly and join the royal army to help guard against Edward of March's advance, and Warwick's. Their troops are coming from all parts of the realm. They seek to gain London.'

Silently she escorted him to the bedchamber. There he stood for a little while looking down at the baby in his cradle. In the next room Thomas cried out sharply in a nightmare. John's tired face relaxed; he sank upon the bed. With difficulty she removed his boots that were stiff and crusted with mud and snow. Almost instantly he was asleep, and she covered him with the quilt. As he succumbed his hand sought hers, and clasped it. So, throughout the remainder of the night, she sat, half-frozen, her fingers bonded in his, her long soft hair falling protectively about his face. She would not lie down. She would watch him until dawn; and how soon that dawn came up! She awakened him with hot wine, fresh clothes, and helped him with his harness. She said little, for there was an air of hushed ceremonial about the proceedings, as well as a heart-tearing regret. He kissed the boys, who were still asleep, and Elizabeth he held for a long moment in which she felt the forbidding chill of his steel breast; and he said, once more: 'Isabella, my heart's joy!' and then, 'Now, we ride.'

Ride then, said her mind. Ride and return, my love. And with the inexorable beat, the dull, living beat of her heart and the diminishing hooves, came the old wedding rhyme.

> The fairest man,
> That best love can,
> Dandirly, dandirly, dandirly, dan!

There was more black ice, more snow. Snow, that had killed the timorous February buds, that swelled the lake to a murky flood. It swirled dark and dangerous, like her own unrest. Where were they now? Two months, two long months. She tried to envisage him, hoping his face had lost that look of bitter trouble; that he rested somewhere during a break in fighting; that the fighting was over. She delved deep, remembering times of gladness, feeding on words and images to soothe the irksome, waiting winter. If she closed her eyes she could recreate his strength, his lips, his hand playing with her hair. And his words: 'My sweet Isabella, my dear Isabella, my douce one, my fair one, my joy!' If she could have a penny for every word that had caressed her, she would buy another tapestry to grace the wall opposite Goliath and David. Sweet fancy ... the tapestry shone the length of the hall. It was the fairest of all her possessions. The might of the giant, the subtle half-naked grace of the young David, the gay colours. Thomas was tugging at her sleeve. He chattered ceaselessly, laughs and cries of temper mingled. All morning he had whined to ride his pony. Elizabeth, or rather the weather, had forbidden it. He was tugging, tugging, trying to pull her across the room.

'Mother! There's a man coming!'

He let go her sleeve and ran to the window, mad with excitement, as well he might be. Since John's departure, not even a dead beggar had visited the manor. Next moment the steward stood in the doorway. His broken arm had healed badly, it was misshapen and ugly; she averted her eyes from it. The man stood looking at the floor, passing his tongue over his lips. Jesu, she thought, this long winter has addled him. I share his vagaries, being fogged by lordlack and ignorance of the realm's affairs. She said, her voice made sharp by this realization: 'Well? What is it, Hal?'

'An emissary from the Queen's Grace, Madame.'

He bowed into the shadows and let another figure through, one as snow-stained and unkempt as any of John's fighting men had been. One whose familiar face brought a urge of inexplicable affection. The graceless face of a court page.

She moved forward swiftly. 'Why, Master Barnaby!'

She waited for him to greet her, Ho, Dame Grey! winking and saucy enough to be whipped, but his insouciance was gone. He must have learned manners, she thought, for he went on his knee on the stone flags and kissed her hand; and he kept his head bent during what even she thought a long homage. She noticed that the insides of his boots were rubbed almost through, as if he had ridden hard to be with her.

He had caught his neck on a thorn, too, dried blood was patterned on the skin. He was pressing his brow upon her wrist, she felt a wetness on her hand. So, to jostle him from whatever pangs assailed (did the knave dare to love her?) – she said: 'Up, Barnaby! What news from court? Who holds sway there, these perilous days?'

He made a muffled noise. 'Tears, Master Barnaby?' she said mockingly.

Then he rose, thinner, damp-suited, dolorous. Not a vestige of mirth in him, only embarrassment. 'Dame Grey,' he whispered. 'They sent me, for I can ride swiftly. All the way I came, from St. Albans.'

The Queen's image arose, shockingly clear. 'Cursed be the name of St. Albans!' Thomas was ramping round Barnaby, feinting at him with a wooden sword.

'Tell me,' she said.

He stood very straight, as if for execution. 'Sir John Grey is slain, my lady.'

She thought: Barnaby is talking to me of some slain knight. So I must in courtesy ask him details, how this one died, and why. This she did, very calmly.

'He was grievously wounded at the fighting at St. Albans. The Earl of Warwick met Queen Margaret's force in a second battle there, and the Queen was victorious. She called it her vengeance for the first battle when Beaufort was slain. Warwick fled. But Sir John Grey led the last cavalry charge that routed the Yorkists. And he was wounded, and died.'

'Where?'

'In his tent. At St. Albans. Wounded head to foot and bloody. At cursed St. Albans, Sir John Grey, knight, did die.'

But John is not a knight! A frail gladness rose. It is some other, for he is but plain John Grey. Poor John, who ever craves knighthood. Sweet John. He is not dead.

'My husband lives,' she said, greatly relieved. 'There is, to my knowledge, no Sir John Grey.'

Barnaby was weeping copiously.

'They did knight him 'ere he died. For his services in war. They vowed none fought so bravely or with such chivalry, sparing the defenceless, crushing the strong. They gave him a knighthood.'

Outside the snow began again, softly covering the ground. Life struggled beneath, small buds kissed by cold to an infant death. Elizabeth snatched up a cloak. He was wounded; she would bring him to life. She would staunch his blood with her own body. There were elixirs known only to her mother and herself, secrets to heal a man of the most dreadful wound. Thomas was shouting around the room, war-cries, wielding his little sword.

'Saddle me horses. My lord needs me,' she said urgently.

'Madame, your lord is dead!' said Barnaby sadly. He took the cloak from her; it fell to the floor.

She would not scream as Queen Margaret did at the news of cursed St. Albans, or the taste of those screams would be forever in her mouth. With great care she sank to sit upon the floor, while the drain of grief within grew and grew until she felt bloodless from head to foot.

Sir John Grey, knight, is dead. There is no John.

As if the winter had slaked its venom in her anguish, the fierce weather yielded. On the trees' stark limbs tiny tight buds showed themselves again. The lake receded, leaving a vista of cool busy water. And the manor was filled with the presence, the essence of John. It ringed her round with a desperate comfort, retrieving the past to veil her agony. In this unseen nimbus she wandered, lonely and sad as a ghost, speaking rarely, seeing the faces of all who dwelt with her as unreal shadows. Images from a time gone by and. never to come again. So tormented, indrawn, she knew a half-life, and was sustained only by Bradgate's stout walls and vivid furnishings. The meadows, like creatures recovering from long sickness, gained fresh slow colour from the wary assault of spring. She told herself: I shall make Bradgate a shrine to John.

Prostrate before the chapel altar, she heard the thin reedy note of the singing-boys rising, sweet and sour and tender, in the Requiem Mass. She flooded the stones beneath her face with hot tears; the first, last and only tears. It was only a short relief; she wondered: when shall I be done with this witless watching for his return, this night-waking, hungry for his presence? Under the high cold psalm that soared and soared she wept for the waste of a young life, a strong ardent body, a courageous, tender soul. Leaving the chapel, she caressed a stout pillar. Thank you, my lord, my love. Thank you for Bradgate. Always, I shall cherish it for your sake.

Slow as an old woman's steps, March came and went with lengthening days. What to do with those days? those months and years ahead? Only wait for night to come, and then another day, and another. Nothing else; no hooves striking unexpected joy from stones; no moonlit ecstasy, no mellow future. She took needle and thread and a length of stuff and fashioned the widow's barbe and wimple, coiling; her hair so that none of it showed beneath the stark headgear. Now she was a nunly thing of the spirit, pale, the blue eyes darkened with sorrow, her heart often raging and rebellious. And at this time, unknown to her, half England quailed under a fresh battle, and the tide of war turned yet again.

Green April came to mock her with the time when she first rode to Bradgate. That was the same cuckoo, surely, chuckling and invisible in the leafing trees; the same clustered primroses, rising like tiny gold roses where the snowdrops had hung their heads. Yet the air seemed chill; did that fickle sky still herald storm? One day she could bear the sounds of spring no longer. She went to the chapel murmuring within the ghostly halo of candlelight: '*Ipsis, Domine ... et omnibus in Christo quiescentibus ...*' Grant to them, we entreat Thee, a place of cool repose, of light and peace. His face was a. star against her closed lids, his face, its image still sharp enough to turn a knife in her heart. She felt the coolness of the carved prayerstall. Old wood, his heritage, hers, and that of their children. In the quiet that followed the requiem, she heard, very faintly, sounds outside. Horsemen again. A shiver ran through her body. Then, there was a mighty knocking on the outer door. It was like the sound of a judgement. She adjusted the seemly wimple and went to meet whoever it might be; she was pale, unknowing, ready.

There was the steward with his twisted arm, gesticulating, vainly barring the way to a score of armed knights. Their grouped presence made the doorway dark, their plumes wavered in the April breeze. The foremost brushed aside the gibbering steward and entered. He was tall. The light behind him hid his face but she knew him. Ah, she knew him. Tethered near the staircase where she stood were John's two wolfhounds. They were old, but more savage than ever. Her hand went to their collars. She bent, whispered into the pricked ears, smelled the meaty tang of their breath, and struck off their chains. They leaped, roaring, straight for the tall figure who advanced so steadily.

Quickly he stripped his gauntlet and extended his fingers to the hounds and spoke. What he said she never knew, but the hounds became gentle, submissive and dropped their muzzles. To see her weapons thus blunted filled her with fury, new, necessary, warming. He came towards her, doffing his helm. Yes, she knew him. She spoke first, trembling with loathing;

'My lord of Warwick.'

Unhurriedly he bowed and straightened so that he towered above her. He looked older, grimmer, but was otherwise the same as at Eltham.

'Dame Grey,' he said. The large brilliant eyes encompassed her, rageless, calmer than she. She looked over his shoulder and saw the knot of armed men who accompanied him walking the Hall, obviously appraising its trappings. One of them fingered the Goliath tapestry. She said in a cold incredulous voice: 'What means this intrusion?'

'Your dogs are fierce, Dame Grey,' said Warwick calmly. 'And your manners are no better than I remember them. Is it not customary to offer refreshment to guests?'

'Uninvited guests?' she said violently. She saw then that the steward, obviously intimidated, had given orders already; Renée came, white-faced, bearing a flagon of wine and cups. The last of the Rhenish, thought Elizabeth furiously. May it choke this Yorkist swine. Warwick poured wine into two hanaps.

'Will you not drink, Dame?' he said. She took the cup he held, saw his eyes on her shaking hand. Rage, my lord, not fear, she wanted to say, and bit her lip against it.

'Pleasure yourself, sir,' she said shortly. 'Then do me the goodness ...'

Her eyes went again to the soldiers who milled about the Hall. They were examining the furniture. The hounds were growling softly, and Warwick's voice was mixed up in the growl.

'I come to acquaint you with the fortunes of England. You should know, Dame Grey, that York's cause is utterly triumphant. We have crushed the madwoman. That French canker in England's heart is excised at last. I have set Edward of March on England's throne. At the battles of Mortimers Cross and Towton, that proud prince was victorious. Dame Elizabeth–' here, the coldness of his voice was replaced by exaltation – 'we have a new King. King Edward the Fourth, may God preserve him for ever!'

Renée was serving the soldiers with wine; they laughed, they tickled her chin, but at Warwick's words all their mirth vanished. They raised their cups devoutly and drank deep. Elizabeth heard her own voice, asking after Queen Margaret, King Henry.

'The Frenchwoman has fled to Scotland, with her bastard whelp,' said Warwick brutally. 'His Grace King Henry is in London, little better than a drooling idiot. Edward of March is King. And you, my lady, are to forfeit this manor to the Crown.'

He went on, saying that she had profited herself well in her marriage to the dead Lancastrian knight. He told her that her father and brother had tasted his tongue at Calais, being but mean squires and knaves, unfit to have language of princes, such as he, Warwick, and Salisbury and York, God assoil their murdered souls ... And all this might well have been left unsaid, for she heard none of it. His previous sentence had drawn all the breath from her body. Her face, reflected in the polished wine-cup, was yellowish-grey as she stared at it. Even Warwick saw the change in her; he said, more kindly:

'I have an escort outside to take you to Grafton Regis. You may have your maidservant, but the others must stay to help my bailiffs with the inventory.'

Still she could not speak. They were taking down the Goliath tapestry. Four men staggered under its jewelled weight. They rolled it like a corpse; Warwick watched them. 'Forfeit to the Crown,' he said, as if in explanation. Then, holding up his wine-cup. 'Come, Dame Grey! Drink a toast to better days! Will you salute King Edward the Fourth?'

Deeply in his eyes she looked, and the brilliant pupils flickered for a moment as if she had struck him. Then she turned her hanap upside down so that the wine streamed out and splashed his boots.

'Dame, dame,' said Warwick, his voice thickly outraged. 'Did you think it wise to make an enemy of me?'

He had said it before, at Eltham. Had she married Sir Hugh, none of this would have happened. She would have known no love, no happiness, no despair. Bereft, she said the one thing that could wound his chivalry. Out of her humiliation it came, and found its mark.

'I will go then, and make ready. All my black gowns. Do you, my lord, think it brave to persecute widows?'

While the dark flush still bloomed on his neck, she curtseyed, insultingly low. Then, small and upright, she ascended the stairs. Behind her came the sound of Bradgate being stripped to the bones.

She seated herself before her mirror. Her hatred uncoiled like one of the serpents that lie sleeping for centuries to arise at their appointed time. She breathed like a runner over many leagues, like a woman in the throes of love, or labour, or madness. Her lips were stiff. She watched the mirrored ghostly face; it stared her out.

'Grief, misfortune and tragedy attend them for ever,' she said softly.

And the mirrored face was that of Melusine, the serpent. Melusine the beautiful. Melusine the accursed, who, with all her ancient force, now rose to damn the House of York.

They reached Grafton in two days. Renée and the baby went in a litter; Elizabeth, spurning comfort and setting a wild pace, rode her old sorrel, and Thomas jounced at her saddle bow. Warwick's escort were completely silent, like wraiths in harness, eyeless and anonymous behind closed visors.

Jacquetta of Bedford was waiting. She wasted no words; she chivvied Elizabeth's weeping sisters to their lessons and sent the little boys to the nursery. She went then with Elizabeth to the private solar, where she took her daughter in her arms, hiding Elizabeth's face against her heart.

The still-beautiful eyes grew large in powerful thought. The lips moved comfortingly. *Now*, the eyes said. As I forecast. This knight of hers, who was naught, has played his part and is gone. She is despoiled of possessions, also naught, compared with what will be. The time is now, the way is open for our heritage, our destiny among the stars.

She is fairer even than I was, and Edward of March is a lecherous young fool.

Now I can begin.

PART TWO

The Rose of Rouen
1463–78

The Rose came to London, full royally riding.
Two archbishops of England they crowned
the Rose King.
Almighty Lord! save the Rose, and give him
thy blessing.
Edward IV's Coronation Song: Anon.

King Edward the Fourth awoke early on a fine summer's morning.
He was tickled out of a pleasant dream by the sun's rays probing a
chink in the bedcurtains. For some moments he lay stretching his
long limbs and trying to recapture the dream's fleeting savour, but
it was already gone, where all dreams go, back into a world of false
joy. None the less, its essence was sweet enough to bring a smile
to the King's face, a radiance that passed over the strong chin and
sensual mouth until it reached the blue eyes and lineless forehead.
He stretched himself to the full until his six feet four inches were
taut and glowing; he flung out one hand to caress the damask sheet
beside him. Now, in warm and sensuous morning, was the time to
welcome a woman's body with searching fingers. The bed's other half
was barren, however, so he abandoned these thoughts. He moved
his golden brow into the narrow path of sunlight and lay still. Youth
and strength bubbled up in an almost unbearable flood. He was King

of England and Ireland, and, more significantly, he was twenty-one years old.

Beyond his curtained feet he could hear his esquires snoring. They whistled and groaned; his lips twitched in amusement. Sluggards all! He would have them out hunting, straight after Mass. The sombre courtiers too; he would see them horsed and running through briars and bogs, after fox or boar or stag, consummating his own life-lust in their discomfort. He bore them no ill-will, though; he loved them. They had earned his love, through their loyalty to York. They were in the main older than he. He thought on them briefly; Chancellor George Neville, Bishop of Exeter, a powerful, strong-spoken man; John Tiptoft, Constable of England, with his bloody-humoured dedication to duty; Lord Hastings; the Chancellor's brothers, John Neville, Marquis of Montagu, faithful and fierce, and Richard, Earl of Warwick. Warwick, the King's protector and mentor. He who had cloven stoutest during the last few perilous years, and who, by his own acknowledgment had set the crown upon the sovereign's head.

Yes. He loved Warwick, no question of that. By force of arms, by strategy and determination, and by a modicum of luck, Warwick had achieved for York's son what York himself had failed to do. Edward was grateful. Yet his sleepy smile faded a trifle when he remembered that he had promised Warwick an audience in the State Chamber that morning. This would undoubtedly delay the hunting expedition. Concourse with Warwick was inevitably a lengthy affair; matters of state and policy were all meat for his painstaking discussion and advice sprang readily to his lips, as if he still considered Edward his pupil. God's Blessed Lady! thought Edward suddenly. I am the King! Now pupil can bid master come and go!

Although there were facets in Warwick which brought out all Edward's obstinacy, which could be considerable, they were joined by blood. Family ties (the King's mother, Cicely Neville, was sister to Warwick's father, the dead Salisbury) and the sword had brought them closer than brothers. In hard weather and pitiless conditions they had achieved the impossible. Warwick had embraced the future king, a fierce, fatherly embrace, after the battles of Towton Field in Yorkshire and Mortimers Cross in Herefordshire. Mortimers Cross: Edward's face sobered as he recalled his vision there. He had scarcely believed it, then; even now he found it incredible. But others had seen it too. In thought, he was back in the battle tent, rising on the morning which, had he but known it, would give him victory. Victory over the French whore, her bastard son and Henry, that barren twig of Lancaster. He had staggered, sick with cold and sleep, through the tent-flaps, his harness, as he put it on, like pieces of burning ice. His heart was low, not through fear but at the prospect of another day's march, snatched meals, hurried decisions, frustration. Then, more from habit than grace, he looked towards heaven, and saw – three suns. Not one, but three! The men-at-arms, at whom he clutched, crying of his discovery, had seen them too. They swore it. Shattered, inspired, he looked so long upon the fiery triumvirate that it remained imprinted on his eyeballs for hours afterwards. Throughout that day, when nothing could go awry, the day that became truly and irrevocably his.

Blessed be God who sent that sign. He muttered it, lying naked and warm in the great bed, whose hangings bore witness to the miracle, being embroidered with his new device, the *rose en soleil*. A rose within a sun in splendour, for was he not acclaimed the Rose of Rouen, place of his birth? At his coronation (a hurried affair, with less magnificence than he would have wished) they presented him with an anthem versed accordingly by which he had been deeply moved. He was the White Rose incarnate, the only Rose. So warming were these thoughts that his fleeting twinge of impatience at Warwick's ceaseless counselling vanished.

Just then, something unknown touched off an echo of his lost dream. There had been a woman's face, not young, but fair. The lips had moved constantly, and he had struggled vainly to catch at some vital intelligence. Watching those red lips with the lines like parentheses around them, he had felt a queer lift of excitement. He had seen the woman before, actually in waking hours, and her speech then had been equally compelling. Always drawn to older women, he could look on this one strangely without lust, but with a deeper fascination, as if her unheard words held the mystery of life. Who the devil was she? He scratched the night's gold growth on his chin. Recollection came flooding. He spoke aloud and laughed, and his esquires awakened hastily.

'My lady of Bedford! Certes, the lady Jacquetta!'

Pleased, he equated the dream and its reason. Only yesterday he had been re-reading the letter from that same lady, one dated the spring of two years earlier, in which she begged a royal pardon for her husband, herself, and the whole Woodville family. He had sent for this Lancastrian lady straightaway, thinking to rebuke her for her years of treachery. To follow the example of Warwick at Calais, when he had railed at Sir Richard Woodville and the young Anthony, calling them knaves unfit to speak with those of the blood. And Jacquetta had come, very cool, modestly dressed, to confound him at his palace of Westminster.

It was not only her eloquence but something in her eyes that lingered on her mouth. An air worn by soothsayers; a mystical immunity. A warning to cherish her. Whatever it was, before the audience was half done he found himself granting a pardon to all Woodvilles everywhere, and moreover, bestowing upon Jacquetta of Bedford an annual stipend of 300 marks, with 100 livres in advance. The fathomless eyes had warmed like the red embers of a gypsy-fire. Gracefully she vowed her duty. Before leaving she had said, turning to gaze at his antlered trophies on the wall:

'There is good hunting at Grafton, your Grace. In Whittlebury Forest the boar excels. We would deem it honour...'

Bowing those eyes, that mouth, in a deep obeisance, she had left the words trailing mid-air, together with her perfume, musk and jasmine.

He had not spoken of this to Warwick, who would rage at the hated name of Woodville. Yet he had fully intended, one day, to disclose his reason for distributing this bounty. He had not disclosed it; because there *was* no reason. The Duchess's eyes had guided his hand, his seal, had left him ruefully baffled. But what had she told him in the dream? More and more he longed to know.

As the esquires drew back the curtains and bowed, sleep still cracking their joints, he recalled that he had never taken up the Duchess's invitation. Very soon after it had been extended, Margaret of Anjou had set about keeping him busy again. What a dance that vixen had led them, with her capture of Alnwick and Bamburgh, with her Scottish rebels piping for the King of England's head. Daft Harry had been with her again, doubtless singing and talking to himself, as he had been discovered after the last battle of St. Albans, with its frightening rout. The tide had turned though, no doubt of it, although Margaret still hissed from the shallows. This was probably what Warwick wished to discuss. More arrays, more deploying of force. England must be kept secure from the swords of France and Lancaster.

The henchmen knelt, and Edward muttered a benediction, while swift visions crossed his inner sight. His father's head on Micklegate. His own pledge, under the starry banners of Christ in Majesty at Fotheringhay, to avenge that pitiful straw-crowned face, the staring eyes of young Edmund, the blood-stained cheeks of Salisbury. He had honoured them all in a Month's Mind ceremony of remembrance; his brothers, Richard and George had been present. Tall, arrogant George and poor sickly Dickon, who was another reason to cherish Warwick. Dickon was Warwick's sole charge, and now learned the ways of urbanity and nurture at the Earl's bleak castle of Middleham.

He sprang from bed, and the gentlemen rushed upon him with rosewater and herbals. A lutanist appeared as if from the air, singing a sacred summer lay. From a side table pages removed the Night Livery, the bread and wine placed in case the king should hunger. And still the dream's essence remained with Edward, giving him good temper and brilliance. He smacked the esquires on the back, tossed the morning cup of ale down his throat. They dressed him and held the mirror for his approval: satin and velvet in loyalty's blue, with the collar of York, suns and roses alternating in beaten gold. He shone, spare and robust as a god. He liked the image.

Singing and praying, they preceded him to the chapel. Warwick was already in his stall with others of the blood and the principal councillors. Edward strode the nave, inclining his head to some visiting Burgundian knights. They in their turn were admiring the new-painted walls and roof of blue and gold, the repaired rood-screen in holy arbutus wood. Edward, appalled by the dinginess of Daft Harry's court, had made many changes. He strode on and the Burgundians saluted him. To Burgundy he owed his brothers' lives. He had said so to Warwick, and strangely, the Earl's response had been lukewarm. For Warwick had lorded it in Calais and, Edward was privily informed, had corresponded with Louis of France. And Louis would strip and burn Burgundy without a second thought. Yes, Warwick was loyal, but also powerfully ambitious. Kneeling on a gold-cloth prayer stool, Edward mused on loyalty. The Sanctus bell rang, he crossed his breast and thought: Warwick would never betray me. He has a stake in England, and he has charge of my youngest brother. He is Plantagenet. Yet he dubs himself a maker of kings and this new-made king must rule, with or without his approval. The choir's voice, like glittering rain, trembled among the gold and blue. And from somewhere lost and far came the old mysterious echo: 'There is good hunting at Grafton, your Grace.'

The King shivered, blown by an alien wind. He lifted his face from the kiss bestowed on the Book, and looked about him. Nobles surrounded him, their lips moving gently in holiness. Women, too. One, though missing not a word of the breviary, kept her beseeching eyes fixed upon him, and under that look all his fair humour fled. Dame Elizabeth Lucey. Ah yes, my dame. Once you were all I ever desired. He glowered at her over his missal, as if to send the words winging across the aisle. Dame, your husband may have died in battle for my cause, but the arms you offer bring weariness, where once there was joy. Can you never let me go? Somewhere, nurtured by his bounty, were two children. Dame Lucey was lovely, but so wanton, so easy. Once her body had pleased him; now it was a familiar manor, its turrets blasted, its standards fallen. And still her eyes reproached him daily, as surely as the incense, wafting, threatened him with a royal sneeze.

He did sneeze; a gusty, roaring explosion that echoed satisfyingly around the nave. Warwick's eyes slid sideways. Perchance, Edward thought, amused, he is alarmed for my health. I have never ailed, save for the one bout of measles – and that in the middle of an array! But that was witchery; the Frenchwoman laid me low with a curse.

Elizabeth Lucey stared no longer; her downcast eyes appeared to weep. When would women learn that naught could hold a man once desire was dead? Another face rose to haunt him – saintly and more beautiful than Dame Lucey. He shuddered. That was yet another secret from Warwick, to be concealed at all costs.

'May the almighty and merciful God grant us pardon, absolution and remission of all our sins.' Dutifully he muttered, eyes closed, thinking: *Eleanor. My greatest folly. Warwick shall never know about Eleanor.*

There were the usual rolls for signature in the chamber filled with heralds, notaries, clerks. Warwick stood close; Edward experienced a familiar satisfaction when the tall Earl was forced to look up into his King's eyes. Together they dealt with the day's business, Edward signing with flourishes, and tossing parchments swiftly to the Master of the Rolls for the Great Seal's imprint. Only when the representatives of the City of London came forward did his haste abate. He embraced the gildsmen and burgesses, his beloved citizens. These were his supporters, and the purveyors of England's lifeblood. These were the men who through their wool and grain and fish would replenish the debt-ridden Privy Purse, legacy of King Henry, and make England a land once more revered. Practical, honest men, who enjoyed the sweets of life. He, Edward, would restore them; and doubtless they would show their gratitude in a practical, honest way.

Eventually Warwick and he were left alone. The Earl seemed fidgety, and Edward was chafing from the summer sounds outside. Nearly nine! He was determined to be astride his favourite courser within the hour.

'So, Richard, how goes it?'

'Well enough, your Grace,' said Warwick.

Edward gestured impatiently. 'God's Blessed Lady! You know my name well enough. Use it.'

'Ned,' said Warwick. 'Ned, my lord. I have serious matters for your opinion. They can delay no longer.'

'Queen Margaret, no doubt,' said Edward with a sigh. 'Well, where is she today? Harlech, Scotland? Give me your scurriers' news, and I'll summon an array. Although, God's Blood! my armies are marched to death. I had thought we might rest a week.'

'Certes, rest all you wish,' said Warwick unexpectedly. 'My serious matters, if you consider them favourably, may give us rest for our lifetimes.'

Edward sat down in the chair of estate and contemplated his own well-turned thighs. The Earl's next words should not have surprised him, yet they did.

'It concerns your marriage, Ned. England needs a Queen, and you must get an heir.'

'So,' murmured Edward, thinking of his bastards. None could ever doubt his potency. He raised his golden brows. 'Whom have we in mind?'

From his pouch Warwick drew sealed letters. 'I have, your Grace, taken the liberty of securing the hand of the Princess Bona of Savoy. Isabella of Spain would also honour such an alliance, but Savoy is shaped to meet our needs in these precarious times.'

He held the letters out to Edward, who did not move or speak.

'The Princess will come next year to be your bride.'

Suddenly stricken by implication, Edward said: 'The Lady Bona is sister by marriage to Louis of France!'

'Yes,' answered Warwick swiftly. 'And this is three parts of her value. With you wed to Louis's kin, there can be no more assaults from the Frenchwoman. France and England can unite. Think, your Grace! Peace without blood!' He added casually: 'Bona, they say, is very fair.'

Wild thoughts nipped at Edward. He broke into a light sweat. Eleanor. Because of my madness with Eleanor, I can marry none. I always wondered whether Warwick, through his spies, had any knowledge of this; now it is proven that he has not. Nor shall he have. But what of this princess he offers me? Implication, realization, smote at him, making his voice hard in reply.

'Burgundy,' he said.

The Earl spread his hands deprecatingly, and was silent.

'I will not side with France against Burgundy,' said the King tightly. 'Not even for the sake of peace.' Louis would expect, nay, demand, that his new kinsman align himself with him against the hated, coveted realm. 'Christ!' his voice rose. 'I owe Burgundy my brothers' lives. Have you forgotten how Duke Philip cherished them in exile, when the Anjou witch would have had them butchered? I can never repay Burgundy!'

Now he was sure of the truth in the rumours of Warwick's friendship with Louis. He wondered how far it had gone. How ruthless the Earl was, and how short of memory! Coldly, Edward said:

'My lord, I trust you continue to guard my brother Richard as faithfully as Duke Philip did.' He changed tack, and smiled an infuriating smile. 'I, too, have every intent of matchmaking. My sister Margaret shall marry Philip's son: Charles of Charolais. Burgundy shall remain our ally.' Secretly he thought too of the wool trade, the low levies and the desirability of commerce with Burgundy rather than France. Edward did not like France at all.

Warwick chose to disregard this last statement. He said coldly: 'Richard does well at Middleham. He is by far the best of my henchmen. He excels in the arts of war. He is not the weakling we all thought him.'

Tell me what I know not, Edward thought, the last vestige of his good humour gone. I know Dickon's worth: Why else would I make him Admiral of England? He may be only twelve and his brother George topping him by inches, but had I to choose in whose hands to lay my life ...

'And he loves me well,' said Warwick, cool and dangerous. 'He vows I am his second father. As for George, he would ride with me to the earth's end.'

The meaning was obvious. Remain my pupil; do my will, or I will suborn your brothers! Edward had never seen the Earl like this. It was also obvious that he had expected an immediate acceptance of the Savoy proposal. Well, this moment was as good as any. Obduracy flourished in Edward. Now pupil can bid master come and go! He rose.

'Enough,' he said. Outside the day glittered, and the birds were singing like mad angels.

'What am I to tell Savoy, your Grace?'

The King stopped, near the door. Warwick's knee was bent, his head bowed, but a flush of chagrin mounted to his hairline.

'Tell them that I am going hunting.' He went out, brain whirling from the impact of this new Warwick, thoughts stumbling over the impossible prospect of marriage – any marriage. Eleanor. Eleanor, why were you not wanton and easy, like Dame Lucey? Anxieties knotted within him, and were suddenly overlaid by a calm, insistent voice, culled from the crazy patter of a dream: 'At Grafton ... at Grafton ...'

He sent messengers ahead to greet the Duchess of Bedford, to arrive a full day and a half ahead of his party. This would give her time to call in any cattle on Whittlebury Chase; his hounds would bring down anything, even the lion, the unicorn. He decided not to burden the Duchess with providing hospitality for all his train. These isolated manors were usually cheerless anyway. Time enough to think of where to stay when the hunt was over. He ran down the Palace stair, leaving his esquires far behind with each long stride. There, waiting for him was Lord Hastings, solid as granite; a drinker, a wencher, a true fellow about whose neck he flung an arm. And the Earl of Desmond, clad in hunters' green; young, handsome and eager. If any asked, Edward could say with truth that Desmond was the knight he loved best. Desmond was like the spring, bright and promising. He made Edward laugh, he lifted his rare melancholies with warmth and wisdom. He was utterly trustworthy, cultured and noble. For all these reasons Edward had bestowed upon him the Deputy Lieutenancy of Ireland.

'Tom, we're for Northamptonshire!' he cried. Desmond pulled a long face, grumbling that it was the devil of a way to ride merely to chase the boar, and Edward laughed. He began to sing, a coarse verderers' song; he clutched Thomas Fitzgerald Desmond about the shoulders and they sparred together like yokels all the way to the princely stables. The esquires followed, shocked and admiring. Edward lifted his face to the sun and laughed again. He was England's King; he could do as he pleased, and he was going hunting.

He was also disenchanted with Warwick, his one-time guide and mentor. He was ready and ripe to be undone.

She walked through the forest, holding the hands of the little boys, one on either side. The hands were cold; they were hungry and so was she. Despite the day's heat, a chill filled their bellies. Thomas was pale, quieter, beginning at seven years to outstrip his strength by inches. Now and then she stopped to lift Richard into her arms. For all his thinness, he seemed to weigh the earth. A slight, black-robed figure, she went dwarfed by the giant trees while all around the forest sang and scampered, small birds and animals in ceaseless activity. She went slowly, unafraid, for nothing could harm her. Even the wolf and wild boar would pass her by, for her mother had laid the word upon them.

In the past two years she had grown to Jacquetta like ivy to an elm. It had been a long and painful business, with many joltings of her spirit, rebellion and tears, but now the two of them were one in desire. Therefore she walked the appointed way at the appointed time through Whittlebury, and often she smiled. Coupled with her downcast eyes, the smile was strangely sinister. Seldom did she look up; the mossy way, starred with celandine and buttercup, made itself plain and clear before her, like the words of a well-learned text.

'She asked Raymond for as much of the land around the fountain as could be covered by a stag's hide, and she cut the hide into ten thousand strips so that her land extended far beyond the forest. There she built Lusignan...'

A bubble of hunger rose in her throat. At Grafton the household was far too large for comfort, even in her father's absence. He was away mostly, leading a life unknown, not fighting, for since the royal pardon he had eschewed Queen Margaret's cause. But there were the sweet, ever-famished sisters: Catherine, Jacquetta, Anne, Mary, Margaret, Eleanor, Martha. Young Edward was at sea and Lionel in training for holy orders. But there was still Dick, cursing his lack of fine clothes, and nineteen-year-old John, who ate the heartiest of all. Anthony was married to a kinswoman of Ismania Lady Scales and Elizabeth was glad for him. He was Lord Scales in right of his wife and could be summoned to the Parliament. He visited Grafton occasionally, and the fair comeliness of his face reminded her of another, two years dead, and her own insupportable pain.

'There she built Lusignan ...'

But had Melusine loved? Had she lost a husband at the hands of Raymond's kin? These were questions forbidden by the Duchess; locked away since that first intense conversation in Jacquetta's private solar. Then, Elizabeth, laughing and crying, had vowed she would sooner put her head in fire than come within an armsbreadth of any Yorkist murderer. Yet she had been conquered, by one sentence, repeated like a charm.

'Do as I say,' Jacquetta, great eyes burning, whispered. 'Do as I say, and you will hurt my lord of Warwick sore.'

There was the spark to the brand. Since the rape of Bradgate, Elizabeth had lain nightly conjuring tortures for the enemy, torments so real that they disturbed her sleep. Warwick's gouged eyes, his flesh aflame with everlasting fire; Warwick hanged from Bradgate's tower, a spike through his tongue. All these outrageous impossible lusts outmatched so simply by one calm phrase: Do as I say. And she had cried: 'Yes, madame! With my last breath!' And so the fantastic pattern was revealed with all its diabolical nuances. Secrets so black and bloody between herself and Jacquetta and the world, that she often trembled at their implications. Sir Richard Woodville could not know, and the sisters were kept apart. Catherine, the dearest, was hurt and troubled. More acute than the others, she pestered Elizabeth: what was that strange perfume, that ugly herb, gathered by night? and received a curt answer, or none at all.

Catherine had wept over Jocelyne de Hardwycke. Not a month after her exile from Bradgate, Elizabeth had received him; he had sought her out, his face troubled and tender. The facile love-poems were a thing of the past. He knelt, he spoke of the passion that had kept him single for years, recalling episodes: her flight from the Hall under King Henry's displeasure (Jocelyne had wept for her); her beauty at the Christmas disguising. He was not John, but these were John's memories too, brought like a dead bird by a hound. John's bones fed the red earth of England, and Elizabeth, robbed of sense or will, gave Jocelyne her hand. She said: 'I am a dead woman; to which he replied: 'Let me bring you back to life!'

His respectful kiss brought no intoxication. She reminded him that John had not been dead six months. These words brought fresh tears from her, more kisses from him. He begged her to accept his meagre estate, for Hardwycke had suffered too, as a Lancastrian holding. His arms were comforting, and he was kind. Broken, uncaring, she agreed, and sought the Duchess to inform her. It was a moment not to be forgotten. 'We shall not wed until next year,' she finished. 'I will keep John's Month Mind properly, as his widow. Jocelyne will wait.'

The Duchess was writing at her lectern. Slowly she laid down her quill. Even with her face backed by window-light, the white fury stabbed clear, a warning. Confused, Elizabeth thought: Jocelyne should have approached my mother first. His ardour led him into forgetfulness ...

'There's no love between us,' she stammered. 'But I have the little knaves to look to, and . .

The Duchess advanced across the room, a terrible look on her face. Holy Jesu! thought Elizabeth. Is Jocelyne a felon? Has he some great crime? His policies are right; he is of Lancaster ... Then the Duchess struck. Her hand cracked on Elizabeth's cheekbone, making her teeth rattle and her head sing like a hive. Reeling, she tried to speak.

'Madame...'

'Madame me not,' said the Duchess. 'What, madam, have you done this day?'

They stared at each other stonily.

'The truth,' whispered the Duchess. 'Has any priest witnessed your vows?'

'Nay,' said Elizabeth, trembling hard. 'It was a privy matter, decided between Jocelyne and me, on the moment.'

Uncomprehending, she heard the great hiss of expelled breath, saw the colour return to Jacquetta's face. She knelt, and waited.

'He must be forbidden our manor,' said the Duchess. Lost, Elizabeth bowed her head. Presently she felt her shoulder lightly touched and looked up. The Duchess held something under her eyes. It was a wax manikin, and about its head was twined a fuzzy comb of black hair. At its waist was a tiny band of iron, meshed so tightly with the wax that the figure was almost cut in two.

'To sap his strength,' said the Duchess, very low. 'My enemy and yours, child. Soon or late, he will fall. By Mithras, he will perish and die.'

That day was the first she had sworn on the ancient heathen god, in Elizabeth's hearing. She held the figure closer to her daughter's face.

'My lord of Warwick!' she said and hissed, pointing. Fear, and joy worse than any fear, filled Elizabeth.

'Do not marry Hardwycke. Do as I say,' said the Duchess. So the campaign began. Catherine wept; she loved Jocelyne, and thought her sister cruel.

Elizabeth walked on, bending beneath the branches hung with succulent leaf, going deeper into the forest. She felt impelled by a force beyond thought, tied by an invisible thread to her mother's solar, and her steps were guided by that thread's true pull and play. In the dim greenness of Whittlebury's heart, she was conscious of the little cold hands in hers, and the silence, for the birds had stopped singing. All but one, who screamed a constant, urgent warning. There was a vast oak, big enough to house twenty men within its crusted trunk. The unseen thread had loosed its pull. She halted beneath the tree, raising her eyes at last to the trellised blue above. Tom sat down in the elbow of a cavernous root and began to whittle with his knife. Soon she heard the thick hollow moan of the hunting horn. Commanded, she raised her hands to the dusty black wimple and loosed it from her hair.

Less than half a league away the King rode through the forest like a meteor. His legs splashed, his doublet rent, he was gloriously happy. He had brought three horses to exhaustion. He had lost his velvet cap long ago and his bright hair blew tangled as he rode. Desmond galloped his mount beside the King's. Often the two men glanced back and laughed to see the courtiers unhorsed, belabouring baulking horses or caught in thickets and cursing. The huntsman was blowing like one possessed, the sweet language of the chase; the notes long and short: *Trout trout, tro ro rot!* Hastings rode hard behind the King; he waved his whip and smiled. 'There! There!' yelled Edward, pointing at a distant backlash of green branches. *Illoeques, illoeques!* replied the huntsman, signalling the sighting. Twenty couples of sleek hounds poured forward, a mottled river. Edward's spur struck blood as, with Desmond, he plunged after the pack, bending just in time to avoid an overhanging branch. He jerked his mount's head around a bend; there, down a green avenue, bowshot-straight, the quarry, a great bronze stag, fled surgingly. The pack sang and bayed. Edward cried out, joining with the huntsman's scream: *sa, cy, cy, avaunt, sohow!* He had been disappointed to find no boar, but, by the Rood! this was better. From the moment that the limer had tracked down this magnificent beast, and the blood-mad hounds had been uncoupled to run unerringly, every care had dropped from him. He had forgotten Warwick; as for the secret that sometimes plagued him like a hairshirt – it was dead and buried. He smote his horse and rode knee to knee with Desmond. As if he were racing at Smithfield Horse Fair (an unrealized dream). There was so much that kingship forbade.

The stag was cunning, like a lovesome woman. As all women should, it evaded capture until the very last, trying every manoeuvre until that inevitable moment ... but this outshone the pursuit of women. Ahead of the hounds singing their lustful joy, the stag twisted and doubled, plunged through a fat thicket and reappeared further up the glade, its antlers festooned with foliage like a knight's jousting helm. The hounds had lost a little ground. They burst from the bushes, muzzles scratched bloody and surged forward, all bravery, while the kingly beast, for which Edward now felt a passionate love, soared boundingly on. Could the pack be tiring? God's Blessed Lady! he muttered. The stag was fleet, the distance between it and pursuit growing steadily. Edward frowned, gripping his horse between strong thighs: He had never wanted a kill so much in his life. Close behind him rode bowmen, weapons slung and jouncing. A pity to deny the dogs but that hateful gap was lengthening, the gold-bronze, sweated haunches of the quarry lunging powerfully, and the path growing more tortuous. He half-turned in the saddle to yell a command. Several goose-quill arrows thrummed past his ear, falling wide. One or two overshot the running beast; it swerved wildly before racing on.

'Blood!' cried Edward. 'Give me a bow!'

He tore on the reins so that his horse reared and screamed. Behind him, the whole company clashed to a disorderly halt. One of Hastings's henchmen soared over his mount's head into a thornbush and Desmond laughed for joy, but the King's mouth was grim with anguish. He seized the proffered bow, fitted a barb and, standing in his stirrups, discharged one, two, three shots, snatching arrows and loosing them with powerful fluid movements. The first shot bounded off the quarry's antlers, the second missed completely. Then, in the third dart's swift trajectory, he saw the stag waver and plunge. His cry of triumph mingled with arrogant music of the horn, the frenzy of the hounds.

Wounded in the shoulder, the stag still ran under the impetus of its own leaping fear. It would feel no pain yet, only the lust to flee – like a virtuous woman under the first kiss! He called to the half exhausted hounds: *'How amy, swef, amy, sa, sa, sa!'* Time to check them a little, or they would be too run down to effect the consummation.

Churning up bog-mire, tearing through branches, the King's hunt rode. The deep wound was taking its toll of the quarry; it slowed and stumbled now and then. The pack, renewed by joy, was gaining. The hunt thundered across a glade, struggled through a streamlet and up a steep bank. John Neville's mount slid on to its side and brought down four other horses. Terrified birds left their perches with a roar of wings. Overall the horn cried: *Trout, trout, tro, ro, rot!* Covered in mud, thorns in his hair, King Edward chased the stricken animal into a grove of trees. Under his breath he called it endearments. Then the hounds had it by the heels.

It was down, antlers rearing like the mast of a broken ship in a sea of writhing, brindled life. Desmond leaped down to steady the King's horse as, nearly falling from excitement and stiffness of limb, he dismounted. The huntsman came forward with the special weapons of chivalry, each knife honed to separate sharpness, each blade designed for the ritual kill and dismembering. Solemnly Edward took the slaying knife. When the dogs had been whipped from their prey he bent and looked into the brown, fear-glazed eyes. So like a woman's ... he saw his own face, mudstreaked and haloed by the sun, reflected there. Under his hand the great antlers heaved, almost throwing him off balance. He set the knife to the sweating, satiny throat.

Behind him came the murmurs of approval. A good, kingly kill, by a man skilled in venery with strength to sever proud muscle and sinew. A rich jet of blood soared and splashed the King's face, to make patterns with the crusted mud. He straightened his back and sighed. 'A noble beast.' He handed the killing-blade back to the huntsman, feeling drained and holy. He turned to count his followers, to speak to Desmond, to drink in the surrounding greenness and worship the blue day. About a dozen strides away he saw the woman beneath the oak. So still, so small and nunly in her black gown. But the hair that cloaked her to her knees made nonsense of nunliness. Two little boys sat at her feet; he scarcely saw them. He looked at that hair, that face, lit by silver sunlight. And then he knew why he had come to Grafton.

Thomas Fitzgerald Desmond saw her too, and his lips pursed in a little soundless tune, a tribute, courtly and almost mechanical, to her beauty. She was so still; that stillness sent an unexplained shudder over his body. He felt the sweat drying cold upon his neck and face. He knew his King, however, as well as any man can know another. So at his whispered command the other courtiers pulled their horses round and drew off from Edward. They faded, converging about the huntsman and the cadaver of the stag, they became part of the back-cloth of green trees. Their outlines were misty, their voices muted. With steps still unsteady from the ride Edward walked towards the great oak, from whose heart came the liquid piping of one uneasy bird. The King felt himself trembling, and deeply aroused, ridiculously ashamed of this arousal, and subsequently confused. He knew an odd desire to kneel before Elizabeth, which was madness. All these warring emotions made his voice unusually harsh.

'I am Edward Plantagenet.'

There was no need for this; she herself already knelt, pressing the little boys down on either side of her. At this he felt an irrational regret. Looking down upon the crown of her head, which was clothed by finest shining textures impossible for anything but divinity to weave, he said more softly: 'Rise, lady. The ground is damp under trees.'

Slowly she obeyed. She raised her eyes until they were level with his strong sunburned throat, then higher so that they encompassed his face. He was more man than any she had ever beheld. Broad and slender, but so monstrously tall – a giant. After one glance at the mud and blood-splashed face she lowered her gaze again to his neck. Thoughts ran through her like little flames. *This is Edward, the Yorkist butcher!* Then something stilled her inner wildness; a last pull from that invisible thread, reminding her that the struggles and the sacrifices of the past months should not go in vain. A well-shaped hand was extended for her kiss. She tasted sweat, beast's blood, the fading hint of rosewater. She lifted her innocent, starved face and gave the King one crystal look. She ventured timidly (her mother's first injunction – be always douce, he will wish to dominate): 'Your Grace made a fine kill.' And, hearing the distant crack of bones being dismembered: 'A good store of venison. The beast was fat.'

For a moment he was silent, then he said gently: 'Unlike yourself,

Madame, if I may say it. The stag is yours. I will have my grooms deliver it to your manor.'

She bowed her head and smiled. Good. Good. Melusine had asked only for the hide! Already she owned the whole beast. She could feel the King's gaze, hotter than the latticed sunlight.

'Your Grace is generous,' she said soberly, 'and my family is always conscious of past benefits.'

The royal pardon. So it was that he knew her. It could have been none other in any case, he thought, than the daughter of the dream-like Jacquetta, lately of Lancaster. Had his eagerness left room for sense, he might have groaned at the thought. Eleanor had been Lancastrian; these fair women always seemed to embrace foul policy. Still, all that was over; soon all the world would be for York.

Thomas, meanwhile, had been regarding the King with interest. His own head reached only to the top of Edward's thighboot. Rudely piping, his voice floated up.

'Sir, are you really the King?'

Edward cuffed the child's ear gently and laughed.

'Yes! little knave, by God's grace.' He looked down at the smaller, silent Richard, and back to Elizabeth.

'Your sons?'

'My fatherless sons.' She raised sparkling eyes, in the face which she herself thought robbed by privation of much beauty, and which he marked as slender and winsome. A good thing of the spirit, like the Virgin, Our Lady, whom he had adored as a child and swore upon as a man. Yet in this face was something thrillingly at odds with things spiritual, that made his body molten and his face hot. He was the veteran of frightful battles and skilled in political strategy. His hand lay on England's heart. He knew and used women. Yet his voice shook as he asked: 'Have you ever been at court?'

'Yes. With Marguerite ...' She bit her lips. Wrong. A mistaken reminder likely to incense him. Yet he seemed not to have noticed. He became secretly further inflamed, and not with anger. Starkly he wondered what her price was. There were gaps in his imagination that admitted only what he wished to believe.

'You might come to court as our guest,' he muttered. 'There are wondrous sights, and banquets. Things are not as you would remem-ber them.' Henry's piety had forbidden true revelling, and when she saw the new glory that was Edward's, she would be his at once. That slender body could writhe in dances public and private. In his mind all was settled; so he was amazed when she answered:

'Sire, I am widowed, and bound to stay at Grafton. In prayer, and in duty to my mother and my sons. You do me honour which I must sadly decline. Yet ... may I invite you to share our humble joy at the manor?'

This was Jacquetta's second injunction. Bring him under our roof. Let him eat our food, drink our ale and wine. Then the task will be easy. Elizabeth continued: 'We have little to offer a prince. Yet our sun would. shine, reflecting his splendour!'

Her words were spontaneous, yet they could not have been better chosen. She looked into his gratified blue eyes.

'All that we are or ever might be is in your keeping, Sire.'

And, royal cub, may God rot Warwick's soul for Bradgate, and for the death of my love. Come to Grafton, Edward of March! Come, and be entranced! She lifted her face again and smiled, a gentle, loving smile, facsimile of the forgiving Virgin's look, while he began to ask her of her family. Hearing of the many unwed sisters, an understanding pout spread across his face so that he was like a boy aping a wise old man. She touched but lightly on her brothers and scarcely mentioned Anthony, whom Edward and Warwick had once cursed at Calais. Although she felt instinctively that this episode had fled the King's mind, she must do nothing to jolt his sweet mood. Lastly she told him her name: Elizabeth, for the glad and loving Isabella was dead and buried. Immediately Edward christened her anew.

'Bessy,' he said slowly. 'Light and nimble. A name like a piece of silk.'

'Your Grace is a poet.'

'I have inspiration.' His eyes moved over her, lingering at her waist, her thighs. The coarse black habit could have been a sheet of glass. She stood, unworried. *Yes, my lord. Look, and look again. I shall build Lusignan in that look!*

A figure approached behind the King. A young, handsome knight, with a mouth that looked as if it always smiled. Like a sleepwalker, Edward turned to address him.

'Tom,' he said, 'this lady is the daughter of the Duchess of Bedford. Grafton Regis ...' To Elizabeth he explained: 'My lord of Desmond.' The knight made a bow, all flourishes, stood hand poised on dagger, still smiling. 'Greeting, Dame Woodville,' he murmured. The error raised a stab of anger in her. 'My name is Grey,' she said, with a wistful smile.

'Widow of Sir John Grey,' said Edward briskly. 'You remember him, Tom. He was a fine horseman who ran with the wrong pack!'

'Certes, Grey! Like the colour!' Desmond laughed. The laugh tingled down Elizabeth's spine. All her unvented spleen rose to envelop Desmond, while she continued to look meekly downward, smoothing the hair and clothing of the two little boys, by now yawning and fidgeting. The King and his friend moved away a little, conferring. She listened hard; they were speaking of the King's future plans. She heard the word 'Fotheringhay' and the King's deep sigh. He turned slowly and strode back to her. He took her hands, so hard she thought the bones were crushed.

'You offered me your hospitality,' he said, very low. 'But that stag is for you and yours, lady. I would not have it wasted on those who eat venison daily. He gestured towards the straggling knot of courtiers behind him, then looked down kindly at the two little boys. He notes our meagre bodies and our pallor, she told herself. She let her hands tremble in his as if they were too frail for the holding. She whispered something, soft enough for him to bend closer.

'My lady?' His eyes were hot again.

Leaning a little so that her shoulder brushed his upper arm, she whispered: 'If your Grace were ... to come with a smaller entourage. To my shame, Sire, you must know we are very poor at Grafton.'

He drew a quick, exultant breath. He murmured: 'Lady, my lady. I will do better than that. I will come alone.'

Then, like a schoolboy with his first passion, he abandoned kingship. He covered both her hands with kisses. Over his bowed shoulder she saw two things: the stag, now in pieces, being loaded on to mules, and Desmond's face, which raised in her a peculiar hatred.

She stood feeling the King's greedy mouth upon her wrists. She was suddenly transfixed with awe and fear at how easy it had been; then the fear died under a leaping, pitiless joy.

Through that summer and autumn, during winter's clutch and spring's swift renewal, the King came riding. He came as alone as a king can be, with a handful of armed knights, and an esquire or two. These gentlemen respectfully withdrew to the neighbouring hamlet while their sovereign dallied at Grafton.

Elizabeth was a city under siege, her drawbridge bound up tight, enchained by the counsel of Jacquetta of Bedford. Hold back. Once you surrender, all is for naught. There were times when Elizabeth, nerves taut as hemp, would gladly have disobeyed her mother, and been rid of the desirous hands, the hot mouth. The voice which began the day softly, grew impatient, and rose to quarrelling petulance. Often he left her in a foul humour, rode through the gates and returned minutes later to beg her pardon. Each time he vowed his love; he would never desert her as he had other lemen (yes, he admitted past treachery), and once there were tears in his eyes. He knew naught of the flood she herself loosed as soon as he was safely from the manor. Painful tears, legacy of the exhausting battle against his demands. She asked herself: would it be so harmful to yield just once? And the Duchess, knowing her mind, would encompass her with passionate warning.

In September he brought her a device for her throat; diamonds and pale flaming rubies. He sat beside her in the solar and fumbled to place his gift about her flesh. Jacquetta knocked, entered, knelt. Her lustrous eyes, the pupils blackly dilated, signalled to Elizabeth the required response. Obediently there came the downward look, the regretful smile. 'Nay, my liege, I am unworthy!' Edward's barely controlled temper was audible, little gusty breaths. At Christmas came two harriers, lean joyful young dogs, which she returned with the courier who delivered them. The following week she received an angry note, signed only: 'Ned'. He favoured anonymity, yet the sisters, maddened and curious, whispered their own assumptions in private, for there was none like him in the whole of England.

By April, her strength had diminished. Drained by endless assault, there were times when she saw the true end of the campaign as something misty and forgotten. Its purpose was veiled by the constancy of Edward's bruising hands, his pleading, his temper. Although she was but six years older than he, the six seemed sixty. His voice echoed in her dreams. 'Yield, Bessy! Bessy, my heart's lust!' And his near-blasphemies, which should have offended her and strangely did not: 'Forget the priests! True love is past all priestly knowing!' Truly he was a boy, a child, uninitiated, unaware that there were others than God ...

But one such dream made her cry out, mid-April. Faithful Renée ran to her mistress's bedside, while Elizabeth writhed, remembering. She had been riding to Bradgate, John beside her, singing. She turned to kiss him and was engulfed by the King's mouth, that bruised her lips and breast. Desire leaped within her shamefully, while Bradgate's tower soared straight and strong before her eyes. There were the jewels, falling like a rainbow; jewels everywhere, the device she had returned and countless more, pearls for her ears, a girdle studded with sapphire and gold, silver chalices flowing with rich wine, a unicorn's horn filled with emeralds. Then came her mother's voice, that dried the King's kisses and pinned a scowl upon his face. She heard herself crying.

'Get up, daughter.' The feel of her mother's arms, awesomely tender, shocked her awake. 'Be comforted.'

'I thought I was at Bradgate!'

'You shall have Bradgate. You shall have manors by the hundred.'

She said: 'For Jesu's love, madam, how much longer?'

'Not long,' said the Duchess.

I lusted for that necklace,' said Elizabeth. 'I long for Bradgate.'

'All,' replied Jacquetta. 'All shall be yours, and more. He comes today. Prepare for storms, for Mars is in the ascendant! But Venus waits, and Jupiter ...'

She sent Renée away. 'I will attend my lady.' Whispering up and down, like a guttering candle, she ministered to Elizabeth. That face must know no blemish. She took two small vials, the contents of which she applied to her daughter's skin.

'*Lac Virginis*.' It was an incantation. 'Since time unremembered it has been used.' The potion tightened on Elizabeth's face. Litharge of lead, ground on marble into white vinegar with sandiver and settled for a day and a night, filtered into two waters for the application. 'To make ladies beautiful,' said the Duchess with a devilish laugh. 'And used by Queens.' The strong hands massaged, hurting cheekbones too near the skin.

He came at noon, full of golden humour. Among the sweet airs of spring they walked, in Grafton's little pleasaunce. They came to an arbour hung with the green promise of summer. There, he loosened her wimple; he was clumsy as a colt. The silver-gilt hair fell over his hands like a wild river. He began to caress her, his fingers straying to the bounds of propriety. He was so young and clean; she could imagine how others had succumbed. She stared him out with her look of lucent virtue; she rose to pluck a flower. She laughed gently, sighed and withdrew, melted the next moment, only a second later to become adamantine. All afternoon she played a dangerous game, watching his face pale and the muscles of his arms and thighs quiver like those of a man with palsy. This great, royal fish! She played him on her line. Yet he was stronger this day, more stubborn. It had been folly to bring him to the arbour. Away from the house, his fire kindled and blazed. Each long embrace grew more uncontrollable. Her diversions failed; he would not let her rise. His eyes, seen closely, were like an animal's, sick and pleading.

'Bessy, why do you torment me?' he gasped. 'God's Blood, that I should be in this fire. Do you not know–' he shook her fiercely – 'that I am the King of England!'

'And I your loyal subject, Sire.'

He choked on wrath. 'Plague on your loyalty! I would have your love.'

Pinioned, she answered: 'I love you as my King,' the words cut off by a savage kiss that brought blood into her mouth. To quench the pain, she imagined it to be Warwick's blood. Edward's face was against her hair. 'Love me as a man, not a King ... eight months!' He gave a crazed laugh. 'Eight months, in which I have had time to fight against your erstwhile mistress, *la maudite* Margaret – all the while thinking, dreaming of you. Bessy, I would never desert you. You would be cherished unto death. Only give me your body and your heart!'

She heard her gown tear. He would ravish her now, and all lost. She raised one desperate hand and struck him in the face. The next instant he had drawn his knife. Its jewelled hilt flirted with the sun, prisms of blue and gold and green. He set the blade against her throat.

'Yield to me,' he said softly.

A witless laugh trembled within her. She looked into his eyes, riding out their blue storm. The Yorkists killed John – now a Yorkist king kills me. The blade's edge was beginning to burn. She was unready for death; there was so much to gain, Bradgate, jewels, vengeance. And yet she found herself smiling, as if the smile had been painted on by an imp.

He flung down the knife and sprang up. His towering shadow blotted the sun. He cursed her, calling her wanton, bloodless, jade, a whore that should be a nun, though there was no cloister devious enough to hold her. A cheating favour-seller, master and mistress of cruelty and child of Hell. So he railed, while Mars romped in the ascendant. He turned to leave, looking back once, turkey-red, his eyes bloodshot, saying:

'Keep your cursed chastity, Madame. You will not see Edward Plantagenet again.'

She watched him go, riding with savage spurs and oaths for his escort. A qualm of fright gripped her. She stood for a little while, chewing her bruised lips, then walked slowly towards the manor. The Duchess was at her window, watching with a little smile the fading smudge of dust on the horizon.

'The King has left his cloak,' she said. She moved back into the dimness of the solar, and lifted the heavy rich velvet into her arms. All round the collar hairs clung, gleaming like gold-dust. With infinite care Jacquetta plucked them until she had a fistful of shining booty. Over a little flame, a dish of tallow heaved. She watched it and her smile stretched into a snarl. Plenty there, to shape into a gold-headed King.

And she was a craftswoman, she would make this time a better image than the crude Warwick, who lay in his secret coffer, the iron band eating at his vitals. She stole a swift glance at the Earl's spellcast image, before bending to her more special work.

Within five days, the King returned to Grafton.

From the kitchen where lately there had been shouts and snatches of song, came only silence. A cask of spiced mead had been broached for the royal escort, the anonymous men employed for the King's secret forays to Grafton. They had drunk and now lay, oblivious, while their sovereign, supine upon Elizabeth's bed, covered his eyes and groaned softly.

He had touched no wine, but his brain was on fire. He could see the flames; they lapped the pillows, and his upthrown hands had gloves of fire. Desire was stilled for a space, burned by these phantom flames. Faces flowered about him, lambent and terrifying: Warwick, arrogantly ordering his marriage with the Savoy princess; his own mother, the Rose of Raby, beautiful, widowed, spiritual, shaking her head sadly through a mist of fire. Another face, saintly, defiled. A tearstreaked, forgiving face. *Eleanor, my love.* He tried to say it; flames licked his tongue, and the name emerged bewitched.

'Elizabeth!'

'I am here, sweet lord.'

She knelt by the bed, crushing down terror at the sight of his dementia. An hour earlier she had found courage enough to rail at her mother, saying that they would all be hanged in chains. For the King was ill after the strange meal Jacquetta had prepared, the herbal drink stirred in a special way.

'Christ's Blood, madam, he is dying!'

The Duchess took up the bowl that had contained the *amanita muscaria*, its dark fungoid taste masked by basil and cinnamon. 'Go up,' she said calmly. 'Ask him what you would. He will gainsay you nothing.'

So Elizabeth knelt, and took his hand. Down the whole of his body desire rekindled unbearably at her touch. Eleanor faded, his mother faded, and Warwick turned inside out with a sharp 'phut!' vanishing into blackness like a spent firecracker. He had enjoyed the mushroom. An Eastern speciality, she had called it, that old woman of his dream.

She had ministered tenderly to him, topping his hanap with a thick liquid. 'Jupiter's brew,' she said. It was so sweet that he, used to the indulgence of all sweetness, had found it irresistible. It was mixed with the scents of Elizabeth's body, that aroma ...

'Vervain, my lord.' Her voice washed around him, each word a cascade of glittering flame. 'To strengthen the intellect and nervous humours.' (And to restore lust, even in the grave.) 'Ruled by Venus, for merrymaking.'

He tried to laugh. 'I'm far from merry today. So weary ...'

'You are Edward,' she said gently. 'Edward Plantagenet.' *Of the third son of the third Edward, and destined to be mine.* She watched his speedwell eyes, tiny and defenceless as a sparrow's. She suffered his limp hand upon her breast. 'I would have your love,' he said, like a child about to cry. He moved weakly so that there was room beside him on the bed. 'If this is sin, I'll take and eat the sin for your soul's good. There! I offer you not only my love, but absolution. Lie with me.' She drew back only a little, keeping her hand in his. The next words were Jacquetta's, learned by rote.

'My lord,' she said steadily, 'if I am not good enough to be your Queen, I am too good to be your leman. The choice is yours.' She bowed her head.

'So,' he said after a moment. 'You would wed me, Bessy, and be Queen of England.'

She could tell nothing from his faint voice, whether he were angry, amused, or incredulous. She stole a look; his eyes were half closed so that a thread of white showed under the lids. Suddenly ice-cold and commanding, she answered:

'My lord, I am not worthy to be your Queen, but my body is pure. I will be no man's harlot. But to be your loving wife is a dream I have cherished, a dream far beyond me, your Grace. Sweet Ned!'

Out of nowhere came John's face, tenderly, wearily smiling. *O Jesu! Let me hurt my lord of Warwick sore!* She swallowed real tears and continued, dicing on each word.

'Everywhere your Grace goes, my spirit follows. I think of the sweets of love, with the Rose of Rouen ...'

'You think of them!' he said drunkenly. 'Oh God! that you could only be my Queen!'

Very timidly she said, watching the young reed bend: 'I know, your Grace. There are nobles who would cry shame at our union, being as I am so low.' She leaned closer so that the vervain at her breast and armpits drifted to his nostrils. 'I am not ignorant. Your Grace needs the royal blood of Europe to preserve his ancient line, and ...'

'Christ!' he said despairingly. 'Would that it were as simple! I would say hang my nobles and advisers! Bessy, I would wed you tomorrow, save that ...'

In the breath-holding silence, she stroked his hand. 'Save that I am married already,' he said dully.

Time ceased, gathered its wits, and moved on. Her first thought was: so all is lost. Even my mother could not foresee this blight upon our aim. All the months' gruesome wrestling, the outrageous play for naught; the banishment of Jocelyne, to whom I could have grown close; the nightmares and tears ... She looked upon the King who lay now as if in sleep, and her dismay yielded to rage. Willingly she could have killed him. A heavy pillow over the stupefied face ... they would say that he had suffered a seizure and rolled among the bedcovers. Her fingers stole out and wound themselves in a bolster's lace edge, gripping it until the blood thrust from beneath her nails. All for nothing!

He said, with closed eyes. 'I was crazy to marry her. She was chaste, like you, Bessy, and would have me no other way. It has been a secret for three years. She has no royal blood, but – her name is Eleanor Butler, daughter of Talbot ...'

'I knew Lord Talbot,' she said with difficulty ... 'He was killed at Guienne. One of Marguerite's chief officers.'

He smiled. 'Yes! Lancastrian, the whole family. Nell was so saintly, so good. Sudely, curse him, was trying to cheat her of her estates. She was widowed, she came suing to me for restoration. And we were wed.'

'You say it's secret?'

'Only my lady mother knows. Well – she and a very few more. Bishop Stillington, he bound us together. And the nuns of Norwich. Eleanor is in a convent there. It was better so.'

Yes, when you wearied of her, she thought bitterly. And this knowledge challenged her to wish the campaign begun anew. *He would not tire of me! Did Raymond weary of Melusine?* She took Edward's hand and kissed it.

'I shall guard your Grace's confidence with my blood, and pray for you daily. Even though we never meet again.'

She saw then that he wept, one tear trickling from each closed eye, balm to her savage sense of loss and failure. There was a rap on the door; Jacquetta entered, borne on a strong breeze of power, gliding over the polished boards as if on air, smiling, smiling.

'Is my lord refreshed?' With difficulty Edward sat up. 'Your henchmen are without.' She gestured to the door beyond which the escort, sick with mead, straightened their clothing. She continued: 'Will your Grace ride now, while it is light?'

The King wiped tears and sweat from his face and rose from the bed. He did not answer.

'Will your Grace bathe, then? It's warm for April. I have prepared a chamber. And then, supper and entertainment? Dame Grey has a new song for your delight. Whatever you desire.'

'I thank you,' said Edward, ashy pale. 'I will rest here the night, lady.'

He went out, walking like an old man, to the waiting henchmen. The. Duchess watched him dispassionately.

'In a short while he will be renewed. The mushroom sent him visions – horrors mayhap. It sometimes does. It has weakened him like a barbed deer.'

She turned to her daughter. 'Well?'

'The King is married,' said Elizabeth.

The Duchess gave a rasping laugh, and set her arm about Elizabeth's neck.

'You have no faith,' she said. 'Let him lie under our roof this night. Do you think that any earthly bond could hold him from you? Or you from destiny?'

A white moon stood tall in the sky to overlook the Duchess's work. She moved about the sleeping manor and its grounds, followed mutely by Elizabeth. A man came to join them briefly; a pale clerk named Thomas Daunger. Learned in orders holy and unholy, he whispered incantations as he went, for his knowledge began where Jacquetta's skill left off.

There was blood. Before retiring Edward had suffered a nosebleed; he had jested about it, saying that the Duchess's strong wines caused his veins to rejoice and burst their banks. Elizabeth begged pardon for the liquor's treason.

'Give me your kerchief, lord. I will trust it to no wimplewasher.; I'll launder it myself!'

So now the tiny gold-haired image was rosy, the tallow steaked with red like some rare precious stone. Edward Plantagenet lay still within Jacquetta's hands, under the moon's white eye. There was a black candle burning briefly, and more blood, fresh blood, caught before the scream of its small host had died away.

This was the consummation. A night remembered by Elizabeth only in dreams or delirium. A night where fact and fancy were so closely meshed as to be indistinguishable.

When she weakened and trembled, the Duchess fed her drops from a small blue vial, making her sight clearer and yet more treacherous. The hot white night dragged, dry as sand, an eternity of labour and strange sounds, diffused images, voices tirelessly intoning. Towards dawn, when it seemed that a thousand years were running out, the mother and daughter stood, beside Grafton's little lake; Thomas Daunger had departed as silently as he had come. Now there were two moons, one hard and bright and sinking slowly, the other like a soul palely lost beneath the water. Between these two dead fires a light moving mist shimmered, as if the water were boiling, and with it came sights of beauty and terror: a maelstrom of fighting men, forms that sank to dissolution at the touch of Elizabeth's eyes and renewed themselves, changed; ten thousand knights, their screaming mouths silent holes in the mist, and the cruel sting of defeat on their faces. Images that whirled and writhed; the ghostly moon wavered as if it strove to burst the water's skin. In the trees an owl cried, the shriek of a murdered child.

She was afraid. The Duchess stood, her ankles lapped by water and reeds. The small figure of destiny lay between her hands.

'Pray to her, daughter!'

Melusine was with them, strong, her unseen fingers tossing the mist, agitating the water. Within herself Elizabeth felt the change begin, a hardening of thought and will and dispositions, manifesting itself in a marble chill through every vein. She was afraid, and clung to fear as something natural and stable; she tried to call upon the Holy Name. She was dumb and powerless, swept by a change as irrevocable as a tidal bore.

'See!' said the Duchess. 'She'll not fail us!'

Elizabeth lifted her heavy eyes. From the lake a column of mist was rising. It formed a shape she dared not look upon.

All over England they were raising the Maypole. Long before the seashell dawn had cast up the day, there was movement on the roads. Between hawthorn hedges came pedlars, jugglers, minstrels and dancers, bound for the nearest green, the nucleus of gaiety. The cares of winter fell behind. Eagerly the people looked forward to the virile festival, the seal of spring. In every tree small birds sang of maying, and the travellers caught the tune, broke into gruff or warbling song, thinking of the ale, the sports of war or the flesh, the gossip. They wore frail garlands of flowers.

Elizabeth donned her bridal gown. She had fashioned it herself, and nights of lost sleep winked from its lucent damask, the bosom low and fringed with silver thread. Like the day itself, it was a thing of impossible splendour. She treated it cautiously.

She had no doubt that he would come. Carefully, as if each thought were a bubble, she let her mind stray to their last conversation. She had watched disbelievingly while he knelt at her feet and said the words to make her Queen of England. She had thought: he knows not what he says. To be sure, I must remind him...

'The Lady Eleanor Butler.'

His eyes, raised to hers, were glazed, enthralled. In his mind, her words were merely some echo of a life lived long ago. He did not answer. She said then, diffidently:

'My lord ... Earl Warwick – he mislikes my family.'

The eyes cleared, became ruthless, angry.

'Earl Warwick is not my keeper.'

Joy sprang at this; but she was still doubtfilled; for Eleanor was a living, breathing creature, wife to this besotted man. So she spoke her name again, gently. He rose and took her hands. Reverent, lust fled for the moment, he was like a shadow of the hot-breathing Edward.

'Eleanor is with the nuns,' he said. 'And she is sickly, like to die... She will never leave the House of Carmelites. She is dead to me already. Bessy, don't you know you are my fate?'

Incredulous joy gave her a smile like a jewel.

'Yes,' she whispered. 'I am, in truth, your fate!'

Therefore he would come. Even now he was riding, hard and desirous, having left his followers at Stony Stratford. He would tell them he was going hunting, even though they were in the midst of an array. A bubbling laugh escaped her, and was answered by a little sigh from Catherine, who knelt to straighten her sister's gown.

'You are so fair,' she said wistfully. She held the mirror up. Elizabeth's face had a delicate flush, the small red lips were full and pouting. Her eyebrows had been fashionably plucked almost to invisibility; did this account for the change she saw in the eyes? There was something there previously lacking. An echo of mist and water, a fluid, sensuous brilliance that lacked all compassion. A pitiless essence seen in the eyes of an old soul.

She called the other sisters and opened a walnut box. Presents. Gifts, from 'Lord Ned'.

'Ah, Jesu! Will you look!' Like small wild animals they fell upon the coffer. There was a package addressed to each sister. Margaret had a ruby bracelet, Anne a gold muskball; Martha and Eleanor received pearl ear-rings, Jacquetta a jewelled missal, Catherine an emerald necklace, and Mary a sapphire ring. There was a small token packet for Elizabeth too, a harbinger of greater gifts. She unwrapped it. A message in his own hand lay within.

For Dame Elizabeth Grey,
Who grows more like Our Lady every day.

It was a pearl-and-enamel rosary, each pearl as large as her little finger-nail, the crucified Christ worked in red gold, the Five Wounds small rubies. She stared at it; suddenly its beauty repelled her, and she laid it aside. The sisters gloated, pouring their gems from hand to hand, adorning throat and fingers and ears with handfuls of light She watched them, and thought: these are the jewels of my dream, the old dream in John's arms. She thought on him briefly and felt little emotion. Her mind touched on Warwick; the old rage was there, a comforting, everlasting fire. So love had gone, and hatred remained.

The sisters knew nothing of the day's plan. Soon they would be sent, joyous and bemused, out into the May morning to make merry at the fair. They would not return until tomorrow. Ned had insisted on it. None must know; only the Duchess and whatever clergy she might bring in to perform the ceremony. It must be a privy matter for weeks. Until he found the words to inform his Parliament.

'*Must* we stay from home overnight?' Anne moved to her sister's side, breathing the scent of her new muskball. '*Must* we sleep at the nunnery? I never have a full night's rest, thanks to their bell and prayers. And they are always fasting.' She rubbed her small belly comically.

'Mother of God!' cried Margaret; twirling her bracelet. 'Fasting is naught fresh to us, Anne! And to no holy purpose, either!'

Elizabeth longed to say, proudly: Soon, hunger will be a stranger to you all. She chivvied them from the room, just as the sound of horsemen arriving drained the blood from her face and sent her into a flurry of last-minute preparation. There was a step on the stairs, hasty, too light for the King. Neither would the King burst into her bower so, although this one was tall and fair-haired, and swept her up into his arms, as the King might.

'Sweet sister!'

'Anthony!' She kissed him, weeping, for his coming set the seal upon the day. He twirled her about, whistled at her finery like a knavish groom, went on his knee, sprang up and kissed her again.

'What widow's garb is this, my sweet? A wanton widow, by my faith, all Damascus cloth and shining like the sun. What mischief's this? Whatever it is, may it prosper!'

So kind and charming was he that she broke her pledge, and told him. His eyes grew large in disbelief, then jubilation. There was even a kind of envy too.

'By God!' he said, very low. And little more; for the first time ever she saw him speechless.

'Tell none,' she begged.

'Nay, nay,' he said slowly. 'I'd meant to tarry a few days, but I'll go at once, before the bridegroom … Jesu! my mind rocks! … before the *royal* bridegroom comes.'

All gaiety gone, he knelt to her in earnest, pressing his face against the silver hem of her robe.

'I do you homage, Madame,' he said. 'I salute you as Queen of England.'

'Christ's Blood!' she cried. 'Get up, fool! Would you tempt destiny?'

He rose hastily, solemn-faced. 'Bess,' he said tentatively, 'have I always been a good brother to you?'

'Always, dear lord.'

'Then—' sheepishly – 'I pray you, remember me when you come into your glory. Despite my wife's lineage, I have many enemies at court ... a word from the Queen would ransom me from spite and hardship ...'

Again she flinched from the word 'Queen'. Anything could happen, even to the King being killed en route to Grafton by a fall from his horse. Yet the Duchess had bidden her be merry and confident. She took her brother's hand.

'I promise,' she said. 'Now, go at once. We'll meet again.'

'In splendour!' His face was sharply alight. Suddenly she was infected by his ecstasy.

'Anthony, Anthony!' she cried. 'You shall be with me! We will be supreme! More powerful ... than the King himself!'

Young and mocking and handsome, he saluted her, slung his cloak about him and quit the room. Very soon, straining her eyes through the window she saw the little blossomy cloud of dust that heralded the King.

He came into the chapel quite alone. In the gloom his golden head was luminous as the aureole around a painted saint. He was plainly dressed in brown velvet. With the Duchess, Elizabeth stood to welcome him among banked flowers and candles. The smell of the tallow and the spring blooms rose thickly intoxicating and mingled with the cloying incense. Above all was the scent of the peerless vervain with which she had anointed her body, drifting through the chapel like a breath of mysterious song. He saw her and grew pale with longing. More unaccountably, the face of the parish priest waiting at the altar whitened also; he shot one uneasy sideways glance at her and clutched at his breviary. Beside him a boy acolyte stood motionless.

'My love. My fate.' The King's lips were cold upon her hand.

'Edward, our day is come,' she whispered.

'Swear me one thing.'

She nodded, expecting to be asked for assurance of love. The words were ready on her tongue.

'Swear that you, as my Queen, take upon you eternal fealty to the House of York.'

For an instant her mind cried out in rejection. She lowered her eyes. But John was dead, love was dead. And during the past months, perjury had become her bedfellow, and her tongue the tool of blackness.

'I swear. May God preserve York for ever and ever. Amen.'

He gave a little satisfied nod, and from his golden height looked down at her adoringly. She laid her hand on his for their binding.

The boy acolyte began to sing, a high pure cadence of almost pagan sound, like the calling birds outside the high arched window. The music pleasured her; she glanced to thank him with a look, and saw no answering flicker in the sightless eyes. Edward's cold and sweating fingers fumbled with the marriage ring. The Eucharist was raised to heaven; the Blood of Christ burned her mouth. Like a tortured lark, the blind boy sang.

There was darkness as there might be after the end of the world. Darkness and silence. In the hour between dog and wolf, she lay plunged fathoms deep, oblivious of the bed, the world, the great naked body now quiescent beside her. And she dreamed that she was dead, lapped in blissful blackness, all struggles ended.

His voice and hands roused her yet again. The velvet darkness clung as unwillingly she rose from it, her limbs slack with fatigue, like an old woman's. Never had she been so weary, not even after the long travail of bearing the two little boys. Resentment at Edward's vigour trembled on the lip of her mind. But she stretched her leaden arms to him, yielded her body, brittle as an autumn leaf, while somewhere far beyond her consciousness he kissed, and groaned, and possessed. His flesh damp and burning like a marsh-fire, he muttered endearments, striving as though his one desire was to be irretrievably lost within her. The last of the comforting darkness ebbed and she was wide awake to hear him say:

'God, God! I have been in a dream these past weeks, and now the dream is mine.'

She thought irrelevantly of her sisters. Poor Anne, grumbling at the convent bells. The girls would doubtless also be awake at this hour, summoned down draughty cloisters to mouth their sleep-sick prayers and conscious of their yawning bellies ...

'Bessy, Bessy! My lady, my heart!' said the King. 'My poor sisters ...' she murmured.

'Yea! Lovely, lovesome wenches. A nosegay of flowers, and my Bessy the fairest flower of all.'

'I wish they could have shared our wedding feast.'

The supper, prepared by Jacquetta's own hand, had been sumptuous for Grafton. Roast sturgeon, a salmon morteux rich with cream. A syllabub with candied violets.

'Yes, the little doves,' he said foolishly. 'So they should have done.'

She smiled in the blackness. 'My lord, you yourself said ...

'Yes, yes, all must be secret,' he replied hastily. 'It was fitting they should lie from home this night.'

He hugged her closer, stifling her breath.

'Yet even a king can change his whim,' he said.

She laid her lips against his neck.

'Anthony came today,' she said softly.

'Ah, Lord Scales!' he answered after a moment. 'A worthy knight.'

Yes, he had truly forgotten Calais, when he and Warwick called Anthony a knave's son. She went on, softly stroking the muscular plateau of his chest:

'He longs for favour. Would that you knew him better! He is so learned, daring in the joust. He can create a song out of air, and weapons from wit.'

'He shall have my favour,' said Edward.

'And Lionel! He is the most devout in Christendom. For years he has studied the priesthood. And my young brother John! There, sweet lord, you'd find no more worthy courtier. Gracious, cultured. Dick, too ...'

'Lionel, Dick, John,' said Edward. 'Anthony; is there more? You have forgotten Edward, my namesake! God's lady, Bessy! You'll have me jealous of these poxy brothers!'

Although he was jesting, she thought it pertinent to kiss him again, which she did, deeply. It was his turn to smile, unseen. This wife of his was a strategist, and it pleased him. The large and ambitious family of Woodville pleased him too. They were a potential buckler against the power of Warwick. Now the clever Nevilles should dance to the King's air. With this new phalanx of beholden kinfolk about him, he would have his renaissance. Not only at court, but throughout England. Sweep the board clear for a fresh set of chessmen, schooled to his every whim by gratitude. His arms tightened about Elizabeth's frail nudity.

'Which is your favourite sister, honey sweet?'

'Why, Catherine, though Margaret is nearest to me by birth.'

'Have I seen Catherine?' He mused awhile amid the girlish bodies, the shy, perplexed smiles.

'The little, round one.'

'Ah yes. Well, Kate shall have for husband young Harry Buckingham. A Plantagenet of ancient line. Clever. Handsome, too. And Margaret ... she could do worse than Maltravers, Arundel's heir. The others betrothed as I see fit.'

'And my brothers?'

He only kissed her, laughing tormentingly, his dawning beard rasping her throat. His mind went its separate way, gauging the worth of Anthony, Lionel, Richard, Edward, John. Lionel he had heard of already; cunning and glib of tongue. There might soon be a vacancy in the See of Salisbury for such a smart prelate. Edward was a seaman, always useful. Richard? A secretary perhaps. John, nineteen? He almost laughed aloud. Warwick's own aunt, the Dowager Duchess of Norfolk, was lately widowed and very rich. She was eighty if a day; they would call it a marriage made in Hell. But it would benefit Bessy and her family, and it would make Warwick writhe. Was it too cruel? He would see. At the moment he felt too utterly content. Virtue rose and fermented in him. He could even push to the back of his mind his mother's last letter.

'My son, for all we hold most dear, put not your soul in jeopardy for one woman. I beg you to think anew. For bigamy is an odious state and mortal sin, and shall bring ruin and sorrow to our House ...'

Those words, swiftly torn across with the parchment that bore them, had been like a fierce jet of flame. She was so pure, so utterly faithful to York and its old scions. She could not understand his longings that made nonsense of past loyalty. She did not know the wellspring of his dream: the enigma of Jacquetta's eyes; the silver body of Elizabeth. He could not write in reply saying: Mother, I know not why, but I am bound to her. From that sacred moment in the forest, all my life's map lay spread before me, and every path, Elizabeth.

'I was right!' he said out loud.

He crushed her to him, heedless of the thousand love-inflicted bruises. He said thickly: 'And you? What do you desire, my jewel?'

'Bradgate,' she answered mechanically.

He burst out laughing. 'Bradgate! That little cot! Yes, it's yours, sweeting. But there's a house in London for you called Ormond's Inn; its hangings are all gold and gems, it's one of the tallest buildings in town. And there's Sheen for you, and Greenwich, where cursed Margaret once played her wargames; yours, my honey, all yours.'

'Do not forget my mother,' she said, under his mouth.

'Blessed be she who bore you. The world's not wide enough for her deserts.'

Lassitude came on him and he slept. Elizabeth moved cautiously from the slackened circle of his arm. She lay wakeful until dawn delved beneath the threadbare curtains. Tireless now, her mind weaved the trappings for her own coronation; the pitiless change in her achieved completion, making her bright and invincible as the diamonds she planned to wear.

It was as if the years shimmered and slid together, time itself galloping; as if no sooner had she painted all that rich early splendour, out of thought than it was upon her, past and gone. To be relived, two years later, with the same gusto as she had imagined it. Save that it had been far more glorious.

It was February, 1466. Enthroned upon a golden chair in the palace of Westminster, she watched the women dancing. Hawklike, her eyes noted every detail of their apparel (none dared outshine her), and their abject subservience. Their awed faces emphasized her queenliness; every courtly posture before the dais spoke it aloud. They had not forgotten her coronation, and today's ceremony echoed that past glory a thousand-fold. She sat stiffly on the gleaming chair, her hands too weighted with rings to lift easily. She saw all the old nobility dancing to her tune. They were celebrating her deliverance from childbirth. That stiff sharp labour was over and already in the space of days she felt renewed. The accouchement had been vastly different from her struggles to birth Thomas and Dick. This time she had had the most skilled midwifery in the realm; Mother Cobbe. When the old woman's veined hands had drawn a red bawling creature from the Queen, there was a united gasp of disappointment.

'A wench,' said the crone.

Elizabeth only smiled. Outside the door.sat Master Dominic Serigo, physician and astrologer, who had so firmly prophesied a male child. While they lifted her on to the sweet new damask and sponged her with fragrances, she heard scratching on the door. A voice inquired: 'Is it over?'

One of the women opened the door a crack. Master Dominic was maundering: 'What has the Queen's Grace, if you please?' and received the tart reply: 'Whatever 'tis the Queen has in here, sure it is a fool stands without!' Poor Master Dominic! He was full of fear that Elizabeth could not share. For whatever she gave the King seemed to please him mightily. When he came to her bed, his face was full of mooncalf love. He kissed the red roaring babe tenderly.

'My little maid! We will call you Elizabeth! Though you can never match my own, my peerless Elizabeth!'

The babe thrived, seemed strong. This day the Queen had been churched in Westminster and now the court came to thank the Giver of all good gifts for the sovereign's health. Close to the dais knelt Jacquetta of Bedford, the light from a thousand costly candles turning her gem-spiked headdress to a pinnacle of ice. Her straight back quivered a little with fatigue. Elizabeth did not address her during the ceremonial, any more than she acknowledged the rest of the company, and protocol forbade Jacquetta to speak. In this, the Queen found more than a little malicious pleasure and marvelled at herself. No one is greater than the Queen! Yet Jacquetta was cherished and rewarded, rightly so; but by a Queen, and not an obedient daughter. Elizabeth turned her head and nodded to her mother, and the Duchess rose awkwardly, grimacing as the blood returned to her legs. She fixed eyes full of furious pride upon the Queen. Elizabeth spoke at last.

'Madame, what do you desire?'

'To be seated, your Grace.' She smiled grimly through her discomfort. All about them dancers swirled. The court ladies tripped and swooned to the sweet frenzy of viol and rebec and cromorne. There were no knights present; as befitting the honour of childbirth, only women revered the Queen with every tortuous dance-step, each humble gesture. Elizabeth nodded again, and Jacquetta sank once more to her knees. Like a gay bird, bright hair streaming, Margaret Plantagenet, the King's sister, danced before the Queen, and sank in a perfect curtsey before gliding on. Too beautiful, thought Elizabeth. It was well that she would soon be gone to Burgundy, bride for the young Charles of Charolais. Warwick had been sent to negotiate the match. At the thought of Warwick, powerless and sick with rage since that summer day two years earlier, Elizabeth smiled. The company saw that smile, that lit her like a torch; a ripple of tension passed over the dancers. They leaped and spun faster to the strains of the sweating minstrels. When the Queen wore that smile, it was politic to perform one's duty to the letter.

'Speak,' said Elizabeth to the Duchess. 'Tell me what you most desire, this moment.'

'There is an arras,' said Jacquetta. 'In the house of Sir Thomas Cooke, late Mayor of London. Have you seen it?'

The tapestry beggared the glory of Goliath and David at Bradgate. It portrayed the Siege of Jerusalem. Ruby blood spouted from the wounds of golden knights; silver roses climbed each border. Fifty men were needed to lift it. The Duchess said:

'Men say that Cooke has Lancastrian sympathies.' She raised one plucked brow gently. 'Traitors should not own such beauty.' The irony of this made her smile.

The Queen looked away, saying softly: 'The King loved Cooke well, once. There are many whom once he loved.' To herself she added: And I have changed all that!

She decided that her mother should have the arras, as speedily as Cooke should be summarily tried and gaoled. By now she knew whom she could trust to work her will. Upon her advent at court they had gravitated to her like wasps to a comfit-dish; some subtly, some openly, all useful. There was Sir John Fogge, Lancastrian through and through, though none would have guessed it. Lord Stanley and his brother Sir William; they had already shown great eagerness to wield her weapons. And John Morton, a prelate of Marguerite's time. He came and went within the court, and never a word out of place, a dissembler too slippery ever to be marked down. Morton was sometimes here, there, in France, in Scotland, or bowing the knee to Plantagenet and York, and always cloaked by holiness.

And there was Tiptoft, John. They called him the Butcher of Worcester, and his face was enough to frighten the stars from the sky. Eyes that bulged as if a fist thrust at them from behind, a full wet mouth, and hands cold as a winter death. He was Constable of

England, and the Queen's loyal servant. His conversation was somewhat uncomfortable; lovingly he would describe his new method of impaling felons.

'I sever the head first, your Grace. The body is turned upside down and a spike driven upwards through the neck. I place the head between the legs and fasten it there with a further spike. It is a humorous sight.'

The commonalty, she knew, cried outrage on these newfangled methods. But they feared the Butcher.

'I am at your Grace's service,' he had said, when presented. The wet lip dropped upon her hand. She had withdrawn her fingers quickly, thinking to see them bloody from the salute ...

Beside Jacquetta, a diminutive figure was spreading its skirts in homage. Lady Margaret Beaufort, with that plain narrow face old from the cradle. Clever at chess and life alike. Although she was dead Somerset's kinswoman, she had taken the oath of fealty to Edward, and now danced with the rest. Elizabeth beckoned her closer.

'How is your son, Henry Tudor, my lady?'

The narrow black eyes held hers calmly.

'He's well, my liege, and still at Pembroke with his uncle, Jasper. His Latin's good, his Greek could be better, but he's loyal. Loyal to all we revere.'

The last five words spoken so dispassionately brought in a wash of memory, the time of Marguerite. Men said that the French Queen was in Wales; sporadic risings in her favour continued to occur. Elizabeth, Queen of England, gripped the arms of her golden chair. She said coldly:

'I understand that your husband died.'

Lady Margaret inclined her head in its stiff brocade hennin.

'King Henry was graciously pleased to make him Earl of Richmond. I am therefore Countess in his memory. I have a new husband, Henry Stafford; I'm content.'

'So your son is at Pembroke,' pursued the Queen. 'Lord Herbert governs there, does he not?'

'We have much in common, your Grace.' The sharp black eyes were amiable. 'If it be true that your Grace's sister Mary will wed Lord Herbert's son.'

Such a devious wit! thought Elizabeth. I will cherish her; she may one day serve me well. Then she clapped her hands; the music wavered into silence. She rose carefully, lifting the heavy state robe. Ermine facings swelled the bodice and sleeves. She felt the icy bite of diamonds sliding against her neck. She stretched out her hand to Lady Margaret Beaufort.

'We will join the King's court. Madame, you and my mother shall bear my train.'

She descended from the dais and felt the drag of three ells of velvet lifted behind her as she proceeded smoothly across the lozenged tiles. As she passed, the women were like a field of flowers stricken by storm.

Within the King's chambers, the courtiers were gathered, just as they had been for her coronation. Her lightning glance swept the separate features, saw that they all bore that look of stark obeisance overlying duty, indifference, or hatred. She had marked those same faces, with their transparent expressions, before.

Her introduction to court after the Council meeting at Reading when Edward had proclaimed their marriage, had been an ordeal. Edward's younger brother George of Clarence had taken her by the hand. Fair, petulant and plump, his eyes were veiled by outrage, the resentment shared by all the old nobility. At Edward's bidding he had led her before the Council, his hand moist on hers, mumbling oafish response to her own courtesy, and bemused by his brother's apparent madness. At her coronation George had been waiting again, unhappily riding a horse up and down Westminster Hall, with Norfolk, Marshal of England, ready to precede them to the ceremony. Waiting, like the rest of England's peerage, for Elizabeth, the Queen!

She had stood in her place of estate between the Bishops of Durham and Salisbury, her head ringing from the cheers of an obedient multitude, her eyes dazed by the pageant colours that blazed from London Bridge to St. Thomas's Chapel, where the singing soared to split the roof; throat dry from the costly sand sprinkled for her safe coming, she had suffered gladly the weight of the royal purple about her shoulders, the prick of the diadem upon her brow. She would have suffered them had the robe been lead, the diadem fire. If only for the look on Warwick's face! That impotent wrath, sourer than month-old milk; it warmed her with delight.

Anthony her brother had been regal in new velvet, and smiling subtly when she looked his way. The sisters were happy; Margaret was married to Tom Maltravers, and there were betrothals well assured: sweet Kate to Harry Buckingham; Anne to Lord Bourchier, son of the Earl of Essex, Eleanor to Anthony Grey de Ruthyn, son of the Earl of Kent. Mary should have Lord Herbert's heir, and Jacquetta Lord Strange of Knockyn. Martha would be the wife of Sir John Bromley, lord of Bartomley and Wextall in Shropshire.

I wrought all this. So thought Elizabeth, as she extended her hand to William Lord Hastings, the King's close friend, one-time partner in licentiousness. She knew more than they realized; the past drinking forays, the past women. Then Lord Stanley and Sir William knelt to her, their eyes speaking of readiness to serve.

And there was Thomas Fitzgerald Desmond, fresh from Ireland. Even when he had bent to kiss her hand that maddening, mocking smile of his remained. Disproportionate rage made her long to strike it from his face.

They had all been there that day; even Morton with his forked beard, eyes hard as agates and never a word out of place. Today Morton was gone from court, but none knew where, and he was unmissed in the throng that waited to greet their Queen after her deliverance from childbed. She moved through the chamber, and the King came, almost stumbling from his dais in eagerness to greet her. She gave him the meekness that he loved, seeing the courtiers as a blur – Hastings, controlling his spleen with a wavery smile; George of Clarence, trying not to scowl, and, expressionless, the youngest brother, Richard of Gloucester. Fourteen years old and of no account; lately of Warwick's household. She looked swiftly about her for Warwick, seeking to enjoy his tortured rage; but the King was pressing her close, blocking her view. His lips were a warm song on her cheek. 'Blessed be God for your deliverance,' he whispered. He turned, then, and with an arm about her shoulder, her narrow, arrogant shoulder, cried to the assembly: 'Blessed be God!'

Rage was alien to the Earl of Warwick. He was unsure whether to show or to conceal it, to vent it by kicking his hound or his page, or to sublimate it through icy dignity, although the past three years had shown him that dignity was not enough. He was a stone in a millrace, tossed into confusion. All the women he had known – his wife, Neville and Beauchamp of ancient Plantagenet line, his gentle daughters, Isabel and Anne – had set him no pattern for dealing with this particular blight. Little Isabella Woodville. God's Blood! he reminded himself: the Queen of England. Only God could have forecast this. Or the Lord of Evil himself.

He paced the King's antechamber, fingers clasped whitely on his dagger's hilt, and, thought savagely of days when he and Edward together had kept men waiting on audience, just as he, Warwick, was now forced to cool his heels. New fury mingled with old as Westminster Clock boomed twice. A whole hour wasted; Edward was doubtless dallying with – the Queen of England. Like the kiss of plague, the past three years settled on him, striking sickly at his bowels. He sought comfort in the thought of the common people's love. They thronged the streets for a sight of his magnificence. For them his door was ever open on six succulent oxen roasting for a breakfast; his household rule was to turn no man away. All were free to hack their fill. Plump chops, haunches of venison, vanished as under the breath of locusts. It was a small price to pay, for the commons' love. Louis of France had openly called him *'Le conduiseur du royaume'*, but did he still? Louis had been more than annoyed at the betrothal of the King's sister to the heir of Burgundy. And Warwick felt himself to have been used, sent, grim-humoured, as the ambassador for this match. Sentiment ... because the King was indebted to Burgundy. The Earl spat on the floor. God's Blood! He said it aloud this time. There had been no home for sentiment at Towton and Mortimers Cross.

The door opened suddenly and Edward burst in, with his fool and a troupe of minstrels. He was laughing. Warwick bent the knee, and thought: that motleyed jester would wear the crown less lightly ...

He answered the King's greeting, then said abruptly: 'I must speak privily with you,' over the tuneless twanging of the lutanist, the fool's mad rhyming cries.

Edward clapped his hands and the entertainers ran, the drummer rolling his instrument, the fool somersaulting high and cleverly into the air. The King threw himself into a chair, gestured for wine which Warwick poured. The Earl was surprised at the trembling of his own hands.

'Well, my lord!' said the King gently. He was very slightly drunk, flushed and handsome. 'It's months since we had privy audience. Sup with me.'

Warwick shook his head, his mouth tightly drawn. Edward went on pleasantly: 'I'm glad to see you, cousin. We must discuss my sister's wedding. I have commissioned the *New Ellen*; a fine ship, a beautiful vessel, to protect Margaret even against the assaults of the Hanse traders' craft. You shall accompany her to Burgundy.'

The sick feeling in Warwick's belly grew. He said:

'Your Grace knows that this will alienate Louis for ever?'

'Bah!' replied Edward. 'King Spider is all mumblings and threats. Together we can woo him, eh, my lord?'

'It is not only Louis who has ceased to love us,' said Warwick distantly. 'Ferdinand of Spain is still angry.'

More than angry, he added to himself. His emissaries had reported Isabella's curses. Spurned by the English King!

'I have made my match,' said Edward. The smile had left him, and his eyes were stormy. They held Warwick's, a warning. Say no more, my lord. Speak not of my Queen! None the less, the Earl's pride, seething like an ill-digested dinner, rose and fermented. He said: 'By the Rood, Ned! Never did I think you would deal thus with me and mine!'

'How so?' Edward watched Warwick's pacing, strongly irritated. These Nevilles made their own orders of chivalry. Elizabeth's kin would never address him whilst walking about. They, unlike this strutting, choleric minister, revered his kingship.

'Be still, sir,' he cried. 'Address your sovereign.'

Warwick turned on his heel, rich robes lifting like a banner.

'I count it loss,' he said, 'that George, my nephew, should forfeit such estates as belong to the Duke of Exeter's daughter. Can you deny ...'

Icily, Edward cut him short. 'I deny nothing. The Queen's son, Thomas Grey, weds Exeter's maid. Her estates are his by my decree. Concern yourself no more with it.'

'The lady was promised to my nephew. And that's not all. Why was my kinsman Mountjoy asked to resign as Treasurer of England?'

Colder still, Edward said: 'My Queen's father, Earl Rivers, is Treasurer. And he carries the position right well.'

Be gone, Warwick told the violent griping pain in his belly. He stared at the King, who took a pear from a dish and bit into it. Warwick felt his control slipping away under the look from those careless eyes. Pride forbade that he should mention past fellowship, old debts, but these were implicit in his voice.

'I sometimes wonder,' he said slowly, 'how best I may serve your Grace. It seems there are new rules of obedience to the Crown: those who serve it least are best rewarded.'

The King leaped up, throwing the pear away. Sober and furious, he faced the Earl squarely.

'You speak against my Queen's family?'

Warwick, shuddering with the past hour's repressed rage, said thickly: 'Why! I speak against all my mortal enemies, who lie about the King's person. Earl Rivers and his knavish son, Anthony – and John, whom you saw fit to marry to my aged aunt – and Herbert, Devon, scoundrels both! I watch them fawning like curs, draining your strength and treasure. While my own folk go in the shadow, robbed of your Grace's favour through no fault but loyalty ...'

'Enough! God's Blessed Lady!' cried Edward. 'My lord, you strain my mercy to a thread. Never would I have thought you ingrate, traitor ... what of *your* brother, then? Didn't I make him Archbishop of York? Translated from lowly Exeter to please you?'

'To placate me,' said Warwick sullenly.

'And John, your other brother – is he not Earl of Northumberland?'

'Yes, Sire,' said Warwick insolently. 'For a season, mayhap!'

They stared at one another. The Earl had gone further than any dared, gambling on the respect once won in bloody, footsore days. But Edward had other, later memories, and they rankled.

'All know–' fury gathered – 'that after my royal banquet for the Bohemian knights, when fifty courses were eaten, there was one who essayed himself more wealthy than the King. Have you forgotten that?'

Warwick's face reddened darkly. He had been unable to resist temptation, not so much to insult Edward but as a thrust at the flaunting Woodvilles. At his house, the Bohemians, marvelling, had dined on sixty courses. He flew to counter-attack, saying the first thing in his mind.

'Has your Grace forgotten the time and care spent by me in nurturing the Duke of Gloucester?'

He hated saying it. Dickon had been happy at Middleham, confused and shattered to find his time there ending so suddenly. Dickon, the precious pawn!

Coldly the king replied: 'Yes! Well, my brother no longer usurps a place in your house, or eats you out of livelode ...' and wanted to bite back his words. Yet in that instant he recalled a rumour; Warwick had invited Richard and George to a great festival, making much of them, perchance pouring sedition in their ear. George, for one, was very susceptible ... He tore his thoughts back to Warwick's reply.

'Gloucester ate little,' said the Earl. 'It was joy and privilege to have him under my roof.'

The two lordly glances met again, both shadowed with heavy regret. The moment passed.

'We have said enough,' said the King. Warwick bowed; when he straightened Edward was seated again, and the afternoon sun had moved to gild his head. Memory, pride and loss mingled to choke Warwick.

'I would have your Grace's permission to retire to my estates,' he said. 'I have affairs to see to, and the court wearies me.'

'You have my permission,' said Edward stonily. The door closed softly, and he was alone. Had he not been King, he would have rushed after Warwick, crying: 'My lord, come back!' conjuring the old times, sharing laughter, planning fresh feats. But Warwick had slighted Bess's family, and the Devil could have him. I care not, he thought, if he is gone for a twelve-month. Yet some unfinished business lingered with him, stirred by the recent conversation. He summoned a page.

'Bring me the Duke of Gloucester.'

Richard Plantagenet, the King's youngest brother, entered shortly. Young, dark, slender, with an unobtrusive sadness that hung about him like chains. His clothes were shabby and unfashionable; his doe-skin thighboots were rubbed to a sheen. His face betrayed little of the joy he felt at being summoned to the presence. The court had already taught him to conceal emotion.

He had one friend in the household; Francis Lovell, a youth of about his own age. But Francis was away for an indefinite time, at Minster Lovell in Oxfordshire. There was no one, nothing. Only Earl Warwick, adored Warwick, who had cherished him at Middleham; Warwick, who had changed so horrifyingly. Richard kissed his brother's hand and rose, and in the moments before Edward spoke, his thoughts returned to Middleham. The North, the clean, beloved North, with its days of hunting and hawking and prayer amid the sweeping winds. The days of mastery; the French and Latin, the dialectics and the courtly skills. And Anne. Even now she would be waiting for her dancing lesson in the little round turret room. Whom would she dance with now? She would be growing womanly, out of the sight of his loving eyes. There was no one, nothing. The days were gone, and the nights, when he and Warwick would sit man to man before the Hall's bright fire. There they would discuss war and philosophy, strategy and myth, and Warwick had never sneered or patronized Richard's halting theories, being swift to compliment him on any mark of wit or understanding. That Warwick had ceased to exist, the night of the banquet.

He remembered it well; how could he ever forget it? The feast had been in celebration of the enthronement of Warwick's brother as Archbishop of York. Anne and her sister Isabel had been present; their eyes had admired Richard, resplendent in new velvet with the proud order of the Garter shining at his knee and breast. There was a thunderous crowd present and food enough to serve the whole City. Sixty-two cooks had laboured over a hundred roast oxen, six wild bulls, four thousand sheep, pigs and calves, five hundred stags, four thousand swans, and countless sweets and subtleties. Marchpane saints sported upon silver dishes, .and Samson in spun-sugar pulled down a honeycomb temple. Richard realized later how this effigy had symbolized Warwick's own desires: the Earl the Samson and the temple Edward's court.

He had drunk a quantity of wine; Warwick had kept his hanap filled. This was a departure, as the Earl, at Middleham, had lectured him upon the perils of drunkenness. Coupled with the noise, the heat, and Anne's presence by his side, the wine had sent his head spinning. He had smiled at all that Warwick said, until that dreadful, shattering conversation had turned his brain ice-cold.

'Look you, Dickon! The King your brother has no time for us these days. That woman makes him wanton, careless. It's meet you turn your back upon him now and follow me. I'll give you high estates, and more ...'

Then Warwick's piercing, reckless eyes had rested upon Anne, so sweet and unknowing in her green gown.

'It's no secret, Richard, how you love!' said the Earl, laughing.

Then Richard had risen from the board, swaying a little, to say stiffly:

'I must have mistaken you, sir. I thought you to say I should betray the King.' And had sat down again, feeling sick.

Warwick, clasping him about the shoulder, had whispered terrible things, about a new day dawning, and the danger to England through the King's mad policies. That it was left to the Nevilles and their adherents to set the kingdom straight. Plantagenet was fast being disgraced by these Woodville commoners, this machinating Queen. Richard must set spurs and ride after righteousness. He must put off the King. The evening had ended in despair. Writhing, Richard could have taken his dagger gladly and slain Warwick, but chivalry forbade it; he had taken the Earl's meat and drink. Dimly he heard Anne's voice, felt her hand on his.

'Why, Dickon? What ails you, sweet Dickon?'

She was too young; he could not tell her that her father, the man he trusted most, had made nonsense of that trust. Warwick, his god, now gloated on treason. He dragged himself out of these black thoughts; Edward was asking him questions.

'... and have you seen the new babe? Little Bess, the pretty poppet! Have you not a sweet and comely niece?'

He answered with difficulty, thinking of the child, who looked like any other child, and the Queen her mother, whose eyes burned him with contempt. Francis Lovell had said this was purely fancy, but Richard knew otherwise.

Edward looked his brother over carefully. His heart mellowed. He should pass more time with him; the boy looked downcast and his clothes were disgracefully dull. Unlike Tom Grey, Bessy's son, whom he had seen that day arrayed in saffron silk.

'How do you spend your time? In the tiltyard? Shooting? I trust you pay attention to your letters.'

Tilting. Shooting. Yes. In the thrust of the longbow, the thrum of the axe, there was comfort. The other young knights were wary of the skills that Warwick had taught him. Richard fought like the Boar, his own blazon.

'You must have new garments,' said Edward. The boy was the image of their dead father – it made his heart ache briefly, and he wandered among memories.

'Do you remember the gloves I brought you? When you and George were lodging in London with the Pastons?'

'Green,' said Richard. 'With the White Rose on the cuffs. I have them still.'

'How you hated that tutor!' mused the King. 'Blotting your Latin with tears, both you and George ...'

'I have forgotten nothing,' said Richard. 'You brought us gifts and comforted us. You were called by God to win England from Lancaster. At Towton and Mortimers Cross; you were, and are, my loving brother, and praise God, my King.'

He raised eyes black with worship. Edward blinked.

'Aye!' he said, pleased. He wondered whether to ask Richard

about George, who, as everyone knew, hankered after Warwick's eldest daughter Isabel, and whose loyalty was therefore suspect. He decided against it, and said:

'You will soon be grown. Able to minister to my affairs in the courts of justice, and ride on campaign.'

There was that look of gratitude again, almost frightening in its passion. The youth was too serious; no frivolity. To Edward this seemed wrong. He should be dancing, gaming, and soon there should be mistresses. These thoughts brought on a fierce lust for Elizabeth.

'So!' he said, hastily, and stretched his hand again for Richard's salute. 'Be gone, now. Amuse yourself.'

The young Duke left without a word, and Edward extended himself upon a day-bed. Soon, the Queen would enter and come to him. It was uncanny – some days there was no need for him to summon her. It was as if she knew his wishes; the mystical implications of this made his flesh crawl pleasurably.

Within five minutes he was watching her disrobe. The sunlight gleamed upon her whiteness. At his leisure, while the afternoon danced and ebbed like a wanton, he got her again with child.

'Tell me again,' said Elizabeth.

She was fatigued. There had been a revel that evening, and dancing, which her heavy body could not enjoy. Edward was still closeted with her father and brother and the other ministers in the King's privy chamber. She had looked forward to being unrobed by Renée and sinking into sleep. But Margaret Beaufort had craved audience – a matter of urgency, she said – and now sat at the Queen's feet, fresh as if it were dawning, unruffled, keen-witted. She had done with childbearing, she was often heard to declare, as if she were an old woman. Her eyes roved expressionlessly over Elizabeth's heavy roundness.

'Say again, my lady. My wits are dull tonight.' The windows were open but it was still stifling in the Tower apartments. The rooms were too narrow; a pungent mist rose from the summer Thames, but Greenwich and Sheen were being sweetened so she must endure it. Sometimes she thought of Bradgate. Bradgate was hers again, but she had not been back. Lady Margaret leaned close, casting an eye over the attendant ladies. Most of them were dozing or working intently on their tapestry.

'My informant is reliable,' she said softly. 'My clerk.'

'So?'

'Reynold Bray.' The narrow black glance was amused. 'These clerks! They go like church mice, soft and docile. They weasel in and out of the most privy conferences, bringing back tidings like snips of cheese. No great lady should be without them.'

At the news that Elizabeth owned no such servants, she pursed her thin mouth, shocked.

'It would honour me should your Grace require my man at any time to work her bidding, were it in his own blood.'

Elizabeth said carefully: 'Why should I need such service?'

As if in chapel, Lady Margaret bowed her head.

'All have enemies.'

Instantly alert, Elizabeth said: 'Tell me their names,' and Margaret glanced about, maddeningly covert. Whispering, she replied: 'Hastings – he would bring you down an it were possible. And the Deputy Lieutenant of Ireland ...'

Elizabeth froze. So Desmond's laughter was not the mere crackling of thorns; there was real malice beneath it. Small wonder he had incensed her so with his smile; her instinct had not lied.

She said: 'Recount me what your church mouse has learned.'

'Not here, Madame. It's better from his own lips. If your Grace will accompany me ...' She cast waspishly about at the drowsy gentle-women. 'I will support you; 'tis not far.'

Minute and upright, with many obsequious gestures, she led the way to her own apartments. In an antechamber, Bray was writing at a lectern. A pale and shadowy man; anonymous. At the Queen's entrance he dropped his quill, yet neatly so that no ink scattered; he drew a low obeisance, flourishing a soiled kerchief. She looked about her; this day everything revolted – the smell of dust from a pile of parchments in the corner; dog-hairs on a worn cloak. The child kicked fiercely beneath her girdle, as if it were distressed by the smell of sweat and stale beer.

'By St. Denis, Master Bray, you live like a hog!'

He raised a white face, he begged her pardon and that of Lady Margaret.

'Sir,' said the Countess, 'recount to her Grace the conversation between Earl Warwick and Lord Desmond.'

He smirked and twisted his hands together. 'I was saying my morn-ing office,' he began. 'The chapel window was open, likewise that of my lord Warwick ...'

'Come, Sir Clerk!' cried Elizabeth. 'I care not how you heard it. Speak, or I'll have you whipped.'

The smirk vanished. He said quickly: 'Your Grace. My lord spoke first; he said: "Tom" (so he calls Desmond) – "Tom, can you not influence the King? He loves you well and will hearken to you."' He shot a narrow glance upward. 'Your Grace, 'tis almost treason...'

'Would you lose your tongue?' Now she found she could be ruthless and savage, like the Butcher of Worcester.

'He said: "The Queen *wastes* our sovereign. This rift with Spain and Savoy gives me bad dreams. Through her, our realm is plunged into vulnerability. The Queen is an ill-omened person.""

Through her growing rage she felt a little chill. The clerk continued:

'He asked my lord of Desmond if there was any means by which he could persuade the King to ... to put your Grace away.'

'And what said Desmond?'

'I could not hear.'

'But he did not disagree?'

The clerk spread his hands, a yea-nay gesture. She thought, curdled with fury: I'll have Desmond's head, and I will see the blood of Warwick. Cursed Warwick! The child plunged within her as if pricked by memory carried in her own blood: Warwick's men unhanging the Goliath tapestry; Desmond's smile. The two things oddly mingled. Lady Margaret's hard black eyes were upon her, her hand upon her arm.

'Your Grace,' she murmured, 'shall I bid my mouse hide in the wainscot a few more weeks?'

Speechless, she nodded, and quit the chamber where Bray mopped and scraped in duty. Flashes of fire ran through her belly. I must be calm, she told herself. Or I shall miscarry Edward's child. Sometimes she hated him for making her carry the child through the sweltering summer. The burden added viciousness to her thoughts. She felt the weight of enemies all around her, synonymous with this pull of flesh within flesh. Jacquetta of Bedford was constantly at her side, feeding her capers in honey for pains in the womb, and violet syrup for her throbbing head. The King's ardour was undiminished at the sight of her swollen body. He possessed her almost nightly, though now with the tenderness of a nurse. Often she caught herself wanting to scream:

'Leave me be, you lustful Yorkist ram!' She clung to discretion. The glitter in her blue eyes he mistook for love. Jacquetta smiled, mixing little simples, murmuring quiet consolations.

Thomas, the Queen's firstborn, approached manhood, and she saw John in him, a dull, aching memory. But he was arrogant where John had been courteous. He was rumbustious, and bullied the young pages in tiltyard and Hall. He mocked the King's brothers: Richard of Gloucester, and, when he dared, George of Clarence, for Clarence was sixteen and owned his own manor, spending little time at court. One of Warwick's toadies? she wondered, and watched him when she could.

One day Edward, impulsive and restless, burst into her chamber with the announcement that he was riding out. He said it was time to cast an eye over his southern provinces, to attend the *oyer* and *terminer* in a few shires, and to pray at a shrine or two on his progress.

'Would that you were coming with me, sweet heart,' he said. Hands in her hair, warm lips on her throat. She extricated herself with a little laugh, weak with concealed relief.

'Our child must not be born upon the road, Ned,' she agreed. 'How long will you be gone?'

'Oh, weeks, days,' he said vaguely. 'I leave the court in your hands. Send for more minstrels; the Flemish are skilled in song.'

Something awoke in her, and stirred. She said: 'Is there not more to ruling than music, my lord? Are there no matters of policy which I should know? While you're away, should I not be aware of statecraft?'

He laughed indulgently, picked up a tapestry frame in one great hand, admired the birds and flowers, and set the frame down.

'Pretty one,' he said. Then, reconsidering: 'Aye, well. My ministers will attend you daily. I shall take Hastings with me, and your father, and Anthony perhaps. No?' seeing her face fall. 'Very well. Your father shall stay. But there are offices I must confer before I leave – the Deputy Lieutenancy of Ireland for one ...'

She said sharply: 'That is Desmond's commission!'

'Yes. But I intend to confer greater honours upon him. He's wasted in Ireland.'

She said casually: 'Have you thoughts for his successor?'

Laughing at this new interest in policy, he caressed her. 'Have *you*, my love? Come, you shall choose. A worthy supporter of all my causes to rule over those blackthorn bogs. Give me your vote.'

Like a wild vision the ruthless, deathshead countenance of her most faithful servant came to mind.

'Tiptoft is loyal,' she said.

He roared. 'Why, sweeting, a fierce choice. And yet ...' He mused, subtly enlightened, stroking his fair strong chin.

'He would serve you well,' she said almost inaudibly.

For a moment he studied her. She was pale today, her long throat like a windflower stem, her lips like two red petals folded firm. And John of Worcester would and could hold down the chanting peat-bards royally.

'So be it, lady,' he said. 'Tiptoft is our choice. Desmond shall be relieved; he can make merry in his Irish castle until I return.'

She pressed close. 'Return soon,' she said. She yielded her mouth, feeling his hard kiss, warm, insensitive, tasting the salt of his passion on her lips.

At Westminster, she held in her hands the Great Seal. It was heavy, with a solemn dark glow about it, and the arms and images were deeply ingrained like the runes on some mysterious talisman. The Seal! the emblem of omnipotence. The child moved fiercely within her; she saw her pearl-trimmed girdle flutter and rise slightly as if to touch the Seal in approval. About her stood a small and silent assembly: her father, Sir Richard Woodville, new-made Earl Rivers and Treasurer of England; Lady Margaret Beaufort; Doctor Morton; and Jacquetta, with her devil-virgin's smile. Elizabeth looked down. As if at the touch of her eyes the man kneeling before her raised his head and fixed her with that dreadful, thrusting, competent glance.

'Sir John Tiptoft.'

'Your Grace.' He would not release her from that look, or from culmination of a plan that had moved too quickly, burned too savagely. 'All is ready, highness.'

The clerk, familiar, whey-faced Reynold Bray, stepped forward with a long roll of parchment. She cast her eye over it; the word *treason* leaped black and plain to see. It was a most unconstitutional document; but in this she was her own parliament and court of law; vanity was the judge and rage the executioner. And for this end she must know more, hear more. She must feel the spark that lit her tinder. Tell me, Sir Clerk, the words my lord of Desmond lately used to shame us. She must have those words, to counter the Seal's dreadful coolness under her hands.

'My friend (who must be nameless) heard them clearly. They were riding for boar. The beast was grounded in a thicket, and the chase halted. The King was thirsty; he asked Desmond for wine, and they spoke together, merrily.'

She could envisage them: Desmond, handsome, chaffing the King for his want of drink; the white teeth, the laughter.

'His Grace asked Desmond, straight, without dissembling, what he thought of the royal marriage. Desmond answered with a jest, but the King pressed him: "Come, man to man!" Then Desmond said: "Twould have been better had your Grace wed a foreign princess. The barons are wroth at your choice."'

Bray faltered. Elizabeth gripped the Seal's warming roundness.

'It's disrespect to you, my liege.'

'We must hear all,' said Tiptoft commandingly. The whites of his protruding eyes were tinged with red. Bray cleared his throat and continued.

'Desmond said: "Your Grace has laid yourself open to some raillery. The common people speak of the Queen thus: they raise their vessels and drink to the princely stables ..."'

'And?' The Seal seemed alive; it was beginning to burn her hands.

'And ... the King's Grey Mare! It is a jest,' Bray said seriously. 'Rooted in your Grace's first marriage to Lord Grey ... the King's grey mare—' as if explaining to children – 'Mare, hard ridden, nightly.'

Warily he looked at the Queen's face. What he saw there put him swiftly on his knees.

'God's pardon, your Grace,' he whispered. 'You did ask me, and I told all.'

The parchment cracked beneath her fingers. The room spun, and there was a bitter taste in her mouth, shreds of blinding light before her eyes. Through all this her wit told her that it was not so much Desmond's seeking to alienate Edward from her – it was Desmond's laughter. Now he should laugh himself on to a scaffold. Tiptoft was watching her closely. The commission was his; he was ready to leave for Ireland within the hour. She smelled burning wax and watched the gobbet of red fall at the foot of Desmond's death warrant. She firmed the Seal carefully in the red; it spread and hardened, the devices showing plain and unassailable. Tiptoft's bulging eyes sought hers.

'I charge you, Constable, to see this carried out.'

'Within the week, your Grace.'

'Let no more treason such as this come from the lips of his family.'

'He has two sons, my liege. Shall they be punished also?'

She nodded, as the hideous face tipped upwards and the wet lip fastened on her shaking fingers. Then he was gone, swiftly, leaving the chamber still spinning and heaving about her. Heat seared her loins. She felt her mother's arm supporting her. So her time was now, in hot summer. She would soon be rid of her burden, and Desmond, in some lonely Irish cell of execution, of his head. And his two sons punished... but they would be only little boys, younger even that Thomas and Dick! She looked uncertainly towards the door now closed behind the Butcher. Then pain stabbed again, lancing through her groin and stomach. She gasped. The King's Grey Mare! May they all suffer, the pain told her. It is legitimate and right ...

Sir Thomas Cooke, one-time Mayor of London, was an avid patron of beauty. His mansion was crammed with bright manuscripts, rich rugs and furnishings, painstakingly collected over his years in King Edward's favour. He was not a young man, and when Earl Rivers with a score of armed men burst in upon him he was afraid, but he was calm. They came upon him writing at a carved oak table in the solar where slatted sunshine beat through the oriel and danced upon the polished floor. For the sake of his wife and children, huddled terrified behind him, he clung to composure. He had heard enough of the Woodvilles, and of the Queen, to know himself powerless before them, and however guiltless, already guilty. So he laid down his quill gently, and confronted Earl Rivers, father of the Queen. Sir John Fogge, tall and blustering, had a deposition in his hand; impotent as a tossed leaf, Cooke listened to the gale of words.

'And so, sir,' finished Fogge, 'we come to arrest you for your treason.'

Behind his chair Cooke's wife began to weep softly.

'I have always been loyal to King Edward,' said Cooke. 'His Grace will remember, if I am permitted audience.'

Sir Richard Woodville said disdainfully: 'The King is unlikely to visit you in prison. I have warned him on occasion of your Lancastrian sympathies. Now we have evidence of it.'

Sir Thomas smiled palely, wondering who had been bribed to lie against him.

'When may I petition the King?'

'The King is from London.'

Cooke's spirit dived. So this was truly the Queen's doing, and all hope lost. He asked Sir Richard mildly:

'Why is the Queen's Grace so full of hatred?'

Outraged, they thrust him to his feet, and bade him keep his treasonous tongue from the Queen. They forced him down the narrow oak stairs and the sunlight followed sadly, licking the rich carvings, down into the bright Hall. Upon the wall there, the Jerusalem tapestry sprang and glittered. The besieged city of gold shone with an almost holy splendour; the bright knights battled upon it in fierce silence. Sir Thomas thought: fair knights, come to my aid! Against slander and ruin, and the Queen's cruel whim. Sir Richard Woodville also drank in the tapestry, all eight hundred pounds' worth of it. Mentally he set Cooke's trial for the day after tomorrow. There were enough perquisites in this mansion to grease the lawyers. Edward would know nothing but admiration for his ministers' zeal. And Elizabeth! He thought: it will give pleasure to her who has helped us to our height. Turning to the guard, he asked: 'Are the wagons ready?'

The men nodded, and he gestured about him. 'Leave naught. Load up.'

'Where for, my lord?'

'The Jerusalem arras for my lady wife's apartment. All else to the Queen.'

And he smiled at the remembrance of Jacquetta's recent inspiration.

'*Queen's Gold*,' the Duchess had said. 'An ancient due of princes, seldom used these days. See that Cooke is fined and that my daughter profits thereby.'

He had kissed her, marvelling.

'But the tapestry is mine,' she said.

Sir Richard rode back to Westminster, where the Queen was lying-in. The child was another girl, to be named Mary in honour of the Virgin. Outriders were within the Palace with news of the King only a few days' ride away. Alone with her parents, Elizabeth listened from her couch to the tale of Cooke's arrest.

'He, too, clung close to Warwick as well as to the King,' said Earl Rivers. 'Men say he sent messages to France; privy plots. Heads have been lost for less.'

The name of Warwick salved the last infinitesimal pangs of conscience she might have owned over Cooke. She closed her eyes.

'Fine him heavily,' she said.

Two days later, Cooke was committed to King's Bench prison. The sum exacted was eight thousand pounds. And, under the archaic right of England, Elizabeth claimed one hundred marks per every thousand pounds. Queen's Gold.

Every time she passed the costly arras, swaying and shimmering in Jacquetta's apartments, an old sore healed a little. The old, jewelled dreams were crystallized, and the nightmares, together with that day at Bradgate, fled. Even Melusine seemed to be part of the past; as if she had stamped their lives with success and left them, knowing that all would be well. That even Warwick would soon fall. Elizabeth went in daily duty to the Christian offices, and thought no more of Melusine, other than as a thing of improbable mist. On the day of Edward's return she was shaken from this complacency.

He came to her bower like a boisterous warm wind. Among cushions she sat, glowing with the peculiar freshness that follows childbirth. Her long hair fell in two thick braids to her knees, and her gown was a cunning weave of azure and green. Near by the Princess Elizabeth occupied the knee of her nurse, Lady Berners, and the baby Mary mewed softly in her cradle. A trapped bee buzzed drowsily against the oriel and somewhere near a minstrel plucked a gittern. Elizabeth held out her arms.

'Welcome, my lord,' she said softly. Edward looked well, brown from the summer riding, and leaner. He strode to the cradle and surveyed its contents. News of the birth had reached him on the road, and his brief disappointment at another female child was past and over. He tickled the infant, kissed the small Elizabeth, and threw himself down beside the Queen.

'A good sortie! Fine hunting we had,' he told her. 'God's Lady, Bessy; there was a deer as high as a house, and I shot her through the lungs with my first quill. It reminded me of our meeting, sweet heart!'

'And the *oyer* and *terminer*?' She twisted her fingers in his long dagged sleeve. 'Did you find unrest in your shires?'

'Naught to complain of,' he replied. 'I hanged a few, pardoned a score, and lightened the purse of many.' His face was suddenly sober.

'You are sad?' she murmured.

'I heard today about Tom Cooke,' said Edward. 'I'd have staked all on his loyalty; yet your father says ...'

She said quickly: 'My father and his knights have proof, Sire. Cooke was untrue to your cause.' She lowered her lids. 'It's hard to be betrayed, my lord. I feel for you.'

'Yes,' he said heavily. After a moment his humour brightened again. He tipped up her chin; chaffing her, said: 'Feel for me, do you? My cunning, lovely lady!'

'Sire?' (sharply).

'Minx, jade, witty wanton Bess!' He pulled her into his arms, laughing. 'In what law book did you read of that ancient right? Queen's Gold! You mulcted poor Cooke right well – what will you do with all this gold, eh? Buy folderols to send your lord love-crazed ... silk atop, and silk below ...'

His fingers strayed. Lady Berners coughed.

'You are not angry,' Elizabeth murmured, relieved.

'Nay, sweet,' said Edward with a kiss. 'It's fitting; Queen's Gold for a queen. My Queen. My love. My fate.'

'Shall I withdraw, your Grace?' ventured Lady Berners, who had been discreetly watching.

Edward sprang easily up from the cushions. 'Nay, madam, I go myself to find my tardy ministers and see what trials await me in the Council Chamber, what arguments have been afoot in my absence. I'll see you anon, love.'

'Soon?' Her hand detained him.

'Tonight,' he promised. 'We'll have supper together here, to celebrate my safe return. Lord, I've missed you, Bessy.'

'Tonight!' she cried. 'I'll order your favourite dishes – goose patty, heron ...'

'Syllabub! And you!' He kissed her fingers and left. The bee rattled and whined against the window-pane. Elizabeth motioned to Lady Berners to kill it. Then there was a tremulous silence, heavy as the thick sunshine beating in, almost as if the day were waiting upon a judgment. She dismissed a vague unease and summoned her women to make her ready for the King's next visit. Sometimes her toilette took as long as four hours. The long white-gold hair must be combed sleek as a fountain; then there was the skilled application of litharge of lead to combat any rough skin, and the rose water rubbed into every inch of her white body. The small blunt hennin with its gauzy veil must be fitted tightly so that no vestige of hair showed above the domed forehead. In this way, when the King's hands finally loosed that spun silver fall, the effect would be even more startling. This day the Queen had a small eruption on her neck. It filled her with anguish. She bade her sister Catherine fetch a bloom of periwinkle, the Sorcerer's Violet, with which to heal the blemish. She bent to stare into the burnished mirror, satisfied and yet unsatisfied with her image, the mouth like a flower, the cloudless blue eyes. Her breasts, heavy with milk, swelled above the loose gown. The King would be intent on love. She hoped his passion would spend itself swiftly; she needed to talk to him, to learn more of policy, of who was her enemy, who her friend. Especially she needed news of Warwick, so seldom seen at court. She was anxious to know his whereabouts and, if any, his plans.

The tiny pimple worried her, and the feeling of unease returned. Lady Berners brought the swaddled infant for her to bless good night. Then the women dispersed, leaving her within a silken frame of candles that gleamed upon the massed white roses round her couch.

Westminster Clock struck seven, followed fractionally later by other, distant sounds, for Westminster, fittingly, was always first. Sweet chimes, deep voices all over London, tongued the hour. The Council meeting would be ended; in truth, it would have been over for some time. She rose and walked about to calm a ridiculous apprehension. Edward would be here soon; possibly one of his more garrulous ministers, Hastings perhaps, had kept him. Then she heard voices, coming faintly from outside the thick oak door.

'For the love of God, let me pass!'

She clenched her hands. That was Anthony, sounding full of frenzy. She heard the guard telling her brother, with firm reverence, that the Queen had retired. A halberd, struck aside, clanged against the door. She went, opened, and. confronted the two pikemen and her brother. All three knelt.

'Let Lord Scales enter,' she said.

He came in swiftly, white-faced. 'Your Grace,' he gasped.

'Anthony. What's amiss?'

His hands were trembling as he caught her sleeve. A little hound, sharing his fear, slunk at his side.

'Your Grace ... Bess. I had to warn you. The King is angry.'

Her mouth suddenly dry, she said: 'What have you done?' thinking: how can he have offended Edward? Only last month he was made Governor of the Isle of Wight, and Knight of the Garter ... Edward loves him.

His eyes darted about. 'Nay, madam. 'Tis none of my doing – but yours.'

'Mine!'

Then she heard the King's steps in the corridor, felt them too, for they shook the oak. Also another noise, a queer buzzing drone of fury. Outside, the halberds slithered apart, and the King, muttering in his throat like a madman, burst into the room. His face was crimson and stained with tears. He took two paces towards Elizabeth, saw Anthony, and flung out a pointing arm towards the door.

'Leave us, my lord,' he said. But Anthony hesitated, his face more ashen than before.

'Leave us!' cried Edward, choking. The hound crept near his boots and he kicked it viciously. Anthony gave a low obeisance, caught up the dog and backed out of the chamber. Elizabeth felt her heart pounding, the milk pulsing in her breasts. There will be a sick baby tomorrow, I must appoint a wetnurse, she thought with wild irrelevance.

Edward was looking at her with a terrible expression, of contempt and even hatred. Above all, with the look of a small boy whose favourite toy has been wantonly smashed.

'My lord, Edward, my lord,' she whispered.

He made a harsh muffled sound, half oath, half sob. He picked up the first object to hand, a crystal vase containing a single rose, and threw it violently so that it smashed into a million slivers. Then he walked blindly away and buried his face in the bedcurtains. Timidly she approached him and he wheeled to face her, eyes blinded by more tears. To him she was a blur of blue and green and silver. A red thread coursed down her cheek where a flying splinter had struck it. He raised his hand to destroy the blue, the green, the silver and the red, and heard her faint voice.

'Your Grace I am but lately up from child.'

The hand dropped. She thought it prudent to kneel, laying her hand upon his embroidered shoe.

'My lord,' she said softly and quickly. 'I do not know my fault; tell me, so that I may amend it.'

He was like the Edward of Grafton, babbling witlessly, laughing and crying low. He swore on the saints, on God's Body, God's Mother. The storm gave way to his dreadful accusing voice.

'Why, lady, why? Was it not crime enough to steal the Seal for your own purpose? But to take Desmond's life away! Desmond, who never did a knavish thing, or an act that was not knightly ... Desmond, my truest creature in all the world, whom I loved like a brother! Blessed Christ, lady! You chose the right weapon with which to wound me! But why? Why?'

She must answer; silence in this moment was folly. Her mind rippled like a silvery fish through excuse after excuse, flicking them aside as likely to feed wrath. All the while she thought: I repent naught. I did not know the King loved Desmond so much as this. Yet it is right he died. He mocked me.

'Men said Desmond was a traitor to your Grace,' she whispered. It was the best, the only answer.

Edward's lips curled.

'Men *said*' he repeated with contempt. 'Tell me then, lady, were his infant sons traitors too? What evil were they brewing in their schoolroom, that they should also die? Do you know, madam, what your hirelings did? They took them from bed, those two little knaves, and stabbed them! Pray Jesu, madam, you never know the grief that is their mother's now!' He groaned aloud. 'The Butcher did his work – I cannot punish Tiptoft, for he acted under your command in Ireland.' He turned from her. 'Go! I'll not look upon you.'

Suddenly, coldly self-justifying, she said: 'Desmond was hot of tongue, my lord. He spoke words unfitting for a prince's ear. He called me ...'

She said the unforgivable nickname, hating it even in her own mouth. Then she saw the fresh contempt in Edward's eyes.

'Madame,' he said, heavily sarcastic, 'if I were not insulted, neither should you be. 'Twas a jest ...' His face crumpled again. 'Tom loved a jest.'

He wept bitterly. Elizabeth, cold with dread, poured upon him a spate of pleading, promises. She swore it was for his sake that she had acted, that she could not bear to hear their love defiled, not even on the lips of a friend. All these pleas dropped like stones into the torrent of his grief, and left no trace. Finally he faced her again, eyes shadowed with bitterness.

'I fear, Madame,' he said slowly, 'I very much fear, Bessy, that you have become unkind.'

In these almost charitable words there was terror. She would rather he raged again, broke more furnishings, or struck her. The candles were still wavering gently, the white roses banked to perfume their love-pleasure. Was it too late? Yet the weapon of her body seemed blunted. He looked only at her eyes.

'I'll leave you now, lady,' he said, after a while. 'And I advise you to spend your gold on Masses for the soul of Desmond and his boys. Expect me when I choose; it will not be soon.'

Wild, imploring, she said: 'My lord, you have not eaten. You must not ride again without at least a void of wine ...' She picked up a little silver bell.

'I'll not eat or drink with you, lady', said Edward soberly. 'Get to the chapel and pray for Desmond. As for my other pleasures, I'll take them elsewhere.'

Never had he been unfaithful, so closely had she bound him. Now the chain was breaking, and this brought more fear. Was this the moment? The moment when Raymond, hearing that his heirs, the sons of Melusine, had butchered one another, cried: '*Begone, odious serpent! Contaminator of my noble race!*' ?

She held out her hands, but he was already at the door. As if he cursed her, he turned and said,

'I go, to spend my time with a lady who is kinder than you. And should I sire a child on her, this is my will: that the child shall be brought into your household, to attend you. If it is a boy, it shall be named Thomas, in Desmond's memory. If it is a girl, it shall be named Grace, to compensate for your own gracelessness. Whatever it is, it shall be a constant reminder of your evil work this day.'

As he closed the door, he saw her, wraithlike, hands clasped, head still high, and he thought of Elizabeth Lucey. Silly, clinging she might be, but incapable of such acts as the queen had wrought. Then he thought of the woman, lately admired on his progress. There had been promise in those green eyes, compassion on that mouth. Anything, to take his pain away. The sun was not quite down. He would ride from the City.

'Our most good and gracious Queen Elizabeth, Sister unto this our Fraternity of our blessed Lady and Mother of Mercy, Saint Mary Virgin, Mother of God.'

This was her title, bestowed by the Skinners' Guild, who had loaded her shoulders with the pelts of a thousand small beasts. Bright stippled ermine, marten and miniver, she wore them over an azure gown, edged and latched with gold. Here at Fotheringhay she was glad of the furs' warmth. Even in high summer, the ancient castle seemed exposed to the north winds, while the dank breath of the marshes pervaded every room. She stood on the river bank beside the sluggish Nene, and a breeze rippled and flattened the reeds, and her furs, with a silent, wandering hand. She watched the barges carrying the King and his entourage towards the landing stage. They were gold and silver, and all along the prow and sides the Sun in Splendour merged with the White Rose. Standing in the foremost craft Edward towered like a pagan sea-prince behind the curved figurehead shaped like the falcon of York. As the barge drew near, she could see that he was happy. His humours were as fair as on the day he left London to gather an army for his latest campaign.

It was a year since the quarrel, and slightly less since he had returned, strangely sombre, from his unknown leman. That very night he had taken Elizabeth again with a hating passion, resulting in yet another daughter, Cicely. He had not been wroth at this, and had jested, surveying his baby daughters: 'It takes a man to get a girl! And by God's Lady, I am three times a man!' He had gone down in person to Chepe to buy her a necklace and girdle in gem-starred gold; had heaped new honours upon Anthony and Thomas, her eldest son. Staring at the barges, she saw caskets, fardels containing silver and jewels sitting cheek by jowl with the royal library and a cage of singing birds. So he was bringing more gifts, priceless relics from the shrines of Norwich. She caressed one hand with the other, feeling her diamonds ice and the shape of a pigeon's blood ruby. The costly fur blew about her face. Yes, Edward was hers again.

Close by a stern voice spoke, turning her jubilation to impatience.

'He has dallied too long, that son of mine.'

Proud Cis! Be still, arrogant old dame, thought Elizabeth. Yet she turned modestly to acknowledge the presence of the King's mother, that unbending matriarch in whose honour the latest infant had been named. Still wearing her widow's weed, unjewelled, ageless and potent, she stood gazing at the King. Fotheringhay was her demesne; at her waist a vast bundle of keys made music in recognition of the fact. Unease was bred of the old Duchess's presence. Every time the bowed eyes met hers, Elizabeth imagined their accusation: *Unlawful Queen. Remember Eleanor Butler!* No question that the Duchess would ever speak of Eleanor – the succession of York was too precious. Yet always in her mien there was that discomfiting hint of a secret sorely kept.

Together they knelt as Edward leaped on to the little quay. He raised and kissed them, then his approving eye raked the lines of battle-tents set up in the meadow, and the milling hundreds of waged men who had come to his service, in preparation for the affray. With his wife and his mother, he moved across the sward where blown dandelions and buttercups formed a shimmer of misted gold, like froth on metheglin. He talked excitedly of the latest rumours reaching from his northern territories, and seemed amused by the audacity of a nameless rebel.

'Rising against *me*!' he cried. 'Some poxy peasant too cowardly to show his colours. Believe me, madam my mother, and mark well, Bessy. He shall be fried in his own fat.'

'He has wrought much damage, by all accounts,' said the Duchess of York soberly.

'Ah, a few dwellings burned only – more complainings for my *oyer* and *terminer*.'

Elizabeth smiled up into his eyes, wondering how long he could be persuaded to tarry at Fotheringhay. She was unmoved by the rebellion; Jacquetta of Bedford had dismissed it, saying that Mars rode high in the King's favour. Cicely of York said suddenly:

'The Frenchwoman – have her agents to do with this rising?'

'The witch is in France,' replied Edward bluntly. 'Where, like her predecessor in sorcery, she should be put to the fire – for my father's and my brother's deaths.'

'Yes!' said the Duchess sadly. She fingered the great reliquary at her breast. But her eyes were on Elizabeth, a glance like a chill wind.

They ascended the castle steps, ahead of the nobles disembarking from the other barges. Elizabeth felt great satisfaction at entering, with her royal husband, Cicely of York's demesne. Accompanied thus, she lifted her head high and prepared to pass under the portcullis which bore the falcon in the fetterlock, the grim insignia of York. Then someone trod upon her train. She was almost dragged off balance; the gold clasp about her throat bit into the flesh like a ghostly restraint. You have no place here. Somewhere far behind in the ranks she heard a young man's laughter and recognized it as belonging to Sir Francis Lovell; but his was not the offending foot. She swung quickly round, even as the pressure on her garment lifted, and confronted Richard of Gloucester, already on his knee. His head was bowed, his thin restless hands spread behind him in the accepted attitude of supplication.

'God's pardon, your Grace,' he said levelly.

A tart reply sprang to her lips but Edward forestalled it.

He smote the seventeen-year-old Duke on the shoulder and genially bade him rise.

'Guard yourself, Dickon,' he said gaily. 'No brother of mine shall vex a lady!'

The smile that passed between them angered her, for it was token of the things she could not share, and it lay upon the mouths of those who had loved the unspeakable. Yes, Warwick; Gloucester in particular had loved him at Middleham, like a dog. Now, with his gloomy asceticism, he came to haunt her court. She pressed her lips together and moved into the Hall. There was her father, already clad in half-armour, willing to join forces against the tawdry rebellion. And there was young John, similarly arrayed, blond like Anthony, and with the same fine-boned arrogant face. Warmly she pressed his hand. Poor John, who shared a bed with Warwick's aged aunt! Rich John – who had lemen by the score and wealth immeasurable. She smiled at him conspiratorially. He grinned back, cocksure, lithe; her youngest brother. She loved him, with a greedy proprietary love. The clothes he wore, and the new burnished harness were bought and paid for by her body and her wit. He was mischievous, too, a studied breaker of hearts. We are a great family, she thought; we shall endure.

Later at the banquet there was entertainment. The pageantmen appeared in the story of St. Elizabeth. A blond boy knelt in prayer while angels supported by wire and pulley descended with divine tidings. This disguising, by a happy accident, was the same as that performed on her coronation progress; she felt doubly Queen, almost secure. Once or twice she let her eyes wander to her adherents; Sir John Fogge, Lord Stanley and his brother. Dr. Morton, Margaret Beaufort. Tiptoft was there also. Again she marvelled that a year, and the good humour engendered by the prospect of battle, should have so shortened the King's memory. For he had made Tiptoft,

Desmond's executioner, Constable of England for life; free to behead, to impale obscenely, the King's erring and innocent subjects alike.

Close to her chair stood Anthony, in a peacock doublet. She beckoned him, whispered: 'Dear brother! Do you remember the time when you would not take me from Grafton on your charger?' He flushed, answering quickly: 'It was fate, my liege. Fate that you stayed at Grafton, fate that took you to court, returned you home, and gave us these famous days!'

'*Oui, vraiment*,' she answered, for an instant transformed to Marguerite's Isabella, then rushing like a snowball on a slope through the time of widowed, bereft Elizabeth to this high moment. The thoughts made her dizzy. Minstrels were playing a *rondeau* and Edward had given the signal for dancing.

'I will partner our liege sister,' said John, brushing past Anthony's extended hand. She smiled at both brothers, stepped from the dais and began to glide and swoop, curtsey and kiss lightly.

'So, my lord, you are to play the soldier,' she mocked him tenderly, as the viols shrieked and the tabor throbbed like the wings of a captured bird. 'You shall bring me the rebels' heads on a platter.'

'It will be time wasted,' he scoffed. 'All this money and these accoutrements to ride north after a handful of disgruntled serfs. I would liefer hunt bigger game.'

'It's enough, for your first campaign,' she said.

He bowed in the dance, flourishing his long pointed shoe. 'Some there are who prate as if we were to ride against the Turk!' He wagged his chin vaguely in the direction of the royal dais, where one or two of Edward's captains stood awkwardly among the ranks of Woodvilles.

'Richard of Gloucester,' he added disdainfully. 'The King's pet and popinjay. He sickens me with his talk of loyalty, his fussing with weapons, his book-learnt strategy. And Edward listens to him.'

'He loves him,' said Elizabeth, halting suddenly so that the following dancers tripped on their gowns. She looked covertly at Gloucester, then dismissed him from her mind. 'What of Clarence, though? I do not see him here.'

'He has more sense,' said John dourly. 'Doubtless he is hunting on his own manor. There is better sport in stags.'

She danced next with her father. He was as light on his feet as John and, she thought, more handsome than ever. Her feeling of contentment grew. She was flanked by her family, her noble brothers, her pretty sisters like a cluster of bright blossom near the dais. Sir Richard Woodville led her back to Edward's side; the King was dicing with Lord Hastings; Hastings, looking unhappy. He had a weak mouth; somehow this added to her confidence. Edward talked while the dice rattled. He spoke of the proposed affray.

'We shall split into three sections, northerly, ringing the rebels ... thus.' He drew patterns in spilled wine. Richard of Gloucester stood behind him, watching. Once he bent to murmur, and directed the King's carefree finger to an easterly point in the map. Edward looked up, impressed. Irritation was born in Elizabeth.

'You seem skilled in warlike policy, my lord,' she said. 'You are experienced?'

She watched his pallor turn to unhealthy rose. He said softly: 'It's true I've never ridden on campaign, your Grace. But, be it my first or my last, I ride for my King.'

Edward cried: 'Bravo!' spinning the dice, in such a good mood that, thought Elizabeth, had the Devil appeared to mouth platitudes he would have applauded. Quietly she said to Gloucester: 'And your brother Clarence? Why is he not here, putting on harness?'

The blush grew. From her eye's tail Elizabeth saw her father, smiling; behind him, the radiant figure of Anthony, his arm about their sister Catherine, and young John, grinning broadly at Gloucester's discomfiture.

'Is he a traitor?' she pursued.

'He is our brother.'

She raised her plucked brows. 'In the Book, brother shall rise against brother; this, my lord Gloucester, is no warranty of good faith.'

Edward threw down his dice for the last time. 'Soft, Bessy,' he said. 'Clarence is lazy; there's no harm in him.'

'He is loyal, God willing,' said Gloucester. Then he turned and left the dais, thrusting through the skein of dancers and out beneath the stone archway leading from the Hall.

'Such uncourtliness,' said a soft voice. Lady Margaret Beaufort stood beside Elizabeth. Emboldened by the Countess's murmur, the Queen said tightly: 'He had no right to quit my court so ...' Then she saw that Edward watched her. He said casually: 'Gloucester is weary. He is young to wear the duties of a captain.' The eyes warned: Look not with anger upon those I love!

Later, when the fire in their bedchamber was burning down, she stood against the window-slit through which were visible the dusky lines of tents with their tiny glimmering lanterns. The night wind, with its salt marsh tang, blew about her face. Edward's arms came round her from behind, and she turned from the sight of tomorrow's array. Within the resentful walls of the Yorkist stronghold she went to him, glad and lissom as a serpent.

Northbound to Newark, the army left in splendour. The banners flounced above it, screaming colour at the sun. Like a lengendary figure of farewell she stood, while the royal party mounted. The King's stallion was black as Lucifer; against it all the other horses looked pale. Roan and bay, whirling dappled grey, coats like smoke. She kissed her handsome father ardently, and gave a special smile to young John, cool as a pearl on this his first foray. Lord Hastings's mount was wild and kicked up dirt. Richard of Gloucester went by, too preoccupied to give her more than cursory obeisance. Anthony rode behind him, the sun flirting with his silver plumes.

Soon they were only a thin erratic thread on the skyline. With her sisters, Elizabeth moved back into the castle, where she gave orders that her household should remain another week at Fotheringhay. She sent women to prepare her most priceless gowns; she would wear them in hopes of enraging Proud Cis.

One stray thought remained, like a riderless horse. Clarence loved to appear in armour more costly than his brothers' and with weapons polished to an unbelievable glass. Why, why was Clarence absent?

One of the women was screaming, frightened keening yelps like a houseless puppy, and the noise filtered to Elizabeth, sitting very still in Garden Tower apartments. Before her, a courtier was still on his knees, his cloak and boots chalked with riding. His doublet breast was torn where, for safety's sake, he had ripped off the device of Lord Hastings; this, a black belled sleeve on silver, he held in his hand. He had needed to ride thus anonymously through two days and nights, or the rebels would have killed him. She heard him relate this in the same way as she heard the shrieking outside – the shrieking that drifted high about the merlons of the Tower and shivered into silence; she heard and did not hear. Down the corridors of her mind the messenger's first words rolled, like a long echo going away.

There were a lot of names, and all had colours. The King: bright blue and gold, with a cage round it – for Warwick had the King fast a prisoner, having ambushed him in the north ... Hastings, and Richard Gloucester – both dull brown, having fled, escaped. Anthony her brother: a rainbow name shot with fear and hope, for the King had bidden him flee for his life, and where was he now? George of Clarence: over the courier's head, and through the window, she could see ravens; pecking at the battlements. Black. The colour of Clarence, who had allied himself to the foul field. To Warwick, blacker than black.

'None realized that they were so close, my liege,' said the courier promptingly. He wished the Queen would speak. His knees ached; he was broken from fierce riding. 'Clarence took Earl Warwick's daughter in marriage at Great Calais. He is his sworn man.'

There were two other names, names that dripped redness and grief. She saw the face of young John, her brother, smiling in the dance; his body brightly harnessed for campaign. She saw the vivid merciless grace of her father. As if by alchemy she saw change; she witnessed their deaths as clearly as if she had been a bystander. The faces of father and brother were red dripping ruins, held aloft by the hair, while, far below, their bodies leaked more redness into a pile of straw. Warwick himself held a head in either hand, and laughed.

She said: 'Oh, Jesu, mercy.' From the crowding, unquiet throng of her household came whispered amen, like sea on shingle. Emboldened, the courier continued. 'Not only your Grace's father and brother were beheaded, but also Lords Pembroke and Devon. Because Earl Warwick ...'

'Call him not by his name.' The words were like swallowed ice. 'Refer to him, henceforth, as the Fiend.'

'Yes, Madame. All four were beheaded because ... the Fiend vows they were evildoers and succubi, draining the strength from the King and wealth from his coffers. Your Grace,' he said anxiously, 'Lord Hastings sent word that you should take your daughters – and your two sons by Sir John Grey – from the Tower to a place of greater safety. Already Clarence rides on London with Archbishop Neville, Earl ... the Fiend's brother.'

The icy feeling spread and hardened in her breast.

'We shall not leave London,' she said. 'We shall adjourn to our Palace of Westminster.'

As the still tableau of her household began to dissolve, hurrying all ways, she trembled and said softly:

'So! He ranks us with succubi, demons! We, who are descended from the house of Luxembourg, from the blood of a ...'

Margaret Beaufort's narrow face swam into her vision. A small slender hand gripped Elizabeth's sleeve. In the Countesss' black eyes was knowledge, warning. Say naught that can harm you, the eyes pleaded. Then the Countess was whispering, new alarums mixed with advice; There were things undisclosed by the courier, fresh assaults from the foul one. Reynold Bray had been busy with ear and wit. Concerning Jacquetta of Bedford; they must go to her at once.

'My mother?' said Elizabeth, low and harsh.

'She is in danger,' replied the Countess. 'The Fiend seeks to lay her low.'

'Ah, God's blood, he is a canker,' said the Queen. Her feet and hands were icy, as if she had lain for days in snow.

'And we will cut him out!' said Margaret Beaufort, strongly. 'Come, my liege. We must find her before the Archbishop reaches Westminster.'

Jacquetta had been told of her husband's death. The news had robbed her of her wits. In a grim mask of sorrow, her once-clear eyes were opaque and wandering. It was also suddenly apparent that she was no longer young. The Duchess had taken to painting of late, and now the spots of cochineal paste stood out like round wounds on each bloodless cheek. Alarmed, Elizabeth saw her thus and realized that those knowing eyes, that mighty spirit, were for the first time in retreat, and thought: Jesu! what shall I do, without her guidance? and more wildly: How have we offended Melusine ... I have followed her dictates, I have captured and enslaved a prince. I have endowed palaces and colleges with my wealth, and I have spread my stag's hide over the whole of England. I have borne children ... Here the pattern fell to pieces. She bore sons, and what have I? Three frail and pretty wenches. She shook her head involuntarily. This is madness, and no fault of mine. Melusine never had an enemy like the Fiend!

In the chamber corner a stench was rising. It tickled Eizabeth's throat and brought on a genteel fit of coughing from Lady Margaret Beaufort. The latter glanced swiftly about and determined the odour's source – a black candle was alight. She extinguished it and threw it under a deep chest.

'Her Grace becomes indiscreet,' she said softly. Elizabeth turned to her.

'Margaret. How much is known?'

'Too much,' said the Countess. She leaned to where Jacquetta sat glassily and said: 'Your Grace, the images. The waxen images.' Elizabeth looked at her, startled. 'Did you disclose them to anyone?'

In a voice like a sad little wind, the Duchess answered: 'Aye, once. To the nuns of Sewardsley ... they wished for knowledge. There was one whom they would bring down – their Abbess, who used them ill; they sought my secret and I showed them.'

Margaret Beaufort hissed with impatience. Blankly the Duchess looked at her.

'My lord is dead,' she whispered. 'My knight. The handsomest in England ...' Her eyes blurred, went away somewhere far off.

'Madame!' cried Margaret. 'Warwick is upon us ... you are to be tried for sorcery unless we act at once. Your Sewardsley nuns have tongues like clappers, for they even told my clerk! Where are the images now?'

The Duchess sighed, and began talking in a sleepwalker's monotone of her dead knight's grace, treading the ash of lost passions, muttering as if at that moment they bedded together. The frank demented speech of love. For an hour Elizabeth and the Countess rummaged fretfully in chest and coffer, eventually breaking the lock of a tiny box. There, lying unquietly upon a piece of silk was the tiny Edward, streaked with his own blood, and the misshapen facsimile of Warwick, still cinctured with the iron band.

'Make up the fire,' said Elizabeth. From outside came the faint sound of horsemen riding; the sounds of steel and iron and commands. When the flames leaped she took the two figures firmly in her hands. She was more than loath to destroy the King's image, so in precaution she murmured: 'May this heat add only power to the Sun in Splendour,' casting the image into the fire's heart. At the sight of Warwick's little figure her lip curled back like a rabid hound's; she called down a curse upon him for the twentieth time. As she watched him melt and coagulate among the burning logs, a desperate question formed: Will he never die? She turned from the fire to Lady Margaret, whose black eyes net hers calmly, without surprise or censure.

'So, 'tis done. Your Grace, be comforted. Now–' practical again – 'are there witnesses?'

Jacquetta's voice startled them. 'Witnesses ...' she quavered ... 'but no proof. Ah, my sweet lord ...'

She was a shell, bereft. But Margaret Beaufort was doubly strong, immensely comforting, and to her Elizabeth now turned again.

'Margaret. Will the Fiend slay the King?'

'Rumour says yes,' replied the Countess. 'But I think otherwise. Bray says he is at Pontefract, royally housed.' She took Elizabeth's hand. 'Come, my liege. Let us confront Archbishop Neville. Surely,' she mocked; 'the Church will not be a party to the murder of an anointed King!'

With a small entourage the Queen rode to Westminster, mantling her face against curious stares. The streets were black with people. Volatile and distraught, vague news lately in their ears, they ran alongside the train, grabbing at the outriders' stirrups. Was it true that Ned had been beheaded up north? Where was he? Jesu preserve him, wherever he was! Towards Westminster Hall, a knot of people chanted Edward's coronation song. Elizabeth, while motioning to her escort to whip the runners back, was greatly comforted. She alighted outside the Exchequer, and, lifting her velvet robe to plant each small slipper firmly down, mounted the steps to her own Council Chamber. Behind her the mob growled encouragement, and Margaret Beaufort whispered: 'They are loyal to a man, and Burgundy has already sent word promising support.'

There was an armed guard flanking the Chamber door. They wore Clarence's Black Bull upon their livery. The Queen's men marched forward; she heard argument, saw the shaking heads. She threw off the loose velvet hood and stepped forward, small and vital among the tall armoured men. The ranks parted at once, for the guard, unsure, dare not lay hands upon the Queen's person. She entered: the Chamber was bright with new hangings, those of the See of York. Elizabeth's chin went up in cool anger. There upon her dais, sat George Neville, the Archbishop, and this sight fed her wrath. She resolved, glaring at him, to have him down from that perch more speedily than he had ascended to it. Next to the dais stood Clarence. He had put on flesh; uneasy triumph clothed his fair Plantagenet face. As she walked towards him the red vision crossed her mind. The heads of father and brother, weeping blood. Clarence's hands were folded on his sword-hilt; his new wedding-ring was jewelled and prominent. The Fiend's son-in-law! So she marked him down.

Archbishop Neville rose, extending his hand and suddenly full of doubt, as Elizabeth, Queen of England, advanced and outside the walls, loyal London clamoured for their King's return.

For Elizabeth, it was a nightmare test, to be endured not once but many times.

They were felling a tree, with great lusty strokes. She could hear the whine of the falling axe, the crash of the steel on timber. The great bole bled white slivers. They were bringing down the Queen's Oak, while she stood in Whittlebury Forest, watching, powerless. The thunderous blows gained pace and vigour. She flung out her hands and wrenched from the tossing dream. Still sleep-bemused, she lay blinded by a tress of her own hair. The noise went on, and she identified it. She was not in Whittlebury, she was in the Tower state apartments, and someone beat on the outer chamber door. The bolts were drawn; she heard voices – a man's urgent, summoning, and Renée's, as high and hysterical as that day, nearly a year earlier, when they came to tell the Queen that her father and brother were slain.

She slipped from the bed. Fear, odorous and stomach-churning, was all about her once more. She thought, suddenly: Edward is dead! Realizing that which she had always harboured and never dared examine: *Edward's death is my own downfall. Without him ...* She dared think no further. She stood shivering in the curtains' dark velvet cave, her mind racing over the past year, recognizing the mistakes made by the King, and her panic gave way to fury as she remembered how he had ignored her counsel. The resentment shown by the Londoners at their King's imprisonment by Warwick had been shared by the greater part of England. Love Warwick they might – for his ostentatious lordliness and his bonhomie, for his roast oxen and free gifts – yet where the King's person was concerned that love stopped short. Within a month of Warwick's coup, Edward had come riding back unharmed from Yorkshire to a tumultuous welcome from all the prominent Londoners. He had been like a schoolboy, tickled by the jest of outwitting Warwick in popularity. Even then she had had the notion that he took it all too lightly. And he could not resist playing the magnanimous ruler.

She had gone on her knees to him.

'For God's love, Edward, have Warwick beheaded! He has proved himself a traitor, like your brother of Clarence. Kill them.' Her imagination fattened on hatred. 'Let Tiptoft impale them on the highest point of London Bridge!'

Freshly shaven, clad in new white velvet, Edward had listened to her at a banquet ordered in honour of his safe deliverance. He had looked at her with a strangely cynical knowledge.

'Bessy, Bessy,' he said quite gently, 'how you do hate my lord of Warwick!'

She gasped. 'But, Ned! He rose against you! He invaded our Council with his minions. He laid hands upon your sacred person and–' sadly – 'he murdered my father and my brother, both your true men!'

He nodded, briefly commiserating. 'My heart bled for them, in truth. But–' He shook his head decisively, 'I shall not play the tyrant. I have offered Warwick the general pardon, and he will soon come here to accept it.'

Sickly, she said: 'And what of Clarence?'

'Foolish,' said the King. 'Ambitious, disloyal. Yet still my brother.'

And his glance slid upwards to where, left of the dais, Richard of Gloucester stood; she knew then that Gloucester had been Clarence's advocate, as always prating of brotherly love and forgiveness. She looked at the young Duke with a savage steel-blue flicker that carried all her jealous resentment: Edward had spoken for half an hour to the company, praising Gloucester for his courage during the affray and the nobility of his endeavours in obtaining the King's release. Hastings came in for a share of this glory too, and smirked under it.

Elizabeth sought out Anthony. He, praise God, was whole and sound. She embraced him with a lover's fervour.

'Did you do naught to ease the King's plight, sweet lord?'

He shrugged. 'He sent me to Norwich when we were attacked, for my own safety; Warwick hates me most of all. But I would have aided the King, if I could.'

'And now you are Earl Rivers,' she said sadly, and he bowed his head saying: 'Aye, Jesu preserve my murdered father's soul!'

'Thank God I have other brothers.' No more would she think of poor young headless John. She thought of Edward, master seaman, Lionel, now Bishop of Salisbury; Richard. She would look to her own sons, Thomas, newly created Marquis of Dorset; young Richard Grey. Edward's daughters too must be protected from the Fiend. She was indignant that the King had promised Elizabeth, the firstborn, to John Neville's son. This knight, said he, although Warwick's brother, had remained loyal throughout. As if any Neville were less than a demon, a traitor!

'Warwick is not quenched,' said Anthony, voicing her own thought.

She cast a desperate glance towards the King. He had donned the Order of the Golden Fleece, bestowed by Charles of Burgundy. By this token he signified to all that Burgundy was his ally, and to hell with France! There had been more talk of Marguerite, who, it was said, was only awaiting the chance to rise again. But during one of the skirmishes following Edward's release from the northern fortress, King Henry, witless and saintly as ever, had been captured.

'They found him sitting under a tree, singing,' said Anthony. 'While Edward put the enemy to flight. They ran so fast they shed their jackets ... they called it 'Lose-Coat Field'!' He laughed. 'Old Harry came willingly, still whistling the same tune: "if my lords do but love one another ..."'

'"...All will be well," said Elizabeth, but she did not laugh. The certain knowledge of Warwick's undiminished spleen persisted. When Clarence and Warwick came a few days later to bow the knee in contrition, she was doubly certain of his ill-will. Hatefully close to her own small silkclad feet he knelt, and the King took him by the hand. Warwick was leaner, his black curls were traced with silver. The large grey eyes flared to meet Elizabeth's, and she felt the steel of his will. The sight of him hurt her heart. All her curses turned inward and festered impotently. So she turned her uncompromising loathing upon Clarence and saw the meekness on his face give way to bafflement. Self-confessed traitor though he was, the Queen's malevolence startled him.

Warwick would rise again; she knew it. And here, at the Tower, in the quailing oak of her bedchamber, in Renée's yelps, and the slither of a drawn sword, was the proof of her foreboding. She flung on a silk robe and pushed through the bed-curtains, to stand, hard-eyed, while one of two messengers knelt and thrust a parchment towards her. He and his fellow were both pale, scarred by wind and mud. Renée was still volubly dispensing grief. Elizabeth thought fleetingly: she had seen much disaster, both in Marguerite's household and in mine; yet I should be the one to scream! She turned and struck Renée in the face; the screams diminished to a sob. To the messengers she said: 'Tell me, quickly. Is the King dead?' the while unrolling the parchment and seeing, in a quick surge of relief, that part of the letter was written in Edward's own flambouyant hand. Written at Doncaster ...

'He is exiled, my liege,' said the man. 'He and the Duke of Gloucester and your Grace's brother, Earl Rivers; Lord Hastings and others. Warwick's army came upon them by night. John Neville led the rout – he was enraged because the King had taken his earldom away and bestowed it on Lord Percy.'

Yes, she had warned him in vain. Never trust a Neville! She said: 'Where is the King now? I must join him instantly.'

'Your Grace,' said the courier desperately, 'he's half-way to the Low Countries. They took ship at Lynn, with only the clothes on their backs. Read, Madame.'

Candlelight flickered on the message, penned by a panicking clerk, and all ink-blots. Her eyes leaped to the postscript written by Edward.

'Twenty thousand men are at our heels. God keep you, dearest, my Bessy. Get you to Sanctuary with our little maids ...'

Ah God, she thought, he has left me. Left me alone to the Fiend's mercy. Curse him for it. Nay, (hastily) rather Jesu preserve him for without him I am doomed. To Renée she said: 'My clothes, now. We, too, will ride to Lynn; command one of my brother Edward's ships and follow his Grace.'

The courier gave one pitying succinct look at Elizabeth's swollen body. Had the Queen lost her wits? She was seven months gone with child. And she, following his eyes to what she had, for the moment, forgotten, thought in despair: why must I be *enceinte* at such a time as this? Ned takes his pleasure, pardons the Fiend, then puts the North Sea in between us ...

'Madame!' said the bearer, urgently. 'Collect your daughters and let us be gone to Sanctuary. There's a boat waiting below.'

He was no hero, and he wished the Queen would hurry. He had heard enough tales of slaughter to frighten him. Warwick rode on the Tower itself, to rescue witless Harry Six, who had been housed there since after the battle of Lose-Coat Field.

Dressed in her furs, Elizabeth met her household at the steps of the watergate. Through the archway rain fell in drifting spears and the wind moaned up the slime-green stairs leading to the river. A handful of men held torches high, and the flames billowed and swirled with a ghastly leaping light. A flurry of wet dead leaves, blown by a far-off gale, slapped against the portcullis. Agitated by tempest, the swollen river flowed by, black, then red in the cressets' glare. Frightened, the nurse, Lady Berners, was fussing over her three fair-haired charges: Elizabeth, in her fifth year the replica of her father, Mary, a year younger, and eighteen-month-old Cicely. The gentlewomen wore an odd assortment of garments hastily donned, and were shivering with cold and fear. Margaret Cobbe, the midwife, had her little coffer of medicines firmly beneath her arm. Renée was still sobbing. Elizabeth said sharply:

'My mother! Where is the Duchess of Bedford?'

'Here, my liege.' Two more women were supporting Jacquetta along the narrow way. She came like a brittle-winged black bird. The wind tugged her widow's veil, and blew it aside, revealing the crudely rouged cheeks, the vacant stare. Elizabeth set her foot upon the slippery step while the torchbearers milled about her, whispering: 'For God's love, Madame, take care!' their hands trembling protectively about her cumbrous body. She had begun the descent when there was a cry from Renée.

'My liege, wait! We have forgotten someone!'

She stopped, half-turned. The esquires saw her shudder and marked it down to the cold. Oh, Renée, Renée, she thought. I had hoped that none would notice. How the past follows us! One of the men was already running back to the nursery.

'Oh, my liege,' said Renée, laughing and crying. 'We had forgotten Mistress Grace!'

The man returned after a moment. He held a drowsy baby girl clasped against his mud-splashed doublet. Secretly he hoped the Queen might reward him – with a coin, or even a smile – for saving the bastard daughter of King Edward; the child by whom all seemed to set such store; this flaxen mite, who shared the princesses' nursery. But the Queen gave no sign of approval. She looked down once at the yawning infant, drew her furs about her and proceeded down to the waiting boat.

'Rest easy, little maid,' said the esquire kindly. He had six sons and longed for a daughter.

As they rocked on the black water, Elizabeth sat stonily withdrawn. On either bank cressets flamed eerily as Warwick's advance guard entered the City; she saw them, but paid little heed. The cold reproachful wind tossed the dark river around their small craft. Mary was crying, and Jacquetta of Bedford muttered to herself. Elizabeth heard neither of them. Her mind was filled with Edward's angry voice, two years ago, in the chamber with the white roses and the damning grief.

'I go to spend my time with a lady who is kinder than you. And should I get a child upon her ... it shall be a reminder of your evil work this day! Oh Desmond, Desmond ...'

As Westminster Sanctuary loomed ahead, dimly lit by monkish tapers, the Queen glanced down once more at the living token of her guilt. And Mistress Grace, seeing only beauty, stretched out her arms and smiled.

Lancaster! Lancaster!

The name was carried in the beating hoofs, in the hiss of the rain, in the rattle of spur and bridle and arms, as the Earl of Warwick, flanked by a score of harnessed men, rode on London. And he recalled how in his youth, among the fresh winds of Yorkshire, the toast had always been: 'Death to Lancaster!' Now Lancaster was his buckler and battle-cry; it jangled sickly in his ears. The outriders growled it, like a talisman to ward off ill. Warwick rode for Lancaster and yet he rode for England, and at an unthinkable price. Memory rose like bile. As the miles swept by – dull, damp November roads treacherous with leaves – he was back, in thought, at Angers, in high summer. There and then, he had wrought the impossible, for England's good name. He, whom they once called '*le conduiseur du royaume*' had grovelled like the meanest cur. To a woman!

Blood sprayed from his rowels; his horse shrieked and went faster. Riding mechanically, he saw again that French council chamber with its effeminate furnishings: fanciful tapestries, curlicued window-frames. The sun brightened the rich blue and green of the carpet. He had had time to study that carpet minutely, kneeling on it for the best part of an hour before a woman whom he hated more than any other. Save Isabella Woodville, who by her guile had brought him to this.

He knelt before Margaret of Anjou; she who had ridden with fire through England, who had set his own father Salisbury's head on Micklegate. To Margaret, whom he had denounced publicly all those years earlier, he sued for aid. She was his only hope, with her French troops and King Louis (the wily old spider, hand-rubbing upon the dais) ready to uphold his kinswoman in any overthrow of England. Warwick had always found Louis's attentions flattering and it doubled his humiliation that Louis had to witness this sicken-ing confrontation. Yet he, with his long Valois nose for intrigue, had engineered the meeting.

At first Margaret would not speak at all. Her eyes were two cold flames, gazing somewhere rapt and lost. Warwick was null; an entity so loathsome that he had ceased to exist. Yet he persisted; he had rehearsed a speech until it was a second skin on his tongue. A classic paean in which he abjured all his past insults against the Frenchwoman. He debased himself absolutely yet left room for his usefulness to be gauged. He had been careful to ride to Angers escorted by sumptuously armoured men. During his plea, while Margaret stared stonily away, he drew his sword and laid it symboli-cally before her. To all this he added a soupçon of flattery; flattery in truth, for Margaret's beauty was much diminished. At last, one flicker in her eyes showed her resignation to the hideous fact that she and Warwick needed one another.

While Louis, like a pander, washed dry hands and quirked his lip, Margaret deigned to address her old enemy. She berated him in a hoarse and searing voice, opening old wounds – the death of Suffolk, Clifford, Northumberland, and Beaufort of Somerset. He was amazed at her long memory. He knelt abjectly; the carpet's green and blue merged, shimmered. No fury like a woman's, he thought, and was himself angry, his thoughts turning again to the one responsible; the Woodville witch. Sweat trickled down inside his shirt. There was a grinding in his vitals, a constant discomfort around his middle which he had had for a long time and grown used to; this day, however, long kneeling and tension made it unbearable.

His witch-hunter, Thomas Wake, had mentioned waxen images, had repeated the description given him by one of the Sewardsley nuns. No trace of them remained, however, and Wake had seen no physical proof. As for the nuns, they were all under a terrible pen-ance imposed by their bullying Abbess; they could speak to none. He thought: God's Blood! – as Margaret's ranting voice continued – I would fain have seen those Woodville women brought down; the old one walking the streets with a taper, and the other ... the red lips, the sinuousness, the unjust, unholy power of her! Her image wound about him like a doom. Margaret was coughing, a rough draining sound. Beaufort of Somerset the younger stepped forward with wine, and Warwick raised his eyes.

Margaret gulped, taking wine like a man, wrist stiff. She said: 'I have listened. Your words stink in my nostrils. *Non! Jamais!*'

Warwick said, douce as a maiden: 'Most noble Queen of Heaven ...' and she turned, white with fury to Louis.

'Hear how the dog mocks me!'

'It will not hurt to hear him further,' soothed Louis. He found Margaret's histrionics irksome; he had housed and fed her for months and now hoped for some recompense.

'Madame, I come in peace,' said Warwick simply. 'Join forces with me and return with an army. I will help you to claim the throne of England for–' reverently – 'your sacred son.'

A long silence followed. Hope trembled within him. Then Margaret said:

'My son. My prince. Whom you called bastard!'

'Your son, the Prince of Wales by right,' said Warwick. 'His father, noble Henry, lies now in the Tower sorrowing for you.'

Louis interposed. 'To me, the scheme sounds fair. With French and English force, the realm could be snatched from Edward of March. French troops in the majority, though, *monsieur*. We would not wish for another débacle, as when Englishmen refused to follow ...'

Warwick coloured at the barb, controlled himself. He said sagely: 'True, *mon roi.*'

Margaret was waspish. 'My lord Warwick, you are a traitor. Once you upheld Edward of March; how do I know you will not betray me?'

He said steadily and with truth: 'Yes, Madame. I loved Ned of March, and gave him my heart's loyalty. That was before he was ruined by his Queen.'

'Ha!' said Margaret, savagely amused. 'Isabella! I doted on the child. She rose high.' The amusement faded. 'She usurped my own estate!'

'She did, *ma, reine,*' agreed Warwick. 'And now she and her family are no more than night-thieves. They rob, degrade, murder. They must be dispossessed.' His voice shook.

'I do not trouble over which of your barons is robbed or which rewarded,' said the Frenchwoman icily. 'My concern is for my son.' Her voice grew unrecognizably soft. '*Le Cygne d'Argent ... La Fleur d'Anjou!*'

God, let us make an end, thought Warwick; she rambles of silver swans and flowers. He said stoutly: 'The throne is promised to Edward of Lancaster, your son, Madame.'

He fancied she weakened, and again his hope built. 'Well, Madame?'

'Clarence!' she spat the word. 'What of his claim?'

Inwardly he sighed. She knew all. It had been folly, the way he had used Clarence, giving him Isabel, promising him the throne once Edward was deposed. But Clarence could be bribed, blinded with words, fobbed off.

'There is no other heir,' he assured Margaret. 'Only your son, Edward of Lancaster.'

'*Vraiment*.' Then she shook her head. 'I mistrust you, my lord. You will betray me.'

'Madame—' he had this last hurdle already breached — 'I can make surety against that. Let your prince marry my youngest daughter, Anne. Then if I play you false, I butcher my own line!'

The Queen burst into ugly laughter. With renewed venom she beat Warwick with words. She would as lief marry her prince to a pig than to Anne Neville, who was unfit to tie the points of his hose, whose blood was scullions' blood compared to that of the Swan, the Flower. He thought: Margaret of Anjou is mad; a different malady from that of Henry her husband; but mad none the less.

'*Ma reine*,' he said patiently, 'the lady Anne and your son are all slips from the same tree. Are we not all descended from the great Edward Third?'

For a further hour they wrangled. Even Louis's wily calm was tried by their arguments. A distraction was provided in the form of Edward of Lancaster himself. He entered with a train of foppish noblemen. He wore blood-coloured satin and looked older than his seventeen years. Strong and slender, with hard eyes; a warlike mien, Warwick thought approvingly.

'I shall give the Prince Edward my stoutest captains for the affray,' he promised. 'We shall grind York into the dust and Edward of Lancaster shall be immortalized in the annals of chivalry.'

We shall grind York into the dust. The words were iron in his throat. For the first time he looked into his own mind; anguish writhed there like snakes, and every snake a Woodville. Why, oh God, did Edward ever wed her? Those small white hands have stabbed York to the heart.

'Yes!' the Prince was saying, sharp and bright. 'I will ride on England, and claim my throne. I will wed your daughter, *monsieur*, and make England mine for ever!'

Queen Margaret looked appealingly at Louis, who spread his hands, smiled like a depraved cardinal. Warwick carefully rose from his knees.

'It tears my heart, this,' she said, sighing deeply. But I see there is no other way. One thing.' She raised a fierce admonishing hand. 'Your Anne shall have my prince. But they shall not lie together until Lancaster is strong in England. I forbid it!'

She looked ardently at her son. Warwick bowed.

'So be it. When shall the arrangements be made?' Margaret was coughing again. She said: 'I care not; but let us ride on England soon.'

Louis said kindly: 'I will arrange all. The contract shall be solemnized here, in the Cathedral of Angers.'

'*Bien.*' Margaret looked viperishly at Warwick. 'And we will both swear on a piece of the True Cross to keep faith!'

Sweating, Warwick had quit the chamber at last. The pain in his bowels was like pincers. By sheer mental strength he threw it off, and rode to his lodging. Anne waited there for whatever news he brought. Waited patient, helpless, scarcely out of childhood. When he climbed the curling stair to her bower he found her weeping, as if she knew already that her destiny was tied to Lancaster's star. In the next room her sister Isabel, Clarence's wife, lay moaning in child-bed fever, nursed by two unskilled slovenly Frenchwomen. Warwick stood on the doorsill and watched while his youngest daughter dried her eyes. He knew more of her heart than she realized. Long ago at Middleham, when both she and Richard of Gloucester were children, she had given him her heart, lastingly, with every expectation of a happy marriage. Now Gloucester should never have her. Warwick had offered her to him once (at a price) and Gloucester's loyalty had rejected the bribe. Clarence had had no such scruples regarding Isabel. Gloucester, Clarence, Edward! How long since they were all together? And who was it who had slashed that bond to ribbons? The endless permutation. All evil, all disorder, all betrayal. Like a great spider-web, it flung itself over the houses of Plantagenet and York. And inevitably at its nucleus – the divine corruption of Elizabeth Woodville.

So thought Warwick as he rode on London, to the heart-heavy beat of Lancaster! Lancaster! Unknown to him, Edward and Gloucester tossed on the North Sea, exiled into darkness. Something within Warwick brought forth a groan, and muffled words.

'Ah, God, Ned! Once we could have conquered the world, and now I must ride against you!'

Butcher William Gould was on his way to the river. With him went his wife, three prentices, and half a beef and two muttons already rank from hanging in his Chepeside shop. The prentices were a necessary evil, brought along to shoulder the meat, and Mistress Gould had simply refused to stay behind.

'You promised I should see the Queen.' She caught up her kirtle and ran, trying to match her husband's long strides. She was a pretty woman, dressed in her best scarlet houpeland trimmed with rabbit-fur. A snowy wimple starched with arrowroot haloed her small bright face. Gould looked at her indulgently.

'So you shall, dame.' Although, as they fought the seething crush that spilled down Mincing Lane into Tower Street – fishporters, carters, vagrants – he wondered on this score. The last time he had gone to Westminster Sanctuary with the weekly carcasses, the Queen had been closeted; praying, Lady Scrope had told him tartly. Gould had smiled, knowing he had a right to inquire. For he had promised King Edward long ago, that he would succour 'his Bessy' in any emergency. And this was one, in truth.

Warwick's men were conspicuous in the City. Everywhere the Bear and Ragged Staff or Clarence's Bull were blazoned on tabards, carried on banners by small knots of wary-eyed foot-soldiers. Gould grinned as he saw how the Londoners persecuted these men – in little ways subtle enough to ensure impunity – a carelessly outthrust foot, a jostle, a curse half-spoken. Rancour fermented, and lately a lack of hope obtained. Two months had passed since Edward and his followers had been driven from the shores of Norfolk. It seemed that Warwick was master; all the frowns and praying, all the tears (Gould's wife had wept copiously) could not gainsay this. And yet, on neither occasion when he had been admitted to the Queen had Gould seen tears or hopelessness – only a poised tension. Cool she is, the butcher mused, catching his wife's sleeve as she migrated to a pedlar selling ribbons. Was she always? He wondered, unrealistically, what it would be like to bed the King's Grey Mare.

He turned to chivvy the prentices who staggered redfaced beneath the reeking joints of meat. Royal meat! He pushed the youths in front of him so that he could watch their safe progress. At the corner of Tower and Thames Street where the way narrowed and the carved house-gables leaned drunkenly down, Gould's little party was brought to a sudden halt by people sweating, swearing, elbowing. Gould was pressed close against the stinking habit of a friar, whose creeping lice transferred themselves to the butcher's doublet. Incensed, he brushed them off and tried to push on, his passage blocked by a row of broad backs. Something or someone was coming; the people were straining on tiptoe; the hubbub of voices soared a semitone higher. Gould peered over the shoulders of a small fishmonger. From Billingsgate and Petty Wales, from Eastchepe and up from Dowgate on the Thames, folk were crowding towards a procession that filtered slowly from the Tower. The Tower itself looked unreal, an almost luminous grey-white against a hanging pall of fog. Several urchins were clinging on to a water conduit and Gould pulled them down, himself climbing to this vantage point, and craning upwards. The procession struggled nearer; they were Warwick's men, and their coming was halted by a carter's mischievously overturned wain. Vile language drifted through the misty air. Then the company came on, escorting someone who rode in their midst. A ragged cheer went up, followed by shouted insults. Throughout the crowd a shiver of incredulity ran as they saw who came; Gould whistled in amazement.

'Why, the devil damn me!' he cried. 'They've got Daft Harry from his prayers!'

King Henry sat limply upon a spavined horse. A worn velvet robe had been flung about him and the Lancastrian collar of 'S's, green with verdigris, clanked upon his concave chest. He wore his black skull-cap crowned with a tarnished diadem, and in his hand he bore a staff from which three foxtails drooped: the emblem of Agincourt! Gould spat in disbelief. With one flaccid hand King Henry clutched the pommel of his saddle, and now and then looked at his homemade sceptre wonderingly as if it were a mysterious extension of his own arm. His pale face was expressionless, but his lips moved in a ceaseless babble of prayer.

Warwick's henchmen nudged the horses into a trot, and Henry bounced in his saddle like a wooden doll. Trumpeters sounded an untidy fanfare. The leading knight raised his hand to the assembled mob.

'Way for Henry of Lancaster!' he shouted. 'Lancaster for ever!'

He cast a savage look around, and one or two people grudgingly echoed the challenge. They were instantly set upon by the partisans of York. The fighting raised clouds of dirt; a fishmonger, with a crude White Rose sewn on his apron, smacked his neighbour in the face with a great silvery mackerel. Gould hoisted his wife up to watch the fun.

'Lancaster!' bawled the herald again. A storm of jeering arose. Soapy Jack, a great lummox who swept out taverns and sometimes lay day-long crooning in the gutter, bored his way head-first through the crowd. His wide toothless mouth drooled spittle.

'Where's Ned?' he roared, bursting through the ranks of horses and men. 'Where's our Ned, then? You ain't our King!' Heedless of the blows raining down on him from the escort's staves, he forced his way to Henry. Doubling his fist he punched the frail dark-clad figure hard in the thigh.

Henry's sleepwalker eyes swivelled. He looked down in a sad daze at Soapy Jack.

'Forsooth and forsooth,' he observed. 'Ye do wrong to strike the Lord's anointed.'

Gould's wife giggled all the way upriver to Westminster, but the butcher was pensive. He stretched his legs in their fine woollen hose in the bottom of the boat, and mused on prosperity. His own affluence had been brought about by King Edward and none other. Trade was better than he and his fraternity ever remembered it. But if Edward's day were done ... gloomily he recalled the old times, when Henry and his hated French consort sat at Westminster. Then, foreigners would trade rather with the Devil than with England. He looked at the great cranes dipping on either side of the Thames, the galleys and carvels and trawlers, from Flanders and Italy and Iceland. Bringing their treasures in trade for English cloth. Cloth meant beef, and beef meant gold for merchants such as himself, good marriages for his daughters, fine garments. He chewed his thumbnail savagely, and promised he would light a candle to Edward's safe return.

At Westminster Sanctuary they were admitted by a one-legged monk. He hopped nimbly on crutches to where the Queen had her apartments. Inside the gloomy building, Gould shivered. The walls were washed by river-mist, insidious and foul, and several high windows were cracked, inviting a killing draught. As if to darken an already heavy mood, a bell tolled and from the near-by Abbey came the ghostly plainsong of the brothers. Like a thin black rabbit, the lame guide skipped ahead; at the entrance to the Queen's buttery four pages relieved the prentices of their burden.

'Wait here,' Gould instructed his boys. 'Brother! is there a chance that we might see her Grace?'

'She asks to see you,' replied the monk, and led them down a short, fog-filmed cloister. Finally they reached a vast, lead-bound door behind which lay the Queen. They entered; they felt change, smelled perfume instead of incense, trod rushes instead of cold flags. There was a fair degree of warmth, and candles. Women, deployed meekly round the walls, were sewing, and four fair-haired small girls played at their nurse's knee. Prone, Gould heard the Queen's voice.

'Come closer, butcher. I wish to thank you. We should, I vow, have starved without your aid.'

He rose, crimson with pride, and went forward to kiss the cool hand. Mistress Gould curtseyed and hung her head, then as the Queen spoke – words which to her disappointment she did not afterwards recall – looked up, and was bemused. She did not know whether to weep or worship. Mistress Gould had on her best gown and knew she looked well; Queen Elizabeth was not even gaily dressed, she wore plain black wool and no jewels. Her head was loosely bound in a netted coif. None the less, Mistress Gould, looking at that half-turned cheek like a crescent moon, felt herself plump and ruddy and gauche. The Queen was all silver; even her voice, each word high and exact like a lute's song. Gould noticed something else: on his last visit, the Queen had been heavy with child, now she was as slender as a young maid. As if she read his thought, she said:

'Master Gould, we have a most glorious advent to our royal house.' She rose and crossed to the door of an antechamber; moving with a soft hushing of her long black gown. A sudden almost tangible air of joy filled the chamber. The monks' distant devout song rose and fell. The Queen threw open the ante-chamber door.

'Renée, bring in – our prince!'

Tears sprang to Gould's eyes. He brushed them away as a week-old child was carried in. Swaddled like a chrysalis, it bawled loudly, drowning the distant anthem.

'Oh, God,' said the butcher, when he could speak.

'A fair omen, Master Gould,' said Elizabeth softly. 'You may salute the prince. Without your sides of beef I should not have had the strength to carry him.'

Gould, trembling, kissed the tiny hand unwrapped for this purpose. This he would tell his grandchildren ...

'His name is Edward, for his sire,' said the Queen.

'Whom Christ preserve,' said Gould, choking. He had not realized how much York meant to him, and the merchants and goldsmiths and gildsmen all over Engand who loved Ned so much. Mistress Gould stole another peep at the Queen's tranquil silvery face, as Elizabeth repeated: 'A fair omen.' Then the clear voice rose. 'I have a message for all loyal subjects, Master Gould!'

They nodded, waited, scarcely breathing, while she spoke. Master Gould would have given half his estate to turn a somersault on the rushes; Ned was coming home! The Queen had had secret messages ... Ned was safe, in Bruges, and already equipping a fleet to sail home and regain his kingdom.

'Tell only your most trusted friends,' said the Queen. 'It will give them heart to resist – Warwick – to the last ditch.'

When they returned to the City, there was another crowd on Tower Hill. A hot-headed gathering, angry yet pleased to see the execution of one whom they had feared for his cruelty yet revered as Edward's Constable. Butcher Tiptoft. The same herald who had bawled acknowledgment of Lancaster read the indictment. He stood at the foot of the scaffold; its planks were crusted with ancient blood.

'In the name of Richard Neville, Earl of Warwick, representing all the greatness of Lancaster and the Crown, here is condemned to execution by beheading Sir John Tiptoft, Earl of Worcester ... as per the law of this land. For his treason and tyranny ...'

He gave the signal quickly, hearing the uncertain growl of the crowd. Any execution these days was a hazardous affair. But Tiptoft, mounting steps that had run with the blood of many of his own victims, seemed in a leisurely humour. His bulging eyes surveyed the throng hungrily as if regretting the unsevered heads, the unripped bowels ... it was almost, they whispered, as if he took some pleasure in his own execution, and this was too much to contemplate.

He knelt, saying loudly to the headsman: 'I pray you, sever my head in three strokes. In honour of the Blessed Trinity.'

The watchers gasped, terrified by this holy heresy. Was the Butcher immune to pain? Seemingly he was, for he made no murmur as the obedient axe sliced a groove in his spine, then clove half-way so that the neck drooped from a yellow-sinewed stump. The final swing sent Tiptoft's head gushing redly on to the straw. Sorcery, the crowd muttered.

Master Gould gave only cursory attention to this show. He was slipping from friend to friend, seeing smiles, hearing joyful incredulous oaths. Ned was coming home.

He stood before her, a weary Atlas, and her heart leaped upward to greet him. Leaped, as it had done years earlier, through love, for John's return. Edward was greater or lesser than love; he was her salvation. He strode into Sanctuary where for five months she had waited with her needle and bright hessian saints. Ringed by little bursting cries from her women she rose slowly. In the instant before he took her in his arms she noted that his clothes were clean and fresh, and knew that he had been in London for some hours. He lived, and he was safe. Against his strong breast she exhaled her shuddering relief.

Shadows entered through the lead-bound door; courtiers, Abbot Milling and his monks, drawn like moths to the scene. Discreet, still pawns, they stood while Queen met King. She thought: we are all chessmen. And which way will the Hand move us next? And whose is the Hand? The choristers, heard through inches of stone, began their office. That sombre drone which had accompanied her labour. Plainsong and childbirth, combined in memory, oddly unpeaceful to her ears.

They were bringing in the prince. She felt Edward stiffen with excitement; his arm gripped her tightly. The prince. Edward's great golden hand moved waveringly down to the mewling bundle. His fingers signed the tiny bald dome with the Cross. Then he wept. He moved to where the little princesses clung wide-eyed, around Lady Berners. The tiny Elizabeth raised her arms, was caught up and kissed. She was a beautiful blonde rosy child, sweet-temperedly smiling. Edward set her down, then in turn lifted Mary and Cicely. All the time he wept and smiled like a rainbow.

'My lord,' said Elizabeth, wanting his arm about her again, for the strength which had supported her over the past months seemed to have ebbed completely.

'Soft, Bessy, I must greet *all* my little maids!' He bent to the fourth child. To Elizabeth it seemed that his tenderness drew on another dimension, something mystically patterned, hateful.

'Mistress Grace!' He settled the child against his shoulder. She was also blonde, but her eyes were not blue like the others, but a clear vibrant green. Sad, adult eyes, that could have looked upon a time gone by. The time of Desmond's death. The living token of past sin.

'Are you a good maid, my Grace? Are you loyal to me?'

Delighted, the child buried her face in Edward's fur collar. One eye peeped out at the assembly. She was loved. Loved, as she longed to be (the eye rolled, rested on the Queen) by the silver lady.

The women were sobbing with joy, watching the King's demonstrations of tenderness, kneeling while he went among them with embraces; Lady Scrope, Lady Berners, Anne Haute. He kissed their mouths. Jacquetta of Bedford went to him blankly, unable to share joy or sorrow, immersed in senile memory. Lastly Edward returned to the baby prince, and stood, magnificent, his hand upon the cradle, ready to address the company. The shadows took on life, came softly forward; the gaunt Abbot Milling, the white-haired Prior John Esteney, their servants, offering round wine and ale. Anthony Woodville, a little worn from the vicissitudes of exile. At the sight of her brother warmth poured through Elizabeth. Then she saw Richard of Gloucester standing beside Anthony, and her smile died like sun under cloud. She had no reason to dislike him. He spoke seldom and now looked so weary that he might collapse. But Edward was speaking of him this moment, of Richard's courage and integrity, extolling him above the skies. What now had he done to gain such reverence? She felt a scowl set like a mask upon her face. The child Grace was staring at her – this rankled too. Her hand moved in a quick impatient gesture of dismissal. The small face lost its happy light.

'I come to reclaim my kingdom!' declared the King. 'Ah, thanks be to Jesu for the love of English folk, for the generosity of the Seigneur de la Gruythuyse, my mentor in Bruges. Good people, I am once more equipped to crush my foes!'

They had landed at Ravenspur, said the King, with their small army. York had opened to them. Laughing, he said: 'I mounted the plumes of Henry of Lancaster and swore that I came only to regain my Duchy of York! Then southward ... they flocked to my standard. We shall conquer.'

'Amen,' said Richard of Gloucester softly.

Edward, snatched up a cup of the Abbot's flat brewing. He called for a toast – to Burgundy – to all Flemings who now formed part of his army. To his brother Richard who had upheld him, to his brother-in-law Anthony Woodville who had advised him – and to the blessed return to his side of George, his brother of Clarence.

She could scarcely believe it. Clarence, murderer of her father and young brother, again forgiven? Yes, there he was, the black-heart, the ill-omened knave. Having the wisdom to stand a little contritely apart. Armour bright, cheeks pink, helm beneath his arm. And Richard of Gloucester had been, once more, the peacemaker. The blood surged in her temples, throbbing, threatening. The King was relating how Richard had drawn his brother over from Lancaster; George would be welcome back at court. Her court! housing murder, treachery. In that moment she desired most fervently Clarence's death.

Edward took them all from Sanctuary within the hour. She rested easily in the barge, the little prince's cradle close to her feet. She smiled deliciously, her eyes upon Anthony; her beloved brother, whose charm offset the irritating presence of Gloucester, and the insult of Clarence's nearness. The forbidding spires of the Abbey faded behind them. The river was excitable with March tides, the air fragrant with the promise of blown buds. To Baynard's Castle on the Thames they rowed, past the cluttered wharves. Swans skimmed upwards before the craft, and on the banks the fishing-nets dropped jewels.

She lay one night with Edward before he left to gather more men. He was jubilant; the Archbishop of Canterbury had once again touched the crown to his King's brow in Westminster. Yet there was a volatile nervousness about Edward, a creeping doubt. In her arms, he asked if she thought it were sin to do battle at Eastertide.

Have you forgotten Towton?' she said gently. *Eleven years ago, when I was enmeshed in sorrow.* 'It was Palm Sunday when you vanquished Lancaster.' *I remember that winter well; the snow covering Bradgate, the racking grief; the coming of the Fiend.*

'So it was.' Edward sounded relieved. 'A good augury. We put Margaret to flight, then.'

'Now you give battle to ... Warwick.'

'Yes, who has joined with Margaret ... for that boy whom he once called bastard ... Edward, Prince of Wales!' He laughed angrily. 'Our own prince Edward is Prince of Wales, and none other!' He was silent for a moment, then said uncertainly. 'Yet I wonder ... did Holy Harry breed that boy, or did he not?'

She said slowly: 'Marguerite's son *is* bastard. It is no lie.'

He raised himself in the bed to stare at her.

'To fight a traitor,' she continued urgently, 'I would myself do battle on any day. Easter is no sin, if the day falls then. As for Marguerite ...'

She told him. Of the days and nights, the tall figure passing ghost-like to Marguerite's chamber. Her own silent vigilance.

'What? You were there?'

'Yes, Ned. Night after night the Queen took Beaufort of Somerset to her bed. She grieved outrageously when he was slain.'

'So!' Laughing with relief, with mocking triumph, he began to call Margaret whore with doubled venom. He seized and kissed Elizabeth, who, in the darkness lay and thought of Marguerite, who had called her Isabella and been kind. It was all a lost, gone, far-off thing. The vital issue was that Edward should win this battle, that the Fiend should be vanquished. Now that Edward of Lancaster's bastardy was sure in the King's mind, he would go into combat like a lion, certain of God and the right. She had given him this confidence. If only there were some way to ensure his victory! Her head throbbed painfully, her rushing blood made the sound of distant seas. If only the Duchess were still her prop and adviser, instead of the empty husk she had become. Edward was already asleep; she breathed this powerful warmth. Above the coverlet she brought her slender hands together, lay stiffly, entombed in thought.

Her mouth moved in a secret prayer; her ears strained for a silent voice. Within her mind, a swirling mist arose.

Warwick could see nothing. A giant white hand, ghostridden, clustered in blinding pockets about him. It clung to his armour, settled and dripped like tears. He was bleeding where a poignard had pierced his hand. Behind him somewhere in the treacherous whiteness lay the St. Albans road. To his left was the hollow called Dead Man's Bottom, and all around him men fought and swore and struck wildly. He could hear the spectral clangour of their steel. He guessed that the King was in the heart of the affray, and half-knew that his own men and those of the Earl of Exeter were working across to the hollow on the lip of which Richard of Gloucester's vanguard struggled. In the endless unnatural whiteness his own esquire appeared like a spirit wielding an axe, cried briefly on the saints and disappeared again in the chilling milk.

White as a woman's body, white as a funeral candle, mist surged and eddied and closed upon him lovingly. Far behind as through a tunnel, he heard cries, screams, curses. The terrified neigh of horses, the long grunting anguish of a man spitted through the bowels. Easter Sunday. Half past five in the morning when He who died on Tree came again to his fellows. Eleven years ago, when that same Lord had passed through into Jerusalem, Warwick had fought – also in white-ness, the purity of snow. Shoulder to shoulder with Ned of England. As they should be fighting now, were it not for the Woodville – the witch. Fog filled his nose and eyes, fog imbued with silent mocking life, and he knew that his naming of her was correct. In his mind, her sinuousness, smooth forehead and red lips flitted ahead, wreathed by the smoke-like mist, beckoning him to death.

Somewhere, nearer now, fighting desperately against the assaults of Warwick's reserve and Exeter's men, was Richard of Gloucester. Dickon, with whom he had sat for so many hours before the great fire at Middleham; talking of everything under heaven; of love, war, Christ and philosophy, while the charitable flames fell smoothly on the faces of Earl and boy. Dickon, to whom he had, taught every nuance of battle, was holding out against the foe, and had asked for no reinforcements yet. Warwick knew this by the gasped messages from his own scouts. In all his dismay he felt a fierce and searing pride. The curling whiteness swooped to kiss his cheek, like the salute of a corpse. He thought briefly of Anne, his daughter, wedded in her heart to Gloucester, wedded on True Cross to the Frenchwoman's son. His lips curled bitterly. Margaret had not even allowed that son to join the battle, and was keeping him safe at Cerne Abbey. She was only waiting to see whether Warwick kept his pledge. And here he was, staggering in mist, while his armies, selected from the hosts of Lancaster and the adherents of Neville, plunged about him, as lost as he. His esquire emerged again from the chilling blindness.

'What passes?' cried Warwick.

'My lord ... Oxford's men were defecting! They rode south to Barnet, to loot and pillage. The mist has made them mad!'

'And Sir John, my, brother?'

'Lord Montagu makes for Edward's troops – he attacks them from the rear. The Earl of Oxford is driving his men back from the town

... but their defection has cost us sore ...'

'Fools, traitors,' muttered Warwick. We need more men, he thought, and bitterly: would that I had Clarence's sumptuous force with me. But Clarence is once again the King's sworn man, and is he any less for that? Would I be less were I to surrender, now, this minute? The fog swung about him in coils, stinging his eyes. The groans of dying men assailed him. No, no. My followers would have perished for nothing.

He looked wildly about. 'The reserve! Bid them advance to my standard!'

'My lord, my lord,' answered the esquire. The white blanket wrapped him, so that a disembodied voice spoke to Warwick. 'We cannot – they can see no standard clearly.'

Lord Jesus, what a day!'

'The day is witched,' said Warwick softly. Even as he spoke, the mist suddenly rolled back, like a bland tapestry rising. It faded; gold threads of sunlight pierced the last smoky wisps. There was the fierce bray of trumpets, the grunt and thud and steel-swish of combat. Then from the south, a great crying: 'Treason! treason! treason!' The Earl wheeled, sword in hand. Now he could see – grey armour patterned with red, spouting wounds, a carpet of dead men on the periphery of his vision. There was the broken line of Hastings's vanguard reforming, and dangerously close, the great fiery blossom of the King's standard. A courier ran up, his face full of terror.

'My lord, all is lost! In the mist, Lord Montagu's men mistook the standards – they thought that Oxford's Star was the Sun in Splendour ...'

'So they are butchering each other,' said Warwick bitterly, listening to the screams.

''Twas this cursed fog,' said the courier, weeping with fright. Then, half-turning, he gave a shriek: 'Oh, God protect us!'

A solid phalanx of armed men – the Sun flaunting above them in the haze – was bearing down on Warwick's contingent. Struggling out of Dead Man's Bottom was Richard of Gloucester's force, depleted but swearing, and armed like a host of bloodstained killing insects swarming up the slope. The Earl cast a glance around him. While his own armies fought among themselves, while the last flicker of grave-cold mist tongued his neck, he knew defeat. Throwing off as much of his harness as possible, he followed his fleeing force. Dodging a knife-thrust here, and there the swing of a redclotted axe, hearing the deathly thrum and swish of a close arrow, he ran. He, whom they had once named '*le conduiseur du royaume*', fled, towards the dawn-blue shadows of Wrotham Wood. Some half a mile ahead it loomed; dense forest, a sanctuary. Behind him, Ned's armies roared, roared as he had taught them so many years ago. And Dickon of Gloucester came upon him from the right flank, in tight and orderly mesh, his archers firing from behind, his infantry hacking from before. As Warwick had taught him, too, at Middleham.

As he ran, another patch of mist like a low-flying ghoul enveloped him so that he stumbled, his hands thrown out; so that he cried upon the Virgin, and upon his wife, and lastly for mercy upon his King. That the King's hand should be the one to take his life away. For they were upon him from behind, faceless shapes in the solitary swirl of white. He felt a gush of fire in his side, a lancing blow in his loins. He looked down, amazed, at the steel protruding from his belly. Right through his coat of mail; a weakened rivet, he thought foolishly. And yet how strange! Right through his vitals, where that ancient pain had been. He was falling. He saw her then. Trying to rise in the shadow of Wrotham Wood, so far, so near, hands slipping in the mud, he saw her. The silent winding-sheet had a face and coiled about him. The red lips smiled.

Edward of England stood upon a little knoll. The sun had conquered and the damp meadow sprang to greenness in the growing gold. The King lifted his sword high.

'Blessed be God, who sent this day!'

'A ragged, weary cheer arose. In the distance tiny figures still chased the men of Oxford and Exeter. Above, birds broke from the silence of fear and began tentatively to sing. The King clasped his brother and Lord Hastings about the shoulders. Anthony Woodville strode up, smiling.

'Load up the dead!' came the cry.

Stiff, as if already in effigy, they lay on the cold pavement of St. Paul's. Sir John Neville, Marquis of Montagu, was on the left, his brother Warwick on the right. They were draped by thin loincloths and their wounds were terribly apparent. From the great hole in Warwick's side and the gash in his belly, entrails protruded a little. Around the corpses candles had been lit, and someone unknown had laid a nosegay, the pale red dog-rose, between Warwick's rigid fingers. The faces of the two knights were stern and far, detached by death with the look of contempt for things earthly. Throughout the days the people came, some weeping, some openly deriding. A drunken man harangued the world in general, until hustled away by an offended priest. But most folk had little to say. It was the end of the House of Neville, and too big for words.

'He was a proud knight,' remarked Butcher Gould, when his turn came to pass and stare.

'He betrayed the King,' said the little Billingsgate fishmonger behind him.

Gould recalled his prentice days and with a shred of regret the meals he had eaten at Warwick's open door. There was the clattering tread of guards; together with the throng, the butcher was pressed back towards the side aisle. A herald cried: 'Make way!' The Queen entered, with her women. Gould's wife nudged him. 'Look!' she whispered. 'She trembles.'

Elizabeth was trembling with the astonishment of power. Strong, ancient phrases, in themselves meaningless, welled within her. *It is written. In the stars. In all waters, lakes, meres, the sea. Her power was so great that none could withstand it.* Her power is mine. She shook so fiercely that her women had to hold her on either side. A froth of spittle bloomed at the corners of her mouth. All around the voices were soothing, gentle. She was weak from recent childbed; she should not look too long upon the dead. But she did, she looked deeply at that unembalmed side, that gaping wound. She extended a quivering hand, perhaps to delve, but the press of women and courtiers nudged her away from her triumph. *May you roast in the everlasting tortures of all damned souls, Warwick.* The voices cajoled tenderly: 'Come away, come away, your Grace!' *Oh, my Melusine, I thank you.*

Then Richard of Gloucester pushed through the ranks. He was accompanied by two knights: Hastings, and Francis Lovell. Eyes red, and with nervous hands, he stopped before the two Neville corpses, went softly on his knees. She saw the tears falling, the whiteness, the written grief. She heard his aching, brooding voice.

'Jesu give thee rest, my Warwick!' To those who listened he said: 'By St. Paul! I loved him well.'

He had lifted her unspoken curse with his benediction. She looked after him uneasily as he passed on. So Warwick was dead yet undead. His influence remained, heavy as a boding shadow.

All over London the cries resounded. Edward of Lancaster is slain! The French Bitch is vanquished! The cries beat up the walls, touched off mania from the leaning gables, rose and fermented even to the cold palaces of Westminster, Greenwich, Sheen. And at Baynard's Castle, Edward King of England made merry. For the battle of Barnet with its mist which, men said, was sent by God, was all but forgotten. It was eclipsed by the new triumph of Tewkesbury.

Up and down the narrow streets, in the Council Chamber and in a thousand great halls, the flying tales ran; of the day with its fierce May heat and danger, the tide that swept the royal army, turning in its favour at the last. The fall of the Frenchwoman's son, hot-followed in the field; the whelp gone, finished, dead. Clarence preened. It was his men who had struck down the young Lancastrian prince.

Dressed in pale blue sarcenet, Elizabeth sat beneath the royal canopy and listened impassively to the noisy talk. Edward crashed his goblet on the board in the excitement of re-telling. They fought in Tewkesbury Abbey – up and down the nave. They dragged Beaufort of Somerset the younger from behind the altar and shore his head off in the market-place. The whole tale was told in a roar. Edward was like a madman; they were all mad with nervous joy, as if they could not believe their skins were whole. During this saga, Elizabeth glanced across at Lady Margaret Beaufort. Her face was slightly drawn, thoughtful. She would doubtless sorrow in secret for Somerset, her cousin. What did she think of the fate of Marguerite?

Elizabeth beckoned, leaned close. 'So the French Queen is taken,' she said lightly.

They had brought her through London in a chariot, having to hold her down so that she should not throw herself beneath the horse's hoofs. They had taken her to the Tower, where Henry lay, praying and groaning, but the two of them were kept apart. It was reported that Queen Margaret cried day long for *La Fleur d'Anjou*; she would not have it that he was dead. She was therefore a close captive, and something of an embarrassment to King Edward.

'My liege, if you should see Marguerite,' said Lady Beaufort, in Elizabeth's ear, 'pray commend me to her kindly.'

She looked straight ahead while speaking, to where King Edward, now standing in the middle of the Hall surrounded by merry court-iers, relived the battle again, with oaths and sweeping arms.

'Why, my lady,' said Elizabeth, also softly, 'this is Lancastrian talk!'

'All have their privy allegiance.' Lady Margaret's thin lips were amused. Unafraid, she looked at the Queen. Just as she had looked years ago, playing at chess. As if she knew the game would be hers in the end.

'My liege, am I not your true friend and lover?'

Yes, and I need you, thought Elizabeth. As Edward crowed and postured, she looked for her friends. Tiptoft, alas, was no more, but there was Reynold Bray, black-clad and servile in a corner; the Stanleys, who fought on whichever side was best and always seemed to catch up with victory in time. A flash of scarlet silk caught her eye; there was Catherine, and her husband, young Harry Buckingham. She frowned. Harry was too flamboyant to be tasteful, but rich beyond dreams, and generous to Kate. Anthony, dear Anthony; unscathed by battle, witty, elegant, even now penning a rhyme on the table-damask, a poem to the King's glory. Who else? Her glance slid, lithe as a fish. Ah yes, John Morton, Bishop of Ely.

Morton's face was fleshy, all wattles and dewlaps, yet divided by a strangely ascetic nose, scimitar-shaped. His bulky body was covered by coarse black cloth. One lean and shapely hand lay on the giant crucifix at his breast; he looked the true divine. Seeing her eyes upon him, he bowed and with three fingers upraised in blessing, padded softly towards the dais.

'How well your sons look tonight, your Grace,' he remarked, after she had greeted him. Thomas Grey moved nearer to acknowledge the Bishop's compliment; he was dressed in the swaggering doublet of high fashion, the sleeves like bladders, hose tight; a rich red gold chain adorned his chest. Richard, the younger, quieter son, wore the same pale blue as his mother.

'Fine young lords,' said Morton kindly. 'Loyal and obedient, ha, your Grace? No rebellion there, I warrant. True to King and Church alike.' His wattles quivered, his lizard eye slipped sideways, fell upon the knot of courtiers surrounding the King. Prominent there was Clarence, laughing and pantomiming a death-thrust with his poignard. At Clarence, Morton stared severely.

'I very much fear me, Madame,' he said slowly, 'that there are others whose disposition is not so fair. I love our King, and would not see him betrayed anew. And for you, my liege, I make constant intercession that you shall, by God's grace, remain supreme.'

His eyes were hard to see clearly, encased as they were in fatty wattles, but the points of light in them burned bright and alert. He spread his hands flat over his crucifix, and continued softly: 'It is simply this, my liege. With Prince Edward of Lancaster dead, my lord of Clarence stands heir to the throne. During the rising, Warwick named him thus. Parliament gave assent, and the Act was not repealed.'

Anthony Woodville, who had come to stand beside the bishop, drew in a sharp breath; Thomas Grey spoke, manly, tumultuous.

'My lord! He would never dare! Whom could he raise for his ally?'

'There is a figurehead,' murmured Morton. 'A royal and saintly figurehead. A focus of upset, no more no less. In London Tower.'

The Woodvilles looked sharply at one another. Elizabeth's mind raced. Henry. That wretched, other worldly scion of Lancaster. Over a decade, memory skipped like a bouncing bladder to reveal the pointing finger, the hysterical voice. She wore no gauge for Henry, in truth. Haltingly she asked the Bishop: 'Tell me, your Grace. Would you think it safer if ...'

The Bishop bowed his head, raised one shapely finger. 'Madame,' he said sonorously, 'God's ways are wonderful. The person concerned is mindless with melancholy. Maybe ... if God should deliver him from the toils of this life ... but who are we to ask God's plan?'

Anthony spoke, sharp and high. 'Why not?' he demanded. 'For England's sake; would not the cause be just?'

Elizabeth slid out her satin shoe, pressed her brother's foot as hard as possible. Close, stood Richard of Gloucester, pale and sombre, detached from the roisterers, and Lord Hastings, wine-flushed but near enough to listen. The Bishop smiled.

'But of course,' he said loudly. 'Aught for England is just. Or for those—' he bowed to Elizabeth – 'of the blood royal.' Proudly she bloomed. Not until long afterwards did she wonder whether the Bishop had mocked her. With Morton one never knew.

Edward, shocked with the aftermath of battle, grew wilder still. He outdanced men ten years younger than himself; he swept his Queen into the wild salterello, he frightened his eldest daughter with a devil-mask. Again and again his cry resounded: Lancaster is dead! Lancaster is done! He laughed and wept in drunken emotion, recalling his own father, whose delight this day would have been. So afterwards, when the spilled drink and the greasy rushes alone bore witness to revelry in the deserted Hall, his mood was pliant. He sat in the chair of estate, twirling a broken flower in his fingers. He was alone save for Elizabeth and a hound cracking bones beneath the trestle. The summer dusk fell about him, the candles burned down. Through the arched windows came the prick of stars, and in every corner sepia shadows drew in like an ambush.

She shivered. She said simply: 'I am afraid.'

He looked at her admiringly, her pallor, the silken veil of hair. He still desired her, even though her body was familiar. But not this night. He was tired, sad almost. God knew why; but as soon as the dancing finished the triumph in him had been replaced by melancholy.

'There is naught to fear,' he told her.

But she pressed closer, kneeling by his side, whispering the veiled suggestions, the cautions planted by Morton. Edward listened at first with a slightly contemptuous smile, then warily, and when she had finished he was chewing his lip, clear minded, unquiet.

'So you see, Ned, Lancaster is far from done!'

'I also had these thoughts,' he admitted. Then, more vehemently: 'Jesu! the cause is just! Shall all these bloody battles come to naught? Shall another rebellion break around one puling saint?'

He did not say who he imagined the instigator of such rebellion might be. Disappointed, she kept silence, and he continued.

'My stomach goes against it. Yet it is kindness, really … snatch him to heaven 'twixt one psalm and the next. Yes. Bessy, you speak well. If it were not heresy and against nature, I'd say you have a man's mind.'

'A woman's heart, though, my liege,' she answered, but he paid no need. He said only: 'It is settled, then. Henry of Lancaster shall die.'

'And Clarence?' The words came out too eagerly. Edward's eyes grew hard as he looked down at her.

'Who spoke of Clarence?' he demanded. 'He will not transgress; he is pardoned once more forgiven. He is my brother.'

She bit her lip, looked away. Edward, sickened by decision and indecision, surveyed her. In the dusk she seemed fluid, her hair a film of radiance, her whole body diffused, spiritual. Sometimes he felt like crossing himself at sight of her, his Madonna, his goddess. Yet she should not speak as she did. Henry must die, he was of Lancaster; but Clarence, fair stupid Clarence, born of the same womb as himself … No, she should not even think of it. He must remind her of an old lesson. In the corner of the Hall, one of the shadows moved. It was a page, come in to fetch napkins for the laundry. Edward called to him.

'Fetch me Mistress Grace!'

'My liege?' The boy hesitated; he was new to the household and did not know who Edward meant.

'My dear bastard daughter,' said the King.

The youth ran, returning with the infant in his arms. Rosy, half-asleep, she smiled, stretched out her arms – to the golden giant, to the silver lady, who once more turned away. Edward, weary and distraught, took the child in his arms with such roughness that she began to cry. With his lips in the soft curly hair he said:

'Lancaster shall die, Bess. Ah, weep not, Grace!'

Above the child's head, his eyes bored into Elizabeth, and spoke of Clarence. *Be careful, Madame. Do not threaten those I love!* But, as if to an empty room, he repeated:

'Henry shall die. Quietly, swiftly. No need to shrive him. He is without fault.'

The long tide of Jacquetta of Bedford's life was ebbing, leaving a desolate strand of memory and the old shipwrecks of those loved and hated. It was a night of strange winds that shivered the tapestry knights upon the Siege of Jerusalem; from her bed, the Duchess looked cloudily upon that stolen splendour. She lay lapped in goosefeather softness while her mottled hands spread and moulded the coverlet. The kneeling figures about the room were opaque, inconsequential; she had been shriven but Bishop Morton remained, also the clerk Reynold Bray, tongueing prayers in a ceaseless monotone. There were also two nuns, the nuns of Sewardsley, fresh from their penance. Silly, blabbering women! She remembered their betrayal of her over the waxen images and her fierce old heart cast a shred of rancour towards them; it was so tangible that one nun, frightened, looked up from her prayers at the bed where Jacquetta lay, formidable even in death. The Duchess's eyes moved over faces, features, jewels. They loomed large and faded. There was Lady Margaret Beaufort, the clever little wench! The outgoing tide washed up admiration. And Morton, with his crucifix held aloft like some battle trophy. Together Morton and Margaret would guard her dream. That gilded staff of heritage ... there she was; dry-eyed as befits a Queen. Standing straight and slender to watch the bearing out of the longship of Jacquetta's soul. Elizabeth.

The Queen came closer, one hand curved around the bedpost, thinking: so death clears my mother's mind. When I needed her she was somewhere distant, locked away in thought. *Now that the Fiend is no more, she comes to me again, purposeless.* She bent so that her warm cheek almost touched the mother's shrivelled face.

'I cannot hear you, madam.'

'Fair,' said Jacquetta in a breath. She smiled. 'Fair enough to grace the ramparts of Lusignan.'

Suspended in memory, the far-off day took on life. The leafy willows, the green and silver reeds. Two brindled trout lying in the shallows. All beauty and all power, departed now from the old voice murmuring so precisely. One word caught at her ear: 'Danger.'

She answered, very quiet: 'No more, madam. Warwick is gone; he burns in Hell.'

The Duchess writhed to sit up; Margaret Beaufort assisted her. '... Others!' said Jacquetta. The word was wrapped up in the sigh and groan of the wind outside the walls. 'Ned's brothers will harm you. Queens can be brought down. Never doubt it.'

Morton's black shape drew nearer the bed, and the nuns crept close. The Duchess's hand made an angry, serpentine gesture.

'Let them depart!' she said, and a look from the Queen sent the nuns stumbling on their habits, quitting the chamber with a backlash of icy draught. Reynold Bray remained, a fixture, the reek of his clothes and his praying voice tokens of his presence. Morton still held his cross aloft. The Duchess caught at Elizabeth's hand. In a surprisingly strong voice she said, 'Listen, my daughter.' Margaret Beaufort leaned near, and the Bishop, one on either side of Elizabeth.

'Danger ... Clarence.' The words hissed and broke like random rain. 'He will dethrone the King, and you. He suspects, but is not sure.'

'Madame,' said Elizabeth uneasily. The old eyes were as clear as a child's, and full of menace.

'He seeks the truth about the King's marriage to Eleanor Butler. His spies go forth, night and day. Soon he will have his proof, and undo you.'

Elizabeth felt the blood rush up into her face. Her heart pounded; she gazed appalled at her mother, knowing that the closest of all secrets had been torn open wantonly before witnesses. Then the Duchess chuckled, a sickly rasp.

'There's no harm in speaking before the Bishop and Lady Margaret. They are your friends. Am I right, my lord?'

Morton, stroking his crucifix, half-closed his wattled eyes and bowed in assent. Margaret Beaufort's clipped voice said, 'Indeed, your Grace,' and Jacquetta looked up triumphantly, but after a moment her face paled, her hands began to scratch once more at the bedcovers.

'Open the window,' she said faintly. Reynold Bray rose from his corner and threw the casement wide. A fierce gust roared in, lifting the Siege of Jerusalem so that the tassels upon it rattled in a skeleton's dance. The Duchess's voice, much weaker, called to Elizabeth. She leaned, shutting out Morton and Margaret. Very softly Jacquetta said: 'Bury me at midnight!'

She was bewildered, and answered: 'Midnight, madam?'

'Aye, for such as we – you and I, daughter – it is the only time of grace. No demon can attack us at that hour. Bury me then so that I may–' she gasped, retched – 'sit with *her* on the heights of Lusignan.'

I will not, cannot do it, thought Elizabeth. It would cause comment. She wanders, her madness returns. 'Rest, madam.' Her voice was caught up and tossed in the gale through the window. Jacquetta was staring at her, one fading look of pride and warning. The tassels made their bony music, the wind thundered, mingled with the moaning rattle in Jacquetta's throat. Lady Margaret touched the Queen's shoulder.

'She dies.'

Morton was gabbling the last rites and the holy unction trickled on Jacquetta's brows. The casement, torn almost off its hinges by a sweep of wind, hurled open and shut. As if summoned by this, there came priests burning ghostly tapers, the two white-faced nuns, and Anthony, weeping. Catherine, weeping and followed by the other sisters, richly gowned, tired from their corridor vigil. They knelt about the bed, making their soft farewell.

Elizabeth had imagined that perhaps some spirit of water and light would show itself, transfiguring Jacquetta's face. That Melusine herself would manifest her power, bear up her loyalest servant. But there was none of this. There was only stillness; the first hint of waste, corruption. And of the grave, with its toad, its snail, its worm.

Edward was unfaithful. It was his privilege and prerogative. She guessed that he had dallied during the later part of their marriage with a dozen different women. Now he had abandoned any pretence at keeping these matters secret. All wives, she told herself, shared her situation, without complaining, but this philosophy, the very pattern of the times, did not lessen the hurt. Now he had three harlots at court; there was a pale pious girl who spent all her free time in chapel. She shared an apartment in Eltham hunting lodge with the King's second favourite, a black-eyed Flemish slut. Both these women were fed and clothed sumptuously, but were seldom seen in the royal palaces. Jane Shore was different.

A hoyden, no more than seventeen, she was permanently at Edward's side. She laughed incessantly, unprettily, like a corncrake shrieking. She had been plucked from the bed of a dotard husband and brought from Chepeside to the royal apartments. Edward was besotted, not only with her round body but with her constant witticisms. He looked upon her as a female fool, and for all the hours the jest continued, with variations, while Elizabeth listened to the distant, jarring screams and howls. She herself was still visited by Edward; he came often enough to make her almost yearly with child, but no longer did he call her his love, his fate.

She watched Jane with Edward, and with her own son Thomas Grey, Marquis of Dorset. He also, she knew, had enjoyed that plump jesting body, and Jane was in love with him. Not only Thomas would like to cuckold the King. Will Hastings, Lord Chamberlain and secret lecher, also desired Jane, the lowly mercer's wife. Elizabeth watched and held her peace, hugging the hurt close. At Ludlow, she listened to the murmured words of Margaret Beaufort, now her dearest counsellor.

She may be useful, my liege.'

'How? A common whore?' The hurt emerged, red and bleeding, was surveyed by the Countess and vanished unappeased.

'Be kind to her, Madame. She may be useful. See how Hastings lusts after her. Madame, believe me, I would befriend and advise you!'

Elizabeth was only half-listening. She looked out over the green bailey of Ludlow. She and the Countess were standing on the battlements. 'Sweet Margaret,' she said absently. The words emerged oddly like a peace-payment, the diplomacy of necessity, like the words recently penned by Edward to Louis of France. The Treaty of Picquigny was in progress. Peace to all men. Elizabeth looked sideways at the Countess; no, none could call her 'sweet' nor could they apply that to Morton. These days the Bishop was always near, standing even now like a sacred sentry, his robe fluttering in the breeze. The heir to England was at Ludlow, so it was fitting that Morton, so wise and holy, should oversee the little Prince's destiny for a space.

Elizabeth stared out over the merlons at the vista of forest green; it was unbroken save for a silver trickle where the Teme glinted in the shadow of the Welsh hills. The fern-scented air touched her face soothingly. Yet behind her, where the spiral wound down through the intricacies of Ludlow Castle, a colder wind blew. Fraught with uncertainty, unseen future betrayals, it shivered her spirit. It nourished the nagging threat from those unknown, who might now plot and jest and speak her name. She drew her mantle closer. *I am Queen of England.* A wary inner voice answered: for how long? She thought: while Clarence lives, while Clarence's spies go forth, my majesty is null and void.

One name, that of Eleanor Butler, could rip the cover off a bare and bleeding wound. Yet I dare not approach the King again, nor drop poison Clarence's way. She longed to turn to Lady Margaret and say: What think you, my lady? You know of my feigned royalty, and that my queenship hangs by a thread. You know I must be ruthless, perjured, bent on exterminating all who threaten my estate. She looked into the berry-black eyes of the Countess; unknowingly she revealed her own desperation.

'The King loves you well, my liege', said Margaret softly. 'As for his harlots—' she made a disdainful moue – 'men are men. Clarence has several lemen, and even Richard of Gloucester, before he married Warwick's Anne, sired at least two children; a maid, on some country wench, and John of Gloucester, whom he keeps in great estate.'

Elizabeth wasted no thoughts on Richard of Gloucester, who had taken himself off, together with Warwick's daughter, to the north country, and there remained. No, it was Clarence who ate at her peace like the red ant ... the Fiend was dead, but Clarence lived. Moth-light, the Countess touched her sleeve, murmuring a distraction.

'Look!' she pointed below. 'There rides your son, Dorset; how elegant he is, my liege.'

Thomas swaggered in the gallop. He rode a tall chestnut across the bailey. His brother Richard Grey lagged a little, on a slower bay. Thomas was laughing. Dorset, the cuckolder of kings.

'She loves me!' he had crowed, strutting, his rich threads catching the candlelight. 'Jane loves me, Ned loves me, and we all love one another! What better fate?' He was born to sail close to the wind; Elizabeth warned him to keep his triumph more discreetly; he had laughed at her, kissed her. Margaret was talking again, half-heard words.

'I believe your Grace has never seen my son,' she said. 'My Henry Tudor. Descended,' she said proudly, 'from the royal house of France.'

Descended by bastardy, thought Elizabeth, but was suddenly too weary to argue the point. Let Margaret have her pride; she had little else. She folded cold hands inside her sleeves and said: 'You must bring your Henry to court.' Margaret's sallow face leaped into life.

'Your Grace is kind; I'll write to him this day.'

And she told herself excitedly: the tide turns. The Queen, depressed, grows pliant and a little careless. It will augur well for Henry to set foot within the court. Both the Stanleys and Morton agree with me here. And if the Eleanor Butler secret were to be disclosed ... Light surged across the battlements of Ludlow, touched off, in the Countess's mind, by her wild dreams – dreams whispered to her in the passing breeze and fading as the Queen, suddenly brisk, said: 'Come. Let us go down and see the heir of England at his lessons.'

They descended the spiral together. Elizabeth hugged the wall close as it dipped down and down, icy, solid, like the round limb of some long-dead monster. The Queen's little slippers were soundless upon the narrow dizzying stair. The high-fashioned gown she wore concealed her latest pregnancy, being cut with a projecting stomacher and falling fold. As they passed by the King's private chamber there came the chuckling shriek of Mistress Shore.

In the schoolroom, the five-year-old Prince Edward, the heir to England, sat yawning over a vast Book of Hours. Beside him, his tutor, Bishop Alcock, followed, as he read, the arrow-straight margin with the jewel-bright capitals. All the children were there; the living testament of Elizabeth's past decade. Bess was nine, and sat quietly at her broidery frame; she raised her blonde head as her mother entered; she rose, curtseyed formally and sat down again. Mary and Cicely were dressing a baby doll. There should have been another sister, but Margaret had only lived eight months and was already a memory.

The Prince Edward got up at Elizabeth's approach. He was very pale, with bluish marks under his eyes. He smiled sweetly and made a little bow.

'Does he learn well?' Elizabeth asked the tutor. Dr. Alcock inclined his black-capped head.

'He's diligent, madam. Kiss the Queen's hand, your Grace.' She felt moist warm lips on her fingers, and she laid her hand for a moment on the silky head. Her fingers passed downwards, absently, to his face. Like a puppy, he ducked his head to rub against her hand. She felt a sharp regret that she saw so little of him; but he was Anthony's charge. He was the heir to England, and should not leave Ludlow until Anthony, as Governor, saw fit.

'His Grace's brow feels chill,' she remarked, and withdrew her hand. Instantly there was a scramble to close the windows. The ferny scents diminished, to be replaced by dust and ink. Elizabeth felt a tugging at her skirt and looked down. Grinning like a bad angel, her second son, two-year old Richard, Duke of York, confronted her. He brandished a toy dagger. He screwed up his face, plunged his head into the folds of her dress. He whispered an unintelligible secret, then proceeded to run, like a whirligig, round and round the Queen's spread skirts. It made her glad to watch him; he was as robust as his brother Edward was frail. An understudy King! Then, a child's voice, oddly adult, chided the small Duke's rudeness, a hand coaxed the dagger from his grip and straightened his doublet. Elizabeth looked into the green eyes of Mistress Grace; those eyes that stared so, full of the disquieting unknown.

'I'll see you anon, my lord,' she told Dr. Alcock. Without looking back she went alone, to see the Governor of Ludlow Castle.

He did not rise instantly at her entrance, he was so immersed in his work. A Latin copy of the Dictes and Sayings of the Philosophers lay on the table before him. Sheets of translation were scattered on the floor. She looked fondly at his bent head; he was heedless of her so she placed her hand over the page on which he was writing. Frowning, he looked up, then sprang instantly to his feet, full of loving apology. He kissed both her hands, then embraced her heavy body.

'Anthony! Sweet Anthony!' It was months since they had met.

'My liege, Bess. Too long!'

'How does Ludlow suit you?'

He drew her down beside him on a settle, soothing her tense mood with his soft voice, jesting, pleasing her eye with his gold good looks.

'I have just come from the prince,' she said.

'Your prince, my scholar,' he laughed. 'Alcock and I are schooling him in all ways of urbanity and nurture.' A little frown of contempt puckered his brow. 'York could do well with some renewal of elegance. Lately it would seem that York breeds lechers, vulgarians. Bess—' more urgently – 'you must not let the King grow careless. How goes it with France?'

'The Treaty will be signed, although he cleaves to Burgundy still ... ah God!' she said suddenly. 'I am so afraid.'

He looked carefully at her. 'The King loves you,' he said slowly. 'Pay no heed to his diversions ... you have his heart and always will.'

'It is Clarence,' she said, her lips trembling. Anthony smiled.

'Naught to fear, sweet sister,' he said. This was not the Anthony who had been afraid to take her from Grafton Regis when she pleaded with him. This was a man who was erudite, calm, skilled. He said casually: 'I know all Clarence's mind. His murmurings against you and the King grow louder. He is fickle, treacherous and foolish. He will overstep himself, and my agents will see to it that he does, and is condemned for it.'

'You're sure?' she breathed.

'Be patient,' he told her. 'Clarence will be the architect of his own ruin.'

She could have told none the reason why she went to the Tower apartments of Margaret of Anjou. Only the itch of a long memory, or a ripple of forgotten duty unconsciously felt, led her through the cavernous vaults and up the twisted stairs. Margaret's door was properly guarded by pikemen wearing the *rose en soleil*. Waiting while they went inside to prepare the Frenchwoman, Elizabeth conjured memories. That frail, vital face; the eyes that could flash fury or soften with love. That gem-starred blondeness, and the voice douce as a dreaming bird's yet capable of harsh command. She waited, and remembered; then one of the men returned to kneel before her.

'My liege, she will not see you.'

'What?' cried Elizabeth. 'I command ...' A little perplexed, she said: 'Tell her that *Elizabeth* stands without the door!'

'I did, highness. She fancies herself mocked. She is intemperate with grief.' He folded his hands on the haft of his pike. On his wrist the marks of five sharp nails dripped blood.

'She may harm your Grace.'

Elizabeth felt in the pouch at her waist, found the dull coldness of a ring seldom worn. The pearl-and-ruby. The token of past friendship. The talisman of the beloved.

'Show her this. Say I come in kindness.'

The man went in again, and she waited, tapping her foot. Impatience mingled with anxiety. Edward knew nothing of this excursion of hers. It could displease him. And who was Margaret, to gainsay her entry? Sounds crept through the studded oak; a voice raised in a scream, then silence, then sobbing. After a moment the pikemen held open the door. Elizabeth caught up her gown to ascend the worn stone step, curved like a bow from a thousand treadings. The guard said uneasily: 'I must accompany your grace, and lock the door.'

She turned, said crisply, 'Lock it, but wait outside,' then entered, turning the iron ring-latch behind her. In the room there was a foul stench of sweat, and something else, the acrid smell of grief. Disorder reigned: strewn on the carpet, which itself was tracked threadless in one straight line, were torn parchments, letters half-begun. The silk hangings had been wrenched from one wall and lay in shreds. There was an overturned jug of flowers, their petals stamped and bruised to pulp. In one corner was a deep Dutch bed, its covers torn and tousled and bearing the traces of old blood. And, standing by the window-slit, looking towards the light, was Margaret – was Marguerite. The shadow and spectre of Marguerite.

She turned, and her face was visible. A cry of horror leapt in Elizabeth's throat. Margaret walked steadily towards her on the worn path of carpet made by years of pacing. From the ruined face came an unrecognizable voice, cracked and harsh.

'They said it was the Spanish disease, and they called me whore. But now they see it is naught but a deep canker that began in my breast and encompassed me. The legacy of my sorrow. God has seen fit to eat me up.'

One side of the face was clustered and corroded with small tumours, the other emaciated so that even the shape of the teeth was visible. Margaret's skin was yellow as fresh gold. The hair once bound with pearls grew in sparse grey tufts, but half the head was bald. The hellish apparition moved closer to Elizabeth, extending the twisted tragedies of its hands.

'You brought the ring,' she said. 'The ring I gave *la sage Jacquette*, your mother. How does your mother?'

'She is dead,' Elizabeth said faintly.

Margaret said with a ghastly smile: 'She is fortunate then! I should kneel to you, Isabella, but I do not. Will you punish me?' She touched the Queen's rich sleeve. 'So fair, so fine, my Isabella. Queen of Heaven!'

She laughed, she stroked her own dreadful mask with writhing fingers. Elizabeth thought wildly: I was mad to come here. She tried to speak steadily.

'Madame, have you no women, no physicians? You should be nursed.'

'My doctors despaired, and my women left me ... or they died,' said Margaret vaguely. 'They were afraid ... of my great beauty!' Her laughter began again. 'My beauty and my greatness! Behold my greatness!' She coughed, the yellow sinews in her throat straining like cords. Elizabeth felt the burn of tears at the back of her eyes. A false, far image of the lost Marguerite, darting and skimming like a swan in the dance ... the Marguerite of jewels and fire and love. Standing alone in the unused shining armour, braver and more soldierly than many of her courtiers. She said, choking:

'Ah, Madame, that you should have come to this!'

There was something more than pity to make her weep. A prescience of certain doom. As if she had glimpsed, unwittingly, the forecast of a time to come. As soon as this thought arose she pushed it savagely away, construing it as a malaise born of Margaret's dreadful presence.

'I am dying,' said Margaret. 'Betrayed. They all turned upon me – slaughtered my flower in the field, murdered my poor, wandering husband. Did you know? Not a hall's length from here, they snuffed the life from that kingly monk ... *Non!* Isabella, you would not know of this.'

Elizabeth was silent. It was better so; confessions did only harm, and Margaret had shown violence to the guard. She therefore let Margaret talk on, while tears collected in a strange pattern upon the misshapen face. Yet she looked at the hands that had once held her own tenderly while their owner wished her well in marriage; and she murmured: 'They have used you ill, Madame.'

'One especially,' said the Frenchwoman. 'One who promised me the world for my son. Curse Warwick!' Sadly she said: 'Was it my fault? Was it my vanity? *Vanité des vanités, toute la vanité!*'

Which was worse, Elizabeth wondered, the weeping or the laughter? Worst of all was to see Margaret beginning to dance, a few trembling, parodying steps. See, Isabella, I am still fair! She came close, placing her arm about Elizabeth, who shrank in dread. She disengaged herself.

'I am dying,' Margaret said again. 'And I am judged. Remember the old rhyme, *ma belle*? That you read so prettily that day?

'Benedicite, what dreamed I this night?
Methought the world was turned up so down,
The sea had covered both tower and town ...'

I have forgotten it ... ah, yes:

'... I heard the sound
Of one's voice saying: Bear in thy mind,
Thy lady hath forgotten to be kind!'

Perchance I was unkind. Now is my reckoning. So be kind, Isabella. Always ...'

The arm clung again. Elizabeth averted her face. The canker could be carried on a breath. Margaret was singing in a ghost's voice, moving her feet in that travesty of a dancestep.

'We were so gay, in France, when I was a little maid. Oh, Jesu, Isabella, help me!'

'How, Madame?'

She said: 'I do not wish to die here in the Tower. I must go home to France.'

Shivering, Elizabeth said: 'I will speak to Edward.'

'Yea, go to the Yorkist butcher!' said Margaret bitterly. 'He who slew *le pauvre Henri*. You see, Isabella, they did not need to tell me. I knew the day and moment of the deed. I heard Melusine cry on the battlements, and I knew.'

Elizabeth's heart began to beat in slow, thick strokes. The sunken eyes searched her face.

'An old legend, you may not know of it,' said the Frenchwoman listlessly. 'But whenever sorrow strikes a royal house – Melusine wails and weeps nightlong. *You'll* not have heard her, for the world is yours. Queen!' She spat the word.

Yes, Queen, thought Elizabeth, chilled to the bone. *Queens can be brought down.* She looked again at Margaret, at the horrifying translation of her beauty. And they can be brought to this! She glanced quickly towards the locked door. Outside lay freedom, jewels, a soothing posset, music to forget by. No more of this painful, insufferable presence.

'Madame, I leave you now.' But Margaret went with her to the door, hanging desperately on her arm. With difficulty Elizabeth shook her off.

'Give me your word, 'Isabella. I would, I must, die in France.' She began to cough, rasping, weeping. 'If ever you loved me, child; this one favour. Bid the King release me from this place!'

Elizabeth reached the door and hammered upon it.

'Promise!' It was like the high wild cry of a bird.

She looked once more. Frail and ghastly, a living doom, Margaret stood there; also betrayed by Warwick, also a scion of Melusine, and also a Queen. A terrifying mirror image, a living, dying warning. She felt the chamber walls closing about her. For here, unmistakably, was destiny seeking to be placated. She retraced her steps, took Margaret in her arms. She pressed her face against the rotting, tear-wet cheek.

'I promise, *ma reine*,' she said. 'I promise.'

Edward called for wine. More than half-drunk already, he sought in the cup's red heart a panacea for guilt. An end to trouble. He swirled the liquor round, turning the priceless goblet so that fire-fly prisms streaked from the silver. Pretty ... He swallowed wine and motioned blindly for replenishment. He felt the cup's coldness against his mouth; the taste brought Clarence back. He, Edward, drank wine, and wine had drunk Clarence.

The King sat among his court, detached from all by a thin red veil. The faces about his dais were distant and drifted hazily. Their talk, geared to the sovereign's mood, was discreet and soft. He heard their voices but their words were meaningless, for they were overlaid by the hammering echoes of earlier speech. Anthony Woodville's voice, full of rich certainty, regret.

'My heart's blood not to tell you this, Sire. But Clarence is crazed with spleen. He has this day usurped the royal prerogative; accused and, hanged a woman said to have murdered his infant son. On your orders, my liege!'

It must be true, Edward thought. Trusted Anthony had come riding from Ludlow to tell him this. So Edward had seized and hanged two of Clarence's men in retribution. It had not been enough, however.

'Your Grace! Today Clarence burst into Council in your absence and incited the lords to rebellion. He's high in madness. "Twas all they could do to prevent him crowning himself King there and then ...'

His own rage had grown and burgeoned, while he stared into Anthony's clear eyes. Anthony's hand sought his, to steady him for the next phrase. Spoken without a tremor, for Anthony was courageous where the truth was concerned.

'He declared that your Grace is no son of York, but the spawn of a French archer! and that England is ruled by bastards.' The lines on his smooth face deepened in pain as he continued: 'And that your Grace holds consort with witches.'

He had needed that steadying hand, feeling the blood leaping and throbbing in his head, hearing his own roar: 'Enough!' then falling mightily upon a couch. While Anthony bowed devoutly so that his face was hidden. Much later, he heard his own voice saying: 'She was right. Bessy was right, and I would not listen to her.' And fear for the future had stared him in the face, fear that Clarence's wild accusations cloaked a deadlier weapon. Clarence had kept close with their mother. How much had he wheedled from that ageing saint? How much would conscience let her hide? She who was privy to the knowledge of Eleanor Butler ...

Though Eleanor was now dead, she was his first and lawful wife. No Queen's Gold for Eleanor, but Bessy was no more than the King's concubine. The game was too dangerous. So, enough. Now he gripped the cup so that his fingers blenched. Clarence had chosen his own death, and a bizarre, unholy death it was. 'To drown in wine, my brother!' The plump bitter face smiling. 'Can your Grace afford it?'

Nauseous, Edward wondered: had he drunk deep before he died? What was it like to feel such bloodlike redness filling the lungs? How much could a man swallow and remain afloat? And, Jesu preserve us all! What had the everthirsty Tower gaolers done – after they took bloated Clarence from the vat? To cast out horror, he began the mental calculation of the cost of a tun of malmsey given to every child named Edward in the realm ... With the fifty thousand crowns from Louis of France, a pittance. Louis had paid for peace. No battle was joined, although Edward had taken to Picquigny a hundred thousand men at arms. Everything had ended in love and gladness, with Louis's veined and spotted paw clasping the King's upon a fragment of True Cross. All had rejoiced; save Gloucester. The wine-cup was again empty, and here was Gloucester's remembered voice, to torment him.

'For the love of God, Edward, spare our brother of Clarence!'

'Edward, our honour is sacrificed for this shameful truce. Louis will betray us, mark me ...'

'Ned, my brother, let Clarence live!'

Now it was all over. Clarence dead; Louis paid off. Bess, the Princess Elizabeth of York, betrothed to the Dauphin of France as part of the bargain. And Margaret of Anjou sent home to France. He had been amazed by the fervour of Bessy's plea for her release, and had acquiesced, for it was little to him where the dying woman ended her days. Now a chance, perhaps, for peace. He had soon silenced the army who had been cheated of their French battle. A few hangings, beheadings, and they came straight to heel. He was in his thirty-sixth year; middle-aged; time to settle down with a happy land under his gauntlet, his sons growing strong, his daughters beautiful. His Queen content and his mistresses willing. He lifted his heavy head and surveyed the courtiers. They shimmered behind the blood-coloured veil. Thomas and Richard Grey, laughing quietly together. Anthony, unrolling a gay Latin verse for the perusal of the Queen. Hastings, gazing in undisguised longing towards Jane Shore. Jane herself sat at the King's feet, a foreshortened image of golden coiffed hair and two apple-round breasts. He touched her shoulder. She seemed very far away.

'Sing,' he commanded.

High and shrill like an untaught boy, she sang rudely about a lecherous clerk. He grew quickly bored with the ditty. Again the spectre of Clarence arose, bobbing to the surface of the vat like a great wine-bag, and the gaolers crowding with their pannikins held ready ... Gloucester had wept when he learned that his plea for leniency had been in vain. Gloucester seldom wept; he was a good soldier. He had gone home to the North, to his Anne, where he would expunge his sorrow in fighting the Scots.

Edward called for yet more wine. Death drank with him, and the knowledge that Richard of Gloucester had been right – both about the French truce (for Louis could never be trusted) – and about Clarence, whom a spell in the Tower might have tamed. But

Gloucester knew nothing of the dangers. He stretched his hand down to dabble between Jane's breasts.

'Eleanor,' he said softly, drunkenly. 'Eleanor' And the Queen was suddenly at his side, pale, patting Jane's head as she might caress a dog, talking swiftly over the high bawling song.

'My lord, how you do tangle up fair ladies' names! I have a boon to beg, a small one. The Countess of Richmond begs leave to present her son. Henry Tudor.'

In his vision the silvery face swung and dipped. Fighting the dizziness, he said: 'Ha! Tudor cub? Fruit of Lancaster ...' and saw the narrow poised face of Margaret Beaufort, looking shocked. From out of a long tunnel her even voice said: 'Your Grace, my family are all loyal!' Some remnant of sense spoke in his mind, ridiculing the Countess, but the words were too difficult, and he nodded, saying: 'Let him come.'

Behind the great doors, Henry Tudor was waiting. He had been waiting like this for almost all his twenty subservient, repressed years: in the house of Lord Herbert at Pembroke, or under the harsh rule of his Uncle Jasper, or, in exile after Tewkesbury, as a despised nonentity in the court of Francis of Brittany. Even now he had waited a week at Westminster for the royal summons, hearing the whispered instructions of Morton and the Stanleys, seeing the fretful excitement of his mother. And only he was calm. A generation of Welsh and Frankish blood moved softly in him, bidding him gather himself for new beginnings. A native ruthlessness told him that behind those doors he would find a court of fools. He gave a slight shrug to his patched doublet, smoothed his dry, rust-coloured hair. His face was long and lean, his mouth almost lipless. It was the face of a man older than twenty, and in it the eyes were as cold as a preying bird's.

Then he smiled, and was changed. The smile lent wistfulness to his demeanour, so that he looked like a starved infant offering macabre love, and the predatory eyes grew lambent and wise. The mouth slid upwards in a bow and quivered. Before him a light-chink between the doors widened into vast radiance. An usher called his name. Across a mile of lozenged tiles he went, between the candle-flames and diamonds and quizzical stares. Once, the faintest ripple of laughter blew across his path and was unheeded by him. His thin shanks carrying him steadily, he advanced upon the coveted court of the Plantagenets.

He saw a sorry, drunken monarch, great belly straining at velvet, the ruined beauty of his face lapped in red jowls, pigeon's blood rubies on his fat hands and breast. A blonde harlot at his feet. A fair-haired, lovely child (the eldest, Bess of York; his mother had primed him well); a nervous ageing minister; that would be Hastings. Next to him the Woodvilles, handsome Anthony, the sons of Sir John Grey; and Lionel, Bishop of Salisbury, who had the royal favour. Henry reached the dais and heard the King mumbling an uninterested welcome. Now for the obeisance, as he had been schooled. The right knee crooked – no trembling – and down, down to the floor, where the eyes must go. Obeisance. Abasement. The left toe stretched out behind, sliding on the red-black crosswork of the tiles. Now, the plump hand with its engorged veins beneath his lips. Dry lips; treason to leave spittle. Good. Good. Another moment of waiting. 'Courtly manners, my young friend,' said the deep, slurred voice. 'Rise. You may greet our Queen.'

He raised his eyes. They slipped quickly across the intimidating semi-circle of faces, imprinting on his consciousness the friends, the foes, the ones unknown. Unerringly he registered their strengths and their failings. The Woodvilles, for example, were imperious as gerfalcons, and as fine-feathered. If such a bird were stripped, feather by feather, what remained? A bleeding, earthbound ruin, unable to prey. His eyes ceased travelling momentarily to greet the black omnipotence of Morton. The Bishop's white hand lifted slightly; the Bishop's hooded eye blinked in tacit approval.

Lastly, slowly, Henry looked at the Queen. He appraised her silks and furs. He noted that she was jewelled like a pagan princess. He guessed her age, saw that she carried those years well. Yet his unflickering eye marked also her inner disquiet, the torment of her lifelong insecurity. Whispering a humble greeting, he assessed her body and soul. It was as his mother had hinted. Elizabeth, the pawn of Richmond. For all her hauteur, ready to cling and listen and be led.

She, looking for the first time upon Margaret Beaufort's son, experienced a strange recognition. It was like the sensation of meeting John Grey at Eltham. *This is he, at last. Love, you are come.*

But this was not love. It was the unknown, the recognizable unknown. Like the reprise of a song unheard, or the shadow of an unconscious dream. She withdrew her hand from that of the youth. With customary coolness she said: 'We greet you well.'

The feeling remained, astounding in its certainty. As Henry Tudor scraped and bowed and backed from the dais, she knew that here was one of utter significance, for evil or for good.

PART THREE

The Boar of Gloucester

1483-5

O God! What security shall our Kings
have henceforth that in the day of battle
they may not be deserted by their subjects!
The Croyland Chronicle: 1485

Grace Plantagenet stood at the latticed window of the stillroom and watched the sky, where oyster-coloured clouds were palely lit by sun. Between delicate spires and stout turrets she could see distantly the brown, boiling river, flushed with spring tides. Once a bird – blackbird or thrush, too swift to tell – dived straight at the window, then veered off, wheeling up and away over the palace of Westminster. She thought: my father's spirit! But this was foolishness; if Edward had departed as a bird it would be no common warbler but a golden kestrel, or a snowy falcon. The Falcon of York. The ethereal towers blurred suddenly and she dabbed at her eyes with a sleeve. She had sworn to weep no more; rather mourn in silence. The ostentatious wailing and hair-tearing of the women and some of the men repelled her. Many had only courted Edward for his easy favour. She, Grace, came from his royal loins; she had more right to cry than they. Even now in some corridor outside the stillroom she could hear Jane Shore, voluble in grief as in laughter.

Jane. Her thoughts ran back like a silken coil to that night eight days ago. The night before the King had been taken so grievously and suddenly sick. She remembered it well; that night she had attended the Queen in the great chamber where Edward so seldom came of late. To cosset the Queen was Grace's joy. She received no thanks, hardly a look or a word, yet, all the while she basked in inexplicable content. Merely to be in that presence was to bathe in the cool unearthly tranquillity of moonlight. Yes, if Edward was the glowing Sun in Splendour, his consort was the moon.

That particular night had been different, troubling, however. As always, Grace had waited, lying taut and vigilant on her trestle until the breathing in the bed should soften almost to inaudibility. She heard midnight chime; then one, two, three, four hours, and still from above came rustlings, little coughs, sighs. Once she thought she heard a murmured prayer, or the drift of a poem; and fancied that she had fallen asleep and dreamed, and snatched at wakefulness to find the silence more pronounced. Not even a dog barked; the palace seemed fixed in enchantment. A finger of dull starlight shone through a gap in the curtains. Grace, sick with weariness, lay willing the Queen to sleep. Then, a few seconds after the quarter's chime, there was a great commotion as the Queen flung herself out of bed, calling for light. Grace lit candles; their wavering flames showed the Queen's pale face, pale hair streaming, hands that clutched and pleated her damask bedgown. She was angry.

'Holy Jesu!' she 'cried. 'Will she never stop that noise? Hour after hour ... I could tear out her tongue!'

She paced the room, and the silence grew more profound than ever. Grace, shocked and afraid, stared at the Queen, who then, for the first time in months, addressed her directly.

'Is she not possessed?' she demanded. 'Some devil must enter her, bidding her mar my sleep! Have you slept, mistress? Nay, how could you? Listen! she grows louder ... laughing. The King calls her merry. I call her mad!'

The candlelight fluttered; in the corners shadows crept. The Queen ran to the window and threw back the curtains.

'Almost dawn, I swear! There again! You hear her?'

Grace, her teeth chattering, whispered: 'Who, highness?' The silence was caught up in the shadows and licked around them both.

'Why, the creature Shore, of course!' The Queen leaned against the window, peering through. 'It sounds – Jesu! It sounds as if she were making merry on the roof!'

Grace, paralysed with uncertainty, waited close to the Queen's silhouetted shape, watching the perfect profile outlined against candlefire and dawnlight, telling herself: I am deaf, and I am witless. This day I will go to the physician and have him probe my ears, however much it hurts. For before God, I hear nothing.

'Is she laughing?' said the Queen. 'Or is she weeping?' Through the gloom her eyes sought Grace's small upturned face. There had to be an answer. The Queen abhorred laughter; that was well known. In the desperate, clinging silence, Grace said: 'I think ...'

'Well?'

'Weeping, your Grace.'

The Queen was looking away. Slowly the tension left her body, her hands unclenched. 'Ah!' She sighed and shuddered. 'It is finished. Praise God.'

After a while she returned and climbed into the deepsided bed. Grace snugged the coverlet down over the Queen, and extinguished the candles. Although it was mild for April, she felt deeply chill, and lay for a long time, wondering. Finally the Queen's voice reached her, strangely quiet.

'Mistress Grace, will you pray?'

'Yes, highness.'

'Pray for protection.'

Grace slid from the trestle once more, and knelt. '*Libera nos, Domine, ab omnibus malis* ...'

The Queen cut her off short, saying: 'Nay, leave it. I am foolish. I will see the Comptroller this day. My household becomes a beargarden. And I will speak to Mistress Shore.'

Grace was there when Jane was summoned. She came dishevelled, mud upon her gown. The Queen spoke to her kindly, while Jane looked up with artless eyes.

'Can you not temper your merrymaking of a night?'

'Madame?'

'Shrieking – aloft ... where were you last night, Mistress Shore?'

Jane, looking mystified, said primly: 'Madame, I have only just returned from the City. My husband is sick, and sent for me two days ago.'

Both she and Grace saw the Queen's face slacken for an instant, but only Grace heard the word that leaped from the Queen's lips, soft as a breath, a blasphemy. Then Elizabeth made a gesture of dismissal, her smooth features once more expressionless. Following the Queen back to her apartment, Grace saw how slowly she walked. Once she leaned on a pillar, and said clearly:

'When sorrow strikes a royal house ... ah, Jesu!'

It was not the Holy Name she had whispered in that one startled gasp at Mistress Shore. It was a name that Grace had never heard; a liquid, silvery name. Half an hour later, Master Hobbes, the King's physician, came almost demented to say that Edward was ill.

Now he was dead. Rain, an April squall like sudden grief, smacked against the window. Grace turned away at last. She watched Renée preparing a draught of honeyed ale for the Queen. Renée's eyes were red; she looked suddenly very old. To Grace's fourteen years, forty were legion. Yet the Queen, who was even older than Renée, seemed ageless.

'She will find that posset too sweet,' Grace said. Renée answered angrily: 'I need no schoolroom cook to teach me my work!' and Grace's sadness gave way to unease. Now that her father was dead, would people change? They already mocked her for having no husband. Fourteen years old, and the bastard of a King. No beauty – she had decided that for herself long ago. The mirror in the Queen's bower – that mirror girdled with sea-shapes, sirens, fishes – showed her a face too thin, a mouth too full. Under the pointed hennin the blonde curls were scraped back and hidden. She missed the striking loveliness of the brilliant green eyes slanted like a cat's, the lissom waist, the kindly lips. She saw only the defects which made her murmur, for comfort: I am Grace *Plantagenet*.'

Renée was keening to herself, uttering little scraps of thought. Perhaps she did have the right to weep – if only for the twice-widowed Queen; but somehow her sorrow was mechanical.

'She was so happy, so glorious. Only two weeks ago. At that pageant the King arranged, showing that her Grace was descended from the Magi. All three kings came to kneel to her ... and now ... ' She omitted to weep for Edward, who had died in a bloated agony so that some whispered of poison.

'I still say the draught is too sweet,' said Grace. 'She will send it away.'

None the less she took the silver cup covered with fair linen to the Queen's chamber. As she walked, each step was measured by the passing bell. The deep sound had beaten on her brain for so many hours that she thought she would never lose it; like a heartbeat, it would remain until death. All around her was unreality. The stones she trod, the carved columns by which she passed, wavered and were fluid. The men and women whom she met swam silently by like blackclad ghosts. Only at the Queen's door did things solidify, among them the figure of Thomas Dorset, Elizabeth's firstborn. He was standing, hand raised to knock, and upon hearing Grace approach he turned with a smile. Although puffed with weeping, his eyes stripped her naked. He bowed elegantly. He mocked her, through envy of her as a King's bastard, but the courtesy and the wandering eyes were tribute to the challenge of her virginity. After the King, Tom Grey had the monopoly of all the remaining maidenheads at court.

'Beauty. Enter, I pray.'

She answered formally: 'My lord takes precedence,' disliking him. It came to her forcibly that she disliked almost everyone at court. With her father's death, this thought crystallized. Half-way up the spiral stair behind her, she heard Jane Shore wailing for the dead King. Jane could have been kind, but she was too shallow and undependable. Grace stood hesitantly while Dorset bowed and sneered. Through the closed door came voices, among them the sibilant note of Reynold Bray, who, whenever he saw her, exhorted Grace to prayer, while resembling a rat in search of a hen-house. Then she heard the Queen's voice, precise and plaintive; a male answer, indistinct, and the name: 'Gloucester.'

Grace's mood suddenly lifted. Naturally, Richard Duke of Gloucester would be coming south for Edward's burial, and there was the thread of a chance that he would bring with him the one person she most wished to see. Someone near enough her own age to be intelligible; someone whose presence in the past had lightened days which were frustrating, bewildering and often hopeless. John. John of Gloucester. A smile trembled on her lips so that Dorset, encouraged, bent closer. The last time she and John had met was at Eltham by the lake. She had wanted a lily, a lily like a fat, pink-tipped candle. He had waded into the water to pluck it, and had spoiled his forest-green hose; new that day. Then they had walked together the periphery of the lake, their hands lightly clasped. She had been two fingers taller than he. Glancing behind at the grass patterned by his soaked feet, she had teased him.

'Will your father have you beaten?'

'I wish he were more often at home to beat me,' John answered.

'He's always away; fighting.'

She had said, inconsequentially: 'I never knew my mother.'

'Nor I mine.' His clear pale face was thoughtful. 'Richard Plantagenet is father and mother to me; and of course, I have the Lady Anne, his wife.'

It was, she decided, because they were of like station that their affinity grew and blossomed into a mood of ease and comfort. Both royal bastards; both Plantagenet, yet touched by unknown, possibly simple blood. Conceived in a moment of lust, or, boredom, or even revenge. Lately Grace had wondered about her own mother; there must be tacit reason for the Queen's manner – the coldness that should have hurt and sometimes did, the unease which filled the Queen's eyes when they looked at Grace. Although it was of no consequence; so long as she was not sent from that hypnotic, spellbinding presence. Only once had she discussed the Queen with John, and he had said, surprisingly: 'Her Grace dislikes my father. Because Edward loves him so. And because he is married to Anne of Warwick.'

Warwick was a name almost out of Grace's time. Only his castle of Middleham remained, a place steadfast yet wild, and painted with vivid glamour by John. He would talk for hours about the moors of Middleham, a tapestry of hawks and horses and sweeping winds. A place of pagan holiness, he called it. A castle warned by great fires and mirth. And as he talked he himself became imbued with the cold and the crying birds, the bubbling, water-white garths, the warm heathery scents and the haunted mists, making them also a part of Grace. She heard the name 'Gloucester' spoken again, and as Dorset pushed the door open, she twinned a prayer: May the Duke bring John with him to London; and may John not have changed.

The Queen was sitting surrounded by her family. She was in mourning, its doleful black lit by a white barbette beneath her chin. She was pale, with a high flush on each cheek. Her hands were clasped hard together and trembled slightly. Behind her chair stood her brothers, Lionel Bishop of Salisbury and Sir Edward Woodville the sea-captain. Her sister Catherine, also in mourning, knelt at her feet. Bishop Morton stood sombrely by; a great parchment, brightly sealed, drooped from his hand. Without being told, Grace knew instantly that this was the King's last will and testament. Again her vision blurred so that the group of tense faces – Margaret Beaufort, Lord Stanley, Reynold Bray (who stood at a lectern, quill poised) shimmered and gleamed in her sight. She blinked, and a tear fell on the snowy linen covering the cup. Dorset moved swiftly forward from her side and knelt, pressing his forehead to the Queen's fingers. She said: 'Where have you been? I summoned you hours ago.' He murmured excuses which she dismissed turning her face with an odd little gesture sharply to one side, closing her eyes. Grace thought: she seems nervous, changed. She pictured the Queen of, two weeks ago, as lamented by Renée; at the pageant of the Magi. There had been something mystic in that scene; the robes green and gold, the incense rising and the rich gifts. Paradoxical, too. Though everyone knew that in the land of the Magi the river of Paradise rose, there were other opinions: that all evil as well as good came from the East – the devils of the sand, the herbs to drive men mad. It was difficult to decide, but the Queen had seemed well pleased.

Also present were Lord Berners, the Queen's Chamberlain, and his wife, nurse to the Princess. With a stab of sympathy Grace wondered how Bess did. She had not wept at the news of her father's death as had Mary and Cicely. Her wide, rather childish blue eyes had looked puzzled and a little afraid. The babes, Katherine and Bridget, were too young to feel much grief. Nine-year-old Richard Duke of York had stifled sorrow bravely, only to break down in Grace's arms when she dressed him in the black velvet doublet. Mourning put a degree of manhood upon him and stopped his noisy battle-games for a day; the powerful atmosphere of disquiet, acutely felt all over the Palace, made his pert face thoughtful. He said to Grace: 'Now my brother Ned will be King.'

'Yes, yes, my lord.'

He blew his nose, sighed as if released from travail.

'Then I shall see him soon. He seems to have been years at Ludlow.' From that moment he was himself again.

Grace shifted her feet. A small figure among the crowd of nobles, she held the rapidly cooling cup of ale. The Queen was speaking, hard and high, pausing only while Reynold Bray, his nose almost touching the parchment, scratched out a letter with his quill.

'To Sir Anthony Woodville, Earl Rivers, Governor of Ludlow. Right worshipful and well beloved brother, we greet you well. And it is our doleful duty to acquaint you of the passing of our sovereign lord, Edward King of England ...'

A dozen hands made the sign of the cross.

'We as Queen-Regent–' the delicate eyelids fluttered; the voice laid down the words, hard and definite, like coins on a table – 'we, as Queen-Regent, make it known that the said Edward in his last will and testament named as Protector of the Realm his brother Richard Duke of Gloucester, to have sole charge and ruling over our sovereign-elect, our son the Prince Edward of Wales, now in your lordship's care. Having regard for ... for our own standing and fortunes in the realm, we charge you thus.'

She stopped, swallowed. Grace looked uneasily down at the draught she held. The Queen was far from finished; it would have to wait. Hard and cool the words flowed on.

'As Queen-Regent we charge you to be diligent in thwarting this decree, and to bring our son Edward Prince of Wales with all speed to London where he shall be crowned King of England in the presence of his rightful supporters. I pray you spare no cost or effort in hindering the Duke of Gloucester ...'

She turned suddenly to Margaret Beaufort. 'Can I make it plainer?' The Countess, coming closer, answered: 'Madame, Sir Anthony is the cleverest knight in Christendom. The missive is clear enough.'

Reynold Bray finished writing and brought quill and parchment over for the royal signature. The Queen said quickly: 'Master, an addition. Write: Gloucester knows not of the King's death. Delay all messengers. I pray you, fail me not.'

Bray wrote. The Queen dipped the pen and in perfect silence, added 'Elizabeth' – fine and hard, the small round 'e' and wild long-tailed 'z' – the whole underlined by a ripple like a seawave. She looked then at the assembly and, as if daring them to disagree, said: 'You are in accord'?' There was an instant mumble of assent. With a rustle of mourning gowns they knelt and bowed and quit the Chamber. Grace, save for Dorset, was alone with the Queen who continued to ignore her, beckoning her son nearer with a small, frenetic gesture.

'Tom, why did you delay?' she demanded. 'You are vital to this enterprise. You must ride at once to Ludlow with the message. Where is Hastings now? Jesu! I know that he will send the news to Gloucester with all speed. Hastings was one we could not suborn. That stupid, arrogant knight,' she said vexedly.

'Madame,' said Tom Dorset. 'I cannot go to Ludlow. There is much to do here.'

She clenched her hands in irritation. 'Did I make you Constable of the Tower for nothing? Are all your honours in vain?'

He smiled, a little seductive smile. 'Madam my mother, it is *because* I am Constable of the Tower that I must remain. Already my men are preparing the armaments – five thousand handguns, ten thousand longbows, a thousand cannon ... for our endeavour.'

'I pray,' she said uneasily, 'that we need not array ourselves in arms. The Londoners will not love us for it. And Gloucester is a warrior, a strategist ...'

'Madame, be courageous,' said Thomas Dorset, smiling again. 'My swiftest men shall ride to my uncle at Ludlow. Leave the rest to him. It will be but a short battle for this ... this ill-chosen Protector, Gloucester. Short, secret, final.'

'And Hastings?' said the Queen uneasily.

'That,' answered Dorset, 'you may leave to me. There are subtler ways than force. Give me the letter, Madame. Couriers, sworn men, are waiting.'

He took the roll, now sealed, and turned. He saw Grace, and still mocking, yet unquiet, asked her: 'Is that soothing potion cold, mistress? And tell me, do you love our Queen?'

Grace answered instantly: 'Till death.' She knew the Marquis's reasons for asking her allegiance; she was privy to a plan. A plan to kill. Bluntly and unequivocally, a plan to kill the Protector assigned by Edward. It all meant little. She thought: let them kill Gloucester if they must, for although he is my uncle, I scarcely know him. But let them leave his son, my friend, alone.

Dorset left, bound for the chamber of Jane Shore. He had decided to seduce her afresh; for a long time he had resented sharing her with the King. At last Grace could approach the Queen, who was still pale although the fiery spots upon her cheeks had diminished. Grace knelt, and proffered the cup. The honey had congealed on the ale's amber surface.

'Your highness complained of evil of the throat. Dame Renée sent this,' she whispered.

'My throat is better. It was weeping that made it sore.'

Again she had spoken and looked directly. It was happiness of the highest order. Grace raised her eyes to the Queen, who was sipping the fluid delicately. Then Elizabeth said a strange thing.

'There is none to taste this posset for me! I have no Beaufort of

Somerset! Are you poisoning me, mistress?'

It was cruel, like a knife. Yet Grace thought: I answered Dorset truly. I love you. Although you have never been kind, I adore you as a dog loves the only master he has ever known, one who rewards his duty with a kick, his loyalty with blows. Is it because, within you, there are those deep fears, those lost feelings, that I myself own? God save me, silver lady. I love you, and know not why.

With a small entourage Elizabeth moved to Windsor to wait out the days. It was mild enough for her to spend the afternoons in the ripening parkland. Wrapped in fine fur over her black gown, she sat on cushions, her spine supported by an ancient oak. All around was a rising cadence of birdsong; thrush and blackbird and robin shrilled in their small-leafed gallery above her head, and from the forest came the guttural rapping of a woodpecker. On the small mere by which she sat, two moorhens bobbed beneath the flashing splendour of a pair of kingfishers. It was April, cruel green April.

Only by sitting very still could she contain herself. Grief, rage and anxiety warred within her. Over all was a black fear that made her finger constantly the diamonds at her breast, the pearls in her ears, seeking comfort in their cool stability. Now and then the sorrow pried through like an irrelevant toothache. It was April; acutely, when she closed her eyes, she saw Bradgate opening to her round a luscious flower-strewn bend. *Sir John Grey, knight, is dead. As is Edward, King of England.* Strange that I, twice-widowed, should have attended neither of them at the end. I would have staunched John's wounds with my hair. But Edward never even sent for me! She bit her lips. Rage gained sovereignty until ousted by unrest. Why did he not call me? While I waited, sending messages every hour, he preferred the company of my son Dorset, my brother Lionel, and cursed, vacillating Hastings. Were all these nineteen years for naught? I gave him sweet daughters, strong sons. The last, little George, died through no fault of mine. I gave him a Prince of Wales, Ned, made in our image, royal and fair and pale. A stout, rumbustious, merry Duke of York, little Dick. And I closed my eyes to lechery and drunkenness. (A picture of Edward rose, Edward reeling to the vomitorium behind the dais, to spew up a thirty-course dinner so he might dine again.) Then Melusine cried on the battlements and he was gone, without asking for my presence at his side. He rejected me to spare his own immortal soul. He died in sin, in bigamy. Tom whispered that he called for Eleanor at the last. Pray Jesu none heard him. *Let not my glory pass away.*

The only tribute to his consort, a poem penned by a stumbling amateur and written as if from the tomb, was nauseating to her in its irony.

> ...Where is now my conquest and royal array?
> Where be my coursers and horses high?
> Where is my mirth, my solace and my play?
> As vanity is naught, all is wandered away!
> O Lady Bessy! long for me ye may call,
> For I am departed until the doomsday,
> But love ye that Lord who is sovereign of all.

She thought: I am again alone. More than when John died. For then I was four-and-twenty, fruitful, resourceful, with a strength that was doubled by the skill and purpose of my mother. Now I am forty-six, and old. A soft wind blew across the tiny lake, and unexpectedly, incredibly, her spirit lifted. I am Queen-Regent. Behind me lies the power of Cleopatra, or the Queen of Sheba. Even now my son Thomas lays hands upon the treasures of the Tower, the vast fortune amassed by Edward, and the weapons of war to crush any who dare question my might. How can I be alone? She lifted her eyes to the greenness above and smiled faintly. All my enemies are dead; the Fiend rots in earth and writhes in Hell. Clarence will ferret no more for secrets to undo me. Even Desmond's laughter is stilled. His two little knaves also, cut off in play ... The smile fled. That was unlucky. Too late now, to mend that. But Tiptoft should have spared them. Unlucky. She began again, for comfort's sake, to account her benefits. I have Anthony, strong, clever Anthony ...

('Sweet sister, think of me when you come into your glory!'

'Anthony, we shall be supreme! More powerful than the King himself!')

I have Margaret Beaufort, with her man's mind and her unerring judgment. And now she has a new husband, Lord Stanley, well to heel. His was the loudest voice upholding me at the Council meeting, when Edward's last decree was superseded. Edward's last decree! Gloucester shall not have charge of my son, that precious chalice of royal blood, that vessel of power. Gloucester, whom I had almost forgotten, shall die. No doubt he is already dead, if Anthony keeps faith, which he will. Anthony shall be rewarded with a quarter of my treasure from the Tower.

Her busy mind went meticulously on, reliving scenes and conversations like a series of tableaux. The interment of Edward in St. George's Chapel, so near through the trees. The lying-in-state; Edward's great chest and belly exposed above the loincloth, his gross flesh ethereal in the tapers' light, so that he drew on a reminder of his slender sunlit youth. So, he was with his Eleanor now! She thought: I once dreaded his death as the end of my power. But now I know my power begins.

The servants, and the Princess Elizabeth who sat near by, looked at the restless twisting hands, the face that smiled and frowned in turn as assets were reckoned, hazards appraised. She calculated ceaselessly her prizes both monetary and prestigious; she saw the realm like cloth of Arras, starred goldly with her possessions. Her fee-farms by the thousand, acre on acre of sweeping land rich with barley or patrolled by a million wool-bearing sheep. Her scores of royal chases thronged with venison and birds to grace a paladin's table. The gold, the silver and jewels, the horses, hawks and weapons, the fabulous furnishings and tapestries in fifty or more palaces. And beside all these the ocean of wealth amassed for Thomas and Richard Grey, for Anthony. She nodded, a gesture weird to the watchers, as she thought: I acted well over Exeter's daughter. Even when she died after a year's marriage to Tom I prevailed on Edward for those vast estates to remain my son's. Clarence's bounty, too. All mine, ours. Earldoms and duchies and marquisates. My brother Edward in charge of a mighty fleet, lying off the French coast. Even Calais mine one day ...

I asked for as much of the land around the fountain that could be covered by a stag's hide. Then I cut the hide into strips so that my land extended far beyond the forest.

The pattern goes on. Even in my widowhood there is naught to fear. Only Hastings, with whom Tom has promised to deal speedily. And Richard Gloucester ... What possessed Edward? To pronounce as Protector of the Realm, a brother whom he scarcely ever saw, one content to rusticate in the soulless North. But Anthony would put him down. The Council should issue all writs *in aurunculus regis uterinus* and *frater regis uterinus*. In the name of the Queen's brother and son.

As for Edward Prince of Wales, he was the greatest asset of all. A pocket King of England, more biddable than the weakest of grown monarchs. Edward should stay at his lessons until he was twenty-one!

Queen's College, Cambridge. Mine. Endowed and refounded to my honour. What Marguerite began I finished, far more gloriously.

Elizabeth, Princess of York. Young Bess. Out of the tail of her eye she could see her, sitting on spread cloth-of-gold; tall and blonde, wistful in her black. A royal prince for her! More glory for the house of Woodville. All the crowned heads of Europe would be present, the jewelled banners would lift, and foreign chroniclers would gape at the marriage of Bess, daughter of the most powerful Queen in Christendom. She who had breasted the tide of humiliation, who herself had snared a king, and had seen her enemies fall like flowers. Twenty bishops would witness a second generation's rise to royal heights.

The bishops. Again, her face sobered. The courtiers did her will, but that covey of wily, guilt-ridden old men were yet to be sounded. Russell, Bishop of Lincoln and Keeper of the Privy Seal; Story, Bishop of Chichester and King's Executor; Bourchier, Archbishop of Canterbury. Thomas Rotherham, Archbishop of York. Bishop Morton of Ely was already hers, through the gracious intercession of Margaret Beaufort. Her own brother Lionel had the see of Salisbury in his grip. One thing was clear; the bishops needed the patronage and favour of the Crown. They were only too conscious of the ritual squabbling in their ranks, the obloquy in which the Church was held by the laity, to the extent of physical assault on clergy. Yes, the Church would soon come begging for the Queen-Regent's assent. And they should have it. She liked the new bidding-prayer already written: 'for our prince, the lady Queen Elizabeth his mother, all the royal offspring, the princes of the King, his nobles and people'. This augured well; she was not to be overpassed as the mothers of previous infant kings had been; Joan of Kent, mother of Richard II, or Katherine, who bore crazy Henry. Then Councils had reigned and lesser Queens embraced obscurity.

She flicked back over her thoughts as one turning the pages of a book. Katherine of France took a lover, Owen Tudor. Bore Edmund Tudor, Margaret Beaufort's first husband. They in turn begat young Henry. Strange young Henry, of the deep curtsey and cadaverous smile. She looked idly across at the little lake; irrelevantly Henry's smile seemed to wink from it. Such manifestation meant that the person concerned was thinking of you. But according to Margaret Beaufort, and Lord Stanley, Henry's new stepfather, this was unlikely. Henry was again in Brittany, thanks to Edward's hectoring of him some years previously; the King had mumbled vaguely about the aspirations of bastard Welshmen. She had paid little heed, but remembered that Henry had been chased to St. Malo by some Yorkist fleet with little else to do. Yet she remembered his smile; that look from the wise, heavy eyes. He could only have been admiring her.

He had looked long at the Princess Elizabeth too. Almost as if he lusted for her. It was impossible to associate such gross emotions with the son of the nunly Countess. Last year Margaret had come to beg the royal licence to her third marriage. Elizabeth had said politely: 'God send you many children.'

The bright black eyes were primly amused. 'Madame, I have told you I am done with childbearing. My marriage to Stanley will be one of the mind.' To this, Stanley showed no objection. He and Margaret were alike, cool and quiet and unfleshly. Margaret made all the decisions, still signing herself Countess of Richmond, a pretension to which she had no vestige of right. This had annoyed Edward, but Elizabeth had been amused. Let Margaret deck herself with small honours like bracelets; the title of noble blood had escaped her. Like all the Beauforts, she was merely the offshoot of old Gaunt's sinful liaison with Katherine Swynford. *She* had no enchanted heritage ... Elizabeth's thoughts rustled on, like the bird-haunted trees.

A commotion reached her. Across the parkland came shouting and the baying of dogs. Around the Queen, the circle of grooms, falconers, guards, rose to attention. Hunting was forbidden during the period of royal mourning, yet there appeared to be a chase in progress, not a quarter-league distant. Then, bursting from a covert of briars, appeared what seemed to be a bundle of rags. It leaped nimbly towards the Queen's little camp of pleasaunce. It was an old woman, running like a hare. Tatters and thorns encompassed her; her face was streaked with blood and filth. Bounding close behind her were a half-dozen sleek, snarling wolfhounds, followed more clumsily by a group of yeomen from Windsor. The woman ran on, mouth gasping in terror, hands clawing the air. She ran straight into the royal circle, throwing herself with one last lunge past the servants who tried to grasp her. She fell face down at the Queen's feet.

Like creatures of Hell, the hounds were close, eyes bloodshot, jaws gaping. Princess Elizabeth screamed. The Queen's women clutched at one another in terror, while several brave pages threw themselves forward to grapple with the rearing beasts. The yeomen raced up and, with difficulty, put the dogs on leash. Baulked, they whined and slavered over the prone woman. Elizabeth, who had not moved, said coldly: 'What is the meaning of this entertainment?'

To the woman she said: 'Get up.' As soon as the eyes in the caked disfigured face met hers, she knew recognition and this worried her. Soon, she thought, I shall be seeing acquaintances in the bole of a tree or the shape of a flower. First, Henry Tudor's smile in the lake, and now this wretched vagrant. One of the men trying to calm the hounds spoke hastily.

'Highness, forgive us. We tried to stop her. She was too fleet. She wished to see your highness. Whitefriar here—' he soothed a hound – 'nearly had her. One more moment and she would not have troubled you'.

Bloody teethmarks stained the woman's brown bare heel. Rough and indistinct, she spoke. She addressed Elizabeth directly; too old, too poor to acknowledge fear.

'Oh, lady,' she said. 'Do you remember Eltham?'

An instant engulfing wave, memory rose. No trick then, no false recollection. Eltham; the day of the joust, of John. The rolling train of festive knights and ladies. The Countess of Somerset, dozing in the litter. The Tudors, Jasper and Edmund, sweeping on to the tiltyard. The coming of York, and the Fiend, to discomfit King Henry. And the old woman (old even then!) whose skull Barnaby craved to break ... Here was certainty that memory was unimpaired, save for deeds born to be forgotten.

A royal prince, fair lady, shalt thou wed,
But trouble dire shall fall upon thine head ...

Then, she had thought the rhyme glib, and suspect. But how true it had become!

Bone of thy bone shall by a future fate
With blood of these three houses surely mate ...

But which three houses? Her mind groped. She had been saying the rhyme out loud, while the gypsy followed her with little nods and smiles.

'Lady,' she said softly, 'the first two are York and Lancaster ...

'And the third?'

The woman laughed. 'Lady,' she said with finality, 'that is for you to decide.' Her deep, lined eye swivelled to rest upon the Princess Elizabeth, still trembling from her recent fright.

'*She*, lady.'

'My daughter? What of her?'

In the eyes there were traces of tears that might have been seen in the gold-framed eyes of ancient Egypt; the tears of dead kings doomed by their enemies to be unremembered.

'She will be Queen of England. God have mercy.'

It is favourable, Elizabeth thought joyfully, disregarding the last strange phrase. My destiny comes to the full. Bess will be a Queen and twenty bishops shall bow to the crowning of a Woodville. And yet – Queen of England? What of Ned, who even now rides to London in Anthony's care? To be crowned king, to be ruled by our Council for years until the name of Woodville is as rooted as Plantagenet ... How can Bess supersede her brother, or his brother, Richard of York? She felt the skin stretch tight over her face.

'Then this means, dame–' she addressed the gypsy courteously but each word slid like ice – 'that my sons will never rule England?'

The woman inclined her head.

'They will ... die young?'

'They will.'

She felt her own senses rejecting the answer almost before it was out. She saw also that the dogs had done more mischief than was earlier evident; blood ran down the woman's legs. The sight of it stole away some magic; this, then, was no seer. Only a wretch who lived on her wits. London, England, abounded with false prophets. Yet she leaned forward again, and said: 'Tell me ...'

Then Whitefriar, the largest hound, slipped his chain from the inattentive hand of a groom and sprang. The stench of blood led him to his duty. He was trained for the throat, and all was quickly over. One stifled shriek, a flurry of torn clothing, brown flesh bursting into red, and silence. Elizabeth sat frozen for a moment, watching Whitefriar whipped and chivvied into subservience, then fondled, then cuffed again by men uncertain of the Queen's humour. Then she rose, carefully pulling her gown away from the woman's body where it lay. I might have kept her to be my soothsayer, she thought, then, looking down: foolishness. How could this mangled bone-bag have had the gift of sight? She saw that the Princess was milk-faced and shuddering; this annoyed her. She moved swiftly to her daughter's side and pinched her wrist, hard.

'Be still,' she commanded. 'Are you some half-wit, to snivel at death?' To herself she added: when I was seventeen no sight disturbed me! She listened impatiently to the girl's stammering reply.

'It was her words, Madame ... she said ... she said ... Madame, I do not want to be Queen of England! I would liefer marry for love!'

'Jesu, God!' cried Elizabeth. She could have boxed Bess's ears. Resisting the temptation she turned with an imperious look to the assembled company and said:

'We have tarried long enough here. We shall return to our Palace of Westminster.'

'Mistress Grace!' Rough hands, rough voice, roused her from sleep. The flickering gold of a cresset pried through her darkness. She moaned with fatigue and sat up in bed. In the communal chamber, the other women were awakening too. Renée's cross voice said: 'What is it?' Grace, suddenly wide awake, peered into the face of a guard.

'Mistress. Rouse the Queen.'

He turned away as she fumbled for her clothing, her body like lead from the exhaustion born of the last few days. The Queen's tense mood had sapped vitality from all the women. It seemed only five minutes since Grace had taken the last cup of cordial into the royal chamber, returning to fall into deepest sleep.

'What time is it?'

'Just on midnight. Hurry, mistress.'

She shivered, wrapping a robe about her, and thought: Today is the third of May. The day for which my Queen has waited and wished. The young king must have arrived, with his uncle Anthony. Today he will be crowned. Grace wished that they had chosen a time other than midnight to arrive. She wished also that she was not always the one to fetch and carry, to be roused because her trestle bed lay nearest the door, or was it because she was the youngest in the chamber? But she was the Queen's servant; this thought renewed her.

'You may turn round, Master Jack,' she said to the guard. 'What is the message for the Queen?'

'Desperate and urgent. Bishop Morton waits outside. I have bidden him to the Queen's Council chamber. For God's love, there is no time to lose.'

Why this frenzy, if the Prince were here? She looked once more at the man's taut face and hurried through into the Queen's bed-chamber. Grace's candle illuminated the unforgettable face, deeply dreaming. As she watched, the broad white forehead creased, the lips puckered in some unknown distress. Tenderly, Grace awakened her.

'He is here,' the Queen murmured, drugged with sleep. 'Is the fighting over? John, you have come ...'

The utterance of that name bred warmth in Grace. John of Gloucester would surely be brought to London now. If they had killed his father as planned, he would be of as little account as any royal Plantagenet bastard. One who lived between dark and light, humbled one day, revered the next. She thought, with unconscious callousness: we shall be even more in sympathy; he will no doubt sorrow for his father, and I will comfort him. To the Queen she said softly: 'Bishop Morton begs audience.' Instantly alert, Elizabeth threw off the bedcovers and said sharply: 'Morton? Why?'

She slipped her feet into high wooden chopines, snatched up a black houpeland with a cowl and swathed her slenderness in its dark folds. The hood fell about her brow. She looked like a pure youth about to take holy orders. So enraptured was Grace by this sight that she fell dumb. Elizabeth's unexpected slap stung her cheek. So be it: that's a caress. I love and serve her.

'Will you speak?' said the Queen. 'Why is Morton here? Have they arrived from Ludlow? Great God! I'll see for myself!'

They passed through the room full of drowsy robing women who knelt before the Queen as she went, the black gown blowing about her swift walk. Her lips were set, her eyes as clear as if they had never closed in sleep. Grace followed a pace behind along tortuous ways stone cold with the night's chill, and entered on the breeze of powerful black into the Queen's council chamber, which was day-bright with torches, and choked with the ambience of disquiet. Several people were there; Morton dominated. He had come fast from Holborn through the night. Thomas Dorset had been roused from the bed of Jane Shore. Catherine Woodville was weeping into her sleeve. Margaret Beaufort and her husband Stanley were present, standing with Thomas Rotherham, Archbishop of York. Yet the Queen addressed Morton alone.

'What news, your Grace?'

Before, the Bishop could reply, Dorset ran forward, sank on his knee before his mother. He was almost in tears.

'The worst possible news, Madame. The Protector ...'

'Who?' The Queen's voice was outraged.

'Gloucester. He intercepted Anthony upon the road. The ambush failed, and he's read your letters, even the one bidding his death. He has taken Edward, our prince, and rides on London with him.'

Morton spoke, sonorously calm against Dorset's hysteria.

'Lord Anthony, your Grace, has been taken north in captivity, for acting under your orders. Likewise imprisoned is your son, Lord Richard Grey; also the Prince's companions, our allies Vaughan and Haute. It seems ...'

Dorset interrupted. '... that we are culpable of high treason!' He gave a short bark of laughter. 'In that we did disobey the King's last decree! Gloucester came riding almost from Scotland. He would never have known of our plan had not cursed Hastings sent couriers straightway to him. He would never have conquered Anthony, had not Harry Buckingham ridden to him with reinforcements.' The Queen looked at Catherine.

'Sister, come here, I pray.'

Catherine, weeping, fell upon her knees.

'Ingrate,' said the Queen softly. 'Your own husband has betrayed me. Did I marry you to Harry Buckingham so that he might use me thus? Are you my sister and cannot sway a man?'

'Your Grace,' blubbered Catherine, 'he did as he liked. And he told me he was going on pilgrimage, for our late King's soul!'

'I fear, Madame—'. Morton's voice rolled like a stroked drum – 'that we have little time. Gloucester is full of righteousness. Remember, he holds York more dear than anything else. What your Grace may have planned against his own person is a grain of sand in the desert of York's betrayal. York, to Gloucester, is God. That decree of Protectorship from Edward's dying mouth – that was no less than God's ordinance.'

'The Devil's ordinance!' she said savagely. 'That any should usurp my heritage. The Prince is mine! Mine! Ours, to be ours in might!'

Grace wondered whether the Queen might fall in a fit. Beside herself, she spilled out tantrum.

'Shall the blood of my inheritance go unrewarded? Shall all my work be unfulfilled? Who is this Gloucester, to take in charge the crown of my estate? You, my lord Morton! Why could you not prevent it?' Morton spread his hands, smiled a sorry ecclesiastical smile. 'You, Catherine, who have shared my splendour – without me you would be mouldering still at Grafton Regis! You, Thomas! Why could you not forestall this plague!'

As Dorset stammered nonsense, the door was flung open. Breathless and dishevelled, Lionel Woodville, Bishop of Salisbury, entered.

'You have heard all?' the Queen demanded.

He nodded, his heavy face flushed. 'My man rode in five minutes ago. Our brother with your son and his followers have been taken to Yorkshire. Their soldiers turned straight to Gloucester, who pardoned them for their part in the affair and sent them home. Gloucester came in mourning, with a mere six hundred men. He ordered a requiem for our late sovereign in York. On reaching Northampton he met Buckingham who informed him of the ambush. Gloucester caught our party at Stony Stratford. Another half a day and the Prince would have been here, and crowned.'

'Crowned and ours,' she said furiously. 'What does Gloucester, now?'

'He brings the Prince, but to be crowned under his Protectorship. He adheres to Edward's decree – that his Council shall govern for the child until he is grown. He has sent barrels of harness on into London so that the people may see the proof of our conspiracy.'

'The arms show our blazon!' said Dorset feverishly. 'They declare us traitors to the Crown ...'

'The people have never loved us,' trembled Catherine. 'Because we are for Lancaster.'

'My lord Bishop,' said the Queen to Morton. She spread her hands; the wide black sleeves fell in a graceful imploring gesture. 'My lord, what now?'

'Take your son,' said Morton unhesitatingly. 'Your youngest son, Richard Duke of York. Take your daughters and your women and go at once into Westminster Sanctuary.'

Grace saw the Queen's face set like an effigy, and she herself viewed the prospect of Sanctuary without relish. To her, it was a vague time of chanting monks, of cold and sparse food, a time when she, a tiny girl, cried outside the door where the Queen laboured to bring Prince Edward into the world. This prince over whom men now fought like curs with a carcass.

'We are to retreat?' said the Queen. Morton smiled. 'For the nonce, highness. It is politic to have no discussion with Gloucester or his creatures. All is far from lost. Sir Edward Woodville still anchors in the Channel, does he not?'

'Yes, with much treasure,' said Dorset, brightening.

'My daughter,' the Bishop swung round to address Grace. She had not realized he was even aware of her presence. 'My child, fetch the Duke of York. Don't alarm him. Remember he is only a little knave.'

'Madame, let me come with you into Sanctuary!' Catherine ran forward to the Queen.

Coldly she replied: 'You are a traitor and a fool, but you are still my sister. Make ready.'

'And I?' Dorset said unsteadily.

'No, you will be more useful in London. Watch Hastings, Gloucester, Buckingham. Send me all news, discreetly ...' She turned and quit the chamber so swiftly that she left her son gaping and the three Bishops drawing together grave-faced, with whispers.

Grace awakened the small prince and helped him to dress. Hand in hand they walked to the outer gate of the Palace. A rosy-pale May dawn was streaking the horizon. Scores of serving men ran across the cobbled strip which divided the Palace from the Abbey precincts. The sound of the monks' morning office came faintly; soft light waxed and waned behind the arched windows as the unseen chanters processed, each carrying a flame. Outside the activity was frenzied. Grooms and servants, each laden with a box, or a pile of richly bound books, or a sheaf of silk garments, ran like madmen towards the Sanctuary door. One man carried two brachets slung over his shoulders. Their jewelled collars flashed like swords in the dawn light. Bumping down the Palace stair came the larger chattels; fardels crammed with gold plate, coffers so full of jewels that the lids were bursting open. A gold chain slithered like a serpent on to the cobbles. One man ran with a vast bundle of cloth-of-gold on his head; six others struggled with a carved table of Spanish chestnut.

The Queen's gold-framed mirror, Turkish carpets, rainbow-coloured and rolled like battering-rams, were borne into the Sanctuary. In went the Queen's prie-dieu, studded with sapphires and diamonds, and two Flemish paintings of the late King. An enormous oak dresser with handles of beaten gold defeated the men. Cursing, they tried all ways to introduce it, finding the arched doorway too narrow. One of the dresser drawers slid open, revealing the flash of diadems, golden wands, necklets, all clumsily, hastily packed.

'It's too big, your Grace!' one man cried.

As if she were commanding a battle, Elizabeth pointed eastward to where the abbey wall was fragmented by arched windows.

'There!' she cried. 'Where it is weakest. Get hammers. Breach the wall!'

Abbot Milling, who had been drawn out into the courtyard by the commotion, looked as if he were about to swoon. 'Madame,' he said diffidently, 'is there no other way?'

'My lord Abbot,' said the Queen, without looking at him, 'I trust you have not forgotten my bequests to your house.' He bowed, and was silent, looking unhappy.

She watched as the last of the movables was rushed from the palace. The Siege of Jerusalem, under whose fabulous weight staggered fifty men. Grace saw the Queen's face – fear and satisfaction and determination all mingling there, and heard the quiet voice say:

'Yes, yes! Break down the wall. They shall not rob me a second time!'

She turned and smiled at Grace, and the dawn rose clear and bright.

'Scream,' Morton ordered. 'When they come, scream and cry.'

Haggardly she looked at him. This ageing prelate, so calm and bland, had in him something of the dead Jacquetta and it gave her confidence. Morton was solid, unlike the vacillating Rotherham, Archbishop of York. How glad she had been to receive, in Sanctuary, the Great Seal from Rotherham's hands. How furious when, panicking, he had demanded it back not twenty hours later. When she had asked his reasons he had said, with a fatuous smile: 'The Lord Protector wishes it.'

Only dignity had held her hand from striking him. Dignity and the knowledge that his behaviour was only to be expected. The Bishops, those fearfilled, conscientious old men, lusted for favour, no matter from what source. Gloucester was supreme in Westminster; therefore it was politic for them to work his will. Not so Morton; he remained her close ally, rich with the wisdom of his years and his skill at being where the grass grew greenest. Although she disliked his appearance; those hard agate eyes among folds of flesh, the forked beard above the dewlapped jowl.

'Madame, hear me,' he repeated. 'When they come to take your youngest son, weep loudly. And let down your hair.'

'My hair?'

'It adds a certain pathos.' he said seriously. 'The brothers in this place go about ... it would be favourable if you were seen to be – persecuted.'

There was no need to question him. Only one question.

'How does my son, the Prince Edward?'

'Fit as a cock,' he answered. 'They plan to crown him on the Nativity of St. John. He is in the royal apartments at the Tower, playing at sovereignty. I wish, though, that we could have kept the little one with us. However ...' he sighed. 'Gloucester vows it is a stain upon his Parliament ...'

'*His* Parliament!' Rage erupted through her.

'Indeed, highness. Unfortunately his claim to the Protectorship is good. As I say, he avers it debases his Council that the king-elect's brother should be absent from the coronation. Like yourself, my lady. He would dearly have you present.'

'I shall not leave Sanctuary,' she said, through her teeth.

Morton looked about, at the stones where damp trickled, at the cracked panes through which a breeze cavorted, and pursed his lips.

'As you will. You are wise. Never fear. The day will come when you dance again in Westminster Great Hall. For now, let them have young Dick. But scream, claw him to your bosom. Let them tear him bodily away.'

'Is Gloucester's wife with him?' she said suddenly.

'She is to join him soon. At present she is ailing, at home in the north. Like their son, Edward, she is frail and sickly ...'

She found herself averse to hearing more about the Fiend's daughter, and shut off her mind to Morton's talk. When next she gave him her attention he was saying:

'Your son the Prince has a will of his own. It is his doing as well as the Parliament's that the other boy joins him.'

'Yet he is not strong enough to defy the Protector,' she said bitterly.

'Or Buckingham; for Buckingham is the spokesman always in this affair,' said Morton. At that unfortunate moment Catherine chose to appear, and the Queen turned on her.

'You hear that? Have you naught to say? Your husband, ranged against our blood!'

Placatingly Catherine held out a sealed roll.

'A letter, Madame.'

Elizabeth broke the seal quickly, cried: 'From Anthony!' She read avidly, laughed, raised feverish eyes. 'Clever,' she murmured. 'He bribed the guard at Pontefract to let this bill through. He says he is safe and well. Our adherents are everywhere. Thomas has already bidden him good cheer by letter. Hastings is the key. The weak link in the chain. Hastings blows where he lists and has not yet chosen his allegiance.' She looked up, scornfully. 'Yes! for years I watched him, wantoning with the King in evil company. Now, for all his love of the Protector, he finds old ties, of lust, of drinking, to be slender things ... he would join us, if he dared.'

Avidly she looked at Morton. 'Is there salvation, my lord?'

He bowed. 'I have examined the situation, highness. With your brother and Sir Richard Grey still in captivity, I admit the cause has its limitations. But as your brother Sir Anthony reveals, your friends are legion, waiting to support you. Let us consider. Gloucester comes to uphold the Crown, the focus of his battle-cry and *credo*. He burns with his late brother's ordinance. You and your kin, Madame, are disliked by the old nobility. Forgive me, but it is so. Factions are bound to arise over the ruling of a child king. Gloucester feels therefore compelled to form a strong Council to uphold what he deems the right. The old nobility are with him. But you, Madame, have a subtler strength. All the families of Lancaster who strive, quietly, in the shadow of your power. Your power, soon to be restored.'

He went on: 'Let us count your allies: Rotherham; he grew frightened, but he is still yours. Salisbury, yours by blood. Lord Stanley ...'

She frowned. Stanley was another gall-bitter disappointment. Lately she had learned that he, Margaret Beaufort's husband, cherished the Protector, and sat on his Council. But Morton murmured: 'do not fear. Stanley can feign love for the most suspicious heart. He pays lip service to the new order, but he dreams of your inevitable majesty.'

As he spoke, the Bishop moved towards the window, seeing white seabirds wheeling beyond the high cracked panes. Where? Across the North Sea perchance, to France, to Brittany? Where the true saviour waited. The one who, without doubt, would value Morton as he deserved. The one in whose service he could rise to magnificence and terrible power. The only one; the master chosen long ago. He kept his back daringly turned on the Queen, while excitement boiled within him. I am an old man, he thought, but I must not die until our hopes are fruited. Until Henry Tudor reigns in England. Meanwhile I must cherish this foolish woman. By my own hand must I move these pawns of state. He turned back slowly, saying:.

'It is better that I do not visit you again here, my liege. All our plans are *en train*. Dorset will suborn Hastings. You know, Madame, where Mistress Shore is now?'

Startled, she said: 'Shore? What has a cackling harlot to do with our plight?'

'She is with your son, Dorset, hidden deep in London. He is teaching her – how to render an ageing lecher witless. Surely, Madame, you have not forgotten Adam's Fall?'

There was knocking, faintly heard, upon the postern door of the Sanctuary. The voice of Abbot Milling echoed in the passage outside.

'I fancy this is Cardinal Bourchier,' said Morton. 'Make ready your son, Madame.'

He was poised to leave, unseen, through the intricacies of cloister and watergate. She said quickly: 'You have given me comfort, my lord. But what of Gloucester?'

'Gloucester will be murdered, as planned previously,' said the Bishop, half-way through the door. 'They come, Madame. Let down your hair.'

The night sounds of Southwark rose and filtered through the upper window of the inn room. From the street where hanging gables and a hot white moon made patterns on the ground, came a snatch of a drunken song. A dog howled gruesomely for minutes on end until quenched by a blow or a caress. Running feet and the jangle of steel told of the night watch pursuing a miscreant. Someone threw a metal canikin from a window and a woman yelled shrewishly. Further down the street someone else was noisily sick.

In the inn's best bed, Jane Shore lay watching the cockroaches. Two were parallel, neck-and-neck, and Jane curled her toes under the coarse sheet, willing the one she had christened Dorset to win. It was through Dorset she was here at all. For him she had temporarily abandoned luxury and lay in this miserable abode of illicit love with the late King's Lord Chamberlain. She turned her head on the pillow and looked at him. Hastings was fast asleep, breath bubbling gently. He looked younger in the moonlight; the greyish stubble on his chin looked almost fair. Jane sighed gently, and glanced back at the roaches. The smaller one had spurted ahead and Dorset was at least an inch behind. This was dull sport. She thought tenderly of her last meeting with Tom Dorset when he had promised her the world. She decided, when this tiresome half-understood affair was over, that she would ask him to take her to the horseraces at Smithfield. Hastings would not take her anywhere – he would not even lie with her in the Palace. 'Too dangerous, my heart.' Too old, too dull. The satisfaction of raising him to a pitch of undreamed-of ecstasy had soon palled for Jane, but this she kept to her practised professional self. Dorset had bidden her, and she would obey to the letter. Dorset was her sky and stars, her daily bread, her master. And her work was nearly at an end.

Day after day, robed in a nun's habit, she had gone meekly through the cloister of Westminster Sanctuary, past the grim grey arch with its vine-leaf capitals, walking like a penitent yet wanting to scream with laughter. In her sleeve she usually carried a packet, writings of instruction, warning, information. Once inside with the Queen, she could throw off the seemly hood, smile brightly into the tense white face, and take wine. Often there would be a present for her, a small gold nouche for her bosom, trinkets insignificant enough to be worn unnoticed. When it was time to return and wait for Hastings at the inn, she had to commit to memory a message. The Queen would never touch pen to paper in this enterprise. So Jane would take her measured murmuring way from the sanctuary like the holiest nun treading out a psalm. Half the messages meant nothing to her; that was why she needed to repeat them over and over. Some were mere fragments.

Tell him – Stanley is with us now in spirit.

The Bishop approves.

Sometimes the Queen's face was terrible. Jane had always been afraid of her, and muttered the messages more fervently in consequence.

We shall be victorious. This latest blight is doomed.

There was mention of the Queen's relatives; sweet Tom's uncle and brother.

Anthony is full-fettled. He awaits your men to help his escape.

Sir Richard Grey has his captor's ear. They will drop the bridge at your captains' signal. Pray reply soon.

Bishop Rotherham is mine again.

This last made Jane chuckle. It was a succession of riddles; yet the Queen had never shown more tolerance of Jane. No raised voices, no wounding waspish chiding of Jane's noisiness. Today, after the weeks of trudging back and forth, the lesson had been easy; it made sense.

Tomorrow, Friday 13th June. Stand ready. Kill Gloucester and Buckingham. Bring out my sons from the Tower and meet with me at Westminster.

She slid cautiously from the bed and crept across the moon-dappled floor to drink wine from a pitcher. King Edward had taught her to drink. Burgundy wine like rubies; the fiery cornelian of good Clary; sack possets heavy with curdled cream, mace and nutmeg. The breath-taking hypocras, burning with aqua vitae and pepper. Last November they had toasted La Mas-Ubel, patron of seeds and fruits, in a great bowl of strong ale in which six roasted apples swam in raw sugar and ginger. They had taken it piping hot and later Edward had tumbled her on the floor of the chamber. A florid, laughing giant, ogreish with fat. She had never loved him, but she had liked him and she missed him sorely. Were it not for Dorset, her life's light, she would be quite alone. The Palace was shrouded in mourning and preparation for the young King's coronation; all was lawyers' talk, work, no gaiety. The most commanding voice was that of Buckingham, so haughty that he had dissolved Jane in tears. Gloucester seemed not to notice her at all. But between the two of them they ruled Westminster, and the happy drinking days were fled.

She stole back to bed, her long, sweat-damp hair stranded over her naked body. Hastings was awake and watching her.

'My Jane,' he said, sleepily reproachful. 'Why did you leave me?'

She wound her arms about him, feeling the slack, old man's flesh, suffering the rasp of his beard on her breast. 'Sleep, my lord. You were so peaceful.'

'No, I had a dream–,' he said uneasily. 'An awful vision.'

She crooned to him. 'Dreams are airy stuff, the work of devils trying to frighten bliss. Sleep, lord.'

'Then stay close, Jane.' He stroked her shoulder with a thin veined hand. 'Holy Jesu! Never did I think these times would come ...'

'You and I together, dear lord?' she said artfully. He was so often tongue-tied with her; she had to shape the words for him.

'Nay ... yea! Truly, Jane, I never thought I should have you – I watched you with Ned – I longed, imagined. I turned from my good wife, Kate. I behaved like a heretic and would not lie with her. You've bewitched me, Jane. Or someone has,' he said in a quieter voice.

Tomorrow, his thoughts ran. Tomorrow, tomorrow, like the tick of a clock, or the frantic riding of an army.

Tomorrow I shall engineer the killing of one who was dear to me, to a man I loved. One who himself loved me well, who rode with me against Lancaster, when he was a sickly stripling youth. Gloucester, who took my hand, not two moons ago – Jesu! who took my hand *today*! – saying: 'Thank God for you, Will Hastings. Thank God for you, in these times of strife and madness.' Tomorrow Gloucester's blood will stain this loving clasping hand. And Elizabeth, upon whose coming I once looked with spleen and disapproval, shall be again supreme. Elizabeth, who put down venom like a ratcatcher throughout the court. Elizabeth, whose policies are loathed by me. She who broke her sovereign's heart with Desmond's death, and used her brother like the most skilled provocateur to bring wretched Clarence to a bubbling end. Elizabeth, who split the soul of Warwick until he knew neither day from night, nor friend from foe. Elizabeth, whose messages. I meekly bear, whose will I wreak! Cloudily her face swam before his mind; the lazy-lidded eyes, the tight red mouth. Woodville and Lancaster wench, you never warmed my lust. Yet to Edward, you were Bathsheba, Salome ...'

He turned closer to Jane, burying his tired slack flesh against her, weary, cold of conscience. She murmured, 'Yes, my lord,' and, 'There, my lord!' while the inn's lath-and-plaster quaked with the quarrels and lovemaking of others, and they lay tightly within it, part of a corporate squalidity.

He slept and dreamed anew. He awoke shouting, beating the bed-covers. From sheer terror, Jane swore at him, using the coarse expressions of her early life in Chepeside. Sticky with sweat he clung to her, the pupils of his eyes distended and black in the moonlight.

'Holy God!' he gasped. 'First, a boar – Gloucester's Boar, a device of unsurpassed might. But worse! Christ protect me! It came out of the sea ...'

His hands hurt her; she listened. 'Monstrous, shining like harness, plated with gleaming scales. It took me about the neck, each scale like a barber's knife. Jane! Jane ...'

Tomorrow is cursed. Friday, the thirteenth of June. I have schemed against the Protectorship. Will the Queen save me now? Or Morton, or Stanley? Or Rotherham? Or Anthony Woodville, Richard Grey, and the others who like myself are embroiled blood-deep in this treason? All these weeks I have been blinded and by what? For what? For the love of a foul-mouthed whore whom my great family would not have used in their kitchens ... He turned upon Jane, but she had left his side.

'Be comforted, sweet Will,' she cried, anxious to amend the oaths she had hurled at him. Look!' She began to writhe and cavort in the moonlight, as the King had loved her to do. 'Look! I'll dance for you!'

She danced, and another danced with her, a shadow whose hair was long and streamed like fern, whose hips and thighs undulated, whose whole outline bore an unearthliness beyond thought. Fresh sweat gushed on Hastings's brow. He rose, clumsy with fright, tangling his feet in the bedclothes and falling on the filthy boards. He scrambled and groped; broken with panic he found his clothes at last. The fine velvet doublet and the shirt in fair Rennes cloth, the plumed bonnet with the pendent diamond, the hose, the piked brocade shoes. Jane became still. Her full face regarded him quizzically. The King had had these strange humours too, leaping up in dead of night to leave her; these hauntings which she did not try to understand.

'I must go back to Westminster,' he muttered, fumbling to fasten his cloak, and making for the door.

'You will have to cross the river,' said Jane. 'And no boatman will bear you at this hour.'

His face livid, he wheeled once more to face her, made an inarticulate noise and plunged through the doorway. After a moment Jane crawled back into bed. Light-headed, lightminded and calm as ever, her last thought before sleeping was that tomorrow all would be well. No more of this fleahouse. No more coaxing of an old man's stubborn pizzle. The Palace again, and sweet Thomas in her arms.

Anthony Woodville, Earl Rivers, sat writing at a small table. Meticulously he shaped his work, giving to each initial letter a thick downstroke and to the tails a delicate grace so that they hung like cats on a wall. Sunlight pooled on his bent head and touched sparks from the jewel on his hand as it moved elegantly across the parchment. He looked up, and, half-blinded by radiance, saw, through stout bars, the surging green world outside. The bailey of Pontefract Castle lay below his window; by craning a little he could see, beyond the wall, the wild north country rioting in summer. Things too distant for his eye he imagined: the dales, green upon green, tracts of mighty oak, fells assaulted by torrents of white water. From far away came the sound of a hunting horn. He bent again to his work. Scholar, aesthete, courtier, Earl and Duke, he wrote; and so doing, saw visions.

> I fear, doubtless
> Remediless
> Is now to seize
> My woeful chance.
> For unkindness
> Withoutenless
> And no redress
> Me doth advance.

'Advance!' he said softly, and laid the quill aside. The horn became a trumpet, with acid, flaunting bray. His sister sat before him. Every detail of her burned his sight with its impeccable loveliness. Her high crown had rich closed arches, each point diademed with a fleur-de-lys. Suncoloured brocade clothed her; striped and slashed with the royal pattern, her sleeves were gold and blue, the rich dark azure of the Garter. Broad strips of ermine crossed her bodice to fall in rouleaux over her shoulders. More ermine bloomed on the hem of her gown and ran like the tail of a beast along the immensities of the train, a fold of which she held looped over her wrist. Her hair was loose and she was smiling, a little smile directed at the points of her tiny shoes. He knelt. He stretched out both hands, and laughed as she did, a sound of ecstasy and triumph. 'Queen! Queen of England and of France!' said Anthony and bent his head, his bedizened bonnet held in courtly fashion in one hand swept out behind him. A wind blew about him; a perfumed tempest emanating from a dozen costly gowns; a hectic breeze of laughter. All his sisters and other ladies of the court surrounded him – fair as flowers – their shining heads auburn and black and gold. With their chattering mirth they engulfed him. He felt a soft fumbling about his thigh, looked down and saw a gold token clasped there; a priceless garter ingrained with sapphires. From its centre hung an enamel flower of rosemary; the whole garter was fashioned in the double 'S', the one-time device of Lancaster.

Elizabeth said softly: '*Souvenance*, my dear lord. A token of my remembrance and of yours.'

One of the ladies roguishly said: 'Sir! Look in your hat!' and he felt inside its velvet rim, and drew out a letter bound with gold thread, bearing the same emprise of remembrance, with a jewel for a seal.

The Queen bent forward. 'The articles of combat, sir. You shall do me honour in the tourney.'

'My adversary?' he said.

'De la Roche.' Her eyes gleamed, flickering a pattern of joy across the vibrant air. The look caught him up and spun him round. De la Roche was grounded already, brought grunting to the turf by one lance-thrust. To your great honour, Madame!

'*Souvenance*,' she said again. 'Remember me.' Her eyes were bright, too bright to gaze on longer, and he wrote again, steadily.

> With displeasure
> To my grievance
> And no surance
> Of remedy.
> Lo, in this trance,
> Now, in substance ...

The vision changed. A pale girl leaned dangerously far from a window above him. Tears lined her cheeks. Beneath his body he felt his horse curvet and plunge. Be careful! he wanted to cry. It is a long way down! Her lips moved, but he could hardly hear her. Take me away. Take me with you! He shivered, shook his head, saw his own bony boyish wrists straining at the taut bridle.

'No.' He turned from her. 'Make the best of it.'

'I will repay you,' she wailed. 'If it's the last thing I do in life!'

Nay, Bess. I am today repaid. He took up the pen afresh. That was the only time, Madame, that I did not your will. The rest of my days have been yours, inspired by you; your wit, your will was mine.

> Lo, in this trance,
> Now in substance,
> Such is my dance,
> Willing to die.

He had jousted with De la Roche. He had fought him with broadsword, lance and axe, horsed and on foot. The loges all around were crammed with screaming exaltation. The sound of excitement drowned the blaze of the clarions and the silken throb of the great standards flying over the royal canopy. He had beaten De la Roche into the ground, then, full of delight, had made the Bastard of Burgundy eat earth; had struck a secret blow for France, and for Lancaster. For the old days of his heritage, for his parents' pride. Above all, as in all things, for *her*. He had jousted, he had sung and prayed and had travelled, in the presence of England's flower; he had visited shrines in undreamed places, had crossed the snarling bare mesetas of Spain and the cypressed plains of Italy. His translations, his tracts and verses, lay, revered as genius, in the Palace library. Dancing, jousting, learning, teaching, prayer. Such is one man's life ... along the passage outside he heard unhurried, inexorable steps. In this castle Richard of Bordeaux was done to death, secretly. Yet some said that he still lived, that he was seen twenty years after in the wilds of Scotland ... a bad place, Pontefract.

> Methinks only
> Bounden am I,
> And that greatly
> To be content.
> Seeing plainly
> Fortune doth wry

> All contrary
> From mine intent.

He murmured, as a release from the poem's terse metre:
'Fortune is a woman. She cannot be gainsaid.'

The pale face reappeared, crowned, speaking later words: 'Do my will. Help me, I am afraid. Do my will.' Aghast, he saw the slender figure falling, dropping from the window like a falcon in stoop, landing by chance rather than judgment upon his saddle. The horse bolting, going at a steaming pace through briars and brushes so that their faces, the faces of brother and sister, were torn and their eyes blinded by the wind. Elizabeth laughed, a madwoman, a spirit of air, utterly fey ... In the lock of his cell door a key turned. He wrote on, faster.

> My life was lent
> Me to one intent,
> It is nigh ... spent
> Welcome, Fortune!
> But I never went
> Thus to be shent
> But she it meant
> Such is her custom.

With careful finality he put the quill aside, and smiled. Apt as anything Lucretius wrote. Let those who read it afterwards think I chided Fortune. I, wherever I may be, shall know otherwise. There is but one 'she'. One who breaks the bread of recklessness and holds out a bitter cup. I loved her; I did her will. He rose at the entrance of Sir Richard Ratcliffe, the lawyer and constable sent by Gloucester to oversee this day's work. A chaplain was with him. Ratcliffe said: 'Are you ready, Earl Rivers?'

'I shall never be more or less so.' He smiled, and with lordly hand indicated the pile of neatly tied rolls on the table: his will, several greetings to followers, and an apology to someone wronged long ago.

'You will see to these?'

They bowed in assent and parted for his going from the cell. The barred sunlight lit the grey walls and his erect back with the same impartial joy. As they reached the courtyard he stopped and looked about. There squat and terrible, was the block, and lined up near it with a muttering priest were the Queen's son, Sir Richard Grey, and Thomas Vaughan and Dick Haute, his adherents from Ludlow. Grey and Vaughan were composed, but Haute looked as if he were about to vomit up his fear. Along the wall of the bailey a little detachment of Yorkshire infantry stood at attention. A drum crackled and throbbed. Anthony turned to Ratcliffe and said 'Then we are all to die?' The herald began his proclamation: 'In the name of Richard Duke of Gloucester, Earl of Cambridge, Constable of England, Lord Protector of the Realm ...' and Ratcliffe inclined his dignified head.

'What of the others?' said Anthony.

'I may tell you now, my lord. Lord Stanley is confined in the Tower of London, as is also Archbishop Rotherham. Bishop Morton is in the custody of the Duke of Buckingham at Brecon. William Lord Hastings is sentenced to death.'

So this was where conspiracy had led them all. They had been so confident, Buckingham and Gloucester as good as dead and the whole house of Woodville reunited in triumph. They had reckoned without Buckingham's tireless agents by whom the whole conspiracy had been smelled out. Buckingham and Gloucester had acted swiftly and ruthlessly.

The sun crept behind a cloud. 'For great treason against the Crown of England!' The herald's voice broke harshly upon the last syllable. Anthony went forward to the block. He smiled, partly to comfort Grey, Haute and Vaughan, partly because he remembered his poem.

Such is her custom

When he knelt, the white-hot sun appeared again, so that ripples of livid light, drifting, coruscating, gilded the axe. The steel fell swiftly, like the plunge of a great silvery fish.

Mistakenly she thought the worst to have befallen. When they brought the news of the utter collapse of all she had striven for, she fell into a rare swoon. Recovering to the sound of her daughters' sobbing, she stared about her, temporarily witless. The familiar chamber with its stark holiness seemed to shrink into a prison. Even the sound of Abbot Milling's monks, droning their ceaseless praise, was a salute to the Protector's power. With one sweep five of her most precious pawns were scattered from the board, lost irrecoverably. Anthony – a thought not to be borne; Richard, John's son. Vaughan and Haute were more dispensable, Hastings a mere broken tool. Dead, all dead, none the less; no more could she call upon them, mould them, direct them. And Morton, imprisoned in Buckingham's castle — that was a grievous loss, and Stanley, and Rotherham ... She sat among the rushes and held her head, while her women looked on, daring to say nothing. Summer boughs brought in for decoration lay around the hearth. In their greenness she saw the shape of demons. Nothing could be worse than this.

Now she knew. What she had termed the worst was only a rumble forecasting the holocaust. Under the stream of waking thought the fear had always remained no matter how many times she had laid it away like a worn-out gown, telling herself she was done with it. Now, into her sanctuary came that fear, nourishing and well-fanged, with the stem approval of the law behind it. Cardinal Bourchier gave it a voice. Silk-clad and hatted, he entered with his train of priests and lawyers. He unleashed a great vellum, newly sealed, and read from it sombrely.

He read that news had been disclosed to the Council that Edwardus Quartus, late monarch of the realm, did take unlawfully in marriage one Elizabeth Grey, he being already trothplight and married to another, Dame Eleanor Butler, daughter of the old Earl of Shrewsbury. The Cardinal's voice faded, was replaced by Edward's, hoarse and bemused as he rolled on the bed, his brain glittering with herbs of madness. *I am married already.*

'... that they did live together therefore sinfully and damnably in adultery ...'

Eleanor is with the nuns. She will die soon. Bessy, my fate!

Nineteen years of suffering Edward's demands, his boisterousness, his infidelities. Of bearing and burying his children. Of always feeling alone.

'... and that we, the Lords Spiritual and Temporal declare that as the said King stood trothplight and married to another, his said pretended marriage with Elizabeth Grey is null ... that all their issue have been bastards, and unable to inherit or claim anything by inheritance, according to the law and custom of England.'

A shrill voice interrupted; young Bess, running forward, ill-mannered through desperation.

'Eminence! Am I no longer a princess?'

He looked at her severely, yet indulgently, and his voice was quite gentle.

'Madame, you are the Lady Elizabeth Plantagenet, bastard daughter of King Edward.' He then cleared his throat to resume reading from the membrane. A pain gripping her breast, Elizabeth said, before he could continue:

'By whose ordinance is this document signed and sealed? And by whose information are these things said?' She felt her head and face grow hot; the feeling frightened her. She repeated, more quietly: 'Is there proof?'

The Cardinal lowered his roll. 'Madame, the Lords Spiritual and Temporal ordain this statute in accordance with the Three Estates of the realm. It is the most important document of this century. As for the source, there are many witnesses, the most prominent being Bishop Stillington. It was he who performed the marriage ceremony between his Grace and Dame Eleanor Butler.'

Stillington. She wanted to scream and swear. Stillington, whom she had thought dead by now and no danger. Years ago she had instructed Bishop Alcock to keep a close eye on Stillington. The pain in her breast grew stronger, frightening her even more. Death was brought by humours such as these.

'There is more, Madame,' continued Bourchier rather ominously. Without looking at the parchment he said: 'God help you, for there is much talk of sorcery.' To a man, the priests and lawyers crossed themselves. 'That you and the late Duchess of Bedford did ...'

Elizabeth closed her eyes, turned her head sharply to the left, a gesture which silenced the cardinal. The pain receded, leaving a dullness as if a stone lodged in her breast. She counted those who had known about the Duchess's secret campaign. The clerk, Daunger – he was dead. The Sewardsley nuns – they had told Bray. Margaret Beaufort! Yes, so I have lost her too, she thought numbly. She has betrayed me and upholds Gloucester. For the first time she thought of Gloucester not as an obstacle to be slain or thwarted, but as a vastly under-estimated enemy. Worse than the Fiend, more dangerous than babbling, power-crazy Clarence. If she looked through the window over the Abbot's little flower garden she could see Gloucester's fleet anchored in the Thames. He was leaving no hazard open. She had never chosen to know him, but it seemed that he knew her well. Bourchier said: 'Dame Grey. Are you sick, Dame Grey?'

She did not answer. The pain returned, spread from breast to throat to head, gripping with vicious jaw. This was the worst. Worse than any outrage of the Fiend's. Warwick had stripped her only of Bradgate and that had been regained. He had taken only her tapestries, her lands. But Gloucester, who had wept at Warwick's corpse-side, now stripped her of her sovereignty. Dame Grey. Dame Grey. No more Elizabeth, Queen of England. Her head began to shake, as if an unseen hand moved it.

Cardinal Bourchier was alarmed at her appearance. As if by alchemy the contours of her face sank and flattened, the taut jaw dropped. Her colour changed from livid white to fiery red then back to startling pallor. While her mind spun on like a leaf in a vortex. *I am Queen no longer.* Nineteen years for naught. My princes are mere bastards and my princess likewise. No throne now for my son Edward, whom I laboured to bring forth in this same comfortless Sanctuary. She heard herself saying, in a queer rasping voice:

'May I ask who will be King of England now?'

'I am instructed to deliver a copy of this Act,' he said, 'It sets out the Titulus Regius – the Council's findings and decision as to the crowning of our sovereign. It is Parliament's decree to the title of King.'

Her fingers could not grasp the parchment. It slipped down, curling, to lie at her feet like the open horn of a trumpet. Even then, the half-hidden words, plain and black, leaped to her eyes.

'So Gloucester will be King!'

She could not hear how her own wail echoed in the embossed vaultings above, and drifted, lonely, through the open window to where the river lapped and fretted. There was an overpowering drumming in her ears. *Queens can be brought down.* How many had said it, and how often? The Fiend had returned in glory, to mock and cheat her and persecute her. His weapon was the Act of Titulus Regius, defying her own enchanted blood.

Grace Plantagenet stood outside the gate of the Sanctuary. A hard summer shower was falling, taking the starch from her spiked hennin and veil, and staining her gown. One or two monks passed in and out of the postern. Weary, disapproving of the constant upheaval about their demesne, they ignored her, going swiftly by with sandal-slap and the reek of incense and dirt from their habits. She tried to catch the attention of one; he looked sourly at her, muttered a benediction or a curse and went in, slamming the wicket behind him. To Grace's left was the wall with its great raped hole, sketchily shored up with timber. The hole was spacious enough to admit slim Grace, but to what? Only a reprise of a painful scene, perhaps added fury, doubled unkindness. Even now that sudden assault beat at her brain, the more shocking for its very unexpectedness.

She had been working on a tapestry of St. Simon and St. Jude, with her ear and eye alert for any movement or request, her heart beating in time with Elizabeth's tumultuous heart. Elizabeth had raised her head, had studied Grace for several minutes. Then she had spoken, with quiet, savage anger.

'You!'

Grace had risen, eagerly, pushing the tapestry frame away

'Go. Get you from this place, and out of my sight. Do not return'.

The red eyes, the whiteness, had moved Grace to murmur: 'Madame, you are ill. I pray you ...' and to receive the whiplash answer: 'I am not ill. I am invincible. Get out of this house!'

Then Elizabeth had risen, had said loudly to her cowering attendants: 'I dismiss, this day, a bastard. I am done with Plantagenet bastards!' To Grace she said in a low fury: 'You bring me ill luck! Jesu! I should have seen it before.'

Young Bess had spoken up bravely. 'Madam my mother, do not turn away my father's child, my sister by blood!' and Elizabeth had silenced her. 'Ah, God! Edward could sire only bastards. Be still, for you know naught of it!'

Grace had gone, assuming a high dignity she did not feel, out through the grey arch and to the fringe of the frightening outer world. To the edge of a city thronged by turmoil where speculation roared like a milling sea. Taverns were thick with secrets; even the carved gables seemed to take on life, murmurously quivering with various allegiance. Loyalty to Gloucester, to Buckingham; to Tom Dorset, exiled in France; to Sir Edward Woodville, whose spy-ships ran free in the channel; to Lionel Woodville, who had retired to his estates, perhaps to pray; to Morton, silent in the fastness of Buckingham's Welsh castle. And to another, whose unknown voice was a distant clarion, whose face was the gleam of a ghostly banner. In the alehouse certain men clashed tankards and whispered: 'To the Dragon!'

Grace's gown was almost soaked with rain. She moved to stand beneath a projecting buttress. Everywhere people tramped about their affairs; merchants, clerks, hurried in and out of Westminster Hall, where the court was in session. Folk in fine wool, in rags, in velvet, were clotted about the entrance to the chambers. Pedlars and cookboys pranced about, bellowing their wares; beggars whined, fiddlers scraped. A tall, ebony-faced Moor went by with a monkey on his shoulder. Westminster clock spoke like Jehovah; the world rocked. A leering gargoyle spat a mouthful of rain down upon Grace and she shivered. Occasionally through the crowd came the flash of the Watch's uniform. Grace saw herself arrested, declared a vagrant or worse and bundled into the Fleet, where Jane Shore, a branded harlot, lay by order of the Protector.

'But I'm the daughter of a king!' she said loudly. She sat down on a stone from the breached sanctuary wall and began to weep. Now, in all the ballads, a knight would appear. She looked up; there was only a band of urchins, with sly rotten-toothed smiles. One weighed a jagged stone in his hand. Another postured a bow, minced nearer. 'Lady's rich gown is wet', suggested another. The oldest, a boy about Grace's age, said softly: 'My mother lusts for a gown like that!' He had coal-black fingernails and the face of a pirate. They ringed her round, eyes bright, bare toes gripping the cobbles. She opened her mouth, sucked in air and dry panic. Behind her she felt the stone buttress, slippery with rain under her palms. The boys came closer. None of them saw the man approaching. His large purposeful feet slapped spray from the puddles, his broad face was crimson with wrath. He wore a tabard blazoned with a chained white Boar, and he was armed with knife and staff. The latter he used to good effect, laying about him, direct and sure. The clique bolted, heads clubbed bloody. A hand reached out for Grace.

'Art harmed?'

She shook her head. Holding her hand in his vast paw, he spoke to her in a dialect barely comprehensible, yet with the essence of kindness. He chided her for standing unescorted among the rowdy toils of Westminster. All the time his eyes appraised her dress, her white hands, her obvious gentleness.

'Tha' shall be taken to my lady,' he said finally.

'Who?'

'Thou. To the Lady Anne Neville, wife to my lord of Gloucester,' he said, looking down with pride at the device on his tabard. Then she understood. This was one of the Yorkshire yeomen appointed as personal guard to Gloucester's lady. Gloucester's lady! She withdrew her hand from his.

'I can't go with you.'

He looked closely at her face, murmuring how much she reminded him of someone, a sharp resemblance save for the eyes. She told him her name, and that of her father. His face became gravely decisive. He took her hand again.

'Tha' must not stand here one moment longer.' He said, in his tortuous northern speech, 'that my lord of Gloucester would be wroth at such things ... his brother's child crying in the road!' He led her down towards the river. The rain died as they entered the boat; the current rocked them as they passed the high carved merchantmen anchored at every quay, the hundred petermen drawing in nets heavy with salmon and flounder. Supple clouds moved across the river, charmed, elemental shadows changing with each ripple. All the time the Yorkshireman held Grace's hand, speaking only once, when he pointed out banners billowing damply from turret and fortress.

'They are preparing for the coronation. London is ready. Soon, my lord of Gloucester will be King.' Radiance flooded his face; Grace sat silent in the little boat.

On the steps of Baynard's Castle, home of the Plantagenets for centuries, bright-liveried guards stood like granite. Within the great hall, the walls were stiff with gay quarterings; over the fireplace banners proclaimed the heritage of Warwick together with the Griffin of Montagu, the Beauchamp Swan, and Gloucester's Boar. Grace made a muffled sound, and pulled back; the broad hand led her on.

'Come. Come to my Lady Anne.'

As they ascended the stairs she felt a mood so powerful it was as if the walls spoke. An aura of frail, transient joy – a peak of unstable pleasure that swayed the senses. So tangible was it that she lifted her eyes expecting to see, above the solar door, a motto limned in gold, something that might say: All happiness is here. Welcome. Welcome to a joy that does not last!

Outside the rain had ceased completely; the solar which they entered ran with fluid brightness streaming through the diamond panes. Anne Neville sat playing chess at a centre table. She raised her face; it was almost the face of a severely ill child; smooth and veined at the temples and completely guileless as if the sins and strategies of the world were without moment; as if the world itself were too fleeting for anything but tranquillities. As she saw Grace, and as the Yorkshireman began his cumbrous explanation, she smiled very sweetly. She held an ivory man posed over the board; her partner was oblivious to all, pondering his play. All that was visible of him was a slender green velvet back, a fall of black hair and one elegantly hosed leg stretched out to the great danger of passers-by. Anne Neville's smile grew broader; her small white teeth looked very bright between her pale lips.

'I greet you well, mistress,' she said. To Grace's escort: 'Master Walter, you did right to bring her here.' And, to her absorbed partner, 'Sir, leave the game, I beg you. Greet our guest!' The chair flew back and he rose, smiling an apology, turned fully so that Grace saw him dark against the sun. The rippling brightness obscured his features; for a moment she was unsure. Then he took a step towards her.

'Madame,' he said hesitantly. 'Why, Madame ... Grace! Have you forgotten me?'

'John,' she said softly. 'Lord John of Gloucester.'

He came closer, taking her cold damp hand to his warm lips.

'This is good fortune!' he said gaily, and looked down at her. She was confused. The last time they had met, he seemed such a little boy, a gallant little boy. As she did not speak he continued: 'I fear you *had* forgotten me!'

'You've changed. You are taller, bigger – grander!'

'It is the archery,' he answered proudly. 'It stretches a man,' and behind them Lady Anne said, laughing: 'Then, John my love, you should be a giant, by reason of practising night and day!'

'It is my father's wish that I excel in arms,' he said gravely. 'Not only the longbow, but the axe ...'

'Yes, yes,' said Anne, with an amused shudder. 'No more talk of weapons for a while. Embrace your cousin, like a courtier!'

Gravely he bent his head. His lips brushed Grace's mouth. From a bowl of white roses on the table he plucked a bloom and placed it in her hand.

'Madame, my honour and duty,' he said. Anne Neville clapped her hands.

'Perfect, John. Now, mistress, come and greet me. I have not seen you since ...' Her smile faded at some turbulent memory. 'You were very young. You would not remember.'

Grace sank low before the Duchess Anne. Fingers touched her

shoulder and her bent head. Anne cried: 'Why, child, you're wet and cold. John, send for Lady Lovell. Fresh clothes, at once!' She kissed Grace on the brow. Thoughts in chaos, Grace told herself: today, misery and banishment bring me again to John, my dear friend. And I am kissed by Warwick's daughter ... The feeling of disloyalty to Elizabeth gave her great unease, and she turned to look again at John. He was not really changed, only so much taller and broader. His cheeks, tanned by the northern wind, were leaner. He was fashionably dressed in the new tunic with slashed sleeves and a short swirling jacket trimmed with marten. On his fingers he wore several rings, and he was very self-assured. When he had left the room, Anne said: 'He is the image of his father, and my constant companion, my dear foster son. It is a compensation for lacking my own son, Edward, in London.' Her face grey heavy as she spoke.

'I don't like London,' (as if to herself). 'I have been ill, and the journey wearied me. I am often ill, you know. Edward, my little prince, also. Richard is the strong one. He will soon be crowned, and then perhaps we can see Yorkshire again.'

She asked Grace: 'How is Dame Grey?'

Grace looked deeply into the bowl of flowers. In their close snowy shape there was pain. 'She is sick with wrath and despair. You must know this already.'

'Will she attend my husband's coronation?' said Anne quietly. Grace shook her head.

'Will you, mistress?'

'I cannot.' Grace looked directly at Gloucester's lady. 'Any more than can Dame Elizabeth. How could she, madame?' She heard the high thread of her own voice, saying: 'Her heirs have been dispossessed. The crown passes from little Edward to your husband. She is robbed of everything, through Gloucester's will ...' Tears burned her eyes; she stopped abruptly.

'No,' said Anne Neville, after a long time. 'Do you not know, silly child, who brought this day about? None other than Edward Plantagenet, who through his folly cast his whole dynasty into chance and sin? Do you think my husband coveted the crown? In the north, we had our own kingdom. But the Council decreed Richard heir; there was none other, now that the boys are bastard. Even Clarence's son is attainted by way of his father's treason ...' She coughed dryly. 'I will speak of it no further. I am weary of policy, threats, rantings.

I only know that Richard will rule England. I have known him all my life; he will endeavour to do well.'

Her mind sped through the past to Middleham where there was peace and breezes like wine, and the small son who was the light and the beginning of the world; and further back to the time when she, a sixteen-year-old maid, was sold in marriage to the French Queen's son. When he died at Tewkesbury, a virgin knight, I was glad, she thought. Otherwise I would not have known marriage to my sweet, troubled lord, or a return to my home in the blessed North. A further bout of coughing paralysed her momentarily and she was frightened. London! this plagued, unhappy domain; it afflicts my breast. She got up and to ease herself, walked about the room. Melancholy shortened her tone.

'I am sorry that I see you cannot love your new sovereign, or me. I had hoped mistress, that you would stay with us. Any child of Edward Plantagenet is welcome in my lord's house'

Grace watched her. She was so thin; her wrists were tiny, brittle as twigs; her waist a mere wisp of flesh. Her face was like a tragic child's.

'I'll stay, your highness,' said Grace. 'But in fairness, it is because I have nowhere else to go.'

Suddenly the door opened and, to Grace's wonder, Margaret Beaufort entered. She was richly gowned, and carried her breviary like some diligent, knowing, female priest. The sight of Grace, standing now hand in hand with Lady Anne, caused the Countess's mouth to fall agape; only for a moment. She clamped her jaw and bustled forward.

'Well met, mistress,' she said perfunctorily. 'I heard you were with Dame Grey – but you are not. No matter. Greetings, Lady Anne!'

Grace watched the Countess kneel. Anne said softly: 'Mistress Grace Plantagenet is to remain with me for a time. How are you, Lady Margaret?'

'The happiest of women,' replied the Countess. She seized Anne's hand and bestowed on it a dry kiss. 'Today my lord of Gloucester has pardoned my husband Stanley. You, Madame, must have prevailed upon him. God bless you for it.'

'I did naught,' said Anne. 'Richard has promised a pardon to all who swear fealty to the Crown. Stanley and Rotherham have taken the oath; others will follow.'

'And I, my lady,' went on the Countess, mixing meekness and exaltation, 'am to bear your train at your coronation!'

'I know,' said Anne. Her mist-grey eyes looked at and through the Countess. Her thoughts moved fraily on. Oh, Dickon, are you wise? To pardon these traitors, to welcome, with such warmth this woman whom I distrust and dislike so heartily? Night after night, Anne had pleaded with her husband. Day after day, snatching brief moments with him between Council meetings. Grasping at conversations when she could cut through the bray of Harry Buckingham, who from the first had been determined to have Richard on the throne, or die ...

Always, Gloucester had said: 'Sweet Anne, don't trouble yourself. I have a *credo*: trust a man and he'll prove worthy. I must have men about me in this task. This yoke of kingship needs stout steeds to draw the plough. And we shall carve a straight furrow, sown with the pure line of Plantagenet, you'll see ...'

He was so anxious, so obsessed with the laws of God, with the plight of the commons. He had a revolution planned for the Statutes of England; he was bent on changing the old order and undermining the power of the barons. Already he was lauded for his dealings with lesser men. But that was in York, and York was not London. Anne shivered. Margaret's measured voice cantered smoothly on.

'I am to oversee the ladies' wardrobe... twelve hundred lengths of sarcenet, studded with the Rose, the Falcon or the Boar. The skirts must be simply cut, or the Abbey will bust asunder!'

She gave a shrill, unpractised laugh, while Grace stared sombrely at her. She was like a young girl, indecently gay.

'Speaking of gowns,' said Anne. 'John must have forgotten his errand. Go, mistress, and find Lady Lovell. Put on dry clothes, and then, a walk in the sun!'

As the door closed behind Grace, Anne sat down, suddenly exhausted. Listening to the hard cheerfulness of the Countess of Richmond, she thought: Dickon, where are you? Doubtless in Council, when you should be on the moors, or in your own northern court. Are you even now setting a hidden scowl on the barons' faces with your new audacious laws? Come to me soon, for my day is dour without you. In London, this London that I fear will be both our deaths.

Lady Lovell, after searching fruitlessly for a fitting headdress for Grace, advised: 'Leave your hair loose then, *doucette* – so!' She twined a lock, a tendril about Grace's temples and throat. 'So curly!' she murmured. Unfashionable – but it suits you, somehow.' She tugged at the hair until the girl's brow was bare and high; she added a band with a small jewel and retreated to gaze at the result. 'Dulcissima,' she said. She called to the others, old Yorkist ladies unfamiliar to Grace: 'I have made a pretty poppet! What eyes, child!' The Duchess of Norfolk remarked: 'You'll make the wench vain'; and Lady Lovell waved white, frivolous hands, crying: 'Go, child! Into the garden!' So Grace obeyed, stepping slowly so as not to disturb the jewel, and leaving the Duchess muttering, as was their custom, about the ways, the general laxity of modern youth. *They* were never allowed to go unchaperoned, they observed. enviously. But Lady Lovell, who loved to matchmake and who had already seen John of Gloucester go into the garden, silenced their censure with a laugh.

It was a small pleasaunce at the rear of the fortress, and neatly squared with rows of box, paved walks. Beds of little flowers, newly glistening from the rain, glowed like illuminations on a psalter. Blue and yellow iris thrust upward with proud languid lips. A sleek robin pecked and whistled at the flags and from a dovecote in the far corner came an amorous murmuring. Here was the joy again, the unknown, fragile happiness, voiceless yet heard, invisible yet unmistakable; the precious clue, the whisper of new worlds.

He was waiting, he had been watching her as she came. He advanced swiftly, light-footed, his hair falling to his neck like the black folded wings of a bird. She had forgotten the colour of his eyes; it had never seemed important – they were dark blue, and very bright. She had, she knew, mislaid his image altogether. Here was more man than child, and with the bearing of a knight. This made her stiff and formal. Gone were the easy confidences, gone the sympathy, for she thought: my little John is a stranger. He was composed, assured; with light courtesy he complimented her, touching her hands to his lips, and he and she began a slow promenade along the rapidly drying pavement. The robin jeered sweetly at them and flew, swift and gaudy, a little way off, to contemplate them from a rosebush. Deftly, directly, with no art or skirmishing, John's hand took hers. And instantly the old times were back; she could breathe deeply, enjoy the garden scents, be at peace. But as they reached the dovecote, his easy clasp tightened and became a pain. She felt the pressure trembling in his wrist and hers, and his fingers slick with moisture. The white birds whirred and murmured about them. He stopped suddenly.

'Ah, God!' he said. 'If only I were older!'

Surprised, she answered: 'Life's short enough, don't wish it away!' a platitude she had listened to herself, many times.

'None the less, I do,' he said. 'I am an esquire now, you know. The life is hard – look!' He flexed his jaw and turned his head so that a hairline scar showed white. 'It's dog eat dog in Hall,' he said proudly. 'But my adversary's head was addled for two days! And I unhorsed three of my fellows in the tourney. It was only a mock tourney,' he added sadly, 'And yet ... I am not old enough to defend my father!'

'Your father?' So, he was not altogether changed; his favourite topic of conversation was still the same. She felt oddly disappointed; the day was fair, she was fair, and yet he addressed her as if she were a fellow esquire, obsessed only with male chivalry.

'You know,' he said quietly, 'that they tried to assassinate him. Twice.'

She turned her head quickly away, and stared at the doves' wooden house, which was festooned with greyish droppings. The flower-scents faded, leaving the stink of wet wood, of murder.

'My grandfather was slain so' he said. 'By Margaret – and the Woodvilles are partisans of Margaret. I was so afraid – that history would repeat itself; it has an infamous habit of so doing.'

And had this happened, now glibly she had imagined the scene; Gloucester murdered, and how she would comfort little John. Here was John, by now no means little and probably not so easily com-forted. She was at a loss, and sought refuge in gaiety. She disengaged her hand, and took a couple of elegant, dancing steps before him.

'No more! The sun's too beautiful!' she cried. 'Lady Lovell had decked me – like a popinjay. I am a great lady today; not a bastard.' She stopped short, feeling herself blushing.

He looked at her, oddly adult, serious. Then he smiled. 'Is there anything better than a royal bastard? Full privilege, yet unable to claim inheritance. Some might grumble at it, but the calling suits me well. And you ... for we have never known another state. It must be hard, though, for Edward and Richard of York.'

Grace bit her lip, remembering Elizabeth's screams when they came to take Richard of York away. My lady, my cruel, lovely lady, she thought. How are you now? Deep sadness began in her, and faded as John took her hand again.

'Let us walk,' he said, and they went slowly while the sun, washed hotter by rain, burned their brows. He hummed a little song, stroked her first finger with his. She looked down at the brown ringed hand and the white entwined. Perfumed rain trickled from the calyx of an iris. The robin reappeared and tripped staccato along the path.

'Do you remember the lake at Eltham?' she said. 'You brought me a lily.'

'I will do it again,' he said.

'No, you've proved your chivalry once,' she began, and saw him frown.

'I know nothing of chivalry,' he said, and again: 'O Jesu, would that I were older!'

This time, she said simply: 'Why?

'My father led campaigns when he was fourteen. He loved the Lady Anne. He could have married her, but his loyalty forbade it until Warwick was dead.' He stooped, and picked up a pebble. 'Now he will be King.' He pitched the pebble to the end of the walk. 'I made a good *Deo Gratias* for that! But I ... I seem to be merely marking time. I have never fought, nor have I loved ...' As he spoke, he knew this to be nonsense. 'What I mean is ... I have never wooed, paid court, only in my mind, my heart.'

She looked at him quickly. His face was red. He occupied himself with more pebbles, choosing flat ones and skimming them along the smooth pavement. She made a jest of the moment. 'What do you know of love? Tell me, for I know nothing!' Talking, she thought, like a jade, a wanton, like poor Jane Shore, who would speak thus in past days to madden the courtiers. Wretched Jane, now in Fleet prison for her treason, her folly.

John threw one last stone. 'I know all about love,' he said sternly. From the pouch at his waist he drew out a crumpled yellow parchment; a mere scrap, thumbed and ragged. From this he read, self-consciously at first, then clearly and more positively.

'It is not sure a deadly pain
To you I say that lovers be,
When faithful hearts must needs refrain
The one the other for to see?'

259

He stopped and looked at her. She said 'That is a sad song, John.'
A breeze wafted the breath of the iris around them. The white doves
called thoughtfully.

He went on reading aloud, his cheek still darkly flushed the fragment of paper unsteady in his hand.

'If you assure ye may trust me,
Of all the pains that ever I knew
It is a pain that most I rue.'

'A fair, sad song,' she murmured. 'Did you write it?' At Middleham
they were trained to make verses as well as break each others'
heads.

'No, it was written by someone long dead, to soothe my heart
perhaps. When I was parted ... from my lady.'

So he had a love. At Middleham it was fashionable to be in love.
The young ones were encouraged to dance together, in between
learning to wear armour and weave cloth of Arras. There were many
female wards at Middleham. Suddenly she felt old and isolated and
sad. The light faded from her eyes; she looked down at the little
Spanish shoes Lady Lovell had given her. Her downcast face had a
tragic repose about it; John watched it for a long moment. Within
the space of a breath, emotion crystallized in him, making nonsense
of feigned love, killing the painted imagery of his unreal heartaches
at Middleham. The love he had squandered on dreams was here; the
unknown lady was blinding reality. Love, he realized, had always worn
the face of Grace Plantagenet.

'Didn't you know?' he demanded, of himself as much as of her. As
he put his arms about her so roughly that she gasped, he thought:
here is something too precious, too clearly seen to lose. She was sweet
and slender and perfumed against him. He laid his hand tenderly
against her cheek and kissed her.

'My Grace. My lady, my love.'

She tried to answer: John, I have thought of you as a friend, a companion. Never did I dream you were the end of loneliness. But he kissed
the words, and her face, eagerly, inexpertly; startled by love, he looked
into the brilliant green eyes and closed them with his lips. Then extravagantly, hastily, he went upon his knee before her. As if aware of time

obedient to his ever fervent plea and passing more swiftly, he said:

'From this day, this moment, I vow my heart and duty to you. God grant we may be betrothed one day. Soon.'

'We're cousins,' she murmured. (Banned, by the Church ...)

He leaped up, smiled into her face. 'My father and the Lady Anne are cousins,' he said. Again he kissed her; the sun grew brighter, and the flowers blew, and at the parlour window Lady Lovell smiled with delight. While Lady Norfolk muttered dourly of the ways of modern youth.

After many days of endeavour, Butcher Gould had penetrated Sanctuary. He came with only one prentice; of the other two, one had been killed in a Fleet brawl and the other was in Ludgate for striking the Watch. The remaining boy therefore bore the weight of a shoulder of mutton and a brace of pheasants slung about his neck. Garnet drops from their beaks rolled down his soiled jerkin. Master Gould was laden too; under each arm he carried a screaming piglet, and his pockets were crammed with sausages.

'Perchance that's why they cry so lustily,' he observed, glancing down at the writhing animals. 'They smell their ancestors.' Grimly and gloomily he smiled at his own jest. One had to smile; one had to forget: Matilda gone. His pretty, silly, ribboned wife, snatched in a day by the plague, that pustulent curse that emanated from all the open ditches in town. It took friend and foe alike, and left bitterness. He sighed, rapped on the Sanctuary door, his ears deafened by the porcine yells which rose higher than the clochard spire nearby.

He did this for Matilda. So long and so often had she talked of her one sight of the Queen; how she looked, her expression when she showed them the baby prince Edward. Gould thought of his visit to Sanctuary as a kind of Month's Mind celebration – made in remembrance of a day that had brought Matilda joy. He tucked the piglets more firmly beneath his arms, and kicked the door of Sanctuary until at last someone came to admit him. The cloister was as forbiddingly chill as ever. Full of stolid melancholy he stumped through, and swung a further kick at the door outside which Matilda had shivered with excitement. It was opened by the Princess – Lady Elizabeth of York, he reminded himself. She looked ill and bored and weary, and swirled away without a second glance at him. Gould entered and knelt before the lady's mother. Over the screaming of the pigs he uttered: 'Good morrow, your Grace,' and looking up, saw the pale face, scarred by old rages and tears, alight with pleasure at his salutation. All unwittingly he had given the best possible greeting.

'It is good to see you again, Master. Catherine!' She called to her sister, gestured at the piglets. 'Have them taken away and killed. My appetite returns at last.' She beckoned Gould closer; he looked for somewhere to lay the mutton, finally setting it awkwardly down upon a faldstool. From the tail of his eye he saw Catherine Woodville ordering a page to remove the meat, and the pheasants. The world is upside down, he told himself. While Buckingham sits in state at Westminster, here's his wife starving by choice with her sister. For he noticed that all the women looked meagre and poor. He compared them to his trade; he measured their flesh by the pound, and in fantasy saw himself bankrupt.

'Sausages, your Grace.' He emptied his pockets and laid his tribute on the stool. Elizabeth was asking him meanwhile how his wife was. He told her.

'And I lost a daughter too ...'

She answered with what seemed to him disproportionate vehemence.

'A daughter! Master, I have lost father, mother, two brothers, two sons, and two more sons were taken cruelly from me! Locked away!' She began to sob, with such extreme suddenness that he was startled. She wrenched at her hair. A tuft of it drifted down to lie among the foul rushes.

'Tell me, Master; tell me. Have you seen my boys, my kingly heirs?'

'Yes, I've seen them,' he said stolidly. Playing at bow-and-arrow on the ramparts of the Tower.'

'So they are still there,' she murmured, and wept no longer. She was silent then, for such a long time that Gould grew restive.

'Did you see the usurper's coronation?' she said next.

Gould blinked. He said carefully: 'Aye, Madame. It was a great affair. All the nobles of England attended; you could not move for lords and bishops ...'

'Curse the Bishops!' she cried. 'Cursed be that creeping ruin, the Church!'

'Your Grace!' Scandalized, Gould stared, seeing a swift smile replace anger.

'I value you, Master Gould,' she said softly. 'You address me as is my right!'

I fear for her, he thought, bowing his head. Once a bull had been brought to him for slaughter; a breeding bull, a beautiful animal turned savage and impotent. In its eyes had been that same half-human wildness he saw now; in the eyes of Dame Grey, the late King's concubine ...

'I address you so, Madame,' he blundered, 'in memory of our late sovereign lord.'

Succour my Bessy, William. They had been tossing dice together, the King incognito, in one of the lesser stews of St. Mary Woolchurch. Thirteen years ago.

A sudden rap on the door made him start. Elizabeth's frozen gaze passed over his head, behind which came mutterings, shuffling feet, and a voice. 'Madame, may we enter?' Gould saw the white hand wave in dismissal to him or assent to others, impossible to tell. He rose uncertainly and backed against the wall, where he stood scratching his calf with the other foot. A clerk wearing dusty black came stoopingly across the room and bowed before Elizabeth. Following the clerk was a gaunt man in a skull-cap who carried a leather bag.

'May we enter?' repeated Reynold Bray.

Traitor, she said. Traitor and knave. No better than your falseheart mistress, Margaret Beaufort. How dare you show your face?

She and the two men were alone. In her chair she leaned away from Bray, who still stank of sour ale and the reek of a hundred secret parchments.

'What do you want?' she cried with a hating glance. Bray coughed and hawked and looked around the floor with a full mouth. She half-rose, eyes daring him to spit. He swallowed, and with a fidgety motion, indicated the hollow man behind him.

'To present a friend.'

'Are there such things?' said Elizabeth. 'And how, by God's grace, did you pass into Sanctuary?'

'My holy cloth knows no horizon,' said Bray pompously. 'Neither does the majesty of medicine.' He nudged the other man forward.

'So! A doctor!' she said with great scorn. Rising, she stepped up to the gaunt-faced man. 'Heal my sickness,' she commanded. (Heal this sore heart, this burning humiliation. Raise me, through alchemy, again to the heights ...)

'Ach!' said the doctor. 'Madame, I don't know the nature of it.' His voice was so Welsh it sounded like a song.

'He comes from Bishop Morton,' said Bray, squinting about him. 'He has ...'

'A message, my lady,' said the Welshman. 'From the Bishop. For you,' he added, so that there should be no mistake. The corner of his mouth and one eye twitched, as if at some unspeakable jest. It was an affliction he had owned for years, but she was not to know this. Overflowing with temper, she sat and twisted her hands.

'You are no friend,' she said tightly. 'I have never seen you before. As for Master Bray – he can return to his mistress. She who sings Gloucester's praise in Westminster.'

Bray kept silence. He had been warned to expect this lunatic stubbornness. His bones were sore from saddle-hours; he had ridden hard, from Margaret Beaufort to Brecon, collecting the Welsh doctor en route; to the estates of Sir William Stanley, then back to Margaret and her husband again. He had sat up all night penning letters to the Dragon in Brittany. Now Woodville abused him. She was not what she once was, but he must play out his time.

'You and your mistress!' she continued. 'Time-servers both! Once she loved me; now she is Gloucester's toady. So is Stanley ...'

'Madame,' answered the clerk patiently, 'I come only from your loyal lovers and admirers.'

She stood up, frail and terrible. 'I do not trust you.' Bray looked around at the bare discomfort, the dirt, the despair all but written into the grimy walls.

'My lady, may I speak?' intoned the doctor. 'I come from Bishop Morton personally; I am his physician. He sends comfort, and a solution to all your miseries. A promise of better days, Dame Grey.'

Her temper broke absolutely.

'As you see fit to address me thus,' she said, trembling, 'bear this message. Let your master come to me himself. Let him bow the knee. Let him deliver his comfort in person.'

Reynold Bray smoothed the air with his hand. 'Madame, you know that the Lord Bishop is closely immured. It was only by great good fortune that my friend was able to come here this day.'

'I care naught,' she said violently. 'My edict remains unchanged. Let Morton come and tell me this glorious news, the smell of which I distrust already. Can he tell me how my sons are, my Richard, my Edward, in the Tower? Or the whereabouts of my son and lieutenant, Tom Dorset?'

'Your sons are all well,' said Bray quietly. 'Dorset is part of the plan, if you would only listen to it.'

She turned away. 'I'll listen only to Morton.' The Welshman was laughing at her, she knew it; her blood sang with murder.

'Morton is in Buckingham's prison.' As to a child, Bray repeated. 'Buckingham, the King's chief minister ...'

'King!' she cried. 'Usurper!'

She advanced on them like a crazed beast, her face ravaged. 'Leave me!' Her voice cracked, then softened. 'Leave me alone.'

Murmuring together, they left, and she sat still, her body drawn and shuddering. In her mind she turned over half-doubts and suspicions, while her ladies fearfully returned to her side. Out of her tumult, one piece of vital information remained clear. Morton was a prisoner of Buckingham. She beckoned to Catherine, who knelt, ingratiating, cowed.

'Sister–' the drained eyes looked down – 'I have a task for you.'

'Anything. Everything, Bess.'

'Does your husband love you?'

Catherine's face crumpled almost in tears. About her person she carried letters, from Buckingham the adored, Buckingham, whom she sadly missed. Night after night she had toyed with the impossibilities of breaking Sanctuary and rejoining him.

'Tell me. Has he a grudge, even the faintest, against the King?'

Buckingham had, and had only hinted at it in one secret letter, daring her to speak of it. But under the look from Elizabeth's eyes she was powerless, and stammered: 'Yes, Bess. He wished to marry our daughter to Gloucester's son – so that she could be Queen-Consort one day. Gloucester would have none of it. Harry was angry.'

'It is enough.' She plucked vellum and quill from a table. 'Write. Fan your husband's resentment. Sound him out.' She smiled a twisted smile. 'Tell him I shall repay him, one day.'

Catherine busied herself. Once she raised her head and asked anxiously: 'Sister, how shall this bill be carried?'

Elizabeth turned from her pacing. Butchers could go anywhere, welcomed with their priceless cargo. Meat for captor and captive alike. Letters could be carried in a wrapped joint, and no questions asked. She said softly: 'Is Master Gould still within Sanctuary?'

In Bloomsbury, he dismounted to fill her arms with flowers. She sat upon a grey palfrey, skirts neatly falling in rich green folds over the sidesaddle. Lady Anne had given Grace the dress. Green, love's colour. She had smiled as she said it, knowing that their love was child's love and not the love she herself knew. Not the suffering love that devours, that nourishes more pain than pleasure; not the love that feeds on anxiety. Now, in the green of Bloomsbury Grace sat lapped in love, while the bright face turned to hers was full of innocence and faith, and. the day long. He plucked for her tall white daisies, and the gold and cream of cowslip; the delicate-hearted dog-rose with its shades of saffron and pink, and the anemone, with its swift-dying purple. He gathered them in a great sheaf, damp and heavily odorous, and offered them high, a fragile pledge, the essence of summer's love.

She buried her lips in their mixed fragrance and wanted to weep. Tomorrow, John would ride north on the first great progress of King Richard after his coronation, and thereafter to Sheriff Hutton in Yorkshire to resume his knightly training. Through the web of green stems she looked at his slender, fiery face, so full of the joy of life, and at the eyes that held no guilt or guile. She saw there his delight in her presence, and his anticipation for Richard the king, to be followed tomorrow through cheering cities. During their weeks together at Baynard's Castle he had talked ceaselessly of the coronation, the great banquet, the roars of acclaim for his father. The people, free of the turbulent Woodvilles, had welcomed Richard like a god. When John spoke of this, she was forced to turn away to hide her face, for the thought of Elizabeth nagged like the toothache. She saw her ill, raging, smiling, sleeping like a weary child. She imagined her waking frightened in the night; no Grace to mouth a bitten-off prayer for her. Only Renée, slow, and growing deaf, or the sisters, too anxious to be of much use. She called me her ill-luck, thought Grace; yet I was really her talisman against despair.

Across the meadow, the little group of knights and ladies, lately abandoned by John and Grace, were hawking. Lady Lovell had a fierce young merlin, Against a blue sky faintly silvered with cloud, it brought down two clumsy panicking partridge, one after the other. Higher still a tiny sparrowhawk chased a lark almost to infinity. They hung for an instant, remote as stars, then plummeted, a Lucifer-fall charged with tragic beauty. John said softly: 'Love. Love, are you listening?'

She lowered the tender green bouquet and tried to smile. She had not heard a word he said. Yesterday they had looked together at the Titulus Regius, a copy of which had been delivered to every courtier. The stark terrible words of it had given her pain, and John had felt it. Gaily he had tossed the roll into the air, making some jest about dull lawyers' talk; and so dismissing the most important document of the century, had drawn her close, a target for his impetuous, unskilled kisses. Now he mounted his horse so that he could move nearer and take her hand, clasping it over the mountain of flowers.

'You are sad,' he murmured. 'Sweetheart, we have so few moments alone together. Be happy.'

What he said was true. In Lady Anne's household – the new Queen's household – privacy was impossible and chaperonage constant save for snatched moments such as these. To Grace the reason for such surveillance was still not clear. No gossip tarnished her or John. She looked at his worried face and said: 'You are sad, too.'

'Tomorrow is almost with us.' He frowned, chewing a green stalk. 'I could arrange for you to accompany us on the progress. You could stay at Sheriff Hutton, and we need not be parted.'

Violently she shook her head; his face darkened.

'You said that you loved me.' His voice was dangerously quiet. He was a Plantagenet, jealous, volatile, like all the male members of the dynasty. He stared into the green eyes made amber by sunlight, at the sweet brows like birds in flight. Lastly he looked at the small pale mouth, the mouth like honey. He felt a great and hungry tenderness.

'I love you,' he said. 'Most heartily. Come to Sheriff Hutton.'

The fronds were cool against her face, balm to her tears. Thoughts, hidden from John, repeated: I cannot leave her. Not while she might need me, call for me. One day she may forgive me the sin of loving her, and while she lies in Sanctuary I cannot leave London. I am a dog, a bitch, turning to lick the striking hand, grovelling to the beloved's frown.

'Do you love me?' he said. 'If you do not, there are others who will.'

She looked at his anguished, bewildered boy's face, heard his tongue aping cruel adult words.

'I love you, John of Gloucester,' she answered. 'And I shall love none other.'

So he was ashamed, and touched her cheek with shaking fingers. 'I am mad,' he admitted. 'Churlish, too. I've no experience in these matters.' He grinned at her and she felt safe again. 'Today,' he said inconsequentially, 'my father sent me two tuns of malmsey wine. It was a token that he considers me a man. Soon I shall be old enough to serve him. If I do well, he will ordain me Captain of Calais, old Warwick's commission. Ah, love!' Joyful now, all rancour forgotten. 'Love, lovely life!'

The melancholy drew near to Grace again. She imagined the forthcoming progress, the panoply surging northward through England. John in the train with his new livery, his gay shield with the bend sinister across royal quarterings. While she wore out the aimless days in London. Did Elizabeth know of her new allegiance? If so, she would brand her traitor, like Margaret Beaufort. As for John – he would easily forget her. His future beckoned, a time to show his valour; soon her own light image would be buried beneath new faces, new triumphs. Perhaps in a year, he would not even remember her name.

All the time he watched her, astutely guessing her thoughts, and secretly a little angry that she should demean his vows. Yet when he saw the smooth honey of her face tremble in sorrow his annoyance died. He took the flowers from her and threw them down. He lifted her easily from her horse on to his. There, he held her silently, while in the distance the hawks winged like legends, rising in majesty, dropping as if stunned.

'We will meet again soon.' His voice was muffled by her hair. 'All will be well, sweet heart.'

Now the hunting party was preparing to leave, the falconers calling in the birds to the lure, the grooms whistling the dogs and running to fetch horses tethered in a grove of oaks. Lady Lovell was casting anxiously about for Grace and pages were looking for John. A group of riders detached itself from the main party and came at a lilting gallop through the grass, raising crickets and bumblebees, scattering flowerheads. Pages ran leggily at the side of a dozen mounted knights, who came as if blown on a holiday wind, their horses' legs shimmering strongly. The foremost horse was blindingly white. Someone shouted, jesting, indistinct, and the horse's rider laughed.

'O Jesu!' said John, his face crimson. 'It is the King, my father. He must have joined the party lately. Mistress, we must dismount.'

It was not so easy. The palfrey, excited by the oncoming horses, backed into John's mount. Grace struggled to extricate herself from one of John's spurs, caught in the trailing hem of her mantle. The more she tugged the more they were entwined. The horse humped its back and kicked out, and John half-fell to the ground, leaving a long rent in the green skirt. Grace was left trying to curb both horses, while the King's mount, raising a bright pollen-cloud, drew up before them.

'Sire,' said John, on his knees.

King Richard sat and laughed at his son's scarlet cheeks and Grace's pale embarrassment. He surveyed the two smooth faces and his laughter died as a pang of almost unrecognized envy jolted him. He himself had forgotten what it was like to be so young, to play at love. Once, before Edward died, while Warwick lived, there had been days like this for him, at Middleham, with Anne. He had a sudden insane urge to gather blooms for Grace, to wrestle with John. As he would have done twenty years ago, before battle wearied him, and kingship laid its yoke on him. He snapped his long, ringed fingers; a page ran to quieten the horses and lift Grace down. She curtseyed in the bruised grass and said: 'Excuse me, highness.' The King was relaxed, holding the great white destrier with one easy hand on the reins. He had the same dark eyes, fine bones, as John. But John was robust of countenance, whereas the King could often look sick and haggard, his pallor turning to ash, his eyes indrawn. She studied him shyly; Richard in turn, saw a true daughter of Edward Plantagenet, with the gold of Edward before indolence and excess coarsened him.

'Excuse you for what, mistress?' he said softly. For being happy?' At his elbow Lord Stanley said: 'such truth, highness!' Stanley and his brother Sir William were very near, proper and subservient, falling over each other to do the royal bidding. Richard motioned to John and Grace to rise, and suddenly, painfully, he saw them as himself and Anne, standing handclasped in the green-gold day. So long ago. Now Anne was ill, trying to gather strength for the progress and unable to join him even for this brief hour of pleasure. He said abruptly:

'We ride for Westminster now. John, I trust you will be ready for tomorrow?'

'Yes, Sire,' John said eagerly. 'It will be wonderful.'

Richard inclined his head, thinking. Yes, by God's mercy, it will. I shall see York, and my little prince again. I pray Anne will stand the journey, and that Buckingham's temper will improve. There was something amiss with him – an arrant insolence, an ill-covered fermenting of – what? He was almost like a cardplayer who has presented the wrong suit and regrets a better ploy. The King turned his horse. Its pelt flamed white in the sun; its rider's cloak made a purple swirl about the saddle.

'God be with you, mistress,' he said to Grace. To a page: 'Escort and assist her.'

They rode away, in a leaping gallop through the high grass. Lord Stanley's mount switched its quarters from side to side, avoiding rabbit-holes. John took Grace's hands and kissed them solemnly.

'I must follow him. Sweet Jesu Christ keep you always, dearest, dearest mistress.'

She turned from him, from the future Captain of Calais, from the adventurer to be, thinking dully: Why do they sing of love so, if it's as sad as this? Then she felt his arms pulling her to him, a rain of kisses on her face. The next moment he was in the saddle, spurring so that his mount leaped forward in a cloud of petals and the seeds of grass. He was soon diminished; at the edge of the meadow he waved violently before merging with the King's train. Grace murmured to herself:

'Of all the pains that ever I knew
It is the pain that most I rue.'

and found no comfort in it.

As the chariot bearing Bishop Morton through the night skirted St. Albans, the rain began again. A solid fall of black water descended as if someone had emptied a pail from the sky. Frightening in its vehemence, the torrent thundered on the wooden roof of the litter, startling the horses and extinguishing the frail lanterns. Morton lifted the sodden curtain and peered out into the murk. He absently murmured a curse, withdrawing it next minute, for in one way the foul weather was a blessing. Few would brave such a tempest to hunt the Bishop down, fugitive and renegade though he was. The King's men would not look for him tonight and any vigilantes among the people would be busy mending their roofs. Such nights as this had ruined the plans of a month ago; a torrent had fallen ever since Buckingham had engineered the rebellion and Morton had been permitted to escape. Folk were already calling it the year of the Great Water. He sank back on damp cushions and pulled his fur closer, stroking the collar as if it were a docile beast. If the roads were not too foul they would reach their destination in a few hours. Morton's hand, blue with cold, left his collar and caressed the icy gold chain at his breast. Calmly he listened to the curses of the drivers, flogging the horses through thick mud. These men would not fail him – he had paid them handsomely. He had paid Buckingham too – with lies and promises and flattery, although Buckingham had proved, to say the least, unfortunate. He lay now in October clay, headless, with his right hand fashionably struck off to mark his treason against King Richard.

For Morton, this journey was a necessary madness. The Dragon himself had warned him to take care. 'Remember, my lord, I shall need a Cardinal Archbishop!' smiling that swift glassy smile, pressing Morton's hand in his skinny nervous fingers. Yet implicit in that warning had been a command to accomplish what was necessary. The last campaign against that ageing, impetuous Woodville. The final dangling of the mammet. 'I will see her dance,' he muttered to himself. A jet of rain through the storm-tossed curtain soaked his robe. He leaned and shouted to the drivers: 'How goes it? There's a bridge ahead, if my memory serves,' and received back the eldritch cry: 'Rest easy, my lord! We'll have you there by midnight!'

He had said a Mass for Buckingham; the poor fool gone to his end not knowing that he was only a catspaw in a game of such magnitude that death was an integral, even a necessary part of it, like the blood-sacrifice laid beneath the walls of a great abbey; the founding of a dynasty. Morton put his long blue hands together and prayed: 'Let me live for many years. Let me laugh in secret, and don the Cardinal's hat that Richard Plantagenet would now never give me. Let me retrieve the schemes ruined by Hastings's bungling and Buckingham's ill-luck. O Thou, whoever and whatever. Thou art, let me live!' Wind battered rain against the carriage, rippling the curtain and spraying the Bishop with pungent filth.

'The pity of it is, I need her,' he said to himself of Elizabeth while the chariot ploughed lurching on. The Dragon had stipulated his price. And certainly there was sense in it. Sir Edward Woodville, with his stolen fleet, had been of great value, lying ready in the Channel and still ready … Despite the rough ride, Morton slept a little. He dreamed he was eating strawberries at Brecon with Buckingham who had received a secret bill in a pig's trotter; a letter that touched fire to his spleen and made him pliant, ready for rebellion. Morton breathed on the flame. 'Harry, such ingratitude! After all your loyalty! What recompense! But there is one who would not use you so, one who recognizes a good heart.' Buckingham's bright eyes were thoughtful, his bent head listened.

'Sheen, my lord!'

Morton woke up, looked out of the carriage. A light in a tower flickered ahead, a light half-hidden by drenching rain. They were making good time. Stretching his shivering limbs, he wondered how Dorset was. He had hoped originally that Tom might come from his refuge in France to uphold the Dragon's invasion. Since that invasion had proved abortive, the Woodville's son had been, in the event, wise. The litter rolled on through the long wet night. It had been a tortuous journey from Ely; Ely, that cowed diocese that did and was as Morton bade it. Soon he would be in Westminster Sanctuary. He felt for the friar's habit rolled up under his feet; it would soon be time to don the disguise. Shameful? With such a stake? He smiled. Never. With laboured, mudsucking breath the sodden horses ploughed north of Sheen and he caught the first sound of the Thames. He reached down and lifted the friar's mantle.

At Westminster the river had risen, nearly lapping the Sanctuary door. The Bishop's thunderous knock resounded against a carillon of rain from the gushing gargoyles. He wa admitted at once. Despite the friar's habit, the brothers knew him, and Abbot Milling was afraid, lost long ago in the deep waters of conspiracy. The Bishop went in and left a trail of mud along the cloister; he stood dripping while Elizabeth was roused. In the chamber where he waited, a fire still burned in the hearth; a miserable half-dead flicker. He extended his wet foot to it, and was standing thus when Elizabeth entered. Hands clasped inside the sleeves of her gown, she walked towards him. A little shiver ran over her body.

'*Domine vobiscum*,' he said, and threw back his hood. He lowered his hand for her salute, and felt her icy lips on his fingers.

'So you have come at last. My lord–' some irony in her tone amused him – 'how was your stay in prison?'

'Comfortable. I was protected from storms such as these. Such a night!'

'Buckingham let you escape?'

'Ah, Buckingham!' He crossed himself. 'He left this world in a vile humour, cursing the King, cursing me, and cursing you, Madame. He cursed you on the scaffold, for sowing the seed of his revolt. That letter your sister wrote '– those were your sentiments, not hers.'

He saw her face whiten: 'Where is the letter now? If Buckingham cursed me, then I curse him. For his failure to overthrow the usurper and bring back my sons. What incubus thwarted this latest plan?'

'The weather,' said Morton coolly. He bent to feed the sullen fire with a branch. 'The bridges were down, the passes sealed off by storm and Gloucester's armies. As for the letter – do not fear implication this time. I myself saw it burn.'

She was able to smile. 'My lord, I misjudged you.'

He moved to grasp the moment. 'You did not trust my doctor friend. You asked for me in person and here I am, come through a night of devils, Madame.' He watched the hem of his robe steam. During a summer of frustration he had aged somewhat; the blue-white skin hung in folded dewlaps at his throat and eyes. He felt a hand upon his damp sleeve.

'My lord,' she said, 'how can you help me?'

'Shall we be seated?' he said gently. They sat on either side of the fire which shifted, revealing deep red caves, a grey abyss edged with white, a falling tree, a withered serpent. The night grew close and secret about them.

He said: 'There is one whom you would destroy?'

Wariness sprang again in her. Margaret Beaufort had often spoken thus to her, with wisdom and provocative confidence, and where was Margaret now? She let the Bishop answer for her.

'King Richard,' he said, and jetted his spittle into the ashes.

'An anointed king,' she said, without expression, and waited.

'To be ruined and vanquished by you.'

Instantly she was convinced that he was a *provocateur* and said stiffly: 'You think too highly of my power. I am a poor widow.' The tears would come at a thought – no need, these days, for feigning.

'*Madame!*' said Morton with a deep and withering smile 'let us, for Jesu's love, be plain. Have you not been death's instrument, more than once? Have I not been witness to your deeds?'

She was silent. The fire settled itself. A little blaze built up, like Hell-Mouth, in a tunnel.

'Lady,' said the Bishop softly, 'God forbid, I should judge you. You have been sorely tried.'

She lifted her eyes and looked at him directly.

'Richard of Gloucester is young, and a great warrior. He has a certain reputation. You may kill an old man, but not a King like the usurper. Like the Hog!' she said violently.

'Yes, the Boar, the Hog,' the soft hypnotic voice agreed. Morton looked disgustedly about him. 'Devil damn me, this is no place for you! Have I not said you will dance again in Westminster?'

'What is the price of this solution?' she said, surprisingly sharp and cool.

'Your eldest daughter, the Lady Bess. In marriage to Henry Tudor.'

She gasped, her brow wrinkled. 'Tudor!' she said incredulously.

Morton said: 'He will be King of England, at my guess, within a twelvemonth. Your daughter will be Queen, and you Queen-Dowager, with all the pomp and pride you wish. I will help you to a height. Henry Tudor will invade ...'

'With what? Who will follow him?'

'Tudor will conquer with the aid of your forces. Immured in Sanctuary as you are, have you not realized that all of Lancaster is now for Tudor? Sir Edward Woodville's fleet still runs free, with all the treasure amassed by your son Dorset. It is enough to pay for another invasion. There are men in France and Brittany willing to spill English blood for Tudor; Lord Stanley will ...'

'Stanley and his wife have betrayed me. They attend the Council; they gave their hand to Titulus Regius.'

Smiling, shaking his head, the Bishop fingered his gold collar.

'Foolishness,' he murmured. 'Madame, do you not believe me when I say they will not, cannot show their hand yet? Have you forgotten that Tudor is Margaret's son?'

Yes, she had forgotten. Now it seemed that Henry was a figurehead of true power; her solution, as Morton said.

'But why is my daughter so necessary to this enterprise?' she said.

'Tudor will conquer,' said the Bishop. 'But he cannot reign by conquest alone. He needs the seal of Plantagenet blood. He will unite the houses of York and Lancaster, and be beloved for it. He comes from God, a saviour. But he must marry into a royal dynasty.'

Then she remembered.

Bone of thy bone shall be a future fate

With blood of these three houses surely mate.

The old riddle was answered. Lancaster, York and Tudor. Henry Tudor was of Lancaster ... it was an omen. Her shivering had nothing to do with the cold, with the dead fire or the dripping walls of Sanctuary. Against the blackened chimney fresh dreams blazed. A reprieve. A frantic hope. Herself Queen-Dowager and no more plain Dame Grey. She tried to speak calmly.

'It is a fair prospect, my lord Bishop. But you have forgotten something!'

Morton inclined his ear.

'The people love Richard! They love him better than they loved his brother. They admire him for his new statutes and his justice. Whatever the barons say, he has won the people's heart!'

She had heard tales of the progress, how England had shaken with cheers for the Hog, the usurper.

'They love him,' she repeated. 'They will not rise against him. And I am powerless.'

That hateful word. Where was Melusine now? And where the secret doctrines of strength and cunning? As if to catch again at that lost mystery and might, she gazed at the Bishop's white, wattled face. He smiled comfortably.

'All that you say is true, my liege lady,' he murmured, 'The time is full. Now we must turn that love to hate.'

On a day of ribald March winds she arose and came out of Sanctuary, for it was time and more than time for her to do so. She knew that Morton disapproved; this, oddly, added impetus to her step, as she thought: *I am not yet totally his; I am not yet altogether committed.* She stood outside the gate and drew in lungfuls of breath, catching the high-tide smell from the river, the smoke of chimneys, the odour of brawn patties from the cookstalls outside Westminster Hall. Armed with a worn dignity, she stood erect, while behind her young Bess shivered in the unfamiliar gales. The girl's mouth was sullen and her cheeks hollow from months of boredom and privation. Elizabeth, stealing a glance, thought: I myself have looked fairer, but what's to be done? Nearly all the jewels, the gold and the fine clothing so carefully rescued months earlier had been handed over to Morton's keeping to swell the funds for the new campaign. The smaller treasure had gone in barter for food and fuel during the long siege in Sanctuary. So Elizabeth stood, naked of glory, in a long cloak of white wool fastened with a tawdry beryl brooch. Her slim face was resolute, her eyes, now finely lined, full of hard brightness. Several merchants with their prentices passed her without a second glance, and she smiled grimly. This time I am not the bait for a king, she thought. It is Bess who must be cherished. A rare wave of affection moved her to clasp the girl's arm, and they moved in procession with the shabby female entourage down to the quay.

'So, daughter, we're out of prison!'

Bess nodded glumly, her eyes on the cobbles.

'Look up!' said Elizabeth. 'Learn to bear yourself straighter. You will be a Queen.'

Bess had no more tears to shed. She had wept so much since Morton's visit that the cause of her grief had become somehow blunted and confused. She was to marry Henry Tudor. So she was finished with romance, both read and dreamed of. Her father had warned her against Tudor, long ago. She was a little girl, at her first ball and banquet. It was early enough in the evening for Edward to be still coherent. Henry had just bowed and quit the Hall, and everyone was sniggering over his quaint continental manners. But the King had growled: 'He is an enemy of my throne,' and none had heeded this. Bess, feeling sorry for her father, had crept close to him, and he had talked to her for about five minutes, as if she were a wise old courtier. Warning, admonishing her. She had never forgotten it. Now, a look of flat despair lay on her face and moved her mother to say, surprisingly gently:

'Everyone must marry. And Henry Tudor is young, probably biddable. Between us we will pluck his plumes!'

Elizabeth saw herself as the matriarch, the omnipotent Queen-Dowager, exerting subtle pressure on her son-in-law. And this, strangely, gave birth to oblique doubts about the whole affair. What if Henry *were* all that young and biddable! What if Morton were flying so high with ambition that he failed to see certain weaknesses in his protégé. He had promised that Tudor would invade, but what if Tudor and his foreign force were unsuccessful? Henry, apparently, had never fought in battle in his life. Gloucester was a skilled and seasoned warrior, vanquishing even the Scots and proving such a strategist that King Edward at the end had left all campaigns in his brother's sole charge. The wind snatched at her veil, whipping it like a battle standard against her face. No, she was by no means committed to the proposal. Better to wait, and get the measure of the Hog. She was summoned, nay, begged to return to his court. He had forgiven her, and was this not weakness of a different kind?

'I, Richard, promise and swear, *verbo regio*, that if the daughters of Elizabeth Grey, late calling herself Queen of England, will come to me ... then I shall see that they shall be in surety of their lives ... that I shall marry them to gentlemen born, and give in marriage lands and tenements to the yearly value of 200 marks for term of their lives. And such gentlemen as shall hap to marry with them I shall straitly charge lovingly to love them, as wives and my kinswomen, as they will avoid and eschew my displeasure.

'And over this, I shall yearly pay the said Dame Elizabeth Grey ... the sum of 700 marks ...

Strange, to reward treason and hatred thus.

'Moreover I promise to them that if any surmise or evil report be made to me of them by any person, I shall not give thereunto faith or credence ...'

Forgiven, forgiven. His one wish was to live in amity. He was the Fiend's lover, and her greatest enemy. Yet what a fool he was! She wondered, as she wondered every day, whether the whispers had reached him yet; whether love was turned to hate in England. In France, it was certain. The messengers had come and gone between Morton and herself: each step of the campaign was planted firmly. She knew the words of the Chancellor of France almost by heart:

'Listen, I pray you, to the events which have taken place since the death of King Edward *in that country*.' (The sneer in the voice; Guillaume de Rochefort would, like all good Frenchmen, have taken pleasure in it: the barbarism of the English!) 'These beautiful children, King's sons, butchered, and the assassin crowned by the will of the people!'

She even knew the go-between's name. Dominic Mancini, poet and chronicler and fast friend of Morton, had the Chancellor's ear. So the rumours were busy, more than rumours now. Dorset did his part in France, and Sir Edward Woodville, and Reynold Bray, when he could be spared. And Henry Tudor himself; what was he doing now? She knew that on Christmas Day last he had all but proclaimed himself King of England in Rennes Cathedral, swearing with flourishes that he would take Elizabeth of York to wife, and thus unite York and Lancaster. She would have liked to witness that scene; to see how he comported himself, whether his voice shook or if his hands faltered on the holy relics. She would have liked to measure his strength. His cadaverous face flashed before her mind, the grey eyes humbly bowed yet with a strange yellowish spark in their depths. An almost priestly face, its spare outlines softened by some unknown lust or longing. And above all, that weird aura of familiarity. If she but knew him as she thought.

'Madame, can we go in the barge now?' Catherine's plaintive voice jolted her from the torment of musing. The river's surface was broken by a thousand sharp-edged waves. From boats people were alighting, some with pallid, relieved faces. A royal escort stood on the slipway below which rocked a painted craft. The men were tall, and the arms on their livery glowed like jewels. With staves, the escort pressed a way among the disembarking people so that Elizabeth's little train should come unhindered. Folk loitered to look at the sombre procession of women. A murmuring arose, over the hiss of the wind on the waves.

'Look, John!' said a voice almost in Elizabeth's ear. 'Isn't it ...'

'God's robe! So 'tis! The King's Grey Mare!'

Like an ogre's fist, rage gripped and shook her. Her face turned white, then scarlet. One of the royal henchmen saved her dignity, catching her elbow as she swayed. His murmuring respect choked the passion on her lips, or she would have turned and screamed her frenzy into the face of the crowd. Two of the escort lifted her, as if she were crippled, into the barge, setting her down, light as a leaf. The boatmen bowed to the oars, and the craft moved over the choppy currents. Through the forest of cranes dipping industriously, tall buildings rose; the Manse fortress, Coldharbour, the amber needles of churches, and a mile, beyond, the distant whiteness of the Tower. My boys, she thought. My murdered boys. When the usurper is vanquished, you shall be brought to life again. Young Lazarus, both of you. She wondered if they themselves knew of their supposed death. Richard would find humour in it, but Edward was delicate; it might distress him.

Surging towards them suddenly came a lavishly gilded barge. Banners flew from it and in the stern stood a small group of minstrels.

The sound of viols came in squeaky snatches above the rush of tide and air. The craft passed close so that the woman reclining on a canopied couch was visible in detail. She wore rich blue velvet and a gold coif from which depended a drift of white veil. A leather book lay open on her lap, and she drank from a crystal cup. Two pages were draping her shoulders with a fur. She looked up at one of them and laughed. Like a night-bird's shriek the laugh blew away, raucously merry.

'Sweet Jesu!' cried Elizabeth, twisting in the boat to stare as the rich craft shot by. 'Jane Shore!'

One of the royal escort answered. 'Nay, Madame. That is Lady Lynom. She was released from prison last fall. She is married now to the King's Solicitor-General.'

'But she was a traitor! Conspirator and harlot – condemned by the King!'

'He pardoned her,' said the man, dipping his head on his chest as if to weight his words. 'He showed her mercy.'

Elizabeth sank back in her seat. The wind played on her lips, still incredulously parted. Slowly her thoughts reformed themselves. Richard was more than a fool; he was utterly possessed of lunacy. If this treatment of Shore were token of his mercy ... She began to laugh, to hold in laughter, shaking silently, tears spilling down her cheeks. The boat rocked on the wash from Lady Lynom's barge. Young Bess stole a glance at her mother and was alarmed. She touched her hand gently.

'Madame, don't weep,' she whispered. 'I am sure my uncle of Gloucester will take good care of us.'

'Oh, he will,' sobbed Elizabeth. 'On my soul, he will!'

That evening she walked into the hall at Baynard's Castle with downcast eyes, primarily to retain her composure. Were the truth known, she found the sudden warmth and noise and life of the court disturbing after the spectral peace of Sanctuary. Even though there were only about a hundred sitting at table that evening, she felt their presence crowding her, their eyes vying with the thousand firefly candles and seeking her out. The usher's voice rebounded from the walls and the hammerbeam roof: 'Dame Grey! Grey! Grey!' Behind her, so close that she could feel Bess's breath touching her bare neck, came the daughters. The rustle of their new gowns, the hard little slither of their dancing shoes, sounded like a school of adders in stealthy progress. From the corners of her eyes she caught the lazy movement of the White Boar bannner and the fidgeting of a page standing with his fellows against the wall. About fifty of Richard's Council were seated above the salt, whose great silver barrel divided nobles from relatives, henchmen, and hangers-on. Trestles lapped in shining damask flowed past on either side her slow advance to the dais where King Richard sat with his Queen.

She had planned her most obsequious curtsey, thinking to inject mockery into the swept-back skirt, the crooked knee. No sooner had she begun to bend to the throne than Richard rose and came to her on light hurried feet down the two steps; he took her hands, holding her up from the obeisance. His thin grasp was cool and strong. She dipped her mouth to his hand but his arms went about her. He held her stiff, outraged body against him and spoke loudly over her head.

'My lords and councillors! I bid you give welcome heartily to our well-beloved Dame Elizabeth Grey!'

Was he the mocker now? One insult, and she would turn and leave him to humiliation. With her unwilling face grazing his soft velvet doublet she heard him bidding the court rise and salute her. 'Drink, my friends! to her who gave comfort to King Edward for many years.' He released her then, enough to look at her, saying softly:

'Your presence here gladdens me, Elizabeth,' and would have said more but for the shudder of distaste she could not hide. He whispered again, 'Welcome,' and she stared into his dark face. The blue eyes were tired yet vital, but there were ageing marks of stress in his high-boned countenance. She looked, past his dark head with the glittering diadem, to the dais, to her place for so many lost years. Queen Anne was watching anxiously, twisting her hands above her damask napkin. Mortal sickness lay upon her. Her skin was so pale that the blood could almost be seen moving beneath it; on each cheek flew the dangerous bright flag of a wasting disease.

Elizabeth smiled faintly. She raised her lips and gave to Richard a dry and dutiful kiss. In contrast to his hands, his face burned. His whole body was hard and tense and feverish. She thought with sudden clarity: born under Mars, with the Scorpion rising. Mars is burning him up, and the Scorpion will sting him to death. She was instantly assuaged.

A place had been set for her at the top of the right-hand trestle. From it she watched her daughters received in turn, saluted, and presented to the company. Bess was first in line – weeping anew, Elizabeth noted angrily; weeping, casting herself into her uncle's arms so that a pleased indulgent murmur arose from the Hall. Elizabeth was uneasy. For some reason unknown, save perhaps that he had coddled her when she was a child, Bess had always been fond of her uncle. The girl's face was hidden against his shoulder. At any moment she might complain to him about the unwanted Tudor marriage ... dare she? Elizabeth half-rose, but the danger was past, Bess was leaving the dais while Richard embraced her younger sister, Cicely.

As the meal began Elizabeth wondered if it were a celebration – of her own capitulation? A line of butlers served the company with roast swan; the carvers dismembered a dozen roasted oxen. There were wines like liquid jewels, a syllabub covered with coils of spun sugar, and a great subtlety depicting in honied pastry and crystal fruits the Coming of Christ in Majesty. Young Bess fell upon the food, eating until her small belly was as tight as a tabor. Her sisters flirted and giggled with Richard's younger henchmen. Elizabeth stared down at her platter from which rose the smell of well-hung meat and herbs. Famished yet nauseated, she could eat nothing. Despite the concern of Sir Richard Ratcliffe who sat by her, she left all untouched, crumbling her bread-trencher, barely tasting her wine. From a seat across the hall, Margaret Beaufort was trying vainly to catch her eye. Let her wait, she thought. I will make my peace in my own time.

For much of the banquet, and when the board had been cleared for entertainment, she watched Anne Neville. Yes, death sat by her, she coughed and coughed and held her throat, her eyes bright with tears of anguish. As the jugglers strutted, throwing up lighted brands, her colour worsened. A woman came with a consort of viols and sang, piercingly sweet, of love and flowers and destiny. Anne left the dais and slipped away; her physician followed close behind her. The King forced a smile to his lips and looked away down the Hall. Near him Bess, rosy with food, made careless by wine, raised her goblet in a gay salute. Courteously he returned her gesture, while his anxious eyes reluctantly registered her youth, her health. Like a small candle on a dark plain, a thought flickered in Elizabeth's mind and she too smiled at Richard. Across the Hall Margaret Beaufort whispered to Lord Stanley. It was their turn to be uneasy. Later when the guests were dispersing, Elizabeth approached the Duke of Norfolk.

'I wish for an audience with his Grace,' she said, trying to speak kindly. She must bring out of retirement the silver tongue which had seduced Edward, were she to serve his brother likewise.

'I will inquire,' said Jack of Norfolk. *Serpent.* The word hovered with him as he went away. He loved Richard dearly but sometimes thought his actions unfathomable.

They brought her to him after a little while. He was in his private apartments, writing at a table, with a great shaggy hound at his feet. A grim old lady knelt before a prie-dieu in the corner. Her raiment was crow-black and a great bunch of keys hung at her waist. Proud Cis Plantagenet, mother of two kings. She finished her prayer as Elizabeth entered. She rattled her fingers down her rosary with a sound of skeletal menace, and stalked towards the door.

'I shall retire now,' she announced. Richard got up. The hound followed him to where the Duchess of York stood; it waved its long banner of a tail.

'Good night, my son.' Her gaunt face swivelled so that her eyes, deep hollows and black ageless fires, rested on Elizabeth. 'Good night,' she said again. Still looking at Elizabeth: 'May God protect you, Richard, through this night.'

Moving strongly like a black ship, the hound in her wake, she quit the room, and left behind a mood of grave disquiet.

'Be seated, Elizabeth,' Richard said. He had a fair idea of why she had come, and did not delude himself that it was out of affection. Her enmity had communicated itself plainly in that public embrace. In nine months of power he had discovered that people can forgive much, but not the crime of being forgiven. Magnanimity hurts.

'It is a long time since I was here,' she said, laughing nervously. He bowed agreement; sitting, contemplatively turning his finger-rings.

'I fear your lady wife the Queen is sick,' she said next, and saw his face grow more haggard in the space of her words. 'I have no doubt her doctors are skilled' she went on, 'but I have remedies, tried remedies, for evil of the breast.'

Take woodsage, horehound ... It had not cured Marguerite! Neither would it heal the Fiend's daughter.

'God grant that she will recover soon,' she continued, and knew by his expression that he had already given up hope. And the little candle of thought, lit while she watched Bess salute her uncle, smouldered and burnt up brightly. How much better for Bess's bridegroom to be already King! No need to parry then with Tudor and his uncertain conquest ... it would be satisfying, too, to hatch a plan without Morton's knowledge. To serve Richard as her own mother had served Edward – by seduction, witchery, the torments of temptation. It was a thought to be mulled over very carefully. Bess would be Queen of England by some means; Tudor was not the sole solution.

Richard said: 'Madame, I am a little weary, and I must look to the Queen. What is your desire?'

'I came to thank you,' she said, 'for receiving me back into your grace and for the gifts to me and mine. I am conscious of –' it was hard to say, even in feigning – 'of my transgressions against you in the past. I hope these are forgotten out of your great generosity.'

His tired eyes brightened. 'This is more than I hoped for,' he said softly. 'Elizabeth, believe me I spoke truly when I bade you welcome to my household. I wish to live at peace.'

'And I, Sire.' Lids lowered, she smiled her little downward smile, not knowing that it was now a grotesque twitch, unnervingly without appeal.

'I shall while I rule give you every comfort,' he went on. 'None shall harm or mistreat you. Did Nesfield deliver my grant from the Privy Purse?' She nodded. He said: 'And after my time is done, my son Edward will, at my decree, continue to cherish your children. For God's sake, let the next generation use one another more kindly than we have done!'

She exhaled a long sigh that wavered the candles in their sconces. She raised eyes full of blue piteousness.

'My lord, I must speak ... you talk of your son and this grieves me. Sire, I have sons also. This is my request.'

He listened, the candlelight shuddering on his face.

'May it please your Grace to receive back my son, Thomas Grey, Marquis of Dorset. Would you permit him safe-conduct from France?'

It would be wonderful to have Tom near her again. He would be so much more useful than kicking his heels in Henry Tudor's camp. He was the one prop and ally of her blood who was as close as Anthony ... Anthony. She felt her jaw tighten despite herself. She heard the King's quick answer.

'Aye, gladly. Write him tomorrow. He will be welcome as you

are. Certes, bring Dorset home. I harbour no grudges. I will pardon him.'

She thought – how easy it all is! Now for the last and most important gamble. The pin on which all could hinge, if all else failed.

'Your Grace is bountiful.' He waited. 'One more thing. I am certain you have not forgotten the existence of – my other sons. Edward and Richard, in the Tower of London.'

'The Lords Bastard,' he said instantly.

She bit her lip. 'Yes. I would dearly love to have my boys with me again.' Once more, she looked down.

He was silent for a long time while a feeling of sour self-congratulation on his own wit crept over him. For a few moments he had wondered whether he was wrong about Elizabeth's purpose – now it seemed she had only been taking her time. The knowledge that he had read her aright filled him none the less with disillusion. Within him, a second Richard sneered at the first's gullibility. Overall he felt downcast, flattened. He stared at the slender face opposite, willing her to raise her eyes that he might look and be confirmed in that which disappointed him. As if so commanded, the veined white lids flickered upwards, revealing a glittering hardness of purpose which no loving smile could temper.

'May it please your Grace?' she repeated softly.

'Nay, Madame,' he heard himself say. 'No.' He saw the lit eyes dull like two doused fires. He bent and stabbed with a poker at the green logs in the hearth, occupying himself until she should speak again, and thinking: Jesu! we are but two actors in some tawdry play. How often I have foreseen my part, and hers, and this moment. In a blinding instant of clarity such as that experienced in high danger, he saw his own future spread before him like a plain on which grew bloody flowers. A plain, ending in a sheer abyss frighteningly near. The mystic vision appalled him. He straightened abruptly from the fire and heard Elizabeth's voice pathetically say:

'Your Grace, I cannot believe ... for the love of your own son, let me have mine! Must I petition the Queen?'

'The Queen is too ill to be disturbed.'

For the love of Christ, thought Richard. Elizabeth has not seen her one son for years; she knows nothing of the love that Anne and I bear our little prince. These thoughts gave an edge to his voice.

'And she is of like mind with me,' he said. 'We refuse your plea.'

'Why?' she said quietly.

He sighed, and rose. Only the truth would satisfy her, even if it changed her into a foaming wildcat. He took a turn about the room, and said coldly:

'Dame Grey, plain speech does wound, but since you ask it, I will give my reason. I had hoped there would be kindness between us, and pray that I am wrong in my surmise. I think that it is not through maternal affection alone that you wish your sons returned. There are still many ready to rise and unseat me from my throne. Therefore the Lords Bastard must remain my wards until such time ...'

Until you and all the scions of Lancaster and Woodville are dead or quiescent, he thought. He was surprised to hear her answer in a voice still silvery cool.

'My lord, what danger are two little bastard boys?'

He turned to face her squarely. 'They could,' he said quietly, 'with your aid, Madame, raise such a faction to strike blood from England's very core.'

Her lips drew back from her teeth. She seemed to grow immutably old, a being of legend. He almost expected to see flames or bubbling venom issue from her mouth and for an instant was afraid. Her next words, by contrast, seemed ordinary, although he recognized them as more lines from their deathly, deathless play.

'It presumes me to speak of this, Richard,' she said. 'But for your own sake I feel you should know that the people whisper about the safety of my sons. Some even say that you have had them put to death.'

Avidly she watched him, saw the little bitter smile he could not hide and knew that the rumours had reached him already. The secret words nurtured by herself, by Morton, through France and England. And yet he sat, doing nothing. Awed, she stared at him, inwardly fuming the next minute, seeking to attack him from one side or another, seeking weakness in the many-faceted person of the Hog ...

'So, my lady,' he said gently.

'I beg you, Sire, for your honour and the high regard you hold in the realm, and for my own comfort as your kinswoman, produce my sons. Reveal them to the people. Let them ride through London for a week – put an end to these dreadful whisperings!'

A great weariness overtook him. He felt his soul sucked down into some alien marsh, dragged into blackness, oozing, all-encompassing.

He sat staring at his own hands, turning his rings to ward off devils, and knew one lucid thought. God be thanked I had the wit to remove the boys. Now if by some ill chance the Woodvilles broke down the Tower, poisoned the guards – they would not find these small foci of power. *Thank God I sent them north.*

He said, quiet and outwardly tranquil: 'This I'll not do, Madame. There will be no little wars breaking out on Tower Hill – no abductions.' He heard her harshly indrawn breath. 'As for my honour and my high repute, I will gamble these gladly for England's peace.'

She sat on for a few minutes. Neither looked at the other or spoke. Then she rose. The audience was over, and she had failed. The only salvage from this trying hour was the information gleaned. The rumours were flying, even to the King's ear. There was no chance of securing the boys, but their usefulness was far from outworn. And Queen Anne was sick unto death. Bess should have a royal husband yet, of one breed or another.

'If I have spoken uncivilly, forgive me,' she said softly. 'I abide by your decree.'

He did not take her hands or kiss her, but let her swoop down to lip his fingers. He did not pity her, for she was gone beyond pity. He only wondered on her tortured life, and was lost in wonder.

'Good night, highness.'

Outside, racked by sudden nausea, she leaned on the wall, trembling so that her skirts shook upon her thighs. The pitchlight overhead flamed and whispered in sympathy. Gradually she controlled herself, and made her way to her own apartments. She passed by Bess's chambers, from which came muffled laughter; the sisters were all in there together, reliving the banquet. The sound of their weightless youth irked her. She longed desperately for comfort, kindness, a breast on which to cry. To vomit up the tears of centuries until their cause faded like a nightmare.

At her door, a slight figure pulled itself from the shadows. A frightened pulse started up in her head and heart. She cried sharply: 'Who's there?' and the shape moved into the warmly blazing torchlight. The tilted green eyes of Mistress Grace looked up at her. Looked with such imploring anguish that the face could have been a mirror of her own.

She could no more have turned that face away than she could have taken a blade and split her own greedy, lifeloving heart. The chamber door opened and together they went in.

Death struck the King two blows within the year. The first crippled his dynasty; the second destroyed his heart. Both fell in spring, that cruel blossom time. In April at Middleham the small prince Edward burned out his life and so, mysteriously consumed, died in a day upon his nurse's arm. The following March Queen Anne suffered a fatal haemorrhage of the lungs at Westminster. The people muttered of poison, but by whose will administered was not made clear.

Joined like two praying hands, the great roof of Westminster Abbey arched over the mourners. The stone faces, the flowery bosses, the images of saint and martyr and mason gazed impassively down at the black-clad ants in nave and aisles, while the lamenting and the perfumed incense wreathed and whirled hopefully to the feet of God. Possessed of that same granite impassivity, Elizabeth watched the small coffin's entombment; but when the King leaned to drop something after it – a jewel, a flower, a tear? she shivered. Never more than a pace behind, Grace took off her own wool cloak and hung it about her mistress's shoulders. Again, Elizabeth wondered what reward she sought for such devotion. Daily she waited for the whispered request, the shifty boon-begging, but it never came.

With a hand under each elbow, the Duke of Norfolk and Sir Francis Lovell supported the King. Behind them was John of Gloucester, his dark head bowed; as tall as the King now, but broader. Elizabeth looked at him with fleeting favour; he was the proof of Richard's susceptibility, and Bess was more comely than ever these days. Newly robed by the King's bounty, fine-coloured, she was happy to acquiesce in her mother's new desire. There was no more talk of Tudor. From across the nave Margaret Beaufort watched Elizabeth and nudged Stanley, who was weeping into his kerchief.

'I mislike it,' she whispered. The choir began a piercing, heart-tearing motet, rising in a vain hope to touch the essence of God. Stanley shook his head under cover of the fine linen, cocked an eye at his wife.

'She is cold to us,' she muttered. 'She will scarcely speak to me. Never did I think she would go her own way so.'

The *Dirige* and *Placebo* were sung, and the King, pale as marble, walked with his ministers from the Abbey. From that moment choristers would sing a ceaseless Requiem, trusting by their eloquence to waft Anne's soul into the steady gilt presence of the saints. Two processions went on either side of the nave, Dukes and Earls and their ladies. Behind them, some yawning, some weeping, walked their households. Proceeding thus, Grace came level with John of Gloucester.

He had wept for Anne, but he was calm, and the calmness gave him sombre maturity. He was so like Richard in appearance that it was almost comical, until the disparity of grief and years was seen. John's face was young, the King's was a sad skull, and there the jest ended. At the great door John looked and saw Grace. He inclined his head, he smiled. She edged nearer to him, out of the wake of Elizabeth's measured progress. Her shoulder touched his. He whispered: 'God greet you, mistress,' and then: 'My love!'

The anxious months of separation fell away at the sound of his warm voice, at the look in his eyes. It was not even ominous, she thought carelessly, that they should meet again at a funeral. Joy poured into her heart, obliterating her concern for Elizabeth and the vague sadness she felt for dead Anne and her half-dead husband. The procession moved out under the arch and into the milky spring day.

'We are for Eltham Palace,' he whispered. 'Come with us!'

He strode on steadily. Before him, a pack of bishops and priests surrounded the King, offering bleak comforts as droningly intense as the strong arms of the supporting knights. Grace ran a step to keep up with Elizabeth.

'I must go where she goes,' she breathed. John nodded, but he frowned.

'And I must follow him.' He looked towards Richard. 'Come to Eltham, mistress!'

For once, their paths did not divide. Some days later, Elizabeth ordered her household to make ready for Eltham. To Bess, she said: 'Wear your finest gowns, and the jewels Master Nesfield brought for you last week.'

'Everything is ready,' Grace said quietly, an hour later. She tried to strip her tone of gladness in case Elizabeth's whim should go wantoning and the decision be reversed. The glittering blue eyes moved to survey her and a little ironic smile twisted the mouth.

'You work swiftly.' Amazingly: 'Good wench!' She was in an eager humour, determinedly lightened. At one of the gloomy mourning feasts she had laughed aloud, earning the fury of the Duchess of Norfolk. Beneath the black veil Elizabeth was almost radiant, her eyes alive again, her skin rapt and luminous. Silver lady! thought Grace. Her heart turned, just as it did at John's name; the same feeling yet vastly different. Today was well-starred. They were bound for Eltham, Elizabeth was restored in spirit, and John was home from the North. Good had come out of grief.

Grace was not insensitive to the loss of Anne Neville. More than once Anne's face returned to her, and she heard the echo of her voice: 'Why, child, you're wet and cold ...' But Anne was destined for the grave even on that first showery day, and removed by an unknown dimension from things earthly. The hundred kindnesses of Anne diminished beside one smile from Elizabeth.

They rode into Eltham down the greensward leading to the now silent tilting ground. They entered the great hall built by King Edward, where a score of round windows were blazoned with the Falcon, the Fetterlock and the Rose. Grace was dismissed for an hour. Elizabeth was fussing over Bess, straightening the rich gown of black tissue latched with gold. She kissed the girl; Bess, ever prone to weep, burst into tears, then smiles, and Grace went out into the garden alone. She passed through a small stone tunnel, its moist base was thick with violets. On the lake, white swans drifted like petals. Crocuses pushed up their stiff flames around the lake's perimeter. Dying snowdrops hung down their milky hands.

He was there already; unerringly he had known where to find her. The two black figures walked slowly towards one another, she in her high-waisted gown with the jutting stomacher; he in his velvet doublet and jaunty short jacket weighted with a fine gold chain. They walked slowly at first, and then they ran, with arms outheld. They clasped one another breathlessly. His mouth covered hers before she could speak, and she thought: he is more practised – he has been wantoning with others in the North. She was not to know that he had dreamed so often of this kiss that it was merely a practised dream made flesh. He held her, stroking her cheek and her white neck, his fingers, calloused by the handling of horse and weapon, rough on her smooth skin. 'We have only a few days,' he said. 'Then I must return to Sheriff Hutton. My father says that there are troublous times ahead, and he would have me safe. Safe!' he repeated the word disgustedly. 'I am almost done with my training. I am Captain of Calais, and the King's heir.'

She nodded, strained close, as if to expunge the lost months and the turmoils which might keep them apart.

'I know, my love. But surely – the Earl of Lincoln is his heir ... he proclaimed it.'

'I did not mean his royal heir,' he said, laughing. 'A bastard cannot claim the throne. I meant only his heir in love and duty.' His face darkened. 'When his little son died, he was nearly demented ...'

'Hush!' she kissed the taut mouth. 'It's over. Have you spoken to him about our betrothal?'

'What chance?' he said dourly. 'He's full of trouble and policy. What do you know of this Tudor? This whelp who threatens invasion?'

Policy, always policy, when all she needed was to hold him, her love, her lord, during this brief season. As if he had read her thought, he said: 'I love you, lady. There shall be none other, Grace, while I live. And we have no tokens to exchange, have plighted no vows. Can we find a priest in this woodland, I wonder? I would be yours, your true knight and maker, in heart and thought, always.'

'No priest,' she said, laughing gently. 'Is not our word enough?'

The glassy lake, starred by lily-leaves and drifting birds, dreamed on in the chill sunlight. 'Will you take me?' he said. 'With only the swans and flowers for witness? This is a good place. How many lovers I wonder, have here plighted their troth?'

'How many Graces?'

'And how many Johns? They lived, loved, and now ...' He had been merry; now the laughter left him. She was afraid, and moved closer into his arms, feeling his slenderness and strength, and the quick hard beat of his living heart.

'Come,' he said. They walked together to the water's edge and knelt there. Solemnly he snapped off a tall yellow flower and placed it between her folded hands. Then he clasped his own hands together, saying in a loud voice:

'I, John Plantagenet of Gloucester, Captain of Calais, being neither husband nor leman to any, do pledge heart and lands to my dearly beloved Grace Plantagenet, in this place, as God witness my deed. I do so vow my sole regard and affection to her, Grace, this day. I forsake and renounce all other. And should I swerve from her, may God strike me and damn me to eternity.'

At these terrible words she turned sharply and looked at him. His head was bowed, his dark brows drawn together in a grim line.

'Answer!' he said.

She opened her mouth; nothing emerged. Slowly he raised his head.

'Plight me your troth,' he said, soft and savage.

'I cannot!' she whispered.

His colour ebbed. 'So,' he said flatly. 'You don't love me. But you could have spared me this!'

'I love you!' she cried wildly. Desperately she said: 'It is this place. Such vows are wrong, given in a ... a profane place.' She gazed across the lake, as if imploring the water's judgment. 'No good could come of it. Forgive me, love.' She pressed her cheek against his shoulder, and slowly his body relaxed. He stood, drawing her up from her knees, and he smiled faintly.

'You aren't to blame. I was inopportune. There have been too many tales. Such secret pledges are used by lecherous clerks and knaves to draw poor witless maids into a bed that's no marriage-bed ... yet you could not have thought that I would use you thus! Let it rest; I am still plighted to you. One day we shall complete this vow in church. With a shoal of gloomy priests muttering about the sin of cousins marrying!'

He removed a jewel from his thumb. 'Wear my ring, at any rate,' he said. 'Wear it in love of me, and in remembrance, while I am kicking my heels at Sheriff Hutton and you are serving your beloved mistress!'

The ring, like a gold-rimmed bead of blood, was too large. She would need to bind thread round it for safekeeping.

'Yes,' she said absently. 'I must serve my Elizabeth.'

'How you do love her!' he said in a voice so rough and strange that she looked up from caressing the ring. 'Was it from Titulus Regius that you remembered your "profane place"?'

She felt her face grow cold. 'That is cruel.' She walked a few paces away, and he followed her, gnawing his lips. 'I know she did wrong,' Grace said. 'But ...

He was by her side, turning her into his arms with a grasp as rough as his voice. 'Damn the Titulus Regius, and all such documents that hurt you and yours. And forgive me. But do not ask me to love Elizabeth. By that same profane marriage she bastardized the heir of England and set our realm upon its head.'

'And made your father King!' Her green eyes held his steadily.

'Even now, she schemes,' he answered, stung. 'Her latest ploy is to marry Bess to my father. She has already enquired of the papal legate about a dispensation, as they are niece and uncle. It is a heresy, an impossiblity.' He looked hard at her and said: 'Can I believe you live so close to Elizabeth and did not know of this?'

She said dully: 'Why is it an impossibility?'

'Because,' John answered like a lawyer, deadly serious, 'Bess is bastard now, like you, or I. To make her Queen my father would need to reverse the Titulus Regius. This in turn would make Bess's brother King, in Richard's place. The young Edward ...'

'Stop!' Her hands flew to her ears. He pulled the hands away and said relentlessly: 'You know, Grace, in whose grip England would be then – Elizabeth's. The realm would rise in blood against her. God's life, don't you know how the Woodvilles are loathed? Have you not heard Elizabeth mocked and derided?'

His face was flushed. To him the matter was all impartial, crystal logic. To Grace each word was insupportable. Instantly the imprint of her hand flared white on John's cheek. They stared at one another, he bewildered, she panting with rage. Swallowing hard, she said, 'Sir, good day,' and began to walk across the pleasaunce away from him. After a moment she realized the yellow flower still lay within her hand; with great scorn she tossed the bloom into the lake.

'Madame,' said John coldly, and bowed at her retreating back. He watched her walking, so slim and small and furious in her black gown, and a smile pulled at his mouth. A great wave of tenderness rose in him. He stood, feet planted apart, and laughed. He shouted: 'Madame!' Her steps quickened slightly.

He ran after her. She stopped, half-turned, moved forward again.

'Grace!' he bellowed. 'Sweetheart!' Then: 'Madame, farewell! For you, I drown!'

The tremendous splash jerked her about. John was standing, waist-deep in the lake; he was plastered with mud. A swan, disturbed on the nest, was approaching him, its white wings vibrating with rage. It surged towards him, beak opening savagely. He laughed even as it attacked him; it tore a great wedge out of his padded sleeve, but as he threw up his arms to ward off the furious bird, his laughter pealed across the water. All thoughts of the quarrel left Grace. Alarmed, she ran to the water's edge, seizing a fallen branch as a weapon, and wetting shoes and hose among the reeds. She snatched up her gown preparing to wade into the water. 'John! Take care!' The swan hissed, saw her and beat across the lake's surface towards the fresh enemy. John laughed no longer. Shouting to Grace to run, he plunged for shore. His feet were tangled in water-weed, sucked down by mud. He thought of her green eyes blinded by the bill, her limbs broken by the angry wings. It was a nightmare in which he floundered while the great white shape ran at Grace like an outraged angel. An angel with a serpent's head and neck.

She stood still, her arms at her sides. The wings lashed the air, the awkward feet drove the white bulk almost into her face. The graceful neck coiled and shimmered in anger. And John knew how much he loved Grace, more even than he had dreamed; that her destruction meant his own life's ruin. Kicking his feet at last from the clinging slime, he ran towards her, then checked in unbelief. The bird and the girl stood motionless, the attack abandoned, the wings folding, the neck dipping like a sail. Then the swan spread its wings once more, white against the black-clad figure of Grace, spread them in homage and farewell. It turned and waddled back towards its nest.

When he reached her side he was weeping. He gathered her into his arms, leaving smears of mud upon her hands and veil. What he had seen seemed no longer incredible, only a token of her purity, her goodness. What could he fear, when even the wild things revered her?

After a long time she said: 'My hour is almost up. I must go back to my lady.'

'We have wasted it, quarrelling,' he said tenderly. 'Ah, my love, my own dear ...'

'And we have so little time ...'

He held her closer, walking with her, stopping to kiss her in the stone arbour, and parting from her with a sigh. 'Tomorrow. The same hour.'

'My love. My love, yes.'

She fled to Elizabeth's chambers, hearing the rebuking clock boom from the tower and brushing dried mud from her gown. As soon as she entered the apartment she knew that something was amiss. Bess's wild wailing, heard even through a closed bedroom door, told her well enough. What now? she thought, gripped by the old, weary anxiety, She entered to confusion, to the litter of packing cases made ready for a journey. And to the silver lady's face, grey again, and full of demons.

'My lords,' said King Richard. 'It is beyond my comprehension that men give credence to the rumour that I intend marriage with Lady Elizabeth, bastard daughter of Dame Grey. It is so that divers seditious and evil disposed persons enforce themselves daily to sow seed of noise and disclaundre against our person; some by setting up of bills, some by message and sending forth of lies, some by bold and presumptuous speech and communication one with another ...'

He had gone down to the Hospital of St. John in Clerkenwell and had assembled there the lords spiritual and temporal to hear him. His words rejected Bess. Yet underlying them was all his frustrated despair, his stubborn yet veiled denial of all the greater rumour noised against him. He dared not say too much, yet in his impotent frenzy said too little. By reason of this anguish, venom entered his speech and so doing, touched off fresh madness in Elizabeth.

She was like a beast, pacing, raging, ripping her bodice to shreds so that it flowed about her. Her pale hair, now threaded with subtle white, fell about her face, as cursing, she wore out the carpet in her chamber. She threw back her head and cried damnation to the frightened air. She reviled the King while anger hollowed her cheeks and sapped the transient beauty of her face so that she looked old and crazed.

Bess wept in Grace's arms. For her, the slight was more personal. Over and again she said: 'He loved me! I know he loved me!' while Grace, horribly ill at ease, answered: 'Sure, lady, sweet lady, he loves you still; but then he is your uncle, banned from marriage with you by blood!' Bess wept louder, and Grace saw that she was undeceived.

Grace, in her turn, dogged Elizabeth, blown in her wake like a leaf in a hurricane. The unquestioning part of her whispered daily: I love and serve her. On the day of the proclamation Bess was taken away. Her score of new gowns, her lutes and lapdogs were packed and ready when the escort arrived. John of Gloucester was one of the officers commissioned to guard her. In a snatched secret moment he took Grace's hands; he smiled sadly.

'Our time is ended sooner than I deemed,' he whispered.

'Where are you taking my lady?'

'To Sheriff Hutton, for safety, at my father's orders.'

Safety from whom, what? she thought. John looked particularly fine; he wore a long cloak of Kendal green over his trim doublet and doeskin thighboots. His bright eyes were proud with his new commission. Not for the first time, Grace was jealous.

'Guard my sister well,' she murmured mockingly.

'Would to God *you* rode with me.'

He pressed the red-eyed ring she wore with strong fingers. Say nothing, my love, he thought. I know your stubborn allegiance to your dangerous lady. He looked deeply in her eyes; his mouth shaped a kiss. Jesting yet loving and immeasurably sad was that look; and they both grew old upon it. It held all their lost spring days.

'My lord, John!' They called him from the doorway. Farewell again, always farewell. They were gone, slim, gaudy knights shepherding the golden Bess, whose weathervane spirit had swung again to fair; her laughter blew back up the staircase. Farewell, murmured Grace, longing to run to the window, to watch him ride. It was best to remain, however, in line for the next command from Elizabeth. It was not long in coming.

'Bid Lady Margaret Beaufort attend me here.'

Grace needed scarcely a dozen steps for this errand. The Countess and her husband were in the next tower. They were sitting quietly, as if waiting for a boat or a chariot to bear them to a certain destination. When Grace delivered the summons, the Countess smiled a terrible smile. With her and her lord were Stanley's brother Sir William and Reynold Bray; and the look that passed like a lamplighter set itself upon each of the four faces, a mingling of triumph and scorn. The air grew sickly with a sour jubilation.

'Madame,' said Grace unquietly, 'Dame Grey is waiting.'

Margaret turned her face, piously shadowed by a long wimple. It was a brittle face, a stranger to all ungovernable emotion. She answered evenly.

'Mistress Plantagenet, *I* have been waiting for this day for years.'

Then she laughed softly, and Stanley clapped his brother on the shoulder, and Bray, jumping up, plaited his feet in a little jig.

'I should not jest,' said the Countess, rising, 'It is unseemly. We come.'

Grace followed them as they entered to Elizabeth, who moved to stand before her fireplace, hands joined at her breast. Margaret kissed her deliberately, first upon each cheek and then upon the folded hands. Her husband and Sir William did likewise. Bray crooked his knee, hawked and spat, with great delicacy as if this too were part of the ritual.

'Madame,' said the Countess, 'I have hoped and dreamed for this.'

And Sir William looked petulantly at Grace with a raised brow.

'Let her stay,' said Elizabeth, following his glance. 'She loves me.'

'As do we all,' said Lord Stanley.

Wickedly the Countess murmured: 'Our condolences, Madame, on the proclamation; it was unchivalrous ...'

'Have done!' cried Elizabeth, startling them all. 'My daughter shall be Queen of England. I look to you now to supply her King!'

Margaret's black eyes had an almost holy light.

'So you would have my son?'

'Tudor,' said Elizabeth. She clipped the word, as if it hurt her tongue. 'Yes, Henry your son. He shall have my daughter, as Morton advised. He shall wipe out this slur and restore us to the royal table.'

'He shall,' said the Countess, like an amen. The Stanleys bowed, and Bray passed a hand over his own hot face.

'How can I know you will not fail me?' said Elizabeth.

'Tudor will not fail you. He will sweep the past away. He will light a fire in England that you may warm your hands at in old age.'

'I look to Henry Tudor for my vengeance. He must conquer the Hog, the usurper.' There was a tightness in her head; she felt herself beginning to shake and swayed against the chimney-piece. Grace's hand took hers, supporting her.

'He must invade, and be successful,' she continued. 'Morton has my gold; my brother Edward has the ships ...'

'And my son has gathered a force in France and Brittany,' said the Countess. 'Fear naught.'

Reynold Bray spoke. 'Northumberland is ours, too. You recall how King Edward made Gloucester Lord of the North in Northumberland's stead ... the Earl resents him still, and will join our standard.'

'Are you to fight, Master Clerk?' Elizabeth disliked him so much she could not resist a gibe.

'Nay Madame,' (smirking). 'My calling is to help pray for all the dead in King Richard's army.'

'Enough,' said Lord Stanley. He moved swiftly forward to kiss Elizabeth's hand. 'I must be gone. There is much to do. Tudor will come in August. I shall tell the King that I am sick, and must retire to my estates. Leave all to me. God bless you, Madame.'

'One thing.' She stretched out her thin, shaking hand. 'A promise.'

He listened, quiet and grave.

'We have failed before to kill the Hog. At times I think he is immortal. See that he falls this time. And ...'

'My lady?'

'Let him be killed with ignominy,' she said. 'For his insults to me and mine. Let his death be inglorious. Let him be reviled. Do this, Stanley, in remembrance of me.'

He bowed. 'It is done, Madame.'

They went away swiftly. Below, she could hear them calling their esquires, and the noise of hoofs. Margaret Beaufort remained, statuesque, silent, smiling.

'Margaret?' said Elizabeth uncertainly.

'Madame, I feared you had ceased to love me,' said the Countess. She moved rapidly to a flagon on the table, poured red drink into two hanaps, splashing it carelessly. She thrust a goblet into Elizabeth's hand.

'To Henry ap Tydder!' she cried. 'And to the union of the Red and White Roses! To the new dynasty! You and I will build it together!'

Elizabeth set the cup to her lips. Her throat was closed, she regurgitated the wine, turning quickly to spew it into the hearth.

'My lady, you're unwell,' soothed the Countess. 'Attend her, Mistress Grace.' The door closed behind her.

After a while, Elizabeth said: 'I will lie down.'

Grace said tentatively: 'Madame ...'

'Well?'

It came pouring out like that undrinkable toast: if the King were killed, would his son suffer likewise? Would John of Gloucester be safe?

Elizabeth answered with more patience than she had ever shown.

'He will be safe, Grace. He is of no consequence.'

They went then to the bedchamber. Elizabeth slept a little while Grace watched, wanting to weep and knowing no reason for it.

August came in with thunder. Storms the like of which no village ancient could remember crashed over England. Rain burst bridges and laid whole landscapes awash. Daily, white veins of lightning split the heavy sky, striking cattle, firing forest and tenement. The people crossed themselves and looked up aghast for the image of God descending from the clouds to chastise the sins of man. Listening thus for the trumpet, folk cursed the loss to their livelihood, and cursed the King.

'Tis a judgment,' Butcher Gould told his prentice as they hurried along Tower Wharf. He averted his eyes from the fortress etched white against a bursting black cloud. Indignant sorrow fomented in him as he thought of Elizabeth's murdered sons. Smothered or stuck at the orders of the Hog. A friar had muttered the whole tale in the butcher's ear, so it must be right. A rheumy tear filled Gould's eye as he recalled his first sight of the baby prince in Sanctuary. And the Queen – addressing him as her equal: 'Ned is coming home, Master – spread the word!' Now that baby prince was traitorously slain. A fork of fire bisected the heavens, making the prentice leap and howl.

'Nay, not yours, lad,' said Gould grimly. 'The King's judgment. Swine. May he lose his battle.'

The shore of Milford Haven was slippery with rain; Henry's first footstep shuddered and slid. Behind him in the boat his attendants gasped and held their breath. Henry righted himself swiftly. The others, mantling themselves in preparation for stepping ashore, marvelled at the smile he gave them.

'You saw, my lords?' he called. 'I almost fell! Just as the Conqueror did! What better augury that England would have me clasp her?'

The sea-wind blew him, tugging at the fine rust-coloured hair beneath the velvet cap, and whipping colour into his white cheeks. He looked back across the ocean, where, lying a little way out, was the full-masted carrack that had brought him tossing through days and nights from Harfleur. Further out on the horizon was the rest of his fleet. Ships like ghosts, apparently motionless yet making speed to his support. Ships crammed with his fighting men. My beauties! thought Henry, with a grim little smile. He itched at the memory of their lousiness, their scabs. The gaols of Normandy had yielded a fine crop. Scrofulous, ragged (before he clothed them in leather and steel) but strong. More like beasts than men. Murderers trained by circumstance from the cradle and pleased by the bargain that had released them to fight against Plantagenet. He walked a pace to where the ground was firmer and knelt, pressing his face into the sand, feeling the salty grit upon his tongue. Then, raising himself, he cried:

'Oh God! Observe my cause! Uphold me!'

'Amen, amen.' Morton stood at his shoulder. The wind fluttered his robes. He stood, a black carrion crow, crucifix upraised. The breeze smoothed his face to a strange resurgence of youth. He among few had enjoyed the crossing; something in the buffeting waves had called to his own turbulence, had whipped the longings that had gnawed him for so many years. Exaltation rose and he checked it immediately. Time to rejoice when the battle was won. When York and Lancaster were wedded and the succession secure. When the scarlet hat of Cardinal Archbishop lay upon his own head. Yet he sent up one tiny prayer, like a scurrying rat. *Deo Gratias*; I have been spared to see Tudor on England. Even a moment's delay irked him and he touched Henry's arm.

'We should make camp, I think.'

He was unprepared for the look, the answer, both edged with hauteur. Henry's voice had changed. Still quiet, but not diffident as of old; still sibilant, but ringing like brass.

'My lord, do you give orders to your sovereign?'

And Henry smiled. The smile touched every corner of the lean face, drew back the long lipless mouth until a glint of teeth showed, struck yellow fire from the sombre eyes. Obediently the sun emerged from behind a blue cloud and painted Henry's shadow on the sand. Morton, shocked and impressed, said 'Sire,' very humbly. Behind, the lords stepped from the rowing-boat, wetting their feet in the wavelets. Morton turned and gave them a look that bade them clothe themselves in respect. They came quietly to Henry's side. He spoke their names.

'My lord and uncle, Jasper, Earl of Pembroke.'

Jasper Tudor came, no longer young, but tall, wiry and unbowed. He kissed his nephew's fingers.

'John, Earl of Oxford.

'Sir John Cheney.

'Sir William Brandon.'

'Sir Edward Woodville.'

Wet sand stained their hose as they came to kneel like penitents before a shrine. Hot lips, cold lips, touched Henry's hand. He raised his eyes to where dunes soared above the beach. On the ridge a little company of horsemen wheeled about. Their standards blew wildly, wrapping themselves about the staves. Two of the riders broke away from the party and rode jerkily down the slope, their horses' haunches low, fighting the loose sand. Henry stared at the banners. The second was his own; he had dreamed of it. The Red Dragon of Cadwallader, torn and tugged by wind so that it streamed like a flame, like the ancient myth that he had been told surrounded his ancestry. He knew himself the offspring of gods and princes, and his heart shivered in him.

The first standard he did not recognize. To Jasper Tudor he said: 'Who comes?'

'Rhys ap Thomas, Sire. They bring your personal standard. Praised be God, the Welsh chieftains have mustered to our call. And see—' he pointed to the cliff top where more horses were sliding down, urged by their riders — 'Sir John Savage's men.'

'They will all come.' Henry's voice was steady. He sought with his eyes among the whipping cloud of standards, saw, descending, the bucks' heads, the azure and gold of Sir William Stanley's arms, borne by a lieutenant.

'Where is Maredudd?' he said sharply. 'My cousin should be here to greet us. And where is my stepfather?'

Jasper Tudor conferred with the mounted envoys, then turned again to his nephew.

'Stanley awaits us in Denbighshire. He has gathered a great force. He plans to join us on the day of battle; likewise Northumberland. Until then, Richard believes he has their loyalty.'

Henry did not join in the ensuing laughter. *The battle.* Two words to chill his heart, words to be left unfaced until the last necessity. The Dragon fluttered and thrummed above him, and now there was no comfort in it. It was only a strip of coloured silk. God, he thought. Let it be over quickly, and let none see my fear.

'Where is my clerk?' he said abruptly. 'I must write to John ap Marredud at once, and to Gilbert Talbot. Set up camp, my lords.'

Within an hour he was seated in a tent, away from the rush of the waves. The wind had dropped and given way to an oppressive warmth. Out to sea thunder growled, coming nearer. Henry chafed his hands, and began to dictate rapidly, in a clear quiet voice.

'We will ride on Shrewsbury for London, and cross the river at Tewkesbury,' he said. 'Attend me at Shrewsbury.' He raised his eyes and glanced at the attentive faces lining his tent: at Morton, the Welsh chiefs, the Woodville knight. And looking at Sir Edward

Woodville he was reminded of Tom Dorset, his thoughts wandering back to Harfleur. Dorset! What would he not give to be back on his home soil! And how fortunate that he had been apprehended in time. Creeping home to his mother, to follow God knew what whim, what allegiance. Well, Dorset was now a pawn and a pledge to Charles of France; a surety against those thousands of men given to the battle-day. So that Lancaster and France and England could be all one again, and the Yorkist plague forever ended.

'Sire?' said the clerk, waiting.

'Yes.' Henry's face altered, becoming bland and hard as a tombstone effigy. The yellowing light blazed in his eyes. 'Say: 'Attend *us* there.' He rose.

'And head the letter: "*From the King*"'

A vast thunderhead, livid at the edge, rolled westward over England, but the rain held off long enough for Henry's forces to spread, to close up, and to deploy themselves near Redmore Plain, the appointed place of trial. September was nudging August. It was night.

Most of the royal army was asleep, stretched beside their fires, their weapons close at hand. King Richard was wakeful. He stood by his pavilion and watched the sky, the movement of the clouds, the occasional dull flicker of a star. As if it were written in large letters on the sky, the ground, the sleeping tents, he knew this to be his last night on earth. Very strongly he felt the presence of those he had loved; Anne's gentle face, the small laughing Edward, and the larger, the adored golden brother. And Warwick, hands clasped about his knee before the fire at Middleham. The great knight, and himself, the untaught boy. All Plantagenet. All York. All dust.

And he? With the uncanny certainty that comes in lonely, pre-dawn hours, he knew himself a sacrifice, the last offering to a force so strong that no philosophy could reckon it, no priest exorcize it. Gazing at the dark bowl of the sky, he shuddered at the mystique of this knowledge. The clarity of his thought would be gone in the morning, driven off by the primaeval urges of survival and conquest. Yet now he knew himself bought and sold; knew, as surely as Noah anticipated the Flood, that the Stanleys would endeavour to bring about his downfall. He was not afraid, only awed by certainty. He felt destiny rapping at his soul.

A moment's guilt, a moment's pity for the brave men slumbering beside their little fires, brought the sting of tears to his eyes.

'But we will fight, by God!' he said aloud.

He would give this destiny a run for its money. Tudor was the target; if Tudor were slain, this hungry, urgent fate might be appeased.

Yet thinking thus, he knew it vain. As surely as he was born, so would he die, and his dynasty with him.

If only Edward had contained his lust. Had he but married, as Warwick wished, a foreign princess. Or had he but thrown the woman down at Grafton Regis and ravished her, leaving her conquered and himself sated and bored. To Edward all women had been foreign citadels, to be invaded ...

Too late, too late to change the pattern of the years. By that marriage, so secret, so cunningly devised, the houses of York and Plantagenet fell like Sodom, burnt up to ashes. Richard thought: the salt of their wounds is the smile of Elizabeth.

The white-edged thunderhead was dispersing, moving swiftly away. Dawn was coming, hailed by a brave trumpet.

She stirred in her bed, awakened by dream or noise or movement, but unaware of which. The heavy curtains at the window made it impossible to tell whether it was night or day. Grace was still sleeping at the foot of the bed, her breathing so peaceful that Elizabeth was envious. It must surely be dawn. And what would this dawn bring? How many nights lately had she lain in this London bed, fretting the hours until another day of disappointment? Could this one be different at last? Margaret had seemed so sure, so proud and confident. Pressing her hand, whispering as the royal army left a week ago, not to fear because of their great number. Stanley would not fail, even if he came to Henry's aid at the last moment ...

Elizabeth turned her face, seeking coolth from the pillow. A swarm of worries bombarded her. Would Henry conquer? Was he weak? She conjured his face for the thousandth time; so strange, so significant to her. He had never fought a battle in his life. Would Stanley and his brother and Northumberland, and the Welshmen, be strong enough to uphold him? She wound her hands together beneath the covers, imagined disasters spearing her like toothache. There would be no further forgiveness from Richard. Could she pray? Our cause is God's, Margaret had said. Often Elizabeth had prayed to God, and gone away empty. It was not God to whom she had prayed, before the battle of Barnet ...

'Oh, Melusine,' she said very quietly. 'Send me a saviour, Melusine!'

She waited, while faintly a growl of thunder passed over, miles away. Neither omen nor answer; only the ever-present tempest talking to itself.

'My soul in payment!' she said. 'My soul and those of all I love. Aye, and their bodies too!' reckless with anxiety. Then, like a lover: 'Melusine, ah, Melusine ...'

With incredible swiftness sleep took her again. As if drugged she lay fathoms deep, entranced, exhausted. A pleasant dream coiled about her. She walked in a forest; her mother held her hand. Jacquetta, young again, and sumptuously dressed, towered above her, bright eyed. Elizabeth skipped beside her, laughed, listened. Lyrical words accompanied their walk, and the wood thickened, and the treetops closed about their heads. Bright fungi clustered at their feet.

'... and there, she built Lusignan. She bore Raymond children: Urian, with his one red and one green eye; Gedes, of the scarlet countenance; Gyot, of the uneven eyes, Anthony, of the claws and long hair; a one-eyed son; and Geoffrey of the Tooth; he had a boar's tusk.'

The forest grew black, and all about the foliage was on fire. The soft voice repeated the names, over and over; then, without warning, there appeared an abbey, an abbey with wounded firefilled windows, an abbey running red with blood; she knew it to be the monastery of Malliers, where Geoffrey of the Tooth had attacked his brother. There was the abbot, and a hundred monks, bleeding, burning. Shrieking, half weeping, half laughter, filled the air. She looked up at her mother for reassurance and saw a scarlet countenance, one leaking, suppurating eye, a mouth that was no mouth but a hole from which jutted a bloody tusk. The hole spoke:

'See, child! See what you have borne! Monsters all!'

The screams grew louder, lifting her scalp; a cry pitched in ecstasy yet keening like a mourner. High above her bed, above the towers, it tossed and wailed. Her blood heard it, the springing sweat on her face acknowledged it. She plunged in the bed; she cried: 'O Jesu, Jesu ...'

She was dragged from certain disaster by Grace's arms, felt Grace's cheek against her own, and clung desperately.

'Lady, my sweet lady Elizabeth.'

'Is it morning?'

'Yes. Yes. It's morning.'

'Draw back the curtains … Nay, don't leave me!'

They stayed together, Grace on her knees, Elizabeth almost falling from the bed, her hair shrouding them both. Grace stroked the heavy silken mass and kissed it, murmuring little loving words, while Elizabeth leaned shivering on Grace's neck. They stayed thus for some time. Then Elizabeth detached herself with a great sigh.

'Let in the light now, Grace.'

Grace arose and went to the window. She tugged at the drapes and sunlight streamed in. Then she glanced down at the courtyard and was suddenly still.

They were raising the drawbridge. A party of horsemen galloped in, their mounts black with sweat, their gear and their harness visible under their habits mired with blood and mud. Even from the height of the tower she could see their wild faces, and heard indistinctly their shouting.

'What is it?' Elizabeth asked from the bed.

'Part of the army returning.'

'Open the window. Let me look.' She came to stand beside Grace. Across the cobbled yard a figure was running; comically foreshortened, the black-clad tonsured form of Reynold Bray. Joined by half a dozen other men, he rushed towards the knights now swinging down from their punished horses. The cheering rose like smoke. The men were embracing, dancing in the courtyard. Stewards rushed out with flagons as more horsemen surged over the drawbridge; standards flying, men wearing stained liveries, the horned bull of Cheney, the buck of Stanley, the silver crescent of Northumberland; and a score more, Welsh arms, red roses, red dragons, harness red with blood.

Bray turned in the midst of his capering to wave like a boy up at the tower window. He cupped his hands and shouted, then flung out his arms in a wild exultant gesture. Elizabeth murmured in annoyance:

'How can I hear at this distance?'

'The Hog – is – dead!' Bray bawled, long-drawn-out notes. 'Henry lives! *Vivat Rex!*'

'Does he say – is it …' Elizabeth said hesitantly.

Bray, desperate to impart his message, turned and seized a banner from an esquire. A soiled despoiled banner, furled and carried as proof of conquest, as booty. He unrolled it, and for a moment the

White Boar ramped and snarled on an azure ground. Then Bray in savage pantomime, flung it to the cobbles, stamped upon it, and for good measure, spat. Over his head the Red Dragon flamed, tongue and claws like gouts of fire.

Elizabeth turned from the window. Grace looked at her and knew that the warmth, the intimacy between them was over for that day. Triumph and crystal hardness sat on the worn, dewy face.

'Gown me,' she ordered. 'I must look my best. My saviour is come.'

PART FOUR

The Dragon of Wales

1485-7

Jasper will breed for us a Dragon,
Of the fortunate blood of Brutus is he,
A Bull of Anglesey to achieve,
He is the hope of our race ...
Welsh Song (ca. 1484)

The glory was still with him. He sat in the Bishop of London's Palace, while outside, September, as if in penance for wild August, brightened the city with a day of gold. Like a sovereign insect in the hive's deepest cell he sat, able at last to determine the things which excitement and trepidation had snarled together in a wanton skein. For the first time in many days he could catch his breath; the swift nightmare and the ecstasy of conquest were equal; the nightmare fled and the glory remained. Through the high window's diamond panes the sun sparkled. One dusty beam played downward and rested on Henry's head so that he was at the end of a tunnel of light. He felt his mind restoring itself to order and to plan. Part of the glory was that, thanks to the Stanleys, he had quit himself well. In truth they had done it all; they and Northumberland had placed the day in Henry's lap. He thought: I am indebted. A little of the glory fled, leaving watchfulness, and an irony that made his long lips smile. They will expect fair payment, he told himself. And what shall I give them?

Only the honour of being ever under my eyes. For if they betrayed one king, what might they not work upon his successor?

They would do nothing against him, for they would never have the chance. Before him on the table lay Richard's crown, taken from a thorn bush in the field and placed on Henry's head with great drama and reverence by Lord Stanley. Henry took it up and held it in the sun-shaft. It was rather misshapen; the side of the slender ellipse was dented almost beyond repair. There was the half print of a hoof in the soft gold, and one of the delicate trefoils was broken off. Although it had been cleaned it still bore, deeply ingrained, traces of blood and mud. He lifted it higher; it weighed very little; it had been built to circle a battle-helm. The hard joyless glory left him as he stared at the ruined bauble, his imagination augmenting it with a head, a face. A raised visor, a white face distorted with fury. He would not easily forget that face. Richard was dead, hacked almost to pieces by Stanley's men. Yet even thinking of that last charge when the demented figure on the white horse came straight for him, started the sweat upon his hands so that the crown moved in their grasp.

He had been no more than a bowslength away; so near that he could see the hairs on the muzzle of the great white horse, the frog of the deathly hoof raised to strike. He could see the bloody whites of Richard's eyes, the froth-filmed teeth, the razor edge of the whirling axe, that red-edged axe shaped to shear a man in twain. He could hear the screams of 'Richard!' – the tribal cries of the Household – the blind exaltation of the handful of men who rode behind the Boar on that last lunatic charge, their lances like teeth, their armour running blades of light. Across Redmore Plain at him they came, a sweeping wave of menace. He had thought, sharply: So this is my end. Standing on the little knoll whence he had watched the battle thus far in safety, he had clutched at Jasper's mailed arm with frantic fingers. Then Richard was almost upon him; he had felt his tongue cleaving to his palate; shame-fully, secretly, had felt the spurt of wetness on his thigh. He had watched his standard-bearer, William Brandon, go down to meet the charge and be swept away by a blow from that axe, the Dragon falling, undulating gracefully, its scarlet deepened by Brandon's blood. The giant Cheney had stepped out to do battle and Richard had sliced him through the throat. And Henry had taken his first pace, backwards, to fly, anywhere, to bury himself in the bushes, never to see or speak again.

Then Sir William Stanley had come, so tardy that Henry would always resent him for it. At the very last of last moments he had ridden up with a sparkling pristine force, red roses and fresh mounts, like actors on cue but only just. They had smashed into the flank of Richard's little company, translating it in moments from a monster of hell to a toil of severed limbs and massacred flesh. He had not watched while they killed the King; not through any squeamishness but only through the necessity to turn and vomit his relief into the grass. None saw; the pallor he later presented was marked down as reverence to the moment when Stanley crowned him in the field.

He set the crown slowly down upon the table. As soon as it left his fingers he felt warm, for it had been like touching a ghost. He would have a new crown fashioned, a crown of greater magnificence. Emeralds in honour of the Dragon's green ground. He looked up to where his banner hung. The Dragon was so powerful, with its rippling body and serpentine tail, its fierce gory colour. Men said that the Dragon had originally come from the sea; so it possessed all the inexorable tumult of the ocean. Against the sea even fire was powerless.

He pressed his bare bony hands together, and squinted into the floating gold sunlight. Like a myriad motes of debris in the bright ray, the weird talismen and beliefs, his since childhood, arose, pushing back all uncertainty. In one trembling moment omnipotence crystallized, and he was wise enough to know he must work to enslave it. The first lesson was to profit from the mistakes of others. Richard Plantagenet had trusted his ministers and was now bloody defiled carrion in the mean house of the Greyfriars at Leicester. What of his predecessors? Where had their paths forked, their feet trodden in error? Detail, thought Henry, is the great instructor. On the table lay a pile of tomes, heavy ledgers bound with brass. The Household Books, the Grants from the Crown, the Privy Purse. The Docket Book, the Parliamentary Statutes. He pulled one near at random and opened it. The pages smelled musty, with a faint reek of incense. Even without looking at the rusty writing he would have known whose reign this was. From The Issue Rolls he read:

To John de Serrencourt, who came to witness Queen Margaret's coronation and report the same: thirty-three marks.

A hundred pounds to be paid out of the customs on wool and skins at Southampton, to William Andrews, for his services during his attendance on the Queen in foreign parts.

Skipping a few pages, he read:

> To Jean de Jargean, minstrel, 50 livres for his succour of the King in great melancholy.
>
> To the masters of Alchemy, 200l. to the manufacture of gold for the King's pleasure.

Henry opened another book and read from the Acts of the Privy Council:'This day Wm Cleve, King's chaplain and clerk of the works, made supplication for money to pay the poor labourers their weekly wage. This he has the utmost pain and difficulty to purvey.'

Slowly he closed both books. Dust rose and vanished. So, Henry. Men would not hear the later Henry miscall that saint, that dupe. Half-brother to Uncle Jasper, a vein of royalty to be cherished for Lancaster's sake. This did not alter the fact that, according to the Books, he had left the realm almost bankrupt.

He reached for another tome. Gayer writing here, bright with gold leaf

> Writ the feast of St. Crispin and Crispinian, the sixteenth year of King Edward the Fourth:
>
> To John Goddestande, footman, ten marks; for purveying of six ells of sarcenet and three of velvet, and two counterpanes, cloth-of-gold, furred with ermines, for the pleasure of Mistress Shore.

Henry sucked in his lip. Whoremaster. His righteousness was tempered by not a little envy. For a moment he grudged Edward the years of hot beds and willing bodies; he remembered his own stunted youth. He had been driven to learning and piety as a substitute for more earthly pleasures. Always subservient; to Uncle Jasper, Lord Herbert, Francis of Brittany. And yet there had been sweet moments. Maud Herbert had loved him truly, and of her he had had his pleasures, fleeting thing though it was. Maud still loved him and she was here with him in London. He would not, however, like Edward flaunt his concubine to the derision of Europe and the deficit of the Privy Purse. He would never on Crispin's Day, when Harry of Lancaster had done so nobly at Agincourt, defile the Household Book with entries such as these. Particularly when he was wedded to Edward's daughter...

He opened another ledger, thin and small. The reign of King Edward the Fifth. The bastard king; the king that never was. He looked blindly at the expenditure, clothing for knights, grants in preparation for the coronation. He stroked the book, and closed it, drawing another ledger, the latest, towards him, bending to a random page.

An annuity of £20 to Joan Peysmarsh for her good service to King Richard in his youth and to his mother.

To Master John Bently, clerk of poor estate, four pound to defray his expenses at Oxford University.

He pulled the Statute Book towards him. From it he learned that Richard had halved the Crown dues on eighteen cities, had forbidden the benevolence tax begun by Edward the Fourth; had loaded the poor with gifts and so doing had depleted the estate of many barons. He read on and was taken aback by what he saw. The lifting of taxes, together with the financing of Richard's last battle, had brought the country again to the brink of ruin.

To Katherine Bassingbourne, goodwife of York, a pension. For my Lord Bastard, two doublets of silk ...

The Book closed of its own accord as his hand left it. The terrible face snarled under the lifted visor, the death-white horse reared. The bloody axe hung, ready to sever with its aching edge sinew and muscle and nerve. It was full time to forget this demon; this man whose mild writings could bring shameful fear to Henry, the Dragon of Cadwallader. He sat still, calling up his ancestors. The great Uther Pendragon and his greater son, Arthur, not dead but sleeping under green banners and silence. Down through a female line past Owen, the dreamers and warriors of Wales; through Llewellyn, Rhys, Gruffydd, Owain, Maredudd, Hywell, to the misted splendour of Cadell, Rhodri, Merfyn, and last, the Lady Ethil, of the Isle of Man. Although no herald had yet traced it, there was the belief that somewhere beyond Uther, Noah's virtuous blood ran deep. Dragons, two by two ...

'I am immortal!' said Henry the dreamer. While Henry the realist countered: 'So I shall remain!'

A thump on the door made him quickly compose himself. He was reminded by the slither of halberds outside that he was safe in this lodging, as in all his lodgings. At his word a young man entered. He was impeccably liveried, flat cap on his head, high collar cutting into his gullet. On his breast was the royal insignia: H.R. and in his hand he bore a tall pike. Henry looked him over, pleased with his own innovation.

'Well, Master Yeoman Warder?'

'Bishop Morton is here, your Grace.'

Henry frowned. His long face grew lugubrious with annoyance but he did not chide the youth. Though it was vital that his whims, like his orders, should obtain, reiteration in this case served better than scolding.

'Have you forgotten already? We are not 'Your Grace'.'

The warder blushed. He tried to bow, but the stiff collar choked him. Strangling, he said: 'Your Majesty.'

'Yes,' agreed Henry gently. 'The term 'Your Grace' applies to Bishops and Earls and Dukes, a common thing. There is only one Majesty, as there is only one God. Bid the Bishop enter.'

Morton carried a heavy sheaf of papers and a little coffer worked with gold filigree.

'You are tardy, my lord,' said Henry.

'Aye, but through no fault of mine. I thought I had taken the sweating sickness. Praise God, I still am whole.'

'I myself have prayed against this sickness,' said Henry. 'Then, I thought: no Providence could be so cruel ... I stayed here, with faith in my talisman.' He indicated an oblong box, age-mildewed, hanging beneath the Dragon banner.

'What is it, Sire?'

Opened by Henry, the box revealed a brittle bleached bone, with a few fragments of cartilage hanging twisted from one end.

'The leg of blessed St. George.' Morton genuflected dutifully, saying: 'The sickness is bad in all parts; did you know that two mayors have died, and six aldermen? They fall like flowers. Yet I think the worst is over.'

'So I can be crowned.'

'Sire, you must be crowned. But there are certain matters to discuss – some of great importance.'

Henry tapped the Household Books with a forefinger.

'The economy for one, I vow. By the Rood! the country is in a parlous state. You, as my Chancellor, must help me set it right.'

'Taxes,' said Morton succinctly. 'Give me a little time, Sire. Trust my judgment.'

The heavy-lidded eyes and the old wattled ones met briefly. Morton's were the first to look away.

'What have you in your box?' said Henry pleasantly.

'A few of the traitor's jewels.' Morton tapped the rolls of parchment he held. 'And here, the inventory of the larger goods.'

'Let me see.' Henry lifted the coffer's lid. Delving, he said: 'He was enamoured of finger-rings.' He took out rubies, sapphires, enamelled flowers, and fitted them on to his fingers. His hands grew rich; the sunlight sought them out. Silently he heard the screams of the pale war-horse; saw the angry anguished face, the raised axe. He stared at them; they vanished.

He said softly: 'Rings from a rebel. Did you bring my Statutes, Chancellor?'

'I can send for them.'

Henry waved a bright, loaded hand. 'Later. I only wished to see, writ plain, that my reign began the day before the battle. So that the Roll of Attainder on Richard and his followers may be valid.'

'You are King, from the day before the battle, as we said. And I have the notes for the Attainder here, together with the list of those hanged directly after, at Leicester. Or beheaded, according to their station.' Morton extended a roll. 'Here is the list of those you pardoned: Surrey ... Lincoln!'

He looked at Henry. 'I was surprised, Sire. Lincoln was named Richard's heir.'

He said: 'I have offered Lincoln a place on my Council, where I may watch him best, until the day when his ambition brings him down. Lincoln will light the way to all Yorkist traitors still living. My lord, have I not told you...

The sentence drifted. Morton said gently:

'That Tudor will vanquish Plantagenet?'

'That Tudor must destroy Plantagenet,' said Henry gravely. 'Without fear or favour, by order and system. One by one, until, as the dying Cadwallader prophesied, we are supreme in England, and all other is wiped away.'

'The heirs and offshoots are now gathered in,' said Morton. 'Would you learn of their disposal?'

'One by one,' said Henry, sitting back. 'First: Warwick, from Sheriff

Hutton. George of Clarence's boy. How and where is he?'

'The boy is almost an idiot,' answered Morton. 'Simple in the head; attainted for his father's treason, yet a true Plantagenet. At your suggestion, the Tower has him now.'

'Close?'

'Tight guarded.'

'And his cousin, my bride?'

Morton's eye was almost merry. 'I brought her with me today.' He moved to the window and stood bulkily on tiptoe. 'If you crane high, Sire, you will see her, walking in the garden.'

Henry did so, for a long time, his face close to the panes. Below, Bess paced like a sleepwalker; her companion, a tall swarthy girl, had a hand lightly under the Princess's elbow. The first few yellow leaves drifted about them. The girl looked up at the window and Henry raised his hand. It was Maud Herbert; he smiled to see his one-time mistress escorting his future wife. Bess drew out a linen square and wiped her eyes.

'Why does she weep?' he said. Morton muttered.

'She loved the traitor, her uncle,' said Henry. It was not a question. 'God grant that she comes virgin to my bed!'

'I'm sure of it,' said Morton loudly. 'The question is, Sire, does she come to you a bastard? This is the issue. This is why I am here.'

Henry moved back to the table, and looked at the long yellow membrane unrolling in the Bishop's hands. Words flung themselves briskly to his eye.

'... that they lived together sinfully and damnably in adultery ... all their issue being bastard and unable to inherit or claim anything by inheritance ...'

'Yes,' he said after a while. 'The Titulus Regius. I cannot wed a bastard.'

'Yet you must wed Bess of York. To consolidate your claim. It is vital.'

'Therefore I must repeal the Titulus Regius.'

'At once, highness.'

'And by so doing,' said Henry slowly, 'I shall legitimize all Edward's children. I shall therefore restore King Edward the Fifth.'

He rose clumsily, knocking over the little coffer. Jewels flooded the table. He walked to where the Dragon hung, and fixed his desperate eye upon its storm-red curves. Cadwallader, shall all my striving come to naught? And Cadwallader might have answered, writhing his ancient bones: The truth must wound. Our heritage is not great enough to withstand the heirs of Edward the Third ... Henry, your own line is flawed with bastardy.

'The boys' claim is better than my own,' he said.

'The boys are dead,' replied Morton. Henry swung round.

'What?'

'In the mind of the people they are dead,' said the Bishop. 'The mind of the people is your stength. From shore to shore the word was spread. Mancini himself gave it to the Chancellor of France. Did you not hear?'

'I deemed it rumour,' Henry said quietly.

'So it is. A strong rumour with a lion's teeth. Richard Plantagenet, the attained usurper, had them done to death.'

'Where are the boys?'

'I can bring them to you, in a very few days.' Morton picked up a ruby, held it to the light. 'Or ... I can turn rumour into truth.'

The Dragon shimmered, coiled its tail in a little draught. Minutes crawled by, like the slow sand of a dream. Then Morton asked: 'Would you have peace in England?

A faint nod, watched by the Dragon.

'Then Tudor must expunge Plantagenet. Lancaster must exorcize York. Utterly, until there is no figurehead left. No more ruin, no more decimation of the nobles ...'

'Would this happen?' For the moment he was like a schoolboy, begging the answer to a test.

'Children,' said Morton heavily. 'They are the most dire focus for uprising. Powerless yet malleable. And their father was greatly loved.'

'*Children*,' repeated Henry. 'Holy God.' He looked again at the Titulus Regius. Somewhere, Cadwallader's old corpse moved, and he said: 'Do it. Have it done.'

Morton stepped to the door, summoned one of the Yeomen. A sealed writing, prepared weeks earlier by the Bishop, changed hands, and the guard departed.

'I have advised Sir James Tyrrel,' Morton said evenly, returning to Henry's side. 'He is a cool, ambitious man. He will expect the general pardon, and a commission in France.'

'He shall have both.'

He found himself trembling. He said firmly: 'Now ...

'Sire?'

'The Act of Titulus Regius must be repealed *unread* in both Lords and Commons. Its constitution must be forgotten; it solidified Richard's claim. More, the Act must be destroyed.' He went to the window again, beneath which Bess and Maud Herbert still walked. 'Hear me. As Chancellor, you must see to this. All copies of the Act are forfeit from this day. On pain of dire punishment. We will have a great burning.'

'It shall be done.'

'Good.' He turned again with a brittle smile. 'What now? What other bird came within our net this month?'

Morton, peering at his roll, muttered his way down a list of names.

'Sir Francis Lovell ... he escaped the field. Bishop Stillington – half-crazed – to the Tower. Catesby, Speaker of the Commons, caught and hanged at Leicester. The Stafford brothers are in Sanctuary. We cannot touch them – yet. What else? We combed the North ... Bess came from Sheriff Hutton with various women, among them Cicely, her sister. Catherine Woodville is in London. Sir Edward is your loyal man. Dorset (I mistrust him, he clings to his mother) is being brought from France this week. Ah, and there's another royal bastard – John of Gloucester.'

'The traitor's son?'

'Yea, Richard's boy. Seventeen or so; of little note.'

'My lord!' Henry's voice was sharp. 'A *royal* bastard of little note?'

A Plantagenet, a King's son. A livery mocking Henry's claim.

'What manner of youth is he?'

Morton said: 'Hot. Vainglorious. And cast in his father's image, to the life.'

'I do not want him at my court.' To have that face, that facsimile of certain shameful death under his eye; to confront it in hall and corridor would be insupportable.

'Sire, lastly. The Roll of Attainder against Richard. How is it to be worded?'

'All ways,' said Henry rapidly. 'Oppression, tyranny, persecution of the commons, of his wife, betrayal of his friends. See to it.'

'And his greatest crime?' persisted Morton. 'Chapter and verse, your Majesty?'

'No,' said Henry slowly. 'The evidence conflicts. Say only: "guilty of the shedding of infants' blood".'

Morton bowed. He looked at Henry, awed and gladdened. He had made himself a King.

At Greenwich, autumn rioted in parkland and pleasaunce. A dry rain of russet, saffron and rose floated down. The mornings were laden with sharp silver dews, transient mist. Beneath Elizabeth's window a robin sang, bold and confidential, as if for her alone. There had never, she thought, been such a beautiful fall. Yet it seemed to be lasting for a year.

The sweating sickness was the reason why Bray, Morton's spokesman, had advised her to wait at Greenwich. It was not safe yet for her to come again to London; folk were dropping in the streets, and no physician could cure the sickness. It was new; men said that the King's mercenaries had brought it, a gaol-fever from France. Prayers were offered for the King's safety, and Elizabeth added her own.

She learned a kind of patience. The battle was over, the enemy dead, like her rages. So she walked on leaves that were lovely in death, in gardens ravaged by the memory of Marguerite. Elizabeth waited, drawing her spirit into a tight coil until King Henry should bid her to him. Kindness clothed her; she spoke courteously to Grace, to Renée and the other servants. To them she seemed distant, alien; they did not recognize her as she was: a beach recently battered by a tidal wave. Years of longing, and now victory had been too much. One night she cried out from a pain in her head. In the morning her left hand was weak and stricken, her head shaken by occasional spasms. She was still slim and gaunt and burning, but not so brightly as before. Grace was full of fear; the touch of that feeble hand epitomized her own vague terrors. Elizabeth's voice had softened too, feeding the dreadful dark unease, and augmenting another fear, equally strong.

For the twentieth time, she said: 'Madame. Think you that John of Gloucester is safe?'

She could ask her anything now, and have a good reply, yet a comfortless one.

'Mistress, how should I know? Was he in the battle?'

'Nay. His father forbade it.'

'Then he's safe,' said Elizabeth. 'He is of no account, I told you. Stop weeping, Grace.'

Elizabeth gazed over the gold-flecked lawn. There had been tears shed here before, by a Queen whose lover was slain; a Queen comforted by a girl whose husband came running, blood-stained, with bad tidings ... John. Ah, John. Again she put his face, his name away. It was more difficult here, and with this forced inactivity. Marguerite's ghost was lively on the lawn. Through the walled archway she saw banners blazoned with the white daisy-flower and held by tall young men. A woman, small and slight, walked between the escort; the banners were grand, a Queen's banners, and the woman's dress was of fine French cloth, her headdress snowily starched. Elizabeth stared. A verse stole into her head, as if bidden to the moment.

Benedicite, what dreamed I this night ...
Thy lady hath forgotten to be kind ...

The ghost came right up to her, and made itself flesh. For Marguerite at Greenwich had been beautiful. Marguerite would not have carried a breviary wherever she went; more likely a lute, or a sword.

'Greetings,' said Margaret Beaufort, bestowing light kisses.

'Countess.' Elizabeth looked bewildered at the sudden panoply. Marguerites bloomed in profusion on the air. 'I see you bear the daisy ...

'I thought it pretty. For Lancaster triumphant, and of course, for my name.'

Elizabeth took Margaret's arm. 'Come, be refreshed.' The Countess picked delicately through the red leaves as she walked with Elizabeth. Her black eyes missed nothing, the wasted fingers of Elizabeth, the occasional twitch of her head.

'You don't look well, my lady,' she said pleasantly, as, followed by the gaudy entourage, they went into the palace.

'I am exceedingly well,' replied Elizabeth. 'I trust the sickness is over in London. I am anxious to see and rejoice with your victorious son. Felicitations, Madame, on your Henry.'

Margaret sipped a little wine brought to her by a page. She absently opened her breviary, and smiled. 'It was preordained,' she said smoothly. 'Our dynasty shall endure for a thousand years.'

Elizabeth said: 'He will get fine sons upon my daughter.'

Margaret did not answer; she was saying a *Te Deum* under her breath.

'Margaret,' said Elizabeth. 'Countess. You have my word and consent to the marriage. When shall it be?'

'Soon,' said Margaret, gabbling away. Then she closed her breviary with a clap and smiled a sweet, tight smile. She sniffed at her wine-cup and said: 'This drink's too near the lees; is there no Rhenish?'

A steward behind Elizabeth's chair, answered: 'None left, your Grace,' and Margaret raised her brows. Elizabeth thought: has she forgotten that my grant from Richard died with him? The last pension brought by John Nesfield was spent weeks ago. Yet she complains of poor wine in my house. She felt her cheeks flushing and welcomed the spurt of temper like a lover; it signalled the end of a weird apathy.

'Madame!' she said bitingly, 'when my daughter weds your son ...'

'King Henry the Seventh,' Margaret interrupted.

'Yes.' Elizabeth frowned and forgot what she was about to say.

Margaret was glancing about the chamber, at the hangings, the carpets, the servants arrayed mutely at door and wall. She looked at Grace, who was kneeling beside Elizabeth, and gave her a flash of teeth, humourless as a sword.

'Mistress. Do you know where your lady keeps her copy of the Titulus Regius?'

'She does,' said Elizabeth, the healthy rage renewed. 'Grace, take my keys. Fetch the vile thing.'

In the hearth a few logs burned. Margaret, greatly in command, ordered a page to make the flames leap high. Grace returned, carrying the long parchment like a sleeping infant in her arms. 'Throw it in,' commanded the Countess.

Grace set the Act gently on the fire's heart. It smouldered like feathers, then flamed, and the wax upon it ran like spreading veins of blood, blackening, corroding.

'Now, my lady,' said Margaret to Elizabeth. 'By the grace of King Henry the Seventh you are restored. You are Elizabeth, rightful widow of Edward Plantagenet. Parliament has repealed this shameful Act.'

Elizabeth felt tears brimming, burning. She said very softly: 'I would see Henry. I would kiss both his hands.'

'When the time is full,' said Margaret, closing her lips tight.

'Does Bess not please him?'

'The physicians have made their examination ...'

O Jesu! thought Elizabeth suddenly, wildly aghast. She loved her uncle;

he visited her at Sheriff Hutton. Richard has deflowered her, and all is lost. Her head and hand twitched madly, and Margaret looked away.

'They find her strong and goodly proportioned,' she continued. 'She should conceive an heir with no trouble.'

Elizabeth snatched up the despised wine and gulped it down.

The Countess rose. 'Farewell, your Grace,' she said. Elizabeth looked at her with haggard, grateful eyes. Your Grace! That sweet, almost forgotten sound.

'A word,' said Margaret, at the door. 'When you meet His Majesty; let me counsel you on his humour. He is grave and sober, as befits the saviour of England. He would gladly forget the shames that Edward brought on England. Therefore the Titulus Regius no longer exists, and it must never be mentioned. You understand?'

'I do.' Ah, let me kiss his feet!

Margaret drew her mantle about her. 'Also,' she said, leaving, 'he dislikes frivolity. There has been overmuch light-mindedness in past royal households. Go gracefully in his presence, my dame. The King does not jest.'

So, good. I, too, dislike jesters.

Margaret turned outside the door and stepped into the little chariot that had been brought for her. Blazoned on its flank was the White Rose of York, with half its petals painted red, to signify the merging of the Houses. She was already seated when Grace broke from her place beside Elizabeth at the door and ran forward. She clutched at the gold tassels hanging from the side of the litter. The Countess turned to her a frigid face; it blurred and shivered in her sight.

'Madame ... Madame ...' Grace could scarcely speak. 'Is there news ... of my lord of Gloucester?'

'Gloucester is dead,' Margaret said, and laughed. 'His Majesty bravely slew him in the field.'

She saw Grace's cheeks turn to clay. Perhaps the jest was too strong. 'You meant the traitor Richard, of course?' she said curtly.

'No,' Grace whispered. 'His son.'

'Bah!' cried the Countess. 'The boy! Well, to my knowledge he is in London, kindly tended by the King's mercy ...'

She felt Grace's lips, Grace's tears upon her hand. Oddly uneasy, she leaned from the little chariot and called: 'Drive on!' Carriage and escort moved forward, in a storm of golden leaves and marguerites, and roses red and white.

The day was a luminous ghost. Snow blotted the roofs and towers of Westminster and shed broken paleness on courtyard and thoroughfare. Although the weather was warm for January, the snow did not melt. Swiftly London's filth vanished beneath the smooth white silence; footprints, carrion, offal, dung, all were masked and absolved by it. The city's outline blurred. A lucent gloom necessitated the early lighting of torches. The Palace window, behind which Henry dressed for his wedding, flung out a glow mirroring another across the courtyard.

He wished to step to the window and look out curiously at that other light, where Bess underwent the careful ceremonies of preparation. He could hear the jingle of harness as the wedding guests rode into the yard below. He longed to throw open the window and suck in snowflakes, for the chamber was uncomfortably warm. However, this would necessitate treading on a dozen or so henchmen who crowded him, washing him, oiling and dressing him with deliberate formality. He therefore stationed Morton, already in full ecclesiastic regalia, at the window, and fired pleasant questions at him.

'What do you see, my lord?'

The Bishop looked down at the splashed colours, the pennons and banners and quarterings dappled with snow. The yard glowed with the liveries of a hundred visiting knights. A menagerie of blazons filled the air; stags, bulls, wolves, bright birds; azure and gold and gules. Esquires were running to assist dismounting lords; grooms led sleek horses to shelter.

'The Spanish Ambassador, Ayala,' he said. 'And the sub-Prior of Santa Cruz. About thirty in his suite.'

'Spain,' said Henry softly. 'Good. Who goes to meet them?'

'Bourchier,' said Morton, peering. Directly below, the Cardinal Archbishop, looking like a scarlet mushroom, moved to receive the guests. Cardinal Archbishop! A pang of envy, swiftly quelled, shot through him. All will come to pass, he thought.

'Here comes the French contingent,' he said.

I trust we can feed them all, thought Henry. Were four thousand barrels of herring enough? They would surely suffice throughout Lent. The guests were bound to stay until Easter ... The provision accounts were graven on his mind, He had checked them himself. He raised his arms so that two knights could clothe him in a shirt of Rennes cloth of the pale washed-leaf colour called applebloom. And ten thousand barrels of oysters?

'My lord, we must talk again about taxes,' he called, his voice muffled by the shirt over his head.

'Gladly, Sire. But not on your wedding-day!' laughed the Bishop.

Four esquires knelt to adjust the King's hose, lacing the points delicately. Next came the velvet doublet, the colour of claret, and a long mantle one shade paler, faced with whey-coloured ermine soft as down. Henry lifted each foot in turn and was shod in supple red leather. The velvet was heavy; he began to sweat lightly and a page anointed his head with rose-water cologne. There were too many people in the chamber; for instance, de Gigli, the prebendary of St. Paul's, one who fancied himself a poet, stood clutching the endless Latin epithalamium composed for the nuptials. Henry guessed correctly that it would be a flowery piece. It could wait. The servants brought a jewel-coffer; his hands hovered over collars and rings. They winked up at him like knowing eyes.

'Majesty,' said a small voice. Yet another poet, Bernard Andreas, had wormed his way to the edge of the circle of henchmen.

'Will you not hear my anthem? 'Tis only short.'

Henry sighed and nodded.

The poet recited squeakily:

'God save King Henry wheresoe'er he be,
And for Queen Elizabeth now pray we,
And for all her noble progeny;
God save the church of Christ from any folly,
And for Queen Elizabeth now pray we.'

A look of jealous fury passed from de Gigli to Andreas, who bowed, smirking. The King took a ruby from the box and placed it on his forefinger. Of course, the meaning in Andreas's creation was quite plain; a subtle reminder that England expected Bess to be crowned as soon as possible after her wedding. Well, that too could wait. He picked out another ring, a tiny carved skull once belonging to Richard, looked at it and set it down again. Andreas will expect payment, he thought. But he shall have it, the anthem is correct enough and he seems loyal ... savagely he bit his lip at this imbecility. A slip of the mind, in truth. Had he forgotten that none is loyal? Every smile cloaks a traitor; there's no man in this room, this city, this realm, who would not betray me. And my own advantage is this certain truth. He bowed his bony shoulders and received the weight of a gold collar studded with emeralds. Behind him, vassals, like monkeys, plucked invisible fluff off his mantle.

In a corner Reynold Bray was praying for a blessing on the King's marriage. Earlier the clerk had told Henry that the Stafford brothers, still in Sanctuary at Abingdon, were plotting revolt. Henry decided then that he would knight Bray soon. Not for loyalty! but for his tireless, ferreting energy. As for the Staffords – they would be dealt with in his own time. He would make an example of them so that every traitor might know himself under the King's surveillance. One of the pages stood on tiptoe to crown Henry with a velvet cap. A rose, fashioned of red and silver tissue, was pinned to the cap with a jewel. Later, in the Abbey, Henry would wear his crown. They held the steel mirror before him. For a second he thought: that man is pale! not recognizing himself. Then strength flowed into him. The past, with its doubts, died. He thought: I am as glorious as Edward or Richard ever was. More glorious!

And I am careful. I am not prodigal with doubts, money, or my life. All the anthems in the world shall not do justice to the wisdom of Cadwallader's seed! Free now to join Morton at the window, he looked down on the surging panoply, seeing among the standards the silver crescent of Northumberland, who had so nearly betrayed him in the field, coming so tardily to espouse his cause. Reminded by the standard that he had other territories besides London, Henry said: 'I shall ride north after Lent.'

'Is that wise, Sire?' Morton. 'York in particular is still in a ferment of grief over Richard's death.'

Henry looked mildly surprised. 'It must be done. The Yeomen of the Guard will escort me, and a few hundred outriders. Of course we shall go. I will claim my allegiance throughout the realm.'

He looked again at the pale window opposite.

'Is my bride ready?' he mused. 'Who attends her?'

Across that gap of snow-driven air, Bess stood like stone. What seemed a million miles below, wenches crawled fussing with the hem of her gown. Behind her she heard the whispering of her sister Cicely and her aunt Catherine, adjusting her train, a billow of cloth-of-gold. The most prominent of the attendants was Margaret Beaufort, who flitted here and there, advising, admonishing, like an officious gnome. Bess thought: I am a doll, a mammet, being readied for some children's revel. I am no longer Elizabeth of York, for when I donned this shining gown, I relinquished myself. I could no more leave this place than a doll could run from a child's destructive hands. So be it; I will be a doll, inert. So many lectures had been hammered in her ears by Morton, the Countess, and by her constant companion, Maud Herbert, that the advice had mingled in her mind and run away, like rain down a conduit. Be dutiful, Bess. Be obedient. Do not laugh or weep loudly. Above all, be fruitful! Poor Bess, with a wit that astounded even herself, had countered: 'I will be fruitful, if I have a good gardener!'

She felt Grace undo her hair so that it fell almost to her knees, a veil of shining primrose. Poor Grace! she thought absently. So willing and quiet, with her odd little pointed face and those eyes whose colour came as a shock every time they looked at you. Even Grace was changed these days; the hands wielded the comb as efficiently as ever, but her face was indrawn, bleak with some awful distress.

Elizabeth, sitting quietly in the window-embrasure, watched her daughter apparelled. The comb passed through Bess's hair as through water. Maud Herbert took a long strand of sapphires and diamonds and wound it about Bess's head. She pulled it tight, tormentingly tight; it bit into Bess's brow and the nape of her neck. The tension of the past hours overwhelmed Bess; she burst into tears. Instantly Mistress Herbert was contrite, caressing the Princess, whispering unspeakable comforts in her ear.

'Your Grace, don't cry. Marriage is given by God; as to the ... fleshy business – his Majesty will not hurt you!'

Bess spoke, for the first time. 'How should you know?' and turned away, stiff and regal. Maud sniggered and withdrew. 'Let me help,' said Grace gently; arranging the jewelled circlet more comfortably, she was very close to Bess.

'Have you seen John? John of Gloucester?' she whispered.

'He came with me from Sheriff Hutton. They say that Henry has shut him in the Tower, together with my cousin of Warwick; but I don't know ... I don't think so.'

'Was he well?'

'Yes ... no, he was not ...' said Bess. Grace sucked in a harsh breath; next moment the Countess of Richmond descended upon them.

'Are we ready?' she demanded. 'Bess, I vow you are most comely. Dear daughter! *je t'embrasse, je te bénisse* ...' She pecked the girl's cheek. Bess's eyes flicked round the circle of attendant ladies. Fatigue and

323

excitement whitened their faces; the palest was that of her mother, advancing towards her. Elizabeth placed her arms, their flesh fiery, about Bess. The feel of that frail, seething heat was unnerving. 'Madame, are you sick?' she whispered.

'What? On this, our day of days?' said Elizabeth. She held Bess close, kissed her, clung.

'Madame, you will crease my dress.'

'This day,' said Elizabeth almost drunkenly, 'we shall be one family again. Reunited. My dear son Tom, my brothers Edward and Lionel. Your sisters, Cicely here – Kate, Mary, Bridget, for the nuns of Dartford have given her leave. And my little sons whom I have not seen for so long. My Ned, my Richard ...'

She pressed her hot face against Bess's icy gemmed temple. The firm hand of Margaret Beaufort detached them.

'It's time.' She flung open the chamber door. Outside, the snow fell no longer and a pale red sun had appeared. The Yeomen of the Guard were manipulating a golden canopy whereunder Bess might walk. Distant trumpets sounded, and further away, the rhythm of steel on anvil, for men were preparing for the three days' jousting that would follow the wedding. There was the smell of woodsmoke and rubbish burning; it would soon be dusk and the citizens had lighted the first of many bonfires. There would be revelry in the streets; the King had sent messengers abroad, bidding merriment.

The procession gathered. Bishops and Archbishops,. monks and priests and poets; statesmen and nobles, barons and dukes and earls. The bridal party, a shimmering train of rich dress and soaring stand-ards, swayed and converged; as they passed under the gate the entou-rage of York and Lancaster merged in splendour, the white rose and red blossoming athwart one another. Clarions called harshly. There was no question of who should escort the bride. Elizabeth was almost jostled back by the King's mother, and took her place only a few steps before Grace and Catherine. She bade herself have patience. This was the dreamed-of day; Bess will be Queen of England in an hour, and I Queen-Dowager. The past is gone. *Deo Gratias* ...'

'*Deo Gratias!*' The choir strained to the topmost stave, their voice sharp-edged like the silvery vaulting of the Abbey; the singing sof-tened in a dying fall, then rose like the fanned sweep of pillars that dwarfed the congregation. Light, stark yet shadowed, fell upon the couple as they knelt for the final prayer. The choir shrilled to a height again and died, to find breath for the last anthem. Candlelight gleamed upon the wedding-rings. Acolytes raised the great Cross from which fiery prisms smoked down on the bent heads of Henry Tudor and Elizabeth Plantagenet. The Cardinal had officiated at many weddings before, royal weddings, yet he thought: never was there a stranger marriage, for the King's hands had shaken uncontrollably during the exchange of rings, and the maiden was as stiff and waxen as the Virgin in her nearby niche. Faintly there had come sobbing from the nave, from someone unknown, unseen.

Elizabeth's tired eyes ranged over the packed throng. She looked up towards the altar, at the russet hair of Henry under the rich new crown, and at Bess's flaxen fall. Her gaze wandered: stall upon stall was filled, with Tudors, with the old scions of Lancaster, a few of the House of York (Bess's unfortunately and costly blood) – Lincoln and his satellites, Margaret of Salisbury. Again her eyes roved, past shadowed alcoves and through chantrys with their shining leaves of stone, past the dark-blue, the silver and gold, the red of banners, the rose and the dragon; into hollowed darknesses and fraily-lit corners her eyes probed and questioned. They sought answer in the painted face of long-dead knights, the gilded saints, the smoke-grey images, reminders of love and death now cast in clay. Grace was kneeling close behind her. She turned her head and asked:

'Do you see anyone?'

'Who, highness?'

'My sons – Ned and Richard. They must be here.'

She turned fully and saw how Grace's eyes also roved, as they had done throughout the ceremony; they moved about the nave, they strained, with blood-flecks showing, to the chancel and up to the clerestory.

'I see no one, Madame.'

I see no one. I do not see my love. My love, are you imprisoned? If not, why did they forbid you this royal charade?

'I would have thought my sons would be present.'

'Why is John of Gloucester not here?'

They looked at one another as the choir, mad with the wine of heaven, reached an unwavering, heartstopping height and hung upon it. Elizabeth's dull, wasted hand was drooping at her side. Grace's fingers stole out and closed about it. So they remained, as the couple came slowly down towards them, the trumpets sounding for their going out. In the streets, red flame caught the first bonfire, and the cheers of festive London arose.

Leaving the Abbey, Elizabeth slipped on a patch of soft snow. Grace flung out her arms, catching the Queen-Dowager's weight upon her own hip and shoulder. For a moment the two women clung together, while the crowd, yeomen and vassals and merchants, all muffled in their best, watched curiously, but only for a moment; they were avid to drink in the bride. In the dying red rays of the sun, Bess gleamed; her dress, her jewels, her sleek, lambent cheeks. She is like the Queen of Heaven, the watchers murmured, genuinely awed. Henry walked steadily beneath the canopy beside his bride; he was stern and gorgeous. Enthusiasm wafted through the mob; someone took up the cry – God save King Henry! He smiled then; the long lips curved in the calm face, the yellowish eyes sparkled acknowledgment.

'Is all well, Madame?' Grace whispered. Elizabeth held on to her arm.

'Yes. You are good. Grace, you are good to me.'

It was the kindest thing she had ever said to her. Grace seized the hand, the limp wasted hand, and kissed it. Together they moved on to the banquet in Westminster Hall. The King's Yeomen held open the great door, gathering in nobles; finally the door was closed upon the gaping crowd. One last cheer arose, before peasant and pedlar, trollop and friar and prentice turned to one another with shining eyes. A band of fiddlers struck up and a man beat on a drum. The long night was beginning.

'You must bear me sons, Bess.'

Seriously he said it, as if on the moment she could fulfil his command. He stood at the foot of the bed. Propped on pillows, she watched his slender nervousness and the way he twined his hands together. She wondered why he did not come to lie beside her. Twice and thrice he had opened the chamber door to ensure that the Yeoman were vigilant. She could hear the barked orders as they changed duty, and the clash of pikes in salute. She lay, a doll, in a white embroidered high-necked shift and with the long-wheaten sheaf of her hair spread over the coverlet and flung out on the pillows. She was weary past weariness. The banquet had been long and sickly; the toasts had drummed in her dizzy ears. Lancaster! Cadwallader! Tudor! Tudor for ever! Bleakly and vaguely she wondered what her father would have made of it all, then ceased to wonder.

'Bess?' he said again.

'Sire, I will obey to my best endeavour.'

Secretly she thought there must be more to getting children than talking about it. Henry approached and sat on the bed. Blue hollows lay beneath his eyes. There was something he was trying to say, but neither of them knew what it was.

'Did the revel please you?' he said. She nodded.

'I liked the woman who sang with the fiddle,' he continued. (A Welshwoman, with a voice like an icicle to make the blood race like a mountain beck. Two shillings, and cheap at the price.)

'Sire ...'

'For God's love – I am Henry in this chamber.'

She smiled, looked down and began to plait the tassels on the sheet.

'What is it?' he said gently. He began to think she was a simpleton; that was not to her detriment, as long as she bore him strong, clever sons.

'My mother said ...'

The mother; that thin bright desperate face, seen only in a brief moment of greeting before the dais. Well, she had played her part. He would use her kindly, if she gave him no cause to do otherwise. Trust none. The talisman burned his brain. Trust no man, or woman. The face, a dying spark, wavered before him and was still.

'She craved an audience with you,' said Bess's little, dutiful voice. 'She has endeavoured to see you for weeks. Tonight ... Henry, she was disappointed.'

It was the last thing Elizabeth had said to her, before they were parted by a score of priests for the bedding ceremony It would be wrong not to deliver the message.

'Henry?'

He was not listening. There had been a man who ate live coals, and cost six shillings and eight pence. And a little maid who danced – twelve shillings for her. Rather costly; but the Spaniards, full-fed, well-wined, with bulging eyes, had applauded. They would carry back tales of Henry's court, to make a mark with their Isabella. Tomorrow, he thought, I must draw in my horns. The progress north must not be too expensive. I must consult with Morton about taxes.

'... only wishes to thank you. Will you see her?'

'Your mother?' he repeated slowly, returning from his mental account-book. He drew back the covers and hoisted himself into bed. He picked up a shining strand of Bess's hair. It was as healthy and pristine as an ear of wheat, and clung to his fingers.

'What manner of woman is she?' he asked. He had his own thoughts on this, but was none the less open to instruction.

'I don't know. She is ...'

'Proud?' A nod. Of course. Had he not assessed her pride at their very first meeting? 'Strong?' Bess did not answer.

'Not so strong, these days,' he spoke almost to himself. He had guessed she was ill. With characteristic, uncanny intuition, he gave her five years more at best.

'Strong in spirit,' said Bess.

'Ah!' He lifted the tress of hair and set his lips to it. It smelled of gillyflowers, distilled in fatigue and fear.

'She snared that old ram, your father!' he said brutally, and was instantly shocked at himself. One should not speak so ... or was anything permissible these days? In Edward's court, free speech, free doings, had been legion. Curiously he said: 'How was it done?' then, 'Blessed Christ! How should you know?' He laughed and slid an arm about Bess's shoulders.

'She was most beautiful.' It was only a whisper.

'There must have been more than that! Beautiful women were conquered and left by Edward yearly. What more, Bess?'

'He desired her,' said Bess, blushing, and dived under the clothes like a seal.

'What more?' persisted Henry. 'Ah, does it matter?' sliding down under the mounded damask. 'Come, Bess. Let us see if you have inherited your father's lust!'

Shortly enraptured, the cool part of his mind remained to say: There is no witchery here, and so the witch can wait...

The bonfire outside Westminster Hall had melted the snow. The ground was ruddy, fluidly shadowed as the reflected flames leaped and ran between the tossing crowd of dancers. A hundred people capered with linked hands; men and women lifted snow-damp feet and skirts to the squeal of the fiddles and the rabid beating of the drum. Over a lesser fire the hacked remains of two oxen swung on a spit. A gang of prentices were playing football with an empty canikin.

Although some folk were already drifting back to their homes, the noise was still ferocious. It was a wild gaiety; something of blood-sacrifice lay in its note. The joy was desperate, like the last dance before a judgment. The din drifted up the palace walls, drowned the office of the Sanctuary monks, and leaped across the icy river in which, reflected from the further bank, answering fires were seen.

A bevy of ancient men occupied a bench and ruminated over the cups. Wool-muffled lovers played tag and fiercer, hotter games in and out of the shadows. Pickpurses made their own festival among the careless crowd. A whippet, flying in pursuit of a rat, upset a friar into a drift of ale-sodden snow; the prentices left their game to gape at the Church struggling in sodden habit. Above this scene, lights were going out all over the Palace.

The Yeomen of the Guard were allowed no drink, so austere was their destiny, the avid protection of the King's person. However, the gate-ward had had their smuggled fill. If they were careless, it was most ardently concealed. Their backs were as straight as ever; their iron grasp unwavering on their pikes. Yet some joined, under their breath, with the crowd's song, and swayed a very little to the singings.

Rutterkin is come unto our town,

In a cloak without coat or gown,

Save ragged hood to cover his crown,

Like a rutterkin, hoyda, hoyda!

It was an innocent-sounding lay, but it made them wink at one another. Mostly they were young men; when Grace, heavily swathed in a wool houpeland, and hand in hand with Renée, sought to pass through into the street, they knew nothing but pleasure. They chaffed the two women, throwing gaudy compliments. One of the guard put his arm about Grace, mock-sternly demanding her business. She looked up and recognized him: Master Walter, who had rescued her from the urchins outside Westminster Hall, who had taken her to Baynard's Castle, to the warm alien caress of Anne Neville. She noticed he still wore a white rose; it was pinned half-under the facings of his tunic. He remembered her too, after a moment, and with rough tenderness, asked her how she was.

'And you're not going out? Into this?' He gestured towards the revelry.

'*Parbleu!* Why not?' exploded Renée, who had dined well and was in a fierce good-humour. 'We have leave ...'

'The King's leave? The Queen's?' he said. Then, more softly. 'God bless her. Sweet Bess!'

'The Queen-Dowager's leave,' said Renée stiffly. 'I heard that my cousins are come from France. I would find them, and you shall not stop me. Master White Rose!'

'*Red* and White, mistress!' He showed her the other lapel, on which stiff scarlet petals bloomed. He bowed, and let the women pass through. Grace glanced back once; there was omething bleak about him, as if part of him had died.

They descended the steps and crossed the square into the leaping firelight. The people surged like insects, all buzzing song, curses and laughter. As the throng enfolded her she felt stifled. She smelled choking woodsmoke, sour ale, vomit, the void of bladders. She thought of the sweating sicknes and was afraid. A prentice still chasing his canikin dived against her, separating her from Renée. Grace's hood was snatched back by the jostle; her loose bright hair took gold light, red shadows from the fire. The flames sought out the pale pointed face and the green eyes wide with alarm. She felt the buffetings of the people; despite this they seemed like mirages, as if her oustretched hand could pass clean through them. Across her vision passed the figure of the tall Moor, the man with the monkey whom she had seen the day when Walter aided her. He seemed ominous; a figure of fate. Out loud she said the old *raison* of reassurance.

'I am the daughter of a King!'

'Why, here's sport!'

There were four of them, they crowded her, their hot bodies pressing. They were young, their doublets smeared with fat from the wedding roast, their faces flushed with ale. Well met, sweetheart, they said, admiring her, a flower on a dunghill. She shook off a clasp on her arm, twisted from an embrace, felt fingers tickling her neck. There was a red haired girl with them, a pretty girl with a dirty face and a torn bodice half-revealing pearly breasts. She laughed scornfully as one of the youths succeeded in kissing Grace. His wet mouth, burning with ale, engulfed her mouth, nose, cheeks. She dragged her face away, and cried out. Renée turned and blundered back through the mob. With a savage hipswing she knocked the red haired girl aside, and tore Grace from the circle of arms. Her hands boxed, leaving red ears, and she let out a long string of complicated French oaths. A few were directed at Grace herself.

'Could you not keep beside me?' she grumbled as they fled. Damn you, Renée, Grace thought; it was only a favour that brought me with you on this social errand. I would rather have stayed with my lady, sleeping peacefully when last seen, with Catherine at the bed-foot. Sleeping like a child, Christ be praised.

The cousins were discovered drinking wine outside a tavern on the farther side of the square. Renée launched herself at them with tears and kisses and endless questions. They had come from Harfleur with the Tudor guests. Grace found them intimidating, especially Alicia de Serrencourt, who viewed the spectacle of London at play with derision.

'*Alors! Regardez les anglais en fête!*' Her fishy eyes spoke of barbarians. Her husband, who never had the chance to speak, brought Grace a cup of wine, and leaned gloomily against the door-frame of the bustling tavern. The women gabbled – French endearments, congratulation, speculation. Did the King like his bride? What a day for France, and England … Spain too was coming around. Although the reconciliation was begun in Richard's day… ah, *vraiment*. The traitor Plantagenet, gone to his master, Lucifer. Grace clasped her brimming goblet, looked disinterestedly around. The fire was burning down, and even the prentices were wearying of their play. One or two young men, heads throbbing with excess, stood apart, dazedly wondering what had passed during the last few hours. One in particular stood rigidly, his hand resting upon a buttressed wall, as if he sought security in its age and firmness. The dying flames lit up his face.

She dropped the wine-cup and its contents splashed her with a deep red spray. She stared as if her eyes would burst, eyes already filling with tears of joy. She took a step forward and nearly fell. Was he real, or only another fleshly mirage, like the gay, strangely deathly crowd? Two people passed between her and the shadowed sight of him; a vagabond dragging spoils in a sack. Someone threw a broken cartwheel on the fire, and it blazed up anew. She saw him then, truly. He was John, unmistakable, alive, adored.

It took a minute to cross the square; it took an hour, an aeon. A spark from the fire caught her gown as she passed, and someone slapped at it, while she walked on, unheeding. The cobbles were warm under her feet. She walked to him through Hell, she came to him through an inferno of delight. Her whole body grew molten with love; her eyes were washed with joy. 'Mistress, take care, you're on fire!' Minutes later the words came back. Yes. I burn. John, I burn. I never knew until this night, how I do burn. Welldoers pressed about her, dousing her smouldering clothes with the dregs of ale, and unthinkingly she struck off their aid. Hair streaming loose, eyes a green mist of love, she reached his side at last. He turned, and she saw in him a devil.

He was John, yet he was not John. He was made old and terrible and sad, by something manifest in his bitter eyes, in the cruel rancour of his mouth. She fell back as if thrust from him. He had lost much flesh; that was apparent from the cheeks sharp as blades, the harsh clean line of his jaw. But he was still elegant; his shoulders were broad and straight, his hair fell sleekly. It was a forced elegance that shrieked defiance and hatred. Hatred poured from him; an idiot could have sensed it. He smiled at her, a smile so awful that she glanced hastily behind to see who it was incurred his loathing, for she could not believe the look was directed at her. Even while seeing no one there she still did not believe, and she spoke his name in love and joy, while the tears in her eyes loosed themselves and poured.

If he had once borne resemblance to King Richard he was now Richard in facsimile, Richard most troubled, with a ghastly indrawn pallor as if he had been tortured and then starved. The fire shone eerily on the tight planes of cheeks and lit up the malevolence in his eyes. He looked her over steadily, keeping his palm pressed so hard against the wall that his whole arm trembled convulsively. She said, greatly pleading:

'John, my love. John, what ails you?'

Still he looked at her, and presently said in a strong, controlled voice:

'My father is dead,' while tears darkened his eyes and fell smoothly down his face, which was like that of an unknowing sleepwalker who dreams and weeps.

She said, as she had always planned: 'Ah, heart's joy, I know it … be comforted,' and took a step towards him, recoiling at sight of the hand held out against her like a drawn sword.

'Stay from me,' he whispered. 'Do not touch or goad me. Christ help me, I am no more master of myself!'

'For God's love, John!' she said, her voice shaking.

'Go back,' he said. Tears ran down his set face and over his chin.

'Go to your mistress. To the witch, the Woodville, the serpent, the murderess. To the breaker of lives, to the ruiner of dynasties, the shame of thrones. To the poisoner, the widow maker, to Our Lady of Sin. Go to her, Mistress Grace, and kiss her and fawn upon her, and stroke her brow. Succour her so that she may have strength to work fresh evil ... to rob fair knights, fine men, of hope and peace and bring them down to death ...'

'Ah, what are you saying?'

'She killed him.' His voice and rigid face were thick with tears. 'As surely as if she had taken the sword and struck him down. She forecast and ensured his death. And worse than death! Oh, Jesus, God!' He wailed so wildly and suddenly that folk turned to stare. 'Would that for one hour she were a man! They could burn me, hang me, but give me chance to shear that Gorgon's head!'

'For God's love, stop!' she begged. Still he raved, he sobbed.

'You do not know what was done to him!' He beat his head against the stone buttress, drawing blood from his brow.

'It is not my fault.' Timidly she stretched out her hand and with a violent movement he struck it away, hurting her. She said, more wildly: 'Why?'

'Today I watched you. I stood outside Westminster while the devil's spawn married my wretched cousin, Bess. I saw you come out with Woodville, and clasp her in your arms, and lip her hand. She who made my father's flesh bloody filth and his name a pestilence upon the earth. She who comes higher in your heart than any other ... you lie nightly with her ... plotting ... ruin, treachery ...' Choking, he bowed his head.

'I plot with none.' Her body was ice-cold

He spun away from the wall and she shrank. He raised his hands but dropped them quickly before they touched her.

'You love her,' he said, venomously soft. 'Deny it!'

'I do not deny it. Neither do I deny that I love you, John. Always, now and ever.'

'Love *me*!' His face came close. His breath was rank, his wet eyes stared. 'Madame–' with loathing emphasis – 'God curse the day I ever knew you. May He burn me for a fool that I ever gave you my heart. In my folly I overlooked your treason, your false allegiance. To think that I ever held you dear!'

She looked down at her feet. All around was filth; chewed gristle from the roast, sodden straw, black snow-slush. Rags and debris and madness. A cur nosed for scraps, while a ragged infant pushed at it for possession of a bone. Her mind shut itself off, rejected the senseless rage that beat about her. This was not John; he was of the swans and the sun and flowers. Very far away she heard her own voice saying: 'I love you, my lord,' and his loud, heedless answer.

'Why don't you drink, lady? It is the brave Dragon's wedding-day! Drink! Hey, tapster, wine here! Wine for a Woodville-lover!'

He cried this so loudly that across the square the tavern keeper heard him, and flapped his hands in a shop-shutting gesture.

John whirled and cried again: 'Is there no wine? Oh, Jesu, I will give them wine like blood ...'

The prentices' red-haired slut came out of the shadows. She had been an avid if half-comprehending witness and was much amused. She held a half-full tankard.

'Will ale do, sir?'

He saw her and she was translated; with her torn gown and soot-streaked white bosom, she was a sharpened sword, an angel of revenge. Ignorant of his purpose, she had been eyeing him for minutes, his fine clothes, his dark anger, even his tears.

'Drink, sir?' She raised the mug towards him. Untroubled by his fierce eyes she sank back into the buttressed alcove, where the leafy stones leaned down. She smoothed her skirts and measured him, look for look. Grace, watching, began to tremble afresh.

'Is there more of this?' His tone was surprisingly calm.

'Plenty, highness.'

He took the cup, raised it, a sacrament. 'Death to Henry!' He swallowed, his throat moving fast and painfully until the draught was done. Grace caught a look of triumph from under swathed red hair, as John said to the girl: 'Are you for Lancaster, maiden, or for York?' pitifully casual, and the grimy white shoulders rose and fell. ''Tis all the same.' The victor, her eyes moved to Grace. 'So long as I've food in my belly, and a man to pleasure me ...'tis all the same.'

'Your name?'

'No name, sir, 'tis best.' She threw back her head, laughed with surprisingly fair white teeth. 'Does it matter?'

'I'll baptize you,' he said. The marks of tears lay on his gaunt, frenzied face. He sprinkled ale-dregs over the girl's skin. 'Let us call you Elizabeth! Elizabeth, my queen!'

'That is the Queen's name ...' she said in wonder. John began to laugh, and moved forward to clasp her in his arms, in front of Grace's anguish. 'Go!' he called to her over the ragged shoulder. 'Go to your first and best love! Go! Witch!'

Yet he watched her return across the square which she had traversed in such love. He shuddered from the devils in him, heard the woman crooning in his ear, and wished for death.

Grace looked back once. Her sight was almost gone, but she fancied that he either wept or laughed. The red-haired girl was holding him so close, she could not be sure.

'Where, my lord?'

'How should I know?'

Tom Dorset was irritable. The new court was not as he had fancied it to be and lacked something, making him uneasy. He was the Queen-Dowager's son, the Queen's halfbrother, and yet ... He hardly ever saw the King. Henry was inaccessible, as different from Edward and Richard as lord from vassal. Dorset had rank, but he was perplexed. He had not enjoyed his sojourn at the foreign court. There, he had fled after the business with Jane and Hastings, and there he had found himself enmeshed. When he had tried to obey his mother's summons home, he had been waylaid; Tudor's men had come upon him at the moment when he was about to board ship for England; they had haled him back to French Charles, from whose side he had been forbidden to stir, save for occasional close-guarded rides. He had not forgotten. He looked down at Grace. He admired her, but she was becoming a nuisance; he had more on his mind than the whereabouts of lost lovers.

'Ask my mother!' he said.

'She does not know.'

Grace was weeping again. She had wept so much during the past week that her vision was affected; objects were fluid or owned misty, hurting edges. She had collided with Dorset coming round a corner in a deserted part of the Palace of Westminster.

'Why do you wish to know?' he said curiously. 'The sons of dead kings are of no value. Grace ...' he admonished her: 'live for the day. Serve King Henry.'

'Do you, my lord?' She raised her swollen eyes.

'Of course,' he answered swiftly.

'Is John here, somewhere in Westminster?' she said softly. 'Where does he live? You know most things. Everyone says so.'

'Indeed.' He was momentarily flattered. 'Well, lady, not this. I tell you ... ask father Stanley.'

'Father Stanley?'

'Bess calls him so.'

'Bess does not know where John is?'

'Don't worry her for the love of God,' Dorset said hurriedly. 'She is to be left in peace, at the King's wish. You will have us all in mischief. Dear Grace,' he said quite kindly. 'Forget this knave. Find yourself another.'

'I cannot,' she said quietly. 'He is my joy and comfort, my heart's maker.'

Had the red-haired girl stripped him of sorrow? Filled him with drink? Yielded her soft, soiled passion to his desire? Cousin, don't cry, Dorset was saying. Cousin? He is not my cousin – John is my most beloved cousin. Bess, whom I may not approach, my half-sister. Richard, whom they slew, was my uncle, and his brother, who died in ardent fullness, my father. Young Warwick, immured in the Tower, is my cousin too. Anne Neville was my aunt, and she lies deep under leaf-edged stone. Elizabeth is none of my blood, and according to John, is devil and witch, and I love her. Vainly she sought the riddle's answers and sanity in the crazed pattern, in Dorset's dismissive face. The answer did not lie in the hard coolness of the ruby on her hand, John's ring, still hopelessly worn. Nor in the nerveless tear-hung air, nor in the silvery sweep of fanned corridor where she and Dorset stood. Nor in the corridor's successive arches, each like a hungry mouth. Arch upon arch yawned into the distance, ending in the blackest mouth of all, to which, impatient, Dorset pointed.

'Ask to see father Stanley,' he repeated. 'At this hour you will find him in his chambers.'

He bowed and went on his way. Grace started slowly through the chasmic arches. As she walked, a sob burst from her and was caught up in the folds of the impassive stone; it echoed above her head, died and was lost. She wondered: will it return? Will my grief resound in this place after I am dead? It was a sudden, weird thought that amazed her, that dried her tears. She spoke with Stanley's personal esquires outside his apartments, and was admitted rather too soon catching the trail of a dire argument between husband and wife. Stanley's voice, usually mellow with diplomacy, was raised.

'Dame, I tell you I mislike it! It will alienate her.'

Margaret Beaufort's clipped tones were high.

'My lord, she is of no import, no more than a puff of wind. I for one am pleased with the Act of Settlement. Should Bess die, my son is free to suit himself. He can take a Spanish princess ... why should he be bound to Woodville daughters? There is precedent, but precedent is born to be broken ...'

'Margaret, Margaret.' Stanley groaned, and hid his head. He was seated at a table, while his wife worked her tapestry, driving the needle viciously. She looked up and saw Grace.

'Why, welcome, child!' Grace took a step into the room, thinking instantly: why do they call me child? I am a woman, tormented, wise. What passes now between John and me is no children's game. I must not weep before the Countess.

'You come from the Queen-Dowager?' said Margaret.

'I come from myself.'

The steady black eyes held Grace's own. 'Are you well?' said the Countess. 'Do you pray daily? Remember the King in your prayers, for my sake.'

'I pray. Daily.'

'Ask for his safety,' said Margaret. 'He is gone to York, where the people are savages. Pray for his long life and constant welfare.'

'I do.' In secret, she touched the hard cold ruby on her hand. Margaret rose and, smiling, ushered her further into the room. The walls were hung with fresh gold banners. One of them depicted a fat hawthorn bush crowned, a reminder of Bosworth Field. 'Cleave to the Crown though it hang on a bush' ran the *raison*, stitched in claret thread.

Stanley smiled at Grace. He looked pale; there was the same vague *distrait* air about him that Dorset wore. His brow creased as he fumbled to place her, and eventually succeeded. Again, Grace was struck by her own unimportance. If I died, she thought, few would notice. They might say: where is that litle maid – Edward's girl? What girl? How did she look, whom did she serve? They would shrug or feign remembrance for politeness' sake. Again, Grace thought, curtseying before Lord Stanley: How shall any of us be remembered?

By our looks, our actions, our allegiances, our prayers? By none of these. If poets, perhaps by the dusty writings that remain. By power?

Certainly, and by the mark that power made upon us and those who follow us. So that I, who have no power, shall be one of the lost legions. One who struggled and wept and laughed briefly, who loved flowers and beauty, and one man, and one woman. Of less event than a dusky moth, born to dance and die in a night.

The mystic flame touched her mind, clarifying past, present, and future, so that Stanley and his Countess were no longer grown and solid and invincible, but mere children, ghosts, their life-span already done together with that of all others in the world who deluded themselves with thoughts of immortality. This left the taste of urgency; best to speak now.

She stepped up to Stanley's table and said firmly:

'You, my lord, have the control of the Household. I beg knowledge in which apartment John of Gloucester lies. I know he is supported by the King ...'

To conceal his sudden interest, Stanley busied himself with some documents. *Anything*, Thomas, the King had said. Any clue to Plantagenet uprising, any hint that might lead to those Stafford rebels, out of Sanctuary now and likely to raise a force. And Stanley had acquiesced like lightning, driven by an unnamed anxiety to serve. Now here was a Woodville partisan seeking one of the last sprigs of the yellow broom. A strange brewing. Was it worth watching ferment?

'His most gracious Majesty treats the young man kindly,' he said. 'Why would you find him?'

'He has something of mine. It is of value, and I would know it is in safekeeping.'

And not a lie in the whole speech. What else, but my heart? It would be unwise to declare this, however, with holy Margaret only waiting to denounce the flesh.

'So.' Stanley smoothed the curling parchments under his hand. 'Yes. I may tell you. Gloucester is not at court. The King has found him lodgings in the City.' He lifted his hand, and the rolls shot into a cylinder again.

'Where, my lord?' Oh, Jesu! let him not leave it there, so vaguely, in London's teeming maw. Stanley looked once at his wife. She gave a quick moorhen's nod and started again on her sewing.

'Do you know Chepeside? Of course you do,' he said. 'The young man lives with a master butcher, William Gould. Not *with* him, at least, but over his shop. You could send a letter. If you go in person, take one of my men; it is more fitting.'

'I will go alone,' said Grace. The thought of Stanley's henchman witnessing her fresh shames was appalling.

He shrugged. 'As you will. I trust,' with a pallid smile, 'that you recover your property.'

Grace went and kissed his spotted ageing claw. She curtseyed and withdrew under a last smile from Margaret.

'Pay my respects to the Queen-Dowager,' said the Countess.

The door closed behind Grace. Instantly Stanley got up. From an ante-chamber entered Reynold Bray.

'You heard?' said Stanley. 'It may be naught, but all the same ...'

There was one more errand, before she could leave. The need to look upon Elizabeth. This sent her the length of the Palace, crossing broad ways where new arras hung, and dipping her skirts down twisted staircases. Treading cold stones, fresh rushes, she passed scurrying servants and twice saw the Yeomen of the Guard. They spoke Breton or Welsh, an almost identical tongue, and looked as if they never smiled. The Tudor court grew and flourished all about, with an austere and alien richness. Although the court was depleted and Henry absent, his presence lingered, cool and meditative and strong.

Catherine Woodville opened the door of the familiar apartment. She was flushed, and held a letter.

'I'm to marry again,' she announced before Grace could speak. 'I am to marry the King's uncle, the Earl of Pembroke.'

'Jasper Tudor,' said Grace softly. 'He's an old man.'

Catherine's fair face reddened. 'Better old than none!' Scornfully she looked Grace over.

Elizabeth was seated by the window, still, save for the occasional restless flutter of her ruined left hand. Her head was lifted as she gazed through the high panes, and the light fell on the perfect line of her throat. Grace knelt beside her. Absently, as on every day, the hand reached out, and Grace began to rub, to knead and massage the dead-cold flesh, curving her own hands round the flaccid fingers. During this ritual the Queen-Dowager continued to stare up and outwards.

'The King has ridden north.'

'I know, highness.'

'He did not call me to say farewell. I was sorry. May the saints

339

preserve him from all enemies.'

After a long silence she went on, as if musing. 'Yesterday he took back my estates – those I have left – for the Crown.' Grace looked up sharply. Elizabeth was smiling. 'He is to pay me in lieu; I would have it so. I am not so enamoured of travelling, these days.' She looked down, her blue eyes pale, far-off. 'He is to pay me in full.'

Grace went on manipulating the slack fingers.

'We can still go to Greenwich, although it is no longer in my name. We can have clothes, make merry. The King, my saviour, will make me rich.'

It was odd to hear calmness in place of raving; this extremity of peace, as if striving were over and done.

'I shall see him when he returns from his progress,' said Elizabeth. 'He will give me privy audience; I have waited a long time.'

'Madame,' said Grace, during another silence. 'I would beg your indulgence.'

The frail shining cheek inclined towards her. 'You ask leave to go out?' Grace bowed, still stroking and moulding the dead hand. Was there a little warmth, returning? 'You guessed, Madame.'

'You're easy to read; said Elizabeth. 'Take your *congé*, then. But ...'

'My lady?'

'Return to me,' said Elizabeth. 'Be sure that you come back.' Grace's burning brow touched the Queen-Dowager's slender wrists.

'I pledge it.' Then she rose and quit the chamber without a backward look. Yet she felt the eyes upon her, in an unknown, unspeakable plea.

The riverboat journey was easy. Wrapped and hooded in wool she sat in the stern, near to three merchants and their wives and an ancient clerk, whose tonsured skull, thin and veined as a baby's, grew pimples in the stiff breeze. She disembarked with the others near Baynard's, and because the merchants seemed bound for the City she followed unobtrusively a little way behind until the streets narrowed and she was sucked into London's dense, overhung heart. The merchants quickened their pace and turned eastwards up Knightrider Street, and she lost them. She stood looking at the roads and alleys going away from the square, and ahead to where Paul's spire pointed at the sun. The day was cold, with an early spring coldness. The last remnants of snow framed the house-gables delicately and shone on a tavernbush. The deep doorways and courts on either side were dark and kept their secrets. Above, gildsmen's signs swung gently, their shadows gibbet-like across Grace's path. The press of people thickened; two mule-carts trundled by, followed by a line of washer-women with bundles on their heads.

Still she stood there, and people skirted her without word or look, as if she were invisible. For the first time she wondered on her own impulse. She had been turned away and with crazed persistence came courting fresh abuse. None could rightly forgive such words as had been launched her way; yet she realized that they had been forgiven as soon as they were uttered. Whether more could be borne was a different matter. She was here, in chaos, seeking him, and knew herself upon the fringe of madness.

A tall figure came to stand by her, becoming part of her own unreality. She looked up into the rolling white-rimmed eyes of the Moor. He was dressed in gay motley, and his monkey, a gold chain about its narrow hips, sat on its master's nape, holding on to his ears. The ebony face shone down like a black sun. This was the third time she had seen him, and again he seemed ominous. She stepped away a pace and he laughed, a deep rolling drum.

'Which way, little maid?' His voice was courtly, heavily accented, yet she was surprised he knew the English tongue. She noticed how passing people crossed themselves at sight of him. He saw it too, and chuckled more heartily.

'Do not fear,' he told her. 'See how they bless me! Never was man more blessed!' He reached behind his head and unhitched the monkey. It sprang on to Grace's flinching shoulder and pulled back a corner of her hood with its tiny hand.

'She likes you,' said the gleaming face. 'Let us promenade. Thou, and Beauty, and I, Salazar. Whither now, the three of us?'

'Chepeside.' The monkey pressed its cold little face against hers, and nibbled a strand of her hair.

'Chepeside, Beauty!' cried the Moor. A marketing woman glanced at him, flipped out the cross from her bodice and kissed it. 'Chepeside, doña!' Nimbly he twirled on the spot in a fluid, leaping dance-step, sketched a bow, and with his long gay arm indicated the way, as if he made her a present of it.

They walked together yet apart, and the monkey played with Grace's hair, and tugged gently at a pearl in her ear, while the Moor sang in Spanish about two sweethearts who had quarrelled, so he said. When Grace asked if the quarrel was mended, he only laughed. They passed through six streets with a church on every corner, amid brightness and shadow and gilded gables. Soon the smell of garlic and offal mingled with that of hot roast venison and the red-blood tang of the butchers' shops nudging the cookhouses. Chepeside roared, with haggling voices raised across the scream of slaughtered beasts. Whole deer and quartered oxen hung heavily beside slender rabbits with dark, dead-jewel eyes. Blood dripped from the beaks of bright birds. Stiffly the banners of gilds and patrons hung in profusion. All the shops looked the same. Grace stopped, and the monkey gibbered and leaped like a sparrow from her shoulder to the neck of the Moor.

'Whom do you seek? I know them all.'

'William Gould.'

He flourished, rose weightlessly from the ground as if bound for the sky, clapped his heels and alighting, bowed again. He was one of the highest paid entertainers in London, but he liked Grace on sight, and grudged her none of his performance.

'There, *doña!*' It was one of the larger shops. The entrance was dark with sides of beef. The second storey projected far into the street, and had ornately carved pentices. Grace turned to thank the Moor but he and his pet were gone, had faded instantly, almost into another dimension. She approached the shop, seeing that outside hung the Sun in Splendour, as if King Edward were still alive. Gould had insisted on this, and so far none had forced him to take it down. The butcher appeared in the doorway. He had seen Salazar, and hoped that he came to command a big order. Although disappointed, he gave fair greeting to Grace. Introducing herself, she spoke of Lord Stanley.

'So, my lady,' said Gould, impressed. 'You are perhaps a servant of the Countess of Richmond?'

She let it pass. The butcher remained cordial until she told him why she had come. A terrible change assailed his face and he came out of the shop so that he might spit lawfully. He said, thunderously, that he could take no message, wanted no part of the errand, and she argued with him, finding within herself undreamed-of resources.

'He *is* here, though,' she said eventually.

'Aye. The murderer's son is here. God rot him. Only at his Majesty's pleasure do I have him under my roof. 'Tis none of my wish.' And then he stopped, said: 'You are his friend?' Grace answered painfully: 'His acquaintance.' Gould spat again, and said: 'Go up.'

She threaded through bleeding carcasses, and the green birds hung head down and beautiful in death. The butcher waved his gaping prentices aside so that she might pass by the counter to the black studded door that led aloft. 'Have caution, mistress,' he said sourly. 'That one has the devil's temper, but as he came from the devil, who can question it?' He opened the stair door for her, and shut it, so that she was closeted in narrow blackness with a chink of light showing from under another door above. She heard her own breathing, loud and sickly, hemming her in. She lifted her skirt and ascended, knocked and waited, and then the loudest sound in that tomblike space was her own heart, over the rumbling gnaw of the rats.

John opened. As if he had lately been asleep, he was pale and shivering. When he saw her face he made to bang the door swiftly upon it, but like a weasel she nipped inside leaving a shred of her cloak caught by the draught of his vehemence. So she was in his poor and sordid room, with the bed unmade and the shutters half-open, through which came the stench of offal and slaughter, enhancing that of his own desperate grief. Once she was inside he was not angry: his face was closed like a Sunday shop.

'My lord.' He was still so designated, although his Captaincy of Calais had been taken from him. He was the son of a king, as she was the daughter of one. He should not dismiss her today without a fair hearing. Determined, she struck deep and fearfully into the matter's heart.

'My lord, it is more than four months since Bosworth Field.'

'My father is dead.' He did not weep now, only repeated it like a dreadful nervous gesticulation. He walked to the window, pushing the shutter apart. He looked down on the coiling mass of men and women at market. On the corner Salazar was giving a free dance and making his monkey juggle two silver coins. Black Salazar, saying a Spanish prayer under his breath for an unknown maid, whose looks he liked.

'John.' She grew nervous, speaking his name. She had the wit not to call him by any of the endearments that had come to them both, among the flowers, in all their transient meetings. 'Listen to me.' He half-turned from the window, and again she saw his resemblance to the dead King; the sombre eyes, arrogant nose and thin lips. His looks made him a danger to himself. At court, the Tudors would think they came face to face with a ghost, and question their victory ... No wonder he lived in these deep-hidden surroundings. Elizabeth, too: would the sight of him strike up old rancours? This was an unbearable thought; the two people she loved best were mortal enemies. She saw that his hands shook, although he held them hard against his sides. She longed to take his hands to her heart. His fine linen shirt was crumpled and soiled; she longed to make it fresh and fair. Yet there was an extravagance in his attitude; he needed only a smear of ash on his brow, and this emboldened her. She said again, steadily:

'Four moons since the battle, my lord. You cannot grieve forever.'

He turned fully, and his face filled her with awe. It said: I can. I do. I will.

'You are unwell, John,' she said gently. 'Have you food?'

He smiled his awful, remembered smile. 'Why? You are hungry? You see, I have become a hermit and barbarous; My servants will attend you.' He stepped towards the door.

'Your servants?'

'Gould's prentices; they wait on me if I call loudly enough. Surly, greasy slovens ... no! My father loved the common people. Much good did it do him,' he said savagely.

Now she remembered what she had to say. 'John! Kings have died before. Many have died. It is a part of life; to the strong, the victory ...'

He crossed to her and stood so close that their bodies almost touched. His face was masked by loathing, and his lips were white.

'Christ's Passion!' he said softly. 'Of what do you prate, lady? You, who know naught of true princes, or of courage or of despair? The Tudor had no strength. His paid assassins, though sworn men of my father's, did that bloody, day all that was needful. Stanley and his brother – there's a special corner of Hell for them! Northumberland, who jealousy held his hand back from the fight until it was too late. And the others, devils every one, whose poisoned minds kept them from my father's side.'

He spoke then of the battle, quoting the witnessed account given to him by Sir William Stonor, who, wounded ands broken, called at Sheriff Hutton on his way to York. He recounted, word for word, the tale that had almost stripped him of sanity and still haunted his heart.

'... he would have killed Tudor; he was so near. Then Stanley made a flank attack, and the Household, a hundred against two thousand, was shattered, destroyed. Some of the Tudor's men were the gaol delivery from France, desperate villains pardoned so that they might murder the King of England. Chivalry died that day. And the betrayal in battle was the noblest part!'

He swallowed hard, and said:

'They stripped my father and threw him across a mule. They spat on him and struck him even in death. They brought him back, naked through Leicester with a rope about his neck, a rope such as common felons wear. Crossing the bridge, the mule ran amok and broke my father's hanging head upon the wall. With knives they dishonoured his poor flesh ... No more, mistress. Go away.'

He was again at the window, darkly silhouetted. Grace sat down upon the tossed and tearstained bed. Twice she tried to speak and failed. Then a whisper emerged.

'Before God, I did not know of this.'

'Yes, you did,' he said, quite calmly. 'If you live close to the witch, you knew it all.'

Like a blinding blow, remembrance came. She had witnessed Elizabeth, crazed by Richard's rejection of Bess, saying: *Let him be killed with ignominy. Let him be reviled. Do this, Stanley, in remembrance of me.* And Stanley's answer: *It is done, Madame.*

The tired, monotonous voice went on.

'Tudor gave him no grave, no kingly interment. He lay in Leicester's Swinemarket for three days while the flies and the buzzards drank at his wounds and the people came to curse him. Poor naked wretch!'

He made a queer sound, half laugh, half sob.

'Where...' said Grace.

'Where does he lie now? A nun, whose place is sure in Paradise, came and took him away. She and her sisters buried him in their mean and holy house, and bought Masses for him. These were women! Shaped in the same wise as your mistress, and as remote from her as dove from serpent. Yes.' He turned a little towards her. 'Bear back this news, that Richard lies easy. Watch Woodville frown. She cannot touch him now.'

Grace's fingers found the red-eyed ring. Slowly she pulled it off and held it in her palm.

Again John came to stand before her. His eyes were deeply sunken, as if weeping had drained them dry.

'Did you not know she was evil?' he said quite gently. 'She is the canker in the rose, the scourge of dynasties. Men have died for her; men have died through her. Before our time, there was the fierce Queen Margaret. Men said she was of Hell, but beside her handmaid, Elizabeth, she was saintly. Weigh my words, and before you run back to your mistress shed a tear. For England and Plantagenet; their curse is accomplished.'

She was silent. She extended her palm where the ruby glowed. He looked down at it.

'Would to God things had been otherwise,' he said. 'Why were you not born a milkmaid or a tapwench, someone apart from the court? Like that poor maid who guided me when when I wept. I would have loved you as well. Why were you destined to serve my enemy?'

And she knew he was giving her the chance to denounce Elizabeth, to join him in vilification. Wearily, she bowed her head.

'I do not know,' she said. 'Who can measure destiny? I love you, John. And I love Elizabeth.'

'Despite all? Why?'

She looked at him again. 'Would that I could tell you. Perhaps ... because I am her one advocate in all the world!'

'Whom she does not deserve,' he said grimly.

'I have always loved her. I have always been loyal. If I miscall her now, I betray my own loyalty.'

'What is loyalty?' he said slowly.

'Your father's *raison*.' Her eyes were dry. If she must look her last on him; let it be clearly. 'Loyalty binds me. He never swerved. When he had time to talk to me, my father King Edward, used to tell me of this.'

She took the ring, placing it on the carved windowsill between the shutters; it caught the sun, being bright as new blood, with rays of light making it a star.

'Farewell,' she said. 'I sorrow for you, and love you. You need not see my face again.'

As if she walked through water, she crossed the boards of the small and dusty room. Faintness caught her for a moment; she touched the bedpost for support. Farewell, kiss; farewell, unknown joy. This little death has dignity.

'O Christ! I want to die!'

His voice impaled her. She turned and saw him on his knees at the window, the ruby clutched in his hand. His head was bowed, resting on the sill. He trembled so much that one of the shutters, unlatched, swung to with a crash. So she came back to his side, and touched his slender, shaking back, and tried to raise him, but he had deadly heaviness so she knelt with him, and for the first time in months, laid her hand on his and touched his burning face, and kissed him. He whispered: 'Don't ...' and no more.

'Don't stay? Don't go?'

He would never ask, she knew; his shame was great. But his answer was there in the drowning way he clung to her hand, and fumbled with the ring, hurting her finger as he pushed it on again. There was one more thing to say, and still kneeling, she said it, carefully, the private oath.

'I, Grace Plantagenet, being neither wife nor leman to any man and by this reason free, do pledge my heart to my dearly beloved John of Gloucester. In this place, as God witness my deed. And should I swerve from John may God take my life and damn me eternally.'

'Yes,' he said hoarsely. He raised her and took her in her arms, clasping her so hard that they both swayed against the wall, and his kiss brought a drop of blood into her mouth that mingled with their tears.

She had dreamed of love many times, thinking it to be a thing of softness, swift and gay as a butterfly, and as trivial. When he lifted her and took her to the bed it was the death of her dreams, and she was afraid. Love was not kind; it was a driving storm that stripped her spirit naked. Far away she heard her own sobbing and his words of love. He was the wind and she the leaf; in his arms she knew dissolution. She became the altar for his sacrifice, the balm for his wounds.

For a space they were apart from the world. The squalid room floated, a fragile rainbow bubble, and sheltered them.

He slept a little, wrapped in her hair. When he awoke, there was fresh colour in his cheeks, and he was John again. She held him, looking like a madonna down at his face. Outside a little breeze had freshened and the shutters slapped against the casement, creaking like the timbers of a galleon. He took her hand and filled it with kisses, then raised himself to gaze at her.

'My lady.' He looked at the marks of his mouth upon her honey flesh. 'I have dishonoured you.'

She smiled. 'You have bound me to you.'

He sighed, searching her face; she knew his mind. How long before the return to Westminster? The parting kiss, the void, doubly tragic after past joy. As if bidden, the brass note of Paul's struck. Outside the chamber door, the stair groaned as someone trod, listened, and went away.

'The butcher,' said John bitterly 'Or one of his louts. How many hours has that ear been at the door?'

She kissed him. 'When I arrived the bell was sounding.'

'So you must go.' He turned his face away, and waited, holding his breath.

'By my faith, love!' said Grace. 'This bolster is stuffed with rocks, I swear. How can you sleep?'

She felt under the pillows and drew out a leather bag. Gold coins spilled from it and rolled about the bed.

'That is my pension,' John said quietly. 'My pension from the Tudor. Twenty pounds a year. I have not spent one penny, nor shall I, until I can use it against him.'

'God knows,' he went on, 'why he has been so bountiful. Be sure though that he has spread word of his generosity, so that the public may applaud.' He frowned, threw up a gold angel and caught it. Drawing Grace close, he laid his cheek, against hers. 'And yet ... it would pleasure me to spend the money. On you, sweeting. We could be merry with it.'

She closed her eyes. Outside, the quarter boomed. She must dress and leave, or it would be too late. John's voice went softly on.

'I keep it beneath my pillow in the hope that one of Gould's lads might steal it, and then I could be rid of it. Graceless, unkindly fellows ... and Gould hates me. He would poison me if he dared.'

Grace lay, breathing his warmth. Her gown and cloak lay on the floor. It was a hundred miles to walk and pick them up and put them on. Quiet and blissful, John set his lips upon the crown of her hair.

'I am hungry,' he said.

'We have been here most of the day.'

'Yes. And now ...'

'Now.'

'Now you must return to the Palace.' She sat up and looked down at his face, its sadness, the transiency of his joy.

'I cannot marry you,' he said gravely. 'It would mean asking the

Tudor's assent, and I will ask him for nothing.'

She bowed her head, silent.

'Go, go,' he said roughly. 'Already I feel the pain.'

She took his face between her hands, and found herself speaking words that might have been long rehearsed; words without which time itself were void.

'I shall go nowhere without you,' she said. 'Have I not sworn? Never send me away, my dear love.'

Against her breast she felt the quick hard beat of his heart, so vibrantly alive.

'You are sure?'

She nodded, smiling; he leaped up, seizing her discarded gown and bringing it to her where she lay.

'Get up, my love!'

Between tears and laughter she looked at him.

'We'll go out,' he declared. 'To the best cookhouse in London. I shall be a merchant–' he started to fling the gold angels about the bed – 'and you a rich and pampered merchant's wife. I thought I had forgotten how to be happy!'

Naked and laughing, he said, 'Hurry, love; it grows late. Come, love, wife, my honey sweet!' She caught his mood and, sprang up, quickly making herself fine again with the aid of his dingy steel mirror. But when they were ready, a doubt assailed her, and made her new joy bleak and terrible for a moment.

'Elizabeth…' she began, and saw his face change, and went to him, putting her arms about his neck.

'My heart, don't blame me; don't chide me if I speak of her at times.' He sighed, and held her close, saying: 'What then, love?'

'She will be treated fairly? She is in favour with King Henry.' She said it as if to convince herself.

For a moment he was silent. Then he said: 'Doubtless.' He opened the door and Grace went down the dark stairs with a light step. As he followed her, he said softly, for his own peace: 'Elizabeth! Tudor will see you damned!'

'Way for Elizabeth, the Queen-Dowager!'

'Welcome to Winchester, highness!'

The words were gold in her ears. Accompanied by Dorset, she walked into the splendid hall. She told herself: these words mean more than my estates, my jewels, more even than the bounty I have lately surrendered, and for which the King will pay me in lieu. These titles are more than Sheen, through which we passed on the journey, or Greenwich, or the Queens' College, Cambridge, or Windsor, or Eltham.

Queen-Dowager! Highness! These hard-won words that break and vanish like bubbles on the air are more than the seat of princes. Does this mean that I have changed, grown old, less striving? Who knows? I am content with my saviour's ordinance, and I will tell him so, given the chance.

Elegant and emaciated in dark blue, she entered Winchester, allowed for the first time to visit Bess. All around courtiers bowed down, corn in a gale. The familiar feeling of near-divinity touched her. The royal matriarch comes! Winchester itself she did not know well; only now, in Henry's time, did it assume the stamp of majesty. She had visited the cathedral which stood rosily weathered in an emerald close. There, within the holy quiet she had seen the fabulous Round Table, the King's innovation. Painted with the Tudor Rose, it lay beneath the Dragon banners with sunlight shafting down upon twelve empty thrones. Mystic silence surrounded it, as it awaited King Arthur's return.

Summer was nearly over, and Winchester also waited, for Arthur's practical incarnation. Henry's progress was complete. As Elizabeth and Dorset travelled their southerly road, royal courtiers had over-taken them, crying of safety and success. Now, as Elizabeth and her son proceeded up the hall, the King's mother rose to receive them. The Countess was not pleased; but after a summer of asking she could no longer withhold the sight of Bess. She kissed Elizabeth, and gave Dorset a gimlet look. Then she led him to the Queen's apartments. Every door was guarded and the ways were clotted with monks and priests and nurses. Throughout the palace preparation for the King's arrival was apparent. Servants smoothed fresh Arras on the walls, strewed a bushel of gillyflowers, bullied one another. Yet within the Queen's chamber all was peace; an almost unhealthy quiet, a tomblike tranquillity.

Great with child, Bess reclined on a day-bed. Her face was bored and flushed. An abigail fanned her tirelessly. The Queen's hair was loose, and wheaten tendrils waved in the draught. Her boredom deepened visibly at sight of the Countess, but when Elizabeth entered she brightened a little. Margaret bustled forward, dismissing the maid with a sharp handclap.

'Daughter! Still abed! You should stretch your limbs, or the babe will grow stunted. See, I have a visitor for you.'

Bess stretched out her hand to Elizabeth. Her eyes rolled saying: See how I am persecuted! but she smiled.

To the Countess, Elizabeth said: 'I will speak to the Queen alone.'

'Do not weary her,' said Margaret commandingly, and went out.

'Mother, be seated,' said Bess. 'You too, Thomas. Elizabeth took a corner of the bed, and Dorset hitched himself on to an oak chest.

'My daughter,' said Elizabeth. A surprising memory jolted her: Bess in her cradle, with Edward's large sparkling face bending down. *What shall we call you? Elizabeth? Yet not as fair as my own, my peerless Elizabeth!* Moved by her own thought, she leaned to kiss the Queen.

'We have been apart too long,' she said, and realized the truth of it. Had she been dreaming? Where had the summer gone? None had the right to hold her from her daughter, or her sons. Richard and Ned would be grown now, big boys. And Dorset, who did not often follow the train of her thought, said:

'Madame, it's good to be one family again.' Drumming his heels like a schoolboy against the chest, he said: 'How are my little brothers, Dick and Ned?'

Bess reached towards a bowl of fruit, took a peach and examined it. One side was blackly bruised, marring the tawny lusciousness. She threw the peach back into the dish.

'How should I know?' she said, wishing someone would rub her aching back. She raised her blue eyes, smoothed the stomach filled with destiny. 'I thought they were with you.' She found a ripe grape and ate it – content to lie and wait, and reckon nothing.

Henry rode in with Morton an hour later. He flung his reins ro a groom and strode through the portal. He was still grimed from the hasty last stages of his journey, but was anxious to see that all was well with Bess, and went straight to her chamber. He had thought about her constantly on the progress. At Worcester, where the people openly mourned Richard, he had been obliged to hang a score of them on the High Cross – an example more salutary than the five hundred marks he fined them. He had watched them drop and strangle, and Bess's face had intruded, overlaying the spectacle, so that the victims were no more than so many insects brushed by storm. At York, the ordeal of entry under Micklegate Bar was tempered by the thought of Bess. The eyes of hate had been like fireflashes. He had ordained that York's Crown dues should be lowered (better to woo than to war at this juncture); and their resentment sailed over him like migrating birds, even when someone tried vainly to assassinate Northumberland. Bess's swollen body was in the forefront of his mind; a living pledge of new hope, the towering beginning of an everlasting line. Only in Gloucester, the dead King's own Duchy, had a chilling thought struck: what if the child were a girl? He took ironic comfort from an old proverb: it takes a man to get a girl! and he was not, even now, altogether sure of his own manhood.

One of the most satisfying recent events had been the arrest of the Stafford brothers. A minor skirmish was quelled by troops waged by the Yeomen. The elder Stafford had trodden air at Tower Hill. His brother had been pardoned at the last moment; again, an example. He, for sure, would walk warily henceforward.

And Morton was working on a new appraisal of the tax system.

'This came to me, your Majesty; as Chancellor, I shall say: if you spend liberally, you must have money to spare for the King. If you live frugally, you must have saved – money to spare likewise. I will have them in a fork, Sire.'

Henry had weighed the idea. 'It will make us unpopular, my lord.'

Squinting impatiently, Morton answered: 'Maybe. It will also make the Treasury strong again. Is that not your desire?'

Morton was to be Cardinal Archbishop.

Of the other factions that had plagued the King, a few were still in flux; Francis Lovell had escaped the purge levied on the Staffords' adherents and was in hiding, possibly near Oxford. He could wait. John, Earl of Lincoln and Richard's named heir, had accompanied the progress as a member of Henry's Council; not one sneeze had escaped Lincoln without being noted down. Already Henry had seen the restlessness there, but Lincoln was more subtle than most. The King decided to withhold all but the most trivial honours from Lincoln, and see where unrest led. As for Sir William Stanley – he was a born traitor. The way he had betrayed Richard still haunted Henry, and he watched Sir William closely. Had not his astrologer bade the King beware the Buck's Head? So they were all surveyed, measured, hung-over by an invisible Damoclean edge. 'Time, my lord,' the King had remarked to Morton, as they rode down the Fosse Way. 'Time, not death, is the leveller. And I have time aplenty.'

Cadwallader smiled. The seed of Wales stood upright in its mother's womb.

The pattern dovetailed; without Morton there would have been many loose ends. Everything moved with an uncanny progression of rightness. Lesser men than Henry would have been tempted to rest their spirit, to reap enjoyment from sovereignty. Not he. Eternally watchful, mirthless and shrewd, he moved in an aura of calculation, vigilant for the cloaked whisper, the ambiguous word, the lightest warning. Sir James Tyrrel had done his work and gone to a commission in Guisnes. Everything was in place.

The sight of Elizabeth, confronting him as he burst into the Queen's chamber, dislocated these steady thoughts. The Queen-Dowager was on her knees, instantly, her wimpled head bowed with one or two stray locks of silver-gilt, or white, showing beneath the brow-band. Henry strode first to his Queen and set his lips to her forehead, while behind them, Morton raised pale fingers in a general benediction. Then Henry turned and raised the Queen-Dowager. Her eyes were misted with an emotion unknown to him.

'Welcome, welcome, Sire.' He accepted this gravely. He bowed, in the sweated cloth-of-gold habit. One of his finger-rings caught in the Queen-Dowager's trailing dark-blue sleeve as she bent to his hand. She laughed, caught the laugh in a half-sob, and disentangled cloth from jewel.

'An audience with you, Sire; my one request,' she whispered.

In that moment, unknown to both of them, Melusine sparred with Cadwallader. The Dragon coiled about the serpent. She was strong, sinuous, but he had claws and a tongue of flame. A wider ocean engulfed Melusine's little lake. Her twining grip loosed; she fell.

He spent five minutes with Bess and an hour with her physicians. Then, having taken neither food nor drink, he went to confer with Morton. Together they pored over the progress's accounts; the revenues levied and the gifts received and bestowed. Henry was alarmed to see how little profit showed. The waging of troops to crush the

Staffords had marred what might otherwise have been a worthwhile expedition. The royal entourage seemed to have eaten and drunk as if each meal were its last.

He sat on a low gilt throne, cracking his knuckles and listening dismally to Morton reading from his rolls, of vast quantities of beef, eggs, salt and beer. Stationed about the chamber were the Yeomen, and outside the door another gold and scarlet dozen stood, death-still. Henry began to cough. Spring, not crisp autumn, was the season for his tertian fever; yet on a side table lay a covered flagon containing elderflower water to soothe his chest. Morton stopped reading.

'Your cough is worse,' he said. 'Should you not take your ease, now?'

Henry sniffed his own armpit. The cloth-of-gold was rankly soaked. One of the Yeomen went silently to a coffer and began to take out fresh linen. Morton gathered up the parchments that lay like folded lilies about the foot of the dais. It was not easy being Chancellor; every farthing must be accounted for, and if a bill were carelessly written, it must be done again. All over the palace clerks went rubbing finger-joints and red eyes.

'What more of urgency?' asked Henry.

'Only these to see, Sire.'

Henry raked the account with a glance, and scrawled his initials in the Household Book. Then he rose and went to where fresh clothes lay ready for his approval.

'The Queen-Dowager, Sire,' said Morton carefully. 'She has waited rather long.'

Two of the Yeomen peeled away Henry's sweated robe. One whispered: what colour today, dread Sire? and he pointed to a velvet doublet, darkly sheen as a crow's wing. Pages of the bath entered and went through into the next room to prepare a herbal tub. Henry said to the Yeomen standing round the walls: 'Dismiss!' and they filed out.

'I will see her,' he said. 'Bid her to me, in an hour.' He coughed again, and Morton's eyes grew troubled.

'It's nothing,' said the King. 'I shall live for ever.'

She was admitted at the appointed time. When she entered Henry had his back to her, his shoulders a little hunched, and coughing softly. Her first thought was: he has changed his suit, why does he wear black? He should wear more gold, scarlet, to deify and dignify him for the person he is. She knelt. A spasm of twitching seized her head and hand, maddeningly inappropriate at this moment of consummation. She controlled herself with difficulty, while he turned and came to her so that she could take his hands, to which she bent first her lips and then her brow. And she found herself dumb. She had waited too long. Henry was her saviour; anything she might say would be superfluous. Stiffly she rose and swayed a little before him. She said softly: 'Sire, I rejoice in your return, and in the fruitfulness of my daughter's womb. She will, I know, fulfil our destiny.'

This was a mistake; his eyes narrowed. '*Our* destiny, Madame?' She felt a blush warming her neck, as if she were a naughty child caught out in some misdemeanour. Ridiculous, for the King, her son-in-law, was young enough to be her son!

'Destiny, Sire. It was a happy day for me when you won the field.' She smiled. 'You have restored me, and my family. I can never forget it.'

She sought his hands again. They were perfumed from his bath; they were bony and unresponsive. Neither did he speak, but weighed her with his long eyes, the eyes of unknown significance.

'Sire ...' She let her hands slide away. He bowed almost imperceptibly.

'Very well,' he said in his high, measured voice, in which the accents of France and Wales blended. 'So you are pleased, Madame. Was there more you wished to say?'

'No ... only, I await my revenues from the estates you have bought from me.'

'My Chancellor has this in hand.' There was another pause, and he foresaw her departure within a moment. Then she said, casting down her blue-veined lids:

'Sire – I would have my sons with me again. I have not seen Richard for a year and a half; Edward I have not seen for years. I would have them with me, for their nurture and my comfort.'

Henry began to cough, a tight rasping bark, and turned from her, walking to the side table where his medicine stood The cup's cover bore an unbroken seal, testament that the draught had been sampled and found safe. He fingered the cup, contemplated it for three or four minutes. It was as if he had not heard her.

'My sons, highness,' said Elizabeth.

The black velvet shoulders rose closer to his ears as he coughed; he moved his head so that one long sombre eye studied her. Did he not understand her request? Perhaps he had the same fears of her that Richard had had – as if he could ever mistrust her? Words tripped and tumbled from her lips.

'Sire, you must not misconstrue my intent; my allegiance is totally yours and the Queen's, and the new blessed heir when he comes. Do not think that any rebellion will break over the persons of my sons. I myself will keep them in submission. They cannot aspire to the Crown. The Act of Titulus Regius ...'

He turned swiftly. The lean face was tinged with a barbarous outrage, yet he smiled, a smile to be seen on the face of a corpse. Sudden apprehension filled her. *The Act of Titulus Regius did not exist.* Treason to mention it, or even to remember that it had ever existed. Through its repeal Bess was Queen and she herself Queen-Dowager. Yet men had been hanged for whispering of it. Henry picked up the cup of balsam, broke the seal and drank silently. Paralysed with guilt, confused by witless paradox, she watched him; the bony throat moving, the little domestic movements of his hands. Disproportionate fear was born and crouched in her like a beast. At last he set down the cup.

'What do you want, Madame?' he said softly.

A little of her old spirit flared. She would not kneel to him again. Not she, who had had a King weeping and prostrate before her ... Centuries ago. She lifted her sharp chin.

'My sons, Sire. Edward and Richard, my sons.'

There was that chilling smile again. Even more softly, he said:

'But your sons are dead, Madame. The traitor Plantagenet had them murdered, so that he might usurp my throne. Did you not cry of it yourself? Day and night? that Gloucester had them smothered in the Tower?'

For a second she felt her heart stop and begin again with a sickening bound. This a nightmare, from which I soon must wake! Or the King jests with me, giving credence to Monton's lie, which I helped spread in honour of our cause ...

The King does not jest.

She heard her own shrill voice.

'Your Grace!'

Sudden anger lit the yellowish eyes. He said contemptuously:

'Madame, you forget yourself. We are 'your Majesty'!'

Then he quit the room, thin and silent in his black; shoulders lifted like a raven. She was alone, staring blindly, tasting blood where she had bitten her lip.

Throughout the spring and summer, Chepeside seethed about John and Grace, and they were a part of it. During the day they walked the City, preferring this to their small room to which slaughter-house roars and the sound of Gould bullying his prentices ascended. Gould grew sourer than ever; would not even bid good-day, but there was no spoken criticism of the ménage, and none suggested they should leave the lodging. The street itself was quick to gossip, and had cause; John spent like a sailor. Hand in hand with Grace, he walked the murmurous ways, down Poultry, the Vintry, and Jewry with its dark shops and darker proprietors. Along Bread Street and Milk Street the lovers took their way; they entered the best taverns. John dressed like a prince in a long tawny mantle, its sleeves fringed with gold, and wore a black cap with a feather. There was something in his face that made folk step aside and the prentices whistle only at a safe distance. Upon Grace he lavished the King's pension. In Candlewick Street he bought lengths of murrey and wool soft as a cat's back, and he ordered a Flemish seamstress to make them up into the latest fashion. He dressed Grace in green, Kendal green, and sapling green; wearing the hoods and gowns of his choosing, her eyes were like burning jade. Nightly, when the butcher had gone home to his Bishopsgate mansion, and the small upper room was quiet, John peeled the willow strands from their white core. She lay tranquilly lapped in green, flickering, candlelit green, the colour of love and hope. So fair were the nights that she grudged the day beginning. Sometimes she awoke before the night was done and, still gathered close in his sleeping arms, would think: if we could sleep, and never wake! A thought, brought by the dark hours, which struck her as unnatural and morbid. Then her peace and her unrest would battle, and the silver shadow of Elizabeth would intrude, wafting down to light upon the bed.

In the City a bizarre rumour arose. On the corner of Eastchepe and Candlewick a strange knight, coming face to face with John, threw himself on his knees and cried: 'Jesu! Richard liveth yet!' and wept uncontrollably. He was gently disillusioned, but the day ended badly; John neither spoke nor ate, but stood for hours at the open casement, his arms stretched wide on the shutters as if crucified.

Grace sorrowed. She had thought him to be mended.

'Are you happy, my love?' she asked, when the spasm had burned itself away with the dawning.

'Are you?' he said anxiously, as if he feared a parting. At such times she was hard put to express her happiness. Never in her life had such kindness come her way. Now it was loaded upon her in such ardent measure that often she was uncertain what to do with its excesses. They stood together at the window and he held her. The crown of her head was level with his neck. She was so slight she seemed to melt against him. He bent his head to touch his lips to hers.

'Yes. I'm happy. Or I should be the most ungrateful dog in the world,' he said.

Grace leaned from the window. By stretching her hand she could almost touch the gable of the house opposite. There was a woman in the window, who quickly banged her shutters closed. John pulled Grace back into his arms and covered her mouth with his. She was unaware of the street's opinion; that she was called a whore and he a popinjay ... He thought: there are some who see evil and some whom it passes by, invisible as the wind. Whether this is stupidity or saintliness, who knows? I only know that without Grace I should have died.

'What shall we do today, sweeting? There's a cockfight at Southwark, and we could dine at the Tabard. Or we could go to Petty Wales and watch them picking pockets. At Billingsgate the Fishmongers are rehearsing a play. But ...'

'I'd rather stay here,' she said. 'I feel ...' He looked at her sharply. To him she seemed pale.

'You're not sick?' he cried. There were still occasional outbreaks of the sweating sickness in the City. Or ... He looked at her closely. There was a sickness that was no sickness ...

'I am only a little weary,' she said, and laughed. Relief, coupled with a whimsical disappointment, showed on his face. My love, he had said, more than once: if I should get you with child! And: Yes! Let it be, then! Let there be more Plantagenets, for even bastard Plantagenets are better than Tudor's spawn! And his lovemaking had brought fear; fear that swiftly became delight.

Now he said: 'So be it. We'll watch the world from our window. I'll buy mutton from Master Gloom below, and have one of his boys cook it.'

Grace prepared the table, brightening it with kingcups gathered in Paul's churchyard. She and John played cards, made light, teasing love. He had a brittle uneasy merriment, as if his flashing temper were only just held in rein. After an hour, a prentice, carrying a tray, kicked at the door, entered, banged the meal down and left, clumping in his worn-out boots. Grace lifted the cover of the dish; the saddle of mutton was black on one side and raw on the other. When she touched it, it fell apart, white with maggots and stinking like a month-old corpse. John's lips paled with fury.

'Our host has a right merry humour,' he said. He pushed back his chair. 'God's passion! How dare he treat us like this!' He stormed from the room, and she heard him running downstairs, angrily calling the prentice back. His sharp imperious voice and the mumbling replies from the youth rose indistinctly.

'Gould is occupied,' he told her, returning. 'Jesu!–' pacing about with anger – 'I have had my belly full of Gould and this place. Love, how would you like to leave it?'

'Where could we go?' She was surprised.

'To Ireland.' He knelt beside her and took her hands. 'Sweetheart, they would welcome us there. They are still strong for my father. Desmond's kin still live – both your father and mine loved them well.'

'Desmond,' she said slowly. A strange little memory, a cradle-dream, tantalizingly vague, crept in her mind. 'The Earl died before I was born.'

'I will write,' said John. 'A courteous letter; I'll not press or commit them. Come to Ireland!'

The door rattled discreetly; a young man entered bearing a fresh tray. This prentice was fair and sturdy, with melancholy blue eyes in a comely face beneath a straight-cut fringe. Without a word he replaced the stinking mutton with a fair piece of beef, perfectly cooked. The mutton he tossed out of the open window, where it landed in the gutter, to the rapture of a bony cur.

'My thanks,' said John, bewildered.

The youth bowed. 'Your pardon, highness. The other was a mistake. Master Gould is busy, and young Harry does not know bad meat from the Pope's head.'

'I've not seen you before,' said John, frowning.

'I'm new to the trade,' said the prentice, and a cloud crossed his face. 'Moreover, it doesn't suit me. It's a bad trade, with a bad master.

I was to be trained for holy orders, but ... No matter, my lord. Enjoy your dinner.' He bowed again, and stepped back a pace nearer the door.

John, carving-knife poised, said curiously: 'It's a far cry from the priesthood to the slaughter-house ... or is it? What changed your fortunes?'

'My father followed Richard Plantagenet,' said the youth simply. 'The wrong fortunes, therefore; I bore the reprisal ...'

Very carefully John laid down the knife. His voice shook a little as he said: 'You have my sympathy.'

They stared at each other. Then the prentice said, with a kind of shudder: 'My lord, I should beg your pardon for more than the meat!'

'Well?' said John softly.

The young man's eyes were fixed on his. 'Walls are thin sir. My lord, I overheard your conversation. I heard you speak of Ireland. I cannot leave without asking forgiveness for my ears, or without offering my services.'

'What services?'

The prentice wiped his hands on the sides of his apron.

'If you have correspondence for Ireland,' he said very softly, 'I could help you. With this new King–' a look of utter abhorrence crossed his smooth face – 'it is most difficult to transmit bills. His agents are everywhere. Even here.'

Grace spoke, amazing herself: 'This is treason!'

The youth was trembling. 'Lady, lady, I know! But I can help you both. For the love of God, don't refuse my aid. And if you do, I pray you, forget I ever spoke of this.'

'Be still.' John's eyes were far away. Colour stained his cheeks. 'I did not know. Before God, I did not know there were still loyal followers who dared speak their mind. You, for one, risk your life. Gould is Henry's man!'

'The more fool he, to love a tyrant and a usurper.'

'I would make use of your services, your good services,' said John softly. 'Come, sit down. Eat and drink with us.'

The prentice laughed sadly. 'And lose my employment? Later, my lord. Now, we have little time. Listen: I can transmit your bill. My brother is a sea-captain bound for Wexford. He sails next month if the tides be right. Sir,' he said soberly, 'I would take your letter myself if

I could. I long for Ireland ... the White Rose still blooms there. They drink–' he was almost choking – 'to Richard's blessed memory.'

John rose, and embraced the youth, greasy apron and all. When they separated, tears shone in both pairs of eyes.

'Serve me,' he said. 'What is your name?'

'Ralph, sir.'

'Serve me, Ralph, in honour of your brave words. You cannot know what you have brought me this day. The finest dinner in the world – a dinner of hope, of comfort. God bless you, Ralph.'

'And you, my lord.'

'I will write the letter.'

'When shall I come for it? I must not visit you too often. Gould watches constantly, for any covert doings.'

'In a little while. In a week or so. I must think how to write it. It is to friends I have not seen for years, and I do not want them to find me presumptuous. I'll make some excuse to see you, send for you.'

'Yes. Next time I'll drink with you. We'll toast Plantagenet ...' He looked quickly towards the door. 'That is Gould shouting for me. I must go.'

He raised his hand as if in blessing, went swiftly from the room and ran downstairs. Grace rose from the table and put her arms about John. He was weeping, shaking, smiling. He was changed. She had never seen him so happy – at least, not since his father's death.

Dorset was more frightened than he had ever been. His mother had come from the King's privy chamber like a horribly animated doll. Straight past where he waited she walked, with her head held to one side and her face working as if struck by countless little blows. He remembered a tower at Grafton Regis when he was a child; a Jack-o'-the-clock, a small brass man who struck the hour. Like Jack, she went with one thin hand wagging before her; dreadfully stiff and steady she went towards the Queen's room. She was turned away, and Dorset caught up with her, as she fell swooning to the stones.

A physician pronounced the malady a rare palsy. Tincture of yarrow was prescribed, pennywort balm and daily bleeding. Desperate, Dorset followed these instructions faithfully. Gradually Elizabeth's twitching subsided save for an occasional frightful spasm, but she lay without speaking. Dorset sat holding the bowl of trickling rubies. Each drop taken seemed to come directly from her face, and each shade of pallor seemed to drain the years away, so that she looked like a dying young girl. On the seventh day Dorset dismissed the leech. 'Enough. Do you want to suck the soul from her?' He wondered what had passed in the King's chamber to bring his mother to this, and decided that he would rather not know. The Queen's time was near, and Winchester was in a state of preoccupation. Twelve doctors and midwives were in residence and already quarrelling fiercely among themselves. Margaret Beaufort had taken her bed into Bess's room and looked likely to remain there until Doomsday. So Dorset sat, ill-at-ease, in his mother's chamber, his eyes fixed on her waxen catelepsy. Her servants had been changed; Renée had gone to France with a pension from the Countess of Richmond; Catherine, now not quite so complacent, was at Pembroke as wife of Jasper Tudor. Grace he scarcely missed. There were only about half a dozen women who spent their time leaning on walls, watching Elizabeth, and yawning behind-hand. They are waiting for her to die, thought Dorset, and he abused them in an uncourtly manner.

'She will soon be strong again!' he said fiercely. I pray that I am right. Without her I am alone, save for my uncle Edward, always at sea. I would not be alone in a Tudor court. He bent to his mother, stroked and massaged her left hand. She opened her eyes.

'You have come back,' she said. Then her gaze cleared and hardened on Dorset's face. 'Ah. It's you, Tom.'

There was a shiver around the wall as the women assumed attentive attitudes.

'Take me ...' whispered Elizabeth.

'Where, Madam my mother?'

'Take me to Bradgate,' she breathed. Dorset got up to ask the King's assent to their congé. Wildly Elizabeth wagged her stricken head.

'Do not ask him, or tell him. Take me to Bradgate. Do this, Tom, if ever you loved me.'

As it had first been spring, now it was autumn, coloured in sadness. They rounded the bend in the long drive and she leaned and stretched out trembling hands to catch the last leaves before they crackled redly beneath hoof and wheel. Dorset rode a shining horse, its coat the colour of the leaves; behind the carriage came a handful of incurious servants picked and paid by Dorset in a hurry. The escape from Winchester had been delayed.

Bess was brought to bed before her time, on the twentieth of September. Margaret Beaufort took sole charge, and it was only after seven days that the frail Queen-Dowager was allowed to view her puny grandchild. Henry was in the chamber, and scarcely looked at Elizabeth. He loomed lean and very pale over the cradle, and he had been weeping. The child was a boy. Arthur had come again. The token of greatness fleshed; the prophecy fulfilled. Because of this, did Henry acquiesce to Bess's plea that Elizabeth should attend the baptism? Or was it only for appearances' sake that the Queen-Dowager was included in the ceremony? Whatever the reason, before she could go to Bradgate, she endured the five-hour ritual. The baby Arthur had cried dolefully throughout; he had received the blessing of God, Our Lady, St. George, his father and mother, and possibly Cadwallader, for whom he was very nearly named. Once or twice Elizabeth had felt like swooning; only by holding her hands tightly within her sleeves could she control the palsy. She listened to the sonorous blessings and the infant's sad mewling, and she watched Henry. Henry, who should have earned all her hatred, all her destructive powers. She realized numbly that these had been expended on others less worthy of them. Power was gone, leaving only despair.

A gold leaf drifted into her hand. Queen's Gold! The litter halted in the drive which, in spring, had been an artery in a bluebell heart, hymned by birds and festooned with primrose and violet. Like the echoes of a dream, voices sang, a horse tossed its head; John leaned and caressed her. Isabella! My heart's joy! The drive was overgrown with great trailing thorns. Dying blackberries, kissed by the devil, mouldered in a tangle of briars. Decay and desolation answered the same in her heart. While the grooms hacked at the obstruction, she lay back with her thoughts. Some were too terrible; her mind leaped away like a wounded stag. Some were too poignant. She remembered the time when she, a young girl, was transfixed by admiration for the spell-casting Jacquetta, the fire and kindness of Marguerite, later turned warrior and vixen. Her mind moved through ball and pageant, gowns and gossip and aspiration; King Henry gibbered and pointed at her bosom; John was mirrored in Eltham lake ... from this she trembled, sprang forward in time to where Edward, the Rose, kissed and clung and possessed; cried and cursed her over Desmond. The vision changed; the Fiend lay dead with a gaping wound in his side. Richard of Gloucester knelt to bless the corpse. Behind closed eyes she saw George of Clarence flaunting, she heard the whispers of his dreadful end. Marguerite's yellow face and half-bald skull moved in a macabre dance, the hoarse voice sang a warning: *Be kind, Isabella!* Jacquetta whispered: Bury me at midnight. The Titulus Regius unrolled, a redlipped serpent. Hate boiled and bubbled, while Morton, Margaret, Bray, the Stanleys, crowded round, kind, deferential, advising.

Detached she heard far away the grunts and oaths of the grooms, their axes chipping at the great thorns. Her own voice quavered silently. *Have him killed, my lord. Bessy, how you do hate my lord of Warwick! Have Clarence beheaded, Edward! Bessy, look not upon those I love!* Like a sad green bird, the slanted eyes of Mistress Grace flashed across memory's path. Edward dead, and the funeral bell. Proud Cis, Richard's old mother, black-clad with her jangling keys, her rosary. God keep you, Richard, through this night!

Let him be killed, let his death be inglorious.; For his insults to me and mine. It is done, Madame. It is done. Richard, where are my sons? The odd disappointment in his face. The stubborn refusal, lighting fresh fires. *Where are my sons, your Grace? Madame, you forget yourself: We are your Majesty!' It is done, Madame. It is done.*

The path freed, the litter rolled on. Bradgate came into view. She leaned and looked, expecting vastness, soaring towers, a gleaming inland sea fringed by willow and rushes. She gasped. Bradgate was so small! Crumbling. The pleasaunce was untended and rooks occupied the tower, flying in and out with mournful cry. The lake was almost dry. It was shallow, clogged with mud and algae. As Dorset lifted her and carried her into the manor, she looked back wildly seeking the place where, naked, she had bathed in the moon, watching John touched by her own unearthliness. None would believe that night! It was, like herself, a thing of dreams.

Laying her head against Dorset's shoulder, she said: 'Tom, you are good. You shall be rewarded.' With what? Ah yes. The long-awaited pension from Henry, lately bestowed. An ex-gratia payment of 'all profits and issues of all lands, honours and castles lately belonging to Elizabeth' … How generous! she thought wrily. The estates granted to her filled six rolls of parchment, their buying back was contained in one little line. She had signed the receipts under Morton's wattled eye.

'Only live,' said Dorset. *I am afraid.*

Here was the Hall, where the Goliath tapestry had hung. The door, where the steward of the twisted arm had fallen back before the Fiend. The banister, where John's two hounds had been unleashed and calmed by Warwick's wizard hand. The stairs, passing swiftly under Dorset's lightly burdened step. Here she had stood to witness John's last returning. And now the bedchamber, where she had sobbed her last true tears, holding the baby Richard, surveyed by infant Tom. Tom, who now carried the ageing infant who had borne him.

He laid her down. 'Rest a little while.'

A fresh pan had been hastily placed in the bed but it was still damp with unuse. The old faces and voices continued their dance. Little Ned, pale and overworked in his Ludlow schoolroom, Ned, the child come forth in Sanctuary, and the joy of fugitive Edward. Ned, who would have loved her, whom she would have loved, and did, too late. And his brother, young Richard of York – volatile, noisy, with his soldiers and his unfailing quest for mirth. How did they die?

I killed them. She twisted, shuddering. Her hands sprang like a snared rabbit and she caught at it with the other biting her lips till they bled, holding her twitching fingers down in a hurting grasp. I killed them. I among others put them to death by whispers, destroyed my sons through word of mouth. *Away, odious serpent, contaminator of my noble race! Send me a saviour, Melusine.* The Red Dragon flared; midway between heaven and hell, Reynold Bray spat on the Boar, looked up at her tower and laughed like a schoolboy. *The souls of those I love, Melusine! and their bodies too!* I killed them. Like the Greeks, who, to ensure victory, act it out beforehand, I wrote their doom in chapter and verse. I cleared the road for Tudor, Beaufort, Morton. *And the man who kept my sons safe I had killed with ignominy.*

There was torment in the bed. It was still light, the misty light of autumn. Bradgate will make me well again, she had told Tom. I could scream and tear my hair, as Morton once advised, but there would be none to mark it down for posterity. I could hurl myself from the window, but there would be no profit in it. Only a huddled sheath for bones, a triumph for Tudor, in whose side I must be one of the lesser thorns.

She sat up, tall. 'I will live!' she said.

She went stiffly downstairs and summoned lights for the Hall. Dorset sat white and worried beside her at the table. There was bravado in her fragile sway at the board, and the way she lifted her eyes to the roof, the arching walls, sureying the last bastion of her domain. By sheer force of will he sat serenely in Bradgate Hall, while wind got up outside and pried around the crumbling manor like a friendless ghost.

She arose early next morning and bade Dorset find a boat. Humouring her, he searched byre and barn and found a vessel scarcely worthy of water, yet one that floated, and had oars. She sat in the stern, while, knee-deep in mud, servants pushed off the rotting craft. Tom rowed and found deep water. He made towards the further bank where stunted willows grew. Anxiously he watched his mother.

'You once fished in this lake, Tom.'

'Yes, Madame.'

'Do you remember your father?'

Green scum clung to the oars. She looked down into the mysterious depths, the source of might, the fluent vehicle of power. She sighed, and trailed her wasted hand where leaves floated and waterweed wove its net. She gave a sharp cry. The drowned face of a child, with staring eyes and open, pleading mouth, looked at her. She clutched at Dorset and nearly upset the boat.

'Tis only a big carp,' he said softly. 'A dead fish, Madame.'

Other fish were attacking it. Smaller ones struck at the tail so that scales broke off, floating, silvering the clogged green surface of the water.

'Let us go back,' she said.

When they entered the Hall, a man was standing before the fireplace. A stranger, dark, fatigued, cap in hand. Richly dressed, and splashed with the mud of haste. He had the most eager eyes she had ever seen.

'No,' she said. It was evening; the servants had been dismissed. She, and Dorset, and the stranger, sat before the fire. The flames leaped, warm as the stranger's eyes.

'If you would only listen, your Grace.'

'How did you know where to find me?' He smiled, a kind weary smile.

'I see,' she said. 'By now I should have learned that there are no secrets. More folk know Tom Fool than Tom Fool knows.'

'Had I not thought you would listen,' he said quietly, 'I would not be here.'

'You have made a mistake,' she answered coldly. 'I want no part of it.' She looked in his eyes. They were fine eyes, rich brown, intensely gleaming.

'I am too old,' she spoke more patiently. 'Too old for further conspiracies. I am no longer part of this world.'

'We need your Grace's support,' he said.

'I have told you. I have conspired in my time – why should I deny it? And it has brought me to desolation.' She turned her head away; it shuddered slightly.

'My mother has been ill,' said Dorset.

Swiftly the stranger turned his attention on the Marquis.

'Then you, my lord. Will you at least hear me?'

'I have forfeited my sons' lives,' said Elizabeth from the chimney-corner. Her eyes were lambent and sad, strangely youthful in the firelight.

'Not necessarily,' said the stranger, and cracked a twig from the fire beneath his sollaret.

After a while she said: 'Tell me.'

'At least one of them escaped, Madame.'

Pityingly she looked at him. 'Sir, I fear you are a fool, whoever you are. My sons are dead. Henry Tudor is thorough.'

'Then why,' said the stranger softly, '*did he not order for them a Requiem Mass?*'

Yes. Yes, she thought, he would have done it. He was so correct, especially in matters of ecclesiastical procedure. His ancestors' holy disposition called for it. And the boys, being murdered, as the rumour ran, would need especial protection for their souls.

'An amazing oversight,' she said. The fire exploded, sendng up a shower of sparks.

'An oversight without precedent. An oversight beyond belief. Nay, Elizabeth–' she looked up sharply – 'Henry would not say Masses for the living. That is heresy.' She sighed. She folded her suddenly quiet hands in her lap.

'In Ireland there is a boy,' he went on. 'His looks are Plantagenet, and he is fair and comely. He comports himself like a prince. He has ten thousand followers. Margaret of Burgundy has promised to uphold him; to overthrow the Tudor. Lord Lincoln, who sits on

Tudor's Council, is with us too. But we need you, Madame. Your seal and your word are worth that of twenty thousand lesser souls.'

'Which of my sons is it?' she said very softly.

'That, Madame, I do not know. It could be either. Again, it could be the young Earl of Warwick.'

'Warwick is in the Tower!'

He shrugged. 'So men say. The Tower has kept its secrets for centuries. It may be Warwick, it may not. Whoever it is, he will bring down the Tudor.'

She gazed into the fire so hard that the flames hurt her sight. Strange, that she might be called upon to uphold the Fiend's grandson, Clarence's son. Stranger still, that the Fiend was less abhorrent than Tudor, who had dealt her the most dreadful wound. Was it not fitting that she should support Warwick's line in atonement? Atonement for what? For Gloucester's bloody death; he who had loved Warwick and all his kin.

'You say that Lincoln is with you?'

'Yes. He is marshalling a great force, in secret.'

'Lincoln was named King Richard's heir. Does he not covet the crown for himself?'

'He cannot have it, in face of your living son's claim,' said the stranger swiftly. 'Not with the reversal of Titulus Regius Nor, in these circumstances, would King Richard have wished it.'

'So the boy in Ireland *is* my son!'

'Madame. I say only: there is a boy, a Plantagenet. Will you place your trust in him? Will you revenge yourself?'

'Tudor duped me,' she said slowly. 'More thoroughly than any other. Yes, for that ...' She turned to Dorset. 'Thomas?' His cheeks were flushed with excitement.

'Madam my mother,' said he, 'I fear and mistrust Tudor most heartily. I am for this enterprise.'

To the stranger she said: 'What do you want of me?' And turned her face against the firelight. For an instant her old beauty returned, magical and weird. She shimmered, she was fluid, never still.

'Your support, your word; any monies you can spare. Bless you, your Grace.' He knelt to kiss her hands.

'And who *are* you?' she said finally.

From his wallet he took a blazon worked in silver and clipped it to the edge of his collar; a dancing hound. 'Behold my master!'

'Sir Francis Lovell.'

He laughed, though his brown eyes were hard and keen. 'Aye, Dickon's 'brave dog'!'

She remembered Lovell well; a youth laughing at her, or so she had imagined. How much evil had she imagined in the past?

'Support us, Madame,' he said again. 'And we will hang Tudor's bowels on Micklegate Bar!'

Looking at Dorset, she smiled sadly. 'So be it,' she said. 'And I vowed I was done with conspiracy!'

Grace stood behind John, an arm about his neck as he sat in his chair. She watched him write, taking pleasure in the fine italic script, the broad underlinings, the swirling capitals. Each black flowing wave was like a cord binding her tightly to the writer. She felt as if the quill scratched on her own heart. With each dipping stroke of it she saw the sea. The margins on the page were gateways of freedom. The odd manner in which he crossed his 'T's' was a little jest.

''Tis fair!' She rubbed her face against his shining hair. 'Who taught you to write?'

'Ssh!' he said, preoccupied. Then he kissed the fingers against his cheek. 'There. It's done. How long for its despatch, Master Ralph?'

The prentice was still on the bed, a flagon of wine in his hand. He came as often as he dared to the upper room. Sometimes he had a bruised face earned from Gould for shirking a duty. He was always merry these days; the sadness was gone from him as it was from John. It was a merriment verging on mania, none the less. During their brief conversations, the upper room trembled with hope and a deathly excitement. Old catchwords, the *raisons* of loyalty, sang in the air. Ralph would take no payment for his services, waving away John's offered gold, although the prentice was threadbare.

'Ralph, Ralph!' John slewed on the chair to look at him, and laughed. 'How long, I say? Tell me, and I'll broach the other cask!'

The prentice sprang up. He was carelessly gay and had been toasting York and the dead King in an unnervingly loud voice.

'No more wine, my lord.' He walked springily to the window, and drank in a gulp of air. 'As for your letter – my brother sails in a fortnight.'

John went to stand beside the prentice, laying an arm about his neck.

'This is my third letter,' he mused. 'I have had only one reply from Desmond's clerk.'

The prentice's merriment faded. 'Pirates took my brother's ship the first time, I told you. Thank God it was only pirates! I was afraid ... They had to run for it, almost down to Cork, and the couriers' gear was washed overboard. But, my lord, your second bill received a warm reply.'

'A very guarded reply,' said John, and frowned.

'Yes. Well ...'

Ralph scratched his nose which was turned-up, and pink with wine.

'Ralph?'

'It's too dangerous,' muttered the prentice. 'We must be careful.'

'Don't talk in riddles,' said John sharply. 'What have I done, or failed to do?'

The last trace of lightness dropped from Ralph and he looked steadily at John. 'Lord, they need more assurance from you – proof of your genuine allegiance. In Ireland they are nervous – as elusive as ill-trained hawks. Who can blame them?'

'Proof of my allegiance?' said John coldly. 'Have they forgotten whose son I am?'

Ralph nodded, said softly: 'Assuredly not. But their plan is too great to risk any hazard, however slight. They must know that you are with them – to dethrone Tudor. They plan to crown the Boy in Christ Church, Dublin. Burgundy is with them, and they have a commander from Germany, a soldier like Samson – Martin Schwarz. So, my lord–' steadily Ralph looked at John – 'you will not be welcome in Ireland until you state your heart's disposition. Too much hangs in the balance.'

John's eyes were bright. 'By St. Denis, Ralph! I had thought of Ireland as a place to hide my sore heart and be happy with my lady! But now! Now, there's so much more – a chance to fight, to die, to live ... Where's the letter?'

He snatched up the drying parchment and tore it across. 'Give me a quill. I'll write it anew. I'll be guarded no longer.'

He sat down again at the table. Grace and the prentice moved to stand beside him.

'It's danger,' said Ralph. 'But worth it, highness.'

'Not highness, Ralph!' said John, looking up, smiling. Grace watched him, and the smile on the arrogant, fiery face, thinking: I love him. I could die for love of him.

'We are brothers in this, Ralph,' he said. 'Drink!'

Ralph took up the flagon, tipped a long swallow of wine down his throat. He gulped, said: 'That was for the Boy! And this for Henry Tudor's ruin!' There was a long silence while he drained the flagon to the dregs. Grace stole closer to John, kissed his cheek, rubbed the smoothness of his jaw, whispered in his ear. He bore it for a moment, then pushed her away.

'Sweet, my letter will be awry.' Sulking, she went to the window and looked out.

'Why, there's Salazar!' she cried, and waved madly. The gleaming face, wearing new jewelled ear-rings and a wide white laugh, looked up. He lifted the monkey's paw and made it wave. A wind blew up, sudden and fierce and the monkey chattered in fear and clasped its master's ears. The Moor smiled once more at Grace, passed down an alley and was gone from sight.

'We have all manner of allies,' Ralph was saying. 'Even La Woodville is with us!'

Grace's heart lurched, but she kept silent.

John was signing the letter. The sweeping quill made 'J. Gloucester' black and even and fair, with a wild flamboyant tail doubled and redoubled with a knot in the end.

'Shall I take it now?' said Ralph hesitantly.

'Yes, yes. Take it. Keep it hidden until your brother sails.' He stood up and embraced the prentice. 'Ralph,' he said softly. 'You must come with us to Ireland.'

'John,' said the prentice. 'I will be with you until your life's end ... Lord!' He lurched suddenly as he turned to go 'The wine is raging ... I must go.'

'God keep you,' said John.

Ralph lurched again as he went out of the door. Grace thought him more than a little drunk. And he was still holding the letter. Alarmed, she ran to the top of the stairs, and was relieved to see him tuck the letter safely in the breast of his doublet. She returned to John, and to the amazement of both of them, burst into tears. He was with her at once, holding her. She clung to him so tightly that he gasped.

'It is the waiting, sweet,' he whispered, when her hold loosened. 'Soon we shall be in Ireland. Not much longer, my heart.'

His words failed to bring comfort. Again she held him; she could only whimper and hold him. Like Salazar's monkey, caught in a whirlwind. As mindless yet as sentient of doom.

It was spring again, and the tertian fever had Henry in its grip. He moved steadily through his court; he was flanked by the Yeomen wherever he went. His long face and deep eyes were tranquil and watchful and hid all evidence of his sickness. His body could shake in secret coughing but his spirit stepped high, and nowhere more than in the prince's chamber. The court had returned to Westminster. Arthur was five months old, and not as sturdy as the King might wish. Nevertheless Henry could not keep from the child's side, even with his own fever raging. For precaution he took to stuffing his own mouth and nostrils with powdered cinnamon; this gave him an unpleasant appearance. He leaned over the swaddled, grizzling infant and whispered in Welsh; whispered of Llewellyn, of Gladis, of Merfyn and Rhodri, of Iowerth and Gruffydd, of Iago and Cynan; of Noah. In the babe's slit eyes Henry looked for the shades of destiny, the long glittering promise of the future. The homage of foreign lands waited there. One day a grand alliance should make Arthur's England great. The infant sneezed. Henry turned to where Master William Petronus, the astrologer, wound in cabalistic robes, lurked reverently.

'It's Oxford's fault!' he said testily to the sage. 'He kept my son waiting in the cold church for three hours at the christening. I should have punished him. I fear I grow over-merciful.'

By my faith, thought Master Petronus, it is more likely that you yourself have infected the child. Your obsession knows no bounds. And as to your mercy … Discreetly he said: 'Sire, Parliament is gathering and awaits you. Before it meets there is something urgent…'

Reluctantly Henry straightened from the cradle and moved away. He passed through the chamber where a bevy of doctors and nurses did him homage. Among them was his mother, who scarcely left the child, except for visits to Bess, who was far from well with milk-fever and an ague.

'Tell me, then,' said Henry walking on. The court was beginning to fill with noise as the councillors arrived to pay their respects. It would be a heavy Parliament with one or two important faces missing, and he knew why. He knew everything; he could taste, smell, presage, gauge past, present and future. It was high time Master Petronus was retired.

'This year,' said the astrologer, 'there will be attempts upon your Majesty's life.'

Henry nodded. He had faith in the man after all. He had forecast the deaths of Edward and Richard Plantagenet correctly. But the King had more faith in himself. Trust none.

'Your Majesty,' said Petronus, hurrying to keep up with Henry's shambling strides.

'Let none know your mind.'

'Yes,' said Henry.

'Let them think they know your mind,' said the astrologer help-fully.

Henry flashed him a long, shrewd smile. 'There is a proverb, Master: "Who knows not how to dissemble knows not how to reign." Does that match your mood, Master Petronus?'

Defeated, the astrologer bowed and withdrew. Henry went on through brass-bound doors flung wide for his coming, to where Morton and Sir Reynold Bray, his new knighthood sleek upon him, waited. Together they went into Henry's privy chamber. On the walls the Dragon ramped upon his emerald ground.

'You look weary, my lord Cardinal,' said Henry cheerfully. He sat down and blew his nose. A cloud of cinnamon dust soaked his kerchief. 'Your news, now. Already my lord astrologer has wearied me with stale warnings.'

'My news is fresh and warm, Sire.' Morton turned to Bray, who carried the customary sheaf of documents, one of which the Cardinal Archbishop extracted with a bone-like slither of parchment.

'Is this the list of names?' said the King.

'It is, Sire. Lincoln is the most prominent of the rebels; he grew weary of waiting ...'

'I was right,' said Henry without expression. 'Time, my lord. Time levels all, reveals all.'

'Truth is the daughter of time,' observed Bray, and, catching the King's eye, wished he had not spoken.

Morton said: 'Lovell is near Oxford and has charge of one wing of the rebels. Schwarz is their captain. I was surprised at their great number.'

'The patron of York is St. Jude,' said Henry. 'The lost cause saint!'

Morton, taking another roll, said: 'And here is the news from Ireland. The boy's name is Lambert Simnel. He is a blacksmith's son.'

Henry said, intrigued: 'How are you sure?'

Bray and Morton exchanged glances. 'The priest we captured – he was the one who schooled Simnel. He sang us a whole psalter ...

Henry looked quickly up at the Dragon banners. That puissance, that red might calmed him, took the sting from Morton's next sickening words. 'We racked the priest, Sire. The rack is a good invention. Upon it, men have the gift of tongues!'

'Go on,' Henry waved his hand. 'So, they will crown the feigned boy. Jesu! the Irish are madmen. They will crown monkeys next!'

'Speaking of crowns,' said Morton suddenly, 'for policy's sake we must arrange the Queen's coronation. More and more I hear dissent in London. She is much beloved, your Majesty.'

'And am I not?' The deep eyes raked Morton's face. 'She will be crowned,' said Henry. 'When we have finished with Lincoln, Lovell, Lambert Simnel. London shall have their Queen. But first, I will have peace in England! I will have it, and maintain it!' He struck the arm of his chair, startling Morton and Bray with uncharacteristic passion. 'I will have a realm that my son can rule with the grace of Uther Pendragon, of Llewellyn the Great. I will have money in my coffers and the adoration of the world. To the ends of the earth my kingdom shall endure. I will it! It shall be so!'

'Amen,' said Morton softly.

'Well, then,' said Henry, still strangely violent, 'read me the conspirators. Nay, I'll read them myself.' He stretched out his hand. 'The lesser fish first – which came within our net this day?'

There was a pounding on the door, the strident clash of a Yeoman's pike. Henry called: 'Enter!' and a youth came in, and fell in homage. Reynold Bray strode over, raised the prone figure and wagged an admonishing finger.

'You should have waited.'

'Let him come,' said Henry. 'Is that for us?' He pointed to a slender package clutched in the youth's hand. Wordlessly it was tendered, and the prone position resumed. Under a dusty ray of sun and the red and green banners, Henry opened and read, from a slim sheaf of writing. He smiled, looked up and to the youth said: 'Come here.'

Conscious of his need for a change of clothes, for he was still greasy from the shop, Master Ralph moved upwards and forward.

His face felt bruised; he wished that Gould had acted out his part with less pith. He stared at the, King, felt Bray behind him with a finger in his ribs to make him stand up straight.

'You have done well,' said the King. 'We shall not forget.' He looked down at the letters again, and the faint smile pulled at his mouth.

'Why does he cross his 't's' this way?' he said.

After a moment Morton said: 'Shall he be arrested now, Sire?' and Henry shook his head. 'Nay!' he said loudly. 'I will make him a gift – a gift of time. Am I not merciful?' A look almost of regret crossed his face as he tapped the sheaf of letters. 'With these, he has built his scaffold, woven the hemp. Now let him sharpen the knife.' To Ralph he said: 'Dismiss!' as if he spoke to the Yeoman. He did not look at the prentice again. The smell of betrayal hung heavily. Great God! he thought. He must have loved John of Gloucester closely to have these weapons placed within his hand. Jesu preserve me from such men.

'Next,' he said, holding out fingers that trembled slightly. The boom of courtiers' voices sounded outside the chamber. Parliament would soon be in session. 'Swift, now. Let us be done.'

'A fish, Sire,' said Morton, passing the King another deposition. 'A big and a strange fish.'

Henry read, half-hearing Morton's explanation of how his agents had gone to work; pure chance, Sire. No betrayals here, only a whisper near Oxford, a courier drunk with weariness, a sealed letter mislaid, a horse recognized. Pure chance. Good fortune for one; ill for the other. But what ingratitude on the subject's part! What arrant folly!

'Sweet Christ!' said Henry, looking up. 'Why ...'

Why am I surprised? he thought. It makes me afraid that I should be surprised. Carefully, and swiftly, make an end of it now. Speeches prepared, and a different reason for disaffection stated. Tracks covered, like the burning of Titulus Regius; might enforced like the pre-dating of our victory. Have done, Elizabeth. Drown, witch.

He stood up. 'Ride to Bradgate,' he ordered Bray. 'And take armed men. The Queen-Dowager's time is done.'

There was a little knot of people standing outside the Council chamber; among them Margaret Beaufort, who had promised herself that one day she would invade the sanctum of men and have herself a voice; and Maud Herbert, who had not been long enough at court to keep her opinions secret. When Maud saw the Yeomen coming with Elizabeth, she gasped. The men were tall and ungentle; they were half-dragging the Queen-Dowager. Once she slipped and struck her side against a pillar. Maud heard her cry of pain.

'Madame!' She turned, shocked, to the Countess. 'She is the Queen's mother, after all!'

'She is but the Mare,' said Margaret, her eyes like black enamel. 'And her usefulness is outworn.'

Maud closed her lips and looked back at the little company approaching. Behind Elizabeth stumbled Dorset, His hands were manacled and he had a bloody ear. Much to everyone's surprise, he had fought like a tiger when apprehended at Bradgate. Now, he wept, drily, hopelessly. They waited a little while in the corridor until summoned to the Council chamber. Elizabeth's face was yellow, her eyes were glazed. Her headdress had slipped askew and revealed hair lily-white and thin in patches, like melting snow on mottled earth. The silver girl who had ensnared princes was dead. Even the palsy was quiescent; her hand hung still, her head, slightly bent to the side, was like the head of a corpse.

Soon they were admitted, Dorset writhing as if he feared the chamber were some dreadful *oubliette* to plunge them summarily into oblivion. The chamber itself was not large and was made smaller by the great assembly of lords and prelates seated on either side of the long table. Elizabeth stood, swaying a little, facing the King. Her eyes rushed forward to encompass him: his face, the face of unknown significance now plain to her; the delicate face touched by a frailty which in itself was strength; the supernormal aura of wisdom, the awful knowledge surrounding it. It was all there, as she had recalled it in some unrealized, uninterpreted dream. In that moment she was a part of him, and he of her.

He stood leaning against a high gold chair. He was wearing a violet gown lined with cloth-of-gold; a collar of many jewels. On his head lay a dark velvet cap pinned by a large diamond and a price-less pearl. An unassailable power poured from him and was manifest above, in the banners, in the fiery tongue and claws of the Dragon. His long, deeply hooded eyes were bleak and ageless, and visions chased across them in her sight. In the little space before he spoke she remembered vague, irrelevant things ... the Jerusalem Tapestry, and Jacquetta's greedy laughter at sight of it. She heard sounds she had never heard, saw sights she had never seen; through the wizard glass of Henry's eyes, Desmond's boys screamed and pleaded vainly for their lives; Edward wept and Warwick died; Gloucester's head was broken upon Bow Bridge. Her own sons called upon her and God. Their voices were stilled, and merged into Morton's, reading the indictment. Thomas was committed first: '... Marquis of Dorset, for your treason against his most sovereign Majesty to be confined during the King's pleasure in the Tower of London ...'

She came from her glassy trance and looked at Dorset's white face. Swift tears rushed into her eyes. My *son*. My first born son. Tom, the boy conceived in far, lost love; John's son, condemned, committed. Helplessly she stretched her arms out towards him. He tried to smile and she saw that he was grievously afraid. The heavy door closed sternly. Her tears receded; she stood, glacial and still, fighting this new loss, sudden nausea, pain.

Her own arraignment was begun; a long farrago. Treason of course; but what treason? She waited vainly to hear the name of Lovell, or of Lincoln.

'That you, Elizabeth, did so displease his Majesty the King by aligning your loyalty with that of the traitor Plantagenet, Richard of Gloucester, the rebel and usurper. That you did place your daughters under his protection, to the great anger of our sovereign lord.'

She frowned, and made a little uncertain gesture. She said: 'Forgive me, my lords. I do not understand. That was all ... a long time ago.'

Henry waited. There was silence. Then she understood.

'The charge is false,' she said. 'I have displeased your Majesty, and I am glad of it!' Her chin was up, as high as she had ever carried it; there was within her a last surging flicker of strength. 'I have displeased your Majesty,' she said again, 'because you would not give me my sons. I sought to uphold one of my still living sons!'

There was a sharp silence, only momentary, but one which seemed to go on for hours. The King looked towards Morton. An early bumblebee tapped gaily at the window.

'Your sons are dead, Madame,' said the Cardinal Archbishop. He looked at the window, and the bee, as if he were reciting a psalm with half his mind upon it. 'The traitor Plantagenet had them smothered in the Tower.'

'Sire,' said Elizabeth.

'Be still, Madame.' Jasper Tudor's voice; strangely quiet, mingled with the tapping of the bee. 'Be still and hear your sentence.'

'Am I to die?' she said. She looked down the polished length of the table, and up into Henry's eyes. Death. It had a stark and beautiful sound. *Sir John Grey, knight, is dead.*

'You are to be confined for life,' someone said, but she had ceased to listen. Her eyes were fixed on Henry's in fascination. Their glances merged as if welded. They drowned in one another's fluent steel, each seeing pitilessness, fear, and the dread of lost power. In the glitter of his sumptuous jewels she saw her own old insecurities, the lusts and longings, the spitting in the eye of God and Fortune; the fate formed by the writhing forces, one stronger than the other. Melusine – Cadwallader. Melusine had folded her coils and gone, sleeping for another thousand years at the bottom of her lake. Only her fading shadow remained in Henry's eyes. Elizabeth looked, and saw herself.

Bermondsey, they said. The Abbey of St. Saviour, and none to communicate with her on pain of severe reprisal.

Bermondsey, they said. There you will live and die.

She looked at him once more before leaving. It was as if she had borne him, had nurtured and moulded his wit and will until they were the facsimile of her own.

As you wax, Henry, so must I wane.

The November sky was coloured like iron, and the river cloaked by mist. All along the Thames lay tall carracks, weighted with Eastern spice, velvet and perfumes from Genoa, vessels carrying gold and silver from Venice, falcons from Iceland. Outgoing craft shivered at their moorings; the high-masted ships bound for Flanders, with decks hidden beneath sarplers of wool, hemp and flax that gave out a pungent smell over the low-tide stench of the fog. The masts seemed to reach the heavy sky, and from each rode a pennon, clinging twisted about the spidery shrouds. Grace raised her eyes to them, and prayed that they should blow, and carry her and John with them. The eel-boats lay in harbour. Usually there was a crowd of wives eager to board them, but this day the quay was silent. The City had gone to Westminster. Grace looked at the towering, webbed mastheads, about which sad seabirds made their dance. November was a bad month for sailing, yet sail they must; she, and the unknown ships, and John, whose heart was sick again.

When Ralph had brought the news of Lincoln's defeat at Stoke, John had cried out in anguish: Plantagenet dies again! She had felt herself lacking in the words and actions to heal him. She could only hold him, pressing her valueless body to his, watching his new-found health fade from him. He was wild of nights, springing up to cry of battles unfought, bloody deeds only dreamed of, vengeance unwreaked. Frustration rode him, and he grew incautious, speaking loudly of the Yorkist cause to strangers who, cursing him, turned away for their own safety. She saw bitterness where there had been hope, stress in place of calm, and finally this silent apathy which accompanied him upon his walk by the river. In this limbo of distress she led him, trying to divert him, pointing out the beauty of the lacy carved ships with their sails asleep, and the envied seabirds, who darted and screamed about them. Near the Steelyard she stopped and put her arms about him. By now she knew that she was called a harlot in the City; it was of no matter. She took him in her arms and he did not resist.

'My dear love,' she said, 'when shall we take ship for Ireland?'

His eyes were dull. 'Ireland?'

'From Bristol?' she said gently. 'Great ships go from there, John. They search for the isle of Brasil.'

Salazar had told her this, in their daily conversations, and he had laughed to see her eyes wide from his talk of sea monsters. Now she chattered to John about it, while he leaned on her like a tired tree; he, who was always so strong and passionate, now bereft and slack. The failed rebellion had taken away a part of him. Grace longed for escape – forgetting. Her own longings as well as his; Elizabeth still tugged at her. As if Elizabeth were the bell and Grace the tongue; where Elizabeth swayed, Grace sounded and was bruised. She knew that Elizabeth had been arrested, and daily, secretly, she remembered her in her prayers.

'The Boy!' said John, for, the hundredth time. 'He was only a blacksmith's son. Tudor has put him to work in the kitchens. It would have been better had he hanged him.'

'Yes, John,' said Grace, as always. 'He was only a feigned boy. He was not the Earl of Warwick, nor was he one of my father's sons.'

Henry had fetched the true Warwick out of the Tower and had paraded him briefly, slug-pale and mindless from incarceration. Although Clarence's son could hardly tell night from day, the point was taken. Simnel was Simnel, and now washed pots for the King's pleasure.

'John,' she said, 'we are ready for the journey.'

Hopeless yet hoping, she had made sure of this. All the bags packed, the green gowns chested in that lonely upper room. Yet all John could talk of was Lincoln, utterly defeated at Stoke and bloodily dead, and the rising shattered by Tudor's waged men. On London Bridge the rebel heads, stripped by kites, had mouldered weeks ago. More and more Grace longed to leave England. It was nearly six months since Stoke, and she and John still lived untouched, above the butcher's shop. The only change had been Master Ralph's dismissal – for laziness.

'My love.' She laid her face against his smooth velvet shoulder. She glanced up at his eyes, now listlessly fixed upon the tall ships and the dozen barges that suddenly appeared around the curve of the river. Painted barges, gilt banners shuddering limply in the thickening fog.

'Where are they all going?' he asked; apart from the world, no longer a lover but a child, young yet immeasurably old, careworn and drained.

'To the coronation. Bess is to be crowned today.'

This affected him; he showed life, his lips curled. 'The time is full, God knows!' he said scornfully. 'The usurper would have held off another ten years, had not London cried shame ... I love Bess, she is Edward's daughter. Although she is the witch's daughter, too.' He looked at Grace with a tinge of the old hatred. Sadness caught at her heart.

'My lord.' Only a sigh, drifting with the rotting November fog.

'The witch!' he said, cruelly. 'More good men died through her this year. Do not forget that she conspired in the rebellion too. Ralph said ...'

'Unfair!' cried Grace. 'You too would have fought! Did you not write to Ireland, offering your arms? Elizabeth joined your cause ...' She stopped, knowing that whatever Elizabeth did, she could never redeem herself with John. Then she said softly: 'Love, don't miscall her. I can't bear it.'

He looked at her, his woman, in whom he slaked needs, passions, rages. She was the moon to his tides, and still she could not realize it. He lifted her chin and gave her a token she could understand; a hard kiss on her pale mouth. She smiled wanly.

'We have been fortunate,' he said.

Yes. John was as guilty as any of the fleshless rebel heads on London Bridge had been. This renewed her itch of unease. She stared at him, willing his whole attention on her words.

'We must leave England,' she said.

She would carry the bags, arrange for pack-mules to Bristol, or Pembroke, or wherever was necessary. She would take him bodily aboard some rough Irish vessel. In her mind she saw the shore slide away, heard the seabirds shrieking of hope, of peace. Desmond's family would welcome them, cordial and careful, like their last letter. Still John did not answer and a fearful thought occurred: did he court death? As his father had done on Bosworth Field? Men said that Richard cared nothing for life that day, went roaring and singing to his end. Men said many things, and daily the tenor of opinion changed. A great gold boat passed along the river to Westminster; it carried the flaccid banners of the Earl of Pembroke. Jasper Tudor, newly made Earl of Bedford, but keeping his old colours. Pembroke! Yes, Bristol was the safer for her and John to slip from the country. Her unease grew like the fog, and John felt it. He knew it, and suddenly he was back with her, he was the John she knew and loved, and she was once more passive, clinging, guided. His cold fingers crept about her own icy hand. A gang of prentices hastened past, best-dressed, to Westminster, where they would gape and howl and drink too deeply of the Queen's health.

John touched her face, set his lips to the damp curl beneath her hood.

'All my fault,' he said. 'You're sad. When you are sad, my Grace, I want to die.'

I want to die. The words entered her heart; every vein felt squeezed up tight. She stood on the fog-filmed cobbles and longed for a high-masted galley. She would steer it herself in fancy, over the black ocean, into the slack green harbour of Ireland.

'There can be other risings, and you will join them,' she said softly. The mist had a weird effect, as if the gap between them were widening. As if he were slipping away, hold him as she would. And like a soothsayer, he answered her:

'There will be other feigned boys. And none will restore my father's name. Men have cast him into Hell. Yet I know that he drinks of the water of life.'

Closely they began to walk, as if their steps were driven by a lifeless wind. And he began to talk to her, not of war or policy, but as he had rarely talked; of how he loved her, that she was his life's light and salvation, and that without her he was dead and damned. The fog about them became warm, a sheltering balm, the cobbles satin beneath their feet. They joined the crowd hastening towards Westminster, yet they were apart from the people. Dreaming, they went slowly, while merchant and friar, peasant and ale-wife scampered by; while carts and chariots flying bright liveries forced them into doorway and alcove. Pliantly the two of them bent before the onrush of traffic, untouched, invulnerable. They filtered through the pulsing vein of London, his arm about her waist, her head in the hollow of his neck. Baynard's Castle fell behind. There was neither hope nor need of entering the garden with its sweet early memories; the flowers bloomed in the clasp of his hands, her breath on his cheek. As Westminster towers rose before them, in stern yet ethereal greyness, he stopped, touched her mouth with his in the sight of festive London.

'My little maid!' he said, and smiled, a smile to live and die upon. And she babbled again of Ireland and escape; any thing, to keep that smile inviolate, and hers.

'We must leave. Today.'

'Hush!' he said. 'Let us go and see Bess's coronation – let us say a prayer for her as she enters the Abbey.'

There was an immense crowd outside, yet folk let them through as if they were ghosts, and they stood at the forefront of the throng, close to the Abbey's entrance. Covering the flags outside was a great carpet, striped in white and red whereon the Queen would walk under a golden canopy. The carpet's shimmering breadth divided the holiday crowd. People pushed forward, heads turning, craning. Wives and merchants, prentices, clerks and schoolboys lined the carpet's edge; and were controlled by armed men; pikemen and swordsmen wearing the Tudor tabard. Beside Grace a pretty young woman held the hand of a small boy. She drew a long dagger from her belt and gave it to the child.

'Now wait, Robin,' she told him. 'Wait until the Queen has passed, and then go to!'

The little boy smiled up at Grace. 'I am to cut the carpet,' he confided.

'I promised him,' explained the woman. 'But I fear the knife isn't sharp enough!'

All down the line folk were discreetly unsheathing daggers for the timeless privilege of taking a square of the royal cloth, for good luck, as a protection against king's evil, and in sheer joy and reverence.

'I cut the carpet at Queen Anne's coronation,' said the young woman softly. 'But then she and Richard were crowned together.' John's cold hand tightened on Grace's; nearer the flaring bray of trumpets sounded and suddenly out of the hanging mist came the procession. A great cheer arose, caps sailed into the air. An ancient man burst into tears, crying: 'Bess! Jesu preserve you, Bess!' Slowly, gently, the Queen began the long walk up to the Abbey door. Her sister Cicely bore her train. Bess wore a kirtle of purple velvet banded with ermine. Her shining wheaten hair, crowned with pearls and rubies, fell to her hips and rippled as she walked. Her face was pale and thin and serious. Edward's daughter, Elizabeth's daughter, silver and gold, she came graciously on; the mob erupted with delight. The pure profile, the glittering hair passed by, gone in an instant. Bright-eyed, the small boy turned to his mother.

'Now!' she whispered, and he ran forward, waving his dagger. Likewise did a hundred men and women, knives gleaming like fishes slipping through the mist. And the guard moved, too swiftly. The majority of them were Breton; they had never heard of the custom and were desperately afraid of their master's wrath. They did not see the joy or the innocence of the crowd; they saw only knives and sudden movements. Unsheathing their weapons, they laid about them. The cheers, the laughter, turned to screams of anguish. Grace saw an old man clubbed, his delicate skull shattered; a woman trampled. There was the sound of splintering bone, and one rending shriek that rose above all other. The small boy, Robin, was impaled on a guardsman's lance. Within a minute a dozen people lay dying, and the beautiful carpet was more red than white.

At the Abbey's portal, the Queen turned and saw all. Cicely dropped her sister's train and buried her face in her hands. All the Queen's ladies were crying; Jasper Tudor rushed them into the porch. Grace watched the Queen go weeping from dead bodies to her coronation. Her own mind froze; she slid fainting into John's arms.

She found herself lying on a tavern bench. John's face was fogged and strange. He had been trying to dribble wine into her mouth; the bosom of her gown was soaked. She could hear the landlord cursing softly in the background.

'Be still, my love,' John said. She tried to smile; her face was stiff.

'You were right!' he said. She frowned. Objects came clearer, then blurred again as, remembering the massacre, she began to weep. 'We must go away,' he went on. 'After today, I have had enough of Tudor's England. We will leave at once.'

She sat up; her head spun, then quietened slowly. She nodded and rose, wiped away tears. 'I'm ready.'

'I must find horses and a boy to bear our goods,' he said. He crossed to the landlord and spoke swiftly; the man: nodded and went away. 'Then, a ship to carry us. Wait here for me.'

'No!' she cried. 'I'll come with you, don't leave me.'

Seriously he looked at her. He said: 'Never.'

'Let us not return to Gould's. Let's leave everything. I have all that I need.'

'You must take your pretty gowns,' he said, smiling: 'I shall have no more money once we are exiled. I shall need to attach myself to some Irish lord ... come, love. I love you in your pretty gowns.'

When they returned to the butcher's shop, Gould was there alone. He looked at them dourly. When John, stiffly arrogant, informed him that they were quitting the lodging, he only grunted, and began sawing at a haunch of venison on the counter. Hand in hand they went upstairs and entered the small room for the last time. Together they leaned from the window once more. Salazar stood on the corner, teaching his monkey a trick; he was absorbed and did not look up. John touched the dingy walls of the room, the crooked table, found a forgotten doublet in a chest. Everything was very quiet; Gould's sawing and chopping had ceased. John sat on the viciously lumpy bed, and stroked its covers.

'Sweet Jesu! I was happy here!' he said softly. Then, without looking at her: 'My lady. Such as you are given by God.'

Tears stung her eyes. She said shakily: 'We shall be even happier. Look!' Trying to laugh, she nudged the coffer containing her gowns. 'I can't lift it!'

'The boy will be here soon,' he said. He sat quietly, turning the ring upon his finger, looking at the floor. Restlessly Grace walked about. Paul's clock struck its harsh remembered note. She turned and looked at John as he sat there, all darkness and light, with his pallor and his black hair, and the sad tempestuous eyes pensively veiled. Love filled her as she looked.

'Oh, my lord!' she began. There was a noise on the stair, steps forcefully, imperatively advancing. No baggage-boy owned such a tread, or wore mailed shoes, or carried halberds that slithered and struck upon the walls of the narrow staircase. There were at least four, faceless ones, ascending the stair. The small upper room shook. John stood up, crossed easily, deliberately, to where she stood aghast, and drew her to him, covering her face with kisses. He set his mouth on hers in an endless embrace, bending her body to his, almost engulfing it, protectively yet with desire, the wild regretful desire of the condemned.

A weapon crashed once upon the door. Still he kissed her, held her as if to merge her body finally and forever with his. Half-fainting again, she cried in her mind: He knew! He knew they would come for him; he knew and did nothing ...

Then they were in the room; the bright Dragon blazons and the royal insignia; tall men, stooping beneath the lintel, disinterested men come by order of their sovereign. And behind them was Gould, peeping gloomily to see his work accomplished.

'You are John of Gloucester, son of the traitor Plantagenet.'

He had withdrawn from Grace, and was standing respectfully apart. He was smiling.

'I am the son of Richard, rightful king of England.'

'You must come now,' they said, sounding foolish.

'The lady has no part of it, of course,' said John. Still he smiled. They inclined their heads, and accepted this. They had their orders; Grace was invisible.

'The charge is treason?'

'Treasonable correspondence with Ireland.' The pikes were hefted and set to attention with a crash.

'Why did he wait so long?' said John softly.

'Come,' they said. The question was irrelevant; one did not question divinity.

Formally John kissed Grace's hand. 'Remember me,' he said. His eyes smiled as well as his mouth; he was full of tenderness. He was slipping away; the fog of destiny had him. He was gone. Strangely, he said: 'My dynasty is damned. The wheel comes full circle. My lady, my love. Remember ...'

Even when the door had closed and the footsteps had died, she could not move. She stood like a stone, gathering strength against the storm about to break in her. When it did, his smile remained, almost but not quite enough to make the moment bearable.

Although Cardinal Morton now had palaces and mortmains the length of England, he found it sometimes convenient to lodge at his old manor of Holborn. There, in the quiet rooms or the pretty garden with its strawberry beds, he could nod acquaintance to harder times. He sat in his parlour, while a serious-faced boy of nearly nine stood reading from a scroll on a lectern. Morton listened to the fluid Latin cadences approvingly. Thomas More, son of a Lincoln's Inn judge, was the wittiest pupil ever to come the Cardinal's way. The clear voice relaxed Morton; he was feeling his great age. There was still so much to do; to shape the Tudor dream, to instruct what should be remembered and what forgotten. He was annoyed when his clerk and gatekeeper knocked, entered, and knelt to whisper against the folds of the scarlet robe.

'Oh, this is monstrous!' cried Morton. 'It is not fitting for women to enter these precincts. Send her away.'

Thomas More slipped from the lectern stool and left the room. He disliked to hear his master in choler, even though this occurred infrequently.

'Eminence,' faltered the clerk. 'Every day for weeks, she has embarrassed us.' He flushed. When Grace wept, he did not know what to say; when she swooned, he was utterly put out, and let her lie moaning.

'She speaks of going to his Majesty.'

'Foolishness,' said Morton quietly. 'Very well. I will see her. No doubt she wishes to confess her sin. Are there no lesser men to give her an ear?'

He let her wait some minutes more while he occupied himself with the latest problem; the entry in York Civic Records, only lately brought to his notice. It was an old entry, dated 22nd August, two years earlier. He was slightly troubled by it. 'This day was our good King Richard, late mercifully reigning over us, piteously slain and murdered to the great heaviness of this City.' It was full time to stop such rot as this. And the herald, Rous, was due for an audience too; the Rous Roll must be amended for it too spoke glowingly of Henry's predecessor. How should it be re-written? And now he was plagued by the bastard wench of Edward Plantagenet. He looked sternly at her when she was admitted. She did him obeisance.

'Rise, child,' he said impassively. Her lips left the great jewel on his finger and she got up. Her eyes were green a glass, contained a thousand years of sorrow, and discomfited him a little.

'You are penitent?'

'Penitent?' An incredulous breath.

'For your carnality during the past year with the traitor Gloucester. Remember the words of St. Jerome: God can do all things but restore virginity!'

She smiled a little. 'Your Eminence,' she said, 'I come to you because you are of God. I wish to plead for John of Gloucester's life.'

'You are too late,' he said stiffly. 'He has been tried and found guilty. He is sentenced to death.'

Something shifted in the green eyes. Fleetingly he saw how she would be as an old woman; a stranger to smiles, still fair, but almost nunly. Somehow this made him feel older still.

'I shall appeal to the King himself,' she said quietly. Then he thought; she is mad, a heretic.

'The King is not in London. The King sees no one.' He picked up a quill, made a notation on Rous's offending roll.

After a time she said: 'When is the execution to be?' and he told her, not looking up. When he raised his eyes, the room was empty. He sent again for Thomas More.

'Divert me, Tom,' he said. 'I am weary.'

'Alas, my lord.' The boy blushed. 'I have no talent for it.'

'Nonsense.' The fresh young mind was geared to storytelling, and untouched by the past thirty years of war. All More's schooling had been directed by the accession of King Henry, the mystical union of Rose Red and White, like Christ and the Church. Brightly the boy said: 'There is a new troupe of entertainers outside. They will do better than I.'

'While he waited, Morton worried about the herald Rous's roll. Such as he should be interrogated, sounded out. God knew how many little clerks there were, scratching the dangerous truth in hidden corners, fancying themselves chroniclers. Morton's task was to achieve an ellipse, woven of thoughts, images, histories. Impossible to close the mouth of every secret scribe. Better to open them wider with a new tale. But how to bring the pattern to its full? So far the story was good – the shedding of infants' blood – Black Will Slaughter was a fine invention, worthy of Chaucer's genius ... Yet there were too many who remembered Richard – the York epitaph exemplified this. Men lived longer these days, he thought, and despite all, found comfort in it.

The players entered and there was a most hideous hunchback among them. Clever, he told rhymes with tongue-torturing skill. He danced a little hornpipe. Yet freakish chance had loaded his body with a clubbed mass of bone; his arms were longer than his legs. Black flowing hair grew on his face.

'Holy Jesu,' murmured Morton, in wondering distaste, but he applauded the monster's antics graciously. Then, suddenly, watching how, during a rest, the other entertainers ignored their wretched companion, illumination bloomed in the Cardinal's mind. He called the hunchback over to the throne.

'Why do they use you thus?'

The dwarf grinned. 'Why, highness, behold!' He bent double so that the misshapen hump moved beneath Morton's eye. 'I am touched by Lucifer – so men say!'

'And are you?' Morton's heresy-sniffing nose dilated.

The hunchback raised clear eyes, his only beautiful feature. 'No, lord,' he said quietly.

Morton gave the dwarf a broad gold piece on parting. Now he knew how Rous should amend his Roll. He knew exactly.

'Touched by Lucifer,' he whispered, charmed. 'Aye. Touched by Lucifer.'

Salazar was waiting for Grace when she came out of the Holborn mansion. He held two Arabian horses. Grace went and rested her head upon the Moor's motleyed breast.

'It is today,' she said softly. 'At noon.'

The monkey sprang to her shoulder. The Moor was crooning, a little hypnotic song stirred by the waves of an alien sea. He laid one long black hand upon Grace's shivering head.

'I know,' he said. 'Upon Tower Hill. You must not go there.'

'I must.'

'It will bring you pain.' Tenderly he looked down at her, so fair and small against his own dark mystery. She was his bright token, his proxy daughter, his special charm, and he, for months, her unknown amulet and guard.

'You must not go,' he repeated. 'Look at the people!'

They were already hurrying through Holborn, dragging on gowns, eager for the dreadful joy, not far removed from love, of witnessing an execution. The apple-sellers were trundling their wagons through the City. The Londoners, the artisans, mercers, clerks and prentices, always the prentices, ran to watch, to feel their own necks secure and take comfort in vicarious death. John's execution would propitiate each man's especial god.

Salazar said, in his dreaming voice: 'I went yesterday to the Tower.'

Broken, she said: 'Why didn't you tell me? Why did you not take me?'

The stroking hand ruffled her hair, leaf-light. He thought of how he had found her, sitting mutely in the upper room without food or drink for three days; how he had carried her out through the stinking shop. How he had nursed her at his house, listening to her ravings, fed and restored her, talked softly through her anguish while she clung to his hand as her one anchor. He knew all her joys, her loyalties and griefs.

'Did you see him?' she whispered.

'Nay, not I. None could. But he sent you this.' He withdrew from his gold-laced pouch a tiny parchment scrap. She read from it, weeping.

'My dear beloved, stay from me now. Remember that you are Plantagenet, accursed by the witch. Guard yourself. Sweet Christ Jesu send you happy. Written at the Tower by my own hand.'

His hand, the hand of delight, whose writings, like black sea-waves, bound her closer and closer, to what? A twitching body, a lifeless, severed head. She would go to Tower Hill. With fortune, the axe might also find her neck.

'Come, Salazar, let us follow the people!'

He nodded, lifted her on to one of the horses, where she sat, swaying, her head shrouded by mist, her outline blurred. Taking the other mount's bridle, the Moor began to walk. A tavern bush, threaded with dried flowers and ribbon, loomed to the left. He looked at Grace; he was with her in this last tribulation; he knew what he must do.

'It is only eleven,' he said. 'A drink, first. A void, to warn you.'

He took her down, wrapped his long arm about her and guided

her into the deserted inn. He pressed her down into a high-backed settle. She leaned her cheek against the wood. It smelled of cinnamon and musk, a scent lately left by some wealthy wife. Its smell was the smell of grief, its black oak the colour of death. There was a little knot in the grain, and into this she ground her cheek until the bruise broke and blood started. Good. Good pain.

Salazar stood before her, his vastness blotting out the little window over her head. He held a silver cup. It smoked and was aromatic. Her hands steadied about its warmth. She tasted the cup; an unfamiliar taste, it was writhing-sour, like swallowing a serpent.

'Drink,' said Salazar sweetly. The monkey chattered and hung upside down from the back of the booth.

'Drink, *doña*.'

Salazar, tall, and wavering like a tree under storm, stood before her. Her head felt heavy, her eyes pained from the quivering colours of his dress. Her gown was creased and her feet had been arranged neatly upon the settle. The tavern swam. With difficulty she looked past the Moor's head to the window. Through the lattice she saw one star, steadfast and burning bright. She thought: it is the end of the world. Night has come in the morning. She felt a weightless warmth in the crook of her arm. The monkey was there, fast asleep.

'It's over,' said Salazar. 'All over, little one. Quick, and noble.'

She tried to speak, and failed.

'He was not tortured,' said Salazar. 'Nor was he despoiled. One stroke, swift and clean. He smiled on the scaffold. My faith is not yours; yet who knows that we do not all cheat death?'

Then he gathered her to his coloured breast and rocked her, humming his foreign song as if he did not care, for this was the way to heal her; no commiseration, no crying against what cannot be mended.

'Now,' he said at last. 'My time here is done. But you?'

'I do not know,' she answered. 'I do not care.'

'You have a place,' said Salazar. 'Tell me where, and I will take you there.'

'I have nowhere, no one, nothing.'

'Impossible.' His ear-rings gleamed in the candlelight. The inn was filling up; gossip drifted among the high-backed stalls.

'Did you love none but him?' he asked gently. 'No man, woman or child?'

Within her purse, Grace's fingers cracked on the last letter. *Plantagenet, cursed by the witch.* And his words, returning like ghosts: *The wheel comes full circle!* She thought: I have been blind, uncaring, utterly ignorant. That dragging love I felt – it is turned to gall. My only love is dead, headless – accursed like the whole of York and Plantagenet. I have loved evil – the evil of Elizabeth.

'I will go to the witch,' she said softly.

'*Bueño*,' said Salazar, calmly. 'Tomorrow I will speed you there. She lies at Bermondsey.'

'I will be revenged upon the witch,' said Grace, and trembled. Salazar nodded gently.

He paid the boatman and saw Grace embark near Dowgate. He left her and was gone, tall, coal-black and mysterious, more elemental than man. He would return to Spain, where he could report to Ferdinand and Isabella that England was gaining in stability. He watched one of the last victims of that stability sitting muffled in her green hood as the boat struck out across the river. He scratched his monkey's ear, and sighed.

Grace passed through Southwark with its teeming stews and whorehouses and into the quieter area of Bermondsey, where the tower of St. Saviour split the sky and the sound of its mournful bell floated across the river. Water and sky were opaque and each dull flat cloud, each timeless ripple, held a terrible truth. Several times she repeated: 'John is dead!' trying the words out, trying to find in them a clue to rob them of meaning. For the first time in her life she saw the terrible face of hatred and felt its fangs. Now she knew the craving for vengeance that poisons every sight and sound, turns blood acid and stretches the spirit on a subtle rack. She knew what John had felt, and why, unrevenged, he had gone almost placidly to death. Death was better than the insupportable corruption, the lonely sickness of hatred, with each stab of which her memory grew long, bringing old weapons brightly renewed; Elizabeth's coldness, her curses, that slap in the face. All rushed, a ragged army, to fan the fearful power into an inferno. Her mind felt like a swollen serpent's egg, filled with all the clamour of the condemned dynasty, and heavy with its tears. She took the unfamiliar burden of hatred upon her, felt its sourness, shivered in its flame. She looked up at the vast door of Bermondsey Abbey and saw it misted, corroded, red.

She pulled the bell and heard it jangling down catacombs of darkness. She muttered: 'Like a dog, I loved her!' *The wheel comes full circle.* Then again, wearily, as if questioning the dying bell's note: 'John is dead.' Infected by hatred, Grace said loudly: 'I am Plantagenet! and I will rid the world of this pestilence!'

Perhaps she is sick, she thought. Lying defenceless in some rich chamber. It will be easy; she is old and I am young and strong. If she should want a drink, it will be easy to doctor her cup. There are swift poisons and there are slow. Dementedly her lips drew back from her teeth. She tugged the bell again. From within came the slap of sandals, and the grille was slid aside. A monk peered through the aperture and saw a dishevelled woman, green eyes that sparked like the eyes of a demon, a slight body shaking as under a gale.

'What do you want, daughter?'

He had an expressionless voice.

'The Queen-Dowager ...' began Grace softly and stopped. No. This was certain failure. There must be subtlety. She went on her knees on the step.

'Sanctuary,' she said formally. 'I crave Sanctuary for the love of God and King Henry.'

The face disappeared for an instant. The great door opened. The monk was revealed, his pallor disembodied against his robe and the creeping darkness behind him.

'Yes,' he said. 'We are by charter a sanctuary house.' He peered at her. 'In the King's name, what is your crime? Treason?' They were careful at St. Saviour's; the fall of the Abingdon Abbot for having sheltered the Stafford brothers was well known.

'Whoredom,' said Grace dementedly, and laughed. The monk's face grew long, hiding relief.

'Follow me,' he said, and walked away, girdle and keys swinging. She went after him down a cloister so cold that it raised the hair on her scalp, and under forbidding arches, past many doors closed like tombs. A thought came to her in passing: it is not a sanctuary, it is a prison. She looked eagerly at each door, for one of them housed the enemy. She followed the monk into a small round chamber with dim lights set high and deeply into the walls. There, he seated himself at a table, took up a pen, opened a ledger. He asked her name, and when she answered, looked up sharply.

'Your fame is not unknown.' He chewed the quill, indecisive. The

King had given no instructions on this score.

'I will consult my lord Abbot: wait here.' He went out, and Grace stood still, near to the door left ajar, and trembling from the cold, thinking only: Where is she? with her glacial, crescent-moon face, once so beloved. Reclining somewhere, little knowing that today is her last upon this earth. Grace's eyes strayed to the walls. The Abbot, before taking holy orders, had been a fighting man; some of his old weapons were displayed. A tarnished shield, a rusty sword with an ornate hilt, and a delicate poignard studded with three red stones. This last Grace unhesitatingly took down; she thumbed its edge and stared at the starting bead of blood on her flesh. After all the years, the dagger was sharp enough to shear a blade of grass. She tucked it in her belt and arranged her cloak in concealing folds. Somewhere down the cloister a door opened and closed. Grace swallowed, and wiped her wet palms, one with the other. Soon, now, if God were merciful.

The monk came back, entering so softly that her heart shook. He carried a small whip and a rosary in one hand. In the other he held a breviary.

'My lord Abbot is satisfied,' he said. 'I may deal with your penance. Take off your shoes, my daughter.'

Grace knelt and unplaced her little pointed slippers. Looking at the flagstones, she said casually:

'Is it true that the Queen-Dowager is here?'

'She is; the King suggested that she should retire here, for her health and comfort. Are you ready?'

She stood up and the cold leaped to encompass her naked soles. It was like putting her feet in fire. Within seconds, her ankles began to ache; ice shivered her skirts. The monk moved forward, proffered the scourge and the book.

'Now you must walk,' he said gently. 'Fifty times along the cloister. Give yourself five-and-twenty lashes and say fifteen *Aves*. Then I will give the absolution. I must strike the first blow in the name of God.'

Grace knelt again. She pushed back her hood and parted the curling hair in the nape of her neck. The monk said: '*In Nomine Patris, Filii, et Spiritus Sancti*,' and raised the little whip. She waited, oblivious, uncaring. Again, she heard the sound of a door closing in the passage without. Soon, she would find the enemy.

'For God's love! Stop!'

The voice was colder than the stones and filled the chamber, a shriek. It was a voice used to command, yet ghostly, an exhausted voice raised in outrage. Very slowly Grace lifted her head. Out of the corner of her eye she saw a rush of black garments, the monk's hand falling, the knout go spinning to the floor. And the voice spoke again, silver, imperious, yet drained, as if by its first utterance.

'For Jesu's love, Master Dominic! Are you mad? This child ...' The voice broke, on a sob. 'This child is without sin!'

'Madame,' said the monk, bewildered.

'Would to God that my life were hers,' said the sobbing voice. 'And that I had had her charity! Strike *me*, Master Dominic! Strike *me*!'

'Madame,' he said again, deeply shocked.

'Grace!' gasped the voice. 'Like her name ... full gracious, and my true beadswoman and comforter. Kind beyond belief. Would that I had been as kind.'

There was touch as well as a voice. A thin transparent hand with raised blue veins clasped Grace's wrist. An icy, burning hand, that sucked all hatred away into itself. The hand of salvation. Grace looked into the face of Elizabeth. The face came close; she kissed her on the mouth.

'You have come back!'

Hard against her hip Grace felt the poignard. Her fingers found it, drew it from her belt. Elizabeth's tremulous voice went on, addressing the priest.

'This child ... is the reminder of my past sin. She is my living penance, my sin-eater. And you would scourge her, Master Dominic!' He, his narrow life utterly dislocated, was praying to cover the Queen-Dowager's heretical words.

Then Elizabeth saw the knife. Her steady look encompassed it; in her eyes a joyous excitement grew.

'Yes,' she said softly. 'Give me release. Be kind, my Grace. And when your kindness is ended, pray for my soul. Your prayers were always the most efficacious.'

The dagger slipped from Grace's hand and shivered on the floor, its blade pointing away. Brother Dominic picked it up and, his face a mask of disapproval, replaced it on the wall. Still muttering a psalm he strode from the chamber. Grace began to cry, in long shuddering sobs. Elizabeth wrapped her thin arms about her. Embraced, they knelt upon the freezing floor, beside the tokens of penance, the rosary, the book, the scourge.

'Pray for me,' Elizabeth whispered. 'Be merciful; be my living token of grace.'

'Madame,' said Grace, weeping. 'Isabella.' She did not know why she used the name. It was a name heard long ago, a courtly name, an infant's memory; even perhaps a name unheard. Fitting, anyway, for this re-baptism of Elizabeth. The name said farewell to hatred. The hatred that rocks worlds and ruins kings and kills the common man.

'Protect me from Melusine and all her works,' said the Queen-Dowager. Grace held her close. Elizabeth was skeletal, her flesh alternately freezing and burning. She had shrunk in stature; her face was yellow. She wore the wimple of deep mourning.

'I am not without sin,' said Grace. 'But I will pray for you and guard you. I will not leave you.'

The sad, perished face lightened a trifle.

'Stay,' said Elizabeth. 'Stay until I am dead.'

Grace raised the Queen-Dowager and helped her to a stance. Very slowly they left the chamber together. The November evening gathered. A ray of misty light peeped through the windows and touched the rusted weapons of war, hanging still and silent on the walls.

Epilogue

1492

AND now the little flame burned sadly beneath the fair face of
the Virgin, so that the compassionate mouth seemed to smile. The
Matins bell had rung and the deep chanting of the monks had died
away, their office finished. The night was quiet save for a soft breeze
whispering at the window. The chamber was still, waiting, as the
unseen stranger waited. Elizabeth's breath came harshly, ceased for
seconds, then began again, a soft sound that was compounded of
echoes, shadows, the language of the undiscovered land.

All the women except Mistress Grace had gone. The others were
the King's servants, young, and ignorant of the time that was passing
away with Elizabeth. Grace had controlled their gossip and their idle-
ness and had made them serve the Queen-Dowager as was fitting. Yet
there was no place for them now. Dr. Benedictus had made his last
examination and gone away. Elizabeth had been shriven. Even so, it
was doubtful whether she knew that she was dying. She whispered,
spoke names, and held Grace's hand. Lucid if only to herself, she held
conversations, repeated the score of names that lately had narrowed
to one or two. This night she dwelt hour on hour upon one alone.

'John, my lord ...' she said, and smiled with closed eyes.

Grace's head drooped. She rested it upon her clasped hands. Five
years, she thought, and still the name turns a blade in my heart. They
lie, who say that time heals all. Elizabeth is proof of this. It is thirty
years since her fair John was slain. And seven-and-twenty years since
her coronation. And almost as long since Desmond's death. Desmond,
the reason for my existence. A strange story, told during the years of
sorrow at Bermondsey; yet a story which, on first hearing, had seemed
to Grace more like a reprise, a recollection, a legend in her blood.

She raised her head again and looked at Elizabeth. Elizabeth, alone. Brothers and sisters dead, all save Catherine, who never came. The latest victim of circumstance was the seaman-knight, Sir Edward, killed in a skirmish at St. Aubyn du Cormier. The house of Woodville was all but extinguished. As for Elizabeth, the cheerless years at St. Saviour's had killed her slowly, by inches. There had been but one day of parole, an incident that might have been comical but for its irony.

The King had commanded her appearance at court, for the sake of the French Ambassador's visit. Bess had been brought to bed of a daughter, Margaret, and could not attend the reception. The court was greatly changed; folk smiled when the King smiled, walked as if over live coals; and never spoke above a murmur. Holiness, riches and pageantry existed, coldly muted. The Ambassador had seemed impressed, although the sight of Elizabeth, already mortally ill, had disturbed him. The King too had not been unobservant. His incisive glance appraising Elizabeth, he had called his Chancellor to his side.

'An annuity to the Queen-Dowager in her retirement,' he had said vigorously. 'Four hundred livres for life!' There had been a genteel hiss of approbation from Henry's mammets, who danced and sang to his calling.'

The money had not lasted long. Some time before this June night, she had made her will, a pathetic little document witnessed by the Abbot of Bermondsey and Dr. Benedictus.

'In the name of God, 10th April, 1492, I, Elizabeth by the Grace of God Queen of England' (they let this pass) 'being late wife to the most victorious prince of blessed memory, Edward IV ...'

The pride was still. there, but changed, refined. It was lawful, and held no vanity. When she was asked for instruction as to her burial, she said softly: 'Let me be interred with ... my lord.'

'Ah, with Edward at Windsor,' they said. Then she failed again and left the will for an hour, while she fell into the swift delirium that plagued her. They wrote what they thought fitting.

'Item, I bequeath my body to be buried with the body of my lord at Windsor.' Later, recovering, she looked at their writing and nodded sadly, continuing more strongly thereafter.

'... without any pompous interring or costly expenses done thereabout.' Ruefully she said: 'Whereas I have no worldly goods to do the Queen's Grace, my dearest daughter, a pleasure with, neither to reward any of my children according to my heart, and mind, I beseech God Almighty to bless her Grace, with all her noble fame ...'

Then she laughed a little, and said: 'What is my blessing worth, masters?' Dr. Benedictus and the Abbot bowed, without answering.

'I will that such small stuff and goods that I have to be disposed truly in the contentation of my debts and for the health of my soul, as far as they will extend.'

Here she looked at Grace piteously, wishing that there were gold and jewels to leave her, but saying nothing, for there was no need with her hand in the kind hand of Grace, who asked for no reward. When the will was done, the Abbot and Dr. Benedictus signed and affixed their seal and went, bloodless and remote, away. Again her spirit lapsed and she raved softly in the bed, crying of Desmond, of Thomas Cooke, of Gloucester, of Dick and Ned. She was mercurial and strange; one day, fevered, she told Grace: 'Bury me at midnight.'

Grace noted this down faithfully, but said: 'Midnight, sweet dame?' and Elizabeth muttered of Lusignan, dreamed of Melusine and the pool, of Gyot, Gedes, Geoffrey of the Tooth, and woke with a cry. Sometimes she said, fervently: '*In manus tuas, Domine*', and Grace whispered a paternoster, watching Elizabeth, craving her release from the interminable sickness.

And now it was June, in the small and weary hours, and the look on Elizabeth's face was unmistakable. She seemed to grow younger every hour, pale and small and childish, her fluent blood stilling, her quicksilver mind running down like a silent glass, her hands no longer stirred by palsy or pain.

'John. Ah, love ...' she said, and groaned. 'Lusignan ... the monster child destroyed his brother ...'

Her eyes opened on Grace, who said gently:

'Are you still afraid?'

'I have wrought great evil,' said Elizabeth for the hundredth time.

'Ah' said Grace, and kissed her. 'There, Madame. It is finished.' She mused that Elizabeth was only the instrument of something mystic and vast. She thought: Like all of us, she was put upon this earth to tread the written measure of destiny. For I sometimes believe that our life is a map drawn before our conception, our joys and sorrows meted out, far from our consciousness. And how shall we be remembered? Destiny having used us and consigned us to dust, shall we, perhaps, be unremembered? What of our loyalties and our loves, our passions and our tears? Our power is all that might leave a mark upon the world. She looked down at Elizabeth's fading countenance. Where is power now? Gone, together with beauty and riches. She was an instrument. And so was I. I, who loved one man and one woman. Less than a dusky moth, born to dance and die in a night.

Elizabeth whispered: 'You loved me ... does this absolve me?'

'Perhaps I inherited a little of Desmond's soul, Madame. As his death was the reason for my birth, perhaps a little of Desmond forgives you. If not all. Maybe this was my destiny, Isabella, my lady.'

'Grace.' The voice was faint.

'Madame?'

'At my funeral ... I wish twelve poor men of the City to follow me and be rewarded. No pomp or splendour. See to it. We shall go by river to Windsor. Be with me to the end.' She was breathing badly, in quick, tearing gasps.

'I shall be with you,' said Grace steadily. 'And the water will be calm.'

Elizabeth did not hear. Her eyes, their brightness dimmed at last, looked past her companion. She tried to sit up; sudden tremulous joy illuminated her face. It was plain that though her body was willed to lie with Edward, her spirit had its own destination. Grace rose quickly, crossed the room and flung open the window. The night breeze swept in, smelling of June lilies and on the edge of morning, for somewhere a bird awoke with a crystal spray of song.

The breeze gained vigour and curled about the chamber joyfully, like a child at play. In its niche beneath the Virgin, the flame went out.

THE END

399

standing. The fact that humans, even tribes that otherwise are very crude, possess a more or less comprehensive system of such signs, valid within smaller or larger circles, for a long time has been regarded as worthy of admiration and as evidence for the supernatural source of language and thus of the human beings themselves who possess such a precious gift: it was believed that it could be explained only as stemming from a supernatural source. The shallow opinion of those was mocked who ascribed even to language a natural origin by supposing a fictitious assembly which might have decided to call one thing a house, another a table, a third an animal, and so forth. In an argument of this kind, language was shown to be a prerequisite for language, which is an impossibility. Nobody wanted to and nobody was able to acknowledge the simple truth that artificial signs would develop from natural signs, and social signs from individual ones, through imperceptible changes and through gradual growth—and that social will was to come about similarly. One might remember here the sign language of deaf-mutes: partly, gestures are understood by these, as by human beings in general and even by higher animals, for instance, as signs of anger and of benevolence; partly, gestures and what is added to them as the somewhat arbitrary expression of emotions, desires, and expectations through movements of one's movable limbs, especially one's fingers, are interpreted on the basis of their being together and hanging together with other, especially more natural, signs that had been understood previously. The correctness or incorrectness of such interpretations enters into consciousness by way of experience: the correct interpretations will be more easily repeated and become automatic through habit; thus they can be learned.

If in this way a quasi-language of gestures can develop, it is even more likely that the language of words has been developed from elementary beginnings not different from animal cries and from whimpering or faltering sounds. We experience every day how infants announce their feelings, moods, and desires, even though they may be comprehensible only to the mother, and that they learn gradually to understand language and to speak it; only gradually do they enter into the long-existing community of those for whom these sounds have validity and who have, as it were, invented and agreed upon such a system that in its further development becomes more varied and complex. Even an adult, and whoever progresses to improve his education, continues to learn more words and their meaning, and the older child learns foreign languages, at least their elements. Only a certain blindness and man's natural inclination to prefer explanations of natural facts by means of imagined beings to those resulting from real persons or things or processes, which was nurtured assiduously by priests and theologians, could have found the origin and growth of such a system of signs more miraculous than the origin and growth of any organic being, including that of a human being out of something that is not yet a human being. Interpreters of this kind are always ready to assume miracles, that is, divine intervention.

Social signs which mean that something is to be or to happen, to be done or left undone, according to the will of a natural or collective person authorized or believed to be empowered to issue such commandments or prohibitions, lead us into the sphere of social norms: for comparable to individual orders or commandments, social regulations may be made known not only through the general system of language but also by means of special signs, the meaning of which is mutually familiar.

Signs as signals.—Here simple artificial signs for the ear (acoustic) or for the eye (optic) prove to be particularly useful, and therefore may achieve great importance as signals in war on land and sea, but also within a peacetime army or in some other system of communication; the reason being that they are particularly suited to be perceived quickly and distinctly and, after having become known through habit, to be understood clearly and regularly. They are of great value also because of their international intelligibility, as soon as they have become generally accepted. An example is the book of international signals in which signals are compiled that serve to promote communication between ships of various flags on the high seas and between ships and land signal stations. Whereas here, then, a general understanding from man to man, whatever language they may otherwise speak or know, is favored, on the other hand, it is evident that the common language is not discrete enough to be kept concealed from the enemy or from persons whose understanding of it is undesirable or even harmful: especially written words are dangerous because an otherwise strange language, which may be hard to understand if spoken, can be more easily comprehended if transmitted in writing. In such a case, writing in ciphers proves to be the suitable means for keeping secret information secret; a coded dispatch, therefore, is an important instrument in diplomatic relations. Similarly, the use of a foreign language, written or oral, may often be sufficient in safeguarding a secret as long as one is sure that unauthorized persons who may see the document do not understand this language and are not particularly interested in having it interpreted to them.

Signs as documents.—The use of signs has always been considered necessary where authority asserts itself, therefore always where a dispute is decided by the judgment of a court, and where a sentence is passed that inflicts a punishment. Certain forms are always prescribed, and these forms in spoken or written words which have become formulae are the signs for the validity of such decisions. Thus, still today the defendant or accused is called before the court by means of a certain *formula*, and judgment is pronounced to him in certain *formulae;* using certain fixed forms, he may appeal the judgment until it becomes valid through a higher court's decision. All this, at one time prescribed by customary law, is now provided by enacted law. Even a law attains validity only through the observance of fixed forms; certain signs are required which confer legal power. In the course of cultural evolution, all these forms have acquired their regular structure, first in writing, then, after printing became customary, as a printed document. Documents are testimonials, and testimonials, written or oral, serve as proof of facts, especially of such facts that are chiefly facts of validity and therefore not provable by means of visible or other sensual evidence. Every proof requires signs which are meant to bear witness that the more or less firm opinion, at best the conviction, is the result of the truth of an assertion, therefore also of a fact; and vice versa. Thus, testimony before a court of law serves as a means of proof, particularly if its power is augmented by means of forms which are required and accepted as signs of the truthfulness of the witness: the most common expression of the significance of the oath in social life. In all these cases, we deal with the development of communication among men for the purpose of peaceful living and acting (working) together. They become all the more important, the more acting together in closed ranks is required for the sake of unity; therefore especially cooperation in battle. This is the reason why we observe in an army particularly pronounced regulations of commanding and obeying; obeying both general rules and individually issued but socially sanctioned single commands. Therefore, here, too, we see the effectiveness of signs: signs of domination and signs of servitude, expressed partly in words, spoken or written, partly by other, mostly visible, signs. A promise and, in consequence, the solemn vow refer in particular to obedience. Here is the place also of the promising oath and its counterpart: the negative promise of a threat of punishment. This, too, is to be discussed in connection with social norms.

Signs as symbols.—The third and particularly remarkable kind of social signs is symbols. These are visible signs represented by certain objects whose significance is to be understood in such a way that they indicate something that cannot be designated or expressed directly, especially if it must not be mentioned in words. This is the reason why the symbol claims enhanced value and gains its special validity regarding everything that is supposed to be mysterious, for instance, as far as the communication with invisible and unreal beings, such as gods, is concerned, whether they are feared or revered. This is why religious symbols cause a pious shudder in the heart, for the believer a necessary and dutiful effect of the supposed presence of intimate and familiar as well as of ghostlike and uncanny powers. But worldly and visible representatives of power, too, obtain their share, although only more or less so, in such supernatural magnificence. To them, too, symbols are of service, especially on festive occasions when they are called upon to represent gods and to display the splendor of their own power in brilliant guise. This task is the immediate concern of priests, especially high priests, who are believed to be in direct contact with their deity, to know their secrets, and to mediate their power.

The word symbol derives from the Greek, and can be traced to a verb meaning "to throw together," therefore also to put together, to contribute, to communicate, from which is further derived the meaning of "concluding a treaty," and many other related meanings. The important sense of the word derives from the fact that it means two fitting halves of the small plate or ring by which hosts and guests would recognize each other. Thus even in the origin of the word there is an element of something that secretly binds persons; hence it gained the significance that made it develop its particularly religious connotation.

Religious symbols, in the first place, are connected with the worship of images: in the same way that the statue of a god is thought of as being the deity itself or at least as being consecrated by it and as being in magic contact with it, and thus as capable of performing miracles as the deity itself. They are the outcomes of fetishism, which endows some objects with sacred power and which survives among civilized peoples in the shape of charms or amulets. In other words, religious symbols are to a lesser or larger degree inspired by that way of thinking of primitive peoples which is at the bottom of all mysticism, namely, the conviction that nature everywhere is filled with efficacious ghosts, or spirits, and that these spirits haunt, that is, do good or evil to, people according to their whim and mood, that they are always and ubiquitously present, preferably in the dark and at particular places, not only at holy ones but also at some that, on account of their age or because they are the residence of important personages, have gained an uncanny kind of quasi-holiness. There is always a basic desire and endeavor either to banish, to exorcise, or to propitiate and befriend them, and often one kind of spirit has to deter and overcome the other, as the symbol of the Cross overcomes the devil. Of a cruder kind are animalistic symbols, in which may be included phallic ones, the use of which, in the form of mimic acts, images, and symbolic ceremonies, even the real act of coition, is so widely spread that one might be tempted to trace it back to an idea fundamental in ancient religious belief that even the maintenance and increase of nature's and man's fertility were not explainable through natural causes but through supernatural ones, namely the spirits. The idea is that fertility, if desired and longed for, could and should be promoted through spirits.

Although the incantation of spirits by magic words: more or less articulate sounds, incomprehensible and mysterious enunciations and holy names, seems to have the same effect as have symbols, nevertheless these always have a special meaning: they condense into chants, and thus stimulate inspired powers, as the images of the gods inspire the plastic arts. Pictures evolve into script, and letters like spoken words, can become sacred and have a magic effect. They, too, become symbols, especially when, as creedal writings, they are destined to become the expression of the common and obligatory doctrines of a religious union or a church, and when they are believed in as such. From this has developed the meaning which symbols have gained by means of such creedal writings: the body of symbols which Roman Catholicism places under the authority of the Holy Ghost and the Apostolic Office, and which have become an essential and infallible part of ecclesiastical and divine truth: therefrom develops the concept of symbolism as a special theological doctrine, claiming validity as a science.

While symbols easily acquire the character of holiness because ceremonial acts attain through them a particular solemn significance, other signs are related to them which claim an important significance because of their content. Without religious solemnity attached to them, as for instance, acts of state, they achieve special dignity in public and private opinion. Of this kind are distinctions which, as the bestowing of titles and orders, are given as rewards for merits, as compensation for damages suffered, and as a means of creating a serene or at least confident mood in perilous situations or during difficult enterprises. Thus they belong into the larger area of signs by means of which a person in authority may show his approval to those under him and employed by him, so as to encourage them to continued diligence and zeal, whether in his own interest or in a common and worthy cause. Here may be included good grades and school reports, meant to give pleasure to children, just as bad ones make them feel bad, so that they try to improve them.

In all these instances, we have to do with social signs, that is, signs that are meant to be generally understood, partly by means of the words by which they are expressed, partly without words, that is, as decoration: for, like all words, they are easily and frequently misunderstood: not only unintentionally, as in the most numerous misunderstandings, but also intentionally, especially when they are considered to be undeserved and deplored as such—misunderstood insofar as their general validity cannot be contested, for which reason the criticism is often ascribed to envy and grudge. These social signs always retain their significance in a centralized order, therefore chiefly in the army and similarly regulated large administrative bodies where order is definitely based on superordination and subordination, hierarchically descending from the chief to the private. Therefore, the abolition of titles and other decorations, as befits a democratic constitution, is a great risk for the government of a state which rests on such a constitution! It loses a strong instrument of social control, that is, a means of ensuring the cooperation of such persons who have to obey orders continually and more often than giving them, down to the multitude of the lowest category, who have nothing to do but obey. Of course, there are other ways of expressing satisfaction and giving praise, and of showing approval as well as disapproval; but the visible, and, in the case of titles, audible, form, as a rule, is for the consciousness of him who receives such praise of a very special value. In the same way, the privilege of wearing a special garment, even if it is connected with a special duty and especially if the garment is supplied free of charge—the livery—may have the effect of a distinction because the uniform impresses the public as a sign of worth and dignity.

The symbols of power—crown and scepter—designate the monarchic form of government; its decline is symbolized by the fact that, even if this form is still in existence, the crown and scepter are rarely visible any longer. However, like all symbols, they remain alive in the imagination and in art.

12

SOCIAL NORMS:

GENERAL CHARACTERIZATION

Commandments and Prohibitions

BY NORM we mean a general rule of action and of other kinds of behavior: it prescribes, either generally or for certain cases that are definable in advance, what shall happen or not happen, inasfar as this happening is based on the willing of reasonable beings, namely, men for whom the norm is intended to have validity. The essence of the norm may be generally conceived of as negation or inhibition, that is, as a restriction of human freedom; for the positive commandment, too, negates the otherwise existing freedom to act as one pleases, therefore to act differently from what has been commanded, above all, to act contrary to commandments. *Omnis determinatio est negatio.* A prohibition blocks one particular way, permits all others or leaves them open. A commandment blocks all other ways except the one indicated and prescribed which, being the only permitted one, at the same time is the way that one is forbidden not to go. The relation, then, between prohibition and commandment not only is that of contrast, but the commandment, at the same time, is an extended prohibition.

A single prohibition or commandment is not a norm, not even when directed toward many. If "silence!" is commanded at a gathering, or if soldiers are ordered to "stand at attention," this means only that silence or attention is required for a while, not forever, or that it is always to be observed in certain situations. However,

---

Translated from *Einfuehrung in die Soziologie*, book 4, chap. 1, pp. 189–203 (§§34, 35, 36); slightly abridged.

if the order says, "Whistling at a gathering of this kind is prohibited," or "If a soldier is addressed by a superior, he has to
stand at attention," those would be norms. The hallmark of norms
is generality.

Why are some norms called social norms? How are they to
be distinguished from individual but also from asocial or alien
norms? Not because social norms are decreed out of their united
will by several persons who are socially connected with one another—such norms could be alien as well as social norms. Social
norms are distinguished from others because the persons for whom
the norm is meant to have validity are among those who themselves
will and establish them; they are based on autonomy. They may
be based on the autonomy of the participants directly or indirectly.
Directly, if the many are really and fundamentally united in wanting these rules or norms. Indirectly, if the norms that are brought
to them from the outside are acknowledged, affirmed, and agreed
upon by them.

To command and to prohibit are actions arising from volition,
actions evident in the most varied manifestations of social life: they
may be expressed as an individual command or as a norm, as an
alien or as a social norm. We may consider them, first of all, as
applied by one person toward another, an everyday event. Everybody can attempt to restrict everybody else's freedom in this manner and, if the attempt is successful, restrict it actually. Whether
a commandment or a prohibition is successful, that is, whether they
are complied with, does not concern us here for the time being. The
attempt to restrict the freedom of another person in this manner is
one of many forms of the endeavor to influence the will of another
person positively or negatively. Other ways are: request, advice,
admonition, warning, demand, summons, invitation, correction,
instruction, persuasion, recommendation, provocation, encouragement, seduction, bribery—all are attempts to move or to induce
someone to do or not to do something by means of words, spoken,
written, or expressed in some other way. Words may be supported
by actions, their influence strengthened, under certain circumstances even substituted: by means of gestures, by touching the
other person, for instance, the request by means of folded hands,

clasping the other's knees, kneeling down oneself, prostrating oneself. Other examples are: advice by means of a cheerful or thoughtful or sad countenance; admonition through cuffs, ear pullings,
knocks, and hits; recommendation and provocation through effects upon the senses, such as figures, pictures, sounds. All these
could be reinforced by means of words of different content;
through praise and blame, flattering and scolding, but especially
by means of promises and threats. Promises, provided the request,
advice, command, or prohibition, or any other form of influence
has been yielded to, open up the prospect of such activities on the
part of the person who made the promise as are expected to be
desirable to the other; conversely, threats, in case of noncompli-
ance, open up undesirable prospects. The same effect as emphatically promising or threatening words may have hope and fear that
are aroused without such words, be it the expectation of good or
bad results from the requested, advised, ordered, commanded, or
forbidden actions, or perhaps the hope or fear of actions of peti-
tioners, advisers, commanders, and so forth. Especially, such sentiments may lead or contribute to obedience, through fear rather
than hope, if it is assumed that the restriction of freedom is unwelcome and that obedience, therefore, is offered unwillingly. Hope
presupposes a more voluntary decision, joyful obedience, or a
grateful following of advice, stimulation, admonition; fear, on
the other hand, presupposes a somewhat less voluntary action or
omission, a willing under pressure.

What distinguishes command and prohibition from other kinds
of attempts at influencing another person's or several other persons' will? Both command and prohibition are attempts at compulsion, applied with the intention of effecting, by means of words,
an action or an omission as a certain consequence; and this intention is connected with the expectation of rousing in the other, or
others, the feeling of compulsion or of having no choice. The other
person expresses this sentiment not only through "I must" but
even more aptly through the words "I ought," which, apart from
the feeling of necessity, contain the implication that this necessity
has been induced by another will, even though in a derivative way
the actor's own will could be regarded as such another will.

If all negation is considered to be hostile, to command and to prohibit are likewise hostile. All other kinds of attempts at moving the other's will toward something are friendly insofar as they do not disturb the other's freedom to act either according to the influence that is being exerted or otherwise; they are friendly insofar as they merely give expression to selfish or unselfish desires —which the other may or may not fulfill, as he pleases. Even he who tries to bribe or seduce does not claim more than to make his desires more effective by the means and artifices which he applies. To be sure, the one who prohibits, too, expresses a desire, but he combines with it the intention of excluding the liberty to act contrary to his desire.

From whatever cause, or for whatever reason, an order or a prohibition may actually be followed, it is not part of it that the person who obeys concedes to the person who commands a "right," in other words that he grants the permission to give orders— whether in general or in particular; nor is it part of it that he admits a duty, that is, an obligation he agrees with, least of all that he feels it to be his duty to obey.

What is meant by saying that I concede someone a right, that I ascribe a duty to myself? To concede a right is more than to give permission or to leave something to someone's choice. It means the admission that the action I permit is right. . . . An action is correct if it is logically incontestable. It is logically incontestable that man, as far as he possesses reason, is the master of his own actions. To be master of himself also means that he can prohibit himself from doing something: and thus is expressed a fact of our own self-consciousness, which used to be designated as the mastery of the reasonable part of the human soul over its unreasonable parts, namely, its drives and passions. Modern psychology, which covers, or intends to cover, with the concepts of sensory perception and emotion all psychic complexities and which calls compound perceptions ideas or images (*Vorstellungen*), expresses the same fact by asserting the existence of inhibitory ideas, or simply inhibitions, as a criterion of a normal human being, namely, a human being in possession of reason. These inhibitions are of different strengths in different persons, and at different times in the same person. But to the extent of their weakness or failing, a man is a pathological or unreasonable being, regarded from the point of view of the theoretician who takes his measure from a normal human being, that is, one capable of being master over himself. Therefore it is right for me to be master of myself, give myself orders; and if I call this reasonable willing, it is implied that the freedom of will is a right to will, that is, to regulate my actions and thus my body and my limbs; in other words, normal and expected inhibitions are present and effective. If I give someone the right to give me orders—and this is to mean more than that I give him the right to speak ineffective words—then this means that I also will what has been ordered, and if the feeling of "I must" and "I ought" has been roused through the order, then this feeling implies an "I will," that is, over and above the willing of the doing, a willing of what ought to be done (*Sollen*). This means that I am conscious of my duty. If I obey my own command, then the feeling of "I ought" or of being obliged (*das Gefuehl des Sollens*) is directly a sense of duty, for it is not different from the "I will." To the extent that the other person has the right to give me orders and I feel duty-bound to obey, the other's command is the same as if I were to give myself orders. It presupposes a relation between us that approaches more or less that of identification insofar as we are in agreement in relation to what we are willing to do and what we ought to do (*Wollen* and *Sollen*). Inversely, from such positive relations which are, for this reason, called social relations evolves the unilateral or mutual right of prohibition and command and the unilateral or mutual duty of obedience.

Other Varieties and Manifestations of Norms

It is an essential feature of a social relation for two or more persons to move or to endeavor to move each other mutually and constantly toward actions or abstentions from actions. But it is not an essential feature for this to occur in the form of ordering and prohibiting. Other forms, as a rule, may be sufficient to prevent certain actions and to encourage others. Even without any attempts at being effective in this sense, by means of words or actions, the existence of a relationship, especially the presence and closeness of a person to another, or the exchange of letters, may have the same or a similar effect, especially where experience allows one to know or to imagine which actions or omissions are welcome, which ones are unwelcome to one's companion or partner. Further, different forms of expressing wishes sometimes merge or overlap: "Your wish is my command," even if the wish was only guessed by the other's looks. Requests can become so earnest, so urgent, so tormenting, that they are at least as sure of success as an order intends to be, and they may be made with the intention of compelling the person to whom the request is directed. This is all the more so, if the latter is an invisible being, existing only in the imagination, like a god, especially where words are supported by actions such as sacrifices and witchcraft . . .

That requests are powerful is indeed an obvious notion to the pious, childlike mind: if children feel sure that through constant repetition they can soften a benevolent father, and even more the good mother, or, as they call it, make them change their mind, then they ought to be surely successful in changing the mind of a saint or even the all-bountiful god himself, and move him to interfere; because these invisible beings do not scare away or reprimand bothersome supplicants, or attempt to instruct them about the uselessness of their desires. It is well enough known that a power is attributed to prayer which, indeed, it may have in the mind of the supplicant.

The request, as petition, is the natural mode of action of those that are smaller and weaker toward the stronger and bigger. Conversely, on the part of the stronger, the request is often only a polite form of command. If a monarch makes a request, this is, as a rule, understood to mean an order. Even an advice may be equal to an order. If the advisor has the power or is supported by those in power, like the British cabinet, or the prime minister in its name, the counsel given to the sovereign implies such urgent advice to take the advice that approval and agreement are taken for granted. Refusal (a *veto*) does not occur and would be almost ridiculous. But even if the advice has not become a mere form for a binding order, it can be obtrusive and experienced as compulsion. The same applies to the use of other methods of influencing the human will. They are often preferred to the form of an order, (1) because the prospect of seeing the order executed is not good, and the probability of effecting its execution small, (2) because an even more favorable effect in this regard is expected from a milder form such as admonition, warning, request, and because, in contrast, for him who is supposed to obey, there is a special thrill in defying an order; pressure arouses counterpressure; attack, resistance—an order may be taken as a sign of hostility; whether this is the case and to what extent, depends in part on the nature of the social relationship, whether it is communal (*Gemeinschaft*-like) or associational (*Gesellschaft*-like).

Out of every social relationship, therefore also out of every circle (if by that is meant a totality of persons who are connected in social relationships such as the family or a circle of friends), out of every collective and every corporation grow and directly develop rights and duties of their "members," who are given this name insofar as they acknowledge their belongingness to the relationship. Every social relation implies for its members the request to behave and to act according to the norms which prevail in it; consequently, these may be understood to be the will of the relation, collective, or corporation itself, which, even without the form of an order, has the effect of being understood and acted upon accordingly. The meaning of every social relation, at the very least, is to refrain from force as the crudest form of hostility unless this force has been recognized as being rightfully exercised and therefore justified. But the demand for some positive contribution is almost indissolubly connected with it; essentially, the contribution is mutual aid. Thus, the social relation itself imposes prohibitions and commands; it restricts the freedom of the individual. In the final result, it means the same thing when we say that within a relation the companions and partners, one regarding the other, undergo identical restrictions of their freedom. But indeed it makes a difference, whether they do it merely as an expression of their personal desires or in the spirit and for the benefit and, as it were, in the name of the relationship. However, what the relationship demands can be proclaimed by the companions and partners in other ways as wish or desire.

The social norms of every relation, that is, of every social entity, are founded in part on its individual, in part on its general nature. They are conditions of life of the one as of the other, and as such more or less known to the members. The individual nature itself can be determined by general criteria which are not general criteria of the social entity; the purely individual remainder consists in the nature, character, and the way of thinking of the individuals themselves and of individuals in reference to one another. Further, what the social relation between only two persons requires in accordance with its individual nature may take the form of a social norm, but only insofar as it is approved, that is, recognized and willed in this quality by both partners. For instance, every marriage has its very individual existential conditions, so that it may maintain itself and remain healthy; further, it has existential conditions of a relatively general nature; finally, there are general existential conditions, arising from the essence of marriage as a supremely significant communal (*Gemeinschaft*-like) relationship. Individual existential conditions may be based on the state of health of the wife or the husband and on peculiarities of their personalities deriving from it: they require mutual consideration in living together. Relatively general existential conditions are provided, for instance, by a considerable difference in the age of the partners, by a difference in character and mode of thinking, therefore also of religious faith or the lack of it, tribal origin or even "race," descent by estate or class: all these differences require certain concessions, forbearances, and resignations. Finally, the general nature of marriage, which is founded on mutual dependence, bestows upon the spouses rights and privileges relating to one another, and imposes duties upon them which extend to all true marriages, even if they may be in part rendered invalid or modified because of special conditions of life.

Equally, a social circle imposes duties and bestows rights; likewise, a collective: even if membership, for instance, of a party— for example a [Catholic or other] religious party—(*Religions-*

partei)—is usually determined by birth, therefore quite involun-
tary, nevertheless the influence of such a collective and of its
members has the effect that, as a rule, it is felt to be of one's own
choice and based on one's convictions, which, however, have only
been developed by those influences. For, like a social relation,
even if less immediately so, a collective produces a sentiment and
consciousness of duties toward it, especially the duty to be directed by it, to recognize and defend its honor, to observe its interests, and in certain circumstances to do battle for it. Corresponding to these duties are the privileges which are the consequence of
the fact that the same duties are imposed on the other members
of the collective. The collective, then, is based on the extended idea
of mutual aid which is the hallmark of every social relation, thus of
every circle, especially the family. The collective is extended to a
number of personally unknown people, comprising also the deceased, whole former generations who are venerated especially
because they are ancestors and possibly founders and who therefore are celebrated as originators of certain rules, norms, and
regulations that are acknowledged as having binding validity.

Expressed more formally, although frequently far less significant, at times trifling, are the duties and privileges which a corporation may impose and bestow upon its members, by whatever
name it may be established, and there are many that may be given
to it as a fictitious, or moral, or legal person. In the first place, the
corporation rests directly on the common and joint will of its
members, whether they have created it or whether they are acknowledged by their entry and admittance or in certain circumstances by the privilege of birth and sheer existence, as members
by the other members, therefore also by the fictitious person itself.
As a "person," the corporation has the right, as a rule limited but
possibly unlimited, that is, the capacity bestowed upon it, to impose rights and duties upon its members, thus, to command and
prohibit. The further the corporation is removed or different from
other more simply constructed social entities, the more is its function restricted to ordering and prohibiting, in other words, to the
creation of norms; these tend to assume the character of coercion,
which is justified insofar as it corresponds to the mind and will of

those who submit to it. However, this is often based on a mere assumption, and the application of the general assumption to a concrete case may be a disastrous mistake. Good examples of the ideal, or fictitious, person and thus of the corporation itself, existing, as it does, in the first place, and perhaps exclusively, in the consciousness of its members, are the secret societies and conspiracies. In spite of this sole basis of their existence, in spite of their rejection of the more general corporation (for example, the state) on which they rest, by which they are conditioned, and whose authority they acknowledge in their volition and consciousness, these societies exercise great power over their members and impose heavy obligations upon them. They even become masters over the life and death of the conspirators, and, as their lawgivers, they demand continual and unconditional obedience.

Consent as the Prerequisite of a Normative System

We started off with the simplest case of one person giving orders to another, who has acquired the right to do so from the latter, so that consequently the obeying person feels duty-bound to obey. This idea is enlarged with regard to social entities and finds its fulfillment in them. The assumption was made that the command, if it implies a general rule, is to be called a norm, and that it becomes a social norm through the consent of him who conforms to it. A system of social norms presupposes general consent, unanimity of wills among all those for whom it is supposed to have validity, for instance, for a people, even for all mankind, insofar as it is conceived of as civilized mankind and its members as capable of comprehension and communication.

However, consent is something very complex, as is volition in general. The consent which is meant here in particular can extend over a whole scale, from passive tolerance, possibly to a considerable degree unwilling and conceded only reluctantly, to active, emphatic, and even joyful affirmation. Another scale, but connected with the first one, is one from nonrational expression of affirmation to a completely rational one denoting conscious overcoming of repugnance and agreeing to something which for the willing person is the means to a possibly distant though ardently desired end and which thus, in spite of repugnance, may be of decisive value. However, even nonrational willing may occur wholeheartedly, namely, without any thought of contradiction, rather as something taken for granted because it is felt and thought to be altogether wholesome and good, in the sense that it is believed to be morally necessary. Of this kind is consent on the grounds of liking, love, and related sentiments, such as reverence, a sense of one's own weakness and of the need for protection and help. The basis for such sentiments are the aforementioned inequalities: differences in age, sex, and, often connected with them, differences of physical and mental power, especially superiority of knowledge and experience in applying it, but also of all other means of power that one person has while the other person has not, and of which one person has more than another.

An ancient case in this regard is the superior position of the mature man as the *pater familias* and master of the house over a woman or the women, over sons and daughters, servants and maids; consequently also the power of the chieftain over an entire clan, tribe, or people: the picture of patriarchal dominance, often compared to a small kingdom. Conversely, princes may feel like fathers of their subjects and they may claim the dignity of patriarchs, even if they themselves are youths. Patriarchalism is not, as has often been said, something original from which the rule of emperors, kings, and princes has grown organically: this is the doctrine and concept of a people with an old and highly developed civilization, the Chinese, which, however, has had but little influence in Europe. Europe has never allowed this doctrine to prevail completely, although it had the support of the high and religious authority of Jewish tradition—as well as the attestation through the Jewish God of Christianity. This concept passed into Islam and is the basis of ideas about oriental despotism which have become prevalent in Europe since the seventeenth century. The revolution and the Enlightenment, which was the basis of revolution, have identified the absolute monarchy, which by then had glamorously risen in the modern countries, with those despotic systems and rebelled against it. It was a widely accepted but erroneous idea, possibly nourished by reminiscences of the Old Testament, that this free and arbitrary rule was something original and derived from patriarchalism. In actual fact, the European monarchy had always been restricted, and was so even where it appeared to have reached its most completed stage, as in France of the Bourbons.

From early times the cooperative fellowship (*Genossenschaft*) had been in competition with authoritarian rule (*Herrschaft*), and had continued to be alive in the consciousness of the people and therefore in reality. Its historical manifestations were: (1) the fellowship of a clan or sib, the significance of which has declined long since; it survived only among the nobility, part of which used to be the sib called a dynasty; (2) the village community and the larger community of a *Landschaft*, within which the Mark fellowship (*Markgenossenschaft*) maintained itself, even if the village community had been absorbed by the manor and had become subject to the nobility who succeeded in asserting their domination over the egalitarian principle of the fellowship; (3) the city, or urban community, by far the most important and increasingly more powerful configuration of the principle of equality and fellowship, in which some roots of the budding modern state are to be found, whereas other roots took their nourishment from tyranny, as it was developed early in the municipalities of Italy. The idea of a republic has never been alien to the idea of the state. It is an egalitarian idea based on fellowship (*genossenschaftlicher Gedanke*), achieving importance in the participation of the estates in government, most of all in England, where it destroyed, through a conservative rebellion, the already highly developed beginnings of monarchic absolutism. The "State" was a new name for the unity and solidarity of a nation, insofar as the nation had become conscious of constituting and representing a unity and defending and protecting its ancient and common law against the administrative uniformity fostered by the ruler and his statesmen, therefore against a standing army and a police force. Communal (*Gemeinschaft*-like) egalitarian structures survived in the great aristocratic families who, in Scotland more than in England, maintained their ancient constitutions; they survived in village communities and cities—although often in a distorted way. In the state, one great unified egalitarian configuration (*Genossenschaft*), overroofing and overshadowing all other configurations, had come into existence or was about to come into existence. As a corporate body, the state is the antithetic complement of civil society. Therefore it tends to throw off its monarchic shell, which has served its purpose.

13

SOCIAL NORMS: LAW

Law as an Effect of Custom

CUSTOM is social will itself, distilled from habit, usage, and practice. This effect of custom is customary law, which has its equivalent in codified or statute law. In the course of normal development, statute law tends to prevail, although custom, representing a more basic form of social will, actually has a much more far-reaching and penetrating significance. This is because custom is the "law" sanctioned by age, often allegedly by a boundless past which over a long period of time has become firm as a rock and, as long as it lasts, apparently indestructible. It is assumed to be the eternal creation of the sense of justice, the consciousness of right, and of the soul and mind of a people (*Volkseele und Volksgeist*). Statute law (*Gesetz*) is different insofar as it is sanctioned outside of or even against, tradition, only by reasonable design, by its *purpose:* it appears to be something new, looking toward the future rather than the past. If law is given or even forced upon people by a single person or by a few individuals, it may offend the remainder of the people, hurt their sense of justice, and do violence to their conscience. If law is the expression of the will of the majority, then, at least, it is only the minority who suffers because of it; but this minority may comprise elements who have the power to express their disapproval, even their disobedience, effectively. It could happen that for this or other reasons, perhaps because of the weight of their arguments or because of the pressure of chang-

Translated from *Einfuehrung in die Soziologie*, book 4, chap. 3, pp. 209–24 (§§40, 41, 42); some brief passages are omitted, others have been contracted.

ing condtions, the established law and order are imperilled by this resistance. Added to this are the mobility and instability of the majority, especially if its composition changes and if this change is caused by the addition of new elements who had not been committed previously. Any innovation, because of its very nature, is always opposed by habit, tradition, ancient custom, and thus also by customary law. This is why the new likes to dress up as a restoration of the old; conversely, restoration turns against innovation, even if innovation claims, with or without reason, to be, and to stand for restoration of, the yet older.

Innovation in law has a better chance of success, if it can claim, and if it succeeds in convincing people, that it is of supernatural origin: this has had enormous historical importance for all relationships of authoritarian rule (*Herrschaft*), especially if these have prevailed over relationships based on fellowship (*Genossenschaft*). At first it appears to be the natural prerogative of the ruler to issue orders and to establish norms and, in the role of a judge, to make decisions as he sees fit and deems right. Soon, however, habit asserts itself in a large circle of the community, and habit endows law, if it is conditioned by fellowship, with the power of creating a common will, possibly with reference to a precedent: the way in which the predecessor, for instance, the father, has ruled, is said to have been good, and the new ruler is unpopular merely by not being and acting like him: all the more so where there used to be greater respect for tradition. The ruler who is endowed with higher authority needs special accreditation, because he is more remote and less well known. Always the dead prevail over the living, and the visible powers are replaced by invisible ones who are shunned and feared.

The less the ruler is capable of achieving his goals on his own, and the greater the number of innovations he wishes to introduce, the more indispensable is the resort to the gods. If a people in its totality is the subject of custom and customary law, it prevails over, and restricts thereby, the arbitrary power of the ruler; whereupon the ruler soon asserts himself and reinforces his power through religion. Of the judge's authority, the part which is supported by religion enables him most effectively to reform and overcome customary law: the simplest way of achieving this is for the judge's person itself to be endowed with holiness and the splendor of priesthood. This very point can be observed in important manifestations in the life of ancient and highly developed civilizations, as in India and Ireland and many other places where the king was the highest judge, where he was at the same time, either by himself or by the grace of his god, invested with the dignity of a priest or where he could act with the favor and support of the priests. The Indians and the Irish have also in common that priestly wisdom, which included knowledge of law, was taught and transmitted in schools. The importance of these schools was due to the fact that they were run in a familylike, that is, in a communal (*Gemeinschaft*-like), manner; priestly wisdom thus partook of the natural and genuine holiness which distinguishes any piety relationship. It has always been known and confirmed again and again that religion and law are closely related and that they have even merged to the extent of identity. This has perhaps become nowhere as obvious as in ancient India. "A king and a Brahmin who are thoroughly versed in the Veda, these two uphold the moral order," says one of the oldest books of ancient Indian law. Nowhere has the authority of priesthood manifested itself so bluntly, even to the point of elevating itself openly and emphatically above its gods. In the book of law of Vishnu, we read: "The gods are invisible ones. The Brahmins visible ones. The Brahmins support the world. It is by the grace of the Brahmins that the gods live in heaven."

The antique city-states (polis) and, although more reluctantly, Rome, which in the end became the most powerful of them, at an early time separated law from religious creed and cult. This was achieved by granting all superstitious ideas, ceremonies, and rituals, especially sacrifices their impact upon the people, together with a remnant of royal dignity, which had traditional validity. However, the judge, as a civil servant of the republic, was bound even more strictly to the will of the citizenry, as established by customary and statutory law. Totally different was the effect of the system developed in Palestine, which brought the theocratic ideas of the Orient to its greatest perfection. Law and the courts remained undeveloped. People sought justice from the elders, from the king or, preferably, from the priest. This was called, as we see also in the law book of Hammurabi, "To take the matter before God." Sacred law, of course, was entirely in the hands of the priests. As all culture in the newer countries of Europe has been nourished from these two sources, the Roman Empire and late Judaism, from which Christian faith and the Church had sprung, thus it also came about that law and the courts to a great extent fell under ecclesiastical influence. There were, then, these two kinds of law: the native customary law, in its colorful variety, mainly originating from Germanic tradition; and canon law, which is completely based upon alleged revelations and alleged decisions of the head of the Church. Because of the prestige of the ecclesiastical courts and owing to their demands, canon law was extended gradually upon large areas of civil law, especially concerning matrimony, succession, loans, and the taking of interest, which latter was regarded as a mortal sin. These were the very areas in which the Church insisted upon its moral authority, without, however, being able to impede social development; the secularization of these institutions continued irrevocably, just as the secularization of all life, including the Church itself.

Natural Law

A most remarkable and important phenomenon in this area is natural law. As a rule, deliberations about law are left to the special profession of juridical scholars, but natural law is a philosophical discipline which looks for the universal and necessary elements in law. The theory of natural law, as it is nowadays thought of outside Catholic theology, has developed both from and against theological and scholastic natural law. Troeltsch calls this modern natural law profane natural law, which is correct inasfar as it has shaken off ecclesiastical fetters. More adequately, it is called rational natural law, thereby indicating that it has resumed the direction which it had pursued in Greek philosophy and Roman jurisprudence. The decisive innovation in this sense did not emanate from Grotius, as is often asserted, but from Hobbes, although Grotius' treatise on law has indeed been an epoch-making work. It was Hobbes who gave the classical form to this doctrine of natural law around which associational (*Gesellschaft*-like) thinking, which has since grown, has crystallized.

The Hobbesian doctrine starts from the assumption that every man by nature tends to be the enemy of everybody else, because of mutual fear and mutual distrust. Consequently, the natural condition of man must be thought of as a general state of war, a war of everyone against everyone (*bellum omnium contra omnes*). Frequently, this doctrine is misinterpreted and misunderstood, partly because Hobbes himself only gradually became clearly aware of the strictly abstract and schematic character of his own doctrine, and partly because he never quite ceased to connect his abstraction with the development of human civilization out of savagery and barbarism, an idea which was much discussed at that time, when the first circumnavigation of the earth had occurred. He interprets his theory more correctly when he compares a stateless and lawless condition between individual persons with the actually observed condition between individual independent states. He asserts ideal validity (*ideelle Geltung*) for the law of nature, that is, for the sum total of rules of behavior which can be derived from men's own interest by drawing correct conclusions. These rules, however, have only limited and insufficient force, as long as there is no authority which changes this law of nature into positive law, thus enforcing conditions of peace.

Natural law culminates in the statement that reason demands the affirmation of the state or, if it is nonexistent, its creation. Hobbes mentioned only what he might have elaborated upon, namely, that the true meaning of international law lay in its being recognized as an incomplete institutional arrangement among states, similar to the incomplete natural law which was prevalent prior to the existence of states; there is no superstate in existence which would have the recognized authority to decide conflicts between states and the power to prevent violent hostilities, much as a federation might claim legal superiority over member states. . . .

The analogy of international law and rational natural law is part of the thinking of natural law, as is indicated in the customary expression *jus naturae et gentium*. Kant, who in this as in other respects develops his legal theories in close relation to those of Hobbes, introduces international law as follows. A state perceived as a moral person in the condition of natural freedom, and thus also in a condition of constant war, has the right to make war as well as the right to compel others to abolish this condition of war, and thus should make it his task to create a constitution as the foundation for a lasting peace. The distinction from the state of nature of individuals or families was merely that in international law the concern was not only with the relation of one state to another state but also with the relation of individuals of one state toward individuals of another state, and of individuals toward the other state itself. To consider this, only such rules were required as could easily be derived from the concept of the state of nature. Kant therefore presents as the elements of international law: that states exist by nature in a nonlegal condition, thus in a state of war, even though this may not always be war in the sense of actual hostility; that for this reason a league of nations, according to the idea of an original social contract, was needed, "indeed not to interfere with domestic troubles but in order to protect each other against attacks from the outside." Yet, he adds as another element of international law that the league would not have to have sovereign power, as in the constitution of a state, but should form a fellowship, a federation; a union that could be terminated, and thus would have to be renewed from time to time—a right *in subsidium* of another original right, namely, to prevent the degeneration into the condition of actual warfare between the member states. Kant calls this in parentheses a *Foedus Amphictyonum*, thus referring to the coalitions of Greek city-states, which were based partly on international, partly on constitutional law; if he had experienced the *Deutschen Bund* (German Federation), 1815–1866, this might have occurred to him as an example.

Hobbes would have rejected the very thought as completely insufficient [because alliances were exposed to the threat of internal conflict and because one alliance was to call forth a counter-alliance, so that the danger of war would continue to exist and might even increase. This danger could be eliminated only by means of a complete unification, which requirement, in turn, was to make the establishment of an independent, unrestricted, and sovereign organization an absolute necessity. Further, no valid claim against sovereignty could be permitted to exist; as soon as such a right was conceded, the state of nature would be continued —nobody would then be entitled to make the ultimate decision, let alone to enforce it, and the right of self-help, which leaves the ultimate decision to sheer force, would remain in effect or would be reestablished.][1]

Today, Hobbes might refer to the end of the German Federation, as likewise to the terrible Civil War which somewhat earlier tore the "United" States of America into two federations. He would hold the same opinion about the reconstituted federalism in America, as about the present [1930] German *Reich*, although the combination of federalism and centralism in both countries has been changed somewhat toward the latter, that is, from a league of states toward a federal form of government.

Natural Law in Gemeinschaft and Gesellschaft

One may attempt to develop, in contrast to associational or rational (*Gesellschaft*-like) natural law the idea of a communal (*Gemeinschaft*-like) natural law: the task would be to examine whether another basis for the concept of the origin of law could be considered besides the one which opposes individuals to other individuals as isolated persons, that is, as persons who share no common rights, except those which derive from specifically concluded contracts and agreements. Indeed, one is free to assume that men, whether one regards them as equal or unequal, are by nature friendly toward one another; that not war of everyone against everyone but peace of everyone with everyone was the state of nature. To be sure, such an assumption was immanent to the thinking

[1]   In the German text, Toennies refers to Hobbes' position concerning international law prior to referring to Kant's point of view in this regard; the editors have reversed the sequence and abridged the passage dealing with Hobbes. We have also omitted Toennies' reference to the ideas of "Paneuropa" and the "League of Nations" as an exemplification of the Hobbesian argument.—EDS.

of the Middle Ages which Hobbes and his followers attempted to overcome. Regularly, it was associated with the Aristotelian thesis that man is by nature a political being (*zoon politikon*), that is, one destined for life in the *polis*, later expressed by the Latin version indicating that man was a social being (*animal sociale*). Hobbes opposes this view expressly; in the book which has had the greatest effect on world literature, *De Cive*, he attempts to repudiate the Aristotelian idea in detail by maintaining that man in contact with others is not looking for anything but advantage or honor (*Ehre*). Indeed, each needed the help of the other, but whoever was able to would rather strive to rule over others than to ally himself with them; the origin of great and lasting societies was mutual fear, and the origin of mutual fear lay partly in natural equality, partly in the natural inclination to harm one another. However, it is remarkable that in the later great presentation of his theory (*Leviathan*) Hobbes did not return to this kind of reasoning. Besides the three main causes of strife, namely, (1) competition, (2) distrust, (3) vanity, Hobbes maintains, in logical pursuit of his psychological theories, that there are also three "affects that incline men to peace," namely, (1) fear of death, (2) desire of such things as are necessary for commodious living, and (3) the hope of obtaining them by their industry. Here, too, he is looking for a likely transition from the state of nature to the political state without presupposing a natural benevolence of man towards man: man is supposed to be clearly egotistic.

However, it is possible to start from the opposite hypothesis of natural altruism, and from this to arrive at a system of social norms as natural law. It would mean that in every social relationship which is founded on mutual affection and an ensuing feeling of obligation, a germ of objective law is contained and that this germ could grow under favorable circumstances of life and develop into law. One could take one's departure from the actually observable source of communal relationships—whether these are based more on domination (authoritarian) or on fellowship (cooperative). One assumes, even in an attenuated form, a natural inclination of man toward man which makes nonhostile behavior, that is, mutual toleration and peacefulness, possible, as long as there are no particular causes inciting to animosity and violence. Under these assumptions there would be here a germ of law, but with a much diminished chance of growth and development, because it could be suffocated and killed so much easier by counteracting motivations. Within these limits—intimacy among a few, and weak sympathy of every man toward every man—various more or less vital germs of *Gemeinschaft* may be thought to exist. An objective law (*Recht*) derived from such a germ might be designated as communal (*Gemeinschaft*-like) natural law.

But what would be the characteristics of such natural law? It would not distinguish and separate subjective rights from obligations in such a way as is required in associational relationships, where the law of contract contrasts the subjective right or claim of one party with the duty or obligation of the other. On the contrary, the right would directly imply the obligation: the right of dominion (*Herrschaft*) would involve the legal obligation to use it for the benefit of the subjects; the duty of obedience would contain the legal claim to protection and assistance. In cooperative relationships, this reciprocity and unity of right and obligation would be even more obvious as a communal force; rights and obligations would equally and in unison derive from mutual goodwill and the necessity of cooperation. Objective law as a system of social norms in this case would mean that such rules are recognized as natural and necessary, so that the form of control which claims validity as judicial authority would know such rules and apply them when making decisions.

This communal natural law would establish as supreme principle that men, as rational beings, are united in narrower or wider circles, collectives and corporations for protection and defense, that thus all would stand up for one, and one for all. Everybody would be placed in his proper station, with rights and duties connected with it; every man would have a natural right not only of existence but of participation, with corresponding obligations.

Such rules of living together are likely to develop most purely and most completely, because most easily, within the narrowest circles, thus mainly within the family; therefore the first place in civil law would be accorded to marriage and family law, and consequently also to the law of succession insofar as it would be accepted as natural and just. The law of property would be next: here naturally common property and, as far as feasible, common usage and usufruct would have to be assumed as communal natural law; such common property can also be extended for essential and important objects to wider circles and corporations. Common property would always remain necessary and natural insofar as people who live and work together are attached to each other emotionally and perceptively and are determined to let law prevail. They would demand for themselves no more than what is regarded as appropriate for each, assuming that what is to be appropriate had been determined according to mutually acceptable rules. Thus, a nation that would want to be justified in perceiving itself as one large family, as *ein einzig Volk von Bruedern*, ought to submit itself to a natural law which treats land and other essential necessities of peaceful living together as common property, in such a way that it may be disposed of and used according to recognized rules which are regarded as lawful and just.

Besides land, other objects can be administered communally as common means, serving the purpose of common living and working, thus as a means of production, so that these also could be obtained by smaller groups: communities, families, or even individuals as a mediated, conditioned, and revocable possession. This would presuppose that the total labor of such a group, as, for instance, a nation, would be subjected to a suitable regulation which would serve the general welfare but nobody's profit and which would have the purpose of distributing the result of the total thus regulated labor as might be considered proper according to communal (*Gemeinschaft*-like) natural law. The simplest principle of just distribution is absolute equality, which naturally would be modified by given circumstances to relative equality, thus being adjusted to actual inequalities due to ability and achievement.

Thus communal natural law, in this respect not essentially different from associational natural law, would be subsumed under the valid and accepted concepts of reason and wisdom. These are demanding concepts, asking for a—no matter how motivated—measure of self-control and self-restraint in favor of an idea, which even in *Gemeinschaft* would be recognized as ultimately serving the individual's true welfare and benefit. This idea as applied to action, especially the peaceful regulation of man's relation to man, and to things appears as the idea of justice which is inseparable from the idea of natural law. According to the Aristotelian distinction, for associational (*Gesellschaft*-like) natural law, the idea is the justice of exchange: commutative justice, as Greek usage puts it. In communal (*Gemeinschaft*-like) natural law, on the other hand, distributive justice prevails, the justice of fair distribution within the unity of common ownership and common use. The maxim *suum cuique* in the case of *Gesellschaft* means that each member of society shall keep what he has gained, unless it is conclusively proved that it has been earned dishonestly. In the case of *Gemeinschaft*—respecting distributive justice—it means that each member of a community (*Gemeinschaft*) may and shall earn what has been assigned to him by law and equity.

Characteristic for the difference between the two ideas of natural law is thus their relation to moral concepts. This is demonstrated by the different meaning which the concept of justice has in different contexts. The justice of exchange enters into associational relation, as it were, from the outside: it requires merely the conditions of concurring wills and of the proper understanding of the advantages of contracts, in other words, the abstention from force and deceit. On the contrary, the justice of distribution is concerned with the objects themselves; it is, if one may say so, the precondition of life in a *Gemeinschaft*. Corresponding to this difference is the relationship of morality and law within the two systems of natural law. The idea of associational natural law has nothing to do with morality except that it leaves to the latter the problem of evaluating by its norms the actions of its subjects. This includes the actions of judges, insofar as it is assumed that judges ought to be just. Law itself does not claim to be moral in an associational (*Gesellschaft*-like) context. It merely wants to be useful, that is, fitted to a purpose. The purpose is a peaceful living together, without force, but not a living the good life together, replete with goodwill and the desire to provide mutual aid. This is precisely what the idea of communal (*Gemeinschaft*-like) natural law requires. It merges morality and law, but necessarily submits law to morality. Law becomes here an instrument of the spirit of self-control and the limitation of the individual, thus of education for and practice in applying the virtues which are required for a good living together.

The development of the theory of rational natural law has actually meant the separation of law and morality; consequently, the development of law modeled after this kind of natural law means the elimination of the moral elements which had previously been contained in it. It is in this respect exclusively that we shall consider theory. Hobbes had treated natural law as almost identical with morality, so that according to him the individual as a citizen, within the sphere of freedom granted to him by the state, had the obligation to apply rules of honesty as a means of his own self-preservation, just as he who wields political power must shape positive law according to these rules. Christian Thomasius, following Pufendorf, has undertaken a clear and sharp separation of law and morality. Pufendorf tried to mediate in this respect between Hobbes' theory and that of Grotius, which still adhered to the premise of the inherently social nature of man. But Thomasius divided the whole complex of what ought to be into that of *justum, honestum*, and *decorum*. This point of view remained prevalent in the German theory of natural law. The philosophers Kant and Fichte, especially, have insisted upon the strict separation of law and morality. Indeed, Fichte, otherwise Kant's successor and disciple—although his discipleship is of questionable quality—has gone farther than Kant in this respect. The separation is more radical with him. He denies expressly that any legal relationship should be based on morality, that is, on the moral duty to keep one's word. He demands that jurisprudence establish means by which legality can be preserved even if trust and good faith should have disappeared entirely. That is why law ignores morality, and morality even transcends law because the truly moral man does not recognize any law that could compel him.

This theory has become more effective in Kant's rendition. In the most generalized way, Kant distinguishes the idea of legislation as (1) ethical: which makes an action a duty, and this duty the motivating power; and (2) juridical: which does not include the motivation in the law and thus **permits** another motivation than duty. In the same way he differentiates between the morality and legality of actions. Kant, like others, uses as his foremost example that of contract. He maintains that ethics did not comprise a legislation of all duties, although the duties themselves were part of ethics. Thus, ethics demands that an obligation promised in a contract should be complied with, even though the other party might not be able to enforce it. But ethics derives the legal principle that *pacta sunt servanda* and the corresponding duty from jurisprudence and takes it for granted. "It is not a duty of virtue to keep one's promise, but a legal duty, compliance with which may be enforced." This latter attribute has been presented as the distinctive feature of law prior to Kant, as after him, and more recently, by Stammler. On the other hand, on the authority of older concepts of law it is contested that this is an essential feature, although nobody denies that it describes the reality of modern positive law, which is completely determined by the power of the state, and that it postulates in this respect the separation of law from morality: rules of law are enforceable, rules of morality are not. One can say that this separation is part of the modern development of law, although it is not generally sustained. One should, moreover, not overlook the fact that positive morality—that is, public opinion in its communal or associational manifestations—does not lack the means that are necessary to enforce its demands and its judgments, thus to punish transgressions. However, it is certain that the state increasingly has become what it ought to be according to the concept of the younger school of natural law: *the possessor of all enforcement rights.*

14

SOCIAL STRUCTURES OR INSTITUTIONS: GENERAL CHARACTERIZATION

Pairs of Concepts

By SOCIAL STRUCTURES (*Bezugsgebilde*) we mean all institutions and other systems of social action to which social entities refer and in which their more communal or more associational character may be discerned, including the possible transition from one type to the other.

For economic life and, further, for social life in general, places and localities are of the greatest importance because work is performed there, business is engaged in, and all kinds of social activities occur. Village or town—sparse or dense population—small town, medium-sized town, metropolis—these differences shape economic life in various ways; most of the other institutional configurations develop in accordance with these. Recognizing this, Marx writes: "The basis of all highly developed division of labor, which is mediated through the exchange of commodities, is the separation of city and country. One can say that the entire economic history of society is summarized in the movement of this contradiction," to which statement, unfortunately, he adds, "but we are not concerned with that here." (*Das Kapital* I, 4, p. 317, German ed.)

To the separation of city and country correspond the most important differences in political life as well as in spiritual and moral life; to a considerable part these differences arise from the separa-

---

Translated from *Einfuehrung in die Soziologie*, book 5, chap. 1, pp. 261–64 (§51, 52); the first part of §52, apart from the opening sentence, is omitted; the second part follows in the next chapter ("Effectiveness of Factors").

tion of city and country; they are their effect. Separation, antagonism, conflict are always most noteworthy, notwithstanding the fact that all phenomena are interdependent and belong together; this is especially obvious with regard to seemingly purely intellectual differentiations. There, interdependence is noted because fundamentally different movements of thought and action, on the one hand, complement each other, while, on the other hand, they retain liveliness and mobility by means of critique and polemics.

A series of conceptual pairs could be enumerated which would serve to illustrate this kind of differentiation. The facts which correspond to the concepts belong partly to the economic sphere, partly to the political as well as to the spiritual and moral sphere. Only a few of these conceptual pairs are mentioned here. The most important examples are:

1. in economic, that is, in general social life,
   village—town
   small town—metropolis
   mother country—colony
   primary—secondary production
   production—trade
   household—market
   small enterprise—large enterprise
   precapitalistic—capitalistic modes of production and
                              trade

2. in political life,
   folk society—state society (*Volksleben—Staatsleben*)
   aristocracy—democracy
   federalism—unitarism
   conservative parties—mutative parties
   customary law—revolutionary legislation

3. in spiritual-moral life,
   feminine mind—masculine mind
   belief in miracles—knowledge of laws of nature
   religion—scientific way of thinking
   Church—sect
   orthodoxy—heresy
   art—science
   distributive justice—commutative justice

How These Concepts Are Related

It should be understood that all these conceptual pairs are somehow interconnected; most directly those which are vertically aligned, because they belong to the same basic category. But even more important are the interconnections among the basic categories themselves and their reciprocal interaction: partly the general interconnections and interactions, partly the specific ones between corresponding conceptual pairs; finally and especially those within each conceptual pair.

(1) A single conceptual pair should be interpreted in such a way that primarily the necessary and essential *relationship* of its members is open to consideration; this means especially that the second member in the conceptual pair is the younger one, which has developed from the first one and continues to do so. One must therefore be particularly attentive to transitions and connecting links, and generally to the manifold appearance of reality contrasted to the concepts that are not intended to do anything but to represent outstanding phenomena in relatively fixed types. They must never be interpreted otherwise but as means to provide hitching posts to the thinking about things; they offer something like a yardstick, the application of which is supposed to do two things: to clarify the confusion that reigns in the world of experience, and to make the data of experience comparable.

(2) It is important to be cognizant of the differences between the members; they are frequently more striking than the natural unity and the similarity by which they are linked. What is meant here are the relations of the generations of man to one another as well as the relations between whole historical periods that join a series of generations. One might think here, in the first place, of the relation between our European so-called modern era to the so-called Middle Ages, but also of the relation between new countries, especially colonies, to old ones; or of the in many ways analogous relation of late antiquity, in particular that dominated by Rome, to an earlier epoch which culminated in Athenian culture. In some regards, even if the dimensions are totally different, one may think of

the relation between the cultural configuration of northern Europe that had grown out of the decline of the Roman Empire and the older cultural configuration of southern Europe, with its roots in the East, especially in Egypt and Asia Minor.

(3) Another leading consideration is separation and *contradiction*, the latter developing the more easily and strongly the greater the differences are or turn out to be; these contradictions appear in many a shape and form. They are most alive and fraught with fate if they burst into open *conflicts*; these, again, are very varied and can lead to a variety of consequences. They are not always reflected in the subjective consciousness of men as dislike, repulsion, or hatred, but frequently they are, if to a lesser or larger degree. The most significant phenomena of contradiction are closely connected with the reciprocal interactions between the three basic categories.

(4) A reunion or, one even may say, a *reconciliation* of the two diverging and possibly antagonistic wings of a conceptual pair is possible and may at times be desired and attempted. Reconciliation may be understood as a synthesis in the Hegelian sense, succeeding the antithesis and evolving from it. Such a synthesis may have a purely ideological basis and effect, that is, it may arise solely from the desire and will of some persons that participate or do not participate in it. Its strength and effect, however, are much more likely to come to the fore if the inclination toward union arises from the contrast itself, that is, out of contradiction and conflict that are inherent in a situation, like the desire to reestablish a peaceful condition after a long war. This is true even if during wars the desire for the end of hostilities appears to be, or at least is discernible, more strongly on one side, namely, with those who are defeated or about to be defeated; so that what formally seems to be a treaty, in actual fact signifies the victory of one state or principle and the submission of another. As a rule, and most likely, this victory will be that of the more recent reality or idea which, however, at the same time indicates its internal transformation. It is in the nature of things that sooner or later a new split will occur, and therefore possibly a new contradiction.

These developments can be completely described only historically; but this falls outside the frame of a theoretical introduction.

One can merely attempt to clarify typologically the relation of the conceptual pairs and especially the relation of the basic categories to one another. We know of no cultural condition wherein the three basic categories of economic, political, and spiritual life and institutions are not simultaneously present and intermingled.

15

SOCIAL STRUCTURES OR

INSTITUTIONS:

EFFECTIVENESS OF FACTORS

Economic, Political, and Spiritual Aspects of Social Structures

IT MAY reasonably be said: *the economy* is everything, it governs and determines all spheres of human activity. For none can be imagined that is not to a considerable degree economic activity. All kinds of political activities have obvious economic aspects; the same is true of religion and other varieties of spiritual culture, as embedded in ecclesiastical and educational institutions and associations; it likewise applies to all institutions that are devoted to the arts and sciences. They must be served by physical labor, and even more by mental labor, and these constitute elements in the totality of economic life.

In another sense, *politics*, too, may be conceived as a general activity of human reason and volition, as something involved in the regulation of many human activities: in the management of every household, every industrial enterprise, every business becomes discipline, thus leading and following, ordering and obeying, the more necessary, the more the extension of such activites grows: political insight, foresight, cleverness find a place in every kind of administration; it is of the greatest importance in municipal, and even more so in state government. Often, politics has been compared to the art of steering a ship, and certainly the helmsman of a ship, the driver of a car, the railway engineer, to all of whom persons and goods are entrusted, need a certain measure of political reasoning. And finally, in large institutions and organizations that belong to

Translated from *Einfuehrung in die Soziologie*, book 5, chap. 1 (cont'd.) and chap. 2, pp. 267–83 (§§52, 53, 54, 55) ; slightly abridged.

the sphere of the spirit, there is the more scope for politics, the more such an institution represents an organization and system of human activities which resembles the administration of a commonwealth, and the more it requires cleverness, even craftiness and cunning, in order to preserve itself, because its foundation is questionable. The most celebrated case of this kind is the Roman Catholic Church, whose leading minds have long been renowned for being masters in the art of diplomacy and political wisdom. Its system of super- and sub-ordination constituted as a hierarchy has become a model for all governmental organizations, therefore also for the bureaucracy which is characteristic of the modern state.

Finally one may say truthfully: the *spirit* (Geist) is everything. Human living together is spiritual in the most general sense, that is, through language, thought, reason, and by means of deliberation and decision. This is true regarding the simplest and most general economic activity, and even more so the more human labor becomes employed in large and at times gigantic industrial plants; finally, regarding the totality of political activity. Spirit has its own special sphere; the most general in witchcraft and religion, on a different level in educational and instructional processes and in formal schooling, finally, in its most liberal form in the arts and sciences. To be sure, artistic, scientific, and scholarly activities are individualistic to a high degree, and many a person involved in them desires nothing so much as to be left alone. But he is not capable of placing himself outside human interaction; he needs understanding, sympathy, support, often, as a rule even, also of the recipient, of the customer ("the art goes a-begging"). The artist or scientist wishes to preserve his skills and his knowledge, hence to pass it on through disciples and pupils. Often enough he is dependent on the municipality or the state in order to attain the income and honor which his self-consciousness desires. The actual positions of the artist and the man of science in the social life of today are frequently unsatisfactory and are felt to be so. The positions which artists and scientists need in order to have a stimulating effect and to serve as leaders are all too often occupied by those who do not possess the qualifications that are required.

Effectiveness of Factors: Historical Materialism

If, then, economics, politics, and the life of the spirit are always connected and have a unified effect, the question suggests itself: which of the three basic categories is the relatively independent variable, that is, the one most easily, most probably variable, without or even against the influences of the other two? What, on the other hand, are the effects of this variable on the other spheres that orient themselves on the changes of the first, even though they may endeavor to hinder or to reduce it and perhaps follow the road but slowly and reluctantly; in other words, adapt themselves to what is the unalterable new?

This is the field of controversy which, during the past few decades, has stirred up a great deal of discussion and occasioned an immense literature in books, brochures, journals, and newspapers, comparable perhaps only to the discussion around the question of the origin of man some time earlier. Then, as now, a new idea which in both cases was not actually new has collided with a rock of traditional views and obstinate prejudice, without, however, being shattered thereby.

The belief that an idea, or ideas, was something that changed independently, that approached truth more or less closely, that would be transformed into doctrines of faith or into opinions which then would dominate political as well as social and economic life, this was the effect of speculative philosophy in Germany; in other countries, it was rather the remainder of a theological way of thinking. It seemed like a degradation of man when an interpretation of history arose and claimed validity which called itself materialistic and expressly denied the autonomy of ideas by maintaining that the manner how every day's work was conducted was the primary factor and that the changes in the organization of work were a direct expression of the necessary relations of production which corresponded to a certain developmental stage of the material forces of production. The totality of these relations of production, as Marx says in a sketchlike presentation of his theory, makes up the economic structure of society, the real basis upon which the legal and political superstructure develops; certain societal forms of consciousness corresponded to that structure—and with a change in the economic basis, the whole colossal superstructure was bound to be turned over more or less rapidly. The doctrine has often been interpreted as though it meant that only the base, the economic substructure, and the movement of economic phenomena was truly real, and that spiritual phenomena were nothing more than reflex effects of that actual reality. We cannot blame only the sometimes too ardent disciples of the doctrine for these interpretations; its learned originator himself is responsible for the misunderstanding because of his use of the expression "the real basis." Nevertheless, the interpretation is undoubtedly erroneous. In the preface of the short treatise *A Critique of Political Economy* (*Zur Kritik der politischen Oekonomie*), Marx says that, in detaching himself from jurisprudence and Hegelian philosophy, he had endeavored to do justice to French socialism and communism, and that he had come to the conclusion that legal institutions and forms of government could not be conceived either as developing of their own accord or as emanating from the general evolution of the human mind, "but rather that they had their *roots* in the material conditions of life, the totality of which Hegel . . . summarized under the name of civil society." Here he uses another simile than the architectonic ones of foundation and superstructure. It would be odd to present only the foundation as real and the building itself as but a reflex and mere appearance—possibly a case of castles in the air—but it would be clearly nonsensical to declare a tree to be unreal and only its roots to be real. On the other hand, one might say with good reason that law as an order of living together—settling disputes, ensuring discipline, meting out punishment—was of essential significance in every kind of living together insofar as it is a working together, whether these rules among men have their origin in a tacit or emphatic unanimity of the companions or perhaps in the personal will of a chief or of a council of elders in a clan.

Wherever we meet social life, we do in fact find such rules in force: they grow in force through practice, similar to other less severe social norms which we combine with customary law into the general concept of custom. They are the expression of the necessary requirements for living and working together. The requirements have a tendency to expand when men are working together, warlike or peacefully, so that law will more and more take the place of force, especially when peaceful settlement of conflict takes the place of hostilities; thus punishment through organs of the commonwealth replaces the revenge of one clan against the other. Marx clearly expresses this necessity for law when he says that property relations are only a legal expression for the relations of production, and that these, in turn, correspond to a certain stage in the development of the material forces of production. Property relations, therefore, are said to be essentially evolutionary forms of the forces of production. One may argue that this is not a clear way of expressing oneself. But the idea is obviously that *private property*, whether of land, of homes and gardens, tools, implements and instruments, finally, of money, can be useful to society—even after it has become effective as capital in trade and credit operations—in the development of production or in the enlarged and increased production of goods, if the number of socially interacting persons remained equal, and even more so if their number were increasing. Even free and absolute private property might be useful and serviceable as a normal organ of society in a definite if limited epoch of history, if and when it represented a stage in the evolution of the forces of production, that is, as we might say in modern parlance, if it makes sense sociologically.

The Influence of the Economy on Law

Economic life most easily influences politics, therefore public law, which is more order than law; and mostly by this mediation only, economic life influences the real, that is, private law, after it has become differentiated from public law. Like the application of law, and like all life, economic life is in constant movement, therefore changing. Economic life, and this must be emphasized, is more diverse and more comprehensive than the life of law, but it is also more flexible, more fluid, and sometimes even like air: for it is always determined in part by desires and will; by the interests and feelings, then, of innumerable persons, among whom the important ones are of course the strongest; these may be individuals of decisive influence, and they could therefore most easily and effectively change existing institutions. Law, as it is pronounced by the courts, is, like custom, rigid and firm in its original substance, not easily changeable. Even gods and their priests, who are most likely to have the power of changing existing rules, would rather confirm and sanctify what is customary and in effective usage. It is a different matter if the secular rulers, such as kings and their ministers, who can, by means of their power, which is usually enhanced by wealth, disregard law and tradition; if by virtue of their influence upon judges or by means of special orders and decrees, behind which stands not only the power but also the alleged favor of the gods, they can abolish the old and create new law. This may be so on the strength of their irresistible whim and fancy or in the name of the state with which they identify or whose servants they claim to be; the state, they mean, is a master who cannot easily harm them.

In several regards, serious conflicts may develop between customary law, sense of justice, and traditional legal doctrine, on the one hand, and the reason of state (*Staatsraison*), on the other hand, even if reason of state is only the whim of a monarch in disguise, and if, besides the formally established law, mere acts of government and administrative practice take the place of the law. A permanent change in the valid law will be successful only if it corresponds to existing power relations, and the power relations will be at least in part economic power relations, either old and established by tradition or new: struggling, advancing, and endeavoring to manifest themselves in political power. Thus, those at first politically weaker will indirectly become politically stronger if they succeed in winning as an ally or even force into dependence one or several of those political forces which are based on traditional economic conditions; if, for instance, a more recent economic force is capable of splitting the alliance between the aristocracy and its head, the monarchy, which was based on more ancient economic relations of power; if, then, financial power—that of either commercial or industrial capital—strengthens and supports the monarchy, in order to receive favors from it and to be reinforced or, in reverse, if financial power pays for services already rendered.

The one great example of a transformation of law as a result and effect of changes in economic relations and conditions of life is offered by the history of the last few centuries. The underlying cause is the growth of industry, trade, and capitalism, and the urbanization which goes hand in hand with it. When drawing the conclusion that the effects of this development are most obvious in the sphere of public law and, above all, the constitution and the administration of the state, and that subsequently and by means of legislation they gradually extend to and transform all branches of law, we must not conceive of either one or the other effect as having been anything but a long-drawn-out and slow process to which various more or less powerful elements have made their contribution. One of the earliest and at the same time most distinctive phenomena in this regard, in Germany and England as well as in other countries, is the decline of the peasantry in contrast to its previous ascending development, which had been in happy agreement with the growth and prosperity of the cities. The deterioration occurred because of the increasing refinement and urbanization of the nobility, especially where it gathered at the courts and thus developed a greater need of money. "Their" peasants became the obvious object of oppression and exploitation. Heinrich Brunner (*Grundzuege der deutschen Rechtsgeschichte*, p. 216) explains that since the end of the Middle Ages in large parts of the Holy Roman Empire the legal security of the various strata composing the peasantry had been undermined.

Whereas formerly there had been a tendency to convert peasant farms into hereditary possessions, or their de facto heredity was on the way to becoming legal, a regressive tendency asserted itself after the fifteenth century, when the landlords endeavored to abolish the hereditary quality of peasant farms or at least to impede the development of that hereditary quality. This drive was promoted by Romanistic jurisprudence, which, even if not actually hostile to the peasantry, had no use for the complexity of the forms of peasant property in Germanic law. Since for evaluation this Roman law offered only the concepts of hereditary tenure and temporary lease (leasehold), its application had a leveling effect; it forcibly subsumed numerous intermediate forms under the heading of temporary lease.

The adoption (*Rezeption*) of Roman law was another and a new symptom for the preponderance which the Roman cultural inheritance maintained in church, in speech, and in the fictitious continuance of the Roman Empire (which had lost its universal significance in favor of the developing national states long ago).

This spirit was reinforced by the progressive development of the cities, that is, of trade and commerce. This development required, even at that time, a unified civil law; the same necessity became apparent in the nineteenth century. The influence of princely power worked in the same direction, and of all factors of legal life, it was this power that would protect and favor lawyers trained in Roman law and promote their legal interpretation and jurisdiction. This interpretation served imperial privileges, and did not recognize the constitution of the estates (*Staende*) which had developed throughout the Empire. The jurists established the maxim, *Quod principi placuit, legis habet vigorem*, which would please every prince and support him in his struggle against the nobility that limited his power. Paul Laband, the most eminent scholar of political law at the turn of the century, maintained that "the development of the absolute state and the adoption of Roman law in Germany are one and the same historical process." Laband also has drawn attention to the fact that the adoption was accomplished mainly by the princely courts of justice, where the *doctores* soon gained the upper hand. They assumed, as may be read in Janssen's *Geschichte des Deutschen Volkes* (I, p. 560), an attitude of actual hostility toward Germanic law. Brunner, too, admits that Germanic law was pushed aside and neglected by the learned and semilearned jurists who were sitting in the courts. But it was by no means the case that princes and their statesmen always and outright supported the efforts of the nobility to suppress the peasantry, to rule over it at will, to reduce it as they pleased by eviction and by not resettling deserted farms.

However, Roman law has not had the same effect everywhere. Max Weber pointed out (in his posthumous *Wirtschaftsgeschichte*, p. 291) that in France royalty made the eviction of peasants extremely difficult for the landlords, by means of her legists who were trained in Roman law. And in a later phase, German territorial princes, too, occasionally interfered successfully. They had a strong interest in preserving the peasantry; first, because the transformation of peasants' land into seignorial lands rendered it tax-free, since the nobility had retained the privilege of serving on horse for the land which they possessed by feudal law; second, because the peasantry provided the best infantry. From this privilege of the nobility, officership as a chosen profession had emerged, especially service in the cavalry. But that it was possible for the nobility to increase its power over the peasants, and thereby its income to such an extent, was indirectly the result of the long-standing battle which the princes had to fight against the nobility and against the estates (*Staende*) in general until they established, in the words of the soldier king (Frederic I of Prussia), their sovereignty as a *rocher de bronze*. In Brandenburg particularly, as early as the sixteenth century, but more so in the seventeenth, the relationship had developed in such a way that the nobility was forced and often willing to relinquish its previous political privileges and its right to participation in government for private manorial rights and castelike privileges. In the local community the estates retained their magistracy, but in government their power was annulled (Schulze, *Preussisches Staatsrecht*, p. 43). It was a compromise: private privileges were increased in order to decrease public ones. Only after princely power had become sufficiently strong, could it attempt to curtail those private powers again, as happened toward the end of the sixteenth century through forcing resettlement of abandoned peasant farms and through prohibiting the transformation of peasant land into manorial land. And in the territories of the west, where the power of the landed gentry had been defeated earlier by the sovereign, that is, by the central governmental power, this sovereign power had started at an earlier date to assume the role of protector of the peasants versus the manorial lords. However, only after the successes of the French Revolution, did this progress lead to the abolition of the restrictions on transfers of land. (The Prussian edict of 9 October 1807 permitted the free sale of rural property.) This also meant the breakdown of the institution of *Leihezwang*, that is, the protection of peasants. And it is remarkable how by means of this newly established freedom, the power of the estate owners (*Gutsherren*) which they had formerly possessed and claimed as lords of the manor (*Grundherren*), was reestablished.

During the time of general reaction that followed the peace [of Paris, 1815] and the founding of the German Federation (*Deutscher Bund*), the estate owners managed to prevent the so-called regulation of the smaller peasant holdings, with the result that a great number of these were bought by the estate owners in the course of the next generation. Only because of the popular unrest of 1848, unrestricted ownership was legally extended to the smaller holdings that had survived until that time. Just as the regulation of the larger peasant holdings, because peasants had to buy their emancipation by yielding from one-third to one-half of their land, resulted in a considerably enlarged ownership of land by the great landlords and in much reduced holdings by the peasants, so the process which in its beginning the lords had fought against so violently turned out to be definitely in their favor in the end. Knapp indicates through the title of his book *Die Bauernbefreiung und der Ursprung der Land-arbeiter in den aelteren Teilen Preussens* (*The Emancipation of the Peasants and the Origin of Agricultural Laborers in the Older Parts of Prussia*) that the greater part of the owners of the smaller peasant farms and their children became day laborers, and that the great majority of them was left with no land whatsoever. It is well known that in the whole area of Prussia, recently much reduced, east of the River Elbe, the peasantry is of little significance and that this remained or became the area of large estates and of large agricultural enterprises.

In England, the course of development was very different, but a similar goal was reached; the political result was similar to that emerging in Prussia in spite of Prussia's conquest of large, predominantly peasant provinces: the overwhelming influence of the landed gentry upon legislation. As early as in the sixteenth century, the solution of the agrarian problem was effectuated in favor of the economic power of the landlords which then grew—especially after the confiscation of the estates of the monasteries—to greater and greater dimensions. The legal position of the peasants, although practically always personally free, since ancient times had been similar to that of the so-called lassitic farmsteads in Prussia: they were copyholders, in contrast to freeholders, who were in the minority. The right of ownership was doubtful, and different in almost every manor because it was dependent on its particular customary law and on additional statutes. The main question was whether the right of inheritance was protected and the giving of notice admissible.

It was natural that the landlords were in favor of the restriction of peasant prerogatives, but the peasants themselves in every district in favor of the extension or at least preservation of their prerogatives. This class struggle, like others, assumed the form of a struggle between right and right, with the new law (*Recht*) definitely considered to be a wrong (*Unrecht*) in the popular consciousness. Although Roman law was not adopted in England because the London bar rejected it successfully, principles similar to those of the later Roman law were established under the name of Equity, especially at the younger High Court of the King's Bench which has been preserved as an absolutistic element, notwithstanding the victory of the estates over the crown. The inheritance of the peasantry had become the rule, even where it remained rather doubtful legally, as long as it was in the interest of the landlords themselves, and this was the case as long as the lords themselves administered their land, the so-called domain, and therefore depended on the services of the peasants. But as early as in the fifteenth century, because of the increasing significance of the export of wool to Flanders, grazing became more economic than tillage, and the landlords succeeded in asserting their will more and more, although the Courts of Plea in particular often decided in favor of the peasant's right of inheritance, on the ground of the custom of the district. Generally, however, larger acreages of property were established or leased by formal contract, in part long term but mainly in such a way that the lessor reserved the right to annual cancellation or renewal of the contract, the so-called tenancy at will.

Stammler's objection to historical materialism, that some sort of law is inherent, more or less, in all social relations, that the economy is to law as matter to form, is indicated in Marx's own sketch, when he calls property relations nothing but a legal expression of the existing relations of production, and adds that the relations of production change within the property relations, and are, to begin with, developmental forms of the forces of production, even if they may become their fetters.

The true facts, and this is what matters, are not contested, namely, that material relations change sooner than the forms in which they occur or, in other words, that material changes will eventually, even after heavy resistance, be followed by changes of form. Rights will always be fought over, not only in the councils of governments or in parliaments. Courts of law, too, even if the judge is considered to be a person of ideal impartiality, will interpret the law either in favor of the economically strong or in favor of the economically weak. Not infrequently, the judge may be inclined—for reasons of fairness, sympathy, good nature, humanity—to decide rather in favor of the weak and the poor. But by social position he belongs to the ruling class, and will sympathize, although perhaps not consciously so, more with the way of thinking and with the interests of his class. A popular or labor movement will not be likely to rouse his sympathy, not only because of its rough ways but also because of its indifference, if not hostility, toward ideas which are dear to him. Moreover, it is psychologically unavoidable that a judge is influenced in his judgment by the skill and eloquence of an attorney; and it is obvious that the strong are better clients for lawyers than the weak, and therefore in a position to choose the most skillful counsel.

The reality of the relations between the economy and the law, which is not completely identical with, but touches closely on, the dependence of political power on economic power, has been recognized and acknowledged a hundred times, although a fundamental and systematic theory has been shunned and rejected. The idea can be found expressed again in the brilliant inauguration speech by Georg Jellinek, *Der Kampf des alten mit dem neuen Recht* (*The Struggle between the Old and the New Law*) (Heidelberg, 1907); he expects that the future, too, is destined to experience new struggles between the old law and the new. "New historical and social conditions will, in the days to come, as always, produce new systems of law."

The Material Basis of Spiritual Life

Not only the law but also the mind, the spiritual life which is expressed in thought and creation, as well as morality and public opinion—all of this changes along with the economic foundation of social life. The sketchiness of the simile used by Marx becomes more obvious when he speaks of religious, artistic, or philosophical, in short, of ideological, forms, within which men become, as he thinks, aware of the conflict between a state of higher development of the forces of production and the relations of property, and fight out the conflict. For one could call it "fighting"—unless it is done with swords, guns, and cannons—only insofar as it is a *disputare*, a thinking differently, therefore talking and advising differently, and willing differently. Consequently, literature which is more and more written for the day, is the main battlefield where the different tendencies, and thus the social forces, those of conservation and those of change, those of the traditional and those of the new, those ways of thinking based on faith and those based on reason meet, as long as the one has not been silenced or killed off altogether by the other. But total killing hardly ever occurs. Whole generations may be silent and die. But new generations emerge who in part have already received and learned from those preceding them, in part will gain from new facts the same sentiments, impressions, and emotions. Attitudes and convictions are to a high degree hereditary, and so are, therefore, opinions, insofar as they spring from the same social facts, thus also from the same relations of production.

The relationship between the material bases and the higher manifestations of the mind, or spirit, might be conceived perhaps best of all according to the analogy of the relations that can be recognized between, on the one hand, the vegetative system of the human body, and the human needs and passions based on it and, on the other hand, the animal and mental system. This may be expressed in the words of Schiller, the much praised idealist, which he addressed to the Duke of Augustenburg, words that in abridged form are included in his collected works (*Briefe ueber die aesthetische Erziehung des Menschen*), namely: "Man is very little when he lives in a warm abode, and has eaten his fill, but he *must* have a warm abode and enough to eat, if his better self is to stir in him"— a sentence that reappeared later in the epigram "Man's Dignity": "No more of this, I ask you. Feed him, house him! Once you have covered his bareness, dignity comes of its own." Even more impressively he says the same in verse:

> Until philosophy succeeds,
> Nature is ruling with its creeds.
> The motive power she supplies
> By hunger's pangs and lovers' sighs.[1]

In a forceful way, the great poet, whose study of medicine early familiarized him with crime, expresses a similar thought in the violent words, "Something man must call his own, or he will murder and burn."[2]

In political life, the poor and suffering have acquired a voice only since the middle of the nineteenth century, after having been represented possibly in religious disguise or through priestly and, perhaps even more often, secular humanists; or else, they have let off steam directly through revolt and riots. It is part of the obvious advantages of the democratic state that the poor can, and are permitted to, present, in an orderly and regulated manner, their charges and complaints; that they can oppose laws which might make their situation worse, and promote better ones. Thus, only in more recent times, after the right to vote has become universal, do the political parties represent a relatively clear reflection of the economic situation. With all that, the picture is often disarranged and distorted. But whereas at a time when care was taken that the poor should not have any representation, the party of the status quo and the party of reform faced and opposed one another, these former opponents

---

[1]   Friedrich Schiller, *Poetical Works*, translated by E. P. Arnold-Foster, p. 290; wording of translation slightly changed by editors.
[2]   "Etwas muss er sein eigen nennen, Oder der Mensch wird morden und brennen."

now move closer together under the pressure of common troubles and dangers. A powerful voice rises on behalf of the masses from the so far silent campsite, the voice of poverty, the voice of labor, not seldom the voice of despair. In this instance, the truth of historical materialism is most clearly evident, and it is only worthy of contempt if the property-owning classes or their advocates stigmatize the materialism of the have-nots, so as to be able to indulge in their alleged or hypocritical "idealism." The reverse relation is often and to a certain degree more real: the love of pleasurable consumption (*Geniessen*) makes common, and a sumptuous way of living insensitizes one's ears to higher and nobler sounds than those of luxurious enjoyment and greedy desire; poverty and deprivation may create more favorable conditions, for some kind of people at least, to devote effort, labor, and sacrifice to the love of the arts or of knowledge, and to strive for them, as long as hope lights the way. Indeed, often it is this hope in the guise of pure idealism that gives the proletariat its self-confidence and the trust in its advancement.

IV. Empirical Sociology

16

STATISTICS AND SOCIOGRAPHY

EDITORS' NOTE. *The following selection is taken from a paper by the same title in the* Allgemeines Statistisches Archiv. *The first half of the article has been omitted because it deals with a problem that was much discussed in Germany at that time but has little interest for American readers today. The issue was whether statistics was merely a method or a special social science. Toennies as well as the dean of German statisticians, Georg von Mayr, took the latter position. There was, however, disagreement about the substance of this science. Von Mayr claimed that the collection and systematic arrangement of official statistics—of all enumerable and measurable social phenomena —could constitute a scientific discipline. Toennies, on the contrary, wanted to revive an older meaning of statistics; in the eighteenth and early nineteenth century* Statistik *in German meant the* description *of a country, or part of a country, of its natural features as well as of the population, the economy, political organization, military power, and other social institutions, in short, of anything that might be of service to the "statesman." Sometimes figures were given, but that was not essential. This was the real issue in Toennies' controversy with von Mayr.*

Statistik *in the modern sense was for Toennies a method. Realizing that the older meaning of the term could not be resurrected, Toennies adopted the term* Soziographie *from the Dutch sociologist Rudolf Steinmetz. Unfortunately, Toennies remained rather vague and perhaps undecided about the actual content of* Soziographie. *Sometimes he gives the impression that* Soziographie *would comprise empirical, comparative inquiries into social problems, that is, pathological phenomena like crime, suicide, prostitution (*"Moralstatistik," *in* Studien und Kritiken *III. p. 125 f.). At other times he defines the task of*

235

Soziographie, *which he identifies with* Moralstatistik, *as giving a "statistical" picture, in the* old *sense of* Statistik, *of the moral conditions of a people.* "*The highest task is to give* a view of the life of a people *but also to comprehend it by* comparative *methods*" (*"Die Statistik als Wissenschaft," in* Studien und Kritiken *III. p. 95 ff.; emphasis added). These overlapping definitions should be kept in mind by the reader.*

Statistics and Sociography

THOSE SCHOLARS who are mainly interested in understanding social life through observation and investigation of facts—that is, by the inductive method, which finds its expression in the statistical method—might rightfully call themselves empirical sociologists. This would be in accordance with Georg von Mayr, who, in one of the last of his varied statements about this subject, had decided to define statistics in his sense (which I, however, contest) as exact sociology. Certainly, the inductive method must strive to proceed as exactly as possible, and quantitative analysis is more exact than any other method. However, empirical sociology harms itself if it regards as its task, as von Mayr does, studying the *general* social phenomena directly instead of limiting itself *first* to a description and analysis of a certain area; this should, just because of the statistical method, be an area for which uniform statistical data are available through official statistics or would be obtainable privately. This would lead back to the old statistics in which scholars in Germany used to be engaged, describing countries and states under the name *Laender- und Staatenkunde.*

Upon such a solid foundation one could imagine building a general theory of certain social phenomena such as population changes, epidemic diseases, suicide, and crime. But this should not be the first object of empirical sociology; it is, rather, a distant and nebulous aim, like the idea of a general grammar. To know the specific grammar of a given language with which we are familiar, thus especially our mother tongue, is in its finer details already a great

Translated from "Statistik und Soziographie," *Allgemeines Statistisches Archiv* 18 (1929) : 546–58; abridged.

and difficult task. In the same way, for empirical sociological studies, our own country in which we were born and reared will always present itself intellectually as the nearest and most easily penetrable subject, not considering emotional attachment.

Within any larger area there would be ample opportunity for comparisons; indeed, one can arrive at a number of relative generalizations: as a rule, these will soon become weaker and more fluctuating if an attempt is made at comparisons with neighboring countries. It is understood that knowledge of the results of such studies (which one may continue to call statistics) will not only be of great interest and value for empirical sociologists but to a certain extent be indispensable.

What is essential is the starting point, the basic question at issue. Necessarily, one must start from the objective facts, not from the subjective wishes of the scholar. The truth is that the basis of insight into this subject matter must be the sort of knowledge of the country and its people which the scholar possesses either as a native of a particular country, as a citizen of a state, or which he has acquired through a sufficiently long stay in a country, through adequate knowledge of its language, and through diligent study. Only on the basis of such intimate knowledge will he be able to properly understand and apply what he may find as reliable material in official and other sufficiently dependable sources. He will not utilize this in the first place in order to derive general conclusions, that is, for the finding of universal laws in seemingly arbitrary human actions. His first aim must be to describe the inhabitants of a particular country, their characteristics, their living conditions, and their changes—as we actually do when we, for instance, describe the status and movement of a country's population. Even though it seems not only permissible but indicated to combine descriptions of this kind with those of other countries, to examine their similarities and differences, yet the more intimate study of the characteristics of a country or a state, a province, or even a community will always require limitation; the scientific character of such investigations will only benefit from such limitation.

We are unable to assign to "statistics" a particular subject matter. The discipline called statistics could, if it existed, not be limited to statistical method, even though this method should be preferred wherever applicable. But a science cannot emerge from mere application of a particular method. If the description of social reality is the object of such a science, then every available means of analysis ought to be utilized.

If we substitute the word sociography for the word statistics, unquestionably it would become equal in rank with theoretical sociology. However, if one prefers a broader concept of sociology, one would have to subsume under it both theoretical (conceptual) and empirical sociology, which latter I regard as identical with sociography. However, this concept appears less commendable for teaching purposes, and generally for academic planning, than the other one, which at least for these purposes limits the term sociology to its conceptually constructive aspects.

Personally, I frankly confess that I think empirical sociology is just as important as theoretical sociology, although I have become known far more through my work in theoretical sociology than through sociography and statistics in the old sense. Indeed, I recognize sociography as basic concerning the study of facts and their interrelations, thus of cause and effect, which, after all, remains the ultimate goal of knowledge. It is true that this study has to be preceded by groundwork (though not necessarily in the mind of each individual scholar) which must consist essentially in purifying conceptual thinking from the residues caused by using language not specifically made for conceptual thought. Every science simply has to speak its own language in some way—as some of the sciences are already doing in a most pronounced way. The development of the humanistic and social sciences is greatly handicapped because with their subject matter this is exceedingly difficult. Here we cannot avoid using a language overloaded with metaphors and associations and beautified and enobled as the language of literature, on which to some extent scientific thought likewise has to rely.

When in 1909 Max Weber was asked to become a special member of the newly founded Heidelberg Academy of Sciences, he declined this offer, giving as his reason that this academy had been established according to a traditional scheme which necessarily would have to be disadvantageous to the systematic study of the poitical and social sciences. These, he emphasized, were especially in need of support by such foundations, because both the utilization of materials hidden in statistical offices and the collective investigation of new facts were so expensive that the individual scholar could not possibly finance them out of his own pocket. "How much more productive" he wrote, "would it be if a modern academy were to support such pressing investigations which might throw light on the present, instead of exhausting its resources for specialized historical and philological studies, which a single person can so much easier do by himself." This result of an overwhelming historicism appeared to him by its very nature (since the academy owed its existence to the living forces of the present) as a contradiction in itself, and he felt it to be his duty to label it as such.

In his basic thought, Weber had a predecessor in another prominent scholar: Fr. J. Neumann of Tuebingen. He gave a lecture at Basel thirty-eight years earlier, entitled "Our Knowledge of the Social Conditions Surrounding Us." In this lecture he points out, on the basis of his complete mastery of the at that time already abundant statistical material, the lack of solid knowledge, especially concerning the conditions of the laboring classes. He places the responsibility for this lack of knowledge not only on insufficient material but also on the deficiency in studying and utilizing the available material: there would be plenty of urgent tasks before us, if we wanted to achieve a knowledge of social conditions around us, adequate for present needs.

The intention of my present paper points in the same direction, nineteen years after my esteemed friend Max Weber expressed himself; I would like to give to the totality of these studies a more unified character by uniting all of these endeavors around the concept and the word sociography. Its special character would be emphasized if it were recognized and promoted by state and society. Apart from chairs for sociography (although chairs for sociology might be established earlier), special research institutes, which I would like to name sociographic observatories, might be serviceable; I would propose to establish them for areas corresponding to a Prussian administrative district (*Regierungsbezirk*).

The time available for my paper prohibits my discussing why I am not in favor of combining such observatories with the existing statistical bureaus, although I am glad to say that except for this proposition I agree with my colleague Wuerzburger. Neither do I have sufficient time to develop my thoughts on what profound benefits, even blessings, such research and the money dedicated to it could create if the research were done strictly according to scholarly principles, completely independent of any administrative purposes; benefits not only would accrue in material welfare but would also be of a spiritual and moral nature; the observatories would serve the people. I only want to mention the general maxim, valid everywhere, that, in order to improve and heal, one must know the causes of the evil first, and that diagnosis is the most difficult task, as for the physician, so also for the action-oriented social scientist.

For a long time, statistics has provided valuable services in this respect, but has also caused trouble and confusion where it has been applied uncritically. Its transformation into sociography would be more effective in preventing abuse than has heretofore been possible. If statisticians were to adopt the concept and name sociography, their professional status would by no means be degraded but would, rather, be upgraded. To achieve this is the intention of my attempts and of the defense of my position.

17

THE PLACE OF BIRTH OF CRIMINALS IN SCHLESWIG-HOLSTEIN

EDITORS' NOTE. *The following selection from* Deutsches Statistisches Zentralblatt, *is presented as an example of Toennies' empirical studies. To be sure, it is a highly condensed report on one of his major investigations. The research on criminals in Schleswig-Holstein occupied Toennies for many years. The data were collected by Toennies himself in the penitentiaries at Altona and Rendsburg, which served the Prussian province of Schleswig-Holstein. The careful reader who is familiar with Toennies' theory will notice that the classification of criminals by type of place of origin (urban, rural, and by size) reflects the distinction between persons from communal (*Gemeinschaft-*like*) *and associational (*Gesellschaft-*like*) *backgrounds although it is not exactly identical with it; the differentiation between natives and nonnatives is also related to this distinction. The typology of* Frevler *(offender) and* Gauner *(swindler, crook), on the other hand, is based on the assumption that the kind of crimes committed by the former tend to be motivationally related to essential will, the crimes committed by the latter to arbitrary will. All this is not stated in so many words but rather implied. The terms* Gauner *and* Frevler *are Toennies' personal choice. They do not conform to German legal terminology; nor do the English equivalents render Toennies' meaning. The underlying meaning is the distinction between (a) crimes committed with deliberation and (b) crimes committed in emotion or out of passion. As the classification of sex delinquents (sub b) shows, the distinction is not the conventional one between "habitual" and "occasional" offenders, although it comes close to it.*

The Place of Birth of Criminals in Schleswig-Holstein

THE FOLLOWING report summarizes the results of two enquiries; the first concerns 3,500 male criminals who were convicted to death or to the penitentiary by courts in Schleswig-Holstein during the period of 1874–98; the second concerns 2,483 equally defined cases from the period of 1899–1914.

In both series the individuals have been classified in the same way, according to place of birth. The basic assumption is that the place of origin, which with few exceptions indicates also the place of upbringing, is of significant importance for those who become criminals, as it is for everybody. The importance of this factor cannot be tested for each individual, but only by the analysis of larger numbers who in this respect have common characteristics.

(1) We distinguish first between criminals who are natives of Schleswig-Holstein (*Heimbuertige*) and those born outside this region (*Fremdbuertige*); we call them natives and nonnatives. The distinction is not significant for a small proportion of the nonnatives, who stem from neighboring regions, even from enclaves (of the states of Hamburg, Luebeck, and Oldenburg); these may be different from the natives only insofar as they went through different public schools systems. The great majority, however, of the nonnatives are men who have left their place of origin (*Heimat*), in most cases as young men, and very often have not found a new home. These are uprooted individuals, especially if they have not founded a family.

(2) In both cases, natives as well as nonnatives, we distinguish between urban-born and rural-born.

(3) We classify the urban-born by size of city.

Translated from "Ortsherkunft von Verbrechern in Schleswig-Holstein," *Deutsches Statistisches Zentralblatt* 21 (1929) : 146–50. The tables, except table 3, have been rearranged by the editors in conformity with present-day usage.

(4) We classify the rural-born by size of village.[1]

The total number of all criminals is 5,983; of these, 2,271 are natives (37.6 per cent), 3,712 nonnatives (62.4 per cent).[2]

(5) We further differentiate by type of crime: (a) those who were convicted for theft, fraud, or robbery, we call *Gauner* (crooks); (b) those convicted for murder or other violence against persons, for perjury, arson, or sexual offenses, we call *Frevler* (offenders). Of the total of 5,983 criminals, 1,570 or 26.2 per cent are offenders and 4,413 or 73.8 per cent are crooks.

We find significant relations between the type of crime and the origin of the criminal; tables 1 and 2 demonstrate these relations.

TABLE 1

	NATIVES		NONNATIVES		TOTAL	
	N	%	N	%	N	%
Offenders	767	48.9	803	51.1	1,570	100.0
Crooks	1,504	34.1	2,909	65.9	4,413	100.0

TABLE 2

	OFFENDERS		CROOKS		TOTAL	
	N	%	N	%	N	%
Natives	767	33.8	1,504	66.2	2,271	100.0
Nonnatives	803	21.6	2,909	78.4	3,712	100.0

Offenses are more likely to be committed by individuals whose psychic structure is that of native and settled; crook-type delicts, far more likely by nonnative and homeless persons. This is not contradicted by the fact that the number of nonnative offenders surpasses the number of native offenders; the difference is much smaller. Not only the nature of the delicts but also the age and

---

[1] For details see for the first series "Verbrechertum in Schleswig-Holstein" in *Archiv f. Sozialwissenschaft und Sozialpolitik*, vol. 61, 2 (1929), p. 322 ff. and "Uneheliche und verwaiste Verbrecher" in *Kriminalstatistische Abhandlungen*, book 14 (1930); for the second, "Die schwere Kriminalitaet von Maennern in Schleswig-Holstein in den Jahren 1899 bis 1914" (with E. Jurkat) in *Zeitschrift f. Voelkerpsychologie und Soziologie*, vol. 5, 1 (1929), pp. 27–39.

[2] Toennies gives all proportions in pro mille.—EDS.

everything else that is of importance for the psychic structure of the criminal tend to be different for crooks than for offenders.

In order to explain the higher proportion of nonnatives in various crategories of criminals, especially the crooks, the following factors are to be considered.

(1) The frequency distribution of nonnatives in Schleswig-Holstein by age groups; according to the census of 1900, which distinguishes five age groups, this distribution is different from that of the natives. Among the nonnatives we find a high proportion in the second and third age groups. If we relate the criminals to the three middle age groups, we still find a strong prevalence of non-native criminals.

(2) The greater mobility of the nonnative and the recidivity which is characteristic, especially for the crooks, produce constantly a fresh supply of criminal individuals, whereas recidivity among the natives tends to bring identical individuals before the criminal judge.

(3) The higher rate of endogenous criminality in the regions of origin of the nonnatives is hardly a decisive factor, and its effect cannot be measured.

(4) More important is the place of residence of the nonnatives who tend to concentrate in the larger cities of Schleswig-Holstein.

(5) The correspondence between the distance of the place of birth of the nonnative inhabitants of Schleswig-Holstein and the proportion of the nonnatives among the criminals within this province; this holds for the crooks without exception, for the offenders to a lesser extent.

Table 3 shows the percentage of criminals among the aver-

TABLE 3

Zone	Crooks	Offenders
1. Hamburg, Luebeck, Oldenburg, both Mecklenburgs	1.74	0.48
2. Hannover, Bremen, Braunschweig, Westfalen, Lippe, Rheinprovinz	2.42	0.63
3. Provinz Sachsen, Brandenburg, Berlin, Pommern, Anhalt	2.75	0.83
4. Ost-Preussen, West-Preussen, Posen, Schlesien	3.51	0.98
5. Koenigreich Sachsen, Sachsen-Weimar, Thueringen	3.67	0.65
6. Hessen-Nassau, Hessen, Baden, Wuerttemberg, Bayern, Elsass	3.55	0.66

age (1874–1914) number of male natives of the respective region residing in Schleswig-Holstein 1874–1914. [The zones are arranged roughly according to the distance from Schleswig-Holstein.—EDS.] These findings are not affected by the fact that the age distribution of the nonnative population varies with the zone of their origin. The increase of criminality with distance of zone of origin is maintained if we relate the criminals to the nonnative residents (in Schleswig-Holstein) of the three middle age groups.

The same correspondence which exists between the numerical relation of natives to nonnatives and those of offenders to crooks can be found in the relations of rural-born to urban-born individuals among native as well as among nonnative criminals and among "offenders" as well as among "crooks."

Among the total number of criminals, the rural-born prevail: 3,425, as against 2,558 urban-born, or 57.3 per cent, as compared with 42.7 per cent. In evaluating this finding, it must be considered that the latest year of birth of these criminals is 1894, that most were born much earlier, since the majority are more than thirty years old. The median year of birth for the group of 1899–1914 may be assumed to be 1880, and 1860 for the earlier and larger group; we may thus assume 1871 as median year of birth for the total group. At that time about 64 per cent of the population of the German Reich were living in rural communities, statistically defined as places of 2,000 inhabitants or less. Around 1890 the rural-born who survived the twentieth year of life must still have been two-thirds of the population, the urban-born less than one-third (or 67 per cent and 33 per cent respectively). This means that the proportions which we find in our universe of criminals actually indicate a heavier load for the *urban* communities; this holds for the relation of native urban-born to native rural-born (40.4 per cent versus 59.6 per cent) as well as in the case of nonnative urban-born as compared with nonnative rural-born (53.5 per cent versus 46.5 per cent). But the nonnatives are in significantly higher degree urban than the natives; one should, however, remember that in Schleswig-Holstein the proportion of urban-born among the living, especially for the earlier period, must be estimated as far below the average [for the German Reich.—EDS.].

Similar relationships are found for the rural-born crooks as compared with the urban-born crooks and for the urban-born offenders in comparison with rural-born offenders. The proportions for crooks are: rural-born 48.4 per cent, urban-born 51.6 per cent; for offenders, urban-born 39.9 per cent, rural-born 60.1 per cent. Interesting relations analogous to those found by the analysis in terms of rural and urban origin are revealed by the further enquiry into the *size* of places of origin, both cities and rural communities. We define as larger cities all those that (about 1871) had a population of 10,000 or more, and as larger villages all rural communities of 500 inhabitants or more.

The table 5 demonstrates the differences in the proportions of criminals corresponding to the size of communities, urban as well as rural.

The fact that large proportions of native offenders and also of crooks stem from large villages demonstrates the predominant contribution of villagers in general to the criminality of natives (endogenous criminality). The important fact is that among natives as well as nonnatives relatively more crooks than offenders originate in the larger villages and especially in larger cities than in smaller communities [while smaller communities tend to produce larger percentages of offenders.—Eds.]

TABLE 4

	NATIVES				NONNATIVES				TOTAL			
	Offenders N	%	Crooks N	%	Offenders N	%	Crooks N	%	Offenders N	%	Crooks N	%
Urban born	239	31.2	681	45.3	387	48.2	1,597	54.9	626	39.9	2,278	51.6
Rural born	528	68.8	823	54.7	416	51.8	1,312	45.1	944	60.1	2,135	48.4
TOTAL	767	100.0	1,504	100.0	803	100.0	2,909	100.0	1,570	100.0	4,413	100.0

TABLE 5

	NATIVES				NONNATIVES				TOTAL	
	Offenders N	%	Crooks N	%	Offenders N	%	Crooks N	%	Offenders N	Crooks N
URBAN-BORN										
Large	27	11.3	127	18.7	117	30.2	585	36.6	144	712
Small	212	88.7	554	81.3	270	69.8	1,012	63.4	482	1,566
SUBTOTAL	239	100.0	681	100.0	387	100.0	1,597	100.0	626	2,278
RURAL-BORN										
Large	117	22.2	227	27.6	136	32.7	476	36.3	253	703
Small	411	77.8	596	72.4	280	67.3	836	63.7	691	1,432
SUBTOTAL	528	100.0	823	100.0	416	100.0	1,312	100.0	944	2,135
TOTAL	767		1,504		803		2,909		1,570	4,413

V. Applied Sociology

EDITORS' NOTE. *Applied sociology was conceived of by Toennies as a dynamic theory in contrast to, but not always clearly distinguishable from, the static theory which is elaborated in pure sociology. Public opinion, being both a manifestation and a changing aspect of* Gesellschaft, *surely is of a historical character and therefore belongs to applied sociology. The paper on "Power and Value of Public Opinion" is representative of Toennies' varied attempts to come to grips with the concept of public opinion, not to conduct public opinion research. The paper on "Historicism, Rationalism, and the Industrial System" develops in a wide sweep of argument the principles which in Toennies' view govern the emergence of the new industrial society of our time. In its concluding sentences, it reveals Toennies' confidence—so contrary to the general assumption that he is a pessimist—that mechanization and automatization may ultimately be conducive to the liberation of the intimate forces in human nature, which are presently neglected.*

By way of contrast, the paper on "The Individual and the World in the Modern Age," the clearest of Toennies' sociological interpretations of the course of modern history, ends on a note of resignation. What is progress in one regard is decline in another, and the response of the scholar necessarily will be in line with Spinoza's principle: Non lugere, non ridere, neque detestari, sed intelligere.

18

THE POWER AND VALUE
OF PUBLIC OPINION

PUBLIC OPINION is difficult to define; it is more convenient to determine what it appears to be, to find what it is believed to be rather than what it *is*.

Public opinion appears as a power in societal life, a very important power. Ever since the period immediately preceding the year 1789, which was a turning point, this has often been emphasized—most vividly and intensively by the then minister of the treasury, Necker, who played such a great role immediately prior to the French Revolution and during its first phase. Equally emphatic was Jean Joseph Meunier, who publihsed his *Appel au Tribunal de l'Opinion publique* in Geneva in 1790. Also, Abbé Morellet and the famous Abbé Sieyès participated in what one may call the discovery of public opinion; in Germany, one might name Forster, Wieland, Garve, and others. Many writers in the last quarter of the eighteenth century and throughout the nineteenth century followed suit, until in our days the belief that public opinion is strong and forceful has been widely accepted. One can say that this belief has become part of public opinion itself.

Translated from "Macht und Wert der Oeffentlichen Meinung," *Die Dioskuren, Jahrbuch fuer Geisteswissenschaften* 2 (1923) : 72–99; abridged.

Toennies says in a note that the principal ideas of this treatise are likewise contained in his comprehensive work, *Kritik der Oeffentlichen Meinung* (Berlin: Julius Springer, 1929), but that the *Dioskuren* paper represents an independent investigation which may be considered complementary to the larger work.

The power of public opinion is placed side by side with the power of governments or, where governments are dependent on legislative bodies, side by side with these; one frequently even hears it said that public opinion is the supreme and decisive power, at least in democratic countries, and that it is the court of last appeal in important political matters. Public opinion is thought of as a thinking being, and it is frequently either adored or maligned as if it were a supernatural, quasi-mystical being. As the skeptic and cynic Talleyrand put it, "I know someone who is wiser than Voltaire, more intelligent than Napoleon and all the ministers of state that we have had and will have, and that is public opinion." Napoleon himself, after his downfall, bent his knee before public opinion, when he said on Saint Helena, "Public opinion is an invisible and mysterious force that is irresistible; nothing is more mobile, unsteady and powerful; and capricious as it may be, it nevertheless is far more frequently true, reasonable and just than one is inclined to assume." (Las Cases' *Memorial*, I, 452). Herewith, not only the power but also the value of public opinion is affirmed.

Now, does this view imply a clear idea as to what public opinion *is?* To be sure, there are theories of public opinion, and these theories, like others, have their history, which is worthy of a specific treatment. But the general judgment about the power of public opinion knows nothing about these theories. It is satisfied with indistinct and fluctuating ideas. One believes that there are certain signs by which public opinion can be recognized.

Public opinion is recognized by what one *hears* everywhere, if one "talks to people" and is attentive to what they say; especially important is their judgment about a particular event, and especially so if this judgment implies a definitive approval or disapproval and if it appears as an unopposed and unanimous judgment.

Many judgments seem to go without saying, such as, for instance, those pertaining to morality and propriety. Patriotic-political judgments, to be sure, claim universal validity much more rarely. Their intention is to be subjective; they are supposed to express the emotions and the manner of thinking of a people, especially of a politically organized nation, regarding matters that do not concern other nations, do not interest them, and presumably are not understood by them; or that are necessarily negatively evaluated by those whose interests and modes of thinking—which usually are derived from interests—are likely to be opposed to one's own. Consequently, one considers in every country one's own judgment to be the right judgment, and one considers it the duty of one's compatriots, as "good patriots," to share in this judgment, not to contest and not to doubt it; on the other hand, one understands that one's judgment cannot be shared by other nations, or at least that it cannot be shared and affirmed by enemies; one can even understand that the judgment of enemies is of an opposite character. However, hatred of the enemy easily leads to the assumption that he harbors a mean and corrupt manner of thinking and that his adverse judgment is derived therefrom; especially from his ill will "against us," which is manifested in the very maliciousness of his state of mind. Indeed, the common judgments of a collectivity, like the judgments of individuals, are largely based on their common wills, desires, strivings, loves, and hatreds, on the sentiment and consciousness of common needs and interests, insofar as these are shared by an entire people; it would seem that one must expect similarity in judgment as certain or at least as very likely. However, even if this is the case, and if one further assumes the existence of common needs and interests, views will diverge because these are felt in varying strength and gravity, and because the thoughts of men, in the majority of instances, do not widely differ from their emotions. To sum up, a converging and general judgment, even in patriotic-political matters, can be expected with some assurance only where very strong needs and clear interests are felt with elementary force, so that they impose themselves, as it were, on the common consciousness.

Thus far, we have based our consideration on the observation that one believes to be able to recognize public opinion according to what one hears. However, one also believes one can recognize public opinion according to what one *sees*, such as large gatherings of men in the streets, demonstrations, marches, and so forth.[1] One must understand, however, that popular sentiment and public opinion are related, but by no means identical, phenomena. Public

---

1   In this context, Toennies gives a colorful description of collective behavior in time of war.—EDS.

opinion manifests its societal and political power by means of its approval or disapproval of political events, by demanding that the government take a certain position and abolish certain abuses, by insisting on reforms and legislative measures, in brief, by "taking a stand" on certain questions of public policy, after the manner of a spectator or a judge. Public opinion as power is thought of as a court of appeal, placed over and above popular sentiment and separated from it; public opinion may be dependent on popular sentiment, but is essentially an intellectual force.

Public joy and public mourning must not be equated with *the* public opinion. The visible signs of these affects must not be thought of as signs of public opinion, except in the very general sense that every affect contains an opinion and that every opinion, that is, every thought, assumes affective coloring. Accordingly, precisely what one sees is frequently misleading and leads to incorrect judgments. One sees a mass of people in a large city, seemingly, even obviously, caught by one single sentiment, and filled with it. One calls this mass "the people," their assembly within a space holding, say, a thousand persons, a popular assembly. But even if this multitude really represented the "people" of the city, it would not constitute a representative assembly of the population of the city or country. We have a true representative assembly (*Volksvertretung*) only in an assembly based on legally sanctioned elections. Such an assembly is considered with some justification as an organ of public opinion. But by all means not always. Parliament in eighteenth-century England—even the House of Commons—was exclusively an organ of the gentry, while a broadly based (*gemeinbuergerliche*) public opinion was already in evidence, as an indefatigable and strong critic of Parliament. Behind that public opinion stood an invisible assembly of the educated and thinking members of the people.

Third, one believes one can recognize public opinion by what one *reads*. The power of public opinion is frequently equated with the power of the press. Both were called "the sixth great power" as early as in the period (1815–67) when the European concert was performed by five great powers. The power of the press is more obvious than the power of public opinion. The power of the press is especially significant because behind a newspaper, especially a big newspaper, stands the power of a political party, which frequently is also a party of economic and intellectual life or at least is closely connected with these; and a political party exerts a great and often decisive influence upon the workings of government. Behind the party stand strong and influential personalities, overt as well as covert leaders of the party, even whole groups of them; they are strong and influential, partly because of intelligence, knowledge, and experience, partly and more frequently because of wealth; and influential wealth, in turn, is based either on landed property or on mobile capital; and capital has different validity and effectiveness depending on whether it is lending capital, crystallized in banking, commercial and communication capital, especially shipping, finally mining and industrial capital, the latter concentrated in what one calls "heavy industry."

Capital in all its forms has gained predominance within modern states; but industrial capital has become the most characteristic manifestation of the power of capital over men to such a degree that industrial capital frequently has been equated with capital generally; in the same vein, capital has been identified and confused with wealth. Indeed, wealth based on landed estate and wealth based on capital frequently merge and are combined in a few large hands. Especially, great wealth based on land holdings (*latifundia*) participates in a variety of capitalistic enterprises; very great capital wealth, on the other hand, is intent on acquiring landed estate because it is prestigious and, especially in earlier stages, politically influential. With all that, capital enjoys a natural advantage over landed estate with regard to the power of the press for the following reasons: (1) commerce, communication, banking, industry are more intimately connected than is landed estate with the spirit of modernity and thereby with the press; (2) commerce, and capital generally, is closely related to the world of information and communication, which is served by the press and thereby to the doings in national and international politics; (3) the newspaper itself is, and becomes more and more, a capitalistic enterprise; the main business of a newspaper is advertising, which is a tool of commercial and industrial capital; (4) the press is in line with the great body of literature inasmuch as it is carried along by the progress of scientific thinking and stands in the service of a predominantly liberal and religiously as well as politically progressive consciousness; consequently the press *ab initio* has been an effective weapon of the cities, especially the large commercially oriented cities, against the feudal forces that are rooted in dominion over the soil; the press addresses itself primarily and preferentially to an urban, especially a metropolitan, public because this is the public that is most eager to read, most accustomed to and capable of reading, and therefore most inclined to do battle by means of script and speech.

It emerges that the power of the press primarily appears to be a means by which liberal thought and parties exert power over conservative thought and parties; conservative and ecclesiastical thinking are closely related, while liberalism goes hand in hand, partly with a freer and less church-oriented religiosity, partly with an agnostic world view connected with the natural sciences. Now, if and inasfar as public opinion is subject to the same influences and developmental causations as the press, public opinion will be reflected in the press, so that the power of the press expresses the power of public opinion to the extent that the identification of the press (and, indeed, of all means of communication.—EDS.) and public opinion becomes understandable and within certain limits justified. The facts meet this prerequisite to a considerable degree. For public consciousness as we may call the common manner of thinking of those who are supposed to be the representatives of contemporary civilization in the advanced countries of the world, is replete with elements that are the fruits of the Enlightenment: thoughts and judgments which two hundred years ago appeared paradoxical, indeed, were detested and proscribed as atheistic and detrimental to the commonwealth but have finally, after a long-drawn-out struggle, emerged victorious. Opposed to these thoughts and judgments were traditional views, sanctioned by religious faith and scientific doctrines which were in concordance with the requirements of faith: views about what is real and possible, right and good, permitted and commanded that today are rejected, despised, and ridiculed by public opinion. Numerous examples of these transformations in every field of opinion can be given. It must suffice here to remind ourselves of tortures, cruel death penalties, witch hunts, and personal servitude, and to ask the question how any attempt to revive these institutions, which formerly were uncontested and considered indispensable, would be received by contemporary public opinion.

To be sure, conservative thought necessarily advocates the restoration of what once has been, but no conservative spokesman will wish to go so far as to appear "reactionary" and become suspect before the forum of public opinion, as if he intended to bring back the Dark Ages; for outdated privileges and the oppression that goes along with them are laid at the door of the Middle Ages by public opinion, even if most things of this kind have flourished in the garish light of modernity. To these things belongs, among others, the absolute monarchy, an institution which in actual fact is characteristic of the modern age and not of the Middle Ages; in contrast, popular representation on the basis of more or less universal suffrage and a written constitution are considered a lasting and indispensable liberal accomplishment. In all these respects, liberalism has become a constitutive part of public opinion everywhere, except in areas of cultural transition, where it is still in the process of spreading from Europe and America to the much older civilization of the Orient. The power of public opinion can be seen in the fact that such modern thoughts are considered to be like a strong fortress that needs to be guarded and defended. In this regard, the press is believed to be the inseparable organ of public opinion; the power of a unanimous press reflects the power of a unanimous public opinion, and if both follow the same direction they are irresistible. The press, then, is *the* organ of *the* public opinion. It is the power of the "spirit of the age." What we have in mind here is a latent, if rarely realized, unanimity of the press. However, the daily spectacle offered by the press is one of contending opinions, even of bitter conflict. And yet, the press is regarded as the expression and organ of public opinion, almost as identical with it, even if it is the very picture of discordance.

This latter view contains a concept of public opinion which is different from the concept that has served us as a point of departure. Surely, if one conceives of public opinion as the sum total of a variety of expressed opinions which appear in the light of publicity, one can say that the press, especially the daily press, is its true image: the more factions there are, whose particular mentalities are expressed in particular signs, the more varied will be the picture. This sum total of public opinion is a power, too, in the same sense in which a polyphonic scream, against which the voice of the individual attempts in vain to assert itself and become audible, is powerful as such, even if the voices of which it is composed are but a confused and contradictory disharmony. But it is a power of a different kind than the power of a unified harmony of many thoughts and opinions, the power which we have in mind, if we conceive of *the* public opinion as the generalized opinion of a people or a public as a whole; in other words, if we conceive of public opinion as a form of *social volition*, which is manifested as a unified will in all its forms, as if it were the will of a *person*. In this sense, it is customary to speak of public opinion as a personal power which asserts itself in affirmation and negation, acceptance and refusal.

Only differentiating, that is, critical thinking is capable of forging a scientifically usable concept of public opinion as a unified potentiality: a concept of this kind must be related to common linguistic usage, but must simultaneously dissolve and limit such usage and describe the conceived object so clearly and sharply as only a thing of thought can be described. Obviously, it is not by chance that public opinion, in one as well as in the other sense, is named by the same name; it is indeed the same thing in two different manifestations. An assembly or a court of justice is one thing in the condition of deliberation and another when it decides or has decided. In the latter instance, the assembly stands behind the decision as a unified whole or a moral person; in the former instance, the assembly, more often than not, is divided and torn apart by contradictory opinions and perorations. One can compare public opinion with an assembly of this kind, but the comparison must not make us overlook the dissimilarities.

Assemblies are one thing if they assemble by chance or are called together by some people, and an entirely different thing if they are the embodiment of an ideal assembly (*ideelle Versammlung*). The ideal assembly is the organ of a unified will, instituted by statute, legislation, or custom. The actual assembly, whether or not it is the embodiment of an ideal assembly, occupies a particular space and has some duration; the individuals that belong to it are recognizable as members of the assembly, either as active participants or as listeners. An assembly, even if it is merely a consultative assembly, will, and should, appear as some kind of a unified psychological body. As a rule, it is formally opened and closed and a temporarily limited existence is ascribed to it, as if it were a living being. Public opinion, on the other hand, is without limitation in space and time. It cannot be perceived by the senses, and one cannot observe who precisely participates in it. Whoever feels motivated can raise his voice; there is no clearly defined membership. Public opinion, in this sense, can much sooner be compared to a consultative assembly, if in such an assembly a discordance of noisy screams is heard, than to an orderly assembly where a firm chairmanship facilitates the quiet exchange of thoughts and opinion and limits quarrel and violent controversy. But a *unified public opinion*, which must be thought of as an expression of social volition, is to be compared to an assembly that decides or has decided, inasmuch as these decisions have binding power, either exclusively for those assembled or for a larger whole whose "organ" the assembly is supposed to be. In the same way, public opinion claims binding power for itself.

Public opinion in this sense strives for validity, that is, for acceptance, and tolerates contradiction and deviance as little as a religious doctrine which is pronounced a saving truth. In the one as in the other case, the disapproval of error soon becomes a moral reproach, which means to say that to believe in something, to think in a particular manner, is established as an obligation. Initially those who think differently are presumed to be blind: the deviant does not see the truth, he does not comprehend that what I see in the brightest light, what I "show" him, what I demonstrate, is right. Or does he comprehend but does not "want it to be true"? Does he not want to admit that it is true because it is inconvenient, indeed, shameful for him to confess that he has been in error, or because the untruth agrees with what he wishes to be true while the truth is contrary to it? In the latter case, his ill will is obvious and his own conscience must condemn him. However, it is possible, and in many instances probable, that he is simply incapable of comprehending the correctness of my opinion, which is the generally accepted opinion, and that he lives in delusion. Does this, then, mean that he is innocent? Religion, as is known, does not assume this. The doctrine of the obduracy and hard-heartedness of those who close themselves off from revealed truth plays a great role in the history of the Christian churches: heresy is a sin, atheism a mortal sin. In this regard, public opinion resembles religion.

Public opinion may be compared to a dominant faith and, like faith, it is all the more intolerant the more sovereign its rule. This is especially obvious if the dogma is "patriotic" in nature.

Everywhere, patriotism, the belief that one's own country is right and good, is considered obligatory in public opinion, frequently also faith in the constitution, whether traditionally or rationally affirmed, monarchic or republican; finally, hope and confidence in the future of one's country. These sentiments and thoughts are enhanced during a war. . . . There are honest doubters, but as a rule they will be careful not to make their doubts public. "One cannot say that"—at least not say it publicly—but what is meant is: "You must not even think that, your thinking and doubting testify to a deficiency in your conviction." Love, more than faith or hope, is independent of critical thought; it is there or not there, a gift of nature, an organic product that cannot be made or enforced; at best, one can further its growth. And yet, patriotism, the love of one's country, is made obligatory by the public opinion of one's fatherland, as the love of God and his holy Church is made obligatory by religion.

In both instances, the request does not remain without effect. The fear of disapproval and punishment brings it about that at least the expression of the prohibited conviction is repressed; even more so does the desire to find favor with leaders in religious life and public opinion. But the repression of explicit thoughts and sentiments retroacts on the thoughts and sentiments themselves, weakens them and makes them wither; and, as an organ that is not exercised receives insufficient nourishment from the total organism, so atrophies the silenced thought.

The power of public opinion to impose itself stands in direct proportion to the applied energy. The greatest energy is exercised by fanaticism—there is a fanaticism of public opinion, as there is a fanaticism of religion. The power with which these fanaticisms assert themselves internally enhances the power which they exercise externally. But the power of inner cohesion and of outward effect must be kept apart. They may further or hamper each other. To the extent to which cohesion is operative, that is, to the extent to which it is possible to assert the social volition which manifests itself internally as religion or public opinion, to the same extent will this power operate also externally, and vice versa: the more external effect, the more internal repercussion, that is, the more successfully will the social volition impose itself on individual subjects, be they members of a church or religious community or the dispersed individuals of which a public is composed.

Both religion and public opinion are part of the spiritual-moral sphere in social life; they compete within this sphere to the point of conflict. Both exercise the strongest influence on political life, so that *the* religion of a country may become either the only or the most favored, recognized, protected, and supported religion. The public opinion of a country, likewise, is an effective power in political life, and will be recognized as such by other factors especially by the government. Religion as well as public opinion strive to be morally supreme, so that all varieties of religious faith have a powerful tendency to become *the* religion, and all particular expressions of public opinion have the tendency to become *the* public opinion. Both are engaged in propaganda. Public opinion propaganda, especially political propaganda, is modelled on religious propaganda. As religious propaganda propagates faith, so political propaganda propagates opinion.

The means to achieve this end are partly the same, partly different; different also with regard to the historical period wherein one or the other kind of propaganda is predominantly effective. The propaganda of public opinion is highly characteristic for the contemporary period. Its most general and most powerful means is the press, which is engaged in a continuous wrestling match in the arena of public opinion. We observe the continuous effort of the political parties to generalize their opinion into the public opinion of the country; but apart from organized parties, occasionally with their assistance, a variety of domestic and foreign influences are at work in order to bring public opinion to their side, by means of the press. Public opinion is belabored, with the frequent result that *the* public opinion is *made* thereby. It has been said more than once that a particular public opinion has been manufactured, as one manufactures any manner of merchandise. One produces merchandise in order to sell, and one sells in order to make a profit. One produces opinion because one expects an advantage from it if it should come to be shared by many, and this advantage differs little from the profit which the merchant and entrepreneur are seeking. The powers of capital are intent not only to bring about a favorable opinion concerning their products, an unfavorable one concerning those of their competitors, but also to promote a generalized public opinion which is designed to serve their business interests, for instance, regarding a policy of protective tariffs or of free trade, favoring a political movement or party, supporting or opposing an existing government. The government must adapt itself to the interests of capital, submit to them or defend itself against them, always dependent on public opinion, always intent on transforming a possible disfavor into a favorable attitude. In such fashion, every political power, including every political party, whose endeavors usually are intimately tied to economic interests although they are also independently motivated, is conditioned by the enjoyment of power or the desire for it. Consequently, governments as well as parties attempt to influence public opinion in the sense that they seek to transform their particular opinion into *the* public opinion, certainly in matters of considerable impact.

The spiritual-moral powers, likewise, participate in wooing for the favor of public opinion. Organized religion, science, arts, and letters do not merely wish to create a public opinion which is favorably inclined toward their interests and achievements; they want also to influence public opinion with regard to political matters. Public opinion is easily accessible to these influences because it is itself a spiritual force. All powers that attempt to gain the favor of public opinion, avail themselves of the printed [or otherwise communicated—EDS.] word as an effective instrument. It is not the only instrument that can be used, but one that is extraordinarily suitable, extremely flexible, always available for purposes of uninterrupted persuasion, and—according to Napoleon—most effective by means of the most powerful rhetorical configuration, namely, repetition. It happens, however, that public opinion is in evidence *prior* to newspaper propaganda, that it is fixed immediately after an event becomes known, that it becomes virulent *pari passu* with the dissemination of the news. This is most likely where the judgment seems to go without saying, particularly if it is a moral, and even more so if it is a patriotic-moral, judgment; and this is especially so if pre-sentiment and prejudice are ready to believe in the truth of the matter without further ado and to arrive at a particular judgment at a moment's notice. This is most obvious in the case of a negative judgment, a condemnation. That happened in 1894 when French public opinion, along with the verdict of the military court, condemned Captain Dreyfus. It was considered proven that he was a traitor; prejudice against Jews confirmed the conviction; hatred against the victors of 1870 lent to the alleged crime the worst possible coloration, made the very doubt that it had been committed suspicious, rendered contradiction impossible, and unconditional consent a moral duty. Hence, the newspapers had their position staked out for them—it was a command of necessity.[2]

All this illuminates the concept of *the* public opinion. The varieties of motivation and their accompanying sentiments are irrelevant if only the judgment is identical; what is essential, therefore, is the judgment. We further learn from the Dreyfus case, as from others where public opinion appears as a political factor, that unanimity is the unity of those who have a political judgment, that is, those who habitually participate in political life. More precisely, one may say that participation in the formation of public opinion is more effective, the more vivid the political interest, especially if the interest is focused on a particular problem area. Hence, it is stronger with men than with women, stronger with adults than with adolescents; stronger with those whose life chances are touched by

2   Toennies treats as another example, the reaction of German public opinion to the Emperor's political *faux pas* of 1908.—EDS.

the matter in question than with mere spectators; consequently, in economic matters more with businessmen than with scholars, but in spiritual matters the other way round; in purely political matters stronger with urban than with rural people, and strongest with the inhabitants of metropolitan areas. Very generally, one can say that public opinion is the opinion of the educated classes as against the great mass of the people. However, the more the masses move upward and the more they participate in the advance of education and political consciousness, the more will they make their voices count in the formation of public opinion. Always public opinion remains the judgment of an elite, that is, a minority, frequently, to be sure, a representative minority, at times, however, a minority that is entirely out of contact with the mass of the people. The great mass of the people, especially of the rural folk, failed to participate in the Dreyfus affair. In the first place then, if we want to determine what public opinion is, we must be attentive to what is accepted and effective (*was gilt*) as public opinion. For instance, it is obvious that in 1878 the issuance of a particular law directed against the Social-Democratic party was considered to be a demand of public opinion in Germany, although, of course, the Social-Democratic party, and consequently a large part of the industrial working class, rejected and detested the very idea of it.

Even with this limitation, it is not difficult to observe that unanimity in public opinion is a rare phenomenon; and what is effective in it most of the time, in the best circumstances, is only the majority of an elite: the predominant, the most conspicuous, the most vociferous opinion. Rarely can one achieve more in the wrestling for the favor of public opinion than this predominance. Every party in the game strives to increase its weight in the scales of public opinion. This has some affinity with the attempt to influence as many voters as possible and, for this purpose, to have as many "organized" members as possible; but there is a difference. Again, the attempt of a party to gain the favor of public opinion differs from the attempt to establish party opinion as the generally accepted public opinion. The party, convinced of the truth and correctness of its opinion, wants nothing but the recognition of this truth and correctness. But is indeed true and correct what is effectively established as true and correct?

One final comment: the intellectuals are called upon to be the leaders in social life; they cannot fulfill their role better than by trying to care for and improve public opinion. We have mentioned, above, those component parts of public opinion whose maintenance is the task of a humanistic ethics. One can easily establish a catalog of those firmly rooted judgments which not even the most resolute enemy of modernity can wish to do away with. These judgments and yardsticks are the fruits of doctrines which the philosophers of the seventeenth and eighteenth centuries have sown and which were propagated by their numerous disciples, by writers, and by secular as well as ecclesiastical popularizers. The philosophers that came later have modified some of these judgments but have annihilated none of them; even the transvaluation of all values, which we experience, cannot touch them.

19

HISTORICISM, RATIONALISM, AND THE INDUSTRIAL SYSTEM

IN THE FIELD OF LAW the historical approach has replaced the rationalistic approach since the beginning of the nineteenth century. This change took place mainly in Germany and was accompanied by the protest against a civil code [*Allgemeines Buergerliches Gesetzbuch*]; the latter had been demanded by the new and liberated national consciousness. When Savigny denied to his age the authority to codify the law, his line of thought was oddly inconsistent. He contended—in the vein of Schelling's philosophy of nature —that law is "organically connected" with the essence and character of a people. In this organic unity with the character of the people, law, he maintained, is comparable to language; and it is tied together with the language, customs, and institutions of a people by the common bond of shared convictions and a shared sense of inner necessity. This idea should have led Savigny to fight for an unadulterated German law, for its renewal and further development in the indigenous spirit. Yet, knowledge of Roman law being his very domain, and intensification of its study by the practitioner of law being his foremost postulate, he refuted "the bitter complaints about this foreign ingredient of our law." He contended that a common civil law of foreign origin was not considered "unnatural" by modern nations, in the same way in which their religion was not

---

Translated from *Soziologische Studien und Kritiken* 1 (1925): 105–26; first published in *Archiv fuer Systematische Philosophie*, vol. 1 (1894). Toennies gave the paper the shorter title "*Historismus und Rationalismus.*" Some quotations and footnotes as well as some paragraphs and sentences in the text are shortened or omitted. Subtitles are supplied by the editors.

indigenous and their literature was not free from the impact of the most powerful external influences. Thus Savigny endorsed the adoption and adaptation of Roman law and did not realize that it followed the same trend as natural law (which he despised), namely, a rationalistic rather than a historical trend. Nor did he realize that a foreign law can hardly be related organically to the essence and character of a people, just as a foreign language cannot be so related. Savigny's successors are accomplishing the task which he wanted to prohibit. They write a civil code for the present-day German Reich,[1] the first draft of which is provoking anew the familiar bitter complaints that it is conceived in a thoroughly "Roman" spirit and is, naturally, approved by the "old and un-eradicable frame of mind characteristic for natural law which will always prevail among the bulk of the "educated classes" and will also, again and again, shatter the forced historical airs *(Allueren)* of the jurists."[2]

The impact of natural law, as *naturalis ratio*, upon the development of Roman law was comparable to the impact of Roman law, turned universal, upon the formation of German law. Regarding the latter process, not much remained to be done for the new natural law except for a fundamental change in the concepts of public law. Natural law claims to be a private law applicable to the mutual relations and transactions, not merely of men who happen to live within the same political borders but of civilized mankind altogether. In the latest draft of the German civil code, there will, indeed, be found hardly a provision or tenet which could be proven to suit "Germans" while running contrary to the common spirit *(Volksgeist)* of Austrians, Italians, Frenchmen, or Englishmen. In these countries, as well as in Germany, customs are contrary to the code. But few such customs bear a national imprint—national in the sense of modern nations—except, perhaps, the customs of the Anglo-Saxon peoples who have been able to preserve some of the principles of ancient Germanic law. But even so, most of these Anglo-Saxon customs are of a regional or local character. No wonder, then, that nowadays we often *call* "national" that which is in

---

[1]   Observe that this article was written in 1894.—Eds.
[2]   Gierke, in *Schmoller's Jahrbuch fuer Gesetzgebung* etc., XIII, 929.

actual fact cosmopolitan, all present-day national tendencies being nothing but preliminary restricted versions of international ideas generated by worldwide trade and communication. Moreover, the demands of everyday practice urgently require the formation and continuous adjustment of an international private law.

To the present day Roman law serves as common law in German territories. Whenever a special state law or local law proves inadequate, Roman law is applied as a subsidiary. Thus the latter is assumed to be the basic law which has been transformed in various ways according to specific needs. In that case, specialized law is considered of a higher order than general law. If, however, legislation generates a new general law, that law is supreme, and the principle is upheld that federal law breaks local law, general law breaks particular law. Only by an explicit decree can, in this case, provisions of particular law remain in force.

In actual fact, common law has always broken local law, because the jurists—lawyers and judges alike—maintained it was the true and proper law, the *ratio scripta,* as I believe Roman law has been called. According to Savigny, the jurists, in developing the law, represent the people at a stage of cultural advance. He did not even realize that, by virtue of applying Roman law, the jurists had the same revolutionary and leveling effect which he feared would result from a codification of civil law. The trend about which Savigny had no misgivings—in contrast to his predecessor Hugo— and which he did not intend to check, led then and still leads to the lifting of all restrictions on civil law, on arbitrary property, on private contracts. It is a question of minor importance whether prescriptive law undergoes change in this direction as a result of scholarly efforts, of interpretation and reinterpretation, or because of legislative action. And as the mind of the jurist could conceivably follow a different trend, under a different set of circumstances, so can the mind of the legislator tend toward repealing this entire development.

In political economy, too, a "historical" school has long since risen against the rationalist one—initially claiming it would match the achievements of the historical school of law. But the analogy is very inadequate. A precise definition of the shared features has never been reached. And the historical school of economics [*Nationaloekonomie*] lost its self-confidence even earlier than historical jurisprudence. Indeed, its foremost representative characterizes the descriptive works of economic history merely as "building blocks for a theory of economics," and states the "philosophical-sociological character" of today's economics (G. Schmoller, article "Volkswirtschaft" in *Handwoerterbuch der Staatswissenschaften*). Representatives of both historical economics and historical jurisprudence have occasionally tried to replace by an "organic view" of social life the "mechanical" approach of the theories which they oppose. But "to the present day the philosophical mastery of this idea (the idea of historical-organic law) has remained insufficient" (Gierke, *Althusius*, 317), and "so far, the argument in favor of this conception—considering the state as well as the economy as an organism—has been unable to win a broader recognition."[3]

Now, if the historical doctrines had no other intention than to present law and economy in a historical perspective, nobody would deny this to be a significant contribution. However, their cutting edge apparently consists in contending—while forgoing, more or less explicitly, conceptualization and theory—that no other approach is at all possible or fruitful. And yet the champions of historical law and historical economics attempt to draw practical conclusions from their historical views—oddly enough, contradictory conclusions. The historic importance of the historical school of law—which it nowadays renounces—consisted in its opposition to arbitrary action by the state and its insistence on leaving the formation of civil law, in all its essentials, to the people and to its natural organ, the profession of law. The historical school of economics, on the other hand, essentially is a school of social *policy*. It grew out of the opposition against the doctrine that the wealth of a nation would increase most if the state did *not* interfere with the natural fluctuations of trade and commerce but pursued a policy of laissez-faire toward the people and particularly its organ, the entrepreneurs. Everybody knowing his own economic advantage and natural confrontation of supply and demand resulting in

[3]   Cf. v. Scheel in Schönberg, *Handbuch der politischen Oekonomie* I, 104.

an ever renewed balance, the unrestricted competition among sellers would necessarily produce the best and least expensive goods and the greatest economic happiness.

Savigny, referring to history, wants to destroy the erroneous assumption that "under normal conditions all law results from legislation, that is, from explicit prescription by the state." Once such an assumption prevails, it results necessarily in the demand to replace the system of particular and deficient laws by a common and rational law posited by the state. The political economists want to disprove from history the erroneous assumption that free individuals have always been capable of self-regulation in trade and commerce—provided the state protected their lives and property. Rather, they contend, restrictive measures were taken by the authorities, and, given the respective cultural level, these restrictions as a rule, have been beneficial. This historical interpretation easily leads to the postulate that, likewise, with regard to the national economy of today, state intervention be not opposed in principle but that its efficacy be considered as a problem in each specific case—the argument being that the merit of state intervention can be established only by the empirical-inductive method, that is, historically. Thus the historical school of law sees the "organic" element in the people—"the quietly moving forces" [*die still-wirkenden Kraefte*]—and regards the state and its arbitrary action as moved by a rather "mechanical" force. By contrast, the historical school of economics tends to consider the contractual relations of isolated individuals as merely mechanical relations and insists on the "organic theory of the state," sympathizing with the doctrine that the individual can "exist only within the state" and regularly confounding the matter with Aristotle's *zoon politikon*.

We notice here ideas that are matched crosswise. The work of Savigny, as well as that of Adam Smith and the physiocrats, resulted from a reaction against the wisdom of the statesmen who thought they governed the nation according to rational principles, be it in a feudal or a parliamentary regime, during a revolution or in an empire. Both favor societal forces. Savigny wants to counter the government with the rational spirit of the jurists; Adam Smith, with that of the merchants and industrialists, including the farmers. Savigny believed that the unimpeded rationality of the jurists, if intensified through the study of Roman law, would be an essentially conservative force, counteracting the "idea of uniformity" which "in Europe for so long has had an impact of unlimited scope, powerful beyond description" and which "aims at the destruction of individuality in all sectors of life." Adam Smith regarded the entire historical development of economic life as "unnatural." Influenced totally by Quesnay, he was under the illusion that the abolition of all state favors and restrictions would benefit most of all agriculture, this being the most productive trade and, further —as he hints—morally superior to manufacture and commerce. In this particular sense, also Adam Smith must be considered a conservative. He, too, regards the state as a revolutionary force. And yet his ideas are rooted in natural law, as are those of the Physiocrats, while the historical school was violently opposed to natural law. The core of natural law is as follows: it assumes free individuals confronting each other, and the will of the state, resulting from their will, placed above them; and it postulates a correctly calculating reason at work in the contracts between individuals and in state legislation. The doctrines disagree on the boundaries between society—the ensemble of individuals—and the state, the collective person. The historical schools, on the one hand, oppose historical opinions contained in the system—a matter not to be dealt with in the present context—on the other hand, they oppose what they call the rationalistic construct. In doing so, they do not distinguish between rationalism inherent in the object, that is, objective rationalism, and rationalism employed in the method, that is, subjective rationalism. The political economists doubt the rationalism of society, the jurists criticize the rationalism of the state. However, hardly asked and certainly not solved is the question whether there can be any other science in this field (beyond mere description) than one employing a rationalistic construction.

It is my contention that society and state tend intrinsically toward rationalism, that is, toward free utilitarian thought—be it individual or collective—and that the same rationalistic trend belongs to the essence of science, occurring here as the trend toward the free construction of efficacious concepts. Furthermore, I am contending that the "historical" approach represents, apart from whatever else it may mean, also the transition to a new type of rationalistic approach toward the facts of social life. In my opinion, the characteristic feature common to all variations of rationalistic thought and volition is a principle of domination *(Herrschaft)*. Consequently, rationalism aims in every field at expansion and even generalization, be it extensive or intensive. Furthermore, to facilitate domination, the rationalistic approach necessarily subdivides its field, rendering the objects of domination as equal and as independent from each other as possible, so that the units can be combined and arranged at will and brought into systems. But first and foremost, reason itself must get disentangled, emerging victorious and absolute from the network of affiliations in which it is caught up.

Rationalistic Processes in Modern History

The rationalistic tendencies themselves, then, are facts of history, and among the most important. They are manifestations of the movement which runs through the entire social development of all modern peoples, if in various forms. It surmounts most easily the obstacles arising in its very own field, namely, science. Other resistances are harder to overcome. The movement has to defeat all sentiments and interests bent on preserving each historic stage. It is always revolutionary. Its own structures become conservative as soon as they solidify and to the extent to which they have grown rigid. On the other hand, all stabilized powers were once revolutionary, because rational tendencies are never entirely absent wherever a social development occurs. However, different tendencies prevail in different epochs, and this makes for the sharp contrast between epochs. All rationalistic tendencies are being assimilated as long as the prevailing tendencies aim at permanent settlement, the formation and conservation of customs, and faith in the reality of the figments of imagination. But these tendencies diminish as soon as the rationalistic tendencies gain superior strength, liberate themselves, and become dominant. Distinguished from all isolated manifestations of rationalistic trends, there are now evolving the forces that represent social reason per se: society, state, science. All three are merely concepts labeling the tendencies that prevail in the different sectors of social life: in the economic, political, and intellectual spheres. In the economic domain, the rationality of individuals is unleashed by their desire for wealth, which to a larger or lesser degree is present in all men, that is, by their desire to utilize and increase existing possessions. In the political realm, the same effect is brought about by the natural desire or the felt obligation to rule, more precisely: by the task of utilizing and expanding a given power over human beings. In the intellectual field, it is curiosity that engages thought most immediately. Here the most important task is to utilize and extend the calculability of events, the command of nature.

These tasks and tendencies are interrelated. To a certain degree they promote each other. Conflicts between them are secondary.

The societal (*Gesellschaft*-like) process is essentially one of rationalization, and shares fundamental characteristics with science. It elevates the rational, calculating individuals who use scientific knowledge and its carriers in the same way they use other means and tools. An establishment in trade or commerce is comparable to a mechanical construction [*Mechanismus*], the entrepeneurial will being the motor. A mechanism is characterized by the relative independence of its parts and by their concerted action. Theoretically, there is no limit to the scope of such coordination and concerted action of tools arranged by careful design; experience shows its steady increase. Likewise unlimited is the growth of cooperation between human volitions and powers, which is intimately related, in the field of productive work, to the application of tools. The increase in machinery as well as the enlargement of businesses and factories is cause and, at the same time, effect of the victory of the most powerful wills in the competitive struggle. It is irrelevant whether these most powerful wills are actually individual wills or whether they are associated and merely act like individual wills. For, as the particles of unorganized matter join or are being joined to achieve mechanical effects, so it is with human wills and powers, if we consider them apart from their organic context. Their dependent, subordinated, regulated cooperation takes place in factories and shops. Their free, coordinated, associated cooperation can be directed toward any goal, but because the volition is commercial, the goal is essentially commercial also. Another goal is the extension of businesses or factories through the acquisition of further establishments—usually by purchase.

Association can take three forms:

1. the fusion of entire enterprises or establishments. Such an association is often free only in name, while in actual fact a larger establishment absorbs smaller ones;

2. the combination of entire legal persons, that is, of their total capital, for the pursuit of common enterprises;

3. the association of individuals who designate certain limited portion of their capital for common enterprises.

Primarily, the individual businessman or the collective enterprise cause movement, namely, a change of place. The merchant moves himself, objects of every description, human beings of all kinds. Motion is especially important to him for the delivery of information, orders, samples, and so forth by land and by water. He aims at the greatest possible speed, because being first brings him profit. Yet he also generates motion in people who remain in the same place, causing them to move their arms and legs; he becomes a manager of work processes by gathering workers—formerly isolated—under his command, and by directing and arranging them in a common workshop, to parcel out among them a unified production process. This is merely a special form of the purchase of commodities. Purchase in advance amounts to placing orders, ordering turns into order taking and finally into production under the capitalist's own name, production of his own merchandise.

Primarily, societal (*Gesellschaft*-like) rationalism means the unleashing and promotion of production and trade, under the general protection of the law. Its champion is the propertied class, which always consists of three sectors, owning (1) real estate, (2) the means of production, (3) money, that is, capital. In all three sectors, those individuals matter mainly who own the respective means in abundance, next those who are fiercely determined to increase their smaller share. The third sector embodies the general concept of the whole class, money being capable of transformation into real estate or means of production. Money is the absolute means. Real estate and means of production are calculated in terms of money insofar as they are considered as means for the acquisition of money. In a historical perspective, therefore, the merchant is the genuine carrier of rationalism and progress in society. He is accompanied by the less active and less visible money-lending capitalist. At the same time, the businessman represents rational man in general—understood as the human being whose total effort serves as a means to one clearly defined end, namely, his personal advantage, and who consequently degrades everything —objects and men alike—to the level of means. The owner or tenant of a landed estate and the manufacturer become increasingly similar to the merchant the more they aim at the production of commodities, that is, the more their activities become a business. The merchant, on the other hand, can pass into both forms, but more readily into that of the manufacturer. This is so because the manufacturer is socially close to the merchant, and as a rule, both are urban, and because in manufacturing the production of commodities lends itself better to limitless expansion.

The generalization of the commercial or business type is of special importance for social history. It marks a trend that counteracts the division of labor as expressed in its original form in the division of society into estates [*Staende.*] Ruling estates are being replaced by a ruling class. The old aristocracy of the soil, the "landed interest," merges with the new aristocracy of the capital, "the monied interest."[4] The ecclesiastical aristocracy is caught in the middle and is being pushed down from its superior position. A rule of priests becomes the more irksome the more it loses its counterbalance in the form of a secular patriarchalism. Nevertheless, it can maintain its strength to the extent that it either remains powerful through landed property or turns commercial and capitalist itself.

Economic Development and Social Change

Furthermore, the commercial and capitalistic direction of economic processes changes and finally reverses the traditional

---

4   Cf. Knapp, *Die Landarbeiter in Knechtschaft und Freiheit*, dealing with the transformation of the manorial system into one of commercially operated large estates in German territories.

forms of the division of productive labor.[5] It does so in three respects:

(1) *The Commercialization of production.*—The merchant or manufacturer becomes the boss of the combined shops each of which was formerly run by its particular master. Now there is no longer any need for the "practice that makes for mastery," for the taste and cultivation of the mind that in the nobler lines of work used to turn the master artisan into an artist. The businessman is the true jack-of-all trades. His art consists in assigning work, that is, eliciting it from artists and other workers. Very often, however, the individual manufacturer turned merchant serves in actual fact as the technical director of the work processes which he initiated. If acting in this capacity, he does specialized work. But we have to differentiate here between two aspects of his activity. Either he can be concerned with producing goods for consumption, aiming therefore at a product of perfect quality, or he can be preoccupied with producing goods as commodities for exchange, aiming, therefore, at the largest possible quantity of commodities made as marketable as possible. The work of the technician qua technician is intellectual work of the highest caliber. But if done under the second aspect, it is only an offshoot of the businessman's work. Although it may involve a considerable amount of mental work, business activity per se is never a social activity, in contrast to the production of goods as goods and the rendering of service as service—even in a fully developed exchange, or market, economy. Production of goods and services, however, loses that natural quality to the extent that they

[5]   In recent years, rich in sociological inquiries and discussions, attention has focused anew on the division of labor, a *locus communis* in political economy since Adam Smith. It has long been noticed that the term refers to very different social phenomena, and there have been efforts to define the concept more precisely, to differentiate between various kinds of the division of labor, etc. To be noted in particular are G. Schmoller, "Die Tatsachen der Arbeitsteilung" and "Arbeitsteilung und sociale Klassenbildung," *Jahrbuch* XIII, XIV; K. Buecher in *Entstehung der Volkswirtschaft*, p. 119 ff. As far as I can see, neither author has so much as touched upon the *involution* of the division of labor which I am treating in the present article. Nor has Emile Durkheim in his book *La division du travail social*, which deals at length with the moral aspect of the division of labor.

are being pressed into the service of commercial speculation,[6] thus turning into the production of commodities or quasi commodities. This is precisely what happens as they progress along rational lines. Speculation is certainly no particular skill; it is nothing but egoistic thinking—a common human trait.

(2) *The Transformation of the social divison of labor.*—For this very reason, the fully developed production of merchandise tends to negate the division of labor by transforming it and providing it with new features. The trend presented under point (1) is directed against the subjective side of the division of labor while leaving the objective side intact, and even intensifying it. The manufacturer having turned merchant and speculator is no longer a "divided" producer, that is, a specialized and highly competent producer of particular goods. He concentrates his effort on a highly differentiated, most specialized category of commodities, with the intention of unloading them on the market in the largest possible quantity and either as perfect as possible (which is unessential) or as marketable as possible (which is essential). He is not limited in his capability to produce a broad range of goods. But his capital is limited, and the production of specialized goods serves his purpose better, to the extent that it avoids competition and responds to specialized demands. The objective division of labor, as a rational and new method, differs decisively from the old one, which had developed historically. The latter stems from an originally undifferentiated process of labor, which subdivides and becomes structured and, by virtue of this very process, preserves its unity. The former is being devised by entrepreneurs, each of whom selects a part without any other concern for the whole than the intention to convert their respective merchandise into money—money representing all other commodities. All commodities taken together can be considered a whole. It is an ideal whole, a thought product, namely, the joining of all commodities in the market.

The natural whole, by contrast, is an active entity; it is the real economy of a commonwealth, be it a household or a farm, a village or a town community, or an entire people with its national economy. What today is called a national economy (*Volkswirtschaft*)

6   Cf. Goldschmidt, *Handbuch des Handelsrechts*, 2d. edition, pp. 408, 412. See also K. Marx, *Kapital* I, 4th. edition, p. 113, note 4.

"is based . . . on an abstraction"; this national economy "lacks a subject."[7] The true condition of the objective division of labor in the context of a national economy becomes apparent when we realize the following: national economies, particularly the large and important ones, are not self-sufficient, but are necessarily part of a larger, theoretical whole, namely, the world economy (*Weltwirtschaft*): the capitalist mode of production results with necessity in an international division of labor. As the economy in one country becomes predominantly industrial, it needs to be supplemented by the economies of agricultural countries. However, the international division of labor stands in striking contrast to all natural division of labor. The latter may be compared with the organic life process, as contrasted to an utilitarian kind of exchange.[8]

The international division of labor takes place not between the countries but between the manipulators of capital. It is not at all important for the objective capitalistic specialization of labor to separate specialized workshops which are linked solely by means of the market; that is but a historical continuation of the precapitalist stage. Rather, capital tends toward integration of the specialized establishments—and the more so, the more it grows, becomes unified, expands, and emancipates itself from the control of its individual owners. The last traces of the subjective division of labor vanish whenever the individual capitalist is transformed into a corporative capitalist, by way of joint-stock companies. This transformation is also the most convenient way to increase indefinitely the capital employed for identical objectives and—contrary to the objective division of labor—to combine heterogeneous enterprises in a system where they lose their independence. The coalition of homogeneous enterprises, for instance, in trusts or cartels, represents a different process although it moves in a similar direction. The process is different because it eliminates competition, but not the division of labor; after having reached its peak, competi-

[7]   The terms are taken from A. Wagner, *Grundlegung* I, 3d edition, p. 354.
[8]   Cf. Ferdinand Toennies, "Herbert Spencer's Soziologisches Werk," in *SStuKr.* I, pp. 75–104. (First publ. in *Philosoph. Monatshefte* 1888, p. 71 f.)

tion among giant enterprises is abandoned as irrational and harmful; it moves in a similar direction because here, too, the enterprises lose their independence as they combine in a system; their specialization—while possibly facilitated—no longer represents the division of labor on a national or international scale but merely a differentiated part of the parent system. So far the very process of combination can be observed only in its significant beginnings, although it has long been foreshadowed by the indifference of capital regarding the ways in which it is being applied.

The combination of an industrial mode of production and agriculture on large estates is rooted, in part, in earlier conditions.[9] Even if it is not a matter of latifundia which defy the division of labor by virtue of their accumulated wealth, the boundaries between agriculture and industry are, nevertheless, getting blurred, as agriculture gears itself to the world market and increases its internal division of labor. The more agriculture concentrates on growing marketable products and turning them, as much as possible, into commodities ready for export, the more it develops into an industry and becomes alienated even from its orginal purpose of feeding at least its own labor force. But more remarkable in our context is the tendency of centralized capital to abandon the principle of self-restriction basic to the modern objective division of labor. It is already being violated in many instances. The principle "Never produce anything which you can buy" is now being replaced by the principle "Never buy from others what you can produce yourself"[10]—a principle which, once in operation, is capable of limitless consequences. Eventually it would lead to the concentration of all major industries within a smaller or larger economic area under the command of one unified capital. The absurdity of

9   T. W. Teifen, "Das soziale Elend und die 'Gesellschaft' in Osterreich," *Deutsche Worte* XIV, 1.
10   Cf. Sidney Webb, lecture, delivered before the Economics Section and the "*British Association*," Oxford 1894; comments on Webb's lecture by E. Bernstein in *Die neue Zeit*, 1894/95, p. 22 ff.) ; J. A. Hobson, *The Evolution of Modern Capitalism* (London, 1894, p. 93 ff.) ; Ludwig Sinzheimer, *Ueber die Grenzen der Weiterbildung des fabrikmässigen Grossbetriebes in Deutschland* (Stuttgart, 1893), pp. 20–30. Cf. K. Marx's earlier and comparable observation in *Kapital* (4th ed., p. 312).

private property in this very capital would be so heightened thereby that it should become obvious even to the most casual observer. The second principle, then, paves the way for a total national economy planned by society; and this in defiance of the intentions of the individual "bosses," who thus usher in what they abhor.

(3) *The Transformation of the internal division of labor.*— The ultimate and most powerful effect of capital upon the division of labor occurs within the enterprise which is controlled by capital. It parallels the entire social division of productive labor, and is almost from the outset what the latter becomes only in the course of its development: artificial, that is, generated, or at least appropriated and established, by explicit and arbitrary human action. The appropriation is the most convenient form of transition from one system to the other; it occurs whenever the production of use values (for individual customers), which require extensive cooperation, turns into the production of commodities (for the market). Karl Marx, in his classical description of the "dual origin of manufacture," uses as an example the (horsedrawn) carriage, "the joint product of the work of a large number of independent craftsmen."[11] He might just as well have mentioned the house, produced as a commodity of a compound of commodities, although in this case we do not encounter a consolidated, permanent workshop. As long as the house is being built for a specific proprietor or for a municipality, the customer benefits directly from the divided labor— which remains on the level of production commissioned by the customer (*Kundenproduktion*), as Karl Buecher has aptly labeled it. Here the division of labor is not only social, meaning that it sustains independent enterprises, but it also essentially retains its communal (*gemeinschaftlich*) character because it is not yet conditioned by the market-oriented production of commodities. But the speculative production of houses turns the craftsmen in the building trades from household suppliers into servants of capital. While they retain their divided functions, these are no longer relevant to the social division of labor. The market knows only the building industry.

11   K. Marx, *Kapital* I (4th edition, p. 300).

The other root of manufacturing is much more important in our context because it is the true orginator of a new and artificial division of labor, employing it as a means to the end of maximizing the effect of cooperation in favor of quantity or, to put it the other way around, minimizing the amount of labor required for a given product (labor is measured in terms of working time to be paid for). The manufacturer considers the workers, whom he has hired and assembled in his workshop, as his tool and strives to make that tool as effective as possible. Thus he concentrates it and makes it as uniform as circumstances permit. Being unable to weld together physically the workers' bodies, he must be content to amalgamate them conceptually, fashioning a joint worker (*Gesamtarbeiter*) though not a joint man. He does so by directing their combined effort toward a common object—a piece of merchandise to be produced as rapidly as possible. This production process is partly divided into natural stages, and partly it is subdivided arbitrarily. The resulting segments are assigned in part to the natural units (namely, individuals) and in part to the artificial units of the joint worker (namely, groups of individuals). The same individual—and consequently the same group of workers—performs for ever the same segmental operation, acquiring virtuosity in the particular skill that it demands. Formerly the individual worker made a complete product, but could produce its parts only successively; now he becomes a component of a collective worker who produces all these parts simultaneously.

The difference between this artificial division of labor and the natural one has been well noted by more recent authors, while Adam Smith, in his time, nearly overlooked it—which did not prevent his chapter on the division of labor from becoming famous. Yet, as far as I can see, only Karl Marx expressly stresses that the two kinds of division of labor are different not merely in degree but in substance.[12]

While in manufacturing, the "divided" worker always uses a specialized tool for his specialized work, a further change takes place as capitalistically controlled production progresses. Now the

---

[12] K. Marx, *Kapital* I (4th edition, p. 319).

"combined" worker is confronted with a combined tool, namely, the machine or, eventually, a system of machines—belonging not to the worker but to the employer, who also owns the worker's labor power. This presupposes an analysis of the work process, dissecting it into its smallest constituent parts, and, as a consequence, the reduction of divided labor to the handling of the simplest tools possible. "The combination of all tools and their subordination to one single motor power constitutes a machine" (Babbage, *Economy of Manufacture*, 172). Once the machine has grown beyond a certain size, the individual can no longer manipulate it. He can merely perform a particular service at it. Consequently, the artificial division of labor disappears, the machine taking over the specialized labor previously performed by man. Heating the machine, supervising, regulating, feeding, cleaning it, in short, servicing the machine may still be called labor, but it is general, unqualified labor and does not differ subjectively from "personal" services. No human master, however, imposes such steady attention, such monotonous movements as does the "mechanical monster whose body fills entire factories and whose demonic force, first hidden under the almost solemnly measured motion of its giant limbs, erupts in the feverish, frantic whirl of its countless organs of work."[13]

Rationalization Continued: The Processes of Gesellschaft May Result in New Forms of Gemeinschaft

We have seen that societal (*Gesellschaft*-like) rationalism, as it becomes manifest in trade, leads to the reduction and eventual elimination of the subjective division and specialization of labor. It returns men to a state where they are undifferentiated and alike with regard to the work they are able to perform. At one extreme we find the capitalists being unspecified and alike, at the other extreme the workers. If the trend runs its full course, in each of the two categories everybody will be able to do everything, the capital-

[13]   K. Marx, *Kapital* I, p. 345. Extensive quotes from such authors as Ure, Hobson, Schmoller and Justus Moeser follow in the German text, but are omitted here.—EDS.

ists through their command over property and the workers with their bodies, that is, with their labor power, which is considered detachable from the person. Theoretically, women and children within each class participate fully in this equality, although in practice there are modifications and limitations. Between both groups, however, we find the actual managers of productive labor. According to the nature of their work, they belong to labor, representing its highest potential and its natural authority. But social organization makes them serve capital and gives them the appearance of representing capital. In their capacity as *actual* managers they direct the workers, along with the lords of capital, and they rule the working class in the interest of capital. *Ideally*, however, they serve the labor process and consequently the laboring class of which they are a part; if the working class stood in an unmediated relation to the production process, the managers would emerge from it as an organic part of the working class. But we have to make certain distinctions here. Management is divided into commercial and technical managements corresponding to the two aspects of production, namely, the generation of exchange value and use value. To an overwhelming extent, commercial management is determined by its capitalistic nature. As long as that persists, commercial management will dominate over technical management.

If the capitalistic nature of commercial management could be abolished, the relationship would reverse itself, commercial management being reduced to the technical level of bookkeeping and correspondence between the cooperating production plants. The entire group thus wavering between the social classes can be called the group of intellectual workers (*geistige Arbeiter*). They distinguish themselves by new qualifications, not so much in regard to skills as in regard to knowledge. Societal (*Gesellschaft*-like) rationalism, which otherwise is a great leveler, has given this class a very specific physiognomy within the economic process.

From this vantage point one can consider societal (*Gesellschaft*-like) rationalism in its other form, which up to now exists only ideally. It is the logical consequence, as well as the sequence in time, of the first form of societal rationalism which has spoken its last word, as it were, by bringing about the situation outlined

above, namely, the advent of coalitions of competing establishments and of combinations of related enterprises; furthermore,
the transformation—thanks to technology—of the previous system of the division of labor within the workshop. The capitalistic
class tends not toward extension but toward contraction. This is
so despite speculations that it is about to broaden its base. Such
speculations can arise and persist as long as there is merely a
slow pace of social change. They may gain renewed vigor as
often as social change slackens or quickens its pace, both changes
of pace being capable of a reconciliatory effect upon the mind.
Splitting up large estates into individual lots; cooperative involvement of large numbers of people in industrial enterprises; improv-
ing the workers' standard of life through parsimony, birth control,
or finally, strikes concerning wage levels, carried on by trade unions, and so forth—all these are being suggested, more or less in
good faith, as a remedy against absolute plutocracy. But ideas of
this kind carry no weight in the present context because they lack
any principle of fundamental change comparable to the one contained in rationalism, which signals a relentless trend.

The working class aims at generalizing its condition by pursuing the results of capitalistic development to its ultimate consequences, with the hope of thereby reversing their effect. It conceives of a future in which the most progressive relation of the
capitalists to production will have been made universal. The capitalists' income is purely unearned revenue or profit from trade. A
considerable portion of the income of technical managers, likewise, is derived from profit. The capitalistic establishments have
become quite independent from their owners, as is demonstrated
especially by the joint-stock companies. Nevertheless, they are being managed as if their objective were the enlargement of their
owners' fortune and income and its true object, which includes the
production of goods, *were* merely a means to this end.

From the perspective of an entire nation or an international
working class, there is no such relation of means and end. Rather,
the production of goods has its intrinsic value, as far as these goods
answer human needs. Goods do not require being changed into
money and then changing back the money into goods. This is a

detour employed by the capitalistic class, to the end of distributing profit as much as possible to its own advantage; it brings about an increasing involvement of productive labor in the boundless world economy; an adequate food supply for a large population comes to depend exclusively on the fluctuations of international trade, so easily upset in its balance. Yet, a nation that wishes to act intelligently should regard it as its first and foremost economic task to produce the indispensable supplies by its own labor. Although the population has increased and will continue to increase, sufficient food for all could be secured regularly, considering the technical and scientific means provided by our civilization. Industry would in part serve this purpose directly, and in part it would be linked up with it or be based upon it. Manual work, and thereby the arts and crafts, would be reinstated in its rightful place with regard to all goods that need not be produced on a mass scale in order to secure the fundamental requirements of a satisfactory standard of living for the total population. There would be ample time for that kind of work because "crude" labor will be taken care of completely by the machine, the scope of machine work no longer being limited by considerations of private profit but solely by taste and moral judgment. The means of production would be common property. Consumer goods would no longer be produced as commodities, nor would their quantity and distribution be determined any more by the consumption and exchange needs of a tiny minority enjoying the good life. Rather, consumer goods would be distributed according to the principle of justice, proceeding from equality to adequacy. That is, every family employed in the nationwide production enterprise would be entitled to a certain amount of goods representing its share in the annual product of collective labor. It would be up to the individual family to produce with its own tools and means and according to its own taste and mentality —or to obtain through exchange—whatever additional goods it desires for the adornment of life. The effort of the working people, which so far has been stood on its head by the reasoning of the egotists who drained its blood, will be put back on its feet through the reasoning of the people themselves and will thus regain the security of being firmly planted in its natural soil.

These considerations and the enormous problem that they pose take as their point of departure the ascertainable facts and are meant to draw their consequences. The facts are not only those of technology and the scientific mastery of nature but also those of the social order which—having been transformed by technology and science—prepares the way for its own abolition (*Aufhebung*) by precipitating the course on which it is set. The independent establishments on whose privilege and utility that social order is based become less and less numerous because of the increased prevalence of giant-sized enterprises; the remaining few depend no longer on the enterprising spirit and the efficiency of the go-it-alone businessman. Furthermore, they lose their individual character by either joining trusts or combining with other enterprises to form larger systems. Competition in selling one's labor power as a commodity is most readily recognized as absurd and consequently abandoned. The overwhelming majority of the population within a country or a culture area no longer being split by the competitive interests of private business, the field is wide open for considerations of the common interest, and the forces of rationalism are being concentrated on its pursuit.

The further the division of labor—demanding a specialization of skills—recedes, the further disappears the necessity that man be chained for a lifetime to the same segmental job. A change of work becomes psychologically desirable and morally imperative. The differentiation of occupations makes it impossible for the industrial worker to return, temporarily, to agriculture. But as agriculture, too, comes to depend increasingly on machines, and "familiarity with a variety of machines" emerges as "the one and only industrial occupation,"[14] the intermittent return to agriculture becomes a matter of course—all to the good of the worker. A telling controversy has arisen about the effect of fully developed machine labor on the human mind. The prevailing opinion admits that, through its monotony, it exhausts the worker, that it ruins the artistic creativity of a people, and that its moral commands are at least extremely one-sided—such as orderliness, exactness, perseverance,

[14]   P. Lafargue, *Die Neue Zeit*, VI, p. 138.

adjustment to a constraining regularity. Yet, on the other hand, we find also an insistence that machine labor has a favorable effect on the human mind. Here the contention is that the increasing size, power, speed, and intricacy of the machine renders more difficult the job of supervising and servicing it, and requires good judgment, close attention, and technical knowledge. "The machines demand . . . a certain loving care on the part of the worker, his understanding of the ideas of technology incorporated in them . . . ; being miraculous works of the human mind, the machines yield the best results when the laborer working at them rises to the level of intellectual work." As the productivity of the individual worker increases, "his responsibility is increasing also . . . This implies the necessity of a gradual improvement of the laboring classes' standard of living."[15] It is obvious that, in the nature of the matter, favorable effects on the mind are possible, that they are latent in the system but are being curbed by the capitalistic form of production, which, however, the system tends to cast off in the course of economic development—owing to the growing necessity of high wages and short working hours. Thus, in every respect, reason demands that mankind, having so well mastered the forces of nature, now master its own works, which so far it has been obliged to serve.

[15]   G. v. Schulze-Gaevernitz, *Der Grossbetrieb*, pp. 167 f., 171. Cf. also Schoenhof, *The Economy of High Wages* (New York, 1892), and L. Brentano, *Ueber das Verhaeltnis von Arbeitslohn und Arbeitszeit zur Arbeitsleistung* (Leipzig, 1893).

20

THE INDIVIDUAL AND THE WORLD
IN THE MODERN AGE

THERE ARE TWO POINTS OF VIEW from which to look upon the modern age and the preceding one, which we customarily call the Middle Ages. The modern age is the continuation of the Middle Ages. It is marked by increased size and density of the population, especially in the cities, a highly developed commerce linking the continents, the growth of large-scale industry, the tremendous advance of science and, tied to science, of technology; it is an age that augments and refines people's needs, their mores, their living patterns, further removing them from the crudity, poverty, and simplicity of the original folk culture—in brief by "modern age" we refer to all that we know and find so often praised as the progress of civilization. For this is the way of looking at it that

---

Translated from *Fortschritt und Soziale Entwicklung* (Karlsruhe: Braun, 1926). pp. 5–35; slightly abridged. The paper was first published in *Weltwirtschaftliches Archiv* 1 (1913) : 37–66.

Toennies refers in this paper to some of the most prominent social scientists of his day. Of these, Jacob Burckhardt, Henry S. Maine, Albert Schaeffle and Alexis de Tocqueville are widely known. Wilhelm Roscher was the head of the "older" historical school of economics in Germany, Gustav Schmoller was the unquestioned leader of the "newer" branch of that school of thought. Heinrich Dietzel and Lujo Brentano belong to the same group of scholars although the latter's importance rests more with his assertion that trade unionism should be considered as a complement rather than as an impediment to the premises of economic liberalism than with his purely historical work. John A. Hobson was a pioneer of the welfare school of economic thought in England. Eberhardt Gothein was an economic historian, Richard W. Dove a historian of law.

strikes us every day in many ways. Yet, within this development, as well as apart from it, the modern age is something altogether different from the Middle Ages. It contains and signifies a reversal, an upheaval, and a renovation, a new principle that turns the difference into an antithesis (*Gegensatz*). The modern age is revolutionary —in every sense, not in the political sense alone.

The modern age, as we understand it, is not a mere name for the last four centuries of European life. It is a concept whose essence and attributes begin to unfold way back in the Middle Ages. As the Middle Ages have remained alive in the modern age, so is the modern age already alive in the Middle Ages.

It is only in the light of sociological concepts that this process can be correctly understood.

The Modern Age as the Antithesis of the Middle Ages

The reversal consists in the fact that a countermovement sets in and gradually comes to prevail—a movement which, because and insofar as it orginates in the first, the main movement to which it is opposed, must be deduced from the first and explained by it.

The first, the main movement, is the trend to specialization, to differentiation and individualization, which necessarily results from the adjustment of an original equality and universality to different living conditions.

First, the universal is the unity of a *people* structured in tribes and clans that are aware of being linked by consanguinity and by a real or fictitious descent from common forebears. Such a people multiplies, migrates, mingles with other peoples, and displaces them; it conquers territory, settles on it, and in many places becomes one (*verwaechst*) with its abode. This is how peoples come to differ, depending on the influences of the climate and the nature of the land; how they come to be one thing in the south and another in the north, one thing in the mountains and another in the plains, one thing on the banks of rivers and another by the seashore. Corresponding differences arise regarding the cultivation of the soil, the utilization of natural resources, and other activities. Already in gray antiquity an exchange of products was thus conditioned, even over great distances; there has always been an extensive field for commercial activities, even though it remained somewhat limited for a long time. Political and religious motivations and institutions combine with these activities to preserve the cohesion and the communality of a people. And yet, all this is far outweighed by the tendency toward independence, toward the individuality of regions and places—an individuality which, however much the general life keeps pouring into it, constantly tends to isolate itself, to delimit itself, to be self-sufficient and self-contained. This tendency becomes all the more pronounced the more remote such places and regions are, the poorer the soil, and the less tempting, therefore, to the conqueror and the trader. But even fertile lands that allow a denser settlement may be closed to them, naturally or artificially; naturally, if they are difficult of access and if they lend themselves to widely scattered habitation, artificially, inasmuch as they resist the intrusion of strangers, an effort in which comparative affluence may be helpful. On the whole, multiplication, diversification, and the refinement of needs will proceed slowly but constantly under these conditions, owing to population growth, to the improvement of roads and the means of transport, and to advances in the division of labor. Working against stability are wars and endemic diseases, although in certain regards even these will stimulate the process.

Second, the universal is the culture of the past, which remains effective even if it should be in remnants only. For the European Middle Ages the cultural base is Roman; within the Roman mold, the deeper Greek culture is continued; in the last phase of Roman development, an Eastern propaganda religion with a claim to universality is included. At first, therefore, these cultural goods are preserved and impersonated by the priests of the Roman Church. As guardians of a great tradition which is considered a sacred tradition, they continue to represent a common will, a common spirit, and thus exert their authority as the teachers and masters of young barbarian peoples. This universality, too, is differentiated in territorial and local developments, but slowly and only in a minor part. In the end, these very elements of the civilization of antiquity play a powerful role in shattering the walls of the Church; soon even the religious "confession" is multiplied and diversified, and becomes petrified in narrow territorial confines as the credo of "national churches" or scattered congregations. But however deeply the universality of the Christian religion, and especially that of the Roman Church, may be rooted in the Middle Ages, there are a variety of aspects in which it does concur with the new universal, inimical though this may be to the spirit of Christianity. The very internationality of the structure of the Church promotes the internationality of trade, and thus of capitalism.

The local differentiations reach their peak in the establishment of free, powerful, wealthy and self-assured cities. It is at those peaks that they start turning into their opposites. For the movement is never completed. The ruling upper strata do not fully participate in it. They remain in contact with each other; they persist in the universal and represent it, especially on account of their superior historical memory and the fact that they are the keepers of documents. However, the countermovement is never entirely absent. No region, no place is entirely cut off from communication. They all have neighbors and maintain relations with those neighbors; they intermarry, observe holidays, exchange gifts with them, they buy and sell merchandise; besides, there are antagonistic contacts that may turn into outright hostilities and frequently will bring them about. Priests come from afar, as do judges, traders, and other travelers. Some of the natives themselves go abroad, most likely the nobler ones, and on their return they will disseminate the knowledge of, and often the admiration for, strange things. They imitate them, and are themselves imitated by friends, neighbors, and subordinates. The result is an equalization, a leveling, though it may take a long time for the essential and preponderant tendency to differentiation to be finally overcome.

The strongest force working toward this is the interest of individuals who meet as isolated individuals but will combine, if their interests coincide. Individuals do this, possibly without regard to the groups to which they belong by occupation or descent; they are essentially free in the choice of the means to their ends.

The countermovement thus represents a return to universality,

or at least a tendency in this direction. But though the new universality appears to have many points of contact with the old one, it
is essentially different. It issues from the individuals and is in the
main their thought, their idea. The new universal is an ideal construct, whereas the old universal is a reality manifested as such in
the emotions and the thoughts of men.

First and foremost, this reality is primarily (a) the bond of kinship which is alive and maintains itself in the consciousness of a
people, more intensely in that of a tribe or even more so in that of
a gens or clan. Further, it is (b) the land that is jointly inhabited
and appropriated whether it is believed to have been their homeland from time immemorial or whether it has been conquered and
settled by force. The homeland as well as family cohesion is the
source of the concepts of joint title and joint rights which continue
in the village community, the superimposed manorial law and feu-
dalism notwithstanding. Third, however, the old universality and
communality are realized (c) in the deities that are conceived as
real and in their abodes; the faithful pay homage to them. All of
these universalities are differentiated, localized, and thereby intensified. The individual human being, notably the common man, that
is, the one who does not belong to the ruling classes, feels bound
by the rules, customs, and religious precepts that surround and
condition him. The closer they are brought to him each day and
hour, the more entwined they are with the habits of his life and work,
the stronger will be his sense of their binding force. The division
of labor, the separation of classes and estates, the hearth and home
where the individual finds himself embedded—all of these have
this effect.

It is *in* these unions (*Verbindungen*) and *out of* them, but even
more so *alongside* them, that the "individual" evolves in the particular sense that has become a sociological concept: both the individual and individualism. As a rule, to be sure, we do not talk about
individualism as if it were a view, a turn of mind, an idea, or an
ideal, whether we hold it to be true and good or false and repre-
hensible. Of late, it has become fashionable to treat individualism
as a mistake corrected by the deeper insights of today, a mistake
that has brought about many good things, for instance, the uni-

versal acceptance of personal liberty, but that must also bear the blame for evils, such as the predominance of capitalism. Such opinions give expression to an intellectualist prejudice, as if thought were the primary function of the human mind—a prejudice closely related to the pride in the nobility of men and to its theological transfiguration. Even the concepts of socialism and communism that are regarded as the antithesis of individualism, are primarily presented as "systems": imaginary structures and constructions that may, for instance, lead to the strange proposal (by H. Dietzel), to call such systems "socialism" if they are derived from the social principle (*Sozialprinzip*), while the other construction, rooted in the individual principle (*Individualprinzip*) and having the central idea of realizing the common good of all individuals, should be termed "communism."[1]

In a most vigorous contradiction to this approach, I referred in the first edition of my book *Gemeinschaft und Gesellschaft* (1887) to communism and socialism as "*empirical* forms of culture." That is to say, I do not regard them primarily as systems of thought but as systems of life, as realities that rest on man's *essential will* in which thought is included as an organ, or else on thought alone, that is, on *arbitrary will*, which is guided in the first place by thought or reason—but always referring to the thought and volition of their own subjects, not to mere theory that approaches the facts from the outside. As far as the concept of "communism" is concerned, this was not a neology; it is accepted usage to speak of the conditions of property in early stages of civilization as "original communism," "family communism," "agrarian communism," or "primitive communism." Likewise, the institutions under which certain religious communities, like the Oneida or the Dukhobors live, or used to live, in the United States and elsewhere are usually called communism. And does socialism exist only as an idea, a dream, a wish, a goal of human endeavor? Is the cry of "sheer socialism" not raised on all sides and in all countries against all kinds of legislative innovations, against the protection of the working man and social security, against nationalization and com-

[1] H. Dietzel in *Z. f. Lit. u. Gesch. d. Staatswissensch.*, vol. I, 2 art. "Individualismus" in HW[3], p. 591.

munalization? Suffice it to cite so astute a sociologist as Schaeffle, who wrote in the third volume of *Bau und Leben des sozialen Koerpers* (1878):

In Church and state, in education and science, socialism is already tangibly present. What the modern or economic form of socialism represents in regard to the productive and distributive processes of actual social impact is a change that has been taking place in other fields for centuries; the rational meaning of socialism is the transformation of family (private) capital into collective capital, of private services into social services, of private labor into professional labor, of private wages into professional salaries.

And even to this economic socialism, Schaeffle would not have paid such comprehensive attention "if it were not now present among us in flesh and blood." He points to the many communal, state, and federal agencies of an economic nature, from national forests and shipyards to arsenals and governmental magazines, the Reichsbank [comparable to the United States Federal Reserve System—EDS.] and the postal service; today he would be pointing to the draft bill or the (German) government's oil monopoly. In England, the concept of municipal socialism has become as widely accepted as that of state socialism has become everywhere. I summed up my own views as early as 1887, when I wrote that the natural and—for us —past but always fundamental structure of civilization is communistic, while the current and evolving one is socialistic.

And what of individualism? "There is no individualism in history and culture, except as it emanates from *Gemeinschaft* and remains conditioned by it, or as it brings about and sustains *Gesellschaft*. Such contradictory relation of individual man to the whole of mankind constitutes the pure problem." In these words of the preface to the first edition of *Gemeinschaft und Gesellschaft*, I indicated the same view which still seems to me to be the right one today.

I am now modifying the first proposition, however. Now I say: It is in communal unions and organized groups and out of them, but to an even greater extent alongside them, that the individual and individualism evolve—and these are the carriers of *Gesellschaft*.

Like all phenomena of the social entity, individualism manifests itself in economic, political, and moral life. And in each, it evolves in the same threefold fashion: *in* the communal unions and organized groups, *out* of them, and *alongside* them.

Gesellschaft Grows within Gemeinschaft

Within communal unions and associations, the development derives from individuals in positions of power, from the men who thus enjoy the greatest freedom from the outset, as they seek to expand their power and to make it as absolute as possible. To them, the association itself and their subordinates become mechanical tools or means to personal ends.

First and foremost, of course, to the end of *economic* enrichment. Most characteristic in this respect for the transition from the Middle Ages to the modern age is the transformation of the traditional form of the lord-vassal relationship (*Grundherrschaft*) to a master-servant relationship (*Gutsherrschaft*). The lord of the manor had a calling, as knight and ruler; the owner of an estate has a business, he directs an agricultural enterprise. The lord of the manor, too, could itch with acquisitiveness, and there is proof that he did so often enough: he could abuse the powers of his office and seek to raise the services and levies of his peasants, he could devastate their fields as a hunter, and could milk the peasant dry by means of judicial fines, as it happened in England in Wycliffe's day. All these manifestations of tyranny would often lead to peasant uprisings, in Germany at the very threshold of the modern age. They kept recurring again and again: in weaker variants, they continue in our time. But such excesses either leave the social fabric unchanged or constitute mere steps on the way to its destruction. The destruction occurs, indeed, when the peasant is forced off the land or bought out or turned into a modern type of serf, or when the abolition of this serfdom finally transforms him into a free but landless rural day laborer.

The lord of the manor may also become a rentier without either calling or business, one whose individualism shows not so much in direct economic action as in other fields. The dependent peasant will then be a tenant or a sharecropper—the first chiefly in

Great Britain and Ireland, the second mostly in the Latin countries of Europe. Most characteristic of this development is the feudal lord's dissolution of his external relationship to the soil. He no longer lives on his inherited land amidst his vassals; at most he keeps it as a luxury place for the summer or as a hunting lodge, while maintaining a regular residence in the city, as the nobility of northern Italy did in the Middle Ages. Or he goes to live at court, to bask in the sun of princely favor but also to obtain economic advantages, such as sinecures or prebends, and political influence with which to protect his prerogatives—a course typified by the seventeenth- and eighteenth-century French nobility. To be sure, the customs and prejudices of the noble estate restrained its individualism, yet the nobles "lived apart from the middle classes, with whom they avoided to assume contacts, and from the lower classes whose goodwill they had forfeited, and as a result the nobility stood isolated from all the remainder of the nation" (Tocqueville). "Only the nobleman whose fortune was insignificant would still reside in the country" (i.e., in a village). But even these "tree falcons" (*hobereaux*), as they were called, displayed an "absence of the heart" that was imposed on them by the conditions of their social status and that Tocqueville described as more lasting and more effective than physical absence. The British squire, too, has in large part turned into a mere landlord, although a number of them have retained some judicial and administrative functions. In general, the months the landlord spends at his castle mean little to the great mass of the rural population. Many a landowner lives permanently in Paris or in Italy, or otherwise travels abroad as an independent gentleman of leisure; rent collecting is done by his officials. Where the tenants remain poor peasants farming miniature plots, as in Ireland, this absenteeism becomes all the more oppressive. The great landowner of countries not yet emerged from a semi-barbarian state, such as Russia, Poland, or the Balkan countries, is likewise characterized to a high degree by life abroad, as is the American dividend millionaire.

In the *political* area, it is chiefly the prince who makes his weight felt as an individual within the traditional organization he is heading. His aim is to make his sovereignty as absolute as the lord of the manor wants to make his property. He may pursue this aim in the belief that it lies in the general interest, in the interest of the state, as whose servant he regards himself; but, at least if he is an average human being, it is more likely that he will simply wish to enjoy his personal power and to indulge in personal pleasures. For state purposes as well as for the needs of his court, he must strive to squeeze or suck money out of his subjects. Political and economic arbitrariness are inseparable. This is why "finance" was equated with simony, secret tricks and wicked schemes by Luther, and with usury and fraud by others. The most successful secretary of the treasury is the new type of statesman who in Italy has assimilated the principles of Machiavellianism. At first, of course, these were intended for the "tyrant," for the illegitimate usurper who would seize control of a city or a whole country; they are the rules of Caesarism. But they are no less valid for the lawful heir to a throne who in contest with the estates of his realm enforces his will as the supreme law. In part, the *raison d'etat* serves to cloak personal ambition; in part, it is consciously advanced as the maxim of the new political society and thereby in effect comes to be all the more revolutionary, that is, all the more destructive of traditional rights and moral convictions. Hence the currency debasements, the issues of paper money at compulsory valuations, the forced loans, government bankruptcies, and other artifices that corrupt a national economy. Like the prince, so must the state—that is to say, the statesman—wage his fight for self-preservation and self-aggrandizement as much as possible as a free individual. In other words, he must choose to be guided by a loose morality that will at best pay some heed to public opinion.

The organized groups of *moral-spiritual* character, of which the churches are the most influential in our history, exert the strongest control over the individual conscience. But this does not preclude the exploitation and extension by the men who head these organized groups of their power over human souls—on the whole, that is, by the priests of their power over the faithful laymen. As a rule, the clergy is superior in sagacity, or at least in knowledge of the mysteries and the miraculous workings of the cult—in other words, of the means to win or lose the favor of supernatural powers. On this ground alone, priests tend to be more conscious individuals, men who will take the liberties required for successful action. They will break through the barriers that inhibit others, will ignore the qualms of conscience that arise from generally valid moral rules that are confirmed by religious commandments. This may seem to be more difficult for a man supposed to personify the divine commandments, but in reality it is made easier by the fact that he is called upon to interpret and apply the commandments that are given into his hands as raw materials which he may, in some measure, shape at will or, in any event, at the will of his superiors.

In the Roman Catholic Church, this loose morality grew out of penitential practice, as a rich casuistic literature discussed the problems of conscience and increasingly permitted following the laxer view even if it was supported by weak authority. This probabilism was tailored to fit the individual case, the requirements of individuals, especially those in high places, and in the modern age the Jesuits became in many ways its most important representatives. In Catholic countries—for the first three centuries (until 1800) still the main culture carriers—they became the methodical heresy hunters, the champions of papal supremacy and, at the same time, insofar as the two were compatible, of princely absolutism. Generally, they became the ecclesiastic politicians who knew how to adapt spiritual power to modern living conditions that were at odds with it, and how to save or to restore the power of the old ruling classes in the growing modern society as well as in the growing modern body politic. This could be done only by modern means, that is to say, by means of capital; and so we find the Jesuit order playing a large and successful role in world commerce and increasingly in industry. The order used its international connections to build up a vast commercial traffic with countries outside Europe, with Lisbon as the center.

The missions were transformed into trading posts, and a thriving business was carried on in cotton, hides, Paraguay tea. . . . In California they acquired large mines, and their factories and sugar refineries were scattered all over Spanish America; in the eighteenth century their trade in colonial products from the French West Indies came to be of primary importance; the Jesuit colleges became magnificent places of exchange where a traveler could establish credit and whose business deals were not subject to any curbs on the rate of interest. (Dove, "Orden, Geistliche" in *Staatswissenschaftliches Woerterbuch*.)

This is an important example, demonstrating that no matter how clearly capitalism and commerce are forces of the modern age, they also serve as tools and weapons for combating the modern spirit, and that the individualism of the profit motive is not exclusively individualistic and personal in its application. Conceptually speaking, it makes no difference whether I serve a joint-stock company or the Society of Jesus. The Middle Ages had already made the priest a pliant muscle within a large social organism by prohibiting his encumbrance with wife and child. The celibate is always more intensely individual than the family man, and as an individual the unwed cleric is no less at the hierarchy's disposal than a soldier at the general's. "I have neither parents nor family," Loyola bade his disciples say; "to me, my father and mother, my brothers and sisters have died; I have no home, no country, no other object of love and reverence than the Order." As Gothein puts it so well, "It might seem puzzling how one can curb a man's will and reduce him, by his own decision, to an automatic instrument of his superiors, and at the same time require that he expertly trains a variety of talents and develops a personal capacity to make decisions. Yet every modern military education solves this puzzle." (*Kultur der Gegenwart* II, Vol. I, p. 174).

Besides having its place above the people, however, not only a large organization such as the Society of Jesus but a professional entity like the clergy constitutes in itself a community headed by single individuals. It is those individuals who guide and enforce the "policy" of the whole, more or less in the interest of this total entity, but also in their personal interest. In doing this, they may be consciously untruthful, and to highly educated individuals the power which a vicar of divinity naturally wields over the minds of the faithful is a great temptation to use it for the benefit of such a community, and thus for their own benefit. This temptation was so much greater when bishops, notably the supreme bishop, were temporal princes as well—a duality that has so far persisted through most of the modern age. It may be an invention, and yet it is a significant invention which quotes a pope as saying that the legends of Christ are extremely useful for governing human souls. Conscious hypocrisy is rarely recognized as such, but it is one of the crown jewels which on occasion adorned even the three bands of the tiara. Wherever man seeks to buttress and to expand his rule, he will encounter the *raison d'etat* that has always been unscrupulous in choosing its means, or at least has more or less thoroughly overcome its scruples. Financial power, in particular, indispensable for such purposes as for all other desired ends, will ruthlessly develop all the arts of dealing with men: judicial and administrative exploitation, the sale of offices, and the debasement of currencies have been extensively practiced by spiritual and temporal dignitaries. These ills are aggravated wherever favoritism, nepotism, and the influence of mistresses weigh upon the courts. In these respects, an immense influence on national mores and economies has been exerted, especially by monarchic governments, for it is in those that individual needs and individualistic actions have the widest scope, the freest play.

Gesellschaft Grows out of Gemeinschaft

Thus far we have considered individualism within the confines of traditional organization, and it appears that in essence it served to maintain these organizational structures even though their maintenance required changes in form. Manor and guild, feudal monarchy, the Church and its orders—all these are medieval in essence; the modern age works against all of them, undermines and subverts them, attacks them by way of opinions, of laws, of competing institutions. They are thus on the defensive, but since the best defense always and everywhere is the attack, we find all of them advancing as well. Their aggressive tendencies are carried by the systematic consciousness of leaders who know how to adapt themselves, and thus their domains, to the new living conditions; and the main requisite of this adjustment is to know the weapons of one's adversaries and competitors and to learn how to use them.

For a more strongly and originally developing individualism is one that seeks to escape from traditional bonds, one that strives for liberty and liberation, one that breaks the chains which hamper its movements and thoughts.

This individualism ranks foremost among the great movements and cultural processes that mark the modern age: the economic, political, and moral-spiritual processes.

In the economic field, the individualistic development is nothing but the decay of the constitution of the medieval community and the medieval guild, that is, of village and town communities as social forces and realities.

Authoritative and cooperative elements are combined in both constitutions. As a rule, the authoritative element predominated in the communal constitution and in the village community, and the cooperative element in the guild constitution and the town community. Individual liberty rebels against both.

No comparative history of the evolution of the European peasantry has yet been written. There are rudiments, as various authors have described the liberation of the peasant in particular countries. But this does not tell us how much the peasant's own wish and will, his own need and effort contributed to every such liberation, to his release from feudal privileges as well as to that from joint duties and privileges. The peasant is not an economic individual by disposition; but he certainly, and increasingly so, has become one over the centuries. Always and everywhere there must have been some peasants whose stronger acquisitive urge and more conscious pursuit of their own interests made them stand out in comparison to their fellows. Rights of occupancy, which were customarily better protected, the proximity and the influence of lively towns and markets—on the whole, what one may call favorable *opportunity*—all these must at all times have done as much to promote this advance into acquisitiveness as legislative and other activities of the central power, with its fiscal interest in placing the individual upon himself. The peasant develops a certain amount of individualism in his struggle for his rights, in litigation against the lords of the manor and against neighbors. He wants to defend tradition, but bit by bit, notably with the aid of urban lawyers, he learns to interpret tradition in his own way. This trend receives a strong stimulus when the ranks of the landholders themselves are complemented by townspeople, a not infrequent occurrence in the Low Countries as early as the fifteenth century, in France during the eighteenth century, and everywhere in recent times. The size of the unit, on the one hand, and, on the other, such specialties as wine, tobacco, and other staple crops could not but favor the intrusion of a money economy. The restraints of mixed holdings, of neighborhood rights, of pasture privileges came to be burdens on a more intensive cultivation. In England and Scotland, the breaking up of common land by enclosures resulted in enlarged private holdings and in the institution of compact, tenant-farmed units which would gradually grow in size with the turn to a scientifically rationalized type of farming. It is this process—and the displacement of the venerable three-field economy by a system which ever more frankly aimed at the achievement of a net profit and thus, as "free" agriculture, adjusted to every shift in market conditions—which characterizes the still far from complete European development.

In colonial countries, above all in the United States, the farmer has been a businessman right from the start. The farming unit comes to resemble a manufacturing enterprise; agricultural machinery is an American invention. As Hobson puts it, American agriculture tends more and more toward a form in which capital plays an increasingly important role, and labor a relatively less important one. In America, as in Europe, the industrialization of agriculture is not necessarily tied to an enlargement of farming units; by intensive cultivation, smaller areas will be better utilized. However, grain cultivation and a free agriculture which is not dependent on animal power will increasingly demand the establishment of giant farms requiring larger and larger capital investments. Up to that point, of course, the individual manager type will be preserved in agriculture, whether as owner, tenant, or supervising official. Schmoller found that "time and again in agricultural enterprise, even in the most modern, one had to fall back on the individual operator with his wife and children, his farm hands and maids-of-all-work." Schmoller remarks that those who love socialist slogans will describe the modernization replacing this system as the intrusion of capitalism into agriculture; but even those who hate murky slogans will be hard put to find a more illuminating term. It is obvious,

however, that in Europe—with the exception of Great Britain—
the peasantry and peasant economy have retained major significance, though considerably burdened and hampered by such silent
partners as the mortgagee and frequently the holder of promissory
notes. In any case, we see the peasant also learn how to become
more of a businessman, and how to cultivate the capitalistic production of goods in cooperatives at least, if not yet as an individual.
The growing mobility and free divisibility of the land are powerful
contributing factors. Property changes hands at a rapidly increasing pace, especially where ground rents have been raised by legislation, and it does not always change into the hands that manage
most economically, but often from one speculator to the next. The
process affects peasant property as well; sooner or later it can be
expected to result in amassment, and it already has had that result
insofar as landholding is prized as a patrician luxury and a safe investment. As a source of income, urban real estate far surpasses the
rural one, and the commodity quality of the land (*Boden*) is more
strikingly apparent in the urban context. The millionaire peasant
and the real estate speculator are closely akin. It is in this area that
individuals and individual capital holdings will combine in development companies and mortgage banks.

Even so, economic individualism will more quickly and deeply
take root in the field of industrial production, and the application of
industrial techniques to agriculture is merely a consequence. Another significant tendency is to make agrarian products similar to
industrial ones—that is to say, to bring them into forms that are
easier to transport as merchandise and more palatable as consumer
goods.

The great event to which modern industry owes much of its
development is the breakup of the institution of the guild. This had
been preceded by centuries of decay, arrested now and then by
ossification. Within the institution, discontent surely would seldom arise among the masters, at least not if they attained that rank
in time or ahead of time; it came from the journeymen who waited
to become masters and who could grow old without achieving independence. Their religious fraternities turned into journeymen's
leagues which protected their interests even against the masters,

an opposition known to have flared into strikes, indeed into revolts. The journeymen's drive for freedom of trade is not as apparent in history as it might have been expected if they had had a press and other literature; but very early we find traces of a kind of second-class journeymen who did not learn, and were not supposed to learn, the secrets of their trade. In the building trades, these soon came to be numerous. They probably supplied a majority of the "free masters," artisans in small towns and in the countryside who rarely struck it rich, and whom the ban on keeping apprentices and journeymen hampered, even in the cities where they were tolerated. Commonly called bunglers, quacks, troublemakers, interlopers, and often suffering violent persecution, these elements kept multiplying anyway and enjoyed the favor of the authorities and the consumers. As their numbers grew, so did the restiveness within the guilds themselves at their compulsory features—although this opposition movement furnished only auxiliaries for the struggle that terminated the compulsion. Now and then such restive craftsmen were indeed more likely than the guildmasters to think of new techniques and thus to become small manufacturers; in France, new inventions were exempted from the guild regulations as early as 1568. The tendencies that assail the guild system from within a trade must be strictly distinguished from tendencies that fight it from without; and those, in turn, from the ones that undermine it by victorious competition. The result is—as Brentano reports from England—that the guilds slowly wither away without being legally abolished.

Not far removed from the fight for freedom of trade is the progressive ascendancy of individualism in the legal-political sphere, when it rises out of the old political groupings against the ruling estates and the powers that be. The catastrophic event within this uprising is the French Revolution. On the basis of the unfettered civil society—having emerged previously under the tutelage of princely absolutism and a mercantilistic economic policy—the French Revolution establishes the bourgeois state, which does far more for the prevalence of national unity than the *ancien régime* had been capable of doing. In every respect, the sovereignty of the people continued the trends laid out by the sovereignty of the king. The course was set; it would be completed with the absorption by the state of all public law, all public affairs. Within its own centralized power, the state recognizes nothing but the departments and agencies it has established, and within those, the individuals—who are accordingly divided into officials and clients, just as the army, the extract of the state, is divided into officers and men. In the prerevolutionary state, the regulative principle predominated even in the economic system: the guilds were allowed to exist as privileged corporations but shorn of all public significance; their functions were pruned; preference was given to the industry that grew beside them and to the commerce that reduced small craftsmen to dependency. The reason is that these branches of business brought highly welcome funds into the country and into the state exchequer. Thus freedom of trade and free competition were but the last words of a tendency that hitherto had been virulent in a somewhat different manner. The physiocratic argument, denying the possibility of a net yield in industry, underlay the revolutionary legislation needed to achieve industrial power. The physiocrats were more enduringly refuted by Lancashire than by Adam Smith, for the facts speak louder than the most brilliant of writers.

Political individualism means that all citizens are equal. This in turn requires the abolition of any rights of dominion which may be traditional within a state; in essence, therefore, individualism goes against the old ruling estates and the cities as carriers of independent political power. The process has often been called the atomization of the social organism. Roscher takes the view that if the advance of central governmental power entirely dissolves the "smaller groups," if they no longer have a life of their own and if the subjects confront the state as a mere disconnected pile of individuals, the people will, as it were, be pulverized. He relates a favorite metaphor of Napoleon III: that, by dissolving the old estates, the nation had been ground into sand grains, which in isolation are mere dust but can be turned into a rock by a strong state power. As a matter of fact, the picture expresses what any statesman must be driving at, the goal of any purposeful internal policy.

Yet the individualistic evolution is not halted by this "socialistic" tendency. It proceeds within the tendency and alongside it, also in the sense that it is an emancipation.

The labor movement makes demands upon the state, but simultaneously remains a movement aiming at the equalization of the rights of the individual workers with the rights of the individuals of the propertied class. The idea is to win equality of private and political rights, in the state and in the communities. Although achieved in principle and indeed stabilized, private equality constantly has to assert itself against obstructions; the same applies far more to political equality, which to frustrate to the utmost possible extent is one of the arts of government. Beside the labor movement there is the feminist movement, another struggle for emancipation, for private and political rights; the struggles for private rights, too, are essentially political struggles. The emergence of women as individuals surely is a giant final step in the disintegration of age-old communal ties (*Gemeinschafts-Zusammenhang*); it decomposes what had remained an authoritative core in domestic relations. Yet here, too, it is far less the doctrine, the theory, the view that is at fault, if for once we may use this accentuated expression; it is not even women's own will and endeavor so much as life itself, that is, the national economy, capitalism and commercialism, communication, and the need to earn a living. Women already are individuals in economic life, and we see them become more and more so; the fact that they become political individuals as well is a consequence that may, like other consequences, bear within itself the seeds of a sound restoration on a new basis. As pointed out by Tocqueville, a historian who makes profound sense in his research into the nature of revolution, which is the nature of the modern age, "Our forebears did not have the word individualism, which we have coined for our use; the reason is that in their time there was no individual who was not a member of a group, none who might have been thought of as standing by himself alone." Tocqueville has hit the nail on the head here, as on many another occasion.

The social and political struggles are so closely intertwined with moral-spiritual ones that as a rule we regard the latter as the primary phenomena and undertake, for instance, to derive the

French Revolution from the French Enlightenment; also, as mentioned before, we usually view individualism as chiefly an intellectual trend. In fact, the greatest and most momentous phenomenon of the modern age in this very field is the disintegration of a powerful body that has had, and in large part even has retained, an immeasurable import and effect on economic and political life: the disintegration of the Roman Catholic Church. It ruled the Middle Ages, and on the threshold of the modern age it split, with frightful civil wars occurring as a result. From these struggles emerged the modern state, a state which, even where the old Church carried the day, could more freely and strongly confront it—at first in the form of "confessional," that is, Church-related, absolutism. The new national churches tried to restore a divinely warranted authority, though their own roots lay in the denial of that authority, in freedom of conscience, in the right of free examination and interpretation of religious texts.

Time and again the devout individualism of original Christianity would come forth, both within and against the new churches, in pietistic trends and in free congregations (*Gemeinden*) of a more or less revivalist persuasion. Time and again the new churches did as the old ones had done: they would enter the service of princes—in order to dominate them—and in general would seek their points of support among the temporal ruling strata. And yet, the more vigorously Protestantism remains what it is meant to be, the more outspokenly bourgeois is its nature. This is more true of Calvinism than of Lutheranism, more of pietism than of orthodoxy, even though a part of the nobility, its ladies in particular, did feel drawn to pietism by humility and sentiment. A stronger factor was the consonance of pietistic separatism with aristocratic individualism and its claim to be segregated from the common herd; spiritual edification had to vindicate the desire to have one's holy communion, one's holy confession, and one's burial rites to oneself. By and large, however, German pietism was urban, as was British nonconformism. From thoroughly petty bourgeois origins, it rose along with the petty bourgeoisie itself and then turned more or less into Enlightenment and theological rationalism. In its main lines, the struggle for religious liberation parallels the economic and political liberalism of the modern age, and they mutually advance each other. Accordingly, the great colonial country in which political and economic liberties came to unfold most freely is also the country of sects; the Puritans found refuge in New England, the Quakers in Pennsylvania; and the body politic in the American union is essentially neutral, as are its several states. The principle of tolerance, which the more modern type of absolutism had already practiced in Europe, worked the same way: the admission of foreign co-religionists regularly meant an expansion of free trade and commerce.

Gesellschaft Grows alongside Gemeinschaft

The third question to be considered here is how the individual and individualism in the modern age rise and evolve alongside the traditional groupings, again beginning with the *economic* field. There it is the trader who always conducts himself more or less explicitly as an individual toward the other strata, as a person more clearly aware of his own self-interest. He is less settled than the others and, being less tied to the soil, he is not so much tied to place and country either. Travel is part of his business; he visits the marketplaces where all kinds of people meet; even after trade has located in fixed abodes, the trader is often a foreigner. His constant concern, of necessity, is to improve communications. The greater their progress, the more numerously, actively, busily will the traveling merchants be moving to and fro, at home on highways and on waterways, gravitating from the confinement of their towns or villages toward the great field of economic endeavor spreading before their eyes; navigation in particular must serve them. A variant of the merchant is the modern manufacturer—already in the "putting-out" system the merchant is a manufacturer. To run his business, the manufacturer must always be a merchant, and he becomes more and more of a merchant with the mechanization of industry, with growing plant size, with more pronounced capitalistic organization. Less concerned than the merchant pure and simple with unrestricted freedom of trade, the industrialist would rather restrain trade wherever he views it as working more to his detriment than to his advantage; but, like the merchant, he does seek as large a market as possible, at least for his own products, and he therefore joins the merchant in opposing those local and territorial barriers which particular areas would use, and are partly still using, to shut themselves off from the outside world. The merchant, too, tends to be patriotic and conservative if the state power protects and helps him against foreign competition; accordingly, he must set special store by sea power, for trade follows the flag. The representatives of big trade and big industry together form the core of the bourgeoisie that is made up of individuals grown conscious of their property and of their interests. This new economically ruling class confronts, first of all, the nobility and the clergy as the old ruling estates, but then also the old "third estate" consisting of the peasantry and of the artisans and other townsmen. The bourgeoisie is willing and able, through the disposition over capital, to subjugate them all or to attract them to its retinue, to train them in the imitation of its methods and techniques. It thus produces a variety of aides and allies from its own ranks, and it is joined by people who come from other circles.

The merchant approaches the people more or less from the outside, as an alien individual, and everywhere the very strangeness of a stranger has a similarly individualistic effect. It makes for businessmindedness, for the pursuit of one's own advantage; among brothers, comrades, or friends, these tendencies are less likely to find a fertile soil. One stranger meets another at trade fairs and wherever commercial intercourse brings men together, where even men who can communicate only with great effort or through interpreters will feel close to each other simply because they like to trade and to do business—in other words, more probably in towns than in villages, and far more likely in metropolitan centers than in the small country towns where the occasion arises only now and then, if at all; also more probably in colonial countries than in old and closely settled regions. Working always in the same direction are original alien descent and the original or acquired alien religion that often goes with it. This is why such elements usually incline to trade and to free and fairly large-scale industry.

In Europe and in the countries that were colonized from

Europe, the most striking case is that of the Jews. A scattered remnant of the old urban civilization of antiquity, a homeless religious nation dispersed over the whole area of imperial Rome, held together by the belief in their God as by bonds of kinship stretching over vast distances, the Jews were predestined for the role of intermediaries. They knew, appreciated, and possessed money in the form of diverse coin, and consequently the merchandise which the growth of cities and traffic made more and more generally desired was at their disposal. They were hated, feared, and persecuted as medieval civilization had to be ready to do battle with the forces hostile to it, until with the progress of this battle—in other words, with the modern age and initially in Protestant countries—the day of tolerance finally dawned for the Jews. The result was emancipation, meaning legal equality, though counteracted now as before by sentiment and opinion. The conception of what Jews are came to blend so completely with trade, that is, with capitalism, that many traits which we regard as Jewish are in fact characteristic of trade in general—notably of dealings in money and capital—although Jewish peculiarities will often enhance them. On the other hand, their alienation from the "host people" will be preserved and exacerbated as modern communications concentrate masses of Jews in the great cities and as the character of alienation and of the struggle of all against all becomes more general in those cities and in the modern world at large. What shows most clearly in the case of Jewry, however, is also apparent with regard to others that are racial or religious strangers, and even between various Christian creeds, with the smaller groups enjoying the same advantage which marks the Jews: that among themselves they form a community, a sort of conspiracy, increasing their inclination to be somewhat reckless against any but their fellows. Typical as a people are the Swiss, as a sect, the Quakers—both good businessmen also inasfar as their moral-religious principles are reinforced by the insight that honesty is the best policy.

In the *political* field, the universal cultural society prevails beside and beyond all special organized groups. To begin with, this universal society links as with an international bond all individuals who by property and education are disposed to acknowledge each other: within each state it appears as a party. Yet from the commercial circles, in which it originated, this cosmopolitanism shifts more and more to their counterpart: it is the proletariat that develops and cultivates the idea of a superstate, an idea long disseminated by those other circles and now assuming the contours of the socialist world republic. In fact, bourgeois society, in its earlier form which retains individual liberty, already has created a superstate in the essentially international North American union, the most characteristic political structure of the modern age; its future development in a sense will decide the future of European mankind as well. Yet there are also organized groups of a social and economic nature, both national and international, that achieve political power and significance beside the state and may well use them against it.

The third power, the moral-intellectual one, that has arisen beside and above the old contexts and organized groups, likewise is international in essence: it is *science*. In Catholic countries, as in Protestant ones—though more strongly in the latter—it has a steadily disintegrative effect on popular beliefs, on traditional views and mores, but at the same time a newly constructive effect on specifically modern life. Science is the force which transforms men who will give it their wholehearted devotion into free individuals in a higher sense, into freethinkers. It teaches cognition and understanding of the world which, as a unit, is in essence, and thus as a whole, incomprehensible even though all of its parts appear necessarily connected and variously reflect the one law of persistence in change. Comparison is the essence of the scientist's activity, the metrical and numerical expression of relations and equations his supreme goal. As his tools, he must fashion artificial concepts; he must reduce the phenomena to artificial units and subsume them under common denominators. In social life, such artificial units are our concepts of the individuals themselves, because it is the individuals whose isolated existence and evolution we imagine for the sake of explicating all the contexts and combinations from which they arise, as well as all those they produce as new forms.

Economic man, political man, and scientific man *are* these imagined individuals. They touch at many points and interact continually. They share a desire to visualize their ends clearly and to adjust their means accordingly. The course they feel they have to follow is one of cool, calculating thought. They are rationalists and empiricists at once. They take their material from experience and shape it by rational thought. Their thinking serves their willing, but this thinking freely disposes of their motivations—that is to say, it may demand acts of will that can be performed only with inner reluctance and may evoke pangs of conscience. Rational striving by nature is reckless and egotistical, even if the strivings of economic man simultaneously may aim at his family's welfare, those of political man at the welfare of country and state, those of scientific man at the welfare of mankind.

The new universal which the isolated individual relates to, which he affirms in order to acquire it, to conquer it, to control it, is naturally unlimited. It is the world, or mankind, which the merchant in commercial relations, the statesman in world conquest and in the attempt to either subjugate or at least to govern his fellow citizens, strive to make dependent on themselves, and which the man of science wants to understand and even to shape, if, indeed, he intends to be intellectually creative.

Man at the Intersection of Two Worlds, Facing Progress and Decline

Individual man occupies the intersection of two diagonals, which we may conceive of as linking the initial and terminal points of a cultural development. He arises from *Gemeinschaft,* and he forms *Gesellschaft. Gemeinschaft,* essentially, is limited and tends toward intensity; *Gesellschaft,* essentially, is unlimited and tends toward extension. It *is* "the world." The isolated individual essentially is a world citizen. Jacob Burckhardt defines cosmopolitanism as a supreme stage of individualism, a stage whose dawn he thought he was perceiving as far back as in thirteenth-century Italy. Not until the seventeenth century does the term "citizen of the world" seem to have been used to describe a widely traveled, unprejudiced person. The eighteenth century brought the idea of cosmopolitanism to full flower; the nineteenth saw its appearance overshadowed by nationalism, although in fact vastly broadening its real base. The modern nation, notably as represented by a major state, is in large measure a fulfillment of the cosmopolitan quest, though, on the other hand, it curbs that quest and may be viewed as the result of a compromise among contradictory tendencies.

A nation, as distinguished from a people, is a modern formation. Precisely as such, it is an artificial structure, a thought product that has emerged from the consciousness and the political will of many. In the common use of the word, of course, this does not clearly show. We hardly ever even think of nations in pure, un-adulterated fashion. The thought, or concept, of a nation is mingled with a variety of emotions that really belong and adhere to the concept of a people.

To be sure, modern nations do have a basic stock of inhabitants who think of themselves as belonging together by descent, and some of the smaller ones—the three Scandinavian nations, for example—are indeed nothing but enlarged, broadened ethnic units [each of them] held together by the same language, by related mores, and by a unified religious creed. But even among the small nations, there are others, like the Belgian and Swiss, composed of people of greatly divergent origin as well as of different languages and creeds; and the small nations are not the typical nations. The great nations are more or less racially mixed. They keep absorbing foreign elements, notably in their capitals and other metropolitan areas. In part they have conquered and annexed territories inhabited by different nationalities; or they attract foreign workers who will fill gaps in the native labor force or undersell it. There are also more and more wealthy foreigners taking up permanent or temporary residence, with the privilege of naturalization after a certain waiting period granted to everyone who is not deemed a risk to national security. In addition, there is the increase in tourist travel. Large cities grow more and more international and metropolitan. By and large, the modern state is indifferent to descent, but less indifferent to wealth and to the conventional marks that serve to embellish the crudity of wealth: to the right religious denomination, to mastery of the state's official language (or of one of its several languages), to displays of a submissive mentality, and to avoidance of whatever might give offense to the circles that set the tone. Compliance with all these conditions is more pronounced among many foreigners than among most natives; this may be particularly so regarding those who are not really the natives' kind, like the Jews, notably if they discard their inherited faith and duly demonstrate their "national" allegiance in the sense of an adjustment to the ruling powers.

In the New World, the international character of modern nations is more strikingly evident than in Europe, and so is their being conditioned by a common government. The American nation is a compound of settlers come from random nations, of Indians they have assimilated or mixed with, and of freed Negro slaves and their illegitimate offspring. Sir Henry Maine remarked that almost all civilized states derive their national unity from past or present submission to some monarchic power. "The Americans of the United States, for instance, are a nation because they once obeyed a king." I would say that to a far greater extent they are today a nation because they respect and acknowledge the union's democratic constitution as their common element of life. In Europe, to be sure, princely power and greed laid a strong foundation for the process of nation building. The princes used to regard territories as latifundia of which they would seek to gain possession by cunning or force, by marriage or inheritance. This quest, however, would scarcely have met with invariable success, if the quest of a strong and steadily more vigorous stratum, the nascent bourgeoisie, had not coincided with it. That stratum—always headed by the merchants and the manufacturers (with whom progressive farmers make common cause) and by their paid and volunteer attorneys—requires a free and expanding sphere of business. What a trust magnate sees in the state or in the empire is a special association for *his* purposes, contributed to by all citizens—and the foremost of these purposes is to guarantee him a large market and action all around the globe, protectively or even aggressively, in behalf of his interests. However, if the power of the state opposes the power of his company, he must submit to the state or make a deal with it.

There are many points of view from which we can observe the individual and the world—how they mutually challenge and qualify each other, how the nations interpose themselves, as it were, as substitutes for "the world"—and these observations are important to an understanding of the economic, political, and intellectual history of the modern age. Let me stress here only one significant aspect out of many.

The course of development is manifested most clearly with regard to the social values which we may understand as the joint property of mankind in the widest sense of the word. Many things, material as well as ideal goods, remain common to many people; others come to be shared by them—ideal goods by the exchange of thoughts and doctrines, material ones by contracts of varied type. To begin with those, we know that the prevailing tendency is to separate and differentiate, to arrive at an increasingly precise definition of private property. The process is most striking regarding real estate; pure and absolute ownership of landed property is a specifically modern phenomenon. Yet personal ownership shows still more precisely in movable goods, especially in those that can be divided at will and turned into other goods—in other words, in money; property comes to be conceived of quite abstractly as "means," as a person's capacity, unlimited in principle, to dispose of things. As a rule, the person is an individual; but parallel to the evolution of individual means runs the one of social means controlled by associations of individuals. The associations are designed to serve a great variety of ends, above all the profit-making ends of business. Capital is combined so as to be more effective in a unified mass. The enlargement of the territory within which economic activities take place means that common goods will increase in any event, to satisfy common needs—most of them depending on the one need for the greatest possible universality and facility of communication and exchange. In part these common needs will be met by private enterprise, but a larger part requires public, that is, joint arrangements. These can come about in considerable quantity without upsetting the character of a social order based on private capitalism; indeed, they support and promote this order. For no private order is possible without the state and its activities, without a multitude of public institutions and goods.

Analogous to the property of private persons is the territorial sovereignty of states. We use the term international property to describe the relation between state power and state territory. It follows that every state has the right to bar strangers from its territory; and yet, under modern international law, the national territory, as a rule, is open to everyone, for transient as well as permanent residence and for the acquisition of property, including real estate. Potentially the earth is jointly owned by all, that is, by all those who know how to win their place on it. In a more distinct and definite sense, this is true of the fluid portion of the globe, or at least of the great mass of that portion which makes up the high seas. It was the early modern age, the same period in which the more precise individualization of national territories was sought and mostly achieved, that saw the application of the principle of the freedom of the seas. . . .

A distinguishing mark of the modern age in all fields is the invention of suitable means to an end, of means of universal communication and exchange in particular; and in a definite sense these will always be the joint property of mankind because and insofar as they serve universal human ends. In this respect, all norms and rules have a tendency to become international in character.

We have reason to be proud of the mighty European civilization of the nineteenth and twentieth centuries, for all the sufferings and sighs it costs us. It has taken much out of our lives: calm, dignity, contemplation, and a great deal of the quiet beauty we may still sense here and there in a village or in a small town. But it has filled our mental as well as our emotional life with tremendous tensions that lift us above all humdrum routine and even above our delight in beauty and virtue, because we have the great intellectual delight to see farther than any past age was capable of seeing and to find ever new satisfactions for our curiosity and love of knowledge. These tensions uplift us because we bless ourselves for our cognition of the causes and effects of things, for facing the world in all its beautiful and ugly manifestations with admiration, even with some measure of understanding. However, modern civilization is caught in an irresistible process of disintegration. Its very progress dooms it. This is hard for us to conceive, and harder still to acquiesce in it, to admit it and yet to cooperate with it willingly and even cheerfully. We must bring ourselves to look upon tragedy, wrestling with both fear and hope so as to rid ourselves of them, and to enjoy the cleansing effect of the dramatic course of events. Scientific analysis can do this if it has matured and transformed itself into philosophy, that is, into wisdom.

21

THE ACTIVE FORCES OF
SOCIAL DEVELOPMENT
IN THE MODERN AGE

EDITORS' NOTE. *Toennies' last publication,* Geist der Neuzeit, *from which this chapter is taken, presents unusual difficulties to the interpreter. Apparently more a collection of notes written at different times during Toennies' scholarly career than a completed piece of work, it is in part repetitive of what the author had said previously, in part merely indicative of what was on the author's mind. Much must therefore be read between the lines; much that is fragmentary must be filled in. To the seminal ideas that are outlined belongs Toennies' rejection of the conventional trichotomy of (Greek and Roman) antiquity, the Middle Ages, and the modern age. Instead, he suggests that there is continuity between the world of antiquity and the subsequent European cultural development and, further, that each and every era within the entire history of human civilization, figuratively speaking, passes through stages of youth, maturity, and aging, with earlier stages showing a predominance of* Gemeinschaft-*like features, giving way to a predominance of* Gesellschaft-*like features with the passage of time. This development is thought to be inevitable, given the fact that man is by nature an individual who cannot help but relate his experience as well as his needs and desires to his own ego and to seek alliances for self-protection and self-enhancement. But the process by which the more and more non-communal and more and more associational individual develops has been most pronounced in recent centuries, partly within communal relations, collectives, and corporations, partly out of these, liberating the individual from them, and partly beside them, initiating associational relations, collectives, and corporations; and all this in an economic, political, and moral-spiritual context. With this sixfold differentiation in mind, Toennies attempts to develop a typology of individual man in the modern age. Going beyond what he already had formulated in the paper on "The Individ-*

ual and the World in the Modern Age," he outlines the types and role performances of the lord, the subject, the layman, the stranger, and the upstart. These are what one may call real types; the normal concept or ideal type behind all these is the individualist.

This is the background upon which the chapter that is presented here ought to be understood. What makes it particularly interesting is that in it Toennies draws a brief sketch of a possible sociology of war. He sees war as an outgrowth of the individualistic spirit and the "great wars" of the modern age as the culmination of the inexorable drift toward Gesellschaft in a "late" historical development.

Growth of Population

THE PARTICULAR forms of social life in our period or civilization, of which the modern age represents only a relatively small section, have been fertilized and nourished by an earlier period of a highly developed and widely dispersed civilization of *Gesellschaft* character in classical antiquity. For all that, the new and present civilization has arisen from simpler rudimentary conditions, from which it has grown into more and more varied and complex ones. This development has been determined essentially by the increase and the expansion of populations, by their differentiation and by the division of labor. In the modern age—though, in an analogous but less distinct form, already in classical antiquity—it was commerce, hence capitalism, that rose to dominate this development. Under this influence the standards of urban life became more and more generally accepted, and urban life moved further and further away from what may be called its elementary basis in villages and rural communities. This process carried with it and entailed immense consequences for the economic as well as the political and the spiritual-moral constitution of peoples.

Let us consider in this light the historical events of the modern age, first of all, those that have been, and still are, of the greatest significance for the progress of general social, including economic, conditions.

Translated from *Geist der Neuzeit* (Leipzig: Buske, 1935), pp. 167–81; one brief subdivision is omitted.

Historical events of this nature are the dynamics of population, chiefly the basic change that depends on the relative magnitude of the incidence of birth to the incidence of death and, in its positive sense, on the excess of the former. This change is not a steady one, nor is it insensitive over against external causes. On the whole, the change is more favorable, or positive, in rural areas than in towns, even more so in large cities and metropolitan areas. In the former, marriages are more fertile, largely because of the lower age at marriage and the earlier opportunities for children to contribute to the support of the family, and for parents to bring up and look after their children. In the town, infants and toddlers succumb more easily to infirmities and injuries. Certain checks, however, do operate under rural conditions. Peasant holdings must try to remain efficient when they are passed on in inheritance. Marriage in the holding is therefore often possible for only one among several sons, and a large increase of population is avoided because one does not want to see the holding subdivided or heavily mortgaged. Large increases do not matter among the poor—for they have nothing to pass on; but, among them, their very poverty acts in a negative sense, that is, as a check.

In the towns, the relative position of the craftsmen whose work is steady and whose status inheritable, on the one hand, and the unpropertied people, on the other hand, is comparable, although in the more recent centuries a particular check arose from the compulsory membership in craft guilds so long as this rule remained in force; the opportunity of establishing a family was restricted by that traditional institution, which became even more rigid as it grew older. Consequently, the abolition of compulsory guild membership brought about a marked liberation in the natural increase of population. Previously, increases had been widely kept under control, in rural areas purposefully by the interests and the influence of manorial lordship, while in the towns the difficulty of achieving a position as master of a craft meant that nuptiality was to some extent restricted to marriages between older journeymen and the widows of masters or their daughters no longer in their first youth. Freedom of marriage became a fact simultaneously as a matter of social and economic conditions and as a legal right. This freedom now exists to the greatest possible extent in all European countries as well as in colonial areas. But it actually remained subject to economic restrictions—and this means the standard of living in the widest possible sense: depending, as it does, not only on the fertility of the soil and climatic and meterological conditions relating to harvests and crop failures but also, because of the growing complexity of the world economy, on the rising uncertainty of making a living; and, therefore, in the first instance, on the scarcity or the unstable opportunities for employment and the implications of this instability for wage levels. While as late as the eighteenth century the towns grew but slowly, or sometimes even suffered a decline in population as a consequence of the rigidity of the craft guilds, the liberation process, together with the extraordinary improvement in technology, forcing the pace in the development of the capitalistic mode of production, has led, throughout the nineteenth century, and most markedly in its last third, to that rapid urban growth that ushered in a truly metropolitan epoch. This process continues into the twentieth century. At this point a new trend becomes discernible, largely owing to internal resistances. These gained in strength through rising needs, including those of a cultural nature, making smaller families desirable; statutory restrictions on child labor worked in the same direction. This trend was reinforced by the impact of the enormous event of the [First] World War. Ultimately, this is more likely to lead to a decline than to a further increase in population, chiefly in large cities. Hence, it becomes possible, and has in fact been attempted, to make scientific forecasts. These turn out to be unfavorable regarding the growth of population in those countries on which the European civilization is based, and favorable regarding countries which have had, and still have, a lesser share in western civilization.

Technology

The economist Schmoller correctly observed that technology itself is among the causes that determine population density. Technology in general means everything that man can do: what he accomplishes, acquires, and produces. It is, first of all, the work of the human arm, the hands, and the fingers; but always, and increasingly as it passes into the fingers, it is the work of the human intellect, or what is designated as his mind or spirit. Gradually this capacity gains the upper hand. As in the individual manual worker the technical intellect moves hands and fingers, so (in the words of Goethe's Faust) one mind moves a thousand hands. If one considers under this aspect the development of human skills, one notices as a technology practiced from time immemorial, though certainly acquired only in the course of untold generations, the accomplishments of the hunter and the fisherman, the domestication of animals by breeding and training, the locomotion by means of the wheel and the boat, and, finally, the achievements in agriculture, in mining, and in the building of tents and primitive shelters. Relatively late, man developed the technology of handicrafts, which enabled him to build in timber and in stone, to make utensils and—as needed for many other kinds of work—tools and appliances. Thus it was that in classical antiquity and even before it some countries of the East had reached such a high degree of perfection that large numbers of people could live and work together, partly by means of direct production of the means of subsistence, partly by means of the exchange of these with other commodities; which in turn enabled the narrow stratum of lords and masters to live in splendor adorned by a variety of arts; some of these also benefited the common people, particularly by means of the services rendered to their invisible masters, the gods and demons. All of this was connected with many other technologies, which contributed and continue to contribute to the improvement and the facilitation of social life.

For it is in technology that a fund of skills is being passed on and inherited. Very little of it gets lost, certainly not forever, although some techniques may be forgotten; but others are being rediscovered. At any rate, the fund is being enriched by new inventions and, indirectly, by discoveries. Inventions, to a large part, are made in the immediate context of work, and they are as often as not due to an endeavor on the part of the worker to ease, shorten, and speed up his task. The famous example Adam Smith gave for the technical improvement of the steam engine by an automatic device (*Wealth of Nations*, Book 1, Chapter 1) is still the best illustration. In general, however, those improvements and refinements in appliances that resulted directly from work had a deeper significance in that they adorned and refined the product itself. All genuine arts are closely connected with a passion for the ornamental, and are therefore based on esthetic discernment, which forms an important part of the human mind. This does not, of course, render superfluous those rudimentary areas of activity where work is, first and foremost, action of the arms and legs; these are determined less by the needs of the worker himself than by the purpose pursued in the production line, which is known only to, and determined by, foremen and managers. Here is a connecting link to warfare, where even in early times a fairly comprehensive cooperation was practiced. This explains why military technology has always been a technology concerned with the management of masses of men and material by mechanical means and, in that connection, with the direction and planned application of fire power. Military technology has always been a field of rapid technical progress, since it must adapt itself with speed and flexibility to an external purpose. The purpose is predominantly destruction as opposed to production, but that purpose has retroactive effects on production, since it consists in the special application of produced instruments, namely armaments, and thereby calls for intensified production.

In the same way as the activities that are essential for commerce, so are the activities that are essential for war, including those of the political leader, responsible for the conduct of war, rationally conceived activities of a very high order. As such, they are an expression of rational, or arbitrary, will (*Kuerwille*), which plainly subjects all means to the ends it has settled upon in a deliberately planned procedure. The predominance of this rationalism is an outstanding feature of the enormous progress that has been made in the modern age in advance of the Middle Ages and, indirectly, of all previous ages—progress in production and progress in destruction. In terms of human creativeness, this means negative as well as positive progress. However, within each of these two spheres progress may be called positive.

The Great Commerce and the Great War

Commerce is a decidedly peaceful, that is, a socially positive, activity. But it has a good many things in common with war, the clearly asocial activity, and these common features are joined in the concept of rationalism: first, the tendency to accumulate means, in one case, means of production, in the other, means of destruction, and the problem of moving them geographically, so that they can achieve their purpose. Second, mastery over these means requires planning and calculating thought and, accordingly, system and orderliness and, in the disposition over manpower, its distribution and deployment. Third, both trade and war involve a large expenditure of effort, which is most directly represented in the investment of money. As in commerce, the disbursement of money aims at an increased return of money, so is the expectation in the conduct of war that the expenditure should pay off, whether in the form of a successful territorial conquest or in the form of ample recompense through the payment of tribute exacted from the opponent after his defeat, especially if defeat forces upon him a relationship of lasting dependence. Fourth, the danger that the enterprise may fail or miscarry is a common element in both activities, and that risk is being accepted.

Neither commerce nor war is a modern invention. Yet both have immeasurably developed their dimensions in the modern age. Large-scale commerce and large-scale war are modern phenomena. And they are linked in a variety of ways. The typical war of the modern age is a commercial war, fought for the purpose of literally driving the competitor from the field—the field of competition—or of guarding against his further gain in strength, or of forestalling him in the penetration of a territory that is of commercial value. These political interests not only grow with the expansion of world trade but their growth is accelerated as commerce extends to the field of finance and worldwide banking; they reach their highest intensity when commercial interests become the dominant force in the production of commodities, in transport, and in communications, all of which are gradually being integrated in the capitalistic system.

Parallel with the commercial runs the political development, that is, the growth of the modern state. It leads to the combination and unification of a great variety of existing political units into larger, integrated units with a centralized administration. The starting point of the new political entity is the expanding power of the city, which becomes the core of the power of the state; then the larger state arises from the association of smaller states, some of which may have originated in cities, while others may have been the outgrowth of other previously existing political units that were united through the willpower of an outstanding prince or king. Conditions for an association of this kind are favorable when a natural basis exists of ethnic and racial affiliation, or of spatial affinity and neighborliness, or of a variety of common customs and interests, including common religious observances. But the formation of a large state may also be the result of the acquisition or takeover of weaker political units by a stronger unit using force. Both types may operate in combination or reinforce each other.

Again, it is by means of commerce and war that the modern age has been an agent of continual social and political change. Capital and the state are joining hands when reaching out toward faraway lands and across the seas: they bring under their dominion, by means partly of their commodities, partly of their armed forces, whole territories and their inhabitants, even those that set great store by their own independence.

Capital and the state are joined by science as the third specifically modern social force. Science, though fundamentally different from the other two, has many and strong ties with them. These are essentially ties of reciprocal give and take, just as capital and the state, in their reciprocal relationships, continually in many ways, to be sure, obstruct but predominantly strengthen and promote each other. Science, too, must aim at unification and systematic order by simplifying and strengthening its methods; for its law, too, is the economy of effort.

In the modern age, as in former periods, scientific development goes hand in hand with capitalistic and political development; in quite fundamental ways it is conditioned by the efforts and successes of commerce and warfare. Commerce promotes thought and knowledge, and thought, as computation and calculation, is an essential element of science. And knowledge, which is a combined product of thought and experience, is being advanced as experience widens with the movement from one place to another, which is the typical movement of the merchant. The effects of warfare are similar. Its campaigns are movement over territory, admittedly with a destructive aim yet always mindful of the need to maintain and feed its armies; and, once it succeeds in an invasion, it must give thought to maintaining and developing the conquered territory. In the pursuit of these aims, warfare is accompanied by commerce acting in its own interest. But warfare by itself, too, means more thought and more knowledge—thought, insofar as it calls for the comparison of favorable and unfavorable effects of armed action, particularly the losses in men and material it must incur in comparison with the losses of the enemy, at which it is aiming; and knowledge insofar as the strategist must constantly observe how his own actions and those of the enemy are reciprocally conditioned in their very aim of impeding each other and how the changing chances of the final outcome of a struggle may be assessed.

In this way commerce and war depend continually on, among other things, scientific progress and on changes in scientific outlook. The activity that has always been closely related to commerce, and in certain ways has been dependent on it, is movement from one place to another, and especially one such movement, namely, navigation. Now, since early times, navigation has had to rely on the observation and knowledge of the skies; and improvements in astronomy in the modern age, as formerly, have greatly facilitated it. Further, we must remember what has been said previously about the connection between commerce and technology; what is most striking in this respect is the powerful development in mechanical technology, based, in its turn, on the science of mechanics, which got under way in the last centuries of the Middle Ages, to reach perfection only in the modern age. An extraordinarily wide area of constantly renewed activity was opened up thereby for the investment of capital, which led increasingly to the amassment of activities, mass employment of labor, mass production of commodities. As an aid to mechanics and a physics based on mechanical principles, the more recent development of chemistry must here be noted, which, in turn, opened the way for a better understanding of those processes of life that are inaccessible to mechanics alone. In addition, biology has been instrumental for the observation and the understanding of the processes of growth and propagation in plant and animal life. The new knowledge also became relevant for commerce and for war; for commerce as all kinds of products of the earth and their derivatives called for attention and exploitation; and for war as war materials became increasingly, as time went on, not only mechanical but chemical ones; and finally, as the life sciences, particularly the sciences of human life and its conditions, grew in importance even in tasks oriented toward the destruction of life.

Commerce and war, capital and the political state, on the other hand, support and promote scientific endeavor, partly through the realization of what science is achieving and may achieve for them in the future, and partly in quite a different context, which is determined by different factors. Outstanding among these is the enhanced valuation attached to science and the arts as the wealth of nations increases. Let us look here at the more immediate connections. Scientific research closely resembles commerce in that both push into what is distant and pursue what is novel; commerce, for the sake of the profit that so often may be gained by better knowledge; scientific research, for the sake of knowledge itself, even though, in its striving for what is distant, it will put up with a dependence that results from useful endowment. But always scientific endeavor is stimulated by the exchange of ideas and of research results between those working along similar lines, particularly between scientists working under a variety of conditions in different countries. And, as of commerce, so it has always been a function of war to foster progress by intensifying communication between the inhabitants of different countries.

The Large-Scale Enterprise

The forces of the modern age successfully assert themselves in each one of these main areas of activity, although they are constantly held back by surviving medieval attitudes. But they persistently surmount them and gain superiority. First, in the economic area, the distinct character of the Middle Ages is determined by comparatively simple conditions of social life—conditions, in which rural life and agriculture markedly predominate, and continue to do so despite the growth and flowering of numerous cities. Even the most important cities do not exceed fairly moderate limits, but they acquire and maintain a high degree of independence, so that they rise to the status of free republics within the framework of the larger empire to which they belong as subjects. Initially, the city is dominated by the patriciate, whose wealth and power are rooted both in tradition and in landed estate. But the patricians are gradually being replaced by a class of craftsmen, which draws its strength from the guilds, is capable of defending itself as well as to produce, and, in alliance with the lower orders, represents the community and the people. However, the beginnings of production of marketable goods for profit become more pronounced in a variety of ways. For instance, the technical requirements of work in mining favor the development of large-scale enterprise. Generally, the large-scale enterprise is typical of the modern age. It stands for the pronounced domination which commerce exercises over the freedom of rural and urban labor, including such industrial labor as is domiciled in the countryside. Even when industries are established in rural areas, they are essentially urban in character. The large-scale enterprise run on industrial principles gradually adapts and transforms to its image also the agricultural enterprise; but being a less suitable, because less flexible, form of capital investment, its relative economic importance may decline to the point of insignificance.

The Great Power Struggle

As the large-scale enterprise has proved superior to the small enterprise in industry and agriculture, and eventually in commerce, so are in political life the great powers superior to the smaller ones. The great power is, together with the growth of the concept of the sovereign state, one of the most momentous results of the social forces at work in the modern age: and with the superpower, a centralized governmental bureaucracy, which is faced by the problems of general social welfare (*salus publica*). Its administration is under pressure not only from the old "estates" but increasingly from the bourgeoisie; the middle classes have become influential with the rise of commerce and industry, particularly heavy industry, and strive for a commanding political position. But along with the bourgeoisie, and at the same time opposed to it to the point of revolt, grows the working class, the proletariat that has been created by the former. The opposition is both political and economic in character. Its chances of capturing political power are enhanced by those very ideas of political liberty and equality which had inspired the middle classes and, in drawing strength from the support of the working class, gained them a decisive influence in political life.

In this respect, as much as in others, it is obvious that the social forces at work in the modern age are still in their formative stage and have not yet played their part to the end. An attempt at forecasting the final outcome may approximate near certainty inasmuch as a scientific understanding of the phenomena of social life can be achieved by reliable methods, that is, the closer it approximates and resembles knowledge in the natural sciences.

The modern state, in the course of its expansion and consolidation, leads to warfare as an expression of conflict between states, whether between two single powers, or between a coalition and a single power, or between coalitions of powers. The modern age is the age of the great war, in contrast to the Middle Ages, in which only minor feuds and conflagrations were frequent, even if they gradually assumed a wider scope. Further, the great wars are a matter of planned execution, as they are more and more going to be a matter of applied military technology and of the mass destruction of human life and material assets. In addition to external wars between different states, civil wars have emerged as conflicts on a large scale. In brief, war in all its aspects has become an essential element in the development of the modern state; and, because of its immense cost, warfare has brought in its wake the growing importance of public finance and fiscal policies.

Warfare is mainly provoked by the territorial expansion of a particular state, whether in the form of direct occupation or indirect domination. Direct occupation is often being sought for reasons of nationalism, or under the pretext of it, particularly when a case can be made for larger or smaller areas having formerly been part of the territory of the aggressor, or, even more so, when the inhabitants are of the same nationality [or ideology—Eds.]; other reasons for an attempted expansion are a supposedly necessary shortening of frontiers, or the acquisition of one or several ports, or the gaining of direct access to the open sea. On closer investigation, it frequently turns out that the real reason for such tendencies lies in the needs of trade; for commerce is unthinkable without its natural aim to expand and to raise its profit, so that it jealously watches the expanding trade of other countries and understandably enough fears, as the consequence of such expansion, the decline, if not the cessation, of its own trade. For this reason, modern wars predominantly have been economic wars. In addition, a victorious war, the more severe the conditions of the peace which are imposed on the loser, is the more likely to be pregnant with a new war; this is comparable to what happens in primitive societies in which tribal revenge may endlessly continue as the consequence of an inflicted death or injury—until a superior power grows strong enough to enforce a public peace. A good example for the latter process can be observed in the transition from the Middle Ages to the modern age. At the threshold, as it were, of the modern age, when the central power in the Holy Roman Empire began to disintegrate, an attempt was made to terminate incessant feuds, and a "general public peace" (*allgemeiner Landfriede*) became the law of the land; however, the subsequent warfare between the larger territories with the empire, nevertheless, took the form of a lingering civil war. The recent centuries of the modern age witnessed also in the rest of Europe outside Germany and in the United States, this great European colony beyond the seas, serious internal conflicts which, more often than not, made all the heavier the burden of external wars these countries had to shoulder.

Since modern wars regularly arise from urban interests, in particular those of trade, they signify as much as does the central state power, which owes to warfare much of its consolidation, an increasing preponderance of the city over the countryside. Yet warfare, and the government wanting war or being forced into it, needs the countryside and the rural economy for two fundamental reasons. First, the countryside is the producer of soldiers of greater physical strength and endurance, who are more ready to fight; this counts for much, especially so long as armies are recruited by voluntary enlistment. The second reason is that the armed forces must be fed by its own country until, having gained enemy ground, they can be fed by the occupied territory; further, the dependence on their own country's resources is intensified once exchange and communciation with other countries are exposed during the war to temporary or permanent interruptions. As rural areas suffer from enemy invasion, often even from the passage of their own military forces, more directly than the towns; as their fields are laid waste, their draft animals pillaged or killed, their houses and barns burned, and their manpower often pressed into service in the army and navy despite the principle of voluntary service: it would be but natural if the rural population revolted against a war that chiefly serves urban interests—and to an extent this does indeed happen. But such a tendency is being counteracted by the circumstance that it is the rural folks who not only are more fit for military service, hence better soldiers, but who also are more easily taken in by government-inspired propaganda which persuades them of the necessity and the justice of a war that is about to break out. Vistas of lasting prosperity, hand in hand with the prospect of immediate gain, are conjured up before them. In one case, only the necessity of war cannot be gainsaid, that is, when a plain act of aggression must be resisted to protect the nation from the terrifying peril of foreign domination which would amount to nothing less than bondage. However, by crafty blandishment and political artifice, it is easy to create the conviction that a war is just; the true reasons and causes of a war of aggression as an instrument of power politics, as a rule, will be discovered only by means of historical research long after the generation of those who were cruelly deceived has passed away.

The City as a Factor in Spiritual and Moral Development

The nature of the relationship between the city and the countryside manifests itself most clearly in the spiritual-moral sphere of social life. The city stimulates intellectual life, because living conditions in the city bring people closer together and offer greater variety. City life is also a fertile ground for intellectuality, because calculation and computation are necessary skills in a monetary economy, that is, in commercial activities. The style of rural life is rather that of the *Gemeinschaft* mode, being steadier and quieter; with all that, it is not lacking in conflicts and disputes over mine and thine, even within families; and personal hatred, jealousy, and vindictiveness often lead to grievous acts of violence. The style of life in the city is more impersonal and matter-of-fact, and so are its conflicts and controversies; but with the greater emphasis on monetary transactions and private property and, consequently, on claims and debts, controversies become more frequent and more intensive, and more often require settlement by formal judicial decision.

Of great significance in this respect is the change in the attitude to the ruling powers, that is, in historical perspective, to rule by the gentry. The country folks, on the whole, willingly used to submit to them, accepting as they did their superiority and indispensability, which was felt to be divinely ordained. Inseparable from the devoutness of the common people, religion has always provided the stongest support for sheer domination. In the city, too, religion is an influential authority; moreover, city life is a favorable ground for its artistic as well as its intellectual refinement. But with refinement, doubts and better insight are promoted also, so that a sharp contrast comes into view: pious devoutness as an essential trait of rural, critical thinking, of urban life.

This viewpoint enables us to compare the general turn of mind that predominates in contemporary life with the way of thinking that is widely attested to and documented for the Middle Ages. The distance separating them is an appreciable though almost immeasurable one. One can perhaps say that it is the urban disposition, guided by, and relying on, scientific thinking, that by this time provides the keynote; long since it has exercised a pervading influence also on the more fundamental and natural way of thinking that used to be the mark of the countryside. The difference between then and now, that is, between science and simple faith as well as superstition, appears at its most striking when one considers the immemorial belief, common to the human race, in the existence and the appearance of ghosts and specters.

Bibliography

FERDINAND TOENNIES' major writings are arranged chronologically in three sections: History of Ideas (p. 334); Sociology (p. 335); Sociography (p. 339). Sections of the translations of his works (p. 341) and of selected writings about Toennies (p. 341) are arranged alphabetically by translator and by author, respectively.

ABBREVIATIONS OF COLLECTED PAPERS
SStuKr I, II, II = *Soziologische Studien und Kritiken, Erste bis Dritte Sammlung.* Jena: G. Fischer, 1925, 1926, 1929.
FSE = *Fortschritt und Soziale Entwicklung.* Karlsruhe: Braun, 1926.

ABBREVIATIONS OF GERMAN PERIODICALS
AGPh = *Archiv fuer Geschichte der Philosophie*
ARWPh = *Archiv fuer Rechts- und Wirtschaftsphilosophie*
ASGS = *Archiv fuer Soziale Gesetzgebung und Statistik*
ASPh = *Archiv fuer Systematische Philosophie*
AStA = *Allgemeines Statistisches Archiv*
ASwSp = *Archiv fuer Sozialwissenschaft und Sozialpolitik*
DStZ = *Deutsches Statistisches Zentralblatt*
DiJG = *Dioskuren, Jahrbuch fuer Geisteswissenschaften*
JbNS = *Jahrbuecher fuer Nationaloekonomie und Statistik*
KVHS = *Koelner Vierteljahrshefte fuer Soziologie*
PhM = *Philosophische Monatschefte*
SchmJb = *Schmollers Jahrbuch fuer Gesetzgebung, Verwaltung und Volkswirtschaft*
VWPh = *Vieteljahrsschrift fuer Wissenschaftliche Philosophie*
WwA = *Weltwirtschaftliches Archiv*
ZGSt = *Zeitschrift fuer die Gesamte Staatswissenschaft*
ZGStr = *Zeitschrift fuer die Gesamte Strafrechtswissenschaft*
ZV = *Zeitschrift fuer Voelkerrecht*
ZVpS = *Zeitschrift fuer Voelkerpsychologie und Soziologie*

HISTORY OF IDEAS

"Anmerkungen ueber die Philosophie des Hobbes." *VWPh* 3 (1879):
453–66; 4 (1880) : 55–74, 428–53; 5 (1881) : 186–204.

"Studie zur Entwicklungsgeschichte des Spinoza." *VWPh* 7 (1883) : 158–83, 334–64.

"Leibniz und Hobbes." *PhM* 23 (1887) : 557–73.

Editor. *Thomas Hobbes, The Elements of Law Natural and Politic.* Edited with a preface and critical notes, to which are subjoined selected abstracts from unprinted mss. of Thomas Hobbes. London: Simpkin Marshal & Co., 1889; reprinted, Cambridge University Press, 1928, and Frank Cass & Co. Ltd., London, 1970, with introduction by M. M. Goldsmith.

Editor. *Thomas Hobbes, Behemoth or the Long Parliament.* Edited for the first time from the original ms. London: Simpkin Marshall & Co., 1889; reprinted Frank Cass & Co. Ltd., London, 1969, with introduction by M. M. Goldsmith.

"Neuere Philosophie der Geschichte: Hegel, Marx, Comte." *AGPh* 7 (1894) : 486–515.

"Historismus und Rationalismus." *ASPh* 1 (1894) : 227–52 (now *SStuKr* I: 105–26).

Thomas Hobbes: Leben und Lehre. Stuttgart: Frommann, 1896; 2d. ed., *Thomas Hobbes, Der Mann und der Denker,* 1912; 3d. ed., *Thomas Hobbes, Leben und Lehre,* 1925. Reprint with epilogue and bibliography by K. H. Ilting, Stuttgart, — forthcoming.

Der Nietzsche-Kultus, Eine Kritik. Leipzig: Reisland, 1897.

"Zur Theorie der Geschichte: Exkurs" (Review of Rickert, *Die Grenzen der naturwissenschaftlichen Begriffsbildung*). *ASPh* 8 (1901) : 1–38.

"Herbert Spencer (1820:1903)." *Deutsche Rundschau* 118 (1904) : 368–82.

"Hobbes Analekten I." *AGPh* 17 (1904) : 291–317.

"Hobbes Analekten II." *AGPh* 19 (1906) : 153–75.

Schiller als Zeitbuerger und Politiker. Berlin: Verlag der "Hilfe," 1905.

"Simmel als Soziologe." *Frankfurter Zeitung.* October 9, 1918.

Marx, Leben und Lehre. Jena: Erich Lichtenstein; Sozialistische Buecherei, vol. 5, 1921.

"Ferdinand Toennies," in *Die Philosophie der Gegenwart in Selbstdarstellungen* 3:203–44. Leipzig: Meiner, 1923.

"Die Lehre von den Volksversammlungen und die Urversammlung in Hobbes' Leviathan." *ZGSt* 89 (1930) : 1–22.

"Historischer Materialismus," pp. 770–75, in ed. L. Heide, *Internationales Handbuch des Gewerkschaftswesens, 1931.* Berlin: Werk u. Wirtschaft, 1930.

"Hobbes und Spinoza," pp. 226–43, in *Septimana Spinozana.* The Hague: Martinus Nijhoff, 1935.

"Hegels Naturrecht, Zur Erinnerung an Hegel's Tod." *SchmJb* 56 (1932) : 71–85.

"Contributions à l'histoire de la pensée de Hobbes." *Archives de Philosophie* 12 (1936) : 259–84.

"Lettre de M. le professeur F. Toennies, Kiel," pp. xlvi–li, in *Actes du VIIIe Congrès International de Philosophie à Prague 2–7 Sept. 1934.* Prague: Orbit S.A., 1936.

SOCIOLOGY

"Gemeinschaft und Gesellschaft, Theorem der Kulturphilosophie." Ms. 1880–81, first published, *Kant Studien* 30 (1925): 149–79 (now *SStuKr* I: 1–32).

Gemeinschaft und Gesellschaft, Abhandlung des Communismus und Socialismus als empirischer Culturformen. Leipzig: Reisland, 1887; reprint, 1904. Subtitle since 2d. ed., *Grundbegriffe der reinen Soziologie.* Berlin: Curtius, 2d. ed. 1912; 3d. ed. 1920; 4th–5th eds. 1922; 6th–7th eds. 1926. Leipzig: Buske, 8th ed., 1935. Darmstadt: Wissenschaftliche Buchgesellschaft, reprint, 1963, with prefaces to 1st, 2nd, 4th and 5th, 6th and 7th and 8th edition added.

"Herbert Spencers soziologisches Werk." *PhM* 25 (1889): 50–85 (now *SStuKr* I: 75–104).

"Werke zur Philosophie des sozialen Lebens und der Geschichte." *PhM* 28 (1892) : 37–66, 444–61, 592–601; 29 (1893) : 291–309 (now *SStuKr* III: 133–95).

Review of Georg Simmel, *Einleitung in die Moralwissenschaft. Zeitschrift für Psychologie und Physiologie der Sinnesorgane.* 5 (1893) : 627–33.

Review of Georg Simmel, *Die Probleme der Geschichtsphilosophie. Zeitschrift für Psychologie und Physiologie der Sinnesorgane.* 6 (1893): 77–79.

"Jahresbericht ueber Erscheinungen der Soziologie aus den Jahren 1893–4,

1895–6, 1897–8." *ASPh* 2 (1896) : 421–41, 497–517; 4 (1898) : 99–116, 230–49, 483–506; 6 (1900) : 505–40; 8 (1902) : 263–79, 397–408 (now *SStuKr* III: 196–336).

Ueber die Grundtatsachen des socialen Lebens. Bern: Steiger & Cie., Ethisch-socialwissenschaftliche Vortragskurse, Zuericher Reden, VII, 1897.

"Philosophical Terminology" (Welby Prize Essay, 1898), trans. Mrs. Bosanquet. *Mind* n.s. 8 (1899) : 289–332, 467–91; n.s. 9 (1900) : 46–61.

"Zur Einleitung in die Soziologie." *Zeitschrift fuer Philosophie und Philosophische Kritik* 115 (1899) : 240–51 (now *SStuKr* I: 65–74). (French transl. *"Notions fondamentales de sociologie pure."* *Annales de l'Institut International de Sociologie* 4 [1900]: 63–77.)

"The Present Problems of Social Structure" (paper read at the Congress of Arts and Science, St. Louis). *American Journal of Sociology* 10 (March 1905) : 569–88.

"Ammon's Gesellschaftstheorie." *ASwSp* 19 (1904) : 88–111 (now *SStuKr* III: 372–93).

"Sociologie et Psychologie." *Annales de L'Institut International de Sociologie* 10 (1904) : 289–97.

"Die Entwicklung der Technik," pp. 127–48, in *Festgabe fuer Adolph Wagner*, 1905 (now *SStuKr* II: 33–62).

Strafrechtsreform. Berlin: Pan Publ., Moderne Zeitfragen, no. 1, 1905.

"Eugenik." *SchmJb* 29 (1905) : 1089–106 (now *SStuKr* I: 334–49).

"Zur naturwissenschaftlichen Gesellschaftslehre: Die Anwendung der Deszendenztheorie auf Probleme der sozialen Entwicklung." *SchmJb* n.s. 29 (1905) : 27–101, 1283–322; 30 (1906) : 121–45; 31 (1907) : 487–552; 33 (1909) : 879–94; 35 (1911) : 375–96 (now *SStuKr* I: 133–329).

Philosophische Terminologie in psychologisch-soziologischer Ansicht. Leipzig: Thomas, 1906.

Das Wesen der Soziologie. Schriften der Gehe Stiftung. Dresden: Zahn & v. Jentsch, 1907 (now *SStuKr* I: 350–68).

Die Entwicklung der sozialen Frage. Berlin: Goeschen (Sammlung Goeschen), 1907. 4th ed., *Die Entwicklung der sozialen Frage bis zum Weltkriege.* Berlin-Leipzig: de Gruyter, 1926.

"Ethik und Sozialismus." *AswSp* 25 (1907) : 573–612; 26 (1908) : 56–94; 29 (1909) : 895–930.

"Entwicklung der Soziologie in Deutschland im 19. Jahrhundert," in *Festgabe fuer Gustav Schmoller*, 1908 (now *SStuKr* II: 63–103).

Review of G. Ratzenhofer, *Soziologie, Positive Lehre von den menschlichen Wechselbeziehungen. SchmJb* 32 (1908): 329–32 (now *SStuKr* III: 348–52).

Die Sitte. Die Gesellschaft, ed. by Martin Buber, vol. 25. Frankfurt: Ruetten & Loening, 1909.

"Comtes Begriff der Soziologie." *Monatsschrift fuer Soziologie* 1 (1909): 42–50 (now *SStuKr* II: 116–22).

"Wege und Ziele der Soziologie, Rede zur Eroeffnung des Ersten Deutschen Soziologentages," pp. 17–38, in *Verhandlungen des Ersten Deutschen Soziologentages vom 19.–22. Oktober 1910 in Frankfurt a.M.* Tuebingen: I. C. B. Mohr, 1911 (now *SStuKr* II: 125–43).

"Ueber Anlagen und Anpassung." *Frauen-Zukunft* 1 (1910): 483–91, 567–76 (now *SStuKr* II: 155–68).

"Individuum und Welt in der Neuzeit." *WwA* 1 (1913): 37–66 (now *FSE*, 1–35).

"Soziologie und Geschichte." *Die Geisteswissenschaften* 1 (1913): 57–62 (now *SStuKr* II: 190–99).

"Rechtsstaat und Wohlfahrtsstaat." *ARWPh* 8 (1914): 1–6.

Der englische Staat und der deutsche Staat. Berlin: K. Curtius, 1917.

"Der Begriff der Gemeinschaft." *Zeitschrift fuer soziale Paedagogik* 1 (1919): 12–20 (now *SStuKr* II: 266–76).

"Zur Theorie der Oeffentlichen Meinung." *SchmJb* 40 (1916): 2001–30 (no. 4: 393–422).

"Die grosse Menge und das Volk." *SchmJb* 43 (1919): 1–29 (now *SStuKr* II: 277–303).

Hochschulreform und Soziologie. Jena: Fischer, 1920.

Kritik der Oeffentlichen Meinung. Berlin: Springer, 1922.

"Macht und Wert der Oeffentlichen Meinung." *DiJG* 2 (1923): 72–99.

"Zweck und Mittel im sozialen Leben," pp. 235–70, in *Erinnerungsgabe fuer Max Weber: Die Hauptprobleme der Soziologie*, vol. 1. Munich: Duncker & Humblot, 1923. (Now *SStuKr* III: 1–39.)

"Zur Soziologie des demokratischen Staates." *WwA* 19 (1923): 540–84 (now *SStuKr* II: 304–52).

"Hobbes und das Zoon Politikon." *ZV* 12 (1923): 471–88.

"Einteilung der Soziologie," pp. 885–98, in *Atti del V. Congresso Inter-*

nazionale di Filosofia, Napoli, 5–9 maggio 1924. Naples: S.A. Editrice Francesco Perrella, 1926. *ZGSt* 79 (1925): 1–15 (now *SStuKr* II: 430–43).

"Begriff und Gesetz des menschlichen Fortschritts" (paper read at the congress in Rome, April 1924, of the *Istituto Internazionale di sociologia e di reforma sociale*). *ASwSp* 53 (1925): 1–10 (now *FSE*, 36–44). Translated in *Social Forces* 19 (1940): 23–29, by Karl J. Arndt and C. L. Folse, "The Concept and Law of Human Progress."

"Kulturbedeutung der Religionen." *SchmJb* 48 (1924): 1–30 (now *SStuKr* II: 353–80).

"Richtlinien fuer das Studium des Fortschritts und der sozialen Entwicklung," pp. 166–221, in *Jahrbuch fuer Soziologie*, vol. 1, 1925. (Now *FSE*, 45–100.)

Soziologische Studien und Kritiken. Jena: Fischer, *Erste Sammlung* 1925; *Zweite Sammlung* 1926; *Dritte Sammlung* 1929.

"Troeltsch und die Philosophie der Geschichte." *SchmJb* 49 (1925): 147–91 (now *SStuKr* II: 381–429).

Fortschritt und soziale Entwicklung. Geschichtsphilosophische Ansichten. Karlsruhe: Braun, 1926.

Das Eigentum. Vienna and Leipzig: Braumueller, Soziologie und Sozialphilosophie, Schriften der Soziologischen Gesellschaft in Wien, vol. 5, 1926.

"Demokratie," pp. 12–36, in *Verhandlungen des Fuenften Deutschen Soziologentages 27–29, September 1926 in Wien*. Tuebingen: I. C. B. Mohr, 1927.

Wege zu dauerndem Frieden? Leipzig: Hirschfeld, Zeitfragen aus dem Gebiete der Soziologie, third series, no. 2, 1926.

"Demokratie und Parlamentarismus." *SchmJb* 51 (1927): 173–216 (now *SStuKr* III: 40–84).

"Amerikanische Soziologie" (Review of Walter Lippmann, *Public Opinion*). *WwA* 26 (July 1927): 1**–11**.

Der Kampf um das Sozialistengesetz 1878. Berlin: Springer, 1929.

"Soziale Bezugsgebilde in ihren Wechselwirkungen." *Forum Philosophicum* (1930): 143–69.

"Sozialpolitik als soziale Idee." *WwA* 31 (1930): 161*–175*.

Einfuehrung in die Soziologie. Stuttgart: Ferdinand Enke, 1931; Reprint, with an introduction by Rudolf Heberle, 1965.

"Gemeinschaft und Gesellschaft," pp. 180–91, in *Handwoerterbuch der Soziologie*, ed. A. Vierkandt. Stuttgart: Ferdinand Enke, 1931. Translated in ed. Loomis, *Toennies, Community and Society (Gemeinschaft und Gesellschaft)*, pp. 237–59 (see below).

"Eigentum," pp. 106–12, in *Handwoerterbuch der Soziologie*, ed. A. Vierkandt. Stuttgart: Ferdinand Enke, 1931.

"Die moderne Familie," pp. 122–31, in *Handwoerterbuch der Soziologie*, ed. A. Vierkandt. Stuttgart: Ferdinand Enke, 1931.

"Staende und Klassen," pp. 617–38, in *Handwoerterbuch der Soziologie*, ed. A. Vierkandt. Stuttgart: Ferdinand Enke, 1931. Translated in *Class, Status and Power: A Reader*, ed. by R. Bendix and S. M. Lipset, pp. 49–63. Glencoe, Ill.: Free Press, 1953.

"Mein Verhaeltnis zur Soziologie," pp. 103–22, in *Soziologie von heute. Ein Symposium der ZV pS*, ed. R. Thurnwald. 1932.

"Sitte und Freiheit," pp. 7–17, in *Probleme deutscher Soziologie. Gedaechtnisgabe für Karl Dunkmann*. Berlin: Junker u. Duennhaupt, 1933.

"Gemeinwirtschaft und Gemeinschaft." *SchmJb* 58 (1934): 317–26.

Geist der Neuzeit. Leipzig: Buske, 1935.

Posthumous: "Die Entstehung meiner Begriffe Gemeinschaft und Gesellschaft. Fuer Earle Eubank," and "Ueber die Lehr- und Redefreiheit." *Koelner Zeitschrift* 7 (1955): 127–31; 132–41.

SOCIOGRAPHY

"The Prevention of Crime." *International Journal of Ethics* 2 (October 1891): 51–77.

"Das Verbrechen als soziale Erscheinung." *ASGS* 8 (1895): 329–44. "Le crime comme phenomène social." *Annales de l'Institut International de Sociologie* 2 (1896): 387:409.

"Hafenarbeiter und Seeleute in Hamburg vor dem Strike 1896/97." *ASGS* 10 (1897): 173–238.

"Der Hamburger Strike von 1896/97." *ASGS* 10 (1897): 673–720.

"Straftaten in Hamburger Hafenstrike." *ASGS* 11 (1897): 513–20.

"Die Enquete ueber Zustaende der Arbeit im Hamburger Hafen." *ASGS* 12 (1898): 303–48.

"Die Ostseehaefen Flensburg, Kiel, Luebeck," pp. 509–614, in *Die Lage der in der Seeschiffahrt beschaeftigten Arbeiter*, II, Schriften des

Vereins fuer Sozialpolitik, vol. 104, part 1. Berlin and Munich: Duncker & Humblot, 1903.

"Todesursachenstatistik." *Soziale Praxis* 13 (1903) : 260–61.

"Eine neue Methode der Vergleichung statistischer Reihen, im Anschluss an Mitteilungen ueber kriminalistische Forschungen." *SchmJb* n.s. 33 (1909) : 699–720.

"Studie zur Schleswig-holsteinischen Agrarstatistik." *ASwSp* 30 (1910) : 285–332.

"Die Gesetzmaessigkeit in der Bewegung der Bevoelkerung." *ASwSp* 39 (1915) : 150–73, 767–94.

"Die Statistik als Wissenschaft." *WwA* 15 (1919) : 1–28 (now *SStuKr* III: 85–116).

"Korrelation der Parteien, Statistik der Kieler Reichstagswahlen." *JbNS* 67 (1924) : 663–72.

"Verbrechertum in Schleswig-Holstein," parts I, II, III. *TSwSp* 52 (1924) : 761–805; 58 (1927) : 608–28; 61 (1929) : 322–59.

"Moralstatistik," in *Handwoerterbuch der Staatswissenschaften*, 4th ed., 1925. (Now *SStuKr* III: 117–31.)

Der Selbstmord in Schleswig-Holstein, Eine statistisch-soziologische Studie. Breslau: Hirt, Veroeffentlichungen der Schleswig-Holstein-ischen Universitaetsgesellschaft, no. 9, 1927).

"Das Haarlemer Meer, Eine soziographische Studie." *ZVpS* 3 (1927) : 183–96.

"Die eheliche Fruchtbarkeit in Deutschland." *SchmJb* 52 (1928) : 581–609.

"Statistik und Soziographie." *AStA* 18 (1929) : 546–58.

"Die schwere Kriminalitaet von Maennern in Schleswig-Holstein in den Jahren 1899–1914." With Dr. E. Jurkat. *ZVpS* 5 (1929) : 26–39.

"Ortsherkunft von Verbrechern in Schleswig-Holstein." *DStZ* 21 (1929) : 146–50.

"Sozialwissenschaftliche Forschungsinstitute," pp. 425–40, in *Forschungs-institute, ihre Geschichte, Organisation und Ziele.* Ed. L. Brauer, Mendelssohn Bartholdy, and A. Meyer. Hamburg: Hartung, 1930.

Uneheliche und verwaiste Verbrecher, Studien ueber Verbrechertum in Schleswig-Holstein. Leipzig: Wiegandt, Kriminalistische Abhand-lungen, no. 14, 1930.

"Soziographie und ihre Bedeutung." *Deutsche Justiz* 6 (1930) : 70–77.

"Der Selbstmord in Schleswig-Holstein alten Umfanges, 1885–1914."
Nordelbingen 8 (1930) : 447–72.

"Leitsaetze und Vortrag in der Untergruppe fuer Soziographie," pp. 196–
206, in *Verhandlungen des Siebenten Deutschen Soziologentages vom
28 September bis 1, Oktober 1930 in Berlin*. Tuebingen: I. C. B. Mohr,
1931.

"Zur Statistik der Deutschen Reichstagswahlen." *DStZ* 23, no. 2 (March
1931) : 33–40.

Review of Theodor Geiger, *Die soziale Schichtung des deutschen Volkes*.
ZGSt 94 (1933) : 527-30.

"Der Selbstmord von Maennern in Preussen 1884–1914." *Mensch en
Maatschappij* 9 (1933) : 234–54.

TRANSLATIONS OF TOENNIES' WORKS

Borenstein, A. Farrell, trans. *Custom, An Essay on Social Codes*. Preface
by Rudolf Heberle. New York: Free Press of Glencoe, 1961.

Bosse Ewald, trans. *Inledning til Sociologien*. Oslo: Fabricius & Sonner,
1932.

Giordano, Giorgio, trans. *Communità e Società*. Introduction by Renato
Treves. Milan: Editioni di Communita, Classici della Sociologia, 1963.

Leif J., trans. *Communauté et Societé: Categories fondamentales de la
sociologie pure*. Introduction and translation by Leif. Paris: Presses
Universitaires de France, 1944.

Llorens, Vicente, trans. *Principios de Sociologia*. Mexico, D.F.: Fondo
de Cultura Economica, 1942.

Loomis, Charles, trans. *Fundamental Concepts of Sociology (Gemeinschaft
und Gesellschaft)*. Translated and supplemented by Loomis. New
York: American Book Company, 1940. British edition, *Community and
Association (Gemeinschaft und Gesellschaft)*. London: Routledge &
Kegan Paul, International Library of Sociology and Social Recon-
struction, 1955. *Community and Society (Gemeinschaft und Gesellschaft)*. Translated and edited by Charles P. Loomis. East Lansing:
Michigan State University Pres, 1957; Harper Torchbook Edition,
1963.

SELECTED WRITINGS ABOUT TOENNIES

Aron, Raymond, pp. 20–28 in: *La sociologie Allemande contemporaine*

(Nouvelle Encylopedie Philosophique), (Paris: Felix Alcan), 1935; English translation pp. 14–19 in: *German Sociology* (New York: Free Press, 1964).

Bellebaum, Alfred. *Das soziologische System von Ferdinand Toennies unter besonderer Beruecksichtigung seiner soziographischen Untersuchungen.* Meisenheim: A. Hain, Koelner Beitraege zur Sozialforschung und Angewandten Soziologie, herausgegeben von R. Koenig und E. K. Scheuch, vol 2, 1966.

Bluem, Norbert S. *Willenslehre und Soziallehre bei Ferdinand Toennies.* Doctoral dissertation, University of Bonn, 1967.

Cahnman, Werner J., pp. 110–11, 540–41 and *passim* in Cahnman, Werner J. and Alvin Boskoff, *Sociology and History* (New York: Free Press, 1964).

———. "Toennies and Social Change," *Social Forces* 47 (1968) : 136–44.

———. "Toennies und Durkheim: Eine dokumentarische Gegenueberstellung," *Archiv fuer Rechts- und Sozialpilosophie,* forthcoming.

Freyer, Hans. "Ferdinand Toennies und seine Stellung in der deutschen Soziologie." *WwA* 44 (1936) : 1–9.

Heberle, Rudolf. "The Application of Fundamental Concepts in Rural Community Studies." *Rural Sociology* 6 (1941) : 203–15.

———. "The Sociological System of Ferdinand Toennies: Community and Society," pp. 227–48, in *An Introduction to the History of Sociology,* edited by Harry Elmer Barnes. Chicago: University of Chicago Press, 1948.

———. "Das soziologische System von Ferdinand Toennies." *SchmJb* 75 (1955) : 1–18.

———. "Ferdinand Toennies' Contributions to the Sociology of Political Parties." *American Journal of Sociology* 61 (no. 3, 1955) : 213–20.

———. "Toennies, Ferdinand," pp. 98–103. *Handwoerterbuch der Sozialwissenschaften.* Tuebingen, 1959.

———. "Toennies, Ferdinand," pp. 98–103. *International Encyclopedia of the Social Sciences.* New York, 1968.

Hoffmann, Friedrich. "Ferdinand Toennies, im Gedenken seiner heimatlichen Vorbundenheit, zu seinem 100. Geburtstag." *Zeitschrift der Gesellschaft fuer Schleswig-Holsteinische Geschichte* 79 (1955) : 301–16.

Jacoby, E. G. "Ferdinand Toennies, Sociologist: A Centennial Tribute." *Kyklos* 8 (1955) : 144–61.

————. "Zur reinen Soziologie." *Koelner Zeitschrift fuer Soziologie und Sozialpsychologie* 20 (1968) : 448–70.

Jurkat, Ernst, ed. *Reine und Angewandte Soziologie: Eine Festgabe fuer Ferdinand Toennies zu seinem achtzigsten Geburtstag am 26. Juli 1935, dargebracht von Albrecht, Boas et al.* Leipzig: H. Buske, 1936.

Klose, O.; Jacoby, E. G.; and Fischer, I., eds. *Ferdinand Toennies– Friedrich Paulsen Briefwechsel 1876–1908*. Foreword by E. G. Jacoby. Kiel: F. Hirt, Veroeffentlichungen der Schleswig-Holsteinischen Universitaetsgesellschaft, N. F. no 27, 1961.

Koenig, René. "Die Begriffe Gemeinschaft und Gesellschaft bei Ferdinand Toennies." *Koelner Zeitschrift fuer Soziologie und Sozialpsychologie,* 7 (1955) : 348–420. Cf. other contributions in *Koelner Zeitschrift,* same issue.

Leemans, Victor. *F. Toennies et la sociologie contemporaine en Allemagne.* Preface by René Maunier. Paris: Felix Alcan, 1933.

Leif, J. *La sociologie de Toennies.* Paris: Presses Universitaires de France, 1946.

Levi, Albert William. "Existentialism and the Alienation of Man," pp. 243–66, in E. N. Lee and M. Mandelbaum, *Phenomenology and Existentialism.* Baltimore: Johns Hopkins Press, 1967.

McKinney, John C., in collaboration with Charles P. Loomis. "The Application of Gemeinschaft and Gesellschaft as Related to other Typologies," in *Community and Society,* transl. by Charles P. Loomis, pp. 12–29.

Nisbet, Robert A. *The Sociological Tradition,* pp. 71–80 and 208–11 and *passim.* New York: Basic Books, 1966.

Oberschall, Anthony. "Toennies' Social Statistics and Sociography," pp. 51–63, in *Empirical Social Research in Germany in 1848–1914.* Paris and The Hague: Mouton & Co.; Publications of the International Social Science Council, 1965.

Oppenheimer, Franz. "Die moderne Soziologie und Ferdinand Toennies." *WwA* 23 (1926) : 187*–208*.

Palmer, Paul A. "Ferdinand Toennies' Theory of Public Opinion." *The Public Opinion Quarterly* (October 1938) : 584–95.

Pappenheim, Fritz. *The alienation of modern man, an interpretation based on Marx and Toennies.* New York: Monthly Review Press, 1959.

Parsons, Talcott. "Note on *Gemeinschaft* und *Gesellschaft,*" pp. 686–94, in *The Structure of Social Action.* 1st ed. New York and London: McGraw-Hill, 1937.

Rosenbaum, Eduard. "Ferdinand Toennies' Werk." *SchmJb* 38 (1913): 2149–96.

Rudolph, Guenther, "Ferdinand Toennies und der Faschismus." *Wiss Z. Humboldt Univ. Berlin* 14 (1967): 339–45. Cf. Rudolph's review of Bellebaum, *op. cit.*, in *Wirtschaftswissenschaft* (1968): 497–501.

Salomon, Albert. "In memoriam Ferdinand Toennies, 1855–1936." *Social Research* 3 (1936): 348–63.

Striefler, Heinrich. "Zur Methode der Rangkorrelation nach Toennies." *DStZ* 23 (1931): 130–35, 163–68.

Takata, Yasuma. "Die Gemeinschaft als Typus." *ZGSt* 83 (1927): 291–316.

Treves, Renato. "Ferdinand Toennies e la teoria della communità e della società." *Quaderni di Sociologia* 12 (1963): 3–24.

Vierkandt, Alfred. "Ferdinand Toennies' Werk und seine Weiterbildung in der Gegenwart." *Kant Studien* 30 (1925): 299–309.

Von Wiese, Leopold. "Toennies' Einteilung der Soziologie." *KVHS* 5 (1925): 445–55.

Wirth, Louis. "The Sociology of Ferdinand Toennies." *American Journal of Sociology* 32 (1926/27): 412–22.

"Zum Hundertsten Geburtstag von Ferdinand Toennies." *Koelner Zeitschrift fuer Soziologie und Sozialpsychologie.* vol. 7, no. 3 (1955), with contributions by L. V. Wiese, H. Plessner, R. Koenig, J. Leif, R. Heberle, G. Wurzbacher, J. Johannesson, and two posthumous papers by Toennies (see above).

Index of Names

345

Index of Subjects